The number one *New York Times* bestselling author Mary Higgins Clark has written thirty-seven suspense novels; four collections of short stories; a historical novel, a memoir, two children's books, and most recently partnered with Alafair Burke to collaborate on a new series: the *Under Suspicion* novels. With her daughter Carol Higgins Clark, Clark has co-authored five more suspense novels. Her books are international bestsellers with more than one hundred million copies in print in the United States alone.

ALSO BY MARY HIGGINS CLARK

All By Myself, Alone
As Time Goes By
The Melody Lingers On
Death Wears a Beauty Mask
I've Got You Under My Skin
Daddy's Gone A Hunting
The Magical Christmas Horse (Illustrated by Wendell Minor)
I'll Walk Alone
The Shadow of Your Smile
Just Take My Heart
Where Are You Now?
Ghost Ship (Illustrated by Wendell Minor)
I Heard That Song Before
Two Little Girls in Blue
No Place Like Home
Nighttime Is My Time
The Second Time Around
Kitchen Privileges
Mount Vernon Love Story
All Through the Night
Daddy's Little Girl
On the Street Where You Live
Before I Say Good-Bye
We'll Meet Again
All Through the Night
You Belong to Me
Pretend You Don't See Her
My Gal Sunday
Moonlight Becomes You
Silent Night
Let Me Call You Sweetheart
The Lottery Winner
Remember Me
I'll Be Seeing You
All Around the Town

Loves Music, Loves to Dance
The Anastasia Syndrome and Other Stories
While My Pretty One Sleeps
Weep No More, My Lady
Stillwatch
A Cry in the Night
The Cradle Will Fall
A Stranger Is Watching
Where Are the Children

BY MARY HIGGINS CLARK AND CAROL HIGGINS CLARK

Dashing Through the Snow
Santa Cruise
The Christmas Thief
He Sees You When You're Sleeping
Deck the Halls

BY MARY HIGGINS CLARK AND ALAFAIR BURKE

The Sleeping Beauty Killer
All Dressed in White
The Cinderella Murder

MARY HIGGINS CLARK

DADDY'S LITTLE GIRL

I HEARD THAT SONG BEFORE

WHERE ARE YOU NOW?

SIMON & SCHUSTER

London · New York · Sydney · Toronto · New Delhi

A CBS COMPANY

This Mary Higgins Clark bind-up first published in Great Britain by
Simon & Schuster UK Ltd, 2017
A CBS COMPANY

Containing:
Daddy's Little Girl
First published in the US by Simon & Schuster, Inc., 2002
First published in Great Britain by Simon & Schuster UK Ltd, 2002

I Heard That Song Before
First published in the US by Simon & Schuster, Inc., 2007
First published in Great Britain by Simon & Schuster UK Ltd, 2007

Where Are You Now?
First published in the US by Simon & Schuster, Inc., 2008
First published in Great Britain by Simon & Schuster UK Ltd, 2008

1 3 5 7 9 10 8 6 4 2

Simon & Schuster UK Ltd
1st Floor
222 Gray's Inn Road
London WC1X 8HB

www.simonandschuster.co.uk

Simon & Schuster Australia, Sydney
Simon & Schuster India, New Delhi

A CIP catalogue record for this book
is available from the British Library

Australian Trade Paperback ISBN: 978-1-4711-6588-7
Australian eBook ISBN: 978-1-4711-6589-4

Printed and bound in Australia by Griffin Press

DADDY'S LITTLE GIRL

Part One

1

When Ellie awoke that morning, it was with the sense that something terrible had happened.

Instinctively she reached for Bones, the soft and cuddly stuffed dog who had shared her pillow ever since she could remember. When she'd had her seventh birthday last month, Andrea, her fifteen-year-old sister, had teased her that it was time to toss Bones in the attic.

Then Ellie remembered what was wrong: Andrea hadn't come home last night. After dinner, she had gone to her best friend Joan's house to study for a math test. She had promised to be home by nine o'clock. At quarter of nine, Mommy went to Joan's house to walk Andrea home, but they said Andrea had left at eight o'clock.

Mommy had come back home worried and almost crying, just as Daddy got in from work. Daddy was a lieutenant in the New York State Police. Right away he and Mommy had started calling all of Andrea's friends, but no one had seen her. Then Daddy said he was going to drive around to the bowling alley and to the ice cream parlor, just in case Andrea had gone there.

"If she lied about doing homework until nine o'clock, she won't set foot out of this house for six months," he'd said angrily, and then he'd turned to Mommy: "If I said it once, I've said it a thousand times—I don't want her to go out after dark alone."

Despite his raised voice, Ellie could tell that Daddy was more worried than angry.

"For heaven's sake, Ted, she went out at seven o'clock. She got to Joan's. She was planning to be home by nine, and I even walked over there to meet her."

"Then *where is* she?"

They made Ellie go to bed, and, eventually, she fell asleep waking only now. Maybe Andrea was home by now, she thought hopefully. She slipped out of bed, rushed across the room, and darted down the hall to Andrea's room. Be there, she begged. *Please* be there. She opened the door. Andrea's bed had not been slept in.

Her bare feet silent on the steps, Ellie hurried downstairs. Their neighbor, Mrs. Hilmer, was sitting with Mommy in the kitchen. Mommy was wearing the same clothes she had on last night, and she looked as if she'd been crying for a long time.

Ellie ran to her. "Mommy."

Mommy hugged her and began to sob. Ellie felt Mommy's hand clutching her shoulder, so hard that she was almost hurting her.

"Mommy, where's Andrea?"

"We. . . don't. . . know. Daddy and the police are looking for her."

"Ellie, why don't you get dressed, and I'll fix you some breakfast?" Mrs. Hilmer asked.

No one was saying that she should hurry up because the school bus would be coming pretty soon. Without asking, Ellie knew she wouldn't be going to school today.

She dutifully washed her face and hands and brushed her teeth and hair, and then put on play clothes—a turtleneck shirt and her favorite blue slacks—and went downstairs again.

Just as she sat at the table where Mrs. Hilmer had put out juice and cornflakes, Daddy came through the kitchen door. "No sign of her," he said. "We've looked everywhere. There was a guy collecting for some phony charity ringing doorbells in town yesterday. He was in the diner last night and left around eight o'clock. He would have passed Joan's house on the way to the highway around the time Andrea left. They're looking for him."

Ellie could tell that Daddy was almost crying. He

also hadn't seemed to notice her, but she didn't mind. Sometimes when Daddy came home he was upset because something sad had happened while he was at work, and for a while he'd be very quiet. He had that same look on his face now.

Andrea was hiding—Ellie was sure of it. She had probably left Joan's house early on purpose because she was meeting Rob Westerfield in the hideout, then maybe it got late and she was afraid to come home. Daddy had said that if she ever lied again about where she'd been, he'd make her quit the school band. He'd said that when he found out she had gone for a ride with Rob Westerfield in his car when she was supposed to be at the library.

Andrea loved being in the band; last year she'd been the only freshman chosen for the flute section. But if she'd left Joan's house early and gone to the hideout to meet Rob, and Daddy found out, that would mean she'd have to give it up. Mommy always said that Andrea could twist Daddy around her little finger, but she didn't say that last month when one of the state troopers told Daddy he'd stopped Rob Westerfield to give him a ticket for speeding and that Andrea was with him at the time.

Daddy hadn't said anything about it until after dinner. Then he asked Andrea how long she'd been at the library.

She didn't answer him.

Then he said, "I see you're smart enough to realize that the trooper who gave Westerfield the ticket would tell me you were with him. Andrea, that guy is not only rich and spoiled, he's a bad apple through and through. When he kills himself speeding, you're not going to be in the car. You are *absolutely forbidden* to have anything to do with him."

The hideout was in the garage behind the great big house that old Mrs. Westerfield, Rob's grandmother, lived in all summer. It was always unlocked, and sometimes Andrea and her friends sneaked in there and smoked cigarettes. Andrea had taken Ellie there a couple of times when she was babysitting her.

Her friends had been really mad at Andrea for bringing her along, but she had said, "Ellie is a good kid. She's not a snitch." Hearing that had made Ellie feel great, but Andrea hadn't let Ellie have even one puff of the cigarette.

Ellie was sure that last night Andrea had left Joan's house early because she was planning to meet Rob Westerfield. Ellie had heard her when she talked to him on the phone yesterday, and when she was finished, she was practically crying. "I told Rob I was going to the mixer with Paulie," she said, "and now he's really mad at me."

Ellie thought about the conversation as she finished

the cornflakes and juice. Daddy was standing at the stove. He was holding a cup of coffee. Mommy was crying again but making almost no sound.

Then, for the first time, Daddy seemed to notice her: "Ellie, I think you'd be better off in school. At lunchtime I'll take you over."

"Is it all right if I go outside now?"

"Yes. But stay around the house."

Ellie ran for her jacket and was quickly out the door. It was the fifteenth of November, and the leaves were damp and felt sloshy underfoot. The sky was heavy with clouds, and she could tell it was going to rain again. Ellie wished they were back in Irvington where they used to live. It was lonesome here. Mrs. Hilmer's house was the only other one on this road.

Daddy had liked living in Irvington, but they'd moved here, five towns away, because Mommy wanted a bigger house and more property. They found they could afford that if they moved farther up in Westchester, to a town that hadn't yet become a suburb of New York City.

When Daddy said he missed Irvington, where he'd grown up and where they'd lived until two years ago, Mommy would tell him how great the new house was. Then he'd say that in Irvington we had a million-dollar view of the Hudson River and the Tappan Zee Bridge, and he didn't have to drive five miles for a newspaper or a loaf of bread.

There were woods all around their property. The big Westerfield house was directly behind theirs, but on the other side of the woods. Glancing back at the kitchen window to make sure no one had seen her, Ellie began to dart through the trees.

Five minutes later she reached the clearing and ran across the field to where the Westerfield property began. Feeling more and more alone, she raced up the long driveway and darted around the mansion, a small figure lost in the lengthening shadows of the approaching storm.

There was a side door to the garage, and that was the one that was unlocked. Even so, it was hard for Ellie to turn the handle. Finally she succeeded and stepped into the gloom of the interior. The garage was big enough to hold four cars, but the only one Mrs. Westerfield left after the summer was the van. Andrea and her friends had brought some old blankets to sit on when they went there. They always sat in the same spot, at the back of the garage behind the van, so that if anyone happened to look in the window, they wouldn't be able to see them. Ellie knew that was where Andrea would be hiding if she was here.

She didn't know why she felt suddenly afraid, but she did. Now, instead of running, she had to practically drag her feet to make them move toward the back of the garage. But then she saw it—the edge of the blanket peeking out from behind the van. Andrea *was* here! She and her friends would never have left the blankets out; when they left, they always folded them and hid them in the cabinet with the cleaning supplies.

"Andrea . . ." Now she ran, calling softly so that Andrea wouldn't be scared. She was probably asleep, Ellie decided.

Yes, she was. Even though the garage was filled with shadows, Ellie could see Andrea's long hair trailing out from under the blankets.

"Andrea, it's me." Ellie sank to her knees beside Andrea and pulled back the blanket covering her face.

Andrea had a mask on, a terrible monster mask that looked all sticky and gummy. Ellie reached down to pull it off, and her fingers went into a broken space in Andrea's forehead. As she jerked back, she became aware of the pool of Andrea's blood, soaking through her slacks.

Then, from somewhere in the big room, she was sure she heard someone breathing—harsh, heavy, sucking-in breaths that broke off in a kind of giggle.

Terrified, she tried to get up, but her knees slid in the blood and she fell forward across Andrea's chest. Her lips grazed something smooth and cold—Andrea's gold locket. Then she managed to scramble to her feet, and she turned and began to run.

She did not know she was shrieking until she was almost home, and Ted and Genine Cavanaugh ran into the backyard to see their younger daughter burst out of the woods, her arms outstretched, her little form covered in her sister's blood.

2

With the exception of when his team practiced or had a game during the baseball season, sixteen-year-old Paulie Stroebel worked in Hillwood's service station after school and all day Saturday. The alternative was to help out during those same hours at his parents' delicatessen a block away on Main Street, something he'd been doing from the time he was seven years old.

Slow academically, but good with things mechanical, he loved to repair cars, and his parents had been understanding of his desire to work for someone else. With unruly blond hair, blue eyes, round cheeks, and a stocky five-foot-eight frame, Paulie was considered a quiet, hardworking employee by his boss at the service station and something of a dopey nerd by his fcllow students at Delano High. His one achievement in school was to be on the football team.

On Friday, when word of Andrea Cavanaugh's murder reached the school, guidance counselors were sent to all the classes to break the news to the students. Paul was in the middle of a study period when Miss Watkins came into his classroom, whispered to the teacher, and rapped on the desk for attention.

"I have very sad news for all of you," she began. "We have just learned . . ." In halting sentences she informed them that sophomore Andrea Cavanaugh had been killed, the victim of foul play. The reaction was a chorus of shocked gasps and tearful protests.

Then a shouted "No!" silenced the others. Quiet, placid Paulie Stroebel, his face twisted in grief, had sprung to his feet. As his classmates stared at him, his shoulders began to shake. Fierce sobs racked his body, and he ran from the room. As the door closed behind him, he said something in a voice too muffled for most of them to hear. However, the student seated nearest the door later swore that his words were "I can't believe she's dead!"

Emma Watkins, the guidance counselor, already stunned by the tragedy, felt as though a knife had gone through her. She was fond of Paulie and understood the isolation of the earnestly plodding student who tried so hard to please.

She herself was positive that the anguished words he shouted were "I didn't think she was dead."

That afternoon, for the first time in the six months he'd been working at the service station, Paulie did not show up, nor did he call his boss to explain his absence. When his parents got home that evening, they found him lying on top of the bed, staring at the ceiling, pictures of Andrea scattered beside him.

Both Hans and Anja Wagner Stroebel had been born in Germany, and they immigrated to the United States with their parents when they were children. They had met and married in their late thirties and used their combined savings to open the delicatessen. By nature undemonstrative, they were fiercely protective of their only son.

Everyone who came into the store was talking about the murder, asking each other who could possibly have committed such a terrible crime. The Cavanaughs were regular customers at the deli, and the Stroebels joined in the shocked discussion that Andrea might have been planning to meet someone in the garage on the Westerfield estate.

They agreed that she was pretty, but a bit headstrong. She was supposed to be doing homework with Joan Lashley until nine o'clock, but had left unexpectedly early. Had she planned to meet someone, or had she been waylaid on the way home?

Anja Stroebel acted instinctively when she saw the pictures on her son's bed. She swooped them up and put them in her pocketbook. At her husband's questioning glance, she shook her head, indicating that he was to ask no questions. Then she sat down next to Paulie, and put her arms around him.

"Andrea was such a pretty girl," she said soothingly, her voice heavy with the accent that became stronger when she was upset. "I remember how she congratulated you when you made that great catch and saved the game last spring. Like her other friends, you are very, very sad."

At first it seemed to Paulie that his mother was talking to him from a distant place. Like her other friends. What did she mean?

"The police will be looking for anyone who has been a particular friend to Andrea, Paulie," she said slowly but firmly.

"I invited her to a mixer," he said, the words coming haltingly. "She said she would go with me."

Anja was sure her son had never asked a girl for a date before. Last year he had refused to go to his sophomore dance.

"Then you liked her, Paulie?"

Paulie Stroebel began to cry. "Mama, I loved her so much."

"You *liked* her, Paul," Anja said insistently. "Try to remember that."

On Saturday, composed and quietly apologetic for not showing up on Friday afternoon, Paulie Stroebel reported for work at the gas station.

Early Saturday afternoon, Hans Stroebel personally delivered a Virginia ham and salads to the Cavanaugh home and asked their neighbor Mrs. Hilmer, who answered the door, to convey his deepest sympathy to the family.

3

"It's a shame Ted and Genine are both only children," Ellie heard Mrs. Hilmer say a couple of times on Saturday. "It makes it easier when there's a lot of family around at a time like this."

Ellie didn't care about having more family. She just wanted Andrea back, and she wanted Mommy to stop crying and she wanted Daddy to talk to her. He'd hardly said a word to her since she came running home and he grabbed her up in his arms and she managed to tell him where Andrea was and that she'd been hurt.

Later, after he'd gone to the hideout and had seen Andrea, and all the police came, he'd said, "Ellie, you knew last night she might have gone to the garage. Why didn't you *tell* us then?"

"You didn't ask me, and you made me go to bed."

"Yes, I did," he admitted. But then later she heard him say to one of the cops, "If only I had known

Andrea was there. She might still have been alive at nine o'clock. I might have found her in time."

Somebody from the police talked to Ellie and asked her questions about the hideout and about who else went there. In her head Ellie could hear Andrea saying, "Ellie is a good kid. She's not a snitch."

Thinking about Andrea, and knowing that she'd never come home again, made Ellie begin to cry so hard that the police stopped questioning her.

Then on Saturday afternoon a man who said he was Detective Marcus Longo came to the house. He took Ellie into the dining room and closed the door. She thought he had a nice face. He told her that he had a little boy exactly her age and that they looked a lot alike. "He has the same blue eyes," he said. "And his hair is just the color of yours. I tell him it reminds me of sand when the sun is shining on it."

Then he told her that four of Andrea's friends had admitted they went to the hideout with her, but none of them had been there that night. He named the girls, then asked, "Ellie, do you know any other girls who might have met your sister there?"

It wasn't like snitching on them if they had already told on themselves. "No," she whispered. "That was all of them."

"Is there anyone else Andrea might have met at the hideout?"

She hesitated. She couldn't tell him about Rob Westerfield. That would really be telling on Andrea.

Detective Longo said, "Ellie, someone hurt Andrea so much that she isn't alive anymore. Don't protect that person. Andrea would want you to tell us anything you know."

Ellie looked down at her hands. In this big old farmhouse, this room was her favorite. It used to have ugly wallpaper, but now the walls were painted a soft yellow, and there was a new chandelier over the table and the bulbs looked like candles. Mommy had found the chandelier at a yard sale and said it was a treasure. It had taken her a long time to clean it, but now anyone who visited admired it.

They always ate dinner in the dining room, even though Daddy thought it was silly to go to all the fuss. Mommy had a book that showed how to set the table for a formal dinner. It was Andrea's job to set the table that way every Sunday, even when it was just them. Ellie would help her, and they would have fun putting out the good silver and china.

"Lord Malcolm Bigbottom is the guest of honor today," Andrea would say. Then reading from the book of etiquette, she'd place him at the seat to the right of where Mommy would sit. "Oh, no, Gabrielle, the water glass must be placed slightly to the right of the dinner knife."

Ellie's real name was Gabrielle, but no one called her

that, except Andrea when she was joking. She wondered if it would be her job to set the table that way on Sunday from now on. She hoped not. Without Andrea it wouldn't be a game.

It felt funny to be thinking like that. On one hand, she knew that Andrea was dead and would be buried Tuesday morning in the cemetery in Tarrytown with Grandma and Grandpa Cavanaugh. On the other hand, she still expected Andrea to come into the house any minute, pull her close, and tell her a secret.

A secret. Sometimes Andrea met Rob Westerfield in the hideout. But Ellie had crossed her heart and promised not to tell.

"Ellie, whoever hurt Andrea may hurt somebody else if he isn't stopped," Detective Longo said. His voice was quiet and friendly.

"Do you think it's my fault that Andrea is dead? Daddy thinks so."

"No, he doesn't think that, Ellie," Detective Longo said. "But anything you can tell us about secrets you and Andrea shared may help us now."

Rob Westerfield, Ellie thought. Maybe it wouldn't really be breaking a promise to tell Detective Longo about him. If Rob had been the one who hurt Andrea, everybody should know it. She looked down at her hands. "Sometimes she would meet Rob Westerfield at the hideout," she whispered.

Detective Longo leaned forward. "Do you know if she was going to meet him there the other night?" he asked. Ellie could tell that he was excited to hear about Rob.

"I think she was. Paulie Stroebel had asked her to go to the Thanksgiving mixer with him, and she said yes. She didn't really *want* to go with him, but Paulie had told her he knew she was sneaking off to meet Rob Westerfield, and she was afraid he would tell Daddy if she didn't go with him. But then Rob was mad at her, and she wanted to explain to him that that was why she agreed to go out with Paulie, to keep him from telling Daddy. So maybe that's why she left Joan's house early."

"How did Paulie know that Andrea was seeing Rob Westerfield?"

"Andrea said that she thought he sometimes followed her to the hideout. Paulie wanted her to be *his* girlfriend."

4

The washing machine had been used.

"What was so important it couldn't wait until I got back, Mrs. Westerfield?" Rosita asked, her tone a touch defensive, as though fearful she had left a task undone. She had gone out of town to visit her ailing aunt on Thursday. It was now Saturday morning, and she had just arrived back. "You shouldn't bother yourself with wash when you have your hands full decorating all those houses."

Linda Westerfield did not know why a sudden alarm bell went off in her head. For some reason she did not respond directly to Rosita's remarks.

"Oh, every once in a while, if I'm checking on the decorative painting and touch it up myself, it's just as easy to run the paint cloths through the machine as to leave them around," she said.

"Well, judging from the amount of detergent you used, you must have had a whole heap of them. And

Mrs. Westerfield, I heard about the Cavanaugh girl on the news yesterday. I can't stop thinking about her. Who would believe that kind of thing could happen in this little town? It breaks your heart."

"Yes, it does." It had to be Rob who used the machine, Linda thought. Vince, her husband, would certainly not have used a washing machine at any time. Probably didn't even know how.

Rosita's dark eyes glistened, and she dabbed her hand over them. "That poor mother."

Rob? What would be so important for him to wash?

It was an old trick of his. When he was eleven, he'd tried to wash the smell of cigarette smoke from his play clothes.

"Andrea Cavanaugh was the prettiest thing. And her father a lieutenant in the state troopers! Somehow you'd think a man like that would be able to protect his child."

"Yes, you would." Linda was sitting at the counter in the kitchen, going over the sketches she had made for window treatments for a client's new home.

"To think that anybody would smash that girl's head in. Had to be a monster. I hope they string him up when they find him."

Rosita was talking to herself now and didn't seem to expect a response. Linda slipped the sketches into the portfolio. "Mr. Westerfield and I are meeting some friends at the inn for dinner, Rosita," she said as she slid off the stool.

"Will Rob be home?"

A good question, Linda thought. "He went out for a run and should be back any minute. Check with him then." She thought she detected a quiver in her voice. Rob had been agitated and moody all day yesterday. When the news about Andrea Cavanaugh's death flashed through the town, she had expected him to be upset. Instead, he'd been dismissive. "I hardly knew her, Mom," he said.

Was it simply that Rob, like many nineteen-year-olds, could not confront the death of a young person? Was it that somehow he felt as though his own mortality was threatened?

Linda went up the stairs slowly, suddenly weighted down with a sense of impending disaster. They had moved from the townhouse on Manhattan's East Seventieth Street to this pre-Revolutionary house six years ago, when Rob went away to boarding school. By then they both knew that the town where they'd traditionally summered at Vince's mother's home was where they wanted to live permanently. Vince had said that there were great opportunities to make money here, and he had begun investing in real estate.

The house, with its sense of timelessness, was a continuing source of quiet pleasure to her, but today Linda did not pause to feel the polished wood of the banister under her hand or stop to enjoy the view of the valley from the window at the top of the stairs.

She walked directly to Rob's room. The door was closed. He had been gone an hour and would be back from jogging any minute. Nervously she opened the door and stepped inside. The bed was unmade, but the rest of the room was oddly tidy. Rob was meticulous about his clothing, sometimes even pressing slacks fresh from the cleaners to sharpen the crease, but he was downright careless about discarded garments. She would have expected to see the clothes he had worn Thursday and yesterday thrown on the floor, waiting for Rosita's return.

She walked quickly across the room and looked into the hamper in his bathroom. That, too, was empty.

Sometime between Thursday morning, when Rosita left, and early this morning, Rob had washed and dried the clothes he'd been wearing Thursday and yesterday. *Why?*

Linda would have liked to go through his closet but knew she risked having him find her there. She wasn't prepared for a confrontation. She left his room, remembering to close the door, and went down the hall and around the corner to the master suite she and Vince had added when they expanded the house.

Suddenly aware that she might be feeling the

onslaught of a migraine, she dropped the portfolio onto the sofa in the sitting room, went into the bathroom, and reached in the medicine chest. As she swallowed two prescription pills, she looked into the mirror and was shocked to see how pale and anxious she looked.

She was wearing her jogging suit because she had planned to go for a run after she'd worked on the sketches. Her short chestnut hair was held back by a band, and she hadn't bothered with makeup. To her own hypercritical gaze, she looked older than her forty-four years, with tiny wrinkles forming around her eyes and the corners of her mouth.

The bathroom window looked out over the front yard and the driveway. As she glanced out, she saw an unfamiliar car driving up. A moment later the doorbell rang. She expected Rosita to use the intercom to let her know who it was, but instead Rosita came upstairs and handed her a card.

"He wants to talk to Rob, Mrs. Westerfield. I told him Rob was out jogging, and he said he'd wait."

Linda was nearly eight inches taller than Rosita, who was only a shade over five feet, but she almost had to grab the small woman to support herself after she read the name on the card: Detective Marcus Longo.

5

Wherever Ellie went, she felt in the way. After the nice detective left, she tried to find Mommy, but Mrs. Hilmer said that the doctor had given her something to help her rest. Daddy spent almost all the time in his little den with the door closed. He said he wanted to be left alone.

Grandma Reid, who lived in Florida, came up late Saturday afternoon, but all she did was cry.

Mrs. Hilmer and some of Mommy's friends from her bridge club sat in the kitchen. Ellie heard one of them, Mrs. Storey, say, "I feel so useless, but I also feel as though seeing us around may make Genine and Ted realize they're not alone."

Ellie went outside and got on the swing. She pumped her legs until the swing went higher and higher. She wanted it to go over the top. She wanted to fall from the top and hit the ground and hurt herself. Then maybe she'd stop hurting inside.

It had stopped raining, but there still was no sun and it was cold. After a while, Ellie knew that it was no use; the swing wouldn't go over the top. She went back into the house, entering the small vestibule off the kitchen. She heard Joan's mother's voice. She was with the other ladies now, and Ellie could tell that she was crying. "I was surprised that Andrea left so early. It was dark out, and it crossed my mind to drive her home. If only . . ."

Then Ellie heard Mrs. Lewis say, "If only Ellie had told them that Andrea used to go to that garage that the kids called 'the hideout.' Ted might have gotten there in time."

"If only Ellie . . ."

Ellie went up the back stairs, careful to walk very quietly so they wouldn't hear her. Grandma's suitcase was on her bed. That was funny. Wasn't Grandma going to sleep in Andrea's room? It was empty now.

Or maybe they'd let *her* sleep in Andrea's room. Then, if she woke up tonight, she could pretend that Andrea would be coming back any minute.

The door to Andrea's room was closed. She opened it as quietly as she always did on Saturday mornings when she'd peek in to see if Andrea was still sleeping.

Daddy was standing at Andrea's desk. He was holding a framed picture in his hands. Ellie knew it was the baby picture of Andrea, the one in the silver frame that had "Daddy's Little Girl" engraved across the top.

As she watched, he lifted the top of the music box. That was another present he had bought for Andrea right after she was born. Daddy joked that Andrea never wanted to go to sleep when she was a baby, and so he'd wind up the music box and dance around the room with her and play the song from it, singing the words softly, until she dozed off.

Ellie had asked if he did that with her, too, but Mommy said no, because she was always a good sleeper. From the day she was born, she'd been no trouble at all.

Some of the song's words ran through Ellie's head as the music drifted through the room. ". . . You're daddy's little girl to have and to hold. . . . You're the spirit of Christmas, my star on the tree. . . . And you're daddy's little girl."

As she watched, Daddy sat on the edge of Andrea's bed and began to sob.

Ellie backed out of the room, closing the door as quietly as she had opened it.

Part Two
Twenty-three Years Later

6

My sister, Andrea, was murdered nearly twenty-three years ago, yet it always seems as though it was just yesterday.

Rob Westerfield was arrested two days after the funeral and charged with first degree murder. Almost solely from the information I provided them, the police were able to obtain a search warrant of the Westerfield home and Rob's car. They found the clothes he had worn the night he took her life, and though he had thoroughly bleached them, the police lab was able to identify bloodstains. The tire jack that had been the murder weapon was found in the trunk of his car. He had washed that, too, but a tiny strand of Andrea's hair still clung to it.

Rob's defense was that he had gone to the movies the night Andrea was murdered. The cinema parking lot was full, and he left his car at the service station next door. He said that the pumps were closed, but he found

Paulie Stroebel working in the enclosed garage. He said he looked in on Paulie and told him he was leaving the car there and would pick it up after the movies.

He claimed that while he was watching the movie, Paulie Stroebel must have driven to the hideout in his car, killed Andrea, then left the car back at the service station. Rob said he'd left the car at the station at least half a dozen times to get dents fixed, and that on any of those occasions Paulie could have had an extra key made.

He tried to explain away the blood on his clothes and in the ridges of his sneakers by claiming that Andrea had begged him to meet her at the hideout. He said that she had been pestering him with phone calls and phoned him at dinnertime the night she died. She told him that she was going to a mixer with Paulie Stroebel and didn't want him to be mad at her.

"I didn't care who she went out with," Rob explained when he testified at the trial. "She was just a kid in town who had a crush on me. She followed me everywhere. I'd be hanging out in town, and she'd walk by. I'd go bowling, and suddenly she's playing in the next lane. I caught her and her friends hanging out in my grandmother's garage, having a cigarette. I wanted to be nice, so I told her it was all right. She was always begging me to take her for a ride in my car. She was always calling me."

He had an explanation for why he went to the garage-hideout that night. "I got out of the movie," he testified, "and started to drive home. Then I got worried about her. Even though I told her that I wasn't going to meet her, she said she'd wait there for me anyway. I thought I'd better drop by and make sure she went home before her dad got angry. The light in the garage had burned out. I kind of fumbled along and walked around behind the van. That's where Andrea and her friends used to sit on blankets and smoke cigarettes.

"I felt the blanket under my foot. I could just about make out that someone was lying there, and I figured Andrea must have been waiting for me and fallen asleep. Then I knelt down, and I could feel the blood on her face. I ran."

He was asked why he ran. "Because I was scared somebody might think I did it."

"What did you think happened to her?"

"I didn't know. I was scared. But when I found out that the tire jack in my trunk had blood on it, I knew it had to be Paulie who killed her."

He was very slick, and his testimony was well rehearsed. A good-looking young guy, he made a strong impression. But I was Rob Westerfield's nemesis. I remember being on the stand and answering the questions the prosecutor asked.

"Ellie, did Andrea call Rob Westerfield before she went to do homework with Joan?"

"Yes."

"Did he ever make phone calls to her?"

"Sometimes he did, but then if Daddy or Mommy answered, he always hung up. He wanted Andrea to call him because he had his own phone in his room."

"Was there a special reason Andrea called him the night she died?"

"Yes."

"Did you hear the conversation?"

"Just a little of it. I went into her room. She was almost crying. She was telling Rob that she couldn't help it that she was going with Paulie to the mixer, that she had to do it. She didn't want Paulie to tell Daddy that she sometimes met Rob in the hideout."

"Then what happened?"

"She told Rob she was going to Joan's to do homework, and he told her to meet him at the hideout."

"Did you hear him tell her that?"

"No, but I heard her say, 'I'll try, Rob,' and when she hung up, she said, 'Rob wants me to leave Joanie's early and meet him in the hideout. He's mad at me. He said I'm not supposed to go out with anyone else.'"

"Andrea told you that?"

"Yes."

"Then what happened?"

And then on the stand I gave away Andrea's last secret and broke the sacred promise I had made to her—the "cross-my-heart-and-hope-to-die" promise that I would never tell anyone about the locket Rob had given her. It was gold and heart-shaped, and had little blue stones. Andrea had shown her that Rob had had their initials engraved on the back. I was crying by then because I missed my sister so much, and it hurt to talk about her. And so, without being asked, I added, "She put on her locket before she left, so I was pretty sure she would meet him."

"A locket?"

"Rob gave her a locket. Andrea wore it under her blouse so no one could see it. But I could feel it when I found her in the garage."

I remember sitting on the witness stand. I remember trying not to look at Rob Westerfield. He kept staring at me; I could feel the hatred coming from him.

And I swear I could read the thoughts of my mother and father who were sitting behind the prosecutor: Ellie, you should have told us; you should have told us.

My testimony was pounced on by the defense attorneys. They brought out that Andrea often wore a locket that my father had given her, that it was on top of her dresser after her body was found, that I was making up stories or that I was repeating the stories Andrea had made up about Rob.

"Andrea was wearing the locket when I found her," I insisted. "I could feel it." I burst out, "That's why I know it was Rob Westerfield who was in the hideout when I found Andrea. He came back for the locket."

Rob's attorneys became furious, and that remark was ordered stricken from the record. The judge turned to the jurors and told them not to consider it in any way.

Did anyone believe what I told them about the locket Rob gave Andrea? I don't know. The case went to the jury, and they were out for nearly a week. We learned that a few jurors leaned at first toward a manslaughter verdict, but the rest insisted on a murder conviction. They believed that Rob had carried that tire jack into the garage because he intended to kill Andrea.

I reread the transcript of the trial the first few times Westerfield came up for parole, and I wrote vehement letters protesting his release. But since he has served nearly twenty-two years, I knew that this time the parole may well be granted, and that is why I have come back to Oldham-on-the-Hudson.

I am thirty years old, live in Atlanta, and work as an investigative reporter with the *Atlanta News*. The editor in chief, Pete Lawlor, considers it a personal affront if anyone on the staff takes even a yearly vacation, so I expected him to hit the ceiling when I told him I needed a few days off immediately and might need more later.

"You getting married?"

I told him that was the last thing on my mind.

"Then what's up?"

I had not told anyone at the newspaper anything about my personal life, but Pete Lawlor is one of those people who seemed to know everything about everybody. Thirty-one years old, balding, and always fighting to get off those ten extra pounds, he was probably the smartest man I've ever met. Six months after I'd started at the *News* and covered the story of a murdered teenager, he said in an offhand manner, "That must have been a tough one for you to write. I know about your sister."

He didn't expect a response, nor did I give him one, but I felt his empathy. It did help. It had been an emotionally wrenching assignment.

"Andrea's killer is coming up for parole. I'm afraid he may get it this time, and I want to see if there's anything I can do to stop it."

Pete leaned back in his chair. He always wore an open-necked shirt and a sweater. Sometimes I've wondered if he even *owns* a jacket. "How long has he served?"

"Almost twenty-two years."

"How many times has he come up for parole?"

"Twice."

"Any problems while he was in prison?"

I felt like a schoolgirl being grilled. "None that I know of."

"Then he'll probably get out."

"I expect he will."

"So why bother?"

"Because I must."

Pete Lawlor doesn't believe in wasting either time or words. He didn't ask any more questions. He just nodded. "Okay. When's the hearing?"

"The hearing is next week. I get to speak to someone on the staff of the parole board on Monday."

He turned back to the paperwork on his desk, effectively dismissing me. "Go ahead," he said. But, as I turned away, he added, "Ellie, you're not as tough as you think you are."

"Yes, I am." I didn't bother to thank him for the time off.

That was yesterday. The next day, Saturday, I flew from Atlanta to the Westchester County Airport and rented a car.

I could have stayed at a motel in Ossining, near Sing Sing, the prison where Andrea's killer has been incarcerated. Instead I drove fifteen miles further to my old hometown, Oldham-on-the-Hudson, and managed to find the quaint Parkinson Inn that I vaguely remembered as a place where we sometimes went for lunch or dinner.

The Inn was obviously flourishing. On this chilly Saturday afternoon in October, the tables in the dining room were filled with casually dressed people, mostly twosomes and family groups. I felt a moment of acute nostalgia. This is the way I remembered my early life, the four of us having lunch here on Saturday, and then sometimes Dad would drop Andrea and me at the movies. She'd be meeting her friends, but she didn't mind that I tagged along.

"Ellie is a good kid, she's not a snitch," she'd say. If the movie got out early enough, we'd all rush to the garage-hideout where Andrea and Joan and Margy and Dottie would share a quick cigarette before going home.

Andrea had an answer ready if Daddy said he smelled smoke on her clothing. "Can't help it. We had pizza after the movie and a lot of other people were smoking." Then she'd wink at me.

The Inn had only eight guest rooms, but one was still available, a spartan space containing a bed with an iron headboard, a two-drawer bureau, a night table, and a chair. It faced east, the direction where the house we lived in was located. The sun that afternoon was uncertain, slipping in and out of clouds, one moment blinding, the next completely concealed.

I stood at the window, staring out, and it seemed to me I was seven years old again and watching my father holding the music box.

7

I remember that afternoon as the defining day of my life. Saint Ignatius of Loyola said, "Give us the child until he is seven years old, and I will show you the man."

I assume that he meant the woman as well. I stood there, quiet as a mouse, watching the father I worshiped, sobbing and hugging my dead sister's picture against his chest, while the fragile sounds from that music box drifted around him.

I look back and wonder if it ever occurred to me to run to him, throw my arms around him, absorb his grief and let his mingle with mine. But the fact is, even then I understood that his grief was unique and that no matter what I did, I could never really ease his pain.

Lieutenant Edward Cavanaugh, decorated officer of the New York State Police, hero of a dozen life-threatening situations, had not been able to prevent the murder of his beautiful, headstrong, fifteen-year-old daughter, and his agony could not be shared with a fellow mourner, however close by blood.

Over the years I came to understand that when grief is not shared, blame is passed around like a hot potato instead, thrust from one to the other, eventually sticking to the hands of the one least able to throw it away.

In this case, that person was me.

Detective Longo lost no time following up on my violation of Andrea's trust. I had given him two leads, two possible suspects: Rob Westerfield, who used his stunning, sultry, rich playboy persona to turn Andrea's head, and Paul Stroebel, the shy and backward teenager with the crush on the gorgeous band member who had enthusiastically cheered his game-winning performances on the football field.

Root, root, root for the home team—no one was better at that than Andrea!

As Andrea's autopsy results were being studied, and preparations made for her interment in Gate of Heaven Cemetery, next to the paternal grandparents I only dimly remembered, Detective Longo was interrogating both Rob Westerfield and Paul Stroebel. Both protested that they had not seen Andrea on Thursday evening, nor had either made plans to meet her.

Paul was working in the gas station, and although it closed at seven, he claimed he had stayed longer in the shop to complete some minor repairs on several cars.

Rob Westerfield swore that he had gone to the local cinema, and even produced a ticket stub as proof.

I remember standing at Andrea's grave, a single long-stemmed rose in my hand, and after the prayers had been offered, being told to place it on Andrea's casket. I remember, too, that I felt dead inside, as dead and still as Andrea had been when I knelt over her in the hideout.

I wanted to tell her how sorry I was that I had told her secret about her meetings with Rob, and with equal passion I wanted to tell her that I was sorry I hadn't told about them the minute we knew she had left Joan's but not reached home. But of course I said nothing. I dropped the flower, but it slid off the casket, and before I could retrieve it, my grandmother stepped past me to place her flower on the casket and her foot crushed my rose into the muddy earth.

A moment later we filed out of the cemetery, and in that crowd of solemn faces I caught angry stares directed at me. The Westerfields stayed away, but the Stroebels were there, standing on either side of Paulie, their shoulders touching his. I remember the feeling of blame surrounding me, overwhelming me, choking me. It was a feeling I have never lost.

I had tried to tell them that when I was kneeling at Andrea's body, I heard someone breathing, but they were skeptical because I was so hysterical and frightened. My own breathing when I ran from the woods was as labored and rattling as it became during my bouts of croup. But over the years I have been awakened many times by the same nightmare: I am kneeling over Andrea's body, slipping in her blood and listening to the harsh, animal-like breathing and high-pitched giggle of a predator.

I know with the instinct of fear that has saved humankind from extinction that Rob Westerfield has a beast lurking inside him, and if he is freed, he will strike again.

8

When I felt tears stinging the back of my eyes, I turned away from the window, reached for my backpack, and tossed it on the bed. I almost smiled as I unpacked, realizing that I had a nerve to even mentally criticize Pete Lawlor's casual wardrobe. I was wearing jeans and a turtleneck sweater. In the bag, besides a nightshirt and underwear, I was carrying only a long wool skirt and two other sweaters. My favorite shoes are clogs, which is just as well because I'm five feet nine. My hair has kept its sandy shade. I wear it long and either twist it up or clip it at the back of my neck.

Pretty, feminine Andrea resembled Mother. I have my father's strong features, which work better on a man than on a woman. No one would ever call me the star on the Christmas tree.

Tantalizing aromas were drifting up from the dining room, and I realized I was hungry. I'd caught an early flight from Atlanta and, of course, had to be at the airport well ahead of departure time. The food service—excuse me, *beverage* service—had consisted of a cup of bad coffee.

It was one-thirty when I went down to the dining room, and the lunch crowd was thinning out. It was easy to get a table, a small booth near the blazing fire. I didn't realize how chilled I felt until the warmth penetrated my hands and feet.

"May I get you a beverage?" asked the waitress, a smiling gray-haired woman with the name tag "Liz."

Why not? I thought, and ordered a glass of red wine.

When she came back, I told her I'd decided on the onion soup, and she said that it was always a favorite.

"Have you been here long, Liz?" I asked.

"Twenty-five years. Hard for me to believe."

She might have waited on us years ago. "Still fix peanut butter and jelly sandwiches?" I asked.

"Oh, sure. Did you used to have them?"

"Yes, I did." I was immediately sorry I'd mentioned it. The last thing in the world I wanted was for old-timers to realize I was the "sister of the girl who was murdered twenty-three years ago."

But Liz was obviously used to having passersby mention having dined at the Inn years ago, and without further comment she left the table.

I sipped the wine and gradually began to remember

specific occasions when we'd been here as a family, back when we *were* a family. Birthdays, usually, and stopping for dinner after we'd gone for drives. The last time we came here was, I think, during my grandmother's visit after she'd lived in Florida for nearly a year. I remember that my father picked her up at the airport and met us here. We had a cake for her. The pink lettering on the white frosting read, "Welcome home, Grandma."

She began to cry. Happy tears. The last happy tears ever shed in our family. And that thought wrenched me back to the tears shed the day of Andrea's funeral and the terrible public confrontation between my mother and father.

9

After the funeral, we went back to the house. The women in the neighborhood had put together a spread, and a lot of people were there: our old neighbors from Irvington, my mother's new friends from our parish, her Wednesday bridge club members, and her fellow volunteers from the hospital. Many of my father's longtime friends and fellow officers were there as well, some of them in uniform and on duty, able to pause only long enough to offer brotherly solace.

The five girls who were Andrea's particular pals, their eyes swollen with tears, were clustered in a corner. Joan, whose house Andrea had been visiting, was especially distressed and was being comforted by the other four.

I felt apart from all of them. My mother, looking very sad in a black suit, was sitting on the couch in the living room, friends on either side, holding her hand or pressing a cup of tea on her. "It will warm you up,

Genine. Your hands are so cold." She was composed even though her eyes kept welling with tears, and several times I heard her say, "I can't believe she's gone."

She and my father had clung together at the graveside, but now they sat in different rooms, she in the living room, he on the enclosed back porch that had been turned into a sort of den for him. My grandmother was in the kitchen with some of her old friends from Irvington, sadly reliving happier times in their lives.

I wandered among them, and even though there is no question that people spoke to me and told me what a brave little girl I was, I felt acutely alone. I wanted Andrea. I wanted to go up to my sister's room and find her there and curl up on the bed with her while she chatted endlessly on the phone with her friends or with Rob Westerfield.

Before she called him, she would say, "Can I trust you, Ellie?"

Of course she could. He almost never called her at home because she was forbidden to have anything to do with him, and there was always the worry that even if she answered the phone on her extension, my mother or father might pick up downstairs and hear his voice.

My mother or father? Or was it just my father? Would my mother have been upset? After all, Rob was a Westerfield, and both Mrs. Westerfields, senior and junior, occasionally attended meetings of the Women's Club, to which my mother belonged.

We got back to the house at noon. At two o'clock, people started to say things like "After all you've been through, you folks need a rest."

I knew that meant that, having paid their respects to the afflicted, having sincerely grieved, they were ready to go home. Any reluctance in leaving was caused by the fact they were also eager to be in our house the moment any developments in tracking down Andrea's killer were reported.

By then everyone had heard about Paulie Stroebel's outburst in school and knew that Andrea had been in Rob Westerfield's car when it was stopped for speeding on the thruway last month.

Paulie Stroebel. Who would ever have guessed that a quiet, introverted kid like that would have a crush on a girl like Andrea, or that she would have agreed to go to the Thanksgiving dance with him?

Rob Westerfield. He had finished a year at college, and he certainly was no dope—anyone could see that. But the rumor was he'd been asked to leave. Apparently he'd just wasted his whole freshman year. He was nineteen when he noticed my sister. What business did he have fooling around with Andrea, a sophomore in high school?

"Wasn't there some story about his having been

involved in what happened to his grandmother at her house?"

It was precisely as I overheard that particular remark that the doorbell rang and Mrs. Storey from the bridge club, who was already in the vestibule, went to answer it. Standing on the porch was Mrs. Dorothy Westerfield, Rob's grandmother and the owner of the estate with the garage where Andrea had died.

She was a handsome, impressive woman, broad-shouldered and full-bosomed. She stood very straight, which made her seem taller than she was. Her iron-gray hair had a natural wave, and she wore it brushed back from her face. At seventy-three, her eyebrows were still dark and drew attention to the intelligent expression in her light brown eyes. A heavy jaw line kept her from ever having been considered pretty, but on the other hand, it added to her overall impression of commanding strength.

She was hatless and wearing a beautifully cut dark gray winter coat. She stepped into the vestibule, and her eyes swept the interior as she looked for my mother, who by then was pulling her hands away from her friends and struggling to stand up.

Mrs. Westerfield went directly to her. "I was in California and could not get back until now, but I had to tell you, Genine, how heartbroken I am for you and your family. Many years ago I lost a teenage son in a skiing accident, so I do understand what you are going through."

As my mother nodded gratefully, my father's voice rang through the room. "But it wasn't an accident, Mrs. Westerfield," he said. "My daughter was *murdered.* She was bludgeoned to death, and your grandson may have been the one who killed her. In fact, knowing his reputation, you must be aware that he is the prime suspect. So please get out of here. You're damn lucky that you're still alive yourself. You still don't believe he was involved in that burglary when you were shot and left for dead, do you?"

"Ted, how can you *say* that?" my mother pleaded. "Mrs. Westerfield, I apologize. My husband . . ."

Except for the three of them, the crowded house might have been empty. Everyone was frozen in place, as in the statues game I used to play as a child.

My father might have been a figure from the Old Testament. He had taken off his tie, and his shirt was open at the collar. His face was as white as the shirt, and his blue eyes were almost black. He had a full head of naturally dark brown hair, but at that moment it seemed even thicker, as if anger had sent bolts of electricity through it.

"Don't you *dare* apologize for me, Genine," he shouted. "There isn't a cop in this house who doesn't know that Rob Westerfield is rotten through and through. My daughter—*our* daughter—is *dead*. Now you—" he walked over to Mrs. Westerfield—"you get out of my house, and take your crocodile tears with you."

Mrs. Westerfield had turned as pale as my father. She did not answer him, but gave my mother's hand a squeeze and walked unhurriedly to the door.

When she spoke, my mother did not raise her voice, but her tone was a whiplash. "You *want* Rob Westerfield to be the one who took Andrea's life, don't you, Ted? You know Andrea was crazy about him, and you couldn't stand that. You want to know something? You were *jealous*! If you had been reasonable and let her go out with him, or any other boy for that matter, she wouldn't have had to make secret dates . . ."

Then my mother imitated my father's way of speaking: "Andrea, you may only go to a school function with a high school boy. You will *not* drive in his car. I will pick you up, and I will deliver you."

The skin over my father's cheekbones reddened, whether from embarrassment or fury I am still not sure. "If she had obeyed me, she would still be alive today," he said evenly, his voice quiet, but bitter. "If you had not been kissing the hand of anyone named Westerfield—"

"It's a damn good thing you're not investigating this case," my mother said, interrupting him. "What about that Stroebel kid? What about that handyman, Will

Nebels? What about that salesman? Have they found *him* yet?"

"What about the tooth fairy?" Now my father's tone was contemptuous. He turned and went back into the den where his friends were gathered. He closed the door behind him. Finally there was complete silence.

10

My grandmother had planned to stay with us that night, but sensing that it would be better if my father and mother were alone, she packed her bag and departed with a friend from Irvington. She would stay there overnight and be driven to the airport the next morning.

Her hope for some sort of reconciliation between my mother and father after the bitter exchange of words was not to be.

My mother slept in Andrea's room that night and every night for the next ten months, until after the trial, when not even all the Westerfield money and a high-powered defense team could save Rob Westerfield from being found guilty of murder in Andrea's death.

Then the house was sold. My father moved back to Irvington, and my mother and I began a nomadic life, starting in Florida near my grandmother. My mother, who had worked briefly as a secretary before marriage, got a job with a national hotel chain. Always very attractive, she was also smart and diligent, and worked her way up rapidly to being a kind of troubleshooter, which entailed moving every eighteen months or so to a different hotel in a different city.

Unfortunately, she applied that same diligence to concealing from everyone—except me—the fact that she became an alcoholic, drinking steadily each day from the moment she arrived home from work. For years she managed to retain enough control to do her job, with only occasional bouts of "flu" when she needed several days to sober up.

The drinking sometimes made her silent and morose. At other times she became loquacious, and it was during those sessions that I realized how passionately in love she was with my father.

"Ellie, I was crazy about him from the time I first laid eyes on him. Did I ever tell you how we met?"

Over and over again, Mother.

"I was nineteen and had been working six months at my first secretarial job. I bought a car, an orange crate on wheels with a gas tank. I decided to see how fast I could go in it on the thruway. Then all of a sudden I heard a siren and in the rearview mirror saw a dome light flashing behind me, and then a voice on a bull-horn told me to pull over. Your father gave me a ticket and a lecture that had me in tears. But when he showed up for my court date, he announced he was going to give me driving lessons."

Other times she would lament, "He was terrific in so many ways. He's a college graduate; he's got looks and brains. But he was only comfortable with his old friends and didn't like change. That's why he didn't want to move to Oldham. The problem wasn't where we lived. It was that he was too strict with Andrea. Even if we'd stayed in Irvington, she'd still have been making secret dates."

Those recollections almost always ended with "If only we'd known where to look when she didn't come home." Meaning, if only I had told them about the hideout.

The third grade in Florida. The fourth and fifth in Louisiana. The sixth in Colorado. The seventh in California. The eighth in New Mexico.

My father's check for my support arrived without fail on the first of the month, but I saw him only occasionally those first few years and then not at all. Andrea, his golden child, was gone. There was nothing left between him and my mother except bitter regret and frozen love, and whatever he felt for me was not enough to make him desire my presence. Being under the same roof with me seemed to open whatever scar tissue he had managed to grow over his wounds. If only I had told about the hideout.

As I grew up, my adoration of my father was

replaced with resentment. What about asking yourself: If only I had questioned Ellie instead of ordering her to bed? What about that, Daddy?

Fortunately, by the time I began college we had been in California long enough to establish residency, and I went to UCLA as a journalism major. My mother died of liver failure six months after I received my master's degree, and, wanting yet another fresh start, I applied for and got the job in Atlanta.

Rob Westerfield did more than murder my sister that November night twenty-two years ago. As I sat in the Inn and watched Liz place the steaming onion soup in front of me, I began to wonder what our lives would have been if Andrea were still alive.

My mother and father would still be together, would still be living here. My mother had great plans for improving the house, and my father undoubtedly would have settled in. Driving through the town, I observed that the rural village I remembered had grown considerably. It now had the look of an upscale Westchester town, which was exactly what my mother had foreseen. My father would no longer have had to drive five miles for a quart of milk.

Whether or not we had remained here, there was no question that if Andrea had lived, my mother would still be alive. She'd have had no need to find comfort and forgetfulness in alcohol.

My father might even have taken note of my hero worship, and in time, perhaps when Andrea went off to college, he might have given me some of the attention I craved from him.

I sipped my soup.

It was exactly as I remembered it.

11

Liz was back at the table, a basket of crusty bread in her hands. She lingered for a moment. "From what you mentioned about the peanut butter and jelly sandwiches, I guess you used to come here."

I had piqued her curiosity.

"A long time ago," I said, trying to sound casual. "We moved away when I was a child. I live in Atlanta now."

"I was there once. It's a nice city." She drifted away.

Atlanta, the Gateway to the South. It proved to be a good move for me. When so many of my journalism classmates were only interested in breaking into television, I for some reason always knew that the printed word held the greatest attraction for me. And at last I began to develop a sense of permanence.

Fresh-out-of-college employees are not paid much at newspapers, but my mother had a modest life insurance policy that gave me the freedom to furnish a small three-room apartment. I shopped carefully in second-hand furniture stores and at closeout sales. When the apartment was furnished, I was almost dismayed to realize that I had unconsciously recreated the overall effect of the living room of our home in Oldham: Blues and reds in the carpet. A blue upholstered couch and club chair. Even an ottoman, although it was a tight fit.

It brought back so many memories: My father dozing in the club chair, his long legs stretched on the ottoman; Andrea unceremoniously pushing them over and plopping down; his eyes opening, his smile of welcome to his saucy, pretty, golden child . . .

I always tiptoed around when he was napping, not wanting to disturb his sleep. When Andrea and I were clearing the table after dinner, I would listen intently as he began to unwind over a second cup of coffee and tell my mother what had happened that day on the job. I was in awe of him. My father, I bragged to myself, saved people's lives.

Three years after the divorce, he remarried. By then I had paid my second and final visit to him in Irvington. I did not want to go to his wedding, nor did I care when he wrote to tell me I had a baby brother. His second marriage had produced the son I was supposed to be. Edward James Cavanaugh, Jr., is about seventeen now.

My last contact with my father was to write and inform him that my mother had died and I would like to have her ashes shipped to Gate of Heaven Cemetery and interred in Andrea's grave. If that did not meet with his approval, I would have her buried with her own parents in their plot in the cemetery.

He wrote back, expressing sympathy for me, and told me he had made the arrangements I requested. He also invited me to come and visit in Irvington.

I sent the ashes and declined the invitation.

The onion soup had warmed me up, and the memories had made me restless. I decided to go upstairs to my room, get my jacket, and drive around town. It was only two-thirty, and I was already beginning to wonder why I hadn't waited until tomorrow to come here. I had an appointment with someone named Martin Brand at the parole office at ten o'clock on Monday morning. I would make an impassioned effort to convince him that Rob Westerfield should not be released, but as Pete Lawlor told me, it was probably a useless gesture.

The message light on the phone in my room was blinking. I had an urgent message to call Pete Lawlor. He picked up on the first ring. "You seem to have a gift for being in the right place at the right time, Ellie," he said. "It's just coming over the wire services. The Westerfields are holding a press conference in fifteen minutes. CNN is covering it. Will Nebels, the handyman who was questioned in your sister's murder, has just made a statement claiming he saw Paul Stroebel in Rob Westerfield's car the night Andrea was killed. He claims he saw him go into the garage with something in his hand, then run out ten minutes later, get back in the car, and drive away."

"Why didn't Nebels tell that story years ago?" I snapped.

"He claims he was afraid someone would try to blame him for your sister's death."

"How was it that he saw all this happen?"

"He was in the grandmother's house. He'd done some repairs there and knew the code for the alarm. He also knew that the grandmother had a habit of leaving loose cash in drawers around the house. He was broke and needed money. He was in the master bedroom, which has windows overlooking the garage, and when the car door opened, he got a good look at Stroebel's face."

"He's lying," I said flatly.

"Watch the press conference," Pete told me, "then cover the story. You're an investigative reporter." He paused. "Unless it's too close to home for you."

"It's not," I said. "I'll talk to you later."

12

The news conference was held in the White Plains office of William Hamilton, Esq., the criminal attorney retained by the Westerfield family to prove Robson Parke Westerfield's innocence.

Hamilton opened the proceedings by introducing himself. He was standing between two men. One I recognized from his pictures as Rob's father, Vincent Westerfield. He was a distinguished figure in his mid-sixties, with silver hair and patrician features. On Hamilton's other side, a visibly nervous, somewhat bleary-eyed fellow, who could have been anywhere between sixty and seventy, was compulsively opening and closing his interlocked fingers.

He was introduced as Will Nebels. Hamilton gave a brief summary of his background. "Will Nebels has worked in Oldham for years as a handyman. He often worked for Mrs. Dorothy Westerfield at her country home, the one at which Andrea Cavanaugh's body was found in the garage. Along with many other people, Mr. Nebels was questioned as to his whereabouts that Thursday evening when Andrea lost her life. Mr. Nebels claimed at the time that he had dinner at the counter in the local diner and went directly home. He had been seen at the diner, and there was no reason to doubt his story.

"However, when best-selling true-crime writer Jake Bern, who is writing a book about Andrea Cavanaugh's death and Rob Westerfield's claim of innocence, spoke to Mr. Nebels, new facts came to light."

Hamilton turned to Will Nebels. "Will, may I ask you to tell the media exactly what you told Mr. Bern?"

Nebels shifted nervously. He looked uncomfortable dressed as he was in a shirt and tie and suit that I was sure they'd put on him just for the occasion. It's an old defense trick, one I've seen hundreds of times in court. Dress up the defendant, cut his hair, make sure he's clean-shaven, give him a shirt and tie, even if he's never buttoned a collar in his life. The same was often true for defense witnesses.

"I feel bad," Nebels began, his voice hoarse. I noticed how thin and pale he was and wondered if he were ill. I only vaguely remembered him. He had done some odd jobs for us, but I remembered him as being pretty beefy.

"It's something I've been living with, and when the

writer fellow started talking to me about the case, I knew I had to get it off my chest."

He then gave the same story that had come over the wires. He had seen Paul Stroebel drive up to the garage-hideout in Rob Westerfield's car and go into the garage carrying a heavy object. The insinuation, of course, was that the object was the tire jack that had been used to bludgeon Andrea to death, the one that had been found in the trunk of Rob Westerfield's car.

Then it was Vincent Westerfield's turn to speak. "For twenty-two years my son has been locked in a prison cell amidst hardened criminals. He has always protested his innocence in this terrible crime. He went to the movies that night. He parked at the service station next door to the cinema where the family cars are routinely serviced and where the key to his car could easily have been duplicated. It had been in the station at least three times in the previous months to have minor dents removed.

"Paul Stroebel was working there that night. The pumps had closed at seven o'clock, but he was servicing a car in the interior service area. Rob spoke to Paul, told him he was leaving his car in the service lot while he was at the film. We know Paul has always denied this account of events, but now we have proof he was lying. While my son was watching that movie, Stroebel took his car, went to what they called the hideout, and killed that girl."

He drew himself up, and his voice became deeper and louder. "My son is coming up for parole. From what we are led to understand, he will be released from prison. That isn't good enough. With this newly discovered evidence we will seek a new trial, and we believe that this time Rob will be acquitted. We can only hope that Paul Stroebel, the real killer, will be put on trial and placed behind bars for the rest of his life."

I was watching the news conference on a television in the little sitting room on the main floor of the Inn. I was so enraged I wanted to throw something at the screen. For Rob Westerfield it was a win-win situation. If he was found guilty again, they couldn't put him back in prison. He'd already served his sentence. If he was acquitted, the state would never put Paulie Stroebel on trial on the word of an unreliable witness like Will Nebels. Nonetheless, in the eyes of the world, he would be the murderer.

I guess other people had heard about the conference because as soon as I turned it on, they began drifting in. The desk clerk was the first to make a comment. "Paulie Stroebel. Come on, that poor guy wouldn't hurt a fly."

"Well, a lot of people think he did a lot more than hurt a fly," said one of the waitresses I'd noticed in the dining room. "I wasn't here when it happened, but I've heard a lot of talk. You'd be surprised how many people think Rob Westerfield is innocent."

The members of the media at the conference were hurling questions at Will Nebels. "Do you realize you could go to prison for breaking, entering, and perjury?" I heard a reporter ask.

"Let me answer that," Hamilton said. "The statute of limitations has passed. Mr. Nebels is in no danger of incarceration. He has come forward to right a wrong. He had no idea that Andrea Cavanaugh was in the garage that night, nor at the time did he know what had happened to her. Unfortunately, he panicked when he realized that his testimony would put him at the scene of a murder, so he kept quiet."

"Were you promised any money in exchange for this testimony, Mr. Nebels?" another reporter asked.

Exactly my question, I thought.

Again Hamilton took over. "Absolutely not."

Will Mr. Nebels get to play himself in the movie? I wondered.

"Has Mr. Nebels made a statement to the district attorney?"

"Not yet. We wanted the fair-minded public to be aware of his statement before there is any spin put on it by the prosecutor. The point is this—it is a terrible thing to say, but if Andrea Cavanaugh had been sexually molested, Rob Westerfield would have been out of prison long ago on DNA evidence. As it stands, it was his very concern that entrapped him. Andrea had begged him to meet her at the hideout. Over the phone she told him that she had agreed to a date with Paul Stroebel only because she thought he was the last person who would provoke jealousy in a young man like Rob Westerfield.

"The fact is that Andrea Cavanaugh was chasing Rob Westerfield. She called him frequently. He didn't care whom she dated. She was a flirt, boy crazy, a 'popular' girl."

I cringed at the insinuation.

"Rob's only mistake was to panic when he found Andrea Cavanaugh's body. He went home, never realizing that he was transporting the murder weapon in his car and that Andrea's blood was already staining the trunk of that car. That night he put his slacks and shirt and jacket in the washing machine because he was frightened."

Not too frightened to bleach the color out of them in his effort to get rid of bloodstains, I thought.

The cameras switched to the CNN anchor. "Observing this interview with us from his home in Oldham-on-the-Hudson is retired detective Marcus Longo. Mr. Longo, what do you think of Mr. Nebels's statement?"

"It is a total fabrication. Robson Westerfield was found guilty of murder because he *is* guilty of murder. I can understand the anguish of his family, but to try to shift the blame to an innocent, special-needs person is beneath contempt."

Bravo, I thought. The memory of Detective Longo years ago sitting with me in the dining room, telling me that it was all right to give up Andrea's secrets, vividly replayed itself in my mind. Longo was about sixty now, a long-faced man with heavy, dark brows and a roman nose. His remaining hair was a salt-and-pepper fringe around his head. But he had an innate dignity that heightened the effect of his obvious scorn for the charade we had just witnessed.

He still lived in Oldham. I decided that at some point I would call him.

The news conference was over, and people began to drift out of the room. The desk clerk, a studious-looking young man who looked as if he was fresh out of college, came over to me. "Is everything okay with your room, Miss Cavanaugh?"

The waitress was passing the sofa where I was sitting. She turned and looked at me sharply, and I knew she wanted to ask if I was any relation to the young girl who was murdered in the Westerfield case.

It was the first indication that I would have to givc up the personal anonymity I craved if I stayed in Oldham.

So be it, I thought. This is something I have to do.

13

Mrs. Hilmer still lived in the same house down the street from ours. There were four other houses now separating it from the home we had lived in for those few years. It was obvious that the people who now owned ours had fulfilled Mother's dream for it. It had been expanded on both sides and in the back. It had always been a good-sized farmhouse, but now it was a truly lovely dwelling, substantial yet graceful, with gleaming white clapboard and dark green shutters.

I slowed the car as I drove past, and then, because on this quiet Sunday morning I didn't think anyone would notice, I stopped.

The trees had grown of course. It had been a warm autumn in the Northeast this year, and even though it was now downright chilly, there was still an abundance of gold and crimson leaves shimmering on the branches.

The living room of our house had obviously been

expanded. What about the dining room? I wondered. For an instant I was standing there, holding in my arms the box of silver—or was it silverplate—as Andrea carefully arranged the place settings. *"Today Lord Malcolm Bigbottom will be our guest."*

Mrs. Hilmer had been watching for me. The minute I got out of the car, the front door opened. A moment later I felt her fierce hug. She had always been a small woman, cozily plump with a motherly face and vivacious brown eyes. Now her medium-brown hair was completely silver, and there were lines around her eyes and mouth. But basically she was as I remembered her. For years she sent Mother a Christmas card with a long note, and Mother, who never sent cards, would write back, putting a good face on our newest move and saying how well I was doing in school.

I had written to let her know when Mother died and received a warm and comforting note. I did not send her word when I moved to Atlanta, so I imagine any holiday cards or notes she might have sent were returned. The post office doesn't forward mail for too long these days.

"Ellie, you're so tall," she said now with something between a smile and a laugh. "You were such a little bit of a thing."

"It happened somewhere between my junior and senior years in high school," I told her.

There was coffee perking on the stove and blueberry muffins fresh from the oven. At my insistence we stayed in the kitchen and sat at the banquette. For a few minutes she told me about her family. I had hardly known her son and daughter. Both had been married when we moved to Oldham. "Eight grandchildren," she said proudly. "Unfortunately, none of them live around here, but I still get to see a lot of them." I knew she'd been widowed for many years. "The kids tell me this place is too big for me, but it's home and I love it. When I can't get around anymore, I'll sell it, I guess, but not now."

Briefly I told her a little about my job, and then we began to talk about the reason I was back in Oldham. "Ellie, since the day Rob was led out of the courtroom in handcuffs and shackles, the Westerfields have been insisting that he's innocent and have been fighting to get him released. They've got a lot of people convinced of it, too." Her expression became troubled. "Ellie, having said that, I've got to admit something. I'm beginning to wonder myself if Rob Westerfield wasn't convicted partly because of his reputation as a troublemaker. Everybody thought of him as a bad kid and was only too ready to believe the worst about him."

She had seen the press conference. "There's one thing I believe in that speech Will Nebels made," she said flatly, "and that's that he'd go into old Mrs. Westerfield's house to look for money to steal. Was he there that night? It is possible. On one hand, I wonder what they're giving him to tell that story, and on the other, I think how Paulie went to pieces in class when they announced that Andrea was dead. I watched that teacher testify in court. You never saw a more reluctant witness. You could tell how protective she was of Paulie, but she had to admit that she thought when he ran out of the classroom that he had said, 'I didn't think she was dead.'"

"How is Paulie Stroebel now?" I asked.

"Actually, he's been doing very well. For ten or twelve years after the trial he was terribly reticent. He knew that some people believed he had killed Andrea, and that just about destroyed him. He started working in the deli with his mother and father, and from what I understand stayed very much to himself. But since his father died and he's had to take on more and more responsibility, he's really kind of blossomed. I hope this story of Will Nebels's doesn't unravel him now."

"If Rob Westerfield gets a new trial and is acquitted, it will be as though Paulie has been found guilty," I said.

"Would they arrest him, put him on trial?"

"I'm not a lawyer, but I doubt it. Will Nebels's new testimony might be enough to get Rob Westerfield a new trial and an acquittal, but he'd never be considered credible enough to convict Paulie Stroebel. But the damage will be done, and Paulie will be another Westerfield victim."

"Maybe, maybe not. That's what makes it so hard." Mrs. Hilmer hesitated, then went on. "Ellie, that fellow who's writing a book about the case came to see me. Somebody had told him I was close to your family."

I sensed a warning in her words. "What's he like?"

"Polite. Asked a lot of questions. I was careful of every word that passed my lips. But I'm telling you right now that Bern has a point of view, and he's going to make the facts fit it. He asked if the reason your father was so strict with Andrea was that she would sneak off to meet a lot of different boys."

"That's not true."

"He's going to make it seem as if it was true."

"Yes, she had a crush on Rob Westerfield, but at the end she was afraid of him, too." It was something I hadn't expected to say, but when I did, I realized it was true. "And I was afraid for her," I whispered. "He was so angry at her because of Paulie."

"Ellie, I was in your house. I was there when you testified in court. You never said that you or Andrea were afraid of Rob Westerfield."

Was she implying that I might be creating a dishonest memory to justify my childhood testimony? But then she added, "Ellie, be careful. That writer suggested to me that you were an emotionally unstable child. It's something he's going to imply in his book."

So that's the tack he's going to take, I thought: Andrea was a tramp, I was emotionally unstable, and Paulie Stroebel is a killer. If I hadn't been sure of it before, I knew now that I had my job cut out for me.

"Rob Westerfield may get out of prison, Mrs. Hilmer," I said, and then I added firmly, "but by the time I finish investigating and writing about every dirty detail of his rotten life, no one will want to walk down the block with him, day or night. And if he gets a second trial, no jury will acquit him."

14

On Monday morning at ten o'clock I had my meeting in Albany with Martin Brand, who was on the staff of the parole board. He was a tired-looking man of about sixty, with pouches under his eyes and a thick head of gray hair that was overdue for attention from his barber. He had opened the top button of his shirt and pulled the knot of his tie down a few inches. His florid complexion suggested a problem with high blood pressure.

There was no doubt that he had heard many versions of my protest a thousand times over the years.

"Ms. Cavanaugh, Westerfield has been turned down for parole twice. This time it's my guess the decision will be to let him out."

"He's a recidivist."

"You can't be sure of that."

"You can't be sure that he's not."

"He was offered parole two years ago if he'd admit

to killing your sister, accept responsibility for the crime, and express remorse. He didn't take the offer."

"Oh, come on, Mr. Brand. He had too much to lose by being truthful. He knew you couldn't hold him much longer."

He shrugged. "I forgot that you're an investigative reporter."

"I'm also the sister of the fifteen-year-old girl who didn't get a chance to have a sweet-sixteen party."

The world-weary expression left his eyes for a moment. "Ms. Cavanaugh, I have little doubt that Rob Westerfield is guilty, but I think you have to resign yourself to the fact that he's served his time and that, after a couple of incidents during the first years, he's behaved himself."

I would love to have known what those couple of incidents were, but I was sure Martin Brand was not going to share them with me.

"Something else," he went on. "Even if he is guilty, it was a crime of passion directed at your sister, and the odds of him repeating this kind of crime are almost nil. We have the statistics. Incidents of recidivism decline after age thirty and almost vanish after age forty."

"And there are people who are born without a conscience and once they are uncaged become walking time bombs."

I pushed the chair back and got up. Brand stood up,

too. "Ms. Cavanaugh, here's a piece of unwelcome advice. I get the feeling you've lived with the memory of your sister's brutal murder all your life. But you can't bring her back, and you can't keep Rob Westerfield in prison any longer. And if he goes for a new trial and is acquitted, that's the way it is. You're a young woman. Go home to Atlanta and try to put this tragedy behind you."

"That's good advice, Mr. Brand, and I'll probably take it someday," I said. "But not now."

15

Three years ago, after I'd written a series of articles about Jason Lambert, a serial killer in Atlanta, I received a call from Maggie Reynolds, a New York book editor I'd met on a crime panel. She offered me a contract to convert the articles into a book.

Lambert was a Ted Bundy–type killer. He'd hang around campuses, passing himself off as a student, and then trick young women into getting into his car. Like Bundy's victims, those girls simply disappeared. Fortunately, he hadn't had time to dispose of his last victim when he was captured. He's in prison in Georgia now with 149 years left to serve on his sentence and no chance of parole.

The book did surprisingly well, even clinging for a few weeks to the bottom of *The New York Times* best-seller list. I called Maggie after I left Brand's office. After describing the case and the investigative track I intended to pursue, she readily agreed to give me a contract for a book about Andrea's murder, a book that I promised her would conclusively prove Rob Westerfield's guilt.

"There's a lot of hype about the one Jake Bern is writing," Maggie told me. "I'd like to go toe-to-toe on it with a book from you. Bern broke his contract with us after we spent a fortune on publicity on his last book, trying to build him up."

I figured the project would take about three months of intensive research and writing, and then if Rob Westerfield succeeded in getting a new trial, several months beyond that. The Inn would be too confining and too expensive to stay in over the long haul, so I asked Mrs. Hilmer if she knew of any rental apartments in the area. She waved my suggestion away, insisting that I stay in the guest apartment over her garage.

"I put it in a few years ago in case I ever felt I needed someone around all the time," she explained. "Ellie, it's comfortable, it's quiet, and I'll be a good neighbor, not a nuisance who runs in and out."

"You were always a good neighbor." It was a great solution, and perhaps the only drawback was that it meant driving past our old house on a regular basis. I assumed that eventually repetition would dull the instant flash of pain that hit me now as I passed that acre of property.

"God's Little Acre." Mother had laughingly called it that. She was thrilled to have so much property and was determined to cultivate a garden that would be one of the highlights on the Oldham Garden Club spring tour.

I checked out of the Inn, moved into Mrs. Hilmer's guest apartment, and on Wednesday flew back to Atlanta, arriving in the office at quarter of six in the evening. I knew there was no chance that Pete would have gone home. He was married to the job.

He looked up, saw me, grinned briefly, and said, "Let's talk over a plate of spaghetti."

"What about those ten pounds you're trying to lose?"

"I've decided not to think about them for the next couple of hours."

Pete has an intensity about him that sends electric jolts into the people around him. He went with the *News*, a privately owned daily, right out of graduate school, and within two years he was managing editor. By the time he was twenty-eight he was wearing two hats, editor in chief and publisher, and the "dying Daily," as it had been labeled, suddenly had a new lease on life.

Hiring an investigative crime reporter was one of his ideas to rev up circulation, and getting the job six years ago was a stroke of luck for me. I had just been taken on as a cub reporter. When the guy Pete wanted for the position backed out at the last minute, I was told to fill in, but only until a permanent replacement was found. Then one day, without comment, Pete stopped looking for that replacement. I had the job.

Napoli's is truly the kind of neighborhood restaurant you find all over Italy. Pete ordered a bottle of Chianti and grabbed a chunk of the warm bread that had been deposited on our table. My thoughts went back to the semester I had spent in Rome during my college years. It was one of the few genuinely happy periods of my adult life.

My mother was trying to get on the wagon and was doing reasonably well. She visited me there during my spring break, and we had a wonderful time together. We explored Rome and spent a week in Florence and the hill towns of Tuscany. We capped that off with a visit to Venice. Mother was such a pretty woman, and on that trip, when she was smiling, she looked like her old self. By unspoken agreement the names of Andrea and my father never crossed our lips.

I'm glad I have that memory of her.

The wine came, was approved by Pete, and uncorked. I took a sip of it and plunged into what I had to say. "I've been doing a lot of homework. The whitewash job on Westerfield has every possibility of succeeding. Jake Bern is a good writer. He's already done an article on the case that will be coming out next month in *Vanity Fair.*"

Pete reached for another piece of warm bread. "What can you do about it?"

"I am writing a book that will come out in the spring, the same week Bern's is published." I told him about my call to Maggie Reynolds. Pete had met her at the book party she threw for me in Atlanta. "Maggie is doing it, and she'll put me on the fast track for publication. But in the meantime I've got to counteract Bern's articles and the Westerfield family's press releases."

Pete waited. That was another thing about him—he didn't rush to reassure. And he didn't fill in dead spots in the conversation.

"Pete, I'm fully aware that a series of articles about a crime committed twenty-two years ago in Westchester County, New York, might not be of great interest to a readership in Georgia, and anyhow, I don't think it's the right place to publish them. The Westerfield family is identified with New York."

"Agreed. So what do you propose to do?"

"Take a leave of absence if you can give it to me. Or if that isn't feasible, quit, write the book, and take my chances after it's finished."

The waiter came to the table. We both ordered cannelloni and a green salad. Pete hemmed and hawed for a minute, but then decided on Gorgonzola dressing.

"Ellie, I'll hold your job open for you as long as it's in my power to do it."

"What does that mean?"

"I may not be around much longer myself. I've had a couple of interesting offers that I'm considering."

I was shocked. "But the *News* is your baby."

"We're getting too big for the competition. There's real talk of our being bought out for big bucks. The family is interested. This generation doesn't give a damn about the paper; it's only about the revenue."

"Where are you thinking of going?"

"The *L. A. Times* is probably going to make an offer. The other possibility is Houston."

"Which would you prefer?"

"Until there's an offer on the plate, I'm not wasting my time making choices that may not exist."

Pete didn't wait for me to comment before he went on.

"Ellie, I've been doing a little research of my own on your case. The Westerfields are getting good at criminal defense strategy. They have an impressive team of lawyers just waiting to get a chance to earn a fortune. They have that Nebels guy, and, weasel that he is, some people are going to believe his story. Do what you have to, but please, if Westerfield goes to trial and gets acquitted, swear to yourself that you'll walk away from it."

He looked directly at me. "Ellie, I can tell that you're thinking, 'Not a chance.' I wish I could make you understand that no matter what books you and Bern write, some people are going to go to their graves believing that Westerfield got a bum deal, while others will still be convinced that he's guilty."

Pete meant his advice kindly, but that night as I packed the things I needed for an extended stay in Oldham, I realized that even he had the feeling that, guilty or innocent, Rob Westerfield had served his time, that people would think whatever they wanted about the merits of the case, and that it was time for me to drop it.

Nothing wrong with righteous wrath, I thought. Except when it hangs around too long.

I drove back to Oldham, and the following week Rob Westerfield's parole hearing was held. As expected, the parole was granted, and it was announced that he would be released on October 31.

Halloween, I thought. How appropriate. The night that demons walk the earth.

16

Paulie Stroebel was behind the counter when I opened the door of the delicatessen, setting off the jingling of the bell attached to it.

My vague memory of him was centered at the old service station where he'd worked years ago. He would pump gas into the tank of our car and then spray and polish the windshield until it gleamed. I remember my mother saying, "What a nice boy Paulie is," a sentiment that was never again uttered after he came under suspicion in Andrea's death.

I believe my memory of his physical appearance was partially—or perhaps even solely—based on the pictures of him I saw in the newspapers my mother had kept, newspapers that reported every detail of Andrea's murder and the trial. There is nothing that piques the reading public's interest more than having the handsome son of a wealthy and socially prominent family as the defendant in the murder of a lovely young teenager.

Of course, there were pictures accompanying the text: Andrea's body being carried out of the garage-hideout; her casket being carried out of the church; my mother, her hands clasped, her face contorted with grief; my father, his expression agonized; myself, small and lost; Paulie Stroebel, bewildered and nervous; Rob Westerfield, arrogant, handsome, and sneering; Will Nebels, with an inappropriate ingratiating smile.

Photographers hell-bent on capturing raw human emotion had a field day.

Mother had never told me that she had this collection of newspapers or the transcript of the trial. After her death I was shocked to learn that the bulky suitcase which accompanied us in all our moves was actually a Pandora's box of misery. I suspect now that when drink sent Mother into depressed reverie, she may have opened that suitcase and relived her private crucifixion.

I knew Paulie and Mrs. Stroebel must have heard that I was in town. When he looked up and saw me, he was startled, but then his expression became guarded. I inhaled the wonderful mingled aroma of ham and beef and condiments that seems to be indigenous to fine German delicatessens, and we stood there and took each other's measure.

Paulie's stolid body was more appropriate on a mature man than it had been on the teenager in the newspaper photographs. His pudgy cheeks had thinned out, and the expression in his eyes no longer had the bewildered look of twenty-three years ago. It was a few minutes before six o'clock, closing time, and as I had hoped, there were no last-minute customers waiting to be served.

"Paulie, I'm Ellie Cavanaugh." I walked over to him and extended my hand across the counter. He took it, his grasp firm, even uncomfortably strong.

"I heard you were back. Will Nebels is lying. I wasn't in the garage that night." His voice was a hurt protest.

"I know you weren't."

"It's not fair for him to say that."

The door that separated the kitchen from the front of the store opened, and Mrs. Stroebel came out. I had the immediate impression that she was always alert for even a hint that something wasn't going smoothly with her son.

She had aged, of course, and was no longer the apple-cheeked woman I remembered. Her body was thinner now. Her hair was gray, with only a hint of the daffodil shade I recalled, and she walked with a slight limp. When she saw me, she said, "Ellie?" and when I nodded, her concerned expression lightened into a welcoming smile. She hurried around the counter to embrace me.

After I testified in court, Mrs. Stroebel had come up to me, taken both my hands in hers, and, close to tears, thanked me. The defense attorney had tried to get me to say that Andrea was afraid of Paulie, and I guess on the stand I got pretty definite. "I *didn't* say Andrea was afraid of Paulie 'cause she *wasn't*. She was afraid Paulie would tell Daddy that she sometimes met Rob in the hideout."

"It is so good to see you, Ellie. You're a young lady now, and I'm an old lady," Mrs. Stroebel told me as her lips brushed my cheek. The accent of her native land flowed like honey through her words.

"No, you're not," I protested. The warmth of her welcome, like the warmth of Mrs. Hilmer's greeting, was a dart of light flashing through the unshakable sadness that accompanies my every waking moment. It is a sense of coming home to people who care about me. Here in their presence, even after all this time, I am not a stranger and I am not alone.

"Put the 'Closed' sign on the door, Paulie," Mrs. Stroebel said briskly. "Ellie, you will come home and have dinner with us, won't you?"

"I'd love to."

I followed them in my car. They lived about a mile away in one of the older sections of town. The houses were all late-nineteenth-century and relatively small. But they looked cozy and well kept, and I could imagine generations of families sitting on those front porches in the summertime.

The Stroebels' dog, a yellow Lab, greeted our arrival enthusiastically, and Paulie immediately got his leash and took him for a walk.

Their home was just what I'd expected—inviting, immaculate, and comfortable. I vetoed Mrs. Stroebel's suggestion that I sit in one of the overstuffed chairs in the living room and watch the news on television while she prepared dinner in the kitchen. Instead, I followed her there and sat on a stool at the counter, watching her work, offering to help, but confident she'd decline.

"A simple meal," she warned. "I made a beef stew yesterday. I always serve it the second day. Better that way. Much tastier."

Her hands worked swiftly, preparing the last-minute vegetables to add to the stew, rolling dough for biscuits, breaking greens for a salad. I sat quietly, suspecting she wanted to get the dinner on track and then would talk.

I was right.

It was about fifteen minutes later when, with a nod of satisfaction, she said, "Good. Now before Paulie gets back, you must tell me. Can the Westerfields do this? After twenty-two years, can they try again to make my son a killer?"

"They can try, but they won't succeed."

Mrs. Stroebel's shoulders slumped. "Ellie, Paulie has come such a long way. You know when he was a boy, it was so hard for him. He's not a student. There is a kind of knowledge that is not for him. His father and I always worried so much. Paulie is such a sweet, good person. In school he was so lonely except when he played football. It was the only time he felt he was liked."

It was obviously hard for her to continue. "Paulie was on the second team, so he didn't play much. But then one day they put him in the game, and the other team scored and then—I don't understand all about these games; if his father were alive, he could tell you—Paulie at the last minute got the ball and made a touchdown that won the game.

"Your sister was in the band, the prettiest one of all, as I remember. She was the one who grabbed a megaphone and rushed out onto the field. Paulie told me about it over and over—the cheer Andrea led for him."

Mrs. Stroebel paused, cocked her head as though listening, and then, in a low but exuberant voice, sang: "*We'll cheer for Paulie Stroebel, the best of them all. He's merry, he's jolly, we love him by golly, we'll cheer for Paulie Stroebel, the best of them all.*"

Her eyes glistened as she said, "Ellie, that was the most wonderful moment of Paulie's life. You can't know what it was for him after Andrea died and the Westerfields tried to blame him. I believe he would have died to save her. Our doctor was worried that he might do something to himself. When you are a little different, a little slower, it is very easy to become depressed.

"He's been doing so well in the last few years. More and more he makes the decisions in the store. You know what I mean. Like last year he decided we should put in some tables and hire a girl to serve. Just a simple breakfast, then sandwiches in the afternoon. It's been very popular."

"I noticed the tables."

"Paulie will never have it easy. He will always have to work harder than anyone else. He will be okay unless—"

"Unless people actively start to point at him again and wonder if he's the one who should have been in prison for twenty-two years," I said, interrupting.

She nodded. "Yes. That's what I mean."

We heard the front door open. Paulie's footsteps and the Lab's short bark announced their arrival.

Paulie came into the kitchen. "It's not fair of that man to say I hurt Andrea," he said, then abruptly went upstairs.

"It is beginning to consume him again," Mrs. Stroebel said flatly.

17

The day after I saw the Stroebels I tried to reach Marcus Longo, the detective who had investigated Andrea's murder. The answering machine picked up, and I left a message explaining who I was and gave my cell phone number. For a few days I heard nothing.

I was terribly disappointed. After seeing how strongly Longo had expressed himself on television about Rob Westerfield's guilt, I'd thought he'd leap to the phone to get back to me. I'd just about given up on him when, on October 30, my cell phone rang. When I answered, a quiet voice asked, "Ellie, is your hair still the color of sand with sunbeams running through it?"

"Hello, Mr. Longo."

"I just got back from Colorado, which is why you haven't heard from me," he said. "Our first grandchild arrived Tuesday. My wife is still out there. Can you have dinner with me tonight?"

"I'd love to." I told him I was staying in Mrs. Hilmer's guest apartment.

"I know where Mrs. Hilmer lives."

There was the slightest pause as we both thought that of course he did—it's just down the road from our old house.

"I'll pick you up at seven, Ellie."

I was watching for his car and hurried downstairs when it pulled off the road and onto the long driveway. The driveway forks, and the garage with the guest apartment is at the end on the right side. At one time it had been a stable, and it is actually a distance from the house. I didn't want him to take the wrong turn.

There are some people in this world with whom we feel immediately comfortable. That was the way it was with Marcus Longo as soon as I slid into the passenger seat.

"I've thought a lot about you over the years," he said as he made a U-turn. "Have you been to Cold Spring since you've been back?"

"I drove through it one afternoon, but I didn't get out of the car. I remember being there when I was a kid. My mother was always browsing around antique shops."

"Well, it still has those, but now it also has some good restaurants."

Oldham is the northernmost town bordering the

Hudson River in Westchester County. Cold Spring on the Hudson is just over the line in Putnam County, directly across the Hudson from West Point. It is a particularly beautiful town with a Main Street that has the look and feel of the nineteenth century.

I did have strong memories of being there with my mother. In fact, over the years she would sometimes talk about Cold Spring.

"Remember how on Saturday afternoons we would drive down Main Street and stop in all those little antique shops? I was training you girls to have an eye for lovely things. Was that so bad?"

The reminiscences usually began over her second or third scotch. By the time I was ten, I was watering the bottle of Dewar's in the hope of slowing her down. It never really seemed to help.

Longo had made a reservation at Cathryn's, an intimate Tuscan-style grill in a courtyard off Main Street. There, at a corner table, we took each other's measure. Oddly, in person he looked older than he did on television. There were furrows around his eyes and mouth, and even though his body was broad, he did not seem physically strong. I wondered if he had been ill.

"I don't know why I thought you'd be about five feet three," he said. "You were small for your age when you were young."

"I grew quite a bit in high school."

"You look like your father, you know. Have you seen him?"

The question surprised me. "No. And I don't intend to." I didn't want to ask, but I was too curious not to. "Do you see him, Mr. Longo?"

"Please call me Marcus. I haven't seen him in years, but his son, your half-brother, is a terrific all-around athlete. Gets lots of press in the local papers. Your father retired from the state troopers eight years ago when he was fifty-nine. There were some very nice write-ups in the local papers about him. He had an impressive career with the state troopers."

"I assume Andrea's death was mentioned?"

"Yes, and there were quite a few pictures, both recent and from the files. That's how I can see how much you resemble him now."

I didn't answer, and Longo raised his eyebrows. "Obviously that's a compliment. Anyhow, as my mother used to say, 'You grew up nice.'" Abruptly he changed the subject. "Ellie, I read your book and liked it a lot. In it you captured the gut-wrenching pain of the victims' families better than anything I've ever read. I understand where that's coming from."

"I guess you do."

"Why are you here, Ellie?"

"I came because I had to protest against Rob Westerfield getting out on parole."

"Even though you must have known you were wasting your frequent flier miles," he said quietly.

"I knew it was useless."

"Do you feel it necessary to be a voice crying out in the wilderness?"

"My message is not to prepare the way for the Lord. Mine is 'Beware. You're uncaging a killer.'"

"It's still a voice in the wilderness. The doors will open tomorrow morning for Rob Westerfield, and he will walk out of prison. Listen to me carefully now, Ellie. There isn't the faintest doubt that he'll get a new trial. Nebels's testimony will probably be enough to cause reasonable doubt in the jurors' minds, and Westerfield will be acquitted. His record will be expunged, and the Westerfields will live happily ever after."

"That can't happen."

"Ellie, you've got to understand something: The Westerfields need to *make* it happen. Robson Parke Westerfield is the last of the line of what used to be a fine and respected name. Don't be fooled by his father's public image. Behind that philanthropic facade, Vincent Westerfield, Rob's father, is a greedy robber baron, but he craves respectability for his son. And *old* Mrs. Westerfield demands it."

"What does that mean?"

"It means that at age ninety-two she is still as sharp

as a tack and in control of the family fortune. If Rob's name isn't cleared, she's leaving everything to charity."

"Surely Vincent Westerfield has plenty of money in his own right."

"Of course. But nothing compared to his mother's wealth. Mrs. Dorothy Westerfield is a class act, and she no longer has blind faith in her grandson's innocence. Didn't your father throw her out of your house the day of the funeral?"

"Yes, he did. My mother never got over being mortified about that."

"Apparently neither did Mrs. Dorothy Westerfield. Your father publicly confronted her with the fact that the guy who robbed and shot her claimed to be in collusion with Rob."

"Yes, I remember him shouting that."

"And apparently Mrs. Westerfield has remembered it, too. Naturally she has wanted to believe that Rob was wrongly convicted, but I gather the seeds of doubt have always been there and have only grown stronger over the years. Now that she obviously is running out of time, she's put it to the father. If Rob is innocent, see that he's vindicated and the stain removed from the family name. Otherwise, her money, the Westerfield fortune, will go to charity."

"I'm surprised she has that much discretion over it."

"Maybe her husband, Vincent's father, saw something

in his son that caused him to set it up that way. Fortunately for him, he didn't live to see his grandson convicted of murder."

"So the father has to prove Rob's innocence, and suddenly there's an eyewitness who saw Paulie Stroebel go into the hideout. Is old Mrs. Westerfield buying that story?"

"Ellie, what she wants is a new jury to review the case and render the verdict she wants."

"And Vincent Westerfield is going to make sure what that verdict is."

"Let me tell you about Vincent Westerfield. For years he's been hell-bent on destroying the character of the Hudson Valley by getting residential areas zoned for business. He'd put a shopping mall in the middle of the Hudson River if he could figure out how to do it. Do you think he cares what happens to Paulie Stroebel?"

The menus came. I decided on one of the specials, rack of lamb. Marcus ordered salmon.

Over our salads I told him my plans. "When I saw that interview on television with Will Nebels, I originally decided to try to get some investigative articles published. What I've gotten so far is a contract to write a book to refute the one Jake Bern is writing."

"They not only have Bern writing a book but they have a publicity machine geared up and ready to blitz the media. What you saw on television was only the beginning," Longo warned. "I wouldn't be surprised if they suddenly released a picture of Rob in an Eagle Scout uniform."

"I remember my father saying he was rotten through and through. What was the story about the break-in at his grandmother's home?"

Marcus had a cop's memory for crimes. "The grandmother was staying at her house in Oldham. In the middle of the night she heard some kind of noise and woke up. There was a live-in maid, but she was in a separate wing. When Mrs. Westerfield opened the bedroom door, she was shot at point-blank range. She never saw her assailant, but he was arrested a couple of days later. He claimed Rob had put him up to it, said he promised him ten thousand dollars if he finished her off.

"Needless to say, there was no proof. It was the word of a twenty-one-year-old high school dropout with a long juvenile record against a Westerfield."

"What would Rob's motive have been?"

"Money. His grandmother was leaving one hundred thousand dollars directly to him. She thought that sixteen wasn't too young to begin to handle and invest money intelligently. She didn't know that Rob had a drug problem."

"She believed he wasn't involved in the shooting?"

"Yes. Nevertheless, she changed her will. That bequest disappeared."

"So she may have had her doubts about him even then?"

Longo nodded. "And that doubt, combined with the doubt about your sister's murder, has come to a head. In essence she's telling her son and grandson to put up or shut up."

"What about Rob Westerfield's mother?"

"Another very nice lady. She spends almost all her time in Florida. She has an interior design business in Palm Beach. Under her maiden name, I might add. She's very successful. You can look her up on the Internet."

"I've opened a Website," I said.

Longo's eyebrows raised.

"It's the fastest way to spread information. Every day starting with tomorrow and every single day after that I'm going to write about Andrea's murder and Rob Westerfield's guilt on my Website. I'm going to follow up every nasty rumor about him and try to verify each one. I'm going to interview his teachers and classmates from his two prep schools and from his freshman year in Willow College. You don't get thrown out of schools without a reason. It's a long shot, but I'm going to see if I can trace the locket he gave Andrea."

"How well do you remember it?"

"Now, it's blurry, of course. But at the trial I

described it specifically. I have the trial transcript, so I know exactly what I said then—that it was gold, heart-shaped, and had three blue stones in the center, and that the letters R and A were engraved on the back."

"I was in court when you described it. I remember thinking that it sounded expensive, but in reality it was probably one of those twenty-five-dollar pieces of junk that you buy from a cart in a shopping mall. They initial them for a couple of bucks."

"But you didn't believe that I actually touched it when I found Andrea's body in the hideout or that I heard someone breathing near me or that the locket disappeared before the police came?"

"Ellie, you went from hysteria to shock. You testified that when you knelt down, you slid and fell over Andrea's body. I don't think that in the dark, and with what must have been going on in your head, that you could have identified feeling the locket. You said yourself that she always wore it under her blouse or sweater."

"She was wearing it that night. I'm certain of it. Why wasn't it on her when the police came?"

"A reasonable explanation is that he took it after he killed her. His defense was predicated on his claim that she was just a kid with a crush on him and that he had absolutely no interest in her."

"Let's leave it at that for now," I said. "I want to talk

about something else. Tell me about your brand-new grandchild. He's the only baby ever born, I assume."

"Of course he is." Marcus Longo seemed as glad as I to change the subject. Dinner was served, and he told me about his family. "Mark's your age. He's a lawyer. He married a girl from Colorado and got a job with a firm out there. Loves it. I retired a couple of years ago and had heart surgery last winter. We spend most of the cold months in Florida now and are talking about selling out here and buying a little place around Denver so that we can see the kids without crowding in on them."

"Mother and I spent a year or so in Denver."

"You've been in Atlanta for a while, Ellie. Do you consider that home?"

"It's a great city. I have a lot of good friends. I've enjoyed my job, but if the paper I work for is sold as rumored, I don't know that I'll stay there. Maybe someday I'll get that nice feeling of putting down roots and being settled. I don't have it yet. I always feel there is unfinished business. As a kid did you ever go to the movies when you had homework due the next day?"

"Sure."

"You really couldn't enjoy the movie, could you?"

"It's a long time ago, but I guess not."

"I have homework to finish before I can enjoy the movie," I told him.

*

I hadn't turned a light on before I left, and when we got back to Mrs. Hilmer's place, the garage apartment looked dark and lonely. Marcus Longo ignored my protests and insisted on walking me upstairs. He stood there while I fished for my key, and then when I inserted it in the lock and stepped inside, he said firmly, "Double-lock the door."

"Any special reason?" I asked.

"Ellie, to quote you, 'Beware, you're uncaging a killer.'"

"That's right."

"Then listen to your own voice. I'm not telling you not to go after Westerfield, but I *am* telling you to be careful."

I was home just in time to catch the ten o'clock news. The big story was that Rob Westerfield was being released from prison in the morning and that there would be an interview with the press from the family home in Oldham at noon.

I wouldn't miss it for the world, I thought.

18

Sleep did not come easily that night. I would doze and then wake up, knowing that each tick of the clock was bringing Rob Westerfield closer to the moment when he would be released from prison.

I could not take my mind off him or off the event that had kept him behind bars for twenty-two years. In fact, the closer he came to freedom, the more alive Andrea and Mother were to me. If only . . . if only . . . if only . . .

Give it up, part of me screamed. Walk away from it. Put it in the past. I know what I'm doing to my life, and it's not something I want to happen. Somewhere around two o'clock I got up and made a cup of cocoa. I sat by the window as I drank it. The woods that separated our house from old Mrs. Westerfield's estate extend past the Hilmer property and are still there, her privacy buffer. I could slip through them as Andrea did that night, and on the other side make my way to the garage-hideout.

Now there is a tall fence defining the several acres around the Westerfield house. I'm sure there is now a security system that would signal an interloper, or a fifteen-year-old kid. At ninety-two, people don't usually require much sleep. I wondered if Mrs. Westerfield was awake right now, glad to see her flesh and blood released from prison but cringing at the publicity that would accompany it. Her need to clear the family name was as powerful as mine was to see that Paulie Stroebel was not destroyed and that Andrea's name was not dragged in the dirt.

She was an innocent, young kid whose head was turned; then her crush on Rob Westerfield became fear, which was why she went to the hideout that night. She was afraid *not* to meet him when he ordered her to show up.

Sitting in the predawn hours, my subconscious feeling that she was afraid of him, and that I was afraid of him for her, crystallized in my mind. I could vividly see Andrea as she had been that night, clasping the locket around her neck, choking back tears. She didn't want to meet him, but she was caught between a rock and a hard place. And so I added another "if only" to the list. If only she had gone to my parents and confessed to them that she had been meeting Rob.

In that moment we reversed roles, and I became her big sister. I went back to bed and slept fitfully until seven o'clock. I was in front of the television when the media covered Rob Westerfield's exit from Sing Sing prison in a limousine that met him at the gate. The on-the-spot reporter of the channel I watched emphasized that Rob Westerfield had always sworn he was innocent of the crime.

At noon I was back in front of the set for the unveiling of Rob Westerfield to the world.

The interview took place in the library of the family home in Oldham. The sofa on which he sat was placed in front of a wall of leatherbound books, inferring, I assume, his scholarly mind.

Rob was wearing a tan cashmere jacket, an open-necked sport shirt, dark trousers, and loafers. He was always handsome but had become much more so in his maturity. He had his father's patrician features and had learned to conceal the condescending sneer that appeared in all of his early pictures. There was the faintest touch of gray in the roots of his dark hair. His hands were clasped in front of him, and he was leaning slightly forward in a relaxed but attentive pose.

"Good setting," I said aloud. "The only thing missing is a dog at his feet." At the sight of him I could feel the bile rising in my throat.

His interviewer was Corinne Sommers, host of *The Real Story*, the popular syndicated Friday night program. She did a brief intro: "Just released after twenty-two years in prison . . . always protested his innocence . . . will now fight to have his name cleared . . ."

Get on with it, I thought.

"Rob Westerfield, it's an obvious question, but how does it feel to be a free man?"

His smile was warm. His dark eyes under well-shaped eyebrows seemed almost amused. "Unbelievable, wonderful. I'm too big to cry, but that's what I feel like doing. I just go around the house, and it's so wonderful to be able to do normal things, like going into the kitchen and getting a second cup of coffee."

"Then you'll be staying here for a while?"

"Absolutely. My father has furnished a wonderful apartment for me near this house, and I want to work with our lawyers to get a speedy retrial." Now he looked earnestly into the camera. "Corinne, I could have gotten parole two years ago if I'd been willing to say I killed Andrea Cavanaugh and that I regretted that terrible deed."

"Weren't you tempted to do that?"

"Not for a minute," he said promptly. "I have always maintained my innocence, and now, thanks to Will Nebels coming forward, I may at last have a chance to prove it."

You couldn't admit it, you had too much to lose, I thought. Your grandmother would have disowned you.

"You went to the movies the night Andrea Cavanaugh was murdered."

"Yes, I did. And I stayed until the movie was over at nine-thirty. My car was parked at the service station for over two hours. It's only a twelve-minute drive to my grandmother's place from the center of town. Paulie Stroebel had access to the car, and he had been following Andrea around. Even her sister admitted that on the stand."

"The ticket taker at the theater remembers you buying the ticket."

"That's right. And I had the stub to prove it."

"But no one saw you leave the theater at the end of the film?"

"No one *remembers* seeing me," he corrected. "There's a difference."

For just an instant I saw a flash of temper under the amiable smile, and I sat up.

The rest of the interview, however, might have been with a newly returned hostage. "Besides clearing your name, what are you looking forward to doing?"

"Going to New York. Dining in the restaurants that probably didn't exist twenty-two years ago. Traveling, eventually. Getting a job." Now a warm smile from him. "Meeting a special someone. Getting married. Having kids."

Getting married. Having kids. All the things Andrea would never do.

"What are you having for dinner tonight, and who is going to be with you?"

"Just the four of us—my mother, my father, and my grandmother. We just want to be reunited as a family. I asked for a pretty basic dinner: shrimp cocktail, prime rib, baked potato, broccoli, a salad."

How about apple pie? I wondered.

"And apple pie," he concluded.

"And champagne, I imagine."

"Definitely."

"It seems as though you have pretty definite plans for the future, Rob Westerfield. We wish you luck and hope that in a second trial you can prove your innocence."

This is a journalist? I snapped the remote button and went to the table in the dining area where I had my laptop ready and waiting. I got online to my Website and began to write.

"Robson Westerfield, the convicted murderer of fifteen-year-old Andrea Cavanaugh, has just been released from prison and is looking forward to roast beef and apple pie. The sanctification of this killer has just begun, and it will be made at the expense of his young victim and of Paulie Stroebel, a quiet, hard-working man who has had to overcome many difficulties.

"He shouldn't have to overcome this one."

Not bad for a beginning, I thought.

19

Every day Sing Sing Correctional Facility discharges prisoners who have completed serving their sentences or have been paroled. When they leave, they are given jeans, work boots, a jacket, and $40, and unless they are picked up by a family member or friend, they are driven to the bus station or issued a train ticket.

The train station is the equivalent distance of four blocks from the prison. The discharged prisoner walks to the station and takes a train going either north or south.

The train going south terminates in Manhattan. The one going north travels up New York as far as Buffalo.

I reasoned that anyone getting out of Sing Sing at this time would almost certainly have known about Rob Westerfield.

That was why early the next morning I dressed warmly, parked at the station, and walked toward the prison. There is constant activity at the gates. I had checked some statistics and knew there were about twenty-three hundred inmates housed there. Jeans, work boots, and a jacket are not particularly distinctive apparel. How would I be able to tell the difference between someone who might be an employee getting off duty and a newly released inmate? The answer is I couldn't.

Anticipating the problem, I had made a cardboard sign. I stood beside the gate and held it. It read: "Investigative journalist seeking information about just-released prisoner Robson Westerfield. Substantial payment."

Then it occurred to me that someone driving out of the prison in a car or taxi, or someone who did not want to be seen talking to me, might come forward if he could reach me by phone. At the last minute I added the number of my cell phone—917-555-1261—in large, easy-to-read numbers.

It was a cold, windy morning. The first of November. All Saints Day. Since Mother died I've attended Mass only on days such as Christmas and Easter, when even fallen-away Catholics like me hear the bells of a nearby church and reluctantly make our way to it.

I'm like a robot when I get there. I dutifully kneel and stand with the others, never sharing in the prayers. I like to sing, and I can feel throbbing in my throat when the congregation joins the choir. At Christmas it's joyous music: "Hark the Herald Angels Sing" or "Away in a Manger." At Easter the song is triumphant: "Jesus Christ Is Risen Today." But my lips always stay closed. Let others sing in exultation.

I used to be angry; now I am only weary. *One way or another you've taken them all, O Lord. Are you finally satisfied?* I know when I watch television and learn of whole families wiped out in bombings, or see them starving in refugee camps, I should be able to realize how much more I have, how much better off I am. I do grasp that intellectually, but it doesn't help. *Let's make a deal, God. We'll leave each other alone.*

I stood for two hours holding the sign. Most people passing in or out of the gates stared at it, curiosity in their eyes. A few of them spoke to me. A bulky man in his late forties, the earmuffs of his cap pulled down for warmth, snapped, "Lady, haven't you got anything better to do with your time than investigate that creep?" He would only tell me that he worked in the prison, but he refused to give his name.

I did notice, however, that some people, including those who looked like employees, studied the sign as though memorizing my phone number.

At ten o'clock, chilled to the bone, I gave up and walked back to the parking lot at the train station. I was just at the driver's door of my car when a man came up to me. He appeared to be about thirty, rawboned, with mean eyes and narrow lips. "Why are you picking on Westerfield?" he asked. "What's he ever done to you?"

He was wearing jeans, a jacket, and work boots. Had he just been released and followed me? I wondered. "Are you a friend of his?" I asked.

"What do you care?"

We have an instinctive reaction to step back when people get too close to us, when they are literally "in our faces." My back was against the side of the car, and this guy was crowding me. From the corner of my eye I was relieved to see a van pulling into the parking area. The thought rushed through my head that at least if I needed help there was someone around.

"I want to get in my car, and you're in my way," I said.

"Rob Westerfield was a model prisoner. We all looked up to him. He set a great example for the rest of us. Now, how much are you going to pay me for that information?"

"Let him pay you." I turned and shouldered the guy away from me, pushed the remote to release the lock, and yanked the door open.

He did not try to stop me, but before I could close the door again, he said, "Let me give you a little free advice. Burn your sign."

20

When I got back to the Hilmer apartment, I began to peruse the old newspapers Mother had kept. They were a godsend in my research on the life of Rob Westerfield. In several of them I found a mention of the two prep schools he had attended. The first one, Arbinger Preparatory School, in Massachusetts, is one of the toniest in the country. Interestingly, he stayed there only a year and a half before switching to Carrington in Rhode Island.

I didn't know anything about Carrington and looked it up on the Internet. The Website of Carrington Academy made it sound like a country estate where learning, sports, and friendship intertwined to create a sort of paradise. But behind the glowing description of all that it had to offer, the nitty-gritty became obvious: It was a school for "students who haven't realized their academic or social potential," for "students who may have difficulty adjusting to disciplined study."

In other words, it was a place for kids with a behavior problem.

Before I placed an inquiry on my Website, looking for information about Rob Westerfield's school days, from fellow students or former Carrington employees, I decided to see both places for myself. I phoned the schools and explained that I was a journalist writing a book on Robson Westerfield who had been a student there. In both cases I reached the president's office. At Arbinger I was immediately referred to Craig Parshall in the media relations office.

Mr. Parshall told me it was school policy that students, former or present, were never discussed with the press.

I took a stab. "Isn't it a fact that you gave an interview to Jake Bern concerning Robson Westerfield?"

There was a long pause, and I knew I was right.

"There was an interview granted," Parshall said, his voice stiff and condescending. Then he added, "If the family of a present student or a former student grants permission for an interview, we would within reason honor that request. You must understand, Ms. Cavanaugh, that our pupils come from distinguished families, including the sons of presidents and royalty. There are times when it is appropriate to allow carefully monitored media access."

"And of course that publicity enhances the name and

reputation of the school," I said. "On the other hand, if every day on a Website the fact that the convicted murderer of a fifteen-year-old girl had been rubbing shoulders with some of those distinguished students, they and their families might not be too happy. And other families might think twice about sending their sons and heirs to you. Isn't that right, Mr. Parshall?"

I didn't give him a chance to answer. "In fact, it might serve the school much better to be cooperative. Don't you agree?"

When, after a long moment of silence, Parshall responded, he clearly was not a happy man. "Miss Cavanaugh, I will grant your request for an interview. I will, however, warn you that the only information released to you will be the dates Robson Westerfield was a student here and the fact that he requested and received a transfer."

"Oh, I don't expect you to admit that you booted him out," I said scornfully. "But I'm sure you managed to find a little more than that to tell Mr. Bern."

We agreed that I would be in his office at eleven the next morning.

Arbinger is about forty miles north of Boston. I found the town on the map and figured out the best route to take and how much time I'd need.

Then I called Carrington Academy, and this time was passed through to Jane Bostrom, director of admissions. She acknowledged that Jake Bern had been granted an interview at the request of the Westerfield family, and added that without the family's permission she could not grant me an interview.

"Ms. Bostrom, Carrington is a kind of prep school of last resort," I pointed out firmly. "I want to be fair to its reputation, but the reason for its existence is to accept and try to straighten out problem kids. Right?"

I liked the fact that she leveled with me. "There are a lot of reasons why kids have problems, Ms. Cavanaugh. The majority of those reasons have to do with the family. They're kids of divorce, kids with high-powered parents who don't have time for them, kids who are loners or the butt of jokes by their peers. It doesn't mean they're not capable academically or socially. It just means that they're overwhelmed and need help."

"Help that sometimes, no matter how hard you try, you simply can't give?"

"I can give you a list of our graduates who went on to become very successful."

"I can name one who succeeded at the very first murder he committed—or at least the very first he is known to have committed." Then I added, "I don't want to do a hatchet job on Carrington. I want to find out what I can about what Rob Westerfield was up to in his teenage years before he murdered my sister. If you gave a lot of information to Jake Bern, and he can extrapolate the good stuff and leave out the rest, I want the same kind of access."

Since I'd be at Arbinger tomorrow, which was Friday, I made an appointment with Ms. Bostrom at Carrington for Monday morning. I debated about spending some time before the meetings tomorrow and Monday in the neighborhood of the schools. From what I could tell, they both were located in small towns. That had to mean there were places where the kids would congregate, such as a pizza parlor or fast-food joint. Sitting around the local off-campus hangout had worked for me when I did an earlier follow-up article on a kid who tried to kill his parents.

I hadn't run into Mrs. Hilmer in a couple of days, but in the late afternoon she phoned. "Ellie, this is a suggestion more than an invitation. I had one of my urges to cook today and ended up with a roast chicken in the oven. If you don't have plans, would you like to come over for dinner? But please don't say yes if you'd rather just be quiet."

I hadn't bothered to go to the grocery that morning and knew that my at-home choices were an American cheese sandwich or an American cheese sandwich. And I also remembered that Mrs. Hilmer was a good cook.

"What time?" I asked.

"Oh, about seven."

"I'll not only be there, I'll be early."

"Wonderful."

As I hung up I realized that Mrs. Hilmer must think of me as something of a loner. She's partially right, of course. But despite my interior core of isolation, or maybe even because of it, I am a reasonably outgoing person. I enjoy being with people, and after a busy day at the newspaper, I often get together with friends. When I worked late, I'd end up having pasta or a hamburger with whoever was around. There were always two or three of us there who weren't rushing home to the spouse or significant other after wrapping up a story or finishing a column.

I was one of the regulars in that group, and so was Pete. As I washed my face, brushed my hair, and twisted it back up, I wondered when he'd let me know which job he'd taken. I was sure that even if the paper *wasn't* sold immediately, he wouldn't stay at it much longer. The fact that the family was trying to sell it would be enough to make him move on. Where would he end up? Houston? L.A.? Whichever, chances were that our paths wouldn't cross much after the move.

It was a suddenly disquieting thought.

The cozy apartment consisted of a large living room with a galley kitchen at one end and a medium-sized bedroom. The bath was off the short hallway between them. I had set up my computer and printer on the table in the dining area near the kitchen. I'm not a neat worker, and as I was about to put on my coat, I looked around as if with Mrs. Hilmer's eyes.

The newspapers I'd been going through were scattered on the floor in an arc around the chair I'd been sitting in. The decorative fruit bowl and brass candlesticks that had been primly centered on the colonial table were shoved together on the buffet. My appointment book lay open on one side of the computer, and my pen was tossed on top of it. The bulky bound copy of the thick trial transcript, complete with vivid yellow markers, was next to the printer.

Suppose for some reason Mrs. Hilmer walked back with me and saw this mess, I thought. How would she react? I was pretty sure I knew the answer to that question, since there was absolutely nothing out of place in her home.

I bent down, scooped up the papers, and straightened them into something of an orderly pile. Then, on further consideration, I dug out the big duffel bag in which I always carried them and dropped them into it.

The trial transcript followed. I reasoned that the notebook, my pen, and the laptop and printer weren't too esthetically offensive. I moved the fruit bowl and candlesticks back to their decorative positions on the table. I had started to put the duffel bag in the closet when it dawned on me that if the apartment were to catch on fire, I would lose all this material. I dismissed that notion as improbable but nonetheless decided to take the bag with me. I don't know why I did that, but I did. Call it a hunch, one of those *feelings* you just get, as my grandmother used to say.

It was still cold outside, but at least the wind had died down. Even so, the walk from the apartment to the house seemed pretty long. Mrs. Hilmer had told me that after her husband died she had an attached garage added to the house because she didn't want to have to walk back and forth from the old one. Now the old garage beneath the apartment was empty except for gardening supplies and lawn furniture.

Walking to the house in the dark silence, I could well understand why she hadn't wanted to make the trip at night alone.

"Don't think I'm moving in here as well as in the apartment," I told Mrs. Hilmer when she opened the door and spotted the duffel bag. "It's just become my constant companion."

Over a glass of sherry I explained what was in it, then a thought occurred to me. Mrs. Hilmer had lived in Oldham for nearly fifty years. She was active in the parish and in the town activities—meaning she knew everyone. There were local people mentioned in those newspaper stories whose names meant nothing to me, but they would surely be familiar to her.

"I wonder if you'd consider going through these papers with me," I asked her. "There are people quoted whom I'd love to talk to, assuming they're still around. For example, some friends of Andrea's from school, neighbors at that time of Will Nebels, some of the guys Rob Westerfield hung around with. I'm sure most of Andrea's classmates are married, and probably a lot of them have moved away. I wonder if it would upset you to read through these old articles and maybe make a list of the people who talked to reporters who are still around here. I'm hoping, of course, that they may have known something that didn't come out at the time."

"I can tell you about one of them off the top of my head," Mrs. Hilmer said. "Joan Lashley. Her parents retired, but she married Leo St. Martin. She lives in Garrison."

Joan Lashley was the girl with whom Andrea had been doing homework that last night! Garrison was near Cold Spring, only a fifteen-minute drive from here. It was obvious that Mrs. Hilmer was going to be a treasure trove of information about people I might want to see.

While we were having coffee, I opened the duffel bag and put some of the newspapers on the table. I saw the look of pain that came over Mrs. Hilmer's face when she picked up the first one. The headline read, "Fifteen-Year-Old Bludgeoned to Death." Andrea's picture filled the front page. She was wearing her band uniform: a red jacket with brass buttons and a matching short skirt. Her hair was falling around her shoulders, and she was smiling. She looked happy and vibrant and young.

That picture had been taken at the first game of the season in late September. A few weeks later Rob Westerfield first met her when she was bowling with friends at the sports center in town. It was the next week that she went for the drive in his car and he was stopped by the state trooper for speeding.

"Mrs. Hilmer, I warn you," I said. "It's not easy going through this material, so if you think it would be too much for you—"

She interrupted me. "No, Ellie, I want to do it."

"Okay." I took out the rest of the newspapers. The trial transcript was still in the duffel bag. I took it out. "This makes pretty unpleasant reading."

"Leave it with me," she said firmly.

Mrs. Hilmer insisted on lending me a small flashlight for my return to the apartment, and I must say I was glad to have it. The night had continued to clear, and now a sliver of the moon was visible. I guess I was getting fanciful, but I could only think of those Halloween images of black cats sitting on crescent moons, grinning as though they were reveling in some secret knowledge.

I'd left on only a small night-light in the stairwell—again my conscious effort to be considerate of my hostess, this time by not running up her electricity bill. As I walked up the stairs, I suddenly was not sure if it was the best idea to be so frugal. The staircase was dark and shadowed, and it creaked under my steps. I suddenly became acutely aware that Andrea was murdered in a garage very similar to this one. They both originally had been barns. The old hayloft here is now the apartment, but the feeling of the structures is similar.

By the time I was at the head of the stairs, the key was in my hand and with a quick turn of the lock I was inside and had bolted the door. I immediately stopped worrying about running up bills and began to turn on every light I could find: the lamps on either side of the couch, the chandelier over the dining room table, the hallway light, the bedroom lights. At last I was able to draw a sigh of relief and begin to shake off the sense of alarm that had seized me.

The table looked strangely neat, with only the laptop and printer, my pen and appointment book at one end, and the fruit bowl and candlesticks in the center. Then I realized that something had changed. I had left my pen to the right of the appointment book, next to the computer. It was now on the left side of the book, away from the computer. A chill shot through me. Someone had been here and must have moved it. But why? To go through the appointment book and check on my activities—that would have to be the only reason. What else had been examined?

I turned on the computer and rushed to check the file where I kept my notes on Rob Westerfield. Just that afternoon I had jotted in a quick description of the man who stopped me in the parking lot at the railroad station. It was still there, but now a sentence had been added. I had described him as average height, gaunt, with mean eyes and mouth. The new sentence was "Considered dangerous, so approach with extreme caution."

My knees felt weak. It was bad enough that someone had come in while I was with Mrs. Hilmer, but that he would flaunt his presence was frightening. I was absolutely certain that I had locked the apartment door when I left, but the lock was basic and inexpensive, and wouldn't be much of a challenge for a professional burglar. Was anything missing? I ran into the bedroom and could see that the closet door, which I had left closed, was now slightly ajar. My clothes and shoes inside, however, seemed to be exactly as I'd left them. In the top drawer of the dresser I had a leather case of jewelry. Earrings, a gold chain, and a simple long strand of pearls are pretty much all I bother with, but the case also held my mother's engagement ring and wedding band, and the diamond earrings my father had given her for their fifteenth wedding anniversary, the year before Andrea died.

The jewelry was all there, so it was clear that whoever came in was not a common thief. He had been after information, and I realized how blessed I was that I had not left the trial transcript and all the old newspapers there. I had not the slightest doubt that they would have been destroyed. I could replace the trial transcript, but it would take a lot of time and those newspapers were irreplaceable. It was not just the accounts of the trial that the articles contained, but all the interviews and background that would be lost if they were to disappear.

I decided not to call Mrs. Hilmer immediately. I was sure she would be awake all night if she knew that an intruder had been in the apartment. I resolved that in the morning I would take the newspapers and the transcript and have copies made of them. It would be a tiresome job but well worth it. I simply couldn't afford to take a chance on losing them.

I checked the door again. It was bolted, but I wedged a heavy chair against it. Then I locked all the windows except the one in the bedroom that I wanted open for fresh air. I love a cold bedroom and didn't want to be deprived of that pleasure by the unknown visitor. Besides, the apartment is on the second floor, and there's no way anyone could get in through a window without a ladder. I was very sure that if anyone wanted to harm me, he'd find an easier way than dragging a ladder that I might hear. Still, when I finally did fall asleep, I kept waking with a start, always listening intently. But the sounds I heard were simply the wind blowing the few remaining leaves from the trees behind the garage.

It was only at dawn when I woke for the fourth or fifth time that I realized what I should have picked up on immediately: Whoever had gone through my appointment book knew that I had a meeting that morning at Arbinger and another one at Carrington Academy on Monday.

I planned to leave for Arbinger at seven o'clock. I knew Mrs. Hilmer was an early bird, so at ten of seven I called her and asked if I could stop by for a moment. Over a cup of her excellent coffee I told her about the intruder and that I would take the transcript and newspapers and get copies made of them.

"No, you won't," she said. "I have nothing else to do. I'm a volunteer at the library and use the machines there all the time. I'll use the copier in the office. That way no one has to know what's going on. Except Rudy Schell, of course. He's been there forever, and I'd trust him not to say a word."

She hesitated for a moment, then said, "Ellie, I want you to move in with me. I don't want you alone in the apartment. Whoever was in last night might come back, and, anyhow, I think we should call the police."

"No to moving in with you," I said. "If anything, I should leave the apartment." She began to shake her head, and I said, "But I won't. I'm too comfortable being near you. And I've thought about notifying the police and decided it's a bad idea. There's no sign of breaking and entering. My jewelry is still there. If I tell a cop that the only disturbance was that someone moved a pen and added a couple of words to a computer file, what do you think he'll believe?" I didn't wait for her to answer. "The Westerfields are already putting out the scenario that I was an overly imaginative and troubled child, and that my testimony at the trial was unreliable. Can you imagine what they'd make of a story like this? I'd sound like one of those people who send threatening letters to themselves just to get attention."

I gulped the last of the coffee. "There is something you can do, though, if you will. Call Joan Lashley and ask her if I can come and see her tomorrow."

It was comforting to hear Mrs. Hilmer say, "Drive carefully," and feel her quick kiss on my cheek.

On my way around Boston I got caught in some of the commuter traffic, so it was almost eleven o'clock when I drove through the carefully guarded gates of Arbinger

Preparatory School. It was even more impressive in real life than the photographs on its Website suggested. The handsome pink brick buildings looked mellow and tranquil under the November sky. The long driveway through the campus was lined with mature trees that in season must form a lush canopy of leaves. It was easy to imagine why most of the kids who graduate from a place such as this received with their diplomas a sense of entitlement, a feeling of having been made special, of being a cut above the rest.

As I steered the car into the area designated for visitors, I recalled the list of high schools I had attended. Freshman year in Louisville. Second half of sophomore year in Los Angeles. No, I was there until the middle of my junior year. Where was I next? Oh, yes, Portland, Oregon. And finally back to Los Angeles, which for my senior year and the four years of college offered some sort of stability. Mother continued to move around in the hotel chain until I was a senior in college. That was when the damage to her liver became accelerated, and she shared my tiny apartment until her death.

I always wanted you girls to know how to do things nicely, Ellie. That way if you met someone with a very good background, you'd be able to hold your own.

Oh, Mother, I thought as I was admitted to the main building and directed to Craig Parshall's office. The walls along the corridor were lined with portraits of grave-faced figures, and from what I could discern from quick glances, most of them were former school presidents.

Craig Parshall was less impressive in appearance than his cultured voice suggested. He was a man in his late fifties who still wore his school ring. His thinning hair was too perfectly combed—in a vain attempt to conceal the empty space on the dome of his head—and he could not conceal the fact that he was downright nervous.

His office was large and very handsome, with paneled walls, formal draperies, a Persian carpet just threadbare enough to guarantee its antiquity, comfortable leather chairs, and a mahogany desk, behind which he promptly retreated after greeting me.

"As I told you on the phone, Ms. Cavanaugh—" he began.

"Mr. Parshall, why don't we not waste each other's time?" I suggested, interrupting him. "I am totally aware of the constraints on you, and I appreciate them. Just answer a few questions, and I'll be on my way."

"I will give you the dates that Robson Westerfield attended—"

"I'm aware of the dates he was a student here. That came out at his trial for the murder of my sister."

Parshall winced.

"Mr. Parshall, the Westerfield family has a goal in life

and that is to whitewash Robson Westerfield's reputation, have a new trial, and get him acquitted. Success will have the *de facto* effect of having the world believe that another young man—one, I might add, who has neither the money nor the intellectual capacity to walk through these doors—is guilty of my sister's death. My goal is to see that that does not happen."

"You must understand—" Parshall began.

"I understand that you can't be quoted on the record. But you can open some doors for me. By that I mean that I want the list of students who were in class with Rob Westerfield. I want to know if any of them was known to be a particular friend of his—or, better yet, if there was someone who simply couldn't stand him. Who was his roommate? And off the record—and I do mean off the record—why was he kicked out?"

We looked at each other in silence for a long minute, and neither one of us blinked.

"On my Website I could easily refer to Robson Westerfield's exclusive prep school and not name it," I said, "or I could put it this way: Arbinger Preparatory School, alma mater to His Royal Highness Prince Gregory of Belgium, His Serene Highness Prince—"

He interrupted me. "Off the record?"

"Absolutely."

"No naming of the school or of me?"

"Absolutely."

He sighed, and I almost felt sorry for him. "Have you ever heard the quote 'Put not your trust in princes,' Ms. Cavanaugh?"

"As a matter of fact, I'm quite familiar with it— not only the biblical reference, but the way it's been paraphrased to me: 'Put not your trust in investigative reporters.'"

"Is that a warning, Ms. Cavanaugh?"

"If the investigative reporter has a sense of integrity, the answer is no."

"Understanding that, I'm going to put my trust in you, in the sense that I can rely on your discretion. Off the record?"

"Absolutely."

"The only reason Robson Westerfield was accepted here is that his father offered to rebuild the science building. And without a hint of publicity, I might add. Rob was presented to us as a troubled student who was never at home among his grade-school peers."

"He went to Baldwin in Manhattan for eight years," I said. "Were there problems there?"

"None reported to us, except perhaps a peculiarly absent—or listless—endorsement from his teachers and guidance counselor."

"And the science lab here needed rebuilding?"

Parshall looked pained. "Westerfield was from a fine family. His intelligence is in the very superior category."

"All right," I said. "Now let's get down to the nitty-gritty. What was it like having that guy on these hallowed grounds?"

"I had just begun teaching here, so I'm a firsthand witness. It was about as bad as it gets," Parshall said frankly. "I assume you know the definition of a sociopath?" He waved his hands in an impatient sort of gesture. "Sorry. As my wife reminds me, my classroom warm-ups can be quite annoying. I am talking of the sociopath as someone who is born without a conscience, who has a disregard for and is in conflict with the social code as you and I understand it. Robson Westerfield was a poster boy for that kind of personality."

"Then you had problems with him from the beginning?"

"Like so many of his ilk, he is blessed with looks and intelligence. He also is the last of a distinguished family line. His grandfather and father were students here. We hoped that we would be able to bring out whatever good qualities there were in him."

"People don't think much of his father, Vincent Westerfield. What kind of record did he have here?"

"I looked him up. Academically, only fair. Nothing like the grandfather, from what I gather. Pearson Westerfield was a United States senator."

"Why did Rob Westerfield leave in the middle of his sophomore year?"

"There was a serious incident stemming from his losing a starting spot on the football team. He attacked another student. The family was persuaded not to sue, and the Westerfields paid all the bills. Maybe more—to that I can't swear."

It dawned on me that Craig Parshall was being unusually frank. I told him so.

"I do not like to be threatened, Ms. Cavanaugh."

"Threatened?"

"This morning, shortly before you arrived, I received a telephone call from a Mr. Hamilton, an attorney who represents the Westerfield family. I was warned that I should give you no negative information about Robson Westerfield."

They work pretty fast, I thought. "May I ask what kind of information you gave Jake Bern about Westerfield?"

"His sports activities, such as they were. Robson was a powerful young man; even as a thirteen-year-old he was nearly six feet tall. He played on the squash team, the tennis team, and the football team. He was also in the theater group. I told Bern that he was a genuinely talented actor. That was the kind of information Bern was seeking. He managed to elicit some quotes from me that will sound very favorable in print."

I could just imagine how Bern would write the chapter on Rob at Arbinger. He'd come out looking like an all-around preppie in the three-generation family prep school. "How will his leaving Arbinger be explained?"

"He took the second semester of his sophomore year abroad, then decided to switch."

"I realize we're going back nearly thirty years, but could you give me a list of his former classmates?"

"You didn't get it from me, of course."

"That's understood."

When I left Arbinger an hour later, I had a list of the freshmen and sophomores who had been classmates of Rob Westerfield. Comparing them with the active alumni list, Parshall identified ten who were in the Massachusetts-to-Manhattan area. One of them was Christopher Cassidy, the football player Rob Westerfield had severely beaten. He now had his own investment firm and lived in Boston.

"Chris was a scholarship student," Parshall explained. "And because he is grateful for having had the opportunity to attend this school, he is one of our most generous donors. In his case, I don't mind making a phone call. Chris has always been blunt about his feelings about Westerfield. But, again, if I hook you up with him, it has to be confidential."

"Absolutely."

Parshall walked with me to the door. It was break time between classes, and the soft pealing of a bell was followed by a steady stream of small groups of students emerging from various rooms. The current generation of Arbinger scholars, I thought as I studied their young faces. Many of them were destined for future leadership roles, but I couldn't help but wonder if there was also another Robson Westerfield–type sociopath incubating within these privileged walls.

I drove out of the school grounds and along the town's main street, which begins at the school. From the map I could see that it runs in a direct line from Arbinger Prep on the south end of town to Jenna Calish Academy for girls on the north end. New Cotswold is one of those charming New England villages that is built around the schools in its vicinity. It has a large bookstore, a cinema, a library, a number of clothing stores, and several small restaurants. I had given up the thought of hanging around with the chance of learning something from students. Craig Parshall had given me the kind of information that I wanted, and I knew that I'd be better off pursuing Rob Westerfield's classmates than spending more time around Arbinger.

But it was nearly noon, and I realized that I had the beginnings of a headache, partly due to the fact that I was getting hungry and partly because I hadn't slept much the previous evening.

About three blocks from the school I passed a restaurant called The Library. The quaint hand-painted sign caught my eye, and I suspected that it might be the kind of place where the soup was homemade. I decided to give it a try and pulled into a parking space nearby.

Because it was before noon, I was the first lunch customer, and the hostess, a cheery, bustling lady in her late forties, was happy not only to give me my choice of the dozen or so smaller tables, but to fill me in on the history of the establishment. "It's been in our family for fifty years," she assured me. "My mother, Antoinette Duval, opened it. She was always a marvelous cook, and my father, to indulge her, staked her to it. She was so successful, he ended up quitting his job and handling the business end here. They're retired now, and my sisters and I have taken it over. But Mother still comes in a couple of days a week to make some of her specials. She's in the kitchen now, and if you like onion soup, she just made it."

I ordered it, and it was every bit as good as I'd hoped. The hostess came over to check my reaction, and my reassurance that the soup was heavenly caused her to beam with delight. Then, since only a few other diners had arrived, she stood at the table and asked me if I were staying locally or just passing through. I decided to be totally honest. "I'm a journalist, and I'm doing a story on Rob Westerfield who was just released from Sing Sing. Do you know who he is?"

Her expression changed instantly from friendly to

stern and tight-lipped. She turned abruptly and walked away from me. Oh, boy, I thought. It's a good thing I've almost finished the soup. She looks as though she's ready to throw me out.

A moment later she was back, this time with a plump white-haired woman in tow. The older woman was wearing a chef's apron and drying her hands on a corner of it as she came to the table. "Mom," the hostess said, "this lady is doing a story on Rob Westerfield. Maybe you'd like to tell her something."

"Rob Westerfield." Mrs. Duval practically spat out the name. "He's a bad one. Why did they let him out of prison?"

She didn't need encouragement to tell her story. "He came in here with his mother and father during one of the parents' weekends. How old was he? Fifteen, maybe. He was arguing with his father. Whatever happened, he jumped up to leave. The waitress was walking behind him, and he knocked into the tray. The food went all over him. I tell you, Miss, I never saw anything like it. He grabbed that girl's arm and twisted it until she screamed. He's an *animal.*"

"Did you call the police?"

"I was about to, but his mother begged me to wait. Then the father opened his wallet and handed the waitress five hundred dollars. She was just a kid. She wanted to take it. She said she wouldn't press charges.

Then the father told me to add the price of the food that was lost to his check."

"What did Rob Westerfield do?"

"He stalked out and left his parents to deal with the mess. The mother was terribly embarrassed. After the father paid the waitress, he told me that it was all her fault and that his son had reacted that way because he had been scalded. He told me I should train waitresses before I let them carry trays."

"What did you do?"

"I told him that we would no longer continue to serve him and that they should leave my restaurant."

"You can't imagine what Mama is like when she's angry," her daughter said. "She picked up the plates that had just been put in front of them and carried them back to the kitchen."

"But I was very sorry for Mrs. Westerfield," Mrs. Duval said. "She was so upset. In fact, she wrote me a very nice letter of apology. I still have it in my files."

When I left The Library half an hour later, I had permission to tell that story on my Website and a promise that I would receive a copy of the letter Mrs. Westerfield had written to Mrs. Duval. Plus, I was on my way to visit Margaret Fisher, the young waitress whose arm Rob had twisted. She was now a psychologist living two towns away, and, yes, she would be very happy to talk to me. She remembered Rob Westerfield very well indeed.

"I was saving money for college," Dr. Fisher told me. "The five hundred dollars his father gave me seemed like a fortune at the time. Looking back, I'm sorry I didn't sign a complaint against him. The guy is violent, and if I know anything about the human mind, I suspect that twenty-two years in prison didn't change him a bit."

She was an attractive woman in her early forties, with prematurely gray hair and a young face. She told me that she had appointments only until noon on Friday and was just about to leave her office when I phoned. "I saw the interview with him the other night on television," she said. "Butter wouldn't melt in his mouth. It sickened me, so I can understand how *you* feel."

I told her what I was doing with the Website and how I had gone to stand outside Sing Sing with the sign requesting information about Rob's conduct in prison.

"I'd be very surprised if there weren't more incidents there that you may find out about," she said. "But what about the years between the time he was in school here and when he was arrested for your sister's death? How old was he when he went to prison?"

"Twenty."

"With his history, I seriously doubt there weren't other situations that were hushed up or never reported. Ellie, has it occurred to you that you're setting yourself up as a constant menace to him? You tell me that his grandmother is very alert. Suppose she learns about your Website and visits it, or has someone in her employ visit it for her every day. If she reads enough negative facts about him, what's to keep her from deciding to change her will even before Westerfield has a second trial?"

"Wouldn't that be absolutely wonderful!" I said. "I'd love to think that I was responsible for having the family money go to charity."

"I would be *very* careful if I were you," Dr. Fisher said quietly.

I thought about her advice as I drove back to Oldham. There had been a break-in at my apartment and then what amounted to a threat lodged in my computer file. I turned over in my mind the question of whether I should have notified the police. But for the reason I had given Mrs. Hilmer, I knew I was right not to notify them; I wasn't going to put myself at risk of being considered some kind of nut case. On the other hand, I had no right to put Mrs. Hilmer in any kind of jeopardy. I decided I'd have to find another place to live.

Dr. Fisher had given me permission to use her name

when I wrote about what had happened in the restaurant. That was something else I'd do on the Website—invite people to share any problems they'd had with Rob Westerfield in the years before he went to prison.

It was late afternoon when I pulled into the driveway and parked in front of the apartment. I'd stopped at the supermarket in Oldham and picked up some much needed supplies. My plan was to make a simple dinner: a shell steak, baked potato, and salad. Then I'd watch television and get to bed reasonably early. I needed to begin to write the book I had contracted to do about Westerfield, and while the material I used on the Website could be repeated in the book, it would have to be presented differently.

Her house was dark, so I wasn't sure if Mrs. Hilmer was home. I reasoned that her car might be in the garage and that she might not have turned any lights on yet, so I phoned her when I got into the apartment. She answered on the first ring, and I could tell that her voice was troubled.

"Ellie, this may sound crazy, but I think someone followed me today when I went to the library."

"Why do you think that?"

"You know how quiet this street is. But I was hardly out of the driveway when I could see a car in the rearview mirror. It stayed a distance behind me, but it didn't turn off until after I'd turned into the parking area next to the library. Then I think the same car followed me home."

"Did it keep going when you turned off?"

"Yes."

"Can you describe it?"

"It was midsize, dark, either black or dark blue. It was far enough behind me that I couldn't see the driver, but I have the impression that it was a man. Ellie, do you think that whoever was in the apartment last night is hanging around here?"

"I don't know."

"I'm going to call the police, and that means I'll have to tell them about last night."

"Yes, of course." I hated myself for the nervousness I heard in Mrs. Hilmer's voice. Until now, she obviously had always felt secure in her home. I only prayed that by being a lightning rod for trouble I had not destroyed that sense of security for her.

A squad car pulled up at the house ten minutes later, and after debating for a few minutes, I decided to walk over to talk to the police. The officer who looked to be a longtime veteran of the force obviously did not think much of Mrs. Hilmer's suspicions. "Whoever was in that car didn't try to stop you or contact you in any way?" he was asking her when I arrived.

"No." She introduced us. "Ellie, I've known Officer White for many years."

He was a craggy-faced man who looked as though he'd spent a lot of time outdoors. "And what's this about an intruder, Ms. Cavanaugh?"

His skepticism was apparent when I told him about the pen and the entry in the file. "You mean your jewelry wasn't touched and the only evidence you have of someone having been in the apartment is that you think your pen had been moved from one side of your notebook to the other and there are a couple of words in a file in the computer that you don't remember writing."

"That I *didn't* write," I corrected him.

He was polite enough not to contradict me directly, but then he said, "Mrs. Hilmer, we'll keep an eye on the house for the next few days, but my guess is that you were a little nervous after hearing Ms. Cavanaugh's story this morning and that's why you picked up on that car. Chances are it was nothing."

My "story," I thought. Thanks for nothing. But then he said he'd like to examine the lock in the door of the apartment. Promising Mrs. Hilmer that I'd call her, I walked back to the apartment with him. He did take a look at the lock and came to the same conclusion I had reached: It had not been forced in any way.

He lingered for a moment, obviously trying to make up his mind about something, and then he said, "We heard about you being at Sing Sing yesterday, Ms. Cavanaugh."

I waited. We were standing in the hall outside the apartment. He had not asked to see the computer file, which showed just how much credence he had put in my "story." I was not about to invite him in to shrug it off any further.

"Ms. Cavanaugh, I was here when your sister was murdered, and I do understand the pain your family experienced. But if Rob Westerfield did commit the crime, he has served his sentence, and I have to tell you there are plenty of people in this town who had no use for him as a wild kid, but who think he got a bum rap."

"Is that your opinion, Officer?"

"Frankly, it is. I've always thought that Paulie Stroebel was guilty. There was a lot that didn't come out at the trial."

"Such as . . ."

"He'd bragged to a number of kids in school that your sister was going to the Thanksgiving mixer with him. If she told any of them, I mean some of her close friends, that she was going only because Rob Westerfield wouldn't get jealous of a guy like Paulie and it got back to him, he might have gone crazy. Rob Westerfield's car was parked at the service station. You said yourself on the witness stand that Paulie told Andrea he'd followed her to the hideout. And then there was that guidance counselor who swore on the stand that when Paulie heard about Andrea's body being found, she heard him say, 'I didn't think she was dead.'"

"And there was a student nearer to him who swore that he said, 'I can't believe she's dead.' A big difference, Officer."

"It's obvious we're not going to see eye to eye on this, but let me give you a warning." He must have sensed that I stiffened, because he said, "Hear me out. You're in way over your head, carrying signs around Sing Sing. The guys getting out of there are hardened criminals. You're standing there, a young, very attractive woman with a sign giving your phone number and begging them to call you. Half of those bums are going to end up back in there within a couple of years. What do you think goes through their heads when they see a woman like you just begging for trouble?"

I looked at him closely. There was sincere concern on his face. And he certainly had a point. "Officer White, it's you and people like you I'm trying to convince," I said. "I understand now that my sister was terrified of Rob Westerfield, and after what I've just learned about him today, I can understand why. If I'm in any danger, I'll take my chances with the people who saw that sign—unless, of course, they're in any way connected to Rob Westerfield and his family."

That was when it occurred to me to describe the man who had spoken to me in the parking lot of the railroad station. I asked him to see if he could learn whether a prisoner of that description had been released yesterday.

"What would you do with that information?" he asked me.

"All right. Let's forget it, Officer," I said.

Mrs. Hilmer must have been watching for Officer White to leave. My cell phone rang just as the taillights of his squad car disappeared onto the road.

"Ellie," she said, "I made a copy of the newspapers and the trial transcript. Do you need the originals this evening for any reason? I'm meeting some friends for a movie and dinner and won't be back until ten o'clock."

I hated the thought that I was afraid to have both the originals and the copies under one roof, but I was.

"I'll be right over," I said.

"No, I'll call you when I'm leaving. I'll drive past the apartment, and you can run down and get the duffel bag."

She came a few minutes later. It was only four-thirty, but already the sky was dark. Even so, I could see the tension in her face when she opened the window to speak to me.

"Did anything else happen?" I asked.

"Just a minute ago I got a phone call. I don't know who it was. The caller ID was blocked."

"Tell me about it."

"I know it's crazy, but somebody said I should be careful keeping a psycho around me. He said that you'd been institutionalized for setting fire in a classroom."

"That's absolutely untrue. My God, I've never spent a day in a hospital since I was born, never mind an institution."

I knew from the relief on her face that Mrs. Hilmer believed me. But that meant, of course, that she had not instantly disbelieved the caller. After all, the first time I visited her, she had suggested that Rob Westerfield might be innocent and that I was obsessed with Andrea's death.

"But, Ellie, why would anyone say such a terrible thing about you?" she protested. "And what can you do to stop him from saying it to someone else?"

"Someone's trying to discredit me, of course, and the answer is that I can't stop it." I opened the back door of the car and retrieved the duffel bag. I tried to choose my words carefully. "Mrs. Hilmer, I think it's better if I move back to the Inn tomorrow morning. Officer White thinks that I'm going to attract some pretty strange people as a result of standing outside Sing Sing with a sign, and I can't have them finding their way here. I'm safer in an inn, and certainly you'll have your peace back."

She was not dishonest enough to contradict me.

There was relief in her voice when she said, "I think you *would* be safer, Ellie." She paused, then added in all honesty, "I guess I would feel safer, too." After that she was gone.

I walked back up to the apartment, the duffel bag in my hand, feeling almost bereft. In biblical days the lepers were made to wear bells around their necks and to shout, "Unclean, unclean," if anyone happened to wander near them. At that moment I swear I felt like a leper.

I dropped the bag and went into the bedroom to change. I replaced my jacket with a loose sweater, kicked off my shoes, and stuffed my feet into ancient fleece-lined slippers. Then I went into the living room, poured myself a glass of wine, and settled in the big club chair with my feet on the hassock.

The sweater and slippers were my comfort clothes. For a fleeting moment I thought about my old comforter, Bones, the floppy stuffed animal who had shared my pillow when I was a child. He was in a box on the top shelf of a closet in my apartment in Atlanta. He shared the box with other mementos my mother had kept of the past, including her wedding album, pictures of the four of us, baby clothes, and, most wrenching of all, Andrea's band uniform. For a moment I felt a childish resentment that Bones wasn't with me now.

Then, as I sipped the wine, I thought of how often

when Pete and I went out after work we'd linger over a glass of wine before ordering dinner.

Two memories: my mother drinking to seek peace, and Pete and I relaxing and joking about what had sometimes been a wildly busy or frustrating day.

I hadn't heard from him in the ten days since we'd had dinner in Atlanta. Out of sight, out of mind, I decided. Looking for another job. "Pursuing other interests," as the business jargon goes when an executive is told to clean out his desk.

Or when he decides to cut his ties. All of them.

21

An hour later there was a subtle change in the weather. The faint rattle of a loose pane in the window over the sink was the first hint of a shift in the wind. I got up and pushed up the thermostat, then went back to the computer. Realizing that I was in acute danger of feeling sorry for myself, I had begun to work on what would become the opening chapter of the book.

After some false starts, I knew that I should begin with my final memory of Andrea, and, as I wrote, my memory seemed to sharpen. I could see her room with the white organdy bedspread and frilly curtains. I remembered in sharp detail the old-fashioned dresser Mother had so carefully antiqued. I could visualize the pictures of Andrea and her friends stuck in the frame of the mirror over that dresser.

I could see Andrea in tears as she talked on the phone to Rob Westerfield, and then I saw her putting on the locket. As I wrote, I realized that there was something about the locket that still eluded me. I knew that I couldn't positively identify it now if I saw it, but at the time, I gave a clear description of it to the police—a description that years ago had been dismissed as childish fantasy.

But I knew she had been wearing it when I found her, and I was certain I had heard Rob Westerfield in the garage-hideout. Mother told me later that it had taken her and my father ten or fifteen minutes to calm me down so that I was coherent enough to tell them where I had found Andrea's body. Plenty of time for Rob to get away. And he had taken the locket with him.

On the witness stand he claimed that he'd been out jogging at that time and had been nowhere near the garage. Nevertheless, he had washed and bleached the sweats he'd worn that morning, along with the blood-ied clothes from the night before.

Once again I was struck by the terrible risk he had taken in coming back to the garage. Why did he retrieve the locket? Was he afraid that it would be enough to confirm that Andrea was not just a kid with an annoying crush on him? Even as I thought of that morning, and the harsh breathing and the nervous gig-gling sound he had made as he hid on the other side of the van, my hands turned clammy on the keyboard.

Suppose I had *not* slipped through the woods alone

but had brought my father with me? Rob would have been caught in the garage. Did sheer panic bring him back? Was it possible that he needed to confirm to himself that what he had done wasn't just a nightmare? Or, worst of all, had he gone back to make certain Andrea was not alive?

At seven o'clock I turned on the oven and put in the lone potato to bake; then I went back to work. Shortly afterward the phone rang; it was Pete Lawlor.

"Hi, Ellie."

There was something in his voice that immediately warned me to brace myself.

"What's the matter, Pete?"

"You don't waste time on chitchat, do you?"

"We never do. That's our agreement."

"I guess it is. Ellie, the paper is being sold. It's definite now. The announcement will be made on Monday. The staff will be cut to the bone."

"What about you?"

"They offered me a job. I turned them down."

"You said you were going to do that."

"I asked about you, but off the record they told me they don't plan to keep up the investigative reporter series."

I'd been expecting that bit of news, but I realized how suddenly rootless it made me feel. "Have you decided where you're going, Pete?"

"I'm not sure yet, but I may be seeing some people in New York before I decide. Maybe when that happens, I'll rent a car and drive up to see you, or you can meet me in the city."

"I'd like that. I was kind of expecting that I'd get a postcard from Houston or L.A."

"I never send postcards. Ellie, I've been watching your Website."

"There isn't much on it yet. It's sort of like a sign, the kind you put on a shop you've rented. You know what I mean: 'Watch for the grand opening.' But I am digging up a lot of nasty stuff on Westerfield. If Jake Bern tries to portray him as an all-American kid, his book will have to be published as fiction."

"Ellie, it is not in my nature to—"

I cut him off. "Ah, come on, Pete. You're not going to warn me to be careful, are you? I've already been warned by my neighbor—a psychologist—and by a cop. And that's just today."

"Then let me join the chorus."

"Let's change the subject. Have you lost any of those ten pounds yet?"

"I did better than that. I decided I look good just the way I am. Okay, I'll call you when I know I'm coming in. Or you can always call me, you know. Long-distance rates are pretty cheap at night."

He disconnected before I could even say good-bye.

I pressed the "end" button on my cell phone and laid the phone down next to the computer. As I made a salad, the ramifications of losing my job began to sink in. The advance on signing the contract to write my book would keep me going for a while, but what would I do when that was finished and I had given my best shot to torpedoing Rob Westerfield's reinvention of himself?

Go back to Atlanta? But my friends at the paper would be scattered. Another thing to ponder: It isn't that easy to get a newspaper job these days. Too many newspapers have been swallowed up or have folded. And when the book is finished and I've put all this behind me, where did I want to live? It was a question that I kept pondering all through dinner, even as I tried to concentrate on the news magazine I'd picked up at the supermarket.

The cell phone rang again as I was clearing the table. "You the lady who was standing outside the prison with a sign yesterday?" a husky male voice asked.

"Yes, I am." Mentally I was crossing my fingers. The caller ID registered "unavailable."

"I might have something to tell you about Westerfield. How much you gonna pay?"

"I guess it depends on the information."

"You pay first, then you hear."

"How much?"

"Five thousand dollars."

"I haven't got that much money."

"Then forget it. But what I can tell you would put Westerfield back in Sing Sing for the rest of his life."

Was he bluffing? I wasn't sure, but I couldn't take a chance on losing the caller. I thought of my advance. "I have some money coming in the next week or two. Just give me some hint of what you know."

"How's this? When he was whacked out on cocaine last year, Westerfield told me he killed a guy when he was eighteen. Is the name of that guy worth five thousand dollars? Think about it. I'll call back next week."

I heard a click in my ear.

Margaret Fisher had told me only that afternoon that in her professional opinion Rob Westerfield had been guilty of other crimes before he murdered Andrea. I thought of incidents I had heard earlier that day, like the ones at school and at the restaurant. But if he had really murdered someone . . .

Suddenly it was a whole new ball game. If the guy who had just called me was on the level and could give the name of a murder victim I could verify, it would be easy enough to find out the facts of the case. Of course, it might be that this was a hoax, just a way for a crook to make a fast $5,000. I had to decide if that was a risk I was willing to take.

I was standing at the computer, looking down at the

open file. As I read my description of Andrea in those last few moments that I was with her, I knew that to help put Rob Westerfield back in prison was worth every cent I would ever earn in my life.

There was a glass of water at the side of the computer. I picked it up and lifted it in a kind of salute, a toast to Andrea and to the prospect of sending Westerfield back to prison.

I tidied up the kitchen and turned on the TV to watch the local news. The sports editor was showing clips of a basketball game. The winning basket had been made by Teddy Cavanaugh, and as I stared, I saw the face of the half-brother I'd never met.

He was close to being a mirror image of me. He was younger, of course, boyish, but our eyes and noses and lips and cheekbones were the same. He was looking straight into the camera, and I felt as if we were staring at each other.

Then before I could change the station, in a final touch of irony, the cheerleaders began to chant his name.

22

Mrs. Hilmer had told me that Joan Lashley St. Martin lived on the road not far beyond Graymoor, the monastery and retreat house of the Franciscan Friars of the Atonement. When I passed the lovely Graymoor property, I had a vague memory of driving up the winding driveway to attend Mass in the main chapel with my parents and Andrea.

Mother had sometimes reminisced about the last time we were there; it had been shortly before Andrea died. Andrea had been feeling silly that day and kept whispering jokes in my ear; during the sermon, I even laughed out loud. My mother had firmly separated us and after Mass told my father that we should go straight home and forget about having the brunch we'd been looking forward to at the Bear Mountain Inn.

"Even Andrea couldn't charm your father that day," Mother recalled. "Of course when everything happened a few weeks later, I was sorry we didn't have that last happy time together having brunch."

The day before . . . the last happy time . . . I wondered if I'd ever be free of that kind of remark. It certainly won't be today, I thought, as I slowed down to check Joan's address again.

She lived in a three-story frame house in a lovely wooded area. The white clapboard shingles glistened in the sunshine and were complemented by the hunter green shutters framing the windows. I parked in the semicircular driveway, went up the porch steps, and rang the bell.

Joan answered the door. She had always seemed tall to me, but I realized instantly that she hadn't grown an inch in these twenty-two years. Her long brown hair was now collar length, and her thin frame had filled out. I remembered her as being very attractive. I would say the definition still fit, at least until she smiled—she is one of those people whose smile is so vivid and warm that it makes the whole face seem beautiful. As we looked at each other, Joan's green eyes became moist for a moment, then she grasped my hands.

"Little Ellie," she said. "Dear God, I thought you'd be shorter than I am. You were such a tiny kid."

I laughed. "I know. It's the reaction I'm getting from everyone who used to know me."

She put her arm through mine. "Come in, I have a pot of coffee going, and I stuck a couple of bake-and-serve muffins in the oven. No guarantees that they're any good. Sometimes they're fine; other times they taste like lead balloons."

We walked through the living room that ran from the front to the back of the house. It was the kind of room I loved—deep couches, club chairs, a wall of books, a fireplace, wide windows that looked out at the surrounding hills.

We share similar taste, I thought. Then I realized that the similarity also extended to clothing. We were both dressed casually in sweaters and jeans. I had been expecting to see a tall fashionable woman with long hair. In addition to expecting me to be small, I'm sure she also thought I'd be dressed in something frilly. Mother's taste in dress-up clothes for Andrea and me had been very feminine.

"Leo is out with the boys," she said. "Between the three of them, life is one long basketball game."

The table in the breakfast room was already set for the two of us. The percolator was plugged in on the sideboard. The picture window offered a stunning view of the palisades and the Hudson River.

"I would never get tired of looking out this window," I said as I sat down.

"I never do. So many of the old crowd went down to

the city, but, you know something? A lot of them are coming back. The commute into Manhattan is only an hour, and they think it's worth it." Joan was pouring the coffee as she spoke, then abruptly set the percolator back on the sideboard. "Oh, my Lord, it's time to rescue the bake-and-serves." She disappeared into the kitchen.

She may not look as I visualized her, I thought, but one thing hadn't changed! Joan was always fun to be with. She was Andrea's best friend and therefore was in and out of our house all the time. Of course, I had my own friends, but if I didn't have one of them around, Andrea and Joan would let me join them, often to listen to records with them in Andrea's room. Sometimes when they were doing their homework together, they'd let me do mine with them, just as long as I wasn't a pest.

Joan returned triumphantly carrying a plate of corn muffins. "Congratulations are in order, Ellie," she said. "I caught them just before the bottoms started to burn."

I helped myself to one. Joan sat down, cut a muffin open, spread butter on it lightly, tasted it, and said, "My God, it's edible!"

We laughed together and began to talk. She wanted to know about me, what I had been doing, and I briefly sketched in the years between age seven and the present. She had heard of Mother's death. "Your father put a notice in the local papers," she said. "A very sweet one. Didn't you know that?"

"He didn't send it to me."

"I have it somewhere. If you'd like to see it, I can dig it out. It might take a while, though. My filing is about on a par with my baking."

I wanted to say no, don't bother, but I was curious to see what my father had written. "If you come across it, I would like to see it," I said, trying to sound offhand. "But please don't go to any trouble."

I was sure Joan wanted to ask me if I had been in touch with my father, but she must have sensed that I did not want to talk about him.

Instead she said, "Your mother was so lovely. And of course your father was very handsome. I remember that I was intimidated by him, but I think I also had a crush on him. I was so sorry when I heard they separated after the trial. The four of you always seemed so happy, and you did so many things together. I always wished my family would go to Sunday brunches at the Bear Mountain Inn the way you did."

"Only an hour ago I'd been thinking of the brunch that we didn't go to there," I said, and then told Joan about Andrea making me laugh in church.

Joan smiled. "She did that to me sometimes in school assemblies. Andrea could keep a straight face, and I'd get in trouble for laughing when the principal was speaking."

As she sipped her coffee, she reflected. "My parents are good people, but, to be perfectly frank, they're not much fun. We never went out to a restaurant, because my father said the food was cheaper and tasted better at home. Fortunately, he's loosened up a bit now that they've retired to Florida."

She laughed. "But when they go out, the rule is they have to be in the restaurant by five o'clock to get the early bird prices, and if they have a cocktail, they fix it at home and sip it in the van in the parking lot of the restaurant before dinner. Don't you love it?"

Then she added, "I mean, it would be different if he couldn't afford to do otherwise, but he can. Dad is just plain cheap. My mother says he still has his First Communion money."

She poured us a second cup of coffee. "Ellie, like everybody else around here, I saw the Rob Westerfield interview on television. My cousin is a judge. He says there's so much pressure for that second trial that he's surprised they're not already into jury selection. You have no idea how manipulative the father is, and, of course, Dorothy Westerfield, the grandmother, has made *huge* donations to hospitals and libraries and schools around here. She wants the second trial for Rob, and the powers that be want her to have it."

"You'll be called as a witness, of course, Joan," I said.

"I know it. I was the last person to see Andrea alive." She hesitated, then added, "Except for her murderer, of course."

We were both silent for a moment. Then I said, "Joan, I need to know everything that you remember about that last night. I've read the trial transcript over and over, and it strikes me that your testimony was very brief."

She put her elbows on the table and folded her hands together, resting her chin on them. "It *was* brief, because neither the prosecutor nor the defense attorney asked me questions that, looking back, I think they should have asked."

"What kind of questions?"

"About Will Nebels, for one," she said. "You remember how he was a handyman and worked for just about everyone in town at some point. He helped build your porch, didn't he?"

"Yes."

"He fixed our garage door when my mother backed the car into it. As my father used to say, when Will wasn't three sheets to the wind, he was a good carpenter. But, of course, you could never count on him showing up."

"I kind of remember that."

"Something you wouldn't remember was that Andrea and I used to talk about the fact that he was a bit *too* friendly."

"Too friendly?"

Joan shrugged. "Today, knowing what I know, I would say that he was one step away from being a child molester. I mean, we all knew him because he'd been in our houses. But any number of times when we bumped into him in the street, he'd give us each a big hug—although never if an adult was around, of course."

I was incredulous. "Joan, I'm sure even at that age I would have been aware if Andrea had complained about him to my father. I certainly knew when he ordered Andrea to stay away from Westerfield."

"Ellie, twenty-two years ago we kids simply weren't aware that he was potentially more than a nuisance. At that time we told each other how yucky it was when Nebels would give us a hug and call us 'his girls.' 'How do you like the new porch I built with your daddy, Andrea?' he'd say with an overly friendly smile, or 'Didn't I fix your garage good, Joanie?' he'd whine.

"Now understand, he didn't molest us, but in retrospect, he was just a boozy sleaze who had a hell of a nerve, and there was no question in my mind that the one he really had his eye on was Andrea. I remember I joked to your mother and father that Andrea was going to invite Will Nebels to the Christmas dance. They never picked up that there was anything behind the joking."

"My father missed that!"

"Andrea could do a great imitation of Will sneaking beer out of his toolbox and getting bombed while he was working. There was no reason for your father to look behind the joking for a potential problem."

"Joan, I don't understand why you're telling me this now. Are you saying that you think that this story Will Nebels is telling now is anything but an outright lie that the Westerfields are paying him to tell?"

"Ellie, ever since I heard Will Nebels with Rob Westerfield during that interview, I'm wondering if there's *any* truth to what he said. Was he really in old Mrs. Westerfield's house that night? Did he actually see Andrea go into the garage? Well after the fact, I wondered if I'd seen someone coming down the road when Andrea left our house that night. But I was so vague about it when I talked to the police and the attorneys then that it was pretty much dismissed as teenage hysteria."

"What I told them was dismissed as childish imagination."

"I do know for certain that Will Nebels had lost his driver's license at that time and was always wandering around town. I also know he had a thing for Andrea. Suppose she was hoping to meet Rob Westerfield in the garage-hideout and got there early. Suppose Will had followed her there and made a pass at her. Suppose there was a struggle, and she fell backward? That was a cement floor. There was an injury on the back of her head that they blamed on the fact that she'd fallen after she was hit with the tire jack. But isn't it possible she fell *before* she was hit with the tire jack?"

"The blow on the back of her head would only have stunned her," I said. "I know that from the records."

"Hear me out. Let's assume for one single minute that, lowlife that he is, Rob Westerfield's story is true. He parked his car at the service station, went into the movie, and after it was over, drove to the hideout, just in case Andrea was waiting for him."

"And found her dead?"

"Yes, and panicked. Just as he claimed."

She saw the protest forming on my lips and held up her hand. "Hear me out, Ellie, please. It is possible that everyone has told parts of the truth. Suppose Nebels struggled with Andrea, and she fell and hit her head and was unconscious. Suppose he ran inside Mrs. Dorothy Westerfield's house while trying to decide what to do. He had done work there and knew the alarm code. And then he saw Paulie drive up."

"Why would Paulie have taken the tire jack out of the car?"

"Maybe for protection, in case he ran into Westerfield. Remember that Miss Watkins, the guidance counselor, swore Paulie had said: 'I didn't think she was dead.'"

"Joan, what are you telling me?"

"Try this scenario: Will Nebels followed Andrea to the garage and made a pass at her. There was a scuffle. She fell and was knocked unconscious. He let himself into the house, then saw Paulie drive up, get out the tire jack, and take it into the garage. A minute later, Paulie is back in the car and speeding away. Nebels isn't sure if Paulie is going to get the police. He goes into the garage again. He sees the tire jack that Paulie has dropped. Will Nebels knows he's facing prison if Andrea can tell them what happened. He kills her, takes the tire jack with him, and gets out of there. After the movie, Rob drives to the hideout and finds Andrea dead and panics."

"Joan, don't you realize you've omitted something basic?" I hoped I didn't sound as impatient as I felt with her theory. "How did the tire jack get back in the trunk of Rob Westerfield's car?"

"Ellie, Andrea was murdered on Thursday night. You discovered her body on Friday morning. Rob Westerfield wasn't questioned until Saturday afternoon.

It isn't in the trial transcript, but on Friday, Will Nebels was working at the Westerfields', doing odd jobs. Rob's car was in the driveway. He always left the keys in it. Will could easily have replaced the tire jack that day."

"Where did you learn all this, Joan?"

"My cousin, Andrew, the judge, used to be in the district attorney's office. He was there when Rob Westerfield was on trial and was very familiar with the case. He's always felt that Rob Westerfield was a nasty, aggressive, worthless piece of humanity, but he also believed that he was innocent of Andrea's death."

Officer White believed that Paulie was guilty of Andrea's murder. Mrs. Hilmer was still doubtful about Paulie's innocence. Now Joan was convinced that Will Nebels was the killer.

Yet I knew with certainty that Rob Westerfield was the one who had taken my sister's life.

"Ellie, you're dismissing everything I've said." Joan's voice was quiet, her tone regretful.

"No, I'm not dismissing it. I promise you that. And as a hypothetical situation, it fits. But, Joan, Rob Westerfield was in the garage that morning when I was kneeling beside Andrea's body. I heard him breathing and I heard—it's so hard to explain. A giggle is as close as I can get to describing it. It's an odd gasping sound, and I had heard it before, one of the other times I was in his presence."

"How often would you have been in his presence, Ellie?"

"A couple of times when Andrea and I walked downtown after school or on Saturday, when he'd suddenly materialize. How much did Andrea tell you about him?"

"Not much at all. The first time I remember seeing him was at one of the high school games. She was in the band, of course, and really outstanding—she looked so good. I remember that Westerfield came up to her after a game in early October. I was standing with her. He made an outright play for her, saying how pretty she was, how he couldn't take his eyes off her—that kind of thing. He was older and very good looking, and she was flattered, of course. Plus I guess your mother had talked a lot about how important the Westerfield family was."

"Yes."

"He knew that we liked to sneak into his grandmother's garage and smoke. And I mean regular cigarettes, not pot. We thought we were hot stuff, but we weren't into anything illegal. Rob Westerfield told us to consider the place our clubhouse but to let him know when we planned to go over. Then when we did, he'd ask Andrea to get there early. You do realize that she had been friends with him—if you can call it that—for only a month or so before she died."

"Did you ever get the feeling that she had become afraid of him?"

"I got the feeling that something was terribly wrong, but she wouldn't tell me what it was. That last night she called and asked if she could come over so we could do homework together. Frankly, my mother wasn't thrilled. I was behind in algebra, and she wanted me to concentrate. She knew that Andrea and I wasted a lot of time talking when we were supposed to be studying. Also, Mom was going to her bridge club, so she wouldn't be around to make sure we were working."

"Did you finish the homework early, or do you think Andrea used you to get out of the house and meet Rob?"

"I think she intended to leave early all along, so I guess the answer is yes, I was her excuse."

And then I asked the crucial question: "Do you know if Rob ever gave Andrea a locket?"

"No, she didn't mention it to me, and if he *did* give her one, then I never saw it. Your dad gave her a locket, though, and she wore that fairly often."

Andrea had been wearing a heavy V-necked sweater that night. That was why I was so clear about seeing her clasping the locket around her neck. It was on a fairly long chain and rested at the base of the neckline.

"Then to the best of your memory she didn't have any jewelry on when she left your house?"

"I didn't say that. As I remember, she was wearing a thin gold chain. It was short, choker length."

But that's *it,* I thought, suddenly remembering another part of that evening. Her coat was downstairs, and Mother was waiting for her. Before she left the bedroom, Andrea had turned the locket around and let it fall down her back, between her shoulder blades. The effect was one of wearing a choker-length chain.

I had carefully read the description of the clothing Andrea had been wearing when her body was found. There had been no mention of that chain.

I left Joan's house a few minutes later with the sincere promise that I would call her soon. I didn't attempt to tell her that she had unwittingly verified my memory of Andrea putting on the locket.

Rob Westerfield had come back for it the morning after he killed her. I was very sure now that that locket had been too important to risk leaving on her body. Tomorrow I would describe it on the Website as I had described it to Marcus Longo twenty-two years ago.

It's another line to cast, I thought as I again drove

past the Graymoor Monastery. If Rob Westerfield was worried enough to come back and get the locket, somebody out there might be interested in getting a reward to tell me why it was so important to him.

The bells of the Graymoor chapel began to chime. It was noon.

Grammar school. Praying the Angelus at noon. *And the Angel of the Lord announced to Mary*. . . And Mary's response to Elizabeth. *My soul doth magnify the Lord. . . . And my spirit doth rejoice*. . .

Maybe someday my spirit will again rejoice, I thought as I turned on the radio.

But not yet.

23

From the clerk's desk at the Parkinson Inn I could look into the restaurant and see that it was enjoying its usual weekend luncheon crowd. Today's group appeared to be particularly festive. I wondered if the sunny fall afternoon had a cheering effect after the several dreary days in the early part of the week.

"I'm afraid that all eight rooms are booked for the weekend, Ms. Cavanaugh," the clerk told me. "It's been that way every weekend this fall, and will be till Christmas."

Of course, that said it all. There was no use staying here during the week, then moving out for the weekend. I'd have to find another place. The prospect of driving from one inn or motel to another seeking admittance, however, was decidedly unappealing. I decided it would be a lot more efficient to go back to the apartment, get out the phone book, and start making calls to see where I could find housing for the next few months. Preferably I'd find something that wouldn't cost an arm and a leg.

The bake-and-serve corn muffin I'd had that morning was all I'd had to eat so far that day. It was then twenty of one, and I didn't particularly feel like having an American cheese, tomato, and lettuce sandwich, which, to the best of my recollection, was all that I'd find in the apartment.

I went into the restaurant and was promptly seated. Technically it was a table for two, but any person in the other seat would have to be skeletal in dimensions. That chair backed up on a sharp corner of the alcove where I'd been placed, leaving no room. Next to me was a table for six which had a reservation sign propped against the salt and pepper shakers.

In my nomadic wanderings I had been to Boston only once, when I was following up on a news story I was writing. That brief visit had left me with a permanent love of New England clam chowder, which according to the menu was the soup of the day.

I ordered it, along with a green salad and a bottle of Perrier. "I like the soup really hot, please," I told the waitress. While I waited to be served, I nibbled on crusty bread and began to analyze why I was feeling disquieted and even depressed.

It wasn't *that* hard to figure out, I decided. A few weeks ago when I came here, I'd felt like a kind of feminine Don Quixote tilting at windmills. But the sobering truth was that even the very people who I would have thought were as convinced as I was of Rob Westerfield's guilt were not taking my side.

They *knew* him. They knew what he was. And still they thought it was entirely possible he had spent his twenties and thirties in prison an innocent man, himself a victim of this crime. Sympathetic as they were to me, in their eyes I was perceived as the obsessed family member of the dead girl, fixated and unreasonable at best, manic and unbalanced at worst.

I know that in some ways I am arrogant. When I think I'm right, all the forces of heaven and hell won't budge me. Maybe that's why I'm a good investigative reporter. I have a reputation for being able to cut through the obfuscation, target what I perceive to be the truth, and then prove my case. Now, sitting in this restaurant where long ago I sat as the smallest member of a happy family, I tried to be honest with myself. Was it possible, was it *remotely* possible, that the same drive that made me a good reporter was working against me now? Was I doing a disservice not only to people like Mrs. Hilmer and Joan Lashley, but to the man I despised, Rob Westerfield?

I was so intent on my own thoughts that I was startled when a hand came across my vision. It was the waitress with the clam chowder. As I'd requested, steam was rising from the bowl.

"Be careful," she warned. "It's really hot."

Mother used to tell us that it's not appropriate to thank a waiter or waitress for service, but that lesson never took with me. To say "thank you" when something that you wanted is placed in front of you never seemed inappropriate to me, and still doesn't.

I picked up the spoon, but before I could take the first sip, the party arrived for the reserved table next to me. I looked up and my throat went dry—Rob Westerfield was standing beside my chair.

I laid down the spoon. He extended his hand, and I ignored it. He was a stunningly handsome man, even more so in person than he had been on television. There was a kind of animal magnetism about him, a suggestion of strength and confidence that is the trademark of many powerful men I have interviewed.

His eyes were a startling cobalt blue, his dark hair lightly brushed at the temples with gray, his complexion surprisingly tanned. I had seen prison pallor on other men and had the fleeting thought that since his release he must have spent several hours under a sunlamp.

"The hostess pointed you out, Ellie," he said, his voice as warm as though we were acquaintances who happened on each other every so often.

"Did she, indeed?"

"She realized who you are and was quite upset. She

didn't have another table for six and thought I might not want to be seated near you."

From the corner of my eye I could see his companions taking their seats. Two of them I recognized from the television interview—his father, Vincent Westerfield, and his lawyer, William Hamilton. They were looking at me, their expressions hostile.

"Did it occur to her that I might not want to be anywhere near *you*?" I asked quietly.

"Ellie, you are totally mistaken about me. I want to find your sister's murderer and see him punished just as much as you do. Can we get together and talk quietly?" He hesitated, then, with a smile, added, "Please, Ellie."

I realized that the entire dining room had suddenly become quiet. Since everyone seemed to want to be in on our exchange, I deliberately raised my voice so that at least some of them could overhear me. "I'd love to get together with you, Rob," I said. "How about at the garage-hideout? That was a favorite place of yours, wasn't it? Or maybe the memory of bludgeoning a fifteen-year-old girl to death there might be painful even for a consummate liar like you."

I threw a twenty-dollar bill on the table and pushed back my chair.

Without the slightest indication of being upset by what I had said, Rob picked up the twenty and shoved it in the pocket of my jacket. "We have a house account here, Ellie. Anytime you come in, you're our guest. Bring your friends." Again he paused, but this time his eyes narrowed.

"If you have any," he added quietly.

I took the twenty-dollar bill out of my pocket, spotted the waitress, gave it to her, and left.

Half an hour later I was back in the apartment. The kettle was whistling, and I was putting together the previously rejected cheese sandwich, complete with lettuce and tomato. By then the fit of trembling that overcame me in the car had passed, and only my hands, cold and clammy, reflected the shock of seeing Rob Westerfield face to face.

Over and over in that half hour, a scene had been replaying itself in my mind. *I am on the witness stand. Flanked by his lawyers, Rob is sitting at the table reserved for the accused. He is staring at me, his eyes malevolent and sneering. I am sure that in a moment he will spring up and attack me.*

The intensity of his concentration when he was inches away from me in the restaurant was just as absolute as it had been at the trial, and behind those cobalt blue eyes and the courteous tone, I felt and saw the same relentless hatred.

But there *is* a difference, I kept reminding myself, until I began to calm down. I'm twenty-nine, not seven.

And one way or the other, I'll do him more harm now than I did then. After the trial, one of the reporters had written, "The sad and earnest child who testified in court that her big sister was really scared of Rob Westerfield carried great weight with the jury."

I took the sandwich and the tea to the table, got the phone book out of the cabinet, and opened my cellular phone. While I was eating, I decided to go through the Yellow Pages and circle places where I could inquire about a monthly rental.

Before I could begin, Mrs. Hilmer called. I started to explain to her that I was looking for a place to stay, but she cut me off. "Ellie, I just got a call from my oldest granddaughter, Janey. Remember I told you that she had her first baby last month?"

I could hear the strain in Mrs. Hilmer's voice. "Nothing is wrong with the baby, I hope," I said quickly.

"No. The baby's fine. But Janey broke her wrist and could use some help. I'm driving to Long Island this afternoon and will stay a few days. Did you make plans to go to the Parkinson Inn? After what's happened, I worry about your being alone out here."

"I stopped at the Inn, but they're all booked up for the weekend and for the next six or seven weekends as well. I'm just starting to call around to other inns and guest houses now."

"Ellie, I hope you realize that my concern is only for you. Stay in the apartment until you find something suitable, but for God's sake be sure to lock the doors."

"I will, I promise. Please don't worry about me."

"I'm taking the copies of the trial transcript and the newspapers with me. I'll be going over them while I'm in Garden City with Janey. Take down her phone number in case you want to reach me."

I jotted it down and a few minutes later heard Mrs. Hilmer's car headed down the driveway. I will confess that after the shock of seeing Rob Westerfield, I was very sorry that she had left.

"Fraidy cat, fraidy cat." That was how Andrea would tease me when, if our parents were out, we watched movies like *Friday the 13th* together on television. I always closed my eyes and snuggled against her at the scariest parts.

I remember that one night, to get back at her, I hid under her bed, and when she came into the bedroom, I reached out and grabbed her leg. *"Fraidy cat, fraidy cat,"* I chanted when she shrieked.

But Andrea wasn't here to snuggle up to now, and I'm a big girl, used to taking care of myself. I gave a mental shrug and began circling the local guest houses and inns in the Yellow Pages.

Then I started phoning the seemingly likely ones; it proved to be a dismaying task. The few that sounded possible were pretty expensive on a monthly basis, especially when I figured in the price of meals.

At the end of nearly two hours I had a short list of four places and was already looking through the newspaper at the "houses for rent" section. Oldham is pretty much a year-round community, but from the classified section I could see some rentals that appeared to be reasonable.

At three-thirty I was finished; I had six places lined up to see tomorrow. I was glad to be done because I wanted to get to the computer to write notes on my encounter with Westerfield.

There were one or two inns in the area where they said they had a room available immediately. Either one would have been all right on an interim basis, but the last thing in the world I wanted to do now was start packing. I also did not want to start emptying the refrigerator and thoroughly cleaning the apartment.

Mrs. Hilmer had made it very clear that it was my safety she was concerned about and that I was to stay here until I found something suitable. I knew she'd be gone at least three or four days, so I debated with myself, then made a decision: I would stay here for now, at least over the weekend, probably until Monday.

I opened the computer, made notes on the meeting with Westerfield, and then realized I was having a hard time concentrating. My solution was to catch an early movie and afterward have dinner somewhere nearby.

I looked up the movie listings and noted with irony that the film I wanted to see was showing at the Globe Cinema.

That was where Rob Westerfield claimed he had been when Andrea was murdered.

The Globe had obviously been enlarged and updated since I was a child. It now had seven different films being shown. The lobby held a large, circular service counter where brisk sales in candy, popcorn, and sodas were being made.

Even though the early viewers were just arriving, the lobby floor was already beginning to be littered with kernels of popcorn that had spilled from the tops of overfilled paper cones.

I bought Peanut Chews—my favorite candy—and went into cinema 3, which was where the film I'd selected was being shown. It turned out to be not nearly the ballyhooed sensation (*"Now! At last! The picture you've been waiting for!"*) I'd expected, but mostly a mildly entertaining story about a woman who takes on the world, is vilified, and then, of course, conquers all and finds true love and happiness in the husband she'd kicked out three years earlier.

If they're that hard up for ideas, maybe I can sell

them the story of my life, I thought as my attention continued to wander. My life minus the love interest, of course.

I was seated between two couples, senior citizens on my right, teenagers on my left. The teenagers passed the bag of popcorn back and forth, and the girl kept up a running commentary on the film.

She used to be my favorite actress, but now I don't think she's as good as . . .

There was no use trying to pay attention to what was happening on the screen. It wasn't just the kids and the popcorn and the play-by-play comments, or even the slight snore of the elderly man next to me, who by then had dozed off.

I was distracted by the fact that twenty-two years ago Rob Westerfield claimed to be in this theater while Andrea was being murdered, and no one could verify that he'd actually stayed to see the picture. Even with all the publicity the case engendered, not one person ever came forward and said, "He was sitting next to me."

Oldham was a fairly small town at that time, and the Westerfields were well known. Certainly Rob Westerfield, with his good looks and rich-boy attitude, was high profile enough to be known around town. As I sat there in that darkened movie house, I visualized him parking in the service station lot next door.

He had claimed that he spoke to Paulie Stroebel, that he told him he was leaving his car. Paulie absolutely denied that Rob spoke to him.

Then Rob made a point of talking to the ticket seller and to the ticket taker, saying something about how much he was looking forward to the film. "Real friendly," they both testified on the stand, their voices tinged with surprise. Rob Westerfield was not known for being friendly, especially to the working class.

He could easily have established his presence in the theater and then slipped out. I had rented the movie *The Guerrilla Jungle Lord* that he claimed to have seen that night. There are plenty of early scenes where the screen is so dark that someone in an end seat could easily have left without being seen. I looked around, noticed the several side exits that are only supposed to be used in emergencies, and decided to try something.

I got up, mumbled an apology for waking my sleeping neighbor, climbed over his wife, and made my way to the side exit near the back of the room.

The door opened quietly, and I found myself in a sort of alleyway between a bank and the cinema complex. Years ago, the service station, not the bank, had been here. I have copies of the diagrams and photographs that the newspapers printed during the trial, so I remembered the layout of the service station.

The enclosed garage where Paulie had been working

was behind the gas pumps and faced Main Street. The parking area, where cars waiting to be serviced were kept, was behind the station. That area is now a parking lot for bank customers.

I walked down the alley, mentally replacing the bank with the service station. I could even visualize where Rob claimed he had parked his car and where it supposedly sat until the film was over at nine-thirty.

Somehow my footsteps became his, and I was in his mind—angry, bad-tempered, thwarted when the girl he thought he had under his thumb phoned to tell him she had a date with someone else.

Never mind that the someone else was Paulie Stroebel.

Meet Andrea. Show her who's boss.

Why did he take the tire jack into the hideout? I asked myself.

There were two possible reasons. One was that he was afraid that my father had learned Andrea was planning to meet him. I have no doubt that my father would have loomed in Rob's mind as a frightening and formidable figure.

The other reason was that Rob took the tire jack with him because he was planning to kill Andrea.

Fraidy cat. Fraidy cat. Oh, God, how terrified the poor kid must have been when she saw him coming at her, saw him lift his arm, brandishing that weapon. . . .

I turned and literally ran back to the other end of the alley where it joined the street. Gulping for air—because for a moment I had literally felt unable to breathe—I steadied myself and walked to my car. I'd left it in the cinema parking lot on the other side of the complex.

The air was still clear, but like last night, a sharp wind had blown up and the temperature was dropping rapidly. I shivered and quickened my steps.

When I'd looked up the film schedule, I noticed an ad for a restaurant, Villa Cesaere, not far from the theater. The ad had made it sound like the kind of place I enjoyed, so I decided to give it a try. I knew I wanted pasta, and the spicier the better. Maybe shrimp *fra diavolo,* I decided.

I simply had to get rid of the terrible inner chill that was overwhelming me.

At nine-fifteen, fed and feeling somewhat better, I turned the car off the street and onto Mrs. Hilmer's property. Her house was in darkness, and the light at the door of the garage made for a feeble welcome.

I brought the car to a sudden stop. Something was urging me to turn around, to go to an inn or motel and spend the night there. I simply hadn't realized how insecure I would feel here tonight. I'll leave tomorrow, I thought. One more night here won't be so bad. As soon as I'm in the apartment, I'll be all right.

Of course, even that rationalization didn't make sense. While I was having dinner with Mrs. Hilmer the other evening, someone had been in the apartment. But somehow I didn't think I would find anyone waiting for me there now. My current sense of uneasiness came more from the prospect of being alone outside, so near the woods, if only for a few moments.

I turned the headlights on bright and drove slowly down the driveway. I had been carrying the duffel bag containing the trial transcript, newspapers, and my mother's jewelry in the trunk of the car all day. When I left the restaurant, I moved the bag from the trunk to the front seat so that once back at the apartment I wouldn't have to stand outside while I retrieved it.

Now I carefully scanned the area around the garage. There was no one there.

I took a deep breath, picked up the duffel bag, got out of the car, and hurried the few steps to the door.

Before I could insert the key in the lock, a car roared down the driveway and screeched to a stop. A man jumped out and lunged at me.

I stood frozen, sure I was about to see Rob Westerfield's face and hear the giggle-like sound he'd made as I was kneeling over Andrea's body.

But then a flashlight shone on me, and as he came

closer, I could see that the man was wearing a uniform and that it was Officer White.

"I was given to understand that you'd moved, Ms. Cavanaugh," he said, his tone decidedly unfriendly. "What are you doing here?"

24

After a few awkward moments as I explained why I hadn't moved out yet, I insisted that Officer White come up to the apartment and phone Mrs. Hilmer at her granddaughter's house. I had left the number on a sheet of paper next to the computer. He made the call, then put me on with her.

"I'm so embarrassed, Ellie," she said. "I asked Officer White to have the police keep an eye on the house while I was away, and I told him you were leaving, but he certainly should have taken your word that you were still my guest."

You're absolutely right, I thought, but what I said was "He's right to be careful, Mrs. Hilmer." I didn't tell her that, rude as he'd been, I was actually very pleased he was here. It meant I didn't have to enter the apartment alone, and after he left, I would bolt the door.

I inquired about her granddaughter, said good-bye, and got off the phone.

"You'll be leaving tomorrow then, Ms. Cavanaugh?"

Officer White asked. From his tone he might as well have said, "Here's your hat, what's your hurry?"

"Yes, Officer. Don't worry. I'll be leaving tomorrow."

"Have you had any response to that sign you carried outside Sing Sing?"

"As a matter of fact, I have," I said, giving him what Pete Lawlor calls my mysterious, self-satisfied smile.

He frowned. I had piqued his curiosity, which is exactly what I wanted to do.

"It's all over town that you had some pretty nasty things to say to Rob Westerfield at the Parkinson Inn today."

"There's no law against being honest, and there's certainly not one that says you have to make nice with murderers."

His cheekbones reddened as he stood with his hand on the doorknob. "Ms. Cavanaugh, let me give you a piece of advice from the real world. I know for a certainty that with the family money to throw around, Rob Westerfield was able to develop a very loyal following in prison. That's just the way it is. Some of those guys are on the street now. Without even talking to Westerfield about it, one of them may decide to remove a certain irritant as a favor to him, anticipating appropriate gratitude of course."

"Who will free me from this turbulent priest?" I asked.

"What are you talking about?"

"A rhetorical question, Officer. In the twelfth century, Henry the Second made that remark to some of his noblemen, and a short time later Archbishop Thomas à Becket was murdered in his cathedral. You know something, Officer White? I can't be sure if you are warning me or threatening me."

"An investigative reporter should be able to tell the difference, Ms. Cavanaugh."

With that, he was gone. It seemed to me that his footsteps were unnecessarily loud on the staircase, as if wanting me to know that he was making a kind of final exit.

I bolted the door, walked to the window, and watched him get back into his squad car and drive away.

Usually I shower in the morning, and if it's been a particularly stressful day, I shower again before I go to bed. I find it's a great way to get the knots out of shoulders and neck muscles. Tonight I decided to go even further. I filled the tub with hot water and squirted in bath oil. After six months the bottle was still almost full, showing how often I get to laze around in a tub. But tonight I needed it, and it did feel good just to lie there and soak. I stayed until the water began to cool.

I'm always amused when I read ads for seductive and provocative nightgowns and robes. My night attire is nightshirts purchased from an L. L. Bean catalogue. They're roomy and comfortable, and their companion piece is a flannel robe. Topping off that exquisite ensemble are fleece-lined bedroom slippers.

The two-door bureau with the attached mirror in the bedroom reminded me of the one my mother had painted white and antiqued for Andrea's room. As I brushed my hair in front of the mirror, I wondered idly what had become of that bureau. When Mother and I moved to Florida, we brought comparatively little furniture with us. I am certain that nothing from Andrea's inviting room accompanied us. My room at that time had been nice, too, but it was little-girl cutesy, with a Cinderella-motif wallpaper.

Then, in a flash of memory, it came to me that I once told Mother I thought the paper was babyish, and she replied, "But it's almost the same as the paper Andrea had in her room when she was your age. *She* loved it."

I guess even then I realized how different we were. I wasn't into girly things, and I never cared about dress-up clothes. Andrea, like Mother, was utterly feminine.

"*You're daddy's little girl to have and hold. . . . You're the spirit of Christmas, my star on the tree. . . . And you're daddy's little girl.*"

Unbidden, the words of that song ran through my head, and I once again envisioned Daddy in Andrea's room, holding the music box and sobbing.

It was a memory that I always tried to immediately close off. "Finish brushing your hair, girl, and go to bed," I said aloud.

With a critical eye I studied myself in the mirror. I usually wore my hair up, anchored with a comb, but now, taking a good look, I saw how long it had grown. Over the summer it became very blond, and while most of the bleaching from the sun had faded, there were still bright streaks running through it.

I often recalled the remark Detective Longo had made the first time he questioned me after Andrea's body was found. He said that my hair, like his son's, reminded him of sand when the sun is shining on it. That was such a sweet description, and streaked as my hair is now, it felt good to think that it might be true again.

I watched the eleven o'clock news, just long enough to be sure the world outside Oldham was still more or less functioning. Then, after checking the locks on the living room windows, I went into the bedroom. The wind was really blowing, so I opened the two bedroom windows a couple of inches. The cross-breeze was enough to send me scurrying under the covers, dropping my robe on the footboard and kicking off my slippers on the way.

In my apartment in Atlanta I could always fall asleep easily. But of course it was different there. I could hear faint street noises and sometimes music from the apartment of my next-door neighbor, an aficionado of hard rock who sometimes played his CDs at ear-splitting volume.

A friendly thump on our joint wall always brought a quick response, but even so I was sometimes aware of metallic vibrations as I drifted off.

I would not mind a few metallic vibrations that signified the closeness of another human being tonight, I thought as I readjusted the pillow. It seemed to me that my senses were all on high alert—probably caused by the earlier face-to-face with Westerfield.

Pete's sister Jan lives not far from Atlanta in a little town called Peachtree. Sometimes on Sunday Pete would call me and say, "Let's go for a ride to see Jan and Bill and the kids." They have a German shepherd named Rocky who is a wonderful watchdog. The instant we got out of the car, he'd be furiously barking to alert the family to our presence.

I sure wish you were paying me a visit right now, Rocky, old pal, I thought.

I did eventually manage to fall into an uneasy sleep, the kind that makes you wish you could wake up. I was dreaming that there was some place I had to go. I had to find someone before it was too late. It was dark, and my flashlight wouldn't work.

Then I was in the woods, and I could smell a campfire.

I needed to find a path through the woods. There was one, I was sure of it. I'd been on it before.

It was so hot, and I was beginning to cough.

It wasn't a dream! I opened my eyes. The room was in total darkness and I could smell nothing but smoke. I was choking. I shoved back the covers and sat up. I could feel the heat building up around me. I'd burn to death if I didn't get out. Where was I? For a moment I simply couldn't orient myself.

Before I put my feet on the floor, I forced myself to think. I was in Mrs. Hilmer's apartment. The bedroom door was to the left of the bed. It was on a direct line with the headboard. Outside there was the little foyer. The apartment door was just past the foyer, on the left.

It probably took ten seconds for me to think that through. Then I was out of bed. I gasped as my feet touched the hot floorboard. I heard a crackling overhead. The roof was catching fire. I knew I only had seconds before the whole building caved in.

I stumbled forward, groping for the frame of the door. Thank God I had left it open. I felt my way along the foyer wall, passed the open space that was the frame for the bathroom door. The smoke was not quite as dense here, but then a wall of flame burst from the kitchen area of the living room. It illuminated the table, and I saw my computer, printer, and cell phone there. The duffel bag was on the floor next to the table.

I didn't want to lose them. It took a second to pull back the bolt and open the door to the stairs. Then, biting my lips from the pain of the blisters forming on my feet, coughing and gasping, I ran to the table, scooped up the computer, printer, and cell phone in one hand and the duffel bag in the other, and fled back to the door.

Behind me the flames were leaping onto the furniture, and ahead the smoke in the stairwell was thick and black. Fortunately, it was a straight staircase, and somehow I was able to stumble down it. At first the handle of the outside door seemed to be jammed. I dropped the computer, phone, and duffel bag, and yanked and twisted with both hands.

I'm trapped, I'm trapped, I thought as I felt my hair begin to singe. I gave a final desperate twist, and the handle turned. I pulled open the door, bent down and felt for my computer, and phone, and duffel bag, and stumbled out.

As I emerged, a man was running down the driveway and rushed to grab me before I fell. "Is anyone else still in there?" he shouted.

Shivering and burning at the same time, I shook my head. "My wife called the fire department," he said as he pulled me away from the blazing structure.

A car was rushing down the driveway. Only half-conscious, I realized it must have been his wife, because

I heard him say, "Lynn, take her home. She's got to get out of the cold. I'll wait for the fire department." Then to me he said, "Go with my wife. We live just down the road."

Five minutes later, for the first time in over twenty years, I was sitting in the kitchen of my old house, wrapped in a blanket, a cup of tea in front of me. Through the French doors that led to the dining room I could see Mother's beloved chandelier, still in place.

And I could see Andrea and me setting the table for Sunday dinner.

"Lord Malcolm Bigbottom is our guest today."

I closed my eyes.

"It's okay to cry, you know," Lynn, the lady who now lives in my old house, said kindly. "You've had a terrible ordeal."

But I managed to blink back the tears. I felt that if I ever started shedding them, I'd never be able to stop.

25

The fire chief came to the Keltons' house and insisted on having an ambulance take me to the hospital. "You must have inhaled a lot of smoke, Ms. Cavanaugh," he said. "You need to be checked out, if only as a precaution."

Oldham County Hospital kept me overnight, which was just as well since I had no place else to go. When I was finally in bed—after the soot and grime were removed from my face and body, and my blistered feet were bandaged—I gladly accepted a sleeping pill. The room I was in was near the nurses' station, and I could hear the soft murmur of voices and the sound of footsteps.

As I fell asleep, I thought about how a few hours ago I'd been wishing for company. I never expected to have my wish granted this way.

When I was woken by a nurse's aide at seven o'clock in the morning, there wasn't a part of me that didn't ache. She checked my pulse and blood pressure and departed. I pushed back the blanket, swung my legs onto the floor, and, not sure of what would happen, tried to stand up. The soles of my feet were padded with bandages, and putting weight on them was terribly uncomfortable, but other than that I knew I was in pretty good shape.

That was when I began to realize how lucky I had been. Just a few minutes more, and I am sure I would have been overcome by smoke. By the time the Keltons arrived on the scene, it would have been impossible to save me, even had they known I was there.

Was the fire an accident? I knew it wasn't. Although I never looked inside, Mrs. Hilmer had told me that the garage under the apartment had very little in it except gardening tools.

Gardening tools don't burst into flames.

Officer White had warned me that a fellow ex-prisoner trying to curry favor with Rob Westerfield might try to get rid of me for him. I think White had the order of things reversed. I had not the slightest doubt that that fire had been ordered by Westerfield and that he had given the assignment to a former lackey in Sing Sing. It wouldn't surprise me a bit to learn that the guy who spoke to me in the prison parking lot got the assignment.

I was sure that by now Mrs. Hilmer had been

notified of the fire by Officer White—I had given him her granddaughter's phone number on Long Island. I knew how distressing it was for her to learn that the garage with the apartment was gone. It had originally been a barn and had some historic value as a structure.

Mrs. Hilmer was seventy-three years old. The apartment over the garage had been her insurance that if she ever needed any kind of live-in assistance, she had separate living quarters to offer.

I'm sure as well that her granddaughter's accident made her keenly aware of how easy it is to be incapacitated.

Would insurance enable her to rebuild that structure, or would she even want the headache of having the work done? Right now Mrs. Hilmer must be thinking that no good deed goes unpunished, I thought unhappily. I would phone her, but not yet. How do you apologize for something like this?

Then I thought about the duffel bag and my computer, printer, and cell phone. I had made sure they accompanied me to the hospital room, and I remembered that the nurse said something about putting them away for me. Where were they?

There was a locker-style closet in the room. I hobbled over to it, hoping and praying that I'd find them there. I opened the door and was delighted to see them piled neatly on the floor.

I was equally delighted to see a hospital-issue chenille robe on a hanger. I was wearing one of those godforsaken hospital gowns. It was meant for someone the size of a Barbie doll, whereas I am five feet nine inches tall.

The first thing I did was unzip the duffel bag and look inside. The crumbling first page of the *New York Post* with the headline "GUILTY" was on top, just as it had been when I last opened it.

Then I reached into the bag and slid my hand down the side. My fingers groped around. I breathed a sigh of relief when I felt the leather case that I had been seeking.

Yesterday morning, just as I was getting in the car to go to Joan's house, it occurred to me that the next unauthorized visitor to the apartment might rummage around for valuables. I ran back upstairs, took the case from the drawer, and put it in the duffel bag that was already in the trunk.

Now I pulled out the case and opened it. Everything was there—Mother's engagement and wedding rings, her diamond earrings, and my modest collection of jewelry.

Gratefully, I put the case back in the bag, closed it, and picked up the computer. I carried it to the single chair, located by the window. I knew that however long I'd be in the hospital today, I'd spend my time right there.

I turned on the computer and held my breath, exhaling only when the beep sounded, the screen lit up, and I knew I hadn't lost any of the material I had stored in it.

My peace of mind somewhat restored, I hobbled back to the closet, reached for the bathrobe, and went into the bathroom. There was a small tube of toothpaste, a plastic-sealed toothbrush, and a comb on a shelf over the sink. I proceeded to attempt to tidy up.

I know that I was in shock after the fire. Now, as my thinking cleared, I began to realize how very lucky I had been to escape, not only alive, but not seriously burned. I knew also that I would have to be much more vigilant about future attempts to take my life. One thing was certain: I had to be in a place where there would be a desk clerk and other employees around.

When I'd given up trying to pull the small comb through my tangled hair, I went back into the room, settled in the chair, and, since I didn't have pen or paper, opened the computer to make a list of the things I had to do immediately.

I had no money, no clothes, no credit cards, no driver's license—all these had been lost in the fire. I would have to borrow money until I could get duplicates of my credit cards and driver's license. So who would be the lucky recipient of my pleading call?

I have friends in Atlanta, and I have school friends scattered around the country whom I could have phoned for help and received it in a minute. I crossed them off my list, though. I just didn't want to go into a long explanation as to why I was temporarily destitute.

Pete was the only one in Atlanta who knew about Andrea and about why I was here. When I took the leave of absence to come here, my explanation to my coworkers and friends had been "It's personal, guys."

I'm sure the general impression is that Ellie, who's always too busy for a blind date, is involved with somebody special and is trying to work things out with him.

Pete? The thought of having to play the helpless female to his save-the-day hero irritated me. I'd make him the court of last resort.

I'm sure I could have called Joan Lashley St. Martin, but her belief that Rob Westerfield was innocent of Andrea's death made me reluctant to go to her for help.

Marcus Longo? Of course, I thought! He'll stake me, and I'll pay him back within the week.

A breakfast tray came and was picked up an hour later, virtually untouched. Have you ever been in a hospital that actually served hot coffee?

The doctor arrived, checked my blistered feet, told me I was free to go home anytime, and departed. I had a mental image of limping around Oldham in hospital gear, asking for a handout. At precisely that psychologically low moment, Officer White appeared with a sharp-featured man he introduced as Detective Charles Bannister of the Oldham Police Department. A hospital orderly was behind them carrying folding chairs, so I gathered that this was not going to be a quick, cheery bedside visit.

Bannister expressed concern for my well-being and the hope that after the ordeal I was feeling as well as possible.

I immediately sensed that beneath the veneer of concern he had an agenda in mind, and it wasn't a friendly one.

I told him that I was quite well and grateful to be alive, a comment he accepted with a nod of his head. I was reminded of a professor I had in a philosophy course in college. After hearing a particularly stupid observation from one of the students, he would give that same kind of nod with a grave expression.

What it meant was "Now I've heard everything."

It didn't take me long to understand that Detective Bannister had one goal in mind: He was determined to prove his theory that I had made up the initial story about the intruder in the apartment. He didn't put it quite so bluntly, but the scenario he put together went pretty much as follows: After hearing about the supposed intruder, Mrs. Hilmer had been nervous. She only imagined someone had followed her to and from the library. Disguising my voice, I made the phone call warning her that I was unstable.

At that, I raised an eyebrow, but said nothing.

According to Detective Bannister, I had set the fire to gain attention and sympathy for myself, while publicly accusing Rob Westerfield of trying to kill me.

"You were in danger of being burned to death, but according to the neighbor who saw you emerge from the building, you were carrying a computer, a printer, a cell phone, and a large, heavy duffel bag. Most people in an inferno don't stop to pack, Ms. Cavanaugh."

"Just as I reached the door to the stairs, the wall at one end of the living room became a sheet of flames. It illuminated the table where I had left those things. They were very important to me, and I took that extra second to grab them."

"Why were they so important, Ms. Cavanaugh?"

"Let me tell you why, Detective Bannister." The computer was still on my lap, and I pointed to it. "The first chapter of the book I am writing about Rob Westerfield is in this computer. Pages and pages of notes that I have honed from the trial transcript of *The State versus Robson Westerfield* are also in it. I do not have backup. I do not have copies in another place."

His face remained impassive, but I noticed that Officer White's mouth was becoming a thin, angry line.

"I posted my cell phone number on the sign I was carrying when I was outside Sing Sing prison. I'm sure you've heard about my appearance there from him." I jerked my head at White. "I've already received one very interesting phone call from someone who knew Westerfield in prison. That phone is my only chance to stay in contact with him until I can get to a store, buy a new cell phone, and get the number transferred. As for the heavy duffel bag, it's in the closet. Would you care to see the contents?"

"Yes, I would."

I put the computer on the floor and stood up.

"I'll get it for you," he said.

"I prefer to keep it in my own hands at all times."

I tried not to limp as I rushed across the room. I yanked open the closet door, picked up the duffel bag, brought it back, dropped it in front of my chair, sat down, and unzipped it.

I could sense rather than see the startled reaction of the two men as they read the headline "GUILTY."

"I would prefer not to be showing these to you." I spat out the words as I yanked newspaper after newspaper from the bag and tossed them on the floor.

"My mother kept these all her life." I made no attempt to hide my anger. "They are the news accounts—starting with the discovery of my sister's body and including the moment when Rob Westerfield was sentenced to prison. They don't make *pleasant* reading, but they do make *interesting* reading, and I don't want to lose them."

The last of the newspapers was on the floor. I had to use both hands to pull out the trial transcript. I held up the cover page for them to see. "Also interesting reading, Detective Bannister," I said.

"I'm sure it is," he agreed, his face impassive. "Anything else in there, Ms. Cavanaugh?"

"If you're hoping to find a can of gasoline and a box of matches, you're out of luck." I took out the leather case and opened it. "Go through this, please."

He glanced at the contents and handed the case back to me. "Do you always carry your jewelry with you in a duffel bag with newspapers, Ms. Cavanaugh, or only when you suspect there might be a fire?"

He stood up, and White jumped to his feet. "You'll be hearing from us, Ms. Cavanaugh. Are you returning to Atlanta, or will you be staying in the area?"

"I'll be staying in the area, and I will be glad to inform you of my address. Perhaps the police department will keep a better eye on those premises than they did on Mrs. Hilmer's property. Do you think that might be possible?"

Officer White's cheekbones became stained with purple. I knew he was furious and I knew I was being reckless, but at that point I didn't care.

Bannister didn't bother to answer but turned abruptly and left with White at his heels.

I watched them go. The orderly came into the room to collect the folding chairs. His eyes widened as he took in the sight of me with the transcript on my lap, the jewelry case in my hand, the duffel bag, and scattered newspapers on the floor.

"Miss, can I help you gather them up?" he offered. "Or can I get you something? You look kind of upset."

"I am upset," I agreed. "And you can get something for me. Is there a cafeteria in the hospital?"

"Yeah. A real good one."

"Would you consider . . ." I stopped because I was on the verge of hysteria. "Would you consider treating me to a cup of very hot black coffee?"

26

Thirty minutes later I was savoring the last sip of the excellent coffee the orderly had kindly bought for me when I had another visitor, more surprising this time. My father.

The door was partially open. He tapped on it, then walked in without waiting for a response. We stared at each other, and my throat went dry.

His dark hair was now silvery white. He was a little thinner, but held himself as erectly as ever. Glasses accentuated his keen blue eyes, and there were deep furrows in his forehead.

My mother chiding, "Ted, I know you don't realize it, but you've got to stop frowning when you concentrate. You're going to look like a prune when you get older."

He certainly didn't look like a prune. He was still a good-looking man and hadn't lost that aura of inner strength.

"Hello, Ellie," he said.

"Hello, Dad."

I can only imagine what he was thinking when he looked at me garbed in a cheap hospital bathrobe, my hair a mass of tangles, bandages on my feet. Certainly not the shining star of the song on the music box.

"How are you, Ellie?"

I'd forgotten the deep resonance in his voice. It was the sound of quiet authority that Andrea and I had respected as children. We had felt protected by it, and I, at least, was in awe of it.

"I'm very well, thank you."

"I came here as soon as I heard about the fire at Mrs. Hilmer's and learned that you'd been in that apartment."

"You needn't have bothered."

He'd been standing just inside the door. Now he pushed it shut and came over to me. He knelt down and tried to take my hands. "Ellie, for God's sake, you're my daughter. How do you think I felt when I heard that you barely got out alive?"

I pulled my hands away. "Oh, that story will change. The cops think I set the fire as a grandstand gesture. According to *them*, I want attention and sympathy."

He was shocked. "That's ridiculous."

He was so close that I caught the faint scent of his shaving cream. Was I wrong, or was it the same scent

I remembered? He was wearing a shirt and tie with a dark blue jacket and gray slacks. Then I remembered that this was Sunday morning and that he might have been dressing to go to church when he heard about the fire.

"I know you mean to be kind," I said, "but I really wish you would leave me alone. I don't *need* anything from you, and I don't *want* anything from you."

"Ellie, I've seen that Website. Westerfield is dangerous. I'm desperately worried about you."

Well, at least I had one thing in common with my father. We both knew Rob Westerfield was a killer.

"I can take care of myself. I've been doing it for a long time."

He stood up. "That's not my fault, Ellie. You refused to visit me."

"I guess I did, so that means your conscience is clear. Don't let me keep you."

"I came to invite you, to *implore* you, to stay with us. That way I can protect you. If you remember, I was a state trooper for thirty-five years."

"I remember. You looked great in uniform. Oh, I did write and thank you for interring Mother's ashes in Andrea's grave, didn't I?"

"Yes, you did."

"Her death certificate gave the cause of death as 'cirrhosis of the liver,' but I think a more accurate diagnosis would be 'broken heart.' And my sister's death wasn't the only reason for that broken heart."

"Ellie, your mother left me."

"My mother *adored* you. You could have waited her out. You could have followed her to Florida and brought her home—brought *us* home. You didn't want to."

My father reached into his pocket and took out his wallet. I hoped he wouldn't dare to offer me money, but that didn't happen. He pulled out a card and laid it on the bed. "You can reach me anytime, day or night, Ellie."

Then he was gone, but the faint scent of his shaving cream seemed to linger after him. I'd forgotten that sometimes I would sit on the edge of the tub and talk to him while he was shaving. I'd forgotten that sometimes he would spin around, pick me up, and rub his face, thick with lather, against mine.

So vivid was the memory that I reached up and touched my cheek, almost expecting to feel the residue of damp suds. My cheek was wet, but it was with the tears that, for the moment at least, I could no longer deny.

27

I tried to reach Marcus Longo twice in the next hour. Then I remembered that he had said something about his wife not liking to fly alone. I realized that there was a very good chance he had flown to Denver to escort her home, and while there he'd have another adoring visit with his first grandchild.

The nurse popped her head in and reminded me that checkout time was noon. By eleven-thirty I was ready to ask if there was a social services office in the hospital, but then Joan called.

"Ellie, I just heard what happened. For heaven's sake, how are you? What can I do?"

Any pride that I had about refusing help because she didn't believe Rob Westerfield was a murdering animal evaporated. I needed her, and I knew darn well that she was as sincere in her conviction about his innocence as I was in mine about his guilt.

"Actually, you can do a lot," I said. Relief at hearing a friendly voice made my own voice tremble. "You can dig up some clothes for me. You can come and get me. You can help me find a place to stay. You can lend me some money."

"You'll stay with us—" she began.

"Negative. No. That's neither a good nor a safe idea for either one of us. You don't need your house to burst into flames because I'm around."

"Ellie, you don't believe that someone set that fire with the intent of killing you!"

"Yes, I do."

She considered that news for a moment, and I'm sure thought of her three children. "Then where can you stay that you'll be safe, Ellie?"

"An inn is my preference. I don't like the idea of a motel with separate doors to the outside." I thought of something. "Forget the Parkinson Inn. It's booked." And it's a Westerfield hangout, I reminded myself.

"I have a place in mind that I think will work," Joan said. "I also have a friend who's about your height and weight. I'll call her to borrow some clothes. What's your shoe size?"

"Nine, but I don't think I can take the bandages off my feet yet."

"Leo is a size ten. If you don't mind wearing a pair of his sneakers, they might do for now."

I didn't mind.

*

Joan arrived within the hour with a suitcase containing underwear, pajamas, stockings, slacks, a turtleneck sweater, a warm jacket, gloves, the sneakers, and some toiletries. I dressed, and the nurse brought in a cane I could use in walking until my blistered feet began to heal. On the way out, the billing clerk reluctantly agreed to wait for payment until I could have a copy of my medical insurance card faxed to her.

Finally we were in Joan's SUV. My hair was smoothed back and caught at the neckline with a rubber band I had acquired at the nurses' station. A cursory glance in the mirror showed that it looked tidy enough. The borrowed clothes fit quite well, and even though the sneakers looked wide and ungainly, they did a good job of protecting my painful feet.

"I made a reservation for you at the Hudson Valley Inn," Joan told me. "It's about a mile away."

"If you don't mind, I'd like to drive to Mrs. Hilmer's place. My car is still there—or at least, I hope it's there."

"Who would take it?"

"No one would take it, but it was parked about two feet from the garage. I'm keeping my fingers crossed that a beam or some debris didn't fall on it."

There wasn't a wall standing of the structure that had housed the cheery apartment Mrs. Hilmer had so generously lent me. The area around it was cordoned off, and a policeman was standing guard.

Three men in heavy rubber boots were painstakingly examining the rubble and undoubtedly trying to pinpoint the source of the blaze. They looked up when they saw us, but then went back to their probing.

I was relieved to see that my car had been moved about twenty feet toward Mrs. Hilmer's house. We got out of the SUV to examine it. It's a previously owned BMW that I bought two years ago, the first decent car I've ever had.

Of course, every inch of it was grimy with black smoke, and there were some blisters in the paint on the passenger side, but I considered myself lucky. I still had my wheels, even if I couldn't use them yet.

My shoulder bag had been in the bedroom. Along with everything else, my key ring was in it.

The cop on guard came over to us. He was very young and very polite. When I explained that I didn't have the key to the car and would contact BMW for a replacement, he assured me the car would be safe. "One of us will be on the premises for the next few days."

To see if you can pin the fire on me? I wondered as I thanked him.

Whatever lift in spirit I'd felt when I got dressed and left the hospital disappeared as Joan and I started to get back in her SUV. It was a beautiful, clear fall day, but around us the smell of smoke permeated the air. I fervently hoped that it would dissipate before Mrs. Hilmer got back. That was another thing I had to do: phone and talk to her.

I could visualize the conversation.

"I'm really sorry I caused your guest house to burn down. I certainly won't let it happen again."

I could hear the pealing of church bells in the distance, and I wondered if my father went to Mass after he visited me—he and his wife and son, the basketball star. I had thrown away his card when I was clearing out of the hospital room, but I'd noticed he still lived in Irvington. That meant he probably was still a parishioner of Immaculate Conception, the church in which I was baptized.

The godparents who were to assist my parents in reinforcing my religious education and spiritual well-being were my father's close friends, the Barrys. Dave Barry was a state trooper, too, and probably also retired by now. I wondered if he or his wife, Nancy, ever said, "Oh, by the way, Ted, any word from Ellie?"

Or was I a subject too uncomfortable to be discussed? A person to be dismissed with a shake of the head and a sigh. *"It's one of those sad things that happen in life. We just have to put it behind us and go on."*

"You're very quiet, Ellie," Joan said as she turned on the ignition. "How do you feel, really?"

"Much better than I dared hope," I assured her. "You're an angel, and with the money you are so kindly going to lend me, I am buying *you* lunch."

I could see that the Hudson Valley Inn was going to be a perfect spot for me. It was a three-story, wide-porched gingerbread kind of Victorian mansion, and the minute we stepped into the vestibule, the elderly clerk behind the desk was looking us over carefully.

Joan gave her credit card for an imprint, explaining that I'd lost my purse and it would be a few days before I would have new cards issued. That bonded Mrs. Willis, the clerk, to me for life. After introducing herself, she confided that seven years ago, in the train station, she had laid her purse beside her on the bench.

"I turned the page of the newspaper," she recalled, "and in that split second, it disappeared. What a nuisance. I was stranded. I was so upset. Someone had run up three hundred dollars on my card before I could even collect my wits and make the phone call, and . . ."

Maybe because of our shared experience, she went out of her way to give me a particularly desirable room. "It's priced as a room, but it's really a junior suite because it has a separate sitting area with a little kitchenette. And best of all it has a wonderful view of the river."

If there's anything in the world I love, it's a river view. It's not hard to figure out why that is true. I was conceived in the house in Irvington that overlooks the Hudson and lived there for the first five years of my life. I remember that when I was very little, I would pull a chair over to the window and stand on it so that I could catch a glimpse of the river shimmering below.

Joan and I walked slowly up the two flights to the room, agreed that it was exactly what I needed, and made our equally slow passage back to the quaint dining room at the rear of the inn. By then I felt as though all the blisters had given birth to septuplets.

A Bloody Mary and a club sandwich did wonders to restore a sense of normalcy to me.

Then, over coffee, Joan frowned and said, "Ellie, I hate to bring this up, but it's necessary. Leo and I went to a cocktail party last night. Everyone is talking about your Website."

"Go on."

"Some people think it's outrageous," she said frankly. "I understand it was legal for you to register it in Rob Westerfield's name, but a lot of people think that was unfair and totally unnecessary."

"Don't look so worried," I said. "I have no intention of shooting the messenger, and I *am* interested in getting reactions. What else are they saying?"

"That you should not have put those mug shots of him on the Website. That the medical examiner's testimony describing Andrea's wounds make brutal reading."

"It was a brutal crime."

"Ellie, you asked me to tell you what people are saying."

Joan looked so terribly unhappy that I was ashamed of myself. "I'm sorry. I know how miserable this is for you."

She shrugged. "Ellie, I believe Will Nebels killed Andrea. Half this town thinks Paulie Stroebel is guilty. And a lot of other people feel that even if Rob Westerfield is guilty, he has served his sentence and has been paroled, and that you ought to accept that."

"Joan, if Rob Westerfield had admitted his guilt and honestly expressed regret, I still would have hated his guts, but there wouldn't be a Website. I understand why people think the way they do, but I can't stop now."

She reached across the table, and we clasped hands. "Ellie, there's another sympathy vote out there. It's for old Mrs. Westerfield. Her housekeeper is telling everyone who will listen how upset she is about the Website and how she wishes you would at least shut it down until after a new jury has heard the evidence."

I thought of Dorothy Westerfield, that elegant woman, offering condolences to my mother on the day of the funeral, and I remembered my father ordering her from the house. He couldn't tolerate her sympathy then, and I could not allow myself to be swayed by sympathy for her now.

"We'd better change the subject," I said. "We're not going to agree."

Joan lent me $300, and we both managed a genuine smile as I paid for the lunch. "Symbolic," I said, "but it makes me feel better."

We said good-bye in the vestibule at the front door. "I hate to see you having to make that climb upstairs," she said, looking worried.

"It will be worth it just to get there. And I've got my freebie to lean on." I thumped the cane lightly to emphasize my point.

"Call me if you need anything. Otherwise, I'll talk to you tomorrow."

I hesitated about bringing up anything else controversial, but there was one more thing I had to ask her. "Joan, I know you never saw the locket that I insist Andrea was wearing, but are you still in touch with some of the girls who were in school with you and Andrea?"

"Sure. And you can bet I'll be hearing from them, given all that's going on."

"Would you ask them directly if any of them ever saw Andrea wearing the locket I described to you? Gold, heart-shaped, embossed at the edges, small blue stones in the center, and 'A' and 'R,' Andrea's and Rob's initials, engraved on the back."

"Ellie—"

"Joan, the more I think about it, the more I believe that the only reason Rob went back to the garage was that he couldn't afford to have the locket found on Andrea's body. I need to know why, and it would help if someone else confirmed that it existed."

Joan didn't comment further after that. She promised she would make inquiries and then left me to go home to her orderly life with her husband and children. Leaning heavily on the cane, I limped upstairs to the room, locked and bolted the door, carefully removed the sneakers, and sank down on the bed.

The ringing of the telephone woke me up. I was startled to see that the room was in darkness. I struggled up on one elbow, fumbled for the light, and glanced at the clock as I picked up the phone on the bedside table.

It was eight o'clock. I had been asleep for six hours. "Hello." I know I sounded groggy.

"Ellie, it's Joan. Something terrible has happened. Old Mrs. Westerfield's housekeeper went into Stroebel's delicatessen this afternoon and shouted at Paulie, telling him to admit that he'd killed Andrea. She said it was his fault that the Westerfield family was being tortured.

"Ellie, an hour ago Paulie went into the bathroom at home, locked the door, and slit his wrists. He's in intensive care in the hospital. He's lost so much blood that they don't think he's going to live."

28

I found Mrs. Stroebel in the waiting room outside the intensive care unit. She was weeping quietly, the tears running down her cheeks. Her lips were clamped together tightly, as though she was afraid that parting them would release a tidal wave of grief.

Her coat was around her shoulders, and even though her cardigan and skirt were dark blue, I could see dark stains that I was sure had been caused by Paulie's blood.

A large-framed, plainly dressed woman of about fifty was sitting protectively close to her. She looked up at me, a hint of hostility on her face.

I wasn't sure what to expect from Mrs. Stroebel. It was my Website that had triggered the verbal attack from Mrs. Westerfield's housekeeper and Paulie's despairing response to it.

But Mrs. Stroebel stood up and walked halfway across the room to meet me. "*You* understand, Ellie," she sobbed. "You understand what they have done to my son."

I put my arms around her. "I do understand, Mrs. Stroebel." I looked over her head at the other woman. She knew the question my eyes were silently asking and made a gesture with her hand which I took to mean that it was too soon to tell if Paulie would make it.

Then she introduced herself. "I'm Greta Bergner. I work with Mrs. Stroebel and Paulie in the delicatessen. I thought you might be a reporter."

We sat together for the next twelve hours. From time to time we went in and stood at the entrance to the cubicle where Paulie was lying, an oxygen mask over his face, tubes in his arms, heavy bandages on his wrists.

During that long night, as I observed the agony on Mrs. Stroebel's face and watched her lips move in silent prayer, I found myself beginning to pray as well. At first it was instinctive, but then it became deliberate. *If you spare Paulie for her, I'll try to accept everything that happened. Maybe I won't succeed, but I swear I'll* try.

Streaks of light began to penetrate the outside darkness. At nine-fifteen a doctor came in to the waiting room. "Paulie is stabilized," he said. "He'll make it. Why don't you people go home and get some sleep?"

*

I took a cab back from the hospital; along the way I had the driver stop so I could pick up the morning papers. I had only to glance at the front page of the *Westchester Post* to be grateful that in the intensive care unit Paulie Stroebel did not have access to newspapers.

The headline was "Murder Suspect Attempts Suicide."

The rest of the front page was covered with pictures of three people. The photo on the left was of Will Nebels posing for the camera, a self-righteous expression on his weak-featured face. The one on the right was of a woman in her mid-sixties with a worried frown that enhanced her severe features. The center photo was of Paulie, behind the counter of the deli, a bread knife in his hand.

The picture had been cropped so that only the hand holding the bread knife showed. There was no context for it, no baguette being sliced in preparation for a sandwich. He was looking into the camera, his eyebrows drawn together.

My guess is that Paulie had been caught by surprise when his picture was taken. Whatever, the effect was that of a surly man with disturbing eyes brandishing a weapon.

The captions under the pictures were quotes. Nebels's was "I knew he did it." The woman with severe features said, "He admitted it to me." Paulie's caption was "I'm sorry. I'm sorry."

The story was on page 3, but I had to put off reading it; the cab was pulling up to the inn. Once in my room, I turned again to the newspaper.

The woman in the photo on the front page was Lillian Beckerson, Mrs. Dorothy Westerfield's housekeeper of thirty-one years. "Mrs. Westerfield is one of the finest human beings who ever walked the face of the earth," the newspaper quoted her as saying. "Her husband was a United States senator, his grandfather was governor of New York. She's lived with this stain on her family name for over twenty years. Now, when her only grandchild is trying to prove his innocence, that woman who lied on the witness stand as a child is back trying to destroy him again on a Website."

That's me, I thought.

"Mrs. Westerfield was looking at that Website and crying yesterday afternoon. I couldn't take it anymore. I marched myself into that delicatessen and yelled at that man, asking him please to tell the truth, to admit what he had done. You know what he kept saying to me? 'I'm sorry. I'm sorry.' Now, if you were innocent, would you have said that? I don't think so."

You would if you were Paulie. I forced myself to keep reading. I'm an investigative journalist, and I could see that Colin Marsh, the guy who wrote this story, was one of those sensationalists who knows how to elicit and then manipulate provocative quotes.

He had looked up Emma Watkins, the guidance counselor who years ago swore on the stand that Paulie had sobbed, "I didn't think she was dead," when the class was told about Andrea.

Ms. Watkins told Marsh that over the years she always had been troubled by Rob Westerfield's conviction. She said that Paulie was easily agitated and that if he learned that Andrea had been joking when she said she'd go with him to the Thanksgiving mixer, he might have been upset enough to lash out.

Lash out. What a delicate way to put it, I thought.

Will Nebels, that poor excuse for a human being, that sleaze who used to like to hug teenage girls, was extensively quoted in the story. With even more flourish than he had exhibited in the earlier television interview I'd seen, he told Marsh about seeing Paulie go into the garage-hideout that night, carrying a tire jack. He ended by piously lamenting he'd never be able to make up to the Westerfield family that he didn't come forward sooner.

When I finished reading the account, I threw the paper on the bed. I was both furious and worried. The case was being tried in the press, and more and more people were going to come to believe that Rob Westerfield was innocent. I realized that if I had read the story cold, even I might have been convinced that the wrong man had been convicted.

But if Mrs. Westerfield was upset by what she read on my Website, it undoubtedly was having an effect on other people as well. I opened the computer and got busy.

"In a mistaken gesture of loyalty, Mrs. Dorothy Westerfield's housekeeper stormed into Stroebel's delicatessen and verbally attacked Paulie Stroebel. A few hours later Paulie, a gentle man already under great stress thanks to the lies perpetrated by the Westerfield money machine, attempted to commit suicide.

"My sympathy goes out to Mrs. Dorothy Westerfield, by all accounts a truly fine woman, for the pain she has suffered because of the crime committed by her grandson. I believe that she will find peace by accepting the fact that her proud family name may still be respected by future generations.

"All she needs to do is leave her vast fortune to charities that will educate future generations of students and fund medical research that will save the lives of countless human beings. Leaving that fortune to a killer compounds the tragedy that more than twenty years ago took my sister's life and that yesterday very nearly cost Paulie Stroebel *his* life.

"I understand that a Committee for Justice for Rob Westerfield has been formed.

"I invite all of you to join the Committee for Justice for Paulie Stroebel.

"Mrs. Dorothy Westerfield, you first!"

Not bad, I thought, as I transferred the text to the Website. As I was closing the computer, my cell phone rang.

"I been reading the papers." I immediately recognized the voice. It was the man who earlier claimed to have been in prison with Rob Westerfield and said he heard him confess to another murder.

"I've been hoping to hear from you." I tried to keep my tone noncommittal.

"The way I see it, Westerfield's doing a good job of making that looney Stroebel look bad."

"He's not a 'looney,'" I snapped.

"Have it your way. Here's the deal. Five thousand bucks. I give you the first name of the guy Westerfield bragged about killing."

"The *first* name!"

"It's all I know. Take it or leave it."

"Isn't there anything else you can give me? I mean when it happened, where it happened?"

"First name is all I know, and I need the money by Friday."

Today was Monday. I had about $3,000 in a savings

account in Atlanta, and, much as I hated the thought, I could borrow the rest from Pete if the book advance didn't come through by Friday.

"Well?" His voice was impatient.

I knew that there was a very good chance I was being conned, but it was a chance I decided to take.

"I'll have the money by Friday," I promised.

29

By Wednesday evening I was reasonably back to normal. I had credit cards, a driver's license, and money. An advance on the book had been electronically transferred to a bank near the inn. The superintendent's wife in Atlanta had gone to my apartment, packed some clothes for me, and shipped them to me overnight. The blisters on my feet were healing, and I'd even had time to get my hair trimmed.

Most important, I had an appointment on Thursday afternoon in Boston with Christopher Cassidy, the scholarship student at Arbinger who, at age fourteen, had been severely beaten by Rob Westerfield.

I had already put on the Website Dr. Margaret Fisher's account of having her arm twisted by Rob Westerfield and being paid $500 by his father not to press charges.

I e-mailed the text to her before I put it on the Website. She not only okayed it but gave her professional opinion that the hair-trigger temper and violence she had experienced could very well have been the same reaction that caused him to bludgeon Andrea to death.

On the other hand, Joan had been in touch with Andrea's circle of close friends at high school, and she'd reported that not one of them ever saw her wear any locket except the one my father gave her.

Every day I was running a description of the locket on the Website, asking for any information anyone might be able to supply. So far there'd been no results. My e-mail was full of comments. Some praised what I was doing. Others vehemently objected to it. I had my share of weirdos writing as well. Two confessed to the murder. One said Andrea was still alive and wanted me to rescue her.

A couple of the letters threatened me. The one that I believed was genuine said he was very disappointed to see me escape from the fire. He added, "Cute nightshirt—L. L. Bean, wasn't it?"

Had the writer been watching the fire from the woods, or could he be the intruder who had been in the apartment and perhaps noticed the nightshirt on a hanger in the bedroom closet? Either prospect was intimidating, and if I wanted to admit it to myself, both were downright frightening.

I was in touch with Mrs. Stroebel several times a day, and as Paulie started to mend, the relief in her voice became more and more evident. However, so did the concern. "Ellie, if there is a new trial and Paulie has to testify, I am afraid he will do this again to himself. He has told me, 'Mama, in court I can't answer them so that they understand. I worried about Andrea being with Rob Westerfield. I did not threaten her.'"

Then she added, "My friends are calling me. They see your Website. They say everyone should have a champion like you. I tell Paulie about it. He would like you to visit him."

I promised I would go on Friday.

Except for the errands I'd completed, I'd been staying in the room, working on the book and having my meals sent up by room service. But at seven o'clock on Wednesday evening, I decided to go downstairs for dinner.

The dining room here was not unlike the one at the Parkinson Inn, but it had a more formal feeling. The tables were farther apart, and the table linen was white instead of checkerboard red and white. The table centerpiece at the Parkinson was a cheery, wide candle, not a prim little vase of flowers. The diners here were distinctly older—vintage senior citizens, not the exuberant groups that frequented the Parkinson.

But the food was equally good, and after debating between rack of lamb and swordfish, I succumbed to what I really felt like having and ordered the lamb.

I took from my bag a book I'd been wanting to read, and for the next hour enjoyed the combination I love—a good dinner and a good book. I was so deeply into the story that when the waitress cleared the table and then spoke to me, I looked up at her, startled.

I said yes to coffee and no to dessert.

"The gentleman at the next table would like to offer you an after-dinner drink."

I think I knew it was Rob Westerfield even before I turned my head. He was sitting not more than six feet from me, a wineglass in his hand. He raised it in a mock salute and smiled.

"He asked if I knew your name, Miss. I told him, and he wrote this note to you."

She handed me a card with Westerfield's full name embossed on the front, Robson Parke Westerfield. *My God, he's giving it the full treatment* was the thought that ran through my head as I flipped the card over.

On it he had written: "Andrea was cute, but you're beautiful."

I got up, walked over to him, tore up the card, and dropped the pieces in his wineglass. "Maybe you want to give me the locket you took back after you killed her," I suggested.

His pupils widened, and the teasing expression in his cobalt eyes disappeared. For an instant I thought he would spring up and attack me as he had attacked Dr.

Fisher in the restaurant years ago. "That necklace was a big worry for you, wasn't it, jailbird?" I asked him. "Well, I think it still is, and I'm going to find out why."

The waitress was standing between the tables, her expression baffled. She obviously hadn't recognized Westerfield, which made me wonder when she had arrived in Oldham.

I jerked my head back at him. "Bring Mr. Westerfield another glass of wine, please, and put it on my bill."

Sometime during the night the alarm was disabled on my car and the gas tank jimmied open. A very efficient way to destroy a car is to pour sand into the gas tank.

The Oldham police in the form of Officer White responded to my call about my trashed BMW. While he didn't quite ask me where I had obtained the sand, he did mention that the fire in Mrs. Hilmer's garage was definitely set. He also said that the remnants of the gasoline-soaked towels that had started the blaze were identical with the towels Mrs. Hilmer had left in the linen closet of the apartment.

"Quite a coincidence, Ms. Cavanaugh," he said. "Or is it?"

30

I drove a rented car to Boston for my appointment with Christopher Cassidy. I was furious that my own car had been trashed and concerned because I knew there was something else to be faced. I had thought that the intruder in the apartment probably had been looking for material that I might be using on the Website. Now I wondered if his main reason for being there was to steal items that could be used later to set the fire that almost took my life.

I knew, of course, that Rob Westerfield was behind it and that he had thugs like the one who came up to me in the parking lot at Sing Sing to do his dirty work for him. My goal was to prove to the world that an examination of his life would show a pattern of violence in the years that led up to Andrea's death. I further believed that it was his intention that I be the next victim of that violence.

Like the risk in paying $5,000 for the first name of

another possible Westerfield victim, it was a chance I had to take.

Any good reporter has to be compulsively punctual. Not being able to use my own car, waiting for the police to fill out the report, and then going to the rental agency had delayed me. I still would have been comfortably early for my appointment, but then I hit bad weather.

The prediction had been for cloudy skies and possible light snow in the evening. The light snow began fifty miles outside Boston; the result was slippery roads and crawling traffic. As the minutes ticked by, I kept glancing at the clock on the dashboard, agonizing at the traffic's slow pace. Christopher Cassidy's secretary had warned me to be prompt, as he was squeezing time for me into a very full day and was leaving this evening for meetings in Europe.

It was four minutes to two when I arrived breathlessly at his office for the two o'clock appointment. During the few minutes I sat in the handsome reception room, I had to make a determined effort to collect my bearings. I felt flustered and disorganized, plus I had the beginnings of a headache.

Promptly at two o'clock Cassidy's secretary came to escort me to his private office. As I followed her in, I reviewed in my mind everything I had learned about Cassidy. I had known, of course, that he'd been a scholarship student at Arbinger Academy and that he had founded this firm. When I looked him up on the Internet, I learned that he had graduated at the top of his class from Yale, had a master's degree from the Harvard Business School, and had been honored by so many charities that it was obvious he was a generous donor.

He was forty-two years old, married, had a fifteen-year-old daughter, and was an avid sportsman.

Obviously quite a guy.

The minute I entered the room, he came out from behind his desk, walked over to me, and extended his hand. "I'm glad to see you, Ms. Cavanaugh. Is it okay if I call you Ellie? I feel as though I know you. Why don't we sit over here?" He indicated the sitting area near the window.

I chose the couch. He sat on the edge of the chair opposite me. "Coffee or tea?" he asked.

"Coffee, please, black," I said gratefully. I felt that a cup of coffee might clear my head and help me think straight.

He picked up the phone from the table at his elbow. In the brief moment he spoke to his secretary I had a chance to study him; I liked what I saw. His well-cut dark blue business suit and white shirt were conservative, but the red tie with tiny golf clubs suggested a touch of the maverick. He had broad shoulders, a solid but trim body, a good head of sable brown hair, and deep-set hazel eyes.

There was a feeling of crackling energy emanating from him, and I could sense that Christopher Cassidy never wasted a minute.

Now he came directly to the point. "When Craig Parshall phoned, he told me why you wanted to talk to me."

"Then you know that Rob Westerfield is out of prison and probably will get a new trial."

"And that he's trying to blame the death of your sister on someone else. Yes, I do know that. Blaming someone else for what he does is an old trick of his. He was pulling it when he was fourteen years old."

"That's exactly the kind of information I want to put on the Website. The Westerfields have gotten a so-called eyewitness to lie for them. As it stands now, in a second trial they have a good chance of getting an acquittal, and then the record will be expunged. Rob Westerfield becomes the martyr who spent over twenty years in prison for another man's crime. I can't let it happen."

"What do you want me to tell you?"

"Mr. Cassidy," I began.

"Anyone who despises Rob Westerfield calls me Chris."

"Chris, according to Craig Parshall, Westerfield beat

you up pretty viciously when you both were sophomores at Arbinger."

"We were both good athletes. There was one starting spot on the varsity for a running back. We competed for it, and I got it. I guess he was brooding over it. A day or so later I was on my way back to the dorm from the library. I had a load of books in my arms. He came up behind up and punched me in the neck. Before I could react, he was all over me. I ended up with a broken nose and jaw."

"And no one stopped him?"

"He had picked his time. He attacked me when there was no one else around, then tried to say I started it. Fortunately, a senior happened to be looking out the window and witnessed what happened. Of course, the school didn't want a scandal. The Westerfields have been big donors for generations. My father was ready to file charges but was offered a full scholarship for my brother who was then in the eighth grade if he'd reconsider. I'm sure now that the Westerfields paid for that so-called scholarship."

The coffee arrived. Nothing had ever tasted so good. Cassidy looked reflective as he raised the cup to his lips. Then he said, "To the credit of the school, Rob was forced to withdraw at the end of the term."

"May I tell this story on the Website? Your name would add a lot of validity to what I'm trying to do."

"Absolutely. I remember when your sister died. I read every account of the trial because of Westerfield. At the time I wished I could get on the stand and tell them what kind of animal he is. I have a daughter the age of your sister when she died. I can only imagine what your father went through, what your whole family went through."

I nodded. "It destroyed us as a family."

"I'm not surprised."

"Before he attacked you, did you have much contact with him in school?"

"I was the son of a short-order cook. He was a Westerfield. He didn't have time for me until I got in his way."

Cassidy glanced at his watch. It was time to thank him and leave. I had one question, however, that I had to get in. "What about his freshman year? Did you have much contact with him?"

"Not really. We pursued different activities. He went out for the drama club and was in a couple of productions. I saw them, and I have to admit he was very good. He wasn't the lead in either play, but he was voted best actor for one of them, so I guess that kept him happy for a while."

Cassidy stood up, and reluctantly I got up, too. "You've been very kind," I started to say, but then he interrupted me.

"You know, I just remembered something. Westerfield obviously loved the limelight and didn't want to lose his moment of glory. He wore a dark blond wig in that play, and, lest we forget how good he'd been, he used to put it on sometimes. Then he'd put on the mannerisms of the character, and I remember he even signed that character's name when he passed notes in class."

I thought of Rob Westerfield showing up at the inn last evening and giving the waitress the impression he was flirting with me. "He's still acting," I said grimly.

I grabbed a quick lunch and was back in the car at three-thirty. The snow was continuing to fall, and the trip up to Boston began to seem like a picnic compared to the trek back to Oldham. I kept the cell phone next to me on the front seat so I wouldn't miss the call from the guy who'd been in prison with Westerfield.

He had insisted he needed the money by Friday. By now I had a hunch that his information was going to be valuable, and I was anxious that he not change his mind.

It was eleven-thirty that night when I finally got back to the inn. I was just inside my room when the cell phone rang. It was the call I was expecting, but this time the voice I heard was agitated. "Listen, I think I've been set up. I may not get out of here."

"Where are you?"

"Listen to me. If I give you the name, can I trust you to pay me later?"

"Yes, you can."

"Westerfield must've figured I might be trouble for him. He's had a ton of money since he was born. I've had nothing. If I get out of here and you pay me, I'll at least have some. If I don't, then maybe you can get Westerfield for me on a murder charge."

Now I was convinced he was genuine, that he did have information. "I swear to you I'll pay you. I swear to you I'll nail Westerfield for you."

"Westerfield told me, 'I beat Phil to death, and it felt good.' Got that? *Phil*—that's the name."

The line went dead.

31

Rob Westerfield had been nineteen years old when he murdered Andrea. Within eight months, he had been arrested, indicted, tried, convicted, and sent to prison. Though he had been out on bail prior to his conviction, I could not believe that during those eight months he would have risked killing someone else.

That meant the earlier crime had been committed between twenty-two and twenty-seven years ago. I had to cover those five or six years of his life to try to find a connection between him and a dead man whose first name was Phil.

It seems incredible to think that at thirteen or fourteen, Rob might have committed a murder. Or was it? He'd been only fourteen when he viciously assaulted Christopher Cassidy.

I reasoned that in those years he had been at

Arbinger in Massachusetts for a year and a half, then spent six months at Bath Public School in England, two years in Carrington Academy in Maine, and a semester or so in Willow, a nondescript college near Buffalo. The Westerfields have a house in Vail and another in Palm Beach. It seemed to me that Rob must have visited those places. He also may have gone on class trips abroad.

That was a lot of territory to cover. I knew I needed help.

Marcus Longo had been a detective with the Westchester County District Attorney's Office for twenty-five years. If anyone could track down the homicide of a man with only a first name as a clue, my money would be on him.

Fortunately, when I phoned Marcus, I reached him instead of an answering machine. As I suspected, he had flown to Colorado to pick up his wife. "We stayed a few extra days to look at some houses," he explained. "I think we found one."

His tone changed. "I was going to tell you all about the baby, but that can hold. I understand a lot of things have happened since I've been gone."

"I would have to agree with that, Marcus. May I buy you lunch? I need some advice."

"The advice is free. I buy the lunch."

*

We met at The Depot Restaurant in Cold Spring. There, over club sandwiches and coffee, I filled him in on my eventful week.

He stopped me regularly with questions.

"Do you think the fire was set to scare you or actually to kill you?"

"I was more than scared; I wasn't sure I'd get out alive."

"All right. And you say the Oldham police think you set it?"

"Officer White has done everything but cuff me."

"His cousin used to be in the D.A.'s office when I was there. He's a judge now and a member of the same country club as Rob's father. In fairness, he always thought Paulie Stroebel was guilty of Andrea's murder. I bet he's the one who has White riled up about you. That Website is mighty provocative to anyone who's hand-in-glove with the Westerfields."

"Then it's a success."

I looked around to make sure that I could not be overheard. "Marcus—"

"Ellie, do you realize your eyes keep darting around this place? Who or what are you looking for?"

I told him about Rob Westerfield showing up at the inn. "He didn't get there until I'd almost finished dinner," I said. "Someone called him and tipped him off. I'm sure of it."

I knew that next Marcus would either warn me to be careful or ask me to stop putting inflammatory material on the Website. I didn't give him the chance.

"Marcus, I received a call from someone who was in prison with Rob." I told him about the deal I had made to buy information and then about the phone call last night.

He listened quietly, his eyes searching my face.

He heard me out, then asked, "You believe this guy, don't you?"

"Marcus, I knew I might be suckered into losing five thousand dollars. But this is different. This man was in fear of his life. He wanted me to know about Phil because he wanted revenge on Westerfield."

"You say he referred to the sign you were holding up outside the prison?"

"Yes."

"You're assuming he was a convict, so that means he probably was released that day. You were only there once, isn't that right?"

"That's right."

"Ellie, that guy could also be a prison employee who was entering or leaving the prison while you were standing outside. Money buys favors from some guards as well as from other prisoners."

I hadn't thought about that. "I was hoping that you could get a list of the prisoners who were discharged the day after Westerfield. Then you could see if anything happened to any one of them."

"I can do that. Ellie, you realize this also could be some nut playing games."

"I know that, but I don't think so." I opened my pocketbook. "I've made a list of the schools Rob Westerfield attended, both here and in England, and the places where his family has homes. There are databases listing unsolved homicides that took place between twenty-two and twenty-seven years ago, aren't there?"

"Of course."

"Westchester County has one?"

"Yes."

"Can you access it, or get someone else to do it for you?"

"Yes, I can."

"Then it shouldn't be too hard to learn if there's a victim whose name is Phil?"

"No, it shouldn't."

"How about checking an unsolved crimes database in the areas around the schools and homes where Westerfield spent time?"

He looked at the list. "Massachusetts, Maine, Florida, Colorado, New York, England." He whistled. "That's a lot of territory. I'll see what I can do."

"One more thing. Knowing the way Rob Westerfield operates, is there a database for solved crimes that would list Phil as the victim and someone claiming innocence as serving time for it?"

"Ellie, nine out of ten people convicted at trial and behind bars claim somebody else did it. Let's start with unsolved homicides and see where we go."

"Tomorrow I'm going to put Christopher Cassidy's story about Rob on the Website. No one would question Cassidy's integrity, so his account should carry some weight. I never did get up to Carrington Academy. I'll see if I can make an appointment there for Monday or Tuesday."

"Check the student roster for the years Westerfield was there," Marcus said as he signaled for the check.

"I've thought of that. One of the schools might have had a student named Phil who tangled with Westerfield."

"That opens the territory," Marcus warned. "The students in prep school come from all over the country. Westerfield could have followed one of them home to settle a grudge."

"*'I beat Phil to death, and it felt good.'*"

Who were the people who loved Phil? I wondered. Were they still grieving? Of course they were.

The waitress was placing the tab in front of Marcus. I waited until she was gone before I said, "I can call my connection at Arbinger. He's been pretty helpful. When I go to Carrington and Willow College, I'll ask about students from Westerfield's time. Philip isn't that common a name."

"Ellie, you've told me you believe Rob Westerfield was tipped off that you were at dinner the other night?"

"Yes."

"You told me that your informant claimed to be in fear of his life?"

"Yes."

"Ellie, Rob Westerfield is worried your Website could influence his grandmother to leave her money to charity. Now he may be terrified that you could uncover another crime that might send him back to prison. Don't you realize how precarious your situation is?"

"I honestly do, but there's nothing I can do about it."

"Damn it, Ellie, yes you can! Your father was a state trooper. He's retired. You could live in his house. He could be your bodyguard. Trust me, you need one. And something else: If that guy's story is on the level, helping to put Westerfield back in prison would help your father have closure, too. I don't think you understand how tough this has been on him."

"He's been in touch with you?"

"Yes, he has."

"Marcus, you mean well," I said as we stood up, "but I don't think you understand something. My father got his closure when he let us go and never lifted a finger to bring us back. My mother needed and expected him to do that, but he did nothing. Next time he calls, tell him to watch his son play basketball and leave me alone."

Marcus gave me a hug as we separated in the parking lot. "I'll call you as soon as I start getting answers," he promised.

I drove back to the inn. Mrs. Willis was at the desk. "Your brother is waiting for you in the sunroom," she said.

32

He was standing in front of the window, looking out, his back to me. He was a good six feet three, taller than I'd realized when I saw him on television. He was wearing khaki pants and sneakers and his school jacket. His hands were in his pockets, and he was jiggling his right foot. I had the impression that he was nervous.

He must have heard my footsteps because he turned around. We looked at each other.

"*You'll never be able to deny her,*" my grandmother used to joke to my mother about Andrea. "*She's growing up to be the image of you.*"

If she were here, she'd be saying the same sort of thing to us. In appearance, at least, we could never deny each other.

"Hello, Ellie. I'm your brother, Teddy." He walked to me, holding out his hand.

I ignored it.

"Can't I just talk to you for five minutes?" His voice had not yet fully deepened, but it was well modulated. He looked worried but determined.

I shook my head and turned to leave.

"You're my sister," he said. "You could at least give me five minutes. You might even like me if you knew me."

I turned back to him. "Teddy, you seem like a nice young man, but I'm sure you have better things to do than spend time with me. I know you've been sent by your father. He just doesn't seem to get the fact that I never want to see or hear from him again."

"He's your father, too. Whether you believe it or not, he never stopped being your father. He didn't send me. He doesn't know I'm here. I came because I wanted to meet you. I've always wanted to meet you."

There was appeal in his voice. "Why don't we have a soda or something?"

I shook my head.

"Please, Ellie."

Maybe it was the way my name fell from his lips, or maybe I just have a hard time being downright rude. This kid hadn't done anything to me.

I heard myself saying, "There's a soda machine in the hall." I started to dig in my purse.

"I've got it. What kind do you want?"

"Plain water."

"Me, too. I'll be right back." His smile was both shy and relieved.

I sat on the brightly patterned wicker love seat, trying to figure out how to send him away. I didn't want to listen to a pitch about what a great father we had and how I should let bygones be bygones.

Maybe he *was* a great father for two of his children, Andrea and you, I thought, but I slipped between the cracks.

Teddy returned carrying the two bottles of water. I could read his mind as he eyed the love seat and the chair. He made the wise decision and chose the chair. I did not want him to sit beside me. Flesh of my flesh, bone of my bone, I thought. No, that has to do with Adam and Eve, not siblings.

Half siblings.

"Ellie, would you come and see me play basketball sometime?"

It wasn't what I expected.

"I mean, couldn't we be friends at least? I always kept hoping you'd come and visit us, but if you won't do that, maybe you and I can just get together sometimes. I read your book last year, about the cases you've worked on. It was great. I'd like to talk to you about them."

"Teddy, I'm awfully busy right now and—"

He interrupted: "I watch your Website every day. The way you write about Westerfield must be driving him crazy. Ellie, you're my sister, and I don't want anything to happen to you."

I wanted to say, "Please don't call me your sister," but the words died on my lips. I settled for "Please don't worry about me. I can take care of myself."

"Can't I help you? This morning I read in the paper about what happened to your car. Suppose somebody loosens a wheel or a brake in the one you're driving now? I'm good with cars. I could check yours out for you before you go anywhere, or I could even drive you around in mine."

He was so earnest and so concerned that I had to smile. "Teddy, you have school and, I'm sure, plenty of basketball practice. And now I honestly have to get to work."

He stood up with me. "We look a lot alike," he said.

"I know we do."

"I'm glad. Ellie, I'm getting out of your way now, but I'm coming back."

Would to God your father had had the same persistence, I thought. Then I realized that if he had, this boy would never have been born.

I worked for a couple of hours, refining the way I would present Christopher Cassidy's story for the Website. When I thought I had it right, I e-mailed it to his office for his approval.

At four o'clock Marcus Longo called. "Ellie, the Westerfields have taken a page out of your book. They have a Website: comjusrob.com."

"Let me guess what it stands for: 'Committee for Justice for Rob.'"

"You have it. I understand they've taken out ads in all the Westchester papers to advertise it. Basically the strategy is to present touching stories of people who were wrongly convicted of crimes."

"Thereby linking them to Rob Westerfield, the most innocent of them all."

"You've got it. But they've also been doing some digging about you, and they've come up with some unfortunate stuff."

"Meaning what?"

"The Fromme Center, a psychiatric facility."

"I did an undercover story on it. It was a rip-off joint. Paid a fortune by the state of Georgia, and not one legitimate psychiatrist or psychologist on staff."

"Were you a patient there?"

"Marcus, are you crazy? Of course I wasn't."

"Was there a photograph taken of you in the Fromme Center in which you were lying on a bed with your arms and legs in restraints?"

"Yes, there was, and it was taken to illustrate what had been going on there. After the state closed Fromme and moved the patients to other facilities, we did a follow-up story on the way they had kept people shackled for days at a time. Why?"

"It's on the Westerfields' Website."

"Without explanation?"

"Insinuating that you were forcibly held there." He paused. "Ellie, are you *surprised* that these people play dirty?"

"I'd be surprised if they *didn't*, frankly. I'll put the full article, including picture and text, on my Website. I'll do it under a new heading: 'Latest Westerfield Lie.' But I do understand that a lot of people who see his Website may not see mine."

"And the other way around. That's my next concern. Ellie, are you planning to put anything on the Website about the other possible homicide?"

"I'm not sure. On the one hand, someone who sees it might come forward with information about a murder victim. On the other hand, it might tip off Rob Westerfield and in some way help him cover his tracks."

"Or get rid of someone who could give damaging testimony against him. You've got to be very careful."

"That may already have happened."

"Exactly. Let me know what you decide."

I went online and found the new Website of "The Committee for Justice for Robson Westerfield."

It had been handsomely designed with a quotation

from Voltaire under the heading: *It is better to risk saving a guilty person than to condemn an innocent one.*

The picture of a grave and contemplative Rob Westerfield was directly below the quote. It was followed by stories of people who genuinely had been imprisoned for someone else's crime. The stories were well written and pulled on heartstrings. It didn't take a great leap to figure that Jake Bern had been the author.

The personal section on the Website made the Westerfields sound like American royalty. There were pictures of Rob as a baby with his grandfather, the United States senator, and at age nine or ten with his grandmother, helping her cut the ribbon on a new Westerfield children's center. There were shots of him with his parents boarding the *Queen Elizabeth II* and dressed in tennis whites at The Everglades Club.

I guess the idea was to convey that it was beneath the dignity of this privileged young man to take a human life.

I was the star of the next page of the Website. It showed me spread out on the bed in the Fromme psychiatric center, my legs and arms shackled, wearing one of the pitifully inadequate nightshirts that were mandatory for the patients. I was only partially covered by a thin rag of a blanket.

The caption was "The witness whose testimony convicted Robson Westerfield."

I clicked off. I have a mannerism I had picked up from my father. When he was absolutely furious about something, he had a way of biting the right corner of his lip.

I was doing exactly that.

I sat for half an hour trying to calm down as I reviewed the pros and cons, and tried to figure out how to handle publicizing Westerfield's alleged confession of another murder.

Marcus Longo had talked about a territorial problem in trying to track down an unsolved homicide Rob Westerfield may have committed.

The Website was international.

Would I be exposing anyone to risk by putting the name of the supposed victim out there?

But my unidentified caller was already at risk, and he knew it.

In the end I composed a simple entry.

"Somewhere between twenty-two and twenty-seven years ago, it is alleged, Rob Westerfield committed another crime. He is directly quoted as saying when he was high on drugs in prison, *'I beat Phil to death, and it felt good.'*

"Anyone with information about this crime, please e-mail me at ellie1234@mediaone.net. Confidentiality and reward."

I looked it over. Rob Westerfield will certainly read

it, I thought. But suppose he knows there is someone besides my unknown caller who has information that could hurt him?

There are two things an investigative reporter does not do: reveal sources and place innocent people in danger.

I put the entry on hold.

33

On Friday evening I broke down and phoned Pete Lawlor.

"Your call is being forwarded to an answering service . . ."

"This is your former coworker who has enough interest in your well-being to inquire as to your state of mind, job opportunities, and health," I said. "A response will be appreciated."

He called back half an hour later. "You must be hard up for someone to talk to."

"I am. That's why you came to mind."

"Thanks."

"May I ask where you are now."

"In Atlanta. Packing up."

"I gather a decision has been made."

"Yes. A dream job. Based in New York, but with a fair amount of traveling. Reporting from hot spots all over the globe."

"Which newspaper?"

"Negative. I'm going to be a television star."

"Did you have to lose ten pounds before they hired you?"

"I don't remember you as being cruel."

I laughed. Talking to Pete had a way of bringing a dash of amusing, everyday reality into my increasingly surreal life. "Are you joking, or do you really have a job in television?"

"It's for real. It's with Packard Cable."

"Packard. That's great."

"It's one of the newer cable networks, but growing fast. I was about to take the L.A. job even though it wasn't exactly what I wanted, but then they came to me."

"When do you start?"

"Wednesday. I'm in the process of subletting the apartment and putting stuff together to load in the car. I start driving up Sunday afternoon. Dinner Tuesday?"

"Sure. It's good to hear that melodious voice of yours. . . ."

"Don't hang up. Ellie, I've been watching your Website."

"Pretty good, isn't it?"

"If this guy is what you say he is, you're playing with fire."

I already have, I thought. "Promise you won't tell me to be careful."

"I promise. Talk to you Monday afternoon."

*

I went back to the computer. It was nearly eight o'clock, and I'd been working steadily. I ordered room service, and while I was waiting, I did a few stretches and a lot of thinking.

Talking to Pete had, at least for the moment, removed my tunnel vision. For the last couple of weeks I had existed in a world in which Rob Westerfield was the central figure. Now, for just a moment, I was looking past that time, past his second trial, past my ability to prove to the world the depth of his violent nature.

I could dig up and publicize every nasty, rotten thing he'd ever done. Perhaps I could track down an unsolved murder he had committed. I could tell his sorry, dirty story in the book. Then it would be time for me to begin the rest of my life.

Pete was already beginning his—a new base in New York, a new job in a different media.

I locked my hands behind my head and began to twist from side to side. My neck muscles were tight, and it felt good to try to stretch them. What was not so good was the dismaying realization that I missed Pete Lawlor terribly and would not want to return to Atlanta unless he was there.

I spoke to Mrs. Stroebel on Saturday morning. She told me that Paulie was no longer in intensive care and probably would be discharged after the weekend.

I promised to drop by later for a visit, at about three o'clock. When I arrived, Mrs. Stroebel was sitting by Paulie's bed. As soon as she looked up at me, I could see from the concern on her face that there was a problem.

"He developed a high fever around lunchtime. There is an infection in one of his arms. The doctor tells me it will be all right, but I worry. Ellie, I worry so."

I looked down at Paulie. His arms were still heavily bandaged, and he had several IVs dripping from overhead pulleys. He was very pale and kept turning his head from side to side.

"They are giving him an antibiotic plus something to calm him down," Mrs. Stroebel said. "The fever makes him restless."

I pulled up a chair and sat beside her.

Paulie began to mumble. His eyes flickered open.

"I am here, Paulie," Mrs. Stroebel said soothingly. "Ellie Cavanaugh is here with me. She came to pay a visit."

"Hi, Paulie." I stood up and leaned over the bed so that he could see me.

His eyes were glazed with fever, but he tried to smile. "Ellie, my friend."

"You bet I am."

His eyes closed again. A moment later he began to

mutter incoherently. I heard him whisper Andrea's name.

Mrs. Stroebel clasped and unclasped her hands. "That's all he talks about. It preys on his mind so much. He is so afraid they will make him go back to court. No one understands how much they frightened him last time."

Her voice was rising, and I could see that Paulie was becoming agitated. I squeezed her hand and nodded at the bed. She understood what I meant.

"Of course, Ellie, thanks to you, everything will be fine," she said brightly. "Paulie knows that. People come into the store and tell me that they look at your Website where you show what a bad person Rob Westerfield is. Paulie and I looked at the Website last week. It made us very happy."

Paulie seemed to calm down a little, then he whispered, "But, Mama . . . suppose I forget and . . ."

Mrs. Stroebel seemed suddenly flustered. "No more talk, Paulie," she said abruptly. "Go to sleep. You must get better."

"Mama—"

"Paulie, you must be quiet now." She laid a gentle but resolute hand on his lips.

I had the distinct feeling that Mrs. Stroebel was uneasy and wanted me to leave, so I got up to go.

"Mama . . ."

Mrs. Stroebel sprang up with me, blocking access to the bed, as though she were afraid that I would get too close to Paulie.

I couldn't imagine what was upsetting her. "Tell Paulie good-bye for me, Mrs. Stroebel," I said hurriedly. "I'll call you tomorrow to see how he's doing."

Paulie was beginning to talk again, tossing restlessly and mumbling incoherently.

"Thank you, Ellie. Good-bye." Mrs. Stroebel began propelling me to the door.

"Andrea. . ." Paulie shouted, *"don't go out with him!"*

I spun around.

Paulie's voice was still clear, but now his tone was frightened and pleading. "Mama, suppose I forget and tell them about the locket she was wearing? I'll *try* not to tell, but if I forget, you won't let them put me in prison, will you?"

34

"There is an explanation. You must believe me. It is not what you think," Mrs. Stroebel sobbed to me as we stood in the corridor outside Paulie's room.

"We have to talk, and you have to be absolutely honest with me," I said. We couldn't do it then, though—Paulie's doctor was coming down the hall.

"Ellie, I will call you tomorrow morning," she promised. "I am too upset now." Shaking her head as she turned away, Mrs. Stroebel struggled to regain her composure.

I drove back to the inn on automatic pilot. Was it possible, was it *remotely* possible, that all this time I had been wrong? Had Rob Westerfield—and, indeed, his whole family—been victimized by a terrible miscarriage of justice?

He twisted my arm. . . . He came up behind me and punched me in the neck. . . . He said, "I beat Phil to death, and it felt good."

Paulie's response to the verbal attack of Mrs. Westerfield's housekeeper had been to hurt himself, not someone else.

I could not believe that Paulie had been Andrea's murderer, but I was sure that years ago Mrs. Stroebel had kept him from telling something he knew.

The locket.

As I drove into the parking lot of the inn, I was overwhelmed with a crushing sense of the irony of what was happening. No one, absolutely no one believed that Rob Westerfield had given Andrea a locket and that she had been wearing it the night she died.

But now the existence of the locket had been validated by the one person who would be terrified to publicly admit any knowledge of it.

I looked around as I got out of the car. It was a quarter past four, and the shadows were already long and slanting. What was left of the sun was passing in and out of clouds, and a light wind was blowing the remaining leaves from the trees. They made a rustling sound along the driveway, and in my edgy frame of mind they sounded to me like footsteps.

The parking lot was almost full, and then I remembered that I'd noticed preparations for a wedding reception when I left this afternoon. To find a space I had to drive around the bend to the farthest section of the parking area, putting me out of sight of the inn. It was getting to be a chronic state of mind, the feeling that someone might be hanging around, watching me.

I didn't run, but I moved quickly as I made my way through a row of parked cars toward the safety of the inn. As I passed an old van, the door suddenly slid open, and a man jumped out and tried to grab my arm.

I began to run and got about ten feet but then tripped on one of the extra-large moccasins I'd bought to accommodate my bandaged feet.

As one of the shoes flew off, I felt myself falling forward and frantically tried to regain my balance, but it was too late. My palms and body caught the worst of the fall, and literally every ounce of breath was knocked out of me.

The man was immediately down on one knee beside me. "Don't scream," he said urgently. "I'm not going to hurt you; *please don't scream!*"

I couldn't have screamed. Nor could I have gotten away from him and run to the inn. My entire body was shaking in reaction to the severe impact with the hard surface of the ground. My mouth open, I gulped air in great shuddering gasps.

"What... do... you... want?" At last I was able to get out those few words.

"To talk to you. I was gonna e-mail you, but I didn't know who else might sec it. I want to sell you some information about Rob Westerfield."

I looked up at him. His face was very close to mine. He was a man somewhere in his early forties, with thin, not particularly clean hair. He had a nervous way of sliding his eyes around like someone who expects to have to make a run for it at any moment. He was wearing a visibly worn lumber jacket and jeans.

As I began to struggle to my feet, he retrieved my moccasin and handed it to me. "I'm not going to hurt you," he repeated. "It's risky for me to be seen with you. Hear me out. If you're not interested in what I have to say, I'm out of here."

It wasn't rational perhaps, but for some reason I believed him. If he had wanted to kill me, he'd already had all the chance he needed.

"Are you willing to listen?" he asked impatiently.

"Go ahead."

"Would you sit in my van for a couple of minutes? I don't want no one to see me. The Westerfields' people are all over this town."

I could vouch for that, but I wasn't about to get in his van. "Say what you have to say out here."

"I have something that maybe might stick Westerfield with a crime he committed years ago."

"How much do you want?"

"A thousand bucks."

"What have you got?"

"You know that Westerfield's grandmother was shot

and left for dead about twenty-five years ago? You wrote about it on your Website."

"Yes, I did."

"My brother, Skip, he went to prison for that job. He got twenty years. He died after he'd served half his time. Couldn't take it. He was always kind of sickly."

"Your brother was the one who shot Mrs. Westerfield and burglarized her home?"

"Yeah, but Westerfield planned it, see, and hired Skip and me to do the job."

"Why did he do it?"

"Westerfield was heavy into drugs. That's why he dropped out of college. He owed people big time. He'd seen his grandmother's will. She'd left one hundred thousand dollars directly to him. The minute she croaked, it would be in his pocket. He promised us ten thousand dollars to do the job."

"Was he *with* you that night?"

"Are you kidding? He was in New York at a dinner with his mother and father. He knew how to cover his bases."

"Did he pay your brother or you?"

"Before the job he gave my brother his Rolex as security. Then he reported it stolen."

"Why?"

"To cover his tracks after my brother was arrested. Westerfield claimed he met us in a bowling alley the night before the old lady was hit. He said Skip kept eyeing his watch, so he put it in his bag when he started bowling. He told the cops that, when he went to get his watch out of the bag later, it wasn't there and we weren't around. He swore that was the only time he ever saw Skip or me."

"How could you have known about his grandmother without him telling you?"

"There'd been a big write-up about her in the paper. She gave a wing to a hospital or something."

"How did your brother and you get caught?"

"I didn't. My brother was picked up the next day. He had a record and was nervous about having to shoot the old lady. That was the reason he was there, but Westerfield wanted it to look like a burglary. Rob didn't give us the combination of the safe because only the family knew it, and that would have given him away. He told Skip to bring a chisel and knife and scratch up the safe like he tried to force it open and couldn't. But Skip cut his hand and took off his glove to wipe it. He must have touched the safe because they found his fingerprint on it."

"Then he went upstairs and shot Mrs. Westerfield."

"Yeah. But nobody could prove I was there. I was the lookout and drove the car. Skip told me to keep my mouth shut. He took the rap, and Westerfield got off scot-free."

"So did you."

He shrugged. "Yeah, I know it."

"How old were you?"

"Sixteen."

"How old was Westerfield?"

"Seventeen."

"Didn't your brother try to implicate Westerfield?"

"Sure. Nobody believed him."

"I'm not certain about that. His grandmother changed her will. That hundred-thousand-dollar direct grant was taken out of it."

"Good. They let Skip plead to attempted murder with a twenty-year sentence. He could have gotten thirty but he was willing to plead to a max of twenty. The D.A. agreed to the deal so that the old lady wouldn't have to testify at a trial."

The last of the sun had gone totally behind the clouds. I still felt shaken from the fall, and now I was cold, too.

"What's your name?" I asked.

"Alfie. Alfie Leeds."

"Alfie, I believe you," I said. "But I don't know why you're telling me this now. There's never been a shred of evidence to prove that Rob Westerfield was in on that crime."

"I have proof he was involved."

Alfie reached into his pocket and pulled out a folded

sheet of paper. "This is a copy of the diagram Rob Westerfield gave us so that my brother could get into the house without setting off the alarm."

From another pocket he took out a pencil flashlight.

Standing out in the windy parking lot was no place to study a diagram. I looked at the guy again. He was an inch shorter than I am, and he didn't look particularly strong. I decided to take a chance. "I'll get in the van, but only if I sit in the driver's seat," I told him.

"Have it your way."

I opened the driver's door and looked around. There was no one else there. The backseat had been flattened down and contained what looked like paint cans, a drop cloth, and a ladder. He had gone around to the passenger side. I slid in behind the wheel but did not fully close the door. I knew that if this was a setup, I still could get out pretty fast.

In my job as an investigative reporter I've had to meet a number of unsavory characters in places I wouldn't have chosen to visit otherwise. As a result, my sense of self-preservation has become well developed. I decided that allowing for the fact that I was cloistered with a man who'd been part of a murder plot, I was as safe as I could get.

When we were both inside the van, he handed me the paper. The thin beam of the flashlight was enough to enable me to recognize the Westerfield house and driveway. The garage-hideout was even depicted. Below the buildings there was a precise layout of the interior of the mansion.

"See, it shows where the alarm is and gives the code to disarm it. Rob wasn't worried that disarming the alarm would draw attention to himself because a lot of handymen and other employees knew the code too. There's the layout of the ground floor, the library with the safe, the stairs to the old lady's bedroom, and the section off the kitchen that was the maid's apartment."

There was a name printed on the bottom of the page. "Who's Jim?" I asked.

"The guy who drew this. Westerfield told Skip and me that he did some work on the house. We never met him."

"Did your brother ever show this to the police?"

"He wanted to use it, but the lawyer they gave him said forget it. He said Skip had no proof Westerfield gave it to him, and the fact that he even had it just made Skip look bad. He said being that the safe was downstairs and the way the old lady's bedroom is so clearly marked only helped prove that Skip was planning to kill her."

"Jim could have corroborated your brother's story. Did anyone try to find him?"

"I guess not. I've kept the map all these years, and when I saw your Website, I figured this is one more thing you might investigate and hang on Westerfield. Have we got a deal? Will you give me a thousand bucks for it?"

"How can I be sure that this isn't something you drew up yourself to get money from me?"

"You can't. Give it back."

"Alfie, if the lawyer had looked into this guy, Jim, and had told the D.A. about him and had shown the D.A. the sketch, they would have had to investigate the information seriously. Your brother might have gotten a better sentence in exchange for his cooperation, and Westerfield might have paid for his crime too."

"Yeah, but there was another problem. Westerfield hired both my brother and me to do the job. The lawyer told my brother that if the cops would end up arresting Westerfield, he could make his own deal and tell the D.A. that I was involved. Skip was five years older than me and felt guilty about getting me into it."

"Well, the statute of limitations has run out for both you and Rob. But wait a minute. You say this is a copy of the original. Where is the original?"

"The lawyer tore it up. He said he didn't want it to fall in the wrong hands."

"He tore it up!"

"He didn't know Skip had made a copy and given it to me."

"I want this," I said. "I'll have the cash for you in the morning."

We shook hands. His skin felt somewhat grimy, but it was also calloused, which said to me that Alfie did hard, heavy work.

As he carefully folded the paper into neat squares and put it in his inside pocket, I couldn't help saying, "With this kind of evidence I just can't understand why your brother's lawyer didn't try to make a deal with the district attorney. It wouldn't have been hard to follow up on an employee named Jim who drew this diagram. The cops could have squeezed him to give up Rob, and you would have been tried in Juvenile Court. I wonder if your brother's lawyer sold out to the Westerfields."

He smiled, baring stained teeth. "He's working for them now. He's that Hamilton guy, the one who's all over television saying he's going to get a new trial and acquittal for Rob."

35

When I got back to the room, there was a message to call Mrs. Hilmer. I'd spoken to her several times since the fire, and she'd been simply wonderful to me. Her whole concern was about my being okay and she was distressed over my almost being trapped in the fire. You would have thought I'd done her a favor by being the reason the garage and apartment had been reduced to rubble. I agreed to have Sunday dinner with her.

I'd barely hung up when Joan called. I'd also been speaking to her, but we hadn't seen each other during the week and I was anxious to return the money and clothes I'd borrowed. I'd had the slacks, sweater, and jacket cleaned and the lingerie laundered, and I bought a bottle of champagne for Joan and Leo and another for the friend who was my size.

Of course that was not Joan's reason for calling. She and Leo and the kids were going out for dinner to Il Palazzo and wanted me to join them.

"Great pasta, great pizza, a fun place," she promised. "I really think you'd enjoy it."

"You don't have to sell me. I'd love to go."

In fact, I needed to get out. After my parking lot encounter with Alfie, the paramount thought in my mind was of all the people whose lives had been altered or destroyed by Rob Westerfield and by the Westerfield fortune.

Andrea, first, of course. Then Mother. Then Paulie, who was so afraid he'd be tricked into revealing he knew something about the locket. Whatever his knowledge of the locket turned out to be, I would stake my life that it did not tie him to Andrea's death.

Mrs. Stroebel, hardworking and honest, also had been caught in the Westerfield web of misery. It must have been agony for her when Paulie was on the witness stand during the trial. Suppose just one person had believed me when I said that Rob had given Andrea a locket, and then Paulie had been asked about it in court. He easily could have incriminated himself.

I believed everything that Alfie Leeds had told me. I had no doubt that his brother had been a potential killer. He was willing to take Mrs. Westerfield's life and had left her for dead. Bad as he was, though, he was entitled to a lawyer who truly represented him. The lawyer he was assigned sold him out to the Westerfields.

I could visualize William Hamilton, *Juris Doctor,*

seeing that case as his chance to break into the big time. He probably went to Rob's father, showed him the diagram, and was properly rewarded for his cooperation.

Alfie was a victim, too. He'd been protected by his big brother and no doubt was left feeling guilty that he couldn't find a way to nail Rob Westerfield. And then he spent all those years sitting on evidence that he was afraid to show anyone.

The hardest to swallow for me, of course, was the knowledge that if Rob Westerfield had been convicted of planning the attempted murder of his grandmother, he would never have met Andrea.

Now I had another person on my list of people I wanted to nail to the wall: William Hamilton, Esquire.

Anyhow, those were the sad and furious thoughts that were running through my head when Joan called. I definitely needed a break. We agreed to meet at seven o'clock at Il Palazzo.

Tilting at windmills, I told myself as I drove the short distance into the heart of town. I had the feeling that I was being followed. Maybe I should call Officer White, I thought sarcastically. He's terribly worried about me. He'll be here right away, sirens blazing.

Oh, give him a break, I snapped at myself. He's honestly convinced that I'm back in this town to make trouble and that I'm obsessed because Rob Westerfield is a free man.

Okay, Officer White, I'm obsessive on that score, but I didn't burn my feet or ruin my car to prove my point.

Joan and Leo and their three boys were seated at a corner table when I got to Il Palazzo. I vaguely remembered Leo. He had been a senior at Oldham High when Joan and Andrea were sophomores.

It's inevitable that when people from those days see me for the first time, the first thing they think about is Andrea's death. Then they invariably either comment on it or make an obvious effort to ignore it.

I liked the way Leo handled his greeting to me. He said, "I remember you, of course, Ellie. You were over at Joan's house with Andrea a couple of times when I stopped by. You were a solemn little kid."

"And now I'm a solemn *big* kid," I told him.

I liked him immediately. He was about six feet tall, solidly built, with light brown hair and intelligent dark eyes. His smile was like Joan's, warm and all-embracing. He conveyed the immediate feeling of trustworthiness. I knew he was a stockbroker, so I made a mental note to talk to him if I ever had any money. I was sure I'd be comfortable taking his advice on where to invest it.

The boys' ages were ten, fourteen, and seventeen. The oldest, Billy, was a senior in high school and almost immediately told me his team had played basketball against Teddy's team.

"Teddy and I talked about the colleges we're applying to, Ellie," he said. "We're both trying for Dartmouth and Brown. I hope we end up at the same one. He's a nice guy."

"Yes, he is," I agreed.

"You didn't tell me you'd met him," Joan said quickly.

"He stopped in to see me at the inn for a few minutes."

There was a satisfied look in her eye. I wanted to tell her not to set aside any dates for a grand reunion of the Cavanaughs, but then the menus arrived and Leo was smart enough to change the subject.

I did a fair amount of babysitting in my teenage years, and I like being around kids. My job in Atlanta certainly didn't expose me to many of them, so it had been a while. It was a treat to be with these three boys. Pretty soon, over mussels and pasta, they were talking to me about their activities, and I promised Sean, the ten-year-old, that I'd play chess with him.

"I'm good," I warned him.

"I'm better," he assured me.

"We'll see about that."

"How about tomorrow? It's Sunday. We'll be home."

"Oh, sorry, but tomorrow I have plans. Soon,

though." Then I remembered something and looked at Joan. "I didn't put the suitcase I wanted to return to you in the car."

"Bring it tomorrow, and we'll have a game of chess," Sean suggested.

"You have to eat," Joan said. "Brunch about eleven-thirty?"

"Sounds great," I told her.

The bar at Il Palazzo was a glass-paneled section of the dining room, directly off the entrance hall. When I arrived, I hadn't paid attention to anyone in the bar. But I had noticed that during dinner Joan sometimes glanced past me, her expression troubled.

We were sipping coffee when I learned the reason for her concern.

"Ellie, Will Nebels has been at the bar since before you got here. Someone must have pointed you out to him. He's on his way over, and from the look of him, I'd say he's drunk."

The warning wasn't fast enough. I felt arms around my neck, a sloppy kiss on my cheek. "Little Ellie, my goodness, little Ellie Cavanaugh. Do you remember how I fixed your seesaw for you, honey? Your daddy was never any good at fixing stuff. Your mama used to call me all the time. 'Will, this needs to be done. Will—' "

He was kissing my ear and the back of my neck.

"Get your hands off her," Leo said, his voice clipped. He was on his feet.

I was literally pinned down. Nebels's full weight was on me now. His arms were resting on my shoulders; his hands were sliding down, groping inside my sweater.

"And pretty little Andrea. With my own eyes I seen that retard go in that garage carrying that tire jack. . . ."

A waiter was pulling at him from one side, Leo and Billy from the other. I kept trying to push his face away, but to no avail. He was kissing my eyes. Then his moist, beery mouth was pressing against my lips. My chair started to tilt back as we struggled. I was terrified that I was going to slam the back of my head against the floor and end up with him sprawled over me.

But men from nearby tables came rushing over, and strong hands caught the teetering chair before it reached the floor.

Then Nebels was forcibly dragged away and the chair lifted up. I dropped my face into my hands. For the second time in six hours I was trembling so violently that I could not respond to the concerned inquiries coming from all sides of me. The couple of pins that anchored my hair had pulled loose, and it was spilling around my shoulders. I felt Joan stroking it, and wanted to beg her to stop—compassion at that moment would undo me. Maybe she sensed my feeling because she withdrew her hand.

I could hear the manager sputtering apologies. You *ought* to apologize, I thought. You should have stopped serving that drunk long ago.

That flash of anger was all I needed to get me back on course. I raised my head and began to smooth back my hair. Then I glanced around the table at the concerned faces, and shrugged. "I'm okay," I told them.

I looked at Joan and knew what she was thinking. She might as well have been shouting it.

"Ellie, now do you understand what I said about Will Nebels? He's admitted he was in Mrs. Westerfield's house that night. He was probably drunk. What do you think he would have done if he saw Andrea go into that garage alone?"

A half hour later, after a fresh cup of coffee, I absolutely insisted on driving myself home. But on the way I wondered if I had been foolish. I was now positive that I was being followed and was not about to risk being alone again in that parking lot. I therefore did not turn off at the inn but drove past it and called the police on my cell phone.

"We'll send a car," the cop at the desk told me. "Where are you?"

I told him.

"All right. Circle back and turn into the driveway of the inn. We'll be right behind whoever is tailing you.

Under no circumstances get out of the car until we come for you."

I drove slowly, and the car behind me slowed down as well. Now that I knew a squad car was coming, I was glad the car on my tail was still there. I wanted the police to find out who was in that car and why I was being followed.

I was approaching the inn again. I turned into the driveway, but the car behind me kept going. A moment later I saw a domelight flashing and heard the wail of the police siren.

I pulled over to the side of the driveway and stopped. Two minutes later the squad car, its light no longer flashing, drove up behind me. A cop got out and came up to the driver's door of my car. As I rolled down the window, I could see that he was smiling.

"You *were* being followed, Ms. Cavanaugh. The kid says he's your brother and was making sure you got back here safely."

"Oh, for goodness sake, tell him to go home!" I said. Then I added, "But thank him for me, please."

36

I'd planned to call Marcus Longo on Sunday morning, but he beat me to it. When the phone rang at nine o'clock, I was at the computer, with my second cup of coffee on the table beside it.

"I have you pegged as an early starter, Ellie," he said. "I hope I'm right."

"As a matter of fact, I slept late this morning," I said. "Seven o'clock."

"That's about what I would have expected of you. I've been in touch with the office at Sing Sing."

"To see if they learned of any recently discharged convict or prison guard who might have had a fatal accident?"

"That's right."

"You've heard something?"

"Ellie, you were outside Sing Sing on November first. Herb Coril, a convict who at one time was in the same cell block as Rob Westerfield, was discharged that morning. He was staying at a halfway house in lower Manhattan. He hasn't been seen since early Friday evening."

"I got that last call on Friday night about ten-thirty," I said. "Whoever called me was afraid for his life."

"We can't be sure it's the same person, and we can't be sure that Coril didn't just break the conditions of his release and take off."

"What's your guess?" I asked.

"I've never been strong on coincidences, especially one like this."

"Neither am I."

I told Marcus about my meeting with Alfie.

"I only hope nothing happens to Alfie before you get that diagram," Marcus said grimly. "I'm not surprised to hear this. We all thought that Rob Westerfield planned that job. I know what that must be doing to you."

"You mean the fact that Rob might have been in prison and therefore not around here to meet Andrea? That's all I've been thinking about, and it's been torturing me."

"You do understand that even with the copy of the diagram and Alfie making a statement to the D.A., you'll never get a conviction. Alfie was involved himself, and the diagram is signed by someone named Jim whom nobody has ever met."

"I know."

"The statute of limitations on that crime has run out for all of them—Westerfield, Alfie, and Jim, whoever that is."

"Don't forget Hamilton. If I could prove that he destroyed evidence that might have gotten his client a lighter sentence by implicating Westerfield, the ethics committee would be all over him."

I promised to let Marcus see the diagram that Alfie was bringing me. Then I said good-bye and tried to get back to work. It was slow, though, and after getting only a little more done, I realized it was time to drive to Joan's for brunch.

This time I remembered the suitcase and the plastic cleaner's bag with the slacks, sweater, and jacket.

Even before I was near the Franciscan Friars monastery at Graymoor, I knew that I was going to stop there. All week a memory had been slowly emerging from my subconscious. I had visited the place with Mother after Andrea died. She had called Father Emil, a priest she knew. He was going to be at Saint Christopher's Inn that day, and they arranged to meet there.

Saint Christopher's Inn, on the grounds of the monastery, is the friars' home for destitute men who are alcoholics or drug addicts. I had a vague memory of sitting with a lady, a secretary probably, while Mother was in the office. Then Father Emil took us into the chapel.

I remembered that there was a book on the side of the chapel where people could write petitions. Mother wrote something and then gave the pen to me.

I wanted to go there again.

The friar who admitted me introduced himself as Fr. Bob. He didn't question my request. The chapel was empty, and he stood at the door as I knelt for a few minutes. Then I looked around and saw the stand with the ledger-sized book.

I went over to it and picked up the pen.

Suddenly I remembered what I had written that last time: *Please let Andrea come back to us.*

This time I could not force myself to stop crying.

"There have been many tears shed in this chapel." Fr. Bob was standing beside me.

We talked for an hour. When I got to Joan's, I was on speaking terms with God again.

Joan and I respectfully disagreed with each other about Will Nebels's performance the night before.

"Ellie, he was just plain drunk. How many people shoot off at the mouth when they've had too much to drink? My point is that's not when they lie—it's when they're more likely to let slip the truth."

I had to admit that Joan was right on that point. I'd

investigated and written about two cases in which the killer would never have been caught if he hadn't loaded up on scotch or vodka and poured his heart out to someone who immediately called the cops.

"That's not the way I see it, though," I explained to her and Leo. "To me, Will Nebels is a spineless, gutless loser. Think of him as the stuff you pour into a gelatin mold. You plan the shape you want, and then, you have it. He wasn't too drunk to remember that he once fixed my seesaw and that my father wasn't born with a tool in his hand."

"I agree with Ellie," Leo said. "Nebels is more complex than he appears to be on the surface." Then he added, "That, of course, doesn't mean that Joan isn't right. If Nebels did see Paulie Stroebel go into that garage that night, he got smart enough to figure that the statute of limitations had run out and that it was safe for him to make a buck out of it."

"Only he didn't figure this one out himself," I said. "They came to him. He agreed to tell the story they needed, and they paid him to tell it."

I pushed my chair back. "Brunch was wonderful," I said, "and now I feel like winning a chess game from Sean."

For a moment I paused to look out the window. It was the second beautiful Sunday afternoon I'd been in this room at this exact same time. I was aware again of the spectacular view of the river and the mountain from this spot.

In my world, which was so far from peaceful, to experience that view was like being at an oasis.

I won the first chess game. Sean won the second. We agreed to a rematch "really soon."

Before I started home I phoned the hospital and spoke to Mrs. Stroebel. Paulie's fever had broken, and he was feeling much better. "He wants to talk to you, Ellie."

Forty minutes later I was at his bedside. "You look a lot better than you did yesterday," I told him.

He was still very pale, but his eyes were clear and he was propped up with an extra pillow. He smiled shyly. "Ellie, Mama said you know that I saw the locket, too."

"When did you see it, Paulie?"

"I worked at the service station. My first job there was just to wash and clean the cars after they were fixed. When I cleaned Rob's car one day, I found the locket stuck in the front seat. The chain was broken."

"You mean the day Andrea's body was found?" But that doesn't make sense, I thought. If Rob went back for the locket that morning, he never would have left it in his car. Or could he really have been that stupid?

Paulie looked at his mother. "Mama?" he appealed.

"It's all right, Paulie," she said soothingly. "You've

had a lot of medicine, and it's hard to keep track of everything. You told me you saw the locket twice."

I looked sharply at Mrs. Stroebel, trying to decide if she was prompting him. But Paulie nodded.

"That's right, Mama. I found it in the car. The chain was broken. I gave it to Rob, and he gave me a ten-dollar tip. I put it with the money I was saving for your fiftieth birthday present."

"I remember, Paulie."

"When was your fiftieth birthday, Mrs. Stroebel?" I asked.

"It was May first, the May before Andrea died."

"The May before Andrea died!" I was absolutely shocked. Then he *didn't* buy the locket for her, I thought. It was one that some girl may have lost in the car, and he had it initialed and gave it to Andrea.

"Paulie, do you remember the locket clearly?" I asked.

"Yes. It was nice. It was shaped like a heart and it was gold and it had little blue stones in it."

That was exactly the way I had described it on the witness stand.

"Paulie, did you ever see the locket again?" I asked.

"Yes. Andrea was so nice to me. She came up and told me how good I was at football and that I'd won the game for the team. That was when I decided to ask her to go to the mixer with me.

"I walked over to your house, and I saw her going through the woods. I caught up with her outside Mrs. Westerfield's house. She was wearing the locket, and I knew Rob must have given it to her. He's not nice. He gave me that big tip, but he's not nice. His car always had dents in it because he drove so fast."

"Did you see him that day?"

"I asked Andrea if I could talk to her, but she said not then, that she was in a hurry. I went back into the woods and watched her go into the garage. A few minutes later, Rob Westerfield went in."

"Tell Ellie when that was, Paulie."

"It was one week before Andrea died in that garage."

One week before.

"Then a couple of days before she died, I talked to her again. I told her Rob was a very bad person and that she shouldn't meet him in the garage and that I knew her father would be very angry if he knew she went there with him."

Paulie looked directly at me. "Your father was always so nice to me, Ellie. He always gave me a tip for filling the gas tank, and he always talked to me about football. He was very nice."

"When you warned Andrea about Rob, was that the time you asked her to go to the mixer with you?"

"Yes, and she said she would, and she made me promise not to tell her father about Rob."

"And you never saw the locket again?"

"No, Ellie."

"And you never went to the garage again?"

"No, Ellie."

Paulie closed his eyes, and I could see that he was becoming very tired. I covered his hand with mine.

"Paulie, I don't want you to worry anymore. I promise you that it's going to be all right, and before I'm finished, everyone will know how nice and kind and good you are. And you're smart, too. When you were a kid, you could see how rotten Rob Westerfield was. A lot of people around here still can't see through him."

"Paulie thinks with his heart," Mrs. Stroebel said softly.

Paulie opened his eyes. "I'm so sleepy. Did I tell you all about the locket?"

"Yes, you did."

Mrs. Stroebel walked me to the elevator. "Ellie, even at the trial they were trying so hard to blame Paulie for Andrea's death. I was so frightened. That was why I told him he must never talk about the locket."

"I understand."

"I hope you do. A special child will always need to be protected, even as a grown-up. You heard the Westerfield lawyer on television telling everyone that in a new trial he would prove Paulie killed Andrea. Can you imagine Paulie on the witness stand with that man hammering at him?"

That man. William Hamilton, Esquire.

"No, I can't."

I kissed her cheek. "Paulie is lucky he has you, Mrs. Stroebel."

Her eyes lowered to meet mine. "He's lucky he has you, Ellie."

37

At seven o'clock I was on my way to having dinner with Mrs. Hilmer. Of course that meant I had to pass our old house. Tonight it was brightly lit, and with the moon shining over the woods behind it, it could have been on the cover of a magazine. It was the house Mother had visualized, a perfect example of a lovingly restored and expanded farmhouse.

The windows of my room were over the front door, and I could see the outline of a figure moving between them. The Keltons, who now owned the house, were a couple in their early fifties. They were the only people from the house I saw the night of the fire, but they might have adolescent children who had slept through the wailing of the police and fire vehicles. I wondered if whoever had my room liked to wake up early and lie in bed watching the sunrise, the way I had.

Mrs. Hilmer's house was well lit, too. I turned into her driveway, which now had only one destination. My headlights picked up the charred remains of the garage and apartment. For some incongruous reason I thought of the candlesticks and decorative fruit bowl that had graced the apartment's dining room table. They were not valuable, but they obviously had been chosen with taste and care.

Everything in the apartment had been chosen with care. If Mrs. Hilmer chose to rebuild, those were the kinds of items that required time and effort to replace.

With that thought in mind, I entered her home with apologies on my lips, but she would have none of it. "Will you stop worrying about the garage?" she sighed as she pulled my face down for a kiss. "Ellie, that fire was deliberately set."

"I know it. You don't think I was responsible, do you?"

"Good Lord, no! Ellie, when I got back and Brian White came marching in here practically accusing you of being a pyromaniac, I gave him a real piece of my mind. If it makes you feel better, he as much as told me that I only imagined I was followed back and forth to the library that day. I set him straight on that, too. But I tell you, Ellie, it's terrible to think that whoever got into the apartment when you were here for dinner that night actually stole towels from it to make it look as if you set the fire."

"I took towels from the linen closet every day. I never noticed that five or six bath towels were missing."

"How could you? The shelves were stacked with them. I went through a period of not being able to resist a bargain, and now I have enough towels to last me till kingdom come. Well, dinner is ready, and you must be hungry. Let's go right to the table."

Dinner consisted of shrimp creole, followed by a Bibb lettuce salad. It was delicious. "Two good meals in one day," I said. "I'm getting spoiled."

I asked about her granddaughter and learned that her broken wrist was mending nicely.

"It was wonderful to spend time with Janey, and the new baby is adorable. But, Ellie, let me tell you, after a week I was ready to go home. The spirit is willing, but it's a long time since I had to get up to heat a bottle at five a.m."

She said she had been watching my Website, and I could see that any feeling of sympathy she had for Rob Westerfield was crumbling. "When I read that statement from the psychologist, telling how Rob twisted her arm in the restaurant, I was shocked. Janey used to waitress when she was in college, and the thought of some bully manhandling her like that made my blood boil."

"Wait till you read what's coming. He also did quite a job on a fellow student when he was only a sophomore in prep school."

"It just keeps getting worse. I was heartsick to hear about Paulie. How is he doing?"

"He's mending. I went to see him this afternoon." I hesitated, not sure that I wanted to share with her Paulie's revelations about the locket. But then I decided to go ahead. Mrs. Hilmer was absolutely trustworthy and a very good barometer of local opinion. I knew she had always firmly believed that the locket was a figment of my imagination. It would be both interesting and helpful to get her reaction about it now.

Her tea cooled as she listened, and her face became grave. "Ellie, it's no wonder Mrs. Stroebel didn't want Paulie to talk about the locket. That story could easily be turned around so that it hurts Paulie."

"I know that. Paulie admitted having the locket in his possession, giving it to Rob, being upset when he saw Andrea wearing it, and following her to the garage." I paused and looked at her. "Mrs. Hilmer, do you believe it happened like that?"

"What I believe is that with all the Westerfield money, Rob Westerfield is cheap as well as vicious. He gave a gift to Andrea that another girl probably lost in his car. I'll bet he took it to one of those malls, paid a couple of dollars to have it engraved, and then made a big show of it."

"I thought about trying to trace whoever engraved it, but after all these years, that's almost impossible. They do that kind of engraving in those jewelry places in shopping malls all the time."

"So you don't know how to use your information about the locket?"

"No, I don't. I was so happy to have my memory of the locket verified that I haven't even thought that through. The locket is a double-edged sword, and in court Paulie could be the one hurt by it."

I told Mrs. Hilmer about Alfie and the diagram.

"We all felt the attack on Mrs. Westerfield was an inside job," she said, her expression an odd mixture of sympathy and disgust. "Mrs. Dorothy Westerfield is kind, elegant, and gracious. To think that her only grandchild would plan her murder goes beyond belief. I'd see her sometimes in town with Rob before he was arrested. Butter wouldn't melt in his mouth, he was so solicitous of her."

"That story and the diagram go on the Internet if Alfie agrees," I said. "When Mrs. Westerfield sees the diagram, it may help to convince her."

My description of Will Nebels's drunken pawing of me in the restaurant reduced Mrs. Hilmer to sputtering indignation. "You mean to say a man like that would be considered a reliable witness in a new trial?"

"Not necessarily reliable, but he could still do a ton of damage in swaying public opinion against Paulie."

Despite her protests, we cleared the table together

and tidied up the kitchen. "Are you going to rebuild the garage and replace the apartment?" I asked.

As she popped plates into the dishwasher, she smiled. "Ellie, I wouldn't want the insurance company to hear me, but that fire turned out to be a good thing. I was well insured, and now I have an empty second building lot where the garage was located. Janey would love to live up here. She thinks it's a wonderful place to raise her baby. If I give them the lot, they'll build a house, and I'll have my family right next door."

I laughed. "You've made me feel a lot better." I folded the dish towel. "And now I have to be on my way. I'm driving to Carrington Academy in Maine tomorrow, digging up more of Rob Westerfield's glorious past."

"Janey and I read those papers and the trial transcript. It brings back how dreadful that time was for all of you." Mrs. Hilmer walked to the closet with me to retrieve my leather jacket. As I buttoned it, I realized I had not thought to ask her if the name Phil meant anything to her.

"Mrs. Hilmer, in prison, apparently while he was high on drugs, Rob Westerfield may have confessed to beating a man named Phil to death. Did you ever know or hear about anyone by that name from around here who might have disappeared or been the victim of a homicide?"

"Phil," she repeated, looking past me and frowning

in concentration. "There was Phil Oliver who had a terrible run-in with the Westerfields when they wouldn't renew his lease. But he moved away."

"Do you know what became of him?"

"No, but I can find out. He and his family had a couple of good friends here who are probably still in touch."

"Will you check for me?"

"Of course."

She opened the door, then hesitated. "I know something or read something about a young person named Phil who died a while ago . . . I can't remember where I heard about it, but it was very sad."

"Mrs. Hilmer, think. This is so terribly important."

"Phil . . . Phil . . . Oh Ellie, it's just not coming to me."

Of course I had to settle for that. But when I left Mrs. Hilmer a few minutes later, I urged her to stop actively trying to remember the connection, and let her subconscious work on it.

I was closing in on Rob Westerfield. I could feel it in my bones.

The car that was following me tonight was much more subtle than the one Teddy had driven. He rode without lights. I only became aware of his presence when I had to stop to let traffic pass before I could turn into the driveway of the inn, and he was forced to stop directly behind me.

I turned, trying to get a look at the driver. The car was heavy and dark, and I knew it wasn't Teddy.

Another car was coming up the driveway, leaving the inn, and its headlights illuminated the face in the car behind me.

Tonight it was my father who wanted to be sure that I got back to the inn safely. For a split second we looked at each other, then I turned left into the driveway and he kept going down the road.

38

Alfie phoned me at seven o'clock Monday morning. "You still wanna buy it?"

"Yes, I do. My bank is Oldham-Hudson on Main Street. I'll be there at nine o'clock, and you can meet me in the parking lot at five after nine."

"Okay."

As I was leaving the bank, he drove up and parked next to my car. From the street no one would have been able to see what was taking place.

He opened the window. "Let's have the money."

I handed it to him.

After he had counted it, he said, "Okay, here's the diagram."

I examined it carefully. In the daylight it seemed even more chilling when I considered that it had been commissioned by the seventeen-year-old grandson of the potential victim. I knew that I would pay anything Alfie asked to have his permission to put it on my Website.

"Alfie, you know that the statute of limitations has expired. If the cops knew about this, you wouldn't get into any trouble. But if I show it on the Website and write about what you told me, it might make the difference between Mrs. Westerfield leaving her money to charities or to Rob."

I was standing outside the van. He was sitting in it, his hand on the wheel. He looked like what he had become: a hardworking guy who never had much of a break.

"Listen, I'd rather take my chances on Westerfield coming after me than think of him rolling in big bucks. Go for it."

"You're sure?"

"I'm sure. It kind of makes it up to Skip."

After the experience of driving to Boston and getting caught in heavy traffic, I allowed plenty of travel time for the drive to Maine when I rescheduled my appointment with Jane Bostrom, director of admissions at Carrington Academy.

That was why I was in Rockport long enough to stop for a grilled cheese sandwich and Coke at a coffee shop a mile from the school. I now felt prepared to take her on.

When I was escorted into her office, her greeting to me was cordial but reserved, and I was certain that she was going to be less than cooperative in releasing information to me. She was at her desk and offered me the seat facing it. Like many executives she had a visiting area with a couch and several chairs, but I was not invited to join her there.

She was younger than I had expected, about thirty-five, with dark hair and large gray eyes that seemed to be somewhat wary. From our brief conversation on the phone it was evident that she was proud of her school and was not about to have an investigative reporter trash it because of one student.

"Dr. Bostrom," I said, "let me put my cards on the table. Rob Westerfield spent his junior and senior years in Carrington. He was kicked out of his former prep school because he viciously assaulted another student. He was fourteen years old when that incident occurred.

"At seventeen he planned the murder of his grandmother. She was shot three times, and it is a miracle that she survived. At nineteen he bludgeoned my sister to death. I am at present tracking down the probability that there is at least one more person whose life he has taken."

I watched as her expression became dismayed and distressed. She took a long moment before she spoke. "Ms. Cavanaugh, that information about Rob Westerfield is horrifying, but please understand something. I have his file in front of me, and there is absolutely nothing in it that indicates a serious behavior problem while he was here."

"I find it hard to believe that with the violent history I've been uncovering, he was able to spend two years without a major infraction on his record. May I ask how long you have been employed at Carrington, Dr. Bostrom?"

"Five years."

"Then of course the only thing you have to go by is a record that may have been tidied up."

"I am going by the record in front of me."

"May I ask if the Westerfields have made any significant contributions to Carrington Academy?"

"At the time Rob was a student, they helped to renovate and refurbish the athletic center."

"I see."

"I don't know what you see, Ms. Cavanaugh. Please try to understand that many of our students have had an emotionally rough time and need guidance and compassion. Sometimes they've been pawns in nasty divorces. Sometimes one or the other parent simply walked out of their lives. You'd be amazed at what that can do to a child's sense of worth."

Oh, no, I wouldn't be amazed at all, I thought. In fact, I understand perfectly.

"Some of our students are young people who can't

seem to get along with their peer group or with adults or both."

"That would seem to have been Rob Westerfield's problem," I said. "But unfortunately for the rest of us, his family has always tried to either cover up for him or buy him out of trouble."

"Please understand that we run a tight ship here. We believe that an important step in healing an emotional problem is helping to build a sense of self-worth.

"Our students are expected to keep up their marks, take part in sports and other activities, and volunteer for the community programs that our school sponsors."

"And Rob Westerfield achieved all these goals willingly and joyfully?"

I could have bitten my tongue. Jane Bostrom had given me the courtesy of an interview, and she was answering my questions. However, it was clear that if there had been any big problems at this school with Rob Westerfield, they had not been put on his record.

"Rob Westerfield apparently achieved those goals to our school's satisfaction," she said stiffly.

"Do you have a list of the student body while he was enrolled here?"

"Of course."

"May I see it?"

"For what purpose?"

"Dr. Bostrom, when he was high on drugs in prison, Rob Westerfield made a statement to another convict. He said, 'I beat Phil to death, and it felt good.' Since he assaulted a fellow student at his previous prep school, it is not unlikely that while he was here, he had an encounter with a student named Phil or Philip."

Her eyes darkened and became progressively more concerned as she absorbed the implications of what I was saying. Then she stood up.

"Ms. Cavanaugh, Dr. Douglas Dittrick has been with Carrington for forty years. I'm going to invite him to join us. I'll also send for the student roster for those years. I think we'd better go into the conference room. It will be easier to spread out the lists on the table there and go through them carefully."

Dr. Dittrick sent word that he was in the middle of a lecture and would join us in fifteen minutes. "He's a great teacher," Jane Bostrom told me as we opened the rosters. "I think if the roof was falling down, he wouldn't budge until he finished his lecture."

She seemed more comfortable with me by then, and certainly willing to help. "We want to watch for 'Philip' as the middle name as well as the first," she warned. "We have many students who are known by their middle names when they've been named after fathers and grandfathers."

The student body totalled about six hundred during Rob Westerfield's time at Carrington. I quickly realized that Philip was not a common name. The usuals, James and John and Mark and Michael, showed up regularly on the lists.

And a host of others: William, Hugo, Charles, Richard, Henry, Walter, Howard, Lee, Peter, George, Paul, Lester, Ezekiel, Francis, Donald, Alexander . . .

And then a Philip.

"Here's one," I said. "He was a freshman when Westerfield was a sophomore."

Jane Bostrom got up and looked over my shoulder. "He's on our board of trustees," she said.

I kept looking.

Professor Dittrick joined us, still wearing his academic gown. "What's so important, Jane?" he asked.

She explained and introduced me. Dittrick was about seventy, of medium build with a scholarly face and a firm handshake.

"I remember Westerfield, of course. He'd only been graduated two years before he killed that girl."

"She was Ms. Cavanaugh's sister," Dr. Bostrom interjected quickly.

"I'm very sorry, Ms. Cavanaugh. That was a terrible tragedy. And now you're looking to see if someone named Phil who was here around his time became a homicide victim."

"Yes. I do realize it may seem farfetched, but it's an avenue I have to explore."

"Of course." He turned to Dr. Bostrom. "Jane, why don't you see if Corinne is free and ask her to come over. She wasn't the director of the theater twenty-five years ago, but she was on staff then. Ask her to bring playbills from those performances Westerfield was in. I seem to remember that there was something funny about the way he was listed in the program."

Corinne Barsky arrived twenty minutes later. A vivacious, slender woman of about sixty with dark snapping eyes and a rich, warm voice, she was carrying the playbills that had been requested.

By then we had isolated two former students with the first name Philip and one with Philip as a middle name.

The first one we'd found, as Dr. Bostrom had told me, was a current trustee of the school. Dr. Dittrick remembered that the student with the middle name Philip had attended his twentieth class reunion two years ago.

That left only one to check. Dr. Bostrom's secretary ran his name through the computer. He lived in Portland, Oregon, and made annual contributions to the alumni fund. The latest was last June.

"I'm afraid I've wasted a lot of your time," I apologized. "If I can have a quick look at the playbills, I'll be on my way."

In each of them Rob Westerfield played the male lead. "I remember him," Corinne Barsky told me. "He was genuinely good. Very full of himself, very arrogant toward the other students, but a good actor."

"Then you had no problems with him?" I asked.

"Oh, I remember him having a row with the director. He wanted to use what he called his stage name instead of his own name in the show. The director refused."

"What was his stage name?"

"Give me a minute, I'll try to remember."

"Corinne, wasn't there some kind of flap about Rob Westerfield and a wig?" Dr. Dittrick asked. "I'm sure I remember something about that."

"He wanted to wear a wig he used in a performance at his previous school. The director wouldn't allow that, either. During the play Rob would come out of the dressing room wearing his own wig and only switched to the appropriate one at the last second. I understand that he wore his wig around campus as well. He got detention any number of times because of it, but he kept on doing it."

Dr. Bostrom looked at me. "That wasn't in his file," she said.

"Of course his file was sanitized," Dr. Dittrick said impatiently. "How else do you think the athletic center got a total renovation at that time? All it took was President Egan's suggestion to Westerfield's father that Rob might be happier in school elsewhere."

Dr. Bostrom looked at me, alarmed. "Don't worry. I'm not going to print that," I told her.

I looked around for my shoulder bag and fished out my cell phone. "I'm going to get out of your way," I promised them, "but there's one call I'd like to make before I leave. I've been in contact with Christopher Cassidy who was a student at Arbinger with Westerfield. In fact, he's the one Rob beat up in his sophomore year. Mr. Cassidy told me that Rob sometimes used the name of a character he played on stage. He was going to try to find out what it was."

I looked up the number and dialed it.

"Cassidy Investment Firm," the operator said briskly.

I was in luck. Christopher Cassidy was back from his trip, and I was put through to him immediately. "I checked around," he said, sounding triumphant. "I have the name Westerfield used, and it is from one of the plays he was in."

"I remember the name," Corinne Barsky was saying, excitement in her voice.

Cassidy was in Boston. Barsky was a few feet away from me in Maine. But they said it together.

"It's Jim Wilding."

Jim, I thought! Rob had drawn the diagram himself.

"Ellie, I have to take another call," Cassidy apologized.

"Go ahead. That's all I needed to know."

"What you wrote about me for the Website is great. Put it on. I'll back you one thousand percent."

He clicked off.

Corinne Barsky had opened one of the playbills. "You may be interested in this, Ms. Cavanaugh," she said. "The director used to have every member of the cast sign a playbill next to where they are listed in the cast."

She held it up and pointed. With defiant emphasis Rob Westerfield had signed not his own name but "Jim Wilding" instead.

I stared at it for a long minute. "I need a copy of this," I said. "And please take very good care of the original. In fact, I wish you'd lock it in a safe."

Twenty minutes later I was sitting in my car, comparing the signature on the diagram with the one on the playbill.

I'm no handwriting expert, but when I compared the way the name "Jim" was signed on both documents, the signatures seemed identical.

I began the long drive back to Oldham, exulting in the prospect of exhibiting them on the Internet side by side.

Mrs. Dorothy Westerfield would have to face the truth. Her grandson had planned her death.

I must confess I thoroughly enjoyed the benevolent feeling that I was about to make a number of charities, medical facilities, libraries, and universities very, very happy.

39

I keep my cell phone on the other pillow. Tuesday morning it began to ring and woke me up. As I gave a sleepy "Hello," I glanced at my watch and was shocked to see that it was nine o'clock.

"Must have had a night on the town."

It was Pete.

"Let's see," I said. "Driving from Maine to Massachusetts and across New York State. It was the most exciting night of my life."

"Maybe you're too tired to come down to Manhattan."

"Maybe you're trying to wiggle out of the invitation to come to Manhattan," I suggested. By now I was awake and on the verge of being disappointed and angry.

"My suggestion was going to be that I drive to Oldham, pick you up, and we'll find a place for us to have dinner."

"That's different," I said cheerfully. "I have a great spot in mind, and it's only fifteen minutes from the inn."

"Now you're thinking. Give me directions."

I did, and he congratulated me. "Ellie, you're one of the few women I know who can give lucid directions. Is it something I taught you? Never mind answering. I can be there around seven."

Click.

I sent for room service, showered, washed my hair, and phoned a nearby nail salon to make an appointment for four o'clock. I had broken several nails when I fell in the parking lot and wanted to do something about them.

I even took time to study my limited wardrobe and decide on the leaf brown pantsuit with the caracul collar and cuffs. The suit had been an impulse buy at the end of the season last year, expensive even at half price, and I had yet to wear it.

Parading it out for Pete seemed like a good idea.

Actually, it was comforting to have something to anticipate at the end of the day. I knew it was not going to be easy to spend the afternoon writing Alfie's story about the break-in and tying the incriminating diagram to Rob Westerfield's use of the name Jim in school.

By not easy, I meant emotionally not easy, because of the unbearable certainty that if Rob Westerfield had been convicted of that crime, Andrea would not have met him.

He'd have been in prison. She would have grown up and gone to college, and, like Joan, probably gotten married and had a couple of children. Mother and Daddy would still be in that wonderful farmhouse. Daddy would have come to love it as much as she did and by now realized what a great buy it had been.

I would have grown up in a happy home and gone to college. Choosing to study journalism had nothing to do with Andrea's death, so I probably would be in the same kind of job. It's the career that held a natural attraction for me. I still wouldn't be married. I think I always wanted a career before a commitment.

If Rob had been convicted, I would not have spent my life grieving for my sister and yearning for what I had lost.

Now, even if I manage to convince Rob's grandmother and the rest of the world of his guilt, he still will get away with it. The statute of limitations has run out on that crime.

And even if his grandmother changes her will, his father has plenty of money, at least plenty by normal standards, so Rob will live well.

Disgusting liar that he is, in a second trial Will Nebels's story might throw enough doubt in jurors' minds to give Westerfield an acquittal.

Then his record will be expunged.

I beat Phil to death, and it felt good.

There is only one way I can get Rob Westerfield back behind bars and that is to track down Phil, that other person whose life he extinguished. Fortunately, there is no statute of limitations for murder.

By three-thirty I was ready to transfer everything to the Website: Christopher Cassidy's story of being beaten by Rob Westerfield in prep school; Rob's insistence on being called "Jim" because of the character he had played on stage; Rob's role in planning the attempt on his grandmother's life.

I wrote that William Hamilton, Esq., was the court-appointed lawyer who had destroyed the original diagram implicating Westerfield in the crime. I ended the piece with the diagram and playbill displayed side by side. On screen the "Jim" signatures were startling in their similarity.

I kissed my fingers in a salute to the story, pressed the appropriate keys on the computer, and an instant later it was out there on my Website.

40

It was a quarter of five when I got back to the inn. The multibillion-dollar cosmetic industry would go broke if it relied on people like me. What little makeup I had was lost in the fire. I had picked up a compact and lipstick at a drugstore a day or two later, but it was time to spend half an hour replacing items like mascara and blush.

Even though I had slept till nine o'clock this morning, I was still sleepy and wanted to take a nap before it was time to dress for my date with Pete.

I wondered if seeing the finish line felt like this. The athlete runs the marathon and knows the end of the race is near. I've heard that there is an interval of a few seconds when the runner actually slows, regroups, and then goes into the final sprint toward victory.

That was the way I felt. I had Rob Westerfield on the ropes, and I was convinced that I was about to learn the truth of what he had done to Phil and where it had happened. If I was right, it would send him back to prison.

I beat Phil to death, and it felt good.

And then when he had been brought to real justice, when the Committee for Justice for Rob Westerfield had been dissolved and slunk away into oblivion, then and only then, like a newly hatched chicken, would I take my own tentative steps into the future.

Tonight I was meeting someone I wanted to see and who wanted to see me. Whither do we wander? I didn't know and wasn't looking ahead that far. But for the first time in my life I was beginning to anticipate the future with my debt to the past nearly paid. It was a hopeful, satisfying feeling.

Then I walked through the door of the inn, and my half-brother Teddy was standing there waiting for me.

This time he was not smiling. He looked uncomfortable, yet determined, and his greeting to me was abrupt. "Ellie, come inside. We have to talk."

"I invited your brother to wait in the sunroom, but he was afraid that he might miss you," Mrs. Willis said.

You're absolutely right, I *would* have missed him, I thought. I would have been upstairs like a shot if I had known he was waiting.

I didn't want her to hear whatever he was going to say, so I walked ahead of him into the sunroom. This time he closed the door, and we stood facing each other.

"Teddy," I began, "you have to listen to me. I know you mean well. I know your father means well. But you can't be trailing after me. I am perfectly fine, and I can take care of myself."

"No, you can't!" His eyes were flashing, and in that moment he looked so like my father that I was transported back to the dining room at home, and Daddy was telling Andrea that *she was forbidden to ever have anything to do with Rob Westerfield.*

"Ellie, we saw what you put on the Website this afternoon. Dad is beside himself with worry. He said that the Westerfields now have to stop you, and they *will* stop you. He said you've become a terrible danger to them, and in the process you've put yourself in great danger. Ellie, you can't do this to Dad or to yourself. Or to me."

He was so upset, so vehement, that I felt sorry for him. I put my hand on his arm. "Teddy, I don't want to upset you or your father. I'm doing what I have to do. I don't know how many ways to say it to you, but please, just leave me alone. You've gotten along without me all your life, and your father has gotten along without me since I was a small child. What is all this about? I tried to tell you the other day—you don't *know* me. You have no reason to *worry* about me. You're a nice kid, but let's leave it at that."

"I'm not just a nice kid. I'm your brother. Whether you like it or not, I'm your brother. And stop saying 'your father' to me. You think you know everything, but you don't, Ellie. Dad never stopped being your father. He's always talked about you, and I always wanted to hear about you. He told me what a great little kid you were. You don't even know it, but he went out to your college graduation and sat in the audience. He got a subscription to the *Atlanta News* when you started working there, and he's read every article you've ever written. So stop saying he's not your father."

I didn't want to hear it. I kept shaking my head. "Teddy, you just don't understand. When my mother and I went to Florida, he let us go."

"He told me you thought that, but it isn't true. He didn't just let you go. He wanted you back. He tried to *get* you back. The few times you visited him after he and your mother broke up, you never said one word to him and you wouldn't even eat. What was he supposed to do? Your mother told him there was too much grief to contain under one roof, that she only wanted to remember the good parts and go on to a new life. And she did."

"How do you know all this?"

"Because I asked him. Because I thought he'd have a heart attack when he saw the last item you put on the Website. He's sixty-seven years old, Ellie, and he has high blood pressure."

"Does he know you're here?"

"I told him I was coming. I'm here to beg you to

come home with me, and if you won't do that, at least to check out of here and go someplace where nobody except us knows where you are."

He was so earnest, so concerned, so caring that I almost put my arms around him. "Teddy, there are things you don't understand. I knew Andrea might have gone to meet Rob Westerfield that night, and I didn't tell on her. I've had to carry that blame all my life. Now when Westerfield gets his new trial, he's going to convince a lot of people that Paulie Stroebel killed Andrea. I didn't save her, but I have to try to save Paulie."

"Dad told me it was *his* fault that Andrea died. He was late getting home. One of the guys he worked with had gotten engaged, and he had a beer with him to celebrate. He was starting to get suspicious and worried that Andrea was still seeing Westerfield behind his back. He told me that if he had been home earlier, he would never have allowed her to go to Joan's house that night—so instead of being in that garage, she would have been at home, safe."

He believed what he was telling me. Was my memory so distorted? Not completely. It wasn't that simple. But was my abiding sense of guilt—"If only Ellie had told us"—only a part of the total picture? My mother let Andrea go out after dark alone. My father suspected Andrea was still seeing Rob but had not yet actually confronted her. My mother had insisted on moving to what was then a rural and isolated community. My father may have been too strict with Andrea; his attempts to protect her may have made her rebellious. I was the confidante who knew of the secret meetings.

Did the three of us *choose* to harbor guilt and grief within our own souls, or did we *have* any choice?

"Ellie, my mother is a very nice lady. She was a widow when she met Dad. She knows what it is to lose someone. She wants to meet you. You'd like her."

"Teddy, I promise I will meet her someday."

"Someday *soon.*"

"When I've seen this through. It's not going to take much longer."

"You will talk to Dad? You will give him a break?"

"When this is over, we'll have lunch or something. I promise. And listen, I'm going out tonight with Pete Lawlor, someone I worked with in Atlanta. I don't want either one of you following me around. He's picking me up here and will deposit me back here safely, I promise."

"Dad will be relieved to hear that."

"Teddy, I have to get upstairs. There are a couple of calls I have to make before I go out."

"I've said what I have to say. No, maybe I haven't. There's something else Dad told me that you should know. He said, 'I've lost one little girl. I can't lose another.'"

41

If I had expected a hint of romance in our meeting, it was quickly dismissed. Pete's greeting to me was "You look great," accompanied by a quick kiss on the cheek.

"And you're so gussied up, you look as though you won a fifteen-minute shopping spree in Bloomingdale's," I told him.

"Twenty minutes," he corrected. "I'm starving, aren't you?"

I had made a reservation at Cathryn's, and while we were driving over, I said, "Big request."

"Let's have it."

"Tonight I would like not to talk about what I've been doing these past weeks. You watch the Website, so you really know what's going on anyhow. But I need to get away from it for a few hours. So tonight is *your* night. Tell me every single place you've been since I saw you in Atlanta. I want every detail about the interviews you've had. Then tell me why you're so pleased about the job you're taking. You can even tell me if you had a hard time choosing between that very nice, and obviously new, red tie or another one."

Pete has a way of raising one eyebrow. He did that now. "You're serious?"

"Absolutely."

"The minute I saw this tie, I knew I had to have it."

"Very good," I encouraged. "I want to hear more."

At the restaurant we looked at the menu, ordered smoked salmon and a seafood pasta, and agreed to split a bottle of Pinot Grigio. "It's handy that we both like the same entrées," Pete said. "Makes it easier with the wine selection."

"The last time I was here I had the rack of lamb," I told him.

He looked at me.

"I love to irritate you," I admitted.

"It shows."

Over dinner he did open up to me. "Ellie, I knew the paper was on the way out. That happens to any business that's family owned when the present generation is only interested in the dollar sign. Frankly, I was getting itchy anyway. In this business, unless you can see that you have a good reason to stay with a company, you've got to be aware of other opportunities."

"Then why didn't you leave sooner?" I asked.

He looked at me. "I'll take a pass on that one. But when it became inevitable, I knew two things for sure. I wanted either to get with a solid newspaper—such as *The New York Times*, the *L. A. Times*, the *Chicago Trib*, or the *Houston Chronicle*—or to try something else altogether. The newspaper jobs were there, but then that 'something else' opened up, and I went for it."

"A new cable news station."

"Exactly. I'm in on the ground floor. It has risks, of course, but substantial investors are committed to making it happen."

"You said it involved a lot of traveling?"

"By a lot I mean the kind anchormen do when they're onto a big story."

"You're not telling me you're an anchorman!"

"Perhaps that's too grandiose a word. I'm on the news desk. Short, clipped, and hard-hitting is in these days. Maybe it will work; maybe it won't."

I thought about it. Pete was smart, intense, and got to the point quickly. "I think you'll actually be good at it," I told him.

"There's something so touching about the way you lavish praise on me, Ellie. Don't go overboard, please. It might go to my head."

I ignored that. "Then you're going to be based in New York City and you're moving there?"

"I already have. I found an apartment in SoHo. It's not great, but it's a start."

"Won't that be kind of a big change for you? Your whole family is in Atlanta."

"My grandparents were all New Yorkers. I used to visit them a lot when I was a kid."

"I see."

We waited silently while the table was cleared. Then when we'd ordered espresso, Pete said, "All right, Ellie, we've played the game by your rules. Now I get *my* two cents in. I want to hear everything you've been up to, and I mean *everything.*"

By now I was ready to talk about it, so I told him all, including Teddy's visit. When I was finished, Pete said, "Your father's right. You've got to move in with him or at least not be visible around Oldham."

"I think he may be right about that," I admitted reluctantly.

"I have to go to Chicago in the morning for a meeting with the board of Packard Cable. I'll be gone until Saturday. Ellie, please go down to New York and stay in my apartment. You can be in touch with Marcus Longo and Mrs. Hilmer and Mrs. Stroebel from there, and you can keep up your Website as well. But at the same time, you'll be safe. Will you do that?"

I knew he was right. "For a few days, until I can figure out where to go, yes, I will."

When we got back to the inn, Pete left his car in the driveway and walked me inside. The night clerk was on duty. "Has anyone been looking for Ms. Cavanaugh?" Pete asked him.

"No, sir."

"Any messages for her?"

"Mr. Longo and Mrs. Hilmer returned her calls."

"Thank you."

At the foot of the stairs, he put his hands on my shoulders. "Ellie, I know you've had to see this through, and I've understood. But now you can't go it alone anymore. You need us around you."

"Us?"

"Your father, Teddy, me."

"You've been in touch with my father, haven't you?"

He patted my cheek. "Of course I have."

42

I dreamt a lot that night. It was an anxiety-ridden dream. Andrea was slipping through the woods. I was trying to call her back, but I couldn't make her hear me and watched in despair as she ran past old Mrs. Westerfield's house and into the garage. I was trying to shout a warning, but then Rob Westerfield was there and waving me away.

I woke to the faint sound of my own voice trying to call for help. Dawn was just breaking, and I could see that it was going to be another of those gray, cloudy, cold days we get in early November.

Even as a child I found the first two weeks of November unsettling, but after the middle of the month, the festive feeling of Thanksgiving was in the air. But those first two weeks seemed long and dreary. Then, after Andrea died, they became forever linked with the memories of the last days we spent together. The anniversary of her death was only a few days away.

Those were the thoughts in my mind as I lay in bed, wishing for an hour or two more of sleep. The dream wasn't hard to analyze. The imminent anniversary of Andrea's death and the fact that I was acutely aware that Rob Westerfield would be enraged by the latest information on my Website were playing on my mind.

I knew that I needed to be very careful.

At seven o'clock I sent for room service; then I began to work on my book. At nine o'clock I showered, dressed, and phoned Mrs. Hilmer.

I was hoping against hope that her call had been to say she remembered why the name "Phil" was familiar to her. But even as I asked her that question, I realized it was terribly unlikely that she would come up with anything that could be connected to Rob Westerfield's vicious boast.

"Ellie, that name is the only thing I've been able to think about," she said, sighing. "I called you last night to tell you that I checked with my friend who's in contact with Phil Oliver. I told you about him. Phil Oliver is the man who lost his lease and had a pretty ugly confrontation with Rob Westerfield's father. My friend told me that he's down in Florida, likes it well enough, but is still pretty bitter about the way he was treated. He reads your Website and loves it. He says if you want to start a Website to let the world know the kind of man Rob's father is, too, he'll be happy to talk to you."

Interesting, I thought, but not helpful information right now.

"Ellie, the one thing I'm sure of is that whatever I heard or read about 'Phil,' it was only recently. And if this is any help, it made me sad."

"Sad?"

"Ellie, I know I'm not making sense, but I'm working on it. I'll get back to you the minute I piece it together."

Mrs. Hilmer had been calling me on the phone at the inn. I didn't want to explain that I was checking out, or go into detail about Pete and his apartment in New York. "You have my cell phone number, don't you, Mrs. Hilmer?"

"Yes, you gave it to me."

"I'm going to be in and out so much. Will you call me on that number if you come up with the connection?"

"Of course."

Marcus Longo was the next one on my list to call. I thought he sounded subdued, and I was right.

"Ellie, what you put on the Website yesterday is inviting a massive lawsuit from both Westerfield and his lawyer, William Hamilton."

"Good. Let them sue me. I can't wait to depose them."

"Ellie, being right isn't always a provable or

successful legal defense. The law can be very tricky. The drawing you claim is evidence of Rob Westerfield's part in the attempted murder of his grandmother was provided by the brother of the man who shot her. And he admits that he was the driver of the getaway car. He's hardly a stellar witness. How much did you pay him for that information?"

"One thousand dollars."

"Do you know how that would look in court? If not, let me explain it to you. You put up a sign outside Sing Sing. You advertise on the Website. In so many words it says, 'Anyone who knows of a crime Rob Westerfield may have committed can make a quick buck.' This guy could be an out-and-out liar."

"Do you think he is?"

"What I think doesn't matter."

"Oh, but it does, Marcus. Do you believe Rob Westerfield planned that crime?"

"Yes, I do, but then I always thought he planned it. That has nothing to do with the multimillion-dollar slander suit you may be facing."

"Let them sue. I hope they do. I have a couple of thousand dollars in the bank and a car with sand in the gas tank that probably needs a new engine, and I may make some decent money on my book. They're welcome to try to get it."

"It's your show, Ellie."

"Two things, Marcus. I'm checking out of here today and going to stay at a friend's apartment."

"Not around here, I hope."

"No, in Manhattan."

"That is a great relief for me. Does your father know that?"

If not, I bet you'll tell him, I thought. I wondered how many of my friends in Oldham were in contact with my father. "I'm not sure," I said honestly. For all I knew, Pete may have called him last night the minute he left me.

I was going to ask Marcus if he had any success in following up on a homicide with someone named "Phil" as the victim, but he anticipated the question. "So far, zero, blank, nothing to tie Westerfield to another crime," he said. "But I still have a lot of searching to do. We're also following up on that name Rob liked to use in school."

"Jim Wilding?"

"Yes."

We agreed to stay in close touch.

I hadn't spoken to Mrs. Stroebel since Sunday afternoon. I called the hospital, hoping to hear that Paulie had been discharged, but he was still there.

Mrs. Stroebel was with him. "Ellie, he's much better. I stop in around this time each day, then go to the store and come back around noon. Thank God for Greta. You met her the day Paulie was brought in here. She is so good. She is keeping everything going."

"When will Paulie be able to go home?"

"I think tomorrow, but, Ellie, he wants to see you again. He is trying to remember something you said to him that he says was not correct. He wants to straighten it out, but he doesn't know what it is. You understand—he's had so much medication."

My heart sank. Something *I* said? Dear God, was Paulie confused again, or was he going to retract anything he had told me? I was glad I had held off putting on the Website his story connecting Rob to the locket.

"I can come over and see him," I offered.

"Why don't you come around one o'clock? I will be here then, and I think that makes him more comfortable."

More comfortable, I thought, or do you mean you want to be sure he won't say anything that will incriminate him? No, I didn't believe that. "I'll be there, Mrs. Stroebel," I said. "If I arrive before you, I'll wait for you to come before I visit Paulie."

"Thank you, Ellie."

She sounded so grateful that I was ashamed of myself for thinking she might be trying to prevent Paulie from being honest with me. She had been the one to call me, and her life was now split between keeping up the deli and visiting her ailing son. God tempers the wind to the shorn lamb. He does it best when he sends someone like Paulie a mother like Anja Stroebel.

I managed to get two hours' work in, then I checked Rob Westerfield's Website. It still had the picture of me shackled to the bed, and more names had been added to the Committee for Justice for Rob Westerfield. But nothing had been added to refute my story of his involvement in the attempted murder of his grandmother.

I took that to be a sign of consternation in the ranks. They were still debating what to do about it.

At eleven o'clock the phone rang. It was Joan. "Want to have a quick lunch around one o'clock?" Joan asked. "I have some errands to do and just realized I'll be passing your door."

"I can't. I promised to visit Paulie at the hospital at one o'clock," I said, then hesitated. "But Joan—"

"What is it, Ellie? Are you all right?"

"Yes, I'm fine. Joan, you told me you have a copy of the obituary notice my father put in the paper for my mother."

"Yes, I do. I offered to show it to you."

"Can you put your hand on it easily?"

"Yes, I can."

"Then if you're passing the inn, would you mind dropping it off at the desk? I'd really like to see it."

"Consider it done."

When I got to the hospital, there was a buzz of activity in the lobby. I saw a group of reporters and cameramen clustered together at the far end of the room, and I quickly turned my back to them.

The woman next to me on the line to get a visitor's pass told me what had happened. Mrs. Dorothy Westerfield, Rob's grandmother, had been rushed into the emergency room, suffering from a heart attack.

Her lawyer had issued a statement to the media that last evening, as a permanent memorial to her late husband, U.S. Senator Pearson Westerfield, Mrs. Westerfield had changed her will and would be leaving her estate to a charitable foundation that would be charged with dispersing all of it within ten years.

The statement said that the only exceptions were small bequests to her son, some friends, and longtime employees. Her grandson was left only one dollar.

"She was very smart, you know," the woman confided to me, "I heard some reporters talking. Besides her lawyers, she had her pastor, a judge who is a friend, and a psychiatrist as witnesses that she was of sound mind and knew exactly what she was doing."

I'm sure that my gossipy informant did not realize

that my Website probably triggered both the will change and the heart attack. It was a hollow victory for me. I remembered that gracious, stately woman offering condolences for Andrea's death the day of the funeral.

I was glad to escape into the elevator before a reporter recognized me and connected me with the breaking story.

Mrs. Stroebel was already in the corridor waiting for me. Together we went into Paulie's room. His bandages were now much smaller. His eyes were clearer, and his smile was warm and sweet. "My friend, Ellie," he said. "I can count on you."

"You bet you can."

"I want to go home. I'm tired of being here."

"That's a good sign, Paulie."

"I want to get back to work. Were there many people in for lunch when you left, Mama?"

"Pretty good crowd," she said soothingly, with a contented smile.

"You shouldn't be here so much, Mama."

"I won't have to be, Paulie. You'll be home soon." She looked at me. "We have a little room off the kitchen at the store. Greta has put a couch and television in there. Paulie can be with us, do whatever he feels up to in the kitchen, and rest in between."

"Sounds good to me," I told them.

"Now, Paulie, explain what it is that worries you about the locket you found in Rob Westerfield's car," his mother encouraged.

I simply didn't know what to expect.

"I found the locket and gave it to Rob," Paulie said slowly. "I told you that, Ellie."

"Yes, you did."

"The chain was broken."

"You told me that, too, Paulie."

"Rob gave me a ten-dollar tip, and I put it with the money I'd saved for your fiftieth birthday present, Mama."

"That's right, Paulie. That was in May, six months before Andrea died."

"Yes. And the locket was shaped like a heart, and it was gold and it had pretty blue stones in the center."

"Yes," I said, hoping to encourage him.

"I saw Andrea wearing it, and I followed her to the garage and saw Rob go in after her. Later I told her that her father would be angry, and then I asked her to go to the dance with me."

"That's exactly what you said earlier, Paulie. That's the way it happened, isn't it?"

"Yes, but something is wrong. *You* said something, Ellie, that was wrong."

"Let me think." I tried to reconstruct the conversation as best I could. "The only thing I remember that you didn't just mention is that I said Rob didn't even buy Andrea a new locket. He had the initials of their first names, Rob and Andrea, engraved on a locket some other girl had probably dropped in his car."

Paulie smiled. "That's it, Ellie. That's what I needed to remember. Rob didn't have the initials engraved on the locket. They were already there when I found the locket."

"Paulie, that's impossible. I know Andrea did not meet Rob Westerfield until October. You found the locket in May."

His expression became stubborn. "Ellie, I remember. I am sure. I saw them. The initials were already on the locket. It wasn't 'R' and 'A.' It was 'A' and 'R.' 'A.R.,' in very pretty writing."

43

I left the hospital with the sense that events were spinning out of control. Alfie's story and the diagram I had put on my Website obviously had the desired effect: Rob Westerfield had been cut out of his grandmother's will. By doing that, Mrs. Westerfield might just as well have erected a sign saying, "I believe my only grandchild planned the attempt on my life."

That heartbreaking realization and painful decision had undoubtedly caused her to have the massive heart attack. At ninety-two, it seemed unlikely to me that she could possibly survive.

Again I remembered the quiet dignity with which she had walked out of our house after my father ordered her to leave. He was the first to humiliate her because of her grandson. Or was he? Arbinger had been the school that her husband, the senator, had attended. It seemed doubtful that she would have been unaware of the reason Rob was asked to leave there.

The fact that she changed the will and took every precaution to see that it could not be legally challenged meant to me that she not only believed he had planned the attempt on her life, but also at last might even be convinced that Rob was responsible for Andrea's death.

Which of course brought me to the locket.

The locket already had the initials "A" and "R" engraved on it before Rob met Andrea.

That fact was so stunning, so utterly out of context with everything I had been thinking, that for the first few minutes after I left Paulie, I had to let it sit in my mind until I could get used to it.

The gray morning had evolved into an equally gray afternoon. The car was at the far end of the hospital's visitors' parking lot, and I walked briskly to it, my coat collar turned up as protection against the damp, cold wind.

I drove out of the hospital grounds and realized that the beginnings of a headache were being caused by the fact that it was one-thirty, and the last time I'd eaten was seven-fifteen this morning.

As I drove, I began looking for a coffee shop or restaurant and passed several that looked pretty good. The reason I kept passing them became evident when I rejected still another popular luncheon spot. It was because being out in public in Oldham made me feel vulnerable now.

I went back to the inn, glad to be there and equally eager to be on my way to the anonymity of downtown Manhattan. Mrs. Willis was at the desk and handed me an envelope. I knew it was the obituary notice that Joan had left for me.

I took it upstairs, phoned room service, ordered a club sandwich and tea, and then sat down in the chair that overlooks the Hudson. It was the kind of view Mother would have loved, with the palisades rising in the mist, the water gray and restless.

The envelope was sealed. I slit it open.

Joan had clipped the obituary from the *Westchester News*. It read:

> Cavanaugh: Genine (née Reid) in Los Angeles, Ca., age 51. Beloved former wife of Edward and loving mother of Gabrielle (Ellie) and the late Andrea. She was active in her church and community, and created a happy and beautiful home for her family. She will always be missed, always loved, always remembered.

So Mother wasn't the only one who remembered the good years, I thought. I had written my father a churlish note to inform him of Mother's death and to ask if her ashes could be interred in Andrea's grave.

I'd been so wrapped up in my own pain that it never

crossed my mind that the news of her death might affect him deeply.

I decided the lunch with my father that I'd promised Teddy would take place sooner rather than later. I put the clipping in my suitcase. I wanted to pack right away and leave as quickly as possible. Then the phone rang.

It was Mrs. Hilmer. "Ellie, I don't know if this is helpful at all, but I remembered where it was that I read a reference to someone named Phil."

"Where, Mrs. Hilmer? Where did you see it?"

"It was in one of the newspapers you gave me."

"Are you sure?"

"I'm positive. I remember because I was reading it when I was at my granddaughter's house. The baby was asleep, and I was going through those papers for names of people who still lived around here whom you might want to interview. And Ellie, as I told you when we had dinner, reading about the trial brought everything back, and I was crying. Then I read something about Phil, and that was very sad, too."

"But you're not sure what it said about him?"

"You see, Ellie, that's why I think that even if I can find the item, I've probably got the wrong person in mind."

"Why do you think that?"

"Because you're looking for a man named Phil. I read something about a young *girl* who died whose family called her 'Phil.'"

I beat *Phil* to death, and it felt good.

Dear God, I thought, *was he talking about a girl?*

A young girl who was a homicide victim.

"Mrs. Hilmer, I'm going to read every one of those papers line by line."

"That's what I'm doing, Ellie. I'll call you if I come across it."

"And I'll call you if I find it."

I pushed the "end" button to terminate the call, laid the phone on the night table, and grabbed the duffel bag. I unzipped it, turned it upside down, and dumped the yellowing, crumbling newspapers on the bed.

I took the first one that came to my hand, sat down in the chair that faced the river, and began to read.

The hours passed. Every so often I would get up and stretch. At four o'clock I sent for tea. Tea peps you up. Hadn't that been the advertising slogan of one of the tea companies?

It does pep you up. And it helped me to keep focused.

I concentrated intensely, reading line by line the newspapers, reading again in horrifying detail the story of Andrea's death and Rob Westerfield's trial.

"A.R." Was the locket totally unimportant after all? No. Absolutely not. If it was unimportant, Rob would never have taken the chance of going back for it.

Was "A.R." the girl who owned the pretty gold locket, yet another victim of one of his murderous rages?

At six o'clock I took another break and turned on the news. Mrs. Dorothy Westerfield had expired at 3:30. Neither her son nor her grandson had been at her bedside.

I went back to reading the papers. At seven o'clock I found it. It was in the memorial section of the obituary page the day of Andrea's funeral. It read:

> Rayburn, Amy P. Remembering you today and every day. Happy 18th birthday in heaven, our darling Phil.
> Mom and Dad

"*A.R.*" Did the initials on the locket stand for Amy Rayburn? Her middle initial had been P. Could it have been Phyllis or Philomena, shortened to Phil?

Paulie had found the locket in early May. Andrea was dead twenty-three years. If Amy Rayburn had owned the locket, had she died twenty-three and a half years ago?

I called Marcus Longo, but there was no answer at his home. I was frantic to have him check Amy Rayburn's name against homicide reports from that year.

I knew there was a complete Westchester phone book in the drawer of the night table. I pulled it out, opened it, and turned to the "R" section.

There were only two Rayburns listed. One lived in Larchmont, the other in Rye Brook.

I dialed the one in Larchmont. The modulated voice of an older man answered. There was no way to be indirect. "My name is Ellie Cavanaugh," I said. "It is necessary for me to speak to the family of Amy Rayburn, the young woman who died twenty-three years ago."

"For what reason?" The voice had suddenly become frosty, and I knew that I had made contact with someone who was at least a relative of the dead girl.

"Please answer one question of mine," I said, "and then I will answer all of yours. Was Amy the victim of a homicide?"

"If you do not know that already, you have no business calling our family."

The phone was slammed down.

I called back, and this time the answering machine picked up. "My name is Ellie Cavanaugh," I said. "Nearly twenty-three years ago my fifteen-year-old sister was bludgeoned to death. I believe I have proof that the man who killed her is also responsible for Phil's death. Please call me back."

I began to leave my cell phone number, but the phone was picked up on the other end. "I'm Amy Rayburn's uncle," he said. "The man who murdered her served eighteen years in prison. What do you think you're talking about?"

44

The man I had called, David Rayburn, was the uncle of seventeen-year-old Amy Phyllis Rayburn, who was murdered six months before Andrea. I told him about Andrea, about Rob Westerfield's confession to a fellow inmate in prison, about Paulie finding the locket in Rob's car, and about its being taken from Andrea's body.

He listened, asked questions, then said, "My brother was Phil's father. That was Amy's nickname in the family and among her close friends. Let me call him now and give him your number. He'll want to talk to you."

Then he added, "Phil was about to graduate from high school. She'd been accepted at Brown. Her boyfriend, Dan Mayotte, always swore he was innocent. Instead of going to Yale, he spent eighteen years in prison."

Fifteen minutes later my phone rang. It was Michael Rayburn, Phil's father. "My brother told me about your call," he said. "I won't try to describe my emotions or those of my wife at this moment. Dan Mayotte had been in and out of our home since he was in kindergarten; we trusted him like a son. We have had to make our peace with the death of our only child, but to think that Dan may have been wrongly convicted of her death is almost more than we can bear. I'm a lawyer, Ms. Cavanaugh. What kind of proof do you have? My brother talked about a locket."

"Mr. Rayburn, did your daughter have a heart-shaped gold locket with blue stones or gems on the front and her initials on the back?"

"Let me put my wife on."

From the moment she spoke I admired the composure of Phil's mother. "Ellie, I remember when your sister died. It was only six months after we lost Phil."

I described the locket to her.

"That has to be Phil's locket. It was one of those inexpensive trinkets you pick up at a shopping mall. She loved that kind of jewelry and had several chains with any number of pendants she'd slip on them. She would wear two or three at the same time. I don't know if she was wearing the locket the night she was murdered. I never missed it."

"Do you think you might have a picture of Phil wearing it?"

"She was our only child, so we were always taking

pictures of her," Mrs. Rayburn said, and now I could hear tears in her voice. "She was fond of the locket. That's why she had it engraved. I'm sure I can find a picture of her wearing it."

Her husband took the phone from her. "Ellie, from what you told my brother, I understand that the convict who says he heard Westerfield confess to my daughter's murder is missing."

"Yes, he is."

"I have never in my heart believed that Dan could attack Phil so violently. He wasn't a violent person, and I know he loved her. But as I understand it, there is no hard-and-fast proof to actually tie Westerfield to Phil's death."

"No, there isn't, at least not yet. Maybe it's too soon to go to the district attorney with what I know, but if you tell me the circumstances of your daughter's murder and why Dan Mayotte was charged and convicted, I can put it out there on the Website and see if it brings in more information. Can you do that?"

"Ellie, we've been living that nightmare for twenty-three years. I can tell you everything about it."

"Believe me, I understand. The nightmare that my family endured broke up my parents' marriage, eventually killed my mother, and has tortured me for more than twenty years. So, yes, I understand that you're always living it."

"I'm sure you do. Dan and Phil had quarreled and hadn't seen each other in a week. He did tend to be jealous, and Phil had told us that the week before, when they were buying sodas and candy in the lobby before a movie, some guy started talking to her, and Dan got angry. She never described the guy or mentioned his name.

"She and Dan didn't speak for a week after that. Then one day she went to the local pizza parlor with some of her girlfriends. Dan came in with some of his friends and went over to Phil. They talked and I guess began to make up. Those kids were crazy about each other.

"Then Dan spotted the guy who'd been flirting with Phil in the movies. He was standing at the counter."

"Did Dan describe him?"

"Yes. Good-looking, about twenty years old, dark blond hair. Dan said that at the refreshment stand of the movie house, he'd overheard him tell Phil that his name was Jim."

Jim! I thought. That had to be one of the times Rob Westerfield was wearing his dark blond wig and was calling himself Jim.

"Seeing the guy there at the pizza parlor made Dan jealous all over again. He said that he accused Phil of planning to meet Jim there. She denied it and said she hadn't even noticed he was in the place. After that, she got up and stalked out. Everyone could see that she and Dan were angry with each other.

"Phil was wearing a new jacket that night. When she was found there were traces of dog hairs on it that came from Dan's Irish terrier. Of course she'd been in his car many times, but because that jacket was brand-new, the hairs were proof that she'd been in his car after she left the pizza parlor."

"Did Dan deny that Phil got in his car?"

"Never. He said he persuaded her to get in and talk things over. But when he told her it was too much of a coincidence for him to believe that Jim just happened to be in the pizza parlor, she got sore at him again and got out of the car. She told him that she was going back to her friends and for him to get lost. According to him, she slammed the car door and started to walk from the parking lot, heading back to the restaurant. Dan admitted he was furious and said that he gunned the engine and took off.

"Phil never made it to the restaurant. When it started to get late and she hadn't come home, we called the friends she'd gone out with."

Mother and Daddy called Andrea's friends. . . . "They told us she was with Dan. At first we were relieved, of course. We thought the world of him and were glad they'd made up. But hours passed, and when he finally did get home, Dan claimed that he'd left Phil in the parking lot and she was going back to the restaurant. The next day her body was found."

Michael Rayburn's voice broke. "She died of multiple fractures of the skull. Her face wasn't recognizable."

I beat Phil to death, and it felt good.

"Dan admitted that he'd been angry and upset after she got out of his car. He said he drove around for an hour or so, then parked near the lake and just sat there for a long time. But he had no one to back up his story. No one had seen him, and Phil's body was found in a wooded area about a mile from the lake."

"Didn't anyone else see Jim at the pizza parlor?"

"People said they remembered a guy there with dark blond hair. But he apparently didn't talk to anybody, and nobody noticed when he left. Dan was convicted and sent to prison. It broke his mother's heart. She'd raised him alone, and, sadly, she died much too young and never lived to see him paroled."

My mother died much too young as well, I thought.

"Where is Dan now?" I asked.

"He got his college degree in prison instead of at Yale. I've heard he works as a counselor to former inmates. I never in my heart really believed he could do that to Phil. If it turns out that your theory is right, then I owe him a profound apology."

Rob Westerfield owes him a lot more than an

apology, I thought. He owes him eighteen years—and the life he should have lived.

"When are you going to put this on your Website, Ellie?" Michael Rayburn asked.

"As soon as I can write it. That should take about an hour."

"Then I won't keep you. We'll be looking for it. Let me know if any new information comes in."

I knew that I was already in jeopardy from the Westerfields and that by mounting this new assault I was being downright reckless. I didn't care.

When I thought of all the victims Rob Westerfield had claimed, I became enraged.

Phil, an only child.

Dan, his life destroyed.

The Rayburns.

Dan's mother.

Rob's grandmother.

Our family.

I started Phil's story with the headline: "WESTCHESTER DISTRICT ATTORNEY, TAKE NOTE!"

My fingers flew over the keyboard. At nine o'clock it was finished. I read it over once and, with grim satisfaction, sent it to the Website.

I knew I had to clear out of the inn. I closed the computer, packed in five minutes, and went downstairs.

I was at the desk, paying my bill, when my cell phone rang.

I thought it might be Marcus Longo, but it was a woman with a Hispanic accent who responded to my quick greeting.

"Ms. Cavanaugh?"

"Yes."

"I have been watching your Website. My name is Rosita Juarez. I was housekeeper for Rob Westerfield's parents from the time he was ten years old until he went to prison. He is a very bad person."

I gripped the phone and pressed it closer to my ear. This woman had been the housekeeper at the time Rob committed both murders! What did she know? She sounded frightened. Don't let her hang up, I prayed.

I tried to make my voice sound calm. "Yes, Rob *is* a very bad person, Rosita."

"He looked down on me. He made fun of the way I talk. He was always nasty and rude to me. That's why I want to help you."

"How can you help me, Rosita?"

"You are right. Rob used to wear a blond wig. When he put it on, he would say to me, 'My name is Jim, Rosita. That shouldn't be too hard even for you to remember.'"

"You saw him put on the wig?"

"I have the wig." There was sly triumph in the

woman's voice. "His mother used to get very upset when he wore the wig and called himself Jim, and one day she threw it in the garbage. I don't know why I did it, but I took it out and brought it home. I knew it was expensive, and I thought maybe I could sell it. But I put it in a box in the closet and forgot all about it until you wrote about it on your Website."

"I'd like to have that wig, Rosita. I'll be glad to buy it from you."

"No, you don't have to buy it. Will it help to make people believe that he killed that girl, Phil?"

"I believe it would. Where do you live, Rosita?"

"In Phillipstown."

Phillipstown was actually part of Cold Spring, not more than ten miles away.

"Rosita, may I come and get the wig from you now?"

"I'm not sure."

She was starting to sound worried.

"Why not, Rosita?"

"Because my apartment is in a two-story house, and my landlady sees everything. I don't want anyone to see you here. I am afraid of Rob Westerfield."

For the moment all I cared about was getting my hands on the wig. Later, if Rob was put on trial for Phil's death, I would try to persuade Rosita to be a witness.

Before I could try to convince her, she volunteered, "I live only a few minutes from the Phillipstown Hotel. If you want, I could drive there and meet you at the back entrance."

"I can be there in twenty minutes," I said. "No, make it half an hour."

"I will be there. Will the wig help to put Rob in jail?"

"I'm sure it will."

"Good!"

I could hear the satisfaction in Rosita's voice. She had found a way to get back at the nasty teenager whose insults she had endured for nearly a decade.

I rushed to finish paying my bill and quickly put my bags in the car.

Six minutes later I was on my way to acquire the tangible proof that Rob Westerfield had owned and worn a dark blond wig.

I was hoping that samples of Rob's DNA would still be lingering within it. That would be definitive proof that the wig had belonged to him.

45

Some time after dark the light mist had turned into a cold, battering rain. The windshield wipers of the car I had rented needed to be replaced, and before I had driven a mile, I found myself straining to see the road.

The traffic became lighter the farther north I drove on Route 9. I could tell by the readout on the dashboard that the temperature outside was dropping, and within minutes I saw that the rain was turning into sleet. As ice began to collect on the windshield, it became harder and harder to see more than a few yards ahead, and I was forced to stay in the right lane and drive slowly.

As the minutes passed, I became frantic that I would miss Rosita. She had sounded so nervous that I was sure she would not wait around if I didn't show up on time.

I was concentrating all my energy on watching the road in front of me and only gradually became aware that I was starting to go up a hill. It dawned on me that it had been a while since I'd seen any headlights coming from the opposite direction.

I glanced at the odometer. The Phillipstown Hotel was not more than ten miles from the Hudson Valley Inn, yet I had already driven twelve miles and still wasn't there. Obviously, somewhere I had veered off Route 9. The road I was on now was clearly not the main highway and was getting narrower.

I looked in my rearview mirror to check for headlights. There were none. Frustrated and furious at myself, I jammed on the brakes—a stupid thing to do, because I started to skid. I managed to straighten out the car and carefully began to make a U-turn. In that instant a red dome light went on behind me and blinding headlights flashed in my eyes. I stopped the car, and what appeared to be a police van pulled up beside me.

Thank God! I thought. I rolled down the window to ask the cop to please give me directions to the Phillipstown Hotel.

The window of the van rolled down as well, and the man in the passenger seat turned to face me.

Though there was no light directly on his face, I saw immediately that it was Rob Westerfield, and he was wearing a dark blond wig. With an unmistakable Hispanic accent, and with his voice pitched to sound like a woman, he mockingly called, "He was nasty to me. He made fun of the way I talk. He told me to call him Jim."

My heart almost stopped. Horrified, I realized that Rob, pretending to be Rosita, had made the phone call to lure me out. Past him I could just make out the face of the driver—it was the man who had threatened me in the parking lot of the railroad station near Sing Sing prison.

Frantically, I looked around for a way out. I could not get around them. My only hope was to straighten out the car, floor the gas pedal, and keep driving blindly ahead. I had no idea where the road might lead. As I accelerated, I saw that there were woods on both sides of me and that the road was steadily narrowing. The tires were slipping, causing the back of the car to fishtail.

I knew I could not outrun them. I could only pray that I would not end up in a cul-de-sac, that this road might take me toward some kind of highway.

They had turned off the dome light, but their bright headlights were still shining straight into my rearview mirror. Then they began to toy with me.

They pulled up on my left, and the van slammed into the side of the car. The door behind the driver's seat took the impact, and I heard grinding steel as the car lurched and my head banged into the steering wheel.

They dropped back as I skidded from side to side,

trying now to stay in the middle of the road. I knew I was bleeding from a cut on my forehead, but I managed to hang on to the wheel and keep the car on the road.

Then suddenly they shot by me, angling in front of me and tearing the fender off my car as they hit me again. I could hear the fender scraping and dragging as I struggled to stay on the road, praying that soon I'd come upon an intersection or at least see another car coming toward me.

But there were no other cars, and I sensed that a third attack was coming. Clearly they would aim to make it the final one. As the road curved sharply, they slowed and moved fully into the left lane. I hesitated briefly, then accelerated, hoping to break ahead of them again. However, they quickly pulled up even with me again.

For a split second I glanced at them. The interior light was on in the van, and I could see that Rob was waving something at me.

It was a tire jack.

With a final burst of speed, the van cut sharply to the right, directly into my path, forcing my car off the road. Helplessly, I tried to turn the wheel, but I felt the tires losing traction. The car went into a spin and then tumbled down the sloping embankment, heading toward a wall of trees thirty feet away.

I managed to hang on to the steering wheel as the car

turned over several times. I covered my face with my hands as the car, right side up again, slammed into a tree and the windshield shattered.

The sound of crashing metal and glass had been deafening, and the sudden silence that followed was ghostly.

My shoulder hurt. My hands were bleeding. My head was throbbing. But I could tell that by some miracle I had not been seriously injured.

The final impact had caused the driver's door to spring open, and sleet was pelting at me from every side. The cold sting against my face may have kept me from losing consciousness, and suddenly my brain felt clear. It was totally dark, and for a moment, I felt extraordinary relief. I thought that when they saw my car tumbling down the side of the road, they decided that I was finished and had driven away.

But then I became aware that I was not alone. Nearby I heard harsh, labored breathing, followed by the high choking sound that as a child I had described as a giggle.

Rob Westerfield was out there in the dark, waiting for me, just as he had waited for Andrea nearly twenty-three years ago in the darkness of the garage-hideout.

The first blow of the tire jack missed me and hit the headrest behind me. I clawed at the clasp of the seat belt and managed to release it.

As I scrambled over to the passenger side, the second blow came so close that I felt it graze my hair.

Andrea, Andrea, this is the way it was for you. Oh, God, please . . . please help me . . .

I think we both heard it at the same time, a car roaring around that last bend in the road. Its headlights must have caught the wreckage of my car, because it turned and came rushing down the slope to where I was trapped.

Rob Westerfield, the tire jack in his hand, was illuminated in the glare. But so was I, and now he could see exactly where I was.

Snarling, he twisted around and turned back toward me. He leaned inside the car until his face was only inches from mine. I tried to push him away as he raised the tire jack, about to smash it over my head.

I heard the scream of sirens filling the air as I shielded my head with my arms and waited for the blow to land. I wanted to close my eyes, but I could not.

I heard the thud before I saw the look of shock and pain on Westerfield's face. The tire jack fell from his hand onto the seat beside me as he was suddenly thrust forward and disappeared. Unbelieving, I stared out.

The car that had driven down the slope was filling the space where he had stood. The driver had seen what was happening and had done the only thing possible to save my life: He had crashed his car into Rob Westerfield.

As the blazing lights of the police cars turned the area into virtual daytime, I looked into the faces of my rescuers.

My father was driving the car that had hit Rob Westerfield. My brother was beside him. On Daddy's face I saw again the agonized expression that I remembered from when he knew he had lost his other little girl.

One Year Later

I often look back and realize how close I came that terrible night to sharing my sister's fate. From the time I left the inn, Dad and Teddy had been following me from a distance. They had seen what they believed to be a police van behind my car and assumed that I had finally requested protection.

However, they lost me when I veered off the highway, and Dad called the Phillipstown police to be sure the van had stayed with me.

That was when he learned that I had no official escort. The police told Dad where I probably had taken the wrong turn and promised immediate response.

Dad told me that when he came around the turn, the driver of Westerfield's van had started to pull away. He'd been about to follow him, but Teddy spotted the wreckage of my car. Teddy—the brother who never would have been born if Andrea had lived—saved my life. I often reflect on that irony.

Both of Rob Westerfield's legs were broken when he was hit by Dad's car, but they mended in time for him to walk into court for his two trials.

The District Attorney for Westchester County immediately reopened the investigation into Phil's death. He obtained a search warrant for Rob's new apartment and found a cache of his trophies, mementos of his hideous crimes. God knows where he had them stashed while he was in prison.

Rob had kept an album containing clippings of newspaper stories about both Andrea and Phil, starting from the time their bodies were found. The clippings were in sequence, and next to them were pictures of Andrea and Phil, photographs of the crime scenes, the funerals, and the other people caught up in the tragedies, including Paulie Stroebel and Dan Mayotte.

On each page Rob had written comments, cruel and sarcastic commentary on his actions and the people he hurt. There was one picture of Dan Mayotte on the witness stand swearing that a guy named Jim with dark blond hair had been flirting with Phil in the lobby of the movie theater. Next to it Rob had written, "I could tell she was crazy about me. Jim gets all the girls."

Rob had been wearing the dark blond wig when he pursued me. But the most telling proof of his guilt in

Phil's death was that he had kept her locket; it was pasted on the last page of the album. The caption under it read: "Thanks, Phil. Andrea loved it."

The district attorney requested the criminal court judge to vacate Dan Mayotte's conviction and to schedule a different trial: *The People vs. Robson Westerfield.* The charge was murder.

I saw the locket exhibited at the trial, and my mind flew back to that last evening in Andrea's bedroom when, close to tears, she had slipped it around her neck.

Dad was sitting next to me in court and closed his hand over mine. "You were always right about the locket, Ellie," he whispered.

Yes, I was, and at last I have made my peace with the fact that, because I saw her wearing it and believed she had gone to the hideout to meet Rob, I did not immediately tell my parents when she was missing. It may already have been too late to save her, but it is time to relinquish the possibility that it may *not* have been too late, and to stop letting it haunt me.

Robson Westerfield was convicted of the murder of Amy Phyllis Rayburn.

In a second trial Rob and his driver were convicted of attempted murder for their attack on me.

Rob Westerfield's sentences are consecutive. If he lives another 113 years, he will be eligible for parole. As he was being escorted out of the courtroom, after the second sentencing, he stopped for a moment to check his watch against the courtroom clock. Then he adjusted it.

"Don't bother," I said to myself. "Time has no meaning for you anymore."

Will Nebels, when confronted with the evidence of Westerfield's guilt, admitted that he had been approached by Hamilton and offered a bribe to lie about seeing Paulie go into the garage that night. William Hamilton, disbarred attorney, is now serving his own prison term.

My book was rushed out for publication in the spring and did very well. The other book—the sanitized version of Rob Westerfield's sorry life—was withdrawn. Pete introduced me to the Packard Cable executives, and they offered me a job as an investigative reporter. It seemed like a good opportunity. Some things never change. I report to Pete.

But that's fine. We were married three months ago in the St. Christopher Chapel at Graymoor. Dad gave the bride away.

Pete and I bought a house in Cold Spring overlooking the Hudson. We use it on weekends. I never tire of the view—that majestic river framed by the palisades. My heart has finally found its home, the home I have been seeking all these years.

I see Dad regularly. We both feel the need to make up

for lost time. Teddy's mother and I have become good friends. Sometimes we all go up to see Teddy at college. He's on the freshman basketball team at Dartmouth. I am so proud of him.

The circle has taken a long time to close. But it *has* closed, and for that I am deeply grateful.

I HEARD THAT SONG BEFORE

Prologue

My father was the landscaper for the Carrington estate. With fifty acres, it was one of the last remaining private properties of that size in Englewood, New Jersey, an upscale town three miles west of Manhattan via the George Washington Bridge.

One Saturday afternoon in August twenty-two years ago, when I was six years old, my father decided, even though it was his day off, that he had to go there to check on the newly installed outside lighting. The Carringtons were having a formal dinner party that evening for two hundred people. Already in trouble with his employers because of his drinking problem, Daddy knew that if the lights placed throughout the formal gardens did not function properly, it might mean the end of his job.

Because we lived alone, he had no choice except to take me with him. He settled me on a bench in the garden nearest the terrace with strict instructions to stay right there until he came back. Then he added, "I may be a little while, so if you have to use the bathroom, go through the screen door around the corner. You'll see the staff powder room just inside it."

That sort of permission was exactly what I needed. I had heard my father describe the inside of the great stone mansion to my grandmother, and my imagination had gone wild visualizing it. It had been built in Wales in the seventeenth century and even had a hidden chapel where a priest could both live and celebrate Mass in secrecy during the era of Oliver Cromwell's bloody attempt to erase all traces of Catholicism from England. In 1848 the first Peter Carrington had the mansion taken down and reassembled stone by stone in Englewood.

I knew from my father's description that the chapel had a heavy wooden door and was located at the very end of the second floor.

I had to see it.

I waited five minutes after he disappeared into the gardens and then raced through the door he had pointed out. The back staircase was to my immediate right, and I silently made my way upstairs. If I did encounter anyone, I planned to say that I was looking for a bathroom, which I persuaded myself was partially true.

On the second floor, with rising anxiety I tiptoed

down one carpeted hallway after another as I encountered a maze of unexpected turns. But then I saw it: the heavy wooden door my father had described, so out of place in the rest of the thoroughly modernized house.

Emboldened by my luck in having encountered no one in my adventure, I ran the last few steps and rushed to open the door. It squeaked as I tugged at it, but it opened just enough for me to squeeze through.

Being in the chapel was like going back in time. It was much smaller than I'd expected. I had pictured it as similar to the Lady Chapel in St. Patrick's Cathedral, where my grandmother always stopped to light a candle for my mother, on the rare occasions when we shopped in New York. She never failed to tell me how beautiful my mother had looked the day she and my father were married there.

The walls and floor of this chapel were built of stone, and the air I was breathing felt damp and cold.

A nicked and peeling statue of the Virgin Mary was the room's only religious artifact, and a battery-lit votive candle in front of it provided the only dim and shadowy lighting. Two rows of wooden pews faced the small wooden table that must have served as an altar.

As I was taking it all in, I heard the door begin to squeak and I knew someone was pushing it open. I did the only thing I could do—I ran between the pews and dropped to the ground, then ostrichlike buried my face in my hands.

From the voices I could tell that a man and a woman had entered the chapel. Their whispers, harsh and angry, echoed against the stone. They were arguing about money, a subject I knew well. My grandmother was always sniping at my father, telling him that if he kept up the drinking there wouldn't be a roof over his head or mine.

The woman was demanding money, and the man was saying that he already had paid her enough. Then she said, "This will be the last time, I swear," and he said, "I heard that song before."

I know my memory of that moment is accurate. From the time I could understand that, unlike my friends in kindergarten, I did not have a mother, I had begged my grandmother to tell me about her, every single thing she could remember. Among the memories my grandmother shared with me was one of my mother starring in the high school play and singing a song called "I Heard That Song Before." "Oh, Kathryn, she sang it so beautifully. She had a lovely voice. Everyone clapped so long and shouted, '*encore, encore.*' She had to sing it again." Then my grandmother would hum it for me.

Following the man's remark, I could not hear the rest of what was said except for her whispered, "Don't forget," as she left the chapel. The man had stayed; I could hear his agitated breathing. Then, very softly, he began to whistle the tune of the song my mother sang in the school play. Looking back, I think he may have been trying to calm himself. After a few bars, he broke off and left the chapel.

I waited for what seemed forever, then I left, too. I hurried down the stairs and back outside, and, of course, never told my father that I'd been in the house or what I had heard in the chapel. But the memory never faded, and I am sure of what I heard.

Who those people were, I don't know. Now, twenty-two years later, it is important to find out. The only thing that I have learned for certain, from all of the accounts of that evening, is that there were a number of overnight guests staying in the mansion, as well as five in household help, and the local caterer and his crew. But that knowledge may not be enough to save my husband's life, if indeed it deserves to be saved.

1

I grew up in the shadow of the Lindbergh baby kidnapping.

By that I mean I was born and raised in Englewood, New Jersey. In 1932, the grandson of Englewood's most prominent citizen, Ambassador Dwight Morrow, was kidnapped. Furthermore, the baby's father happened to be the most famous man in the world at the time, Col. Charles Lindbergh, who had flown the first solo flight across the Atlantic Ocean in his single-engine plane, the *Spirit of St. Louis*.

My grandmother, who was eight years old at that time, remembers the blazing headlines, the crowds of reporters who congregated outside Next Day Hill, the Morrow estate, the arrest and trial of Bruno Hauptmann.

Time passed, memories faded. Today Englewood's most prominent residence is the Carrington mansion, the stone-castlelike structure that I had stolen into as a child.

All these thoughts went through my mind as, for the second time in my life, I went inside the gates of the Carrington estate. Twenty-two years, I thought, remembering the inquisitive six-year-old I had been. Maybe it was the memory of my father being dismissed by the Carringtons only a few weeks later that made me suddenly feel self-conscious and awkward. The bright October morning had changed into a windy, damp afternoon, and I wished that I had worn a heavier jacket. The one I had chosen now seemed much too light both in color and fabric.

Instinctively, I parked my secondhand car to the side of the imposing driveway, not wanting it to be the object of anyone's scrutiny. One hundred and eight thousand miles on the speedometer takes a lot of starch out of a car, even one recently washed and mercifully free of dents.

I had twisted my hair into a bun, but the wind tore at it as I walked up the steps and rang the bell. A man who looked to be in his midfifties, with a receding hairline and narrow, unsmiling lips, opened the door. He was dressed in a dark suit, and I wasn't sure whether he was a butler or a secretary, but before I could speak, without introducing himself, he said that Mr. Carrington was expecting me and that I should come in.

The wide entrance hall was illuminated by light that filtered through leaded stained-glass windows. A statue of a knight in armor stood next to a medieval tapestry depicting a battle scene. I longed to examine the tapestry, but instead I dutifully followed my escort down a corridor to the library.

"Miss Lansing is here, Mr. Carrington," he said. "I'll be in the office." From that remark I guessed he was an assistant.

When I was little I used to draw pictures of the kind of home I'd love to live in. One of my favorite rooms to imagine was the one in which I would read away my afternoons. In that room there was always a fireplace and bookshelves. One version included a comfortable couch, and I'd draw myself curled up in the corner, a book in my hand. I'm not suggesting I'm any kind of artist because I'm not. I drew stick figures and the bookshelves were uneven, the carpet a splotched multicolored copy of one I'd seen in the window of an antique rug store. I could not put the exact image in my mind on paper, but I knew what I wanted. I wanted the kind of room I was standing in now.

Peter Carrington was seated in a wide leather chair, his feet on a hassock. The lamp on the table beside him not only illuminated the book he was reading but spotlighted his handsome profile.

He was wearing reading glasses, which sat on the bridge of his nose and slipped off when he looked up. Retrieving them, he laid them on the table, removed his feet from the hassock, and stood. I had caught occasional glimpses of him in town and had seen his picture in the papers, so I had an impression of him, but being in the same room with him was different. There was a quiet authority about Peter Carrington that he retained even as he smiled and extended his hand.

"You write a persuasive letter, Kathryn Lansing."

"Thank you for letting me stop in, Mr. Carrington."

His handshake was firm. I knew he was studying me just as I was studying him. He was taller than I had realized, with the narrow body of a runner. His eyes were more gray than blue. His thin, even-featured face was framed by dark brown hair that was a shade long but which suited him well. He was wearing a dark brown cardigan with a rust thread running through the weave. If I had been asked to guess his job from his appearance alone, I would have said college professor.

I knew he was forty-two years old. That meant he would have been about twenty the day that I crept into this house. I wondered if he had been home for that party. It was possible, of course—in late August he might not yet have gone back to Princeton, where he had been a student. Or, if he had already started school, he might have come home for the weekend. Princeton was only an hour-and-a-half drive away.

He invited me to sit down in one of the two matching

armchairs near the fireplace. "I've been wanting an excuse to have a fire," he said. "This afternoon the weather cooperated."

I was more than ever conscious of the fact that my lime green jacket was more suitable to an August afternoon than to midautumn. I felt a strand of hair slip over my shoulder and tried to twist it back into the bun that was supposed to anchor it.

I have a master's in library science, my passion for books having made that a natural career choice. Since graduation five years ago, I've been working at the Englewood Public Library and am heavily involved in our community's literacy project.

Now I was in this impressive library, "with my hat in my hand," as my grandmother would say. I was planning a fund-raiser for the literacy program and wanted to make it spectacular. There was one way I was sure I could get people to pay three hundred dollars for a cocktail reception, and that would be if it were held in this house. The Carrington mansion had become part of the folklore of Englewood and the surrounding communities. Everyone knew its history and that it had been transported from Wales. I was certain that the prospect of being inside it would make all the difference in whether or not we could have a sellout event.

I usually feel pretty comfortable in my own skin, but sitting there, sensing that those gray eyes were taking my measure, I felt flustered and ill at ease. Suddenly I felt, once again, like the daughter of the landscaper who drank too much.

Get over it, I told myself, and stop with the "gee-whiz" nonsense. Giving myself a brisk mental shake, I began my well-rehearsed solicitation. "Mr. Carrington, as I wrote you, there are many good causes, meaning many reasons for people to write checks. Of course it's impossible for anyone to support everything. Quite frankly, these days even well-off people feel tapped out. That's why it's essential to our event to find a way to get people to write a check for us."

That was when I launched into my plea for him to allow us to have a cocktail party in this house. I watched as his expression changed, and I saw the "no" word forming on his lips.

He put it gracefully. "Miss Lansing," he began.

"Please call me Kay."

"I thought your name was Kathryn."

"On my birth certificate and to my grandmother."

He laughed. "I understand." Then he began his polite refusal. "Kay, I'd be happy to write a check . . ."

I interrupted him. "I'm sure you would. But as I wrote, this is more than just about money. We need volunteers to teach people how to read, and the best way to get them is to make them want to come to an affair, and then sign them up. I know a great caterer who has promised to reduce his price if the event is held here. It would just be for two hours, and it would mean so much to so many people."

"I have to think about it," Peter Carrington said as he stood up.

The meeting was over. I thought quickly and decided there was nothing to lose by adding one final thing: "Mr. Carrington, I've done of lot of research about your family. For generations this was one of the most hospitable homes in Bergen County. Your father and grandfather and great-grandfather supported local community activities and charities. By helping us now, you could do so much good, and it would be so easy for you."

I had no right to feel so terribly disappointed, but I did. He didn't respond, and without waiting for him or his assistant to show me out, I retraced my steps to the door. I did pause to take a quick glance to the back of the house, thinking of the staircase I had sneaked up all those years ago. Then I left, sure that I had made my second and final visit to the mansion.

Two days later Peter Carrington's picture was on the cover of *Celeb*, a national weekly gossip rag. It showed him coming out of the police station twenty-two years ago, after being questioned about the disappearance of eighteen-year-old Susan Althorp, who had vanished following the formal dinner dance she had attended at the Carrington mansion. The blaring headline, IS SUSAN ALTHORP STILL ALIVE?, was followed by the caption under Peter's picture: "Industrialist still a suspect in the disappearance of debutante Susan Althorp, who would be celebrating her fortieth birthday this week."

The magazine had a field day rehashing details of the search for Susan and, since her father had been an ambassador, comparing the case to the kidnapping of the Lindbergh baby.

The article included a summary of the circumstances surrounding the death of Peter Carrington's pregnant wife, Grace, four years ago. Grace Carrington, known for drinking heavily, had given a birthday party for Carrington's stepbrother, Richard Walker. Carrington had arrived home after a twenty-three-hour flight from Australia, observed her condition, grabbed the glass out of her hand, dumped the contents on the carpet, and angrily demanded, "Can't you have a little mercy on the child you're carrying?" Then, claiming exhaustion, he went up to bed. In the morning, the housekeeper found the body of Grace Carrington, still dressed in a satin evening suit, at the bottom of the swimming pool. An autopsy showed that she was three times over the limit of being legally drunk. The article concluded, "Carrington claimed he went to sleep immediately and did not awaken until the police responded to the 911 call. MAYBE. We're conducting an opinion poll. Go to our Web site and let us know what you think."

A week later, at the library, I received a call from Vincent Slater, who reminded me that I had met him when I had an appointment with Peter Carrington.

"Mr. Carrington," he said, "has decided to permit the use of his home for your fund-raiser. He suggests that you coordinate the details of the event with me."

2

Vincent Slater put down the phone and leaned back, ignoring the faint squeak of his desk chair, a sound that had begun to annoy him and that several times he'd made a mental note to get fixed. His office in the mansion had originally been one of the seldom-used sitting rooms at the back of the house. In addition to its remoteness, he had chosen it because of the French doors that not only gave a view of the formal gardens but also served as a private entrance from which he could come and go without being observed.

The problem was that Peter's stepmother, Elaine, who lived in a house on the grounds, thought nothing of coming up to his office and entering without knocking. At that moment, she had done exactly that again.

She did not waste time on a greeting. "Vincent, I'm glad I caught you. Is there any way you can persuade Peter to give up the idea of having that charity reception here? One would think that after all the terrible publicity last week in that trashy *Celeb* magazine, rehashing Susan's disappearance and Grace's death, he would know enough to attract as little attention as possible."

Vincent stood up, a courtesy he wished he could forgo when Elaine barged in on him. Now, even though he was intensely irritated by the intrusion, he could not resist noticing begrudgingly how exquisitely attractive she was. At sixty-six, Elaine Walker Carrington, with her ash-blond hair, sapphire blue eyes, classic features, and willowy body, could still turn heads. She moved with the grace of the fashion model she had once been, even as, uninvited, she settled herself in the antique armchair on the other side of Vincent's desk.

She was wearing a black suit that Slater guessed was an Armani, whom he knew to be her favorite designer. Her jewelry consisted of diamond earrings, a narrow strand of pearls, and the wide diamond wedding ring that she still wore even though her husband, Peter's father, had been dead for nearly twenty years. Her faithfulness to his memory, Vincent well knew, had everything to do with the terms of her prenuptial agreement, which allowed her to live here for the rest of her life, unless she remarried, and ensured her a million-dollar-a-year stipend. And, of course, she liked to be referred to as Mrs. Carrington, with all the attendant privileges.

Which does not give her the right to walk in here and act as if I hadn't considered very carefully the pluses and minuses of having a public event in this house, Vincent thought. "Elaine, Peter and I have discussed this thoroughly," he began, his tone revealing his irritation. "Of course the publicity is terrible and embarrassing, which is why Peter has to make some move to show he's not in hiding. That is precisely the perception which must be changed."

"Do you really think that having strangers milling around in this house will change the perception most people have of Peter?" Elaine asked, her tone laced with sarcasm.

"Elaine, I suggest you stay out of this," Slater snapped. "May I remind you that the family company went public two years ago, and there is a negative side to having to answer to stockholders. Even though Peter is by far the largest stockholder, the fact remains that there's a growing opinion that he should step down as chairman and CEO. Being 'a person of interest' in the disappearance of one woman and the death of another is hardly a good image to have as the head of an international company. Peter may not talk about it, but I know he's deeply concerned. That's why, from now on, he's got to be seen as active in community affairs and, even if he hates it, his very generous philanthropies have got to be publicized."

"Really?" Elaine got up as she spoke. "Vincent, you're a fool. Mark my words, this won't work. What you're doing is exposing Peter, not protecting him. Socially, Peter comes across as a zero. He may be a genius at business, but as you certainly know, he isn't comfortable with small talk. Away from the office he's much happier with a book in his hand and the door of the library closed than at some cocktail party or dinner. 'Never less alone than when alone,' as the saying goes. When is this affair going to take place?"

"Thursday, December sixth. Kay Lansing, the woman who's running it, needed about seven weeks lead time to publicize it."

"Is there any limit to how many tickets can be sold?"

"Two hundred."

"I'll be sure to buy one of them. So will Richard. I'm on my way to the gallery. He's having a reception for one of his new artists." With a dismissive wave of her hand, she pulled open the French doors and walked out.

Slater watched her go, his mouth drawn in a thin, tight line. Richard Walker was Elaine's son by her first marriage. She's paying for that reception, he thought. Carrington money has been supporting that loser son of hers since he was twenty years old. He remembered how it drove Grace crazy that Elaine assumed she could walk into the main house anytime she wanted.

The one thing Peter was smart enough to do was to not let Elaine move back in here after Grace died.

Not for the first time, Vincent Slater wondered whether there was more to Peter Carrington's tolerance of his stepmother than met the eye.

3

I was at the library when I received the call from Vincent Slater. It was late Wednesday morning and I was about to commit to having our fund-raiser at the Glenpointe Hotel in Teaneck, a neighboring town to Englewood. I've attended affairs there, and they do a really good job, but I was still disappointed I'd been turned down by Peter Carrington. Needless to say, I was absolutely delighted by Slater's message and decided to share my excitement with Maggie, the maternal grandmother who raised me and who still lives in the same modest house in Englewood where I grew up.

I'm a reverse commuter. I live on West Seventy-ninth Street in Manhattan, in a small second-floor apartment in a converted town house. It's about as big as a minute, but it has a working fireplace, high ceilings, a bedroom large enough for a bed and dresser, and a kitchen area that is separate from the living room. I furnished it from garage sales held in the tonier parts of

Englewood and I love the way it looks. I also love working at the library in Englewood, and, of course, that means I get to see a lot of my grandmother, Margaret O'Neil, whom my father and I have always called Maggie.

Her daughter, who was my mother, died when I was only two weeks old. It happened in the late afternoon. She was propped up in bed nursing me, when an embolism hit her heart. My father called shortly after and was alarmed she did not answer the phone. He rushed home to find her lifeless body, her arms still cradling me. I was asleep, my lips contentedly suckling her breast.

My father was an engineer who, after a year with a bridge-building company, had quit and made gardening, previously his avocation, his full-time career. He used his keen mind to achieve a different kind of engineering triumph in the local estates, creating gardens with rock walls, and waterfalls, and winding paths. Which is why he was hired by Peter Carrington's stepmother, Elaine, who disliked the unyielding rigidity of her predecessor's taste in landscaping.

Daddy was eight years older than my mother, thirty-two when she died. By then he had established a solid reputation in his field. All might have been well enough except that after my mother's death, Daddy began to drink too much. Because of it, I began to spend more and more time with my grandmother. I can remember her pleading with him, "For God sake, Jonathan, you've got to get help. What would Annie think of what you are doing to yourself? And how about Kathryn? Doesn't she deserve better?"

Then one afternoon after Elaine Carrington fired him, he did not come to my grandmother's house to collect me. His car was found parked on a bank of the Hudson River, some twenty miles north of Englewood. His wallet and house keys and checkbook were on the front seat. No note. No good-bye. Nothing to indicate he knew how much I needed him. I wonder how much he blamed me for my mother's death, if he thought that somehow I sucked the life from her. But surely not. I had loved him fiercely, and he always had seemed to love me the same way. A child can tell. His body was never recovered.

I still remember how, when we got home from Maggie's, he and I would cook dinner together. He would reminisce about my mother. "As you well know, Maggie's no cook, Kathryn," he would say, "so your mother opened a cookbook and learned out of sheer desperation. She and I used to try recipes together, and now it's you and me."

Then he would talk to me about my mother. "Always remember, she would have given anything to watch you grow up. She kept the bassinet by our bed for a month before you were born. You've missed so much by not having her, by not knowing her."

I still can't forgive him for not remembering all that when he decided to end his life.

All of these thoughts were going through my mind as I drove from the library to Maggie's house to tell her the news. She has a beautiful red maple tree on her small lawn. It gives a special air to the whole place. I was sorry to see the last of its leaves blowing away in the wind. Without their protection, the house looked somehow exposed, and a bit shabby. It is a one-story Cape Cod, with an unfinished attic where Maggie stores the accumulated paraphernalia of her eighty-three years. Boxes of pictures she's never gotten around to putting in photo albums, boxes of letters and treasured Christmas cards she will never live to wade through, the furniture that she replaced with the contents of my parents' home but couldn't bear to throw out, clothes that she hasn't worn in twenty or thirty years.

Downstairs isn't much better. Everything is clean, but Maggie creates clutter just by walking into a room. Her sweater lies on one chair, the newspaper articles she always means to read on another; books are piled by her easy chair; the shades she pulled up in the morning are always uneven; the slippers she can't find are tucked between the chair and the hassock. It's a real home.

Maggie wouldn't meet Martha Stewart's idea of good housekeeping, but she's got plenty going for her. She retired from teaching to raise me, and still tutors three kids every week. As I found out through experience, she can make learning a joyful thing.

But when I went inside and told her my news, she let me down. I could see the look of disapproval on her face as soon as I mentioned the Carrington name.

"Kay, you never told me you were thinking of asking them to let you hold the literacy fund-raiser in that place."

Maggie has lost a couple of inches in height in the last few years. She jokes that she's disappearing, but as I looked down at her, she suddenly seemed very formidable. "Maggie, it's a great idea," I protested. "I've been to a couple of events in private homes, and they've been sellouts. The Carrington mansion is bound to be a big draw. We're going to charge three hundred dollars a ticket. We wouldn't get that anywhere else."

Then I realized that Maggie was worried, genuinely worried. "Maggie, Peter Carrington couldn't have been nicer when I met with him to talk about the event."

"You didn't tell me you saw him."

Why hadn't I told her? Maybe because I knew instinctively that she would not approve of my going there, and then, when he turned me down, there was no need to talk about it. Maggie was convinced that Peter

Carrington was responsible for Susan Althorp's disappearance, and that he may very well have been involved in his wife's drowning. "Maybe he didn't push his wife into the pool, Kay," she had told me, "but I bet if he saw her fall in, he didn't make it his business to save her. And as for Susan, he was the one who drove her home. I'd bet anything she sneaked out and met him after her parents thought she was going to bed."

Maggie was eight years old in 1932 when the Lindbergh baby was kidnapped, and she considers herself the world's leading expert on that subject, as well as on the disappearance of Susan Althorp. From the time I was little, she had talked to me about the Lindbergh kidnapping, pointing out that Anne Morrow Lindbergh, the baby's mother, was raised in Englewood, not a mile from our home, and that Anne's father, Dwight Morrow, had been ambassador to Mexico. Susan Althorp was also raised in Englewood, and her father had been ambassador to Belgium. To Maggie, the parallels were obvious—and scary.

The Lindbergh baby kidnapping was one of the most sensational crimes of the twentieth century. The golden child of the golden couple, and all the unanswered questions. How did Bruno Hauptmann learn that the Lindberghs had decided to stay in their new country home that evening because the baby had a cold, rather than return to the Morrow estate as initially planned?

How did Hauptmann know exactly where to place the ladder to reach the open window of the baby's room? Maggie was always seeing similarities between the two cases. "The Lindbergh baby's body was found by accident," she would point out to me. "It was terrible, but at least it meant that the family didn't spend the rest of their lives wondering if he was growing up somewhere with someone who might be harming him. Susan Althorp's mother has to wake up every morning wondering if this is the day the phone will ring and it will be her daughter. I know that's the way I would feel if my child was missing. At least if her body had been found, Mrs. Althorp could visit her grave."

Maggie hadn't talked about the Althorp case in a long time, but I'll bet anything that if she was at the supermarket checkout and saw that *Celeb* magazine with Peter Carrington's picture on the cover, she would buy it. Which explains her sudden uneasiness at the thought of my being in his presence.

I kissed the top of her head. "Maggie, I'm hungry. Let's go out and have some pasta. My treat."

When I dropped her home an hour and a half later, she hesitated, then said, "Kay, come back inside. I want to go to that affair. I'll write you a check for a ticket."

"Maggie, that's crazy," I protested. "That's too much money for you."

"I'm going," she said. Her determined expression left no room for argument.

A few minutes later I was driving over the George Washington Bridge, back to my apartment, her check in my wallet. I knew the reason she had insisted on attending. Maggie had appointed herself as my personal bodyguard while I was under the roof of the Carrington mansion.

4

As she waited for her visitor to arrive, Gladys Althorp studied the picture of her missing daughter. It had been taken on the terrace of the Carrington mansion the night Susan disappeared. She was wearing a white chiffon evening gown that clung to her slender body. Her long blond hair, slightly tousled, tumbled onto her shoulders. She had been unaware the camera was on her, and her expression was serious, even pensive. What was she thinking at that moment? Gladys asked herself once again, as her fingers traced the outline of Susan's mouth. Did she have a premonition that something was going to happen to her?

Or did she finally realize that night that her father had been involved with Elaine Carrington?

Gladys sighed as she slowly stood, resting one hand on the armchair for support. Brenda, the new housekeeper, had served her dinner on a tray and then headed back to her apartment over the garage. Unfortunately, Brenda wasn't much of a cook. Not that I'm really hungry, Gladys thought as she carried the tray to the kitchen. The sight of the uneaten food made her feel slightly nauseous, and she quickly scraped it into the compactor, rinsed the dishes, and placed them in the dishwasher.

"Just leave it for me, Mrs. Althorp," she knew Brenda would protest in the morning. And I'll say it only takes a minute to tidy up, Gladys thought. Tidy. That was the way to describe what I'm doing now. Trying to tidy up the most important piece of business in my life before I leave it.

"Maybe six months," the doctors had agreed when they delivered the verdict that she hadn't yet shared with anyone.

She went back into the study, her favorite of the seventeen rooms in the house. I've been wanting to downsize for years, and I know Charles will once I'm gone. She knew the reason she hadn't. Susan's room was here, everything still exactly as it had been when she left that night after knocking on the bedroom door to let Charles know she was home.

I let her sleep late the next morning, Gladys thought, once again replaying that day in her mind. Then, finally, at noon I looked in on her. The bed was still made. The towels in her bathroom hadn't been touched. She must have gone right back out after announcing she was home.

Before I die, I have to try to learn what happened to

her, she vowed. Maybe this investigator can find some answers. Nicholas Greco was his name. She had seen him on television talking about the crimes he had solved. After retiring as a detective from the New York City Police Department, he'd opened his own agency and become well known for solving crimes that initially had seemed unsolvable.

"The families of victims need closure," he had said in an interview. "There's no peace for them until they have it. Fortunately, there are new tools and new methods being developed every day that make it possible to take a fresh look at cases that are still open."

She had asked him to come at eight o'clock tonight for two reasons. That she knew Charles would be out was one of them. The second was that she didn't want Brenda to be around when he was there. Two weeks ago, Brenda had come into the study when she was watching a tape of Greco on television. "Mrs. Althorp, I think the true cases he talks about are more interesting than the ones they make up," Brenda had said. "Just looking at him you can tell he's smart."

The front door chimes pealed promptly at eight o'clock. Gladys hurried to open the door. Her first impression of Nicholas Greco was both comforting and reassuring. From his television appearances, she knew he was a conservatively dressed man in his late fifties, of average height, with sandy hair and dark brown eyes. But meeting him, she liked the fact that his handshake was firm and that he looked her directly in the eye. Everything about him invited trust.

She wondered what his impression of her might be. Probably he'd just see a woman in her midsixties, far too thin, with the pallor of terminal illness on her face. "Thank you for coming," she said. "I know you must have many requests from someone like me."

"I have two daughters," Greco said. "If one of them disappeared, I wouldn't be at peace until I found her." He waited, then added quietly, "Even if what I learned was not what I was hoping to hear."

"I believe that Susan is dead," Gladys Althorp said, her voice calm, but the expression in her eyes suddenly bleak and sad. "But she would not have disappeared on her own. Something happened to her, and I believe that Peter Carrington was responsible for her death. Whatever the truth is, I have got to know it. Are you interested in helping me?"

"Yes, I am."

"I have put together for you all my files about Susan's disappearance. They're in my study."

As Nicholas Greco followed Gladys Althorp down the wide hallway, he managed quick glances of the paintings along the way. Someone in this family is a collector, he thought. I don't know if these are museum-quality, but they certainly are pretty fine.

Everything that he could see in the house had an air of good taste and quality. The emerald green carpet was thick and soft underfoot. The crown molding on the stark white walls provided an added frame for the paintings. The area rug in the study where Gladys Althorp led him contained a mellow red and blue pattern. The shade of blue in the couch and chairs matched the blue in the rug. He saw the picture of Susan Althorp on the desk. To the side was a decorative shopping bag, bulging with legal-sized documents.

He walked over to the desk and picked up the picture. Since deciding to take on the case, he had done some preliminary research and had seen this picture on the Internet. "This is what Susan was wearing when she disappeared?" he asked.

"It was what she was wearing at the Carrington dinner. I was not feeling well and my husband and I left the party before it broke up. Peter promised to drive her home."

"You were still awake when she came in?"

"Yes, about an hour later. Charles had the twelve o'clock news on in his room. I heard her call to him."

"Isn't that a bit early for an eighteen-year-old to be home?"

Greco did not miss the tightening of Gladys Althorp's lips. The question had evoked anger in her.

"Charles was an overprotective father. He insisted that Susan wake him up whenever she came home."

Gladys Althorp was one of many grief-stricken parents Nicholas Greco had encountered in his career. But unlike many of the others, he suspected that she had always managed to keep her emotions rigidly private. He sensed that, for her, hiring him was a difficult step, a quantum leap into frightening territory.

With a professional eye, he observed the extreme pallor of her complexion, the air of fragility about her entire body. He had a strong suspicion that she might be terminally ill, and that that was the reason for her decision to contact him.

When he left half an hour later, Greco was carrying the shopping bag containing files with all the information Gladys Althorp could give him about the circumstances surrounding her daughter's disappearance: the follow-up stories in the newspapers, the journal she had kept as the investigation continued, and the recent copy of *Celeb* magazine with a picture of Peter Carrington on the cover.

In his preliminary research, Greco had taken down the address of the Carrington estate. On impulse, he decided to swing past it. Even though he knew it was not far from where the Althorps lived, he was surprised at how very close the two homes were. It couldn't have taken Peter Carrington more than five minutes to drop her off that night, if that's what he did, and not more than five minutes to get back home. As he drove back to Manhattan, he realized that this case had hooked him already. He was anxious to get started. A classic "corpus delicti," he thought, then remembered the pain in Gladys Althorp's eyes and felt ashamed.

I'm going to solve it for her, he thought grimly as he experienced the familiar rush of energy that came when he knew he was about to begin working on a case that would prove to be fascinating.

5

Gladys Althorp waited in the study for her husband to come in. She heard him opening and closing the front door shortly after the eleven o'clock news began. She switched off the television and hurried down the hallway. He was already halfway up the stairs.

"Charles, I have something to tell you."

His already ruddy face became flushed and his voice kept rising as, after hearing that she had hired Nicholas Greco, he demanded, "Without consulting me? Without considering that our sons will also be forced to relive that terrible time? Without understanding that any new investigation attracts media attention from the rags? Wasn't that disgusting story last week enough for you?"

"I have consulted our sons, and they agree with my decision," Gladys said calmly. "I absolutely must learn the truth about what happened to Susan. Does that worry you, Charles?"

6

The first week of November was balmy, but after that the weather turned sharply cold and drizzly, the kind of clammy days that make you want either to stay in bed or go back to bed with the newspapers and a cup of coffee—neither of which I had time to do. Just about every day, I work out early in a gym on Broadway, then shower, dress, and head for the library in New Jersey. Meetings about the fund-raiser were held after working hours.

Needless to say, the tickets to the event sold fast, which was gratifying, but the rehashed story of Susan Althorp's disappearance had triggered renewed interest in the case. Then, when Nicholas Greco, the private investigator, disclosed on *Imus in the Morning* that hc had been hired by the Althorp family to look into their daughter's disappearance, it became hot news. On the heels of Greco's statement, Barbara Krause, the formidable Bergen County prosecutor, told the press that she would welcome any new evidence that would bring closure to the case. When asked about Peter Carrington, she said cryptically, "Peter Carrington has always been a person of interest in the disappearance of Susan Althorp."

On the heels of that statement, the gossip columns began to print reports that the board of directors of Carrington Enterprises was urging Peter to resign as chairman and CEO, even though he was by far the largest stockholder. According to the reports, the other directors felt that since it was now a publicly traded company, it was not appropriate for anyone designated as a "person of interest" in two potential homicides to continue to head a worldwide multibillion-dollar organization.

Pictures of Peter began appearing regularly in the business sections of major newspapers, as well as in the more sensational magazines.

As a result, all through November, I kept my fingers crossed, expecting to get a call from Vincent Slater any day to tell me that the cocktail reception was off and that they would send a check to compensate for our lost revenue.

But the call never came. The day after Thanksgiving I went to the mansion with the caterer we had hired to go over details for the affair. Slater met us and turned us over to the couple who were housekeepers for the mansion, Jane and Gary Barr. They appeared to be in their early sixties, and it was obvious that they had been with the Carringtons for a long time. I wondered if they had been working at the mansion the night of the infamous dinner, but I didn't have the nerve to ask. I learned later that they had come to work for Peter's father after his first wife, Peter's mother, had died, but then left after Elaine Walker Carrington came on the scene. They were coaxed back, however, after Peter's wife, Grace, drowned. They seemed to know everything about the place.

They told us that the living room was actually divided into two rooms, and that when the pocket doors were opened, the space was sufficient to accommodate two hundred people. The buffet should be laid out in the formal dining room. Small tables and chairs would be set up throughout the ground floor so that people would not have to balance plates. Before we left, Vincent Slater joined us again to say that Mr. Carrington was underwriting all the expenses of the reception. Before I even had time to thank him, Slater added, "We have a photographer who will take pictures. We do ask that your guests refrain from using their own cameras."

"As you probably guessed, we'll give a brief report about the literacy campaign," I told him. "It would mean a lot if Mr. Carrington would say a few words of greeting."

"He's planning to do that," Slater said. Then he added, "Before I forget, it goes without saying that the staircases leading upstairs will be roped off."

I had been hoping to slip upstairs for an adult view of the chapel. Sometimes, over the years, I'd wondered if I should have revealed to Maggie the angry conversation I heard there, but she would have been angry at me for going into the house, and besides, what could I tell her? I had heard a man and a woman quarreling about money. If I thought that quarrel had anything to do with Susan Althorp's disappearance, I certainly would have reported it, even years later. But if there was one thing Susan Althorp would never have had to do, it was to plead for money from anyone. So the only thing my revelation would establish was that I'd been a curious six-year-old.

Before the caterer and I left that day, I did glance down the corridor, hoping to see the door to the library open and Peter Carrington come out. For all I knew, he was halfway around the world. But because many executives take the Friday after Thanksgiving off, I fantasized that if he was in the house, I'd run into him.

It didn't happen. I contented myself with the knowledge that December 6th was less than two weeks away, and I'd get to see him then. Then I tried to push away the realization that if for any reason Peter didn't attend the reception, I would be desperately disappointed. I've been dating Glenn Taylor, Ph.D., associate dean of science at Columbia University, with increasing regularity. We had met while having coffee in a Starbucks, helping that establishment to live up to its reputation as a great place for singles to make friends.

Glenn is thirty-two, transplanted from Santa Barbara, and is about as laid back as any Californian ever born. He even looks as though he's from there—after six years of living on the Upper West Side in Manhattan, his hair still retains a sun-streaked look. He's just tall enough to let me be not quite eye level when I'm wearing heels, and he shares my passion for the theatre. I think in the past couple of years we've gone to most of the Broadway and off-Broadway shows, using discounted tickets of course. No business-page editor ever wrote a story about the year-end bonus a librarian received, and Glenn is still paying off his school loans.

In a way, we love each other and certainly we count on each other. Sometimes Glenn even speculates that, with my side of the brain into literature and his into science, we'd have a chance at producing awesome offspring. But I know that we're not anywhere near the emotional level of Jane Eyre and Mr. Rochester, or Cathy and Heathcliff.

It may be that I've set my standards too high, but ever since I was young, I've been into the classic love stories of the Brontë sisters.

From the beginning, something about Peter Carrington had intrigued me, and I think I began to understand what it was. Seeing him sitting there alone in that crazy castlelike mansion was a haunting image. I wished I had had the chance to see what book he was reading. If it was one I had read myself, maybe I could have lingered for a few minutes to discuss it.

"Oh, I see you have the new biography of Isaac Bashevis Singer," I might have said. "Do you agree with the author's interpretation of his personality? I thought he was a little unfair because . . ."

You can see the way my mind was going.

Then, the night before the reception, I went to Maggie's house to pick her up for one of our regular pasta dinners. When I arrived, she was powdering her nose in the hall mirror, humming cheerfully. When I asked her what was up, she blithely told me that Nicholas Greco, the investigator who was delving into Susan Althorp's disappearance, had called and was coming to see her. She was expecting him any minute.

I was dumbfounded. "Maggie, why in the name of God would that guy want to talk to you?" But even before she had answered, I knew that Greco was coming here because my father had worked for the Carringtons at the time of the Althorp disappearance.

Automatically I began to straighten up the living

room. I adjusted the window shades so that they were at the same level, picked up the newspapers that were scattered around, hung up her sweater in the hall closet, and carried the teacup and plate of cookies that were on the coffee table into the kitchen.

Greco arrived as I was putting some loose strands of silver hair into the bun at the back of Maggie's head.

I'm a Dashiell Hammett fan, and Sam Spade, especially in *The Maltese Falcon*, is the prototype for my mental image of a private investigator. Applying that yardstick, Nicholas Greco was a disappointment. In his appearance and manner he reminded me of the insurance adjuster who came to see me when a pipe broke in the apartment above mine.

That illusion was quickly shattered, however, when, after Maggie had introduced me as her granddaughter, he said, "You must be the one who accompanied your father to the Carrington estate the same day that Susan Althorp disappeared."

When I stared at him, he smiled. "I've been going through the files on the case. Twenty-two years ago your father told the prosecutor's office that he had gone to the estate unexpectedly that day because of a problem with the lighting, and that he took you with him. One of the caterer's workers also mentioned seeing you sitting on a bench in the garden."

Had anyone seen me sneak into the house? I hoped

I didn't look as guilty as I felt when I invited Greco to sit down.

It irritated me to see that Maggie was obviously enjoying herself. I knew that this man—who no longer reminded me of an insurance adjuster—had been hired to prove Peter Carrington had been responsible for Susan Althorp's disappearance, and that upset me.

But his next question startled me. It was not about the Carringtons or the Althorps; it was about my father. He asked Maggie, "Had your son-in-law shown signs of depression?"

"If you call hitting the bottle a sign of depression, I would say so," Maggie said, then glanced at me as though afraid I'd be upset by her answer. She hurried to qualify it. "I mean, he never got over Annie's death. She was my daughter, but when a couple of years had passed after her death, I begged Jonathan to start dating. Let me tell you, there were plenty of women around here who would have jumped at the chance to go out with him. But he never would. He'd say, 'Kathryn's the only girl I need.'" Then she added, somewhat unnecessarily, "When she was ten, Kathryn decided she wanted to be called Kay."

"Then you feel that the excessive drinking was a sign of his depression, and that it led to his taking his own life?"

"He'd lost out on a number of landscaping jobs. I think that being fired by the Carringtons may have pushed him over the edge. His insurance policy was about to expire. After he was declared legally dead, it paid for Kay's education."

"But he did not leave a suicide note, and his body was never recovered. I've seen his picture. He was a strikingly handsome man."

I could see where that line of questioning was going. "Are you suggesting that my father did not commit suicide, Mr. Greco?" I asked.

"Miss Lansing, I'm not suggesting anything. Anytime a body is not recovered, there is always an open question about the manner of death. There are numerous documented cases of people who were believed to be dead, and who showed up or were tracked down twenty or thirty years later. These people simply walked away from a life that had become in some way unbearable. It happens often."

"Then I assume you believe that Susan Althorp may have done the same thing?" I shot back at him. "Her body was never found. Maybe her life was suddenly unbearable."

"Susan was a beautiful, healthy young woman, a gifted student pursuing a fine arts degree at Princeton, and the recipient of a trust fund that meant she would lead a life of wealth and privilege. She was very popular and attracted men easily. I'm afraid I don't see the comparison."

"Peter Carrington did something to that girl. I bet he was jealous of her." Now Maggie sounded like the Lord Chief Justice of the United Kingdom pronouncing a verdict. "I gave him the benefit of the doubt until his wife drowned, but it just goes to show that if you kill someone, you're capable of doing it again. As for my son-in-law, I think he was depressed enough to believe he was doing Kay a favor by insuring her education."

That night the pasta stuck in my throat, and it wasn't any comfort when Maggie rehashed Greco's visit. "He's supposed to be smart, but he was way off the mark in even thinking that your dad would just walk out on you."

No, he wouldn't just walk out on me, I thought, but that's not where Greco is going. He's wondering if Daddy had to stage his own disappearance because of what happened to Susan Althorp.

7

It had begun to snow. Nicholas Greco was barely aware of the light wet flakes that drifted onto his face as he looked up at the windows of the second-floor art gallery on West Fifty-seventh Street, the one that bore the name of Richard Walker.

Greco had done his homework on Walker. Forty-six years old, twice divorced, the son of Elaine Walker Carrington, an indifferent reputation in the art world, and undoubtedly supported by the luck of having his mother marry into the Carrington family fortune. Walker had been at the formal dinner the night Susan Althorp vanished. According to the reports in the prosecutor's files, he had left for his apartment in Manhattan when the party ended.

Greco opened the door to the building, was checked by a security guard, and walked up the single flight of stairs to the gallery. He was immediately clicked inside by a smiling receptionist.

"Mr. Walker is expecting you," she said. "It will be just a few minutes since he's on a conference call at the moment. Why don't you look at our new exhibit? We're displaying a wonderful young artist the critics are raving about."

If ever I heard a canned speech, I'm listening to one now, Greco thought. Walker is probably doing the crossword puzzle in his office. The gallery, dreary to him with its stark white walls and dark gray carpeting, was devoid of visitors. He walked from painting to painting, pretending to study them, all scenes of urban blight. He was at the next to the last of the twenty or so paintings when a voice at his shoulder asked, "Doesn't this one particularly remind you of an Edward Hopper?"

Not even remotely, Greco thought, and with a grunt that could be taken as assent, he turned to face Richard Walker. He looks younger than forty-six—was Greco's first thought. Walker's eyes were his most remarkable feature—sapphire, and set far apart. His features were rugged. He was medium in height, with a boxer's solid body and thick arms. He would not have looked out of place in a gym, Greco decided. Walker's dark blue suit was obviously expensive but with his thick frame was not shown off to advantage.

When it was clear that Greco had no intention of discussing art, Walker suggested they go into his private office. On the way he kept up a running commentary on how many family fortunes were based on people having the ability to spot genius in an unknown painter. "Of course, you hear it in every field," he said as he went around to his desk and waved Greco to a chair opposite it. "My grandfather used to tell the story of how Max Hirsch, the legendary horse trainer, turned down the chance to buy the greatest racehorse in history, Man O' War, for one hundred dollars. Do you enjoy racing, Mr. Greco?"

"I'm afraid I don't have much time for hobbies," Greco said, his voice sounding regretful.

Walker smiled amiably. "Nor for small talk, either, I would gather. Very well. What can I do for you?"

"First I want to thank you for agreeing to let me drop in. As you may know, Susan Althorp's mother has hired me to investigate her daughter's disappearance."

"I'd guess that, at least in Englewood, everybody's heard about it," Walker replied.

"Do you spend much time in Englewood, Mr. Walker?"

"I don't know what 'much time' means. I live in Manhattan, on East Seventy-third Street. As you certainly know, my mother, Elaine Carrington, has a home on the Carrington estate, and I visit her there. She also comes into Manhattan frequently."

"You were at the estate the night Susan Althorp disappeared?"

"I was at the party with some two hundred other people. My mother had married the present Peter Carrington's father three years earlier. The real purpose of the party was that Carrington senior had turned seventy that year. He was very sensitive about the fact that my mother was so much younger, twenty-six years to be exact, so the party wasn't called a birthday celebration." Walker raised an eyebrow. "If you do your arithmetic, you'll see that old man Carrington specialized in young women. He was forty-nine when Peter was born. Peter's mother was much younger as well."

Greco nodded and looked around. Walker's office was not large, but it was tastefully furnished with a striped blue and red love seat, creamy-white walls, and a deep-blue carpet. He found the painting over the couch of old men gathered around a table playing cards more interesting than the scenes of squalor he'd seen in the gallery exhibit. A corner cabinet held several photos of Walker on the polo field, as well as a golf ball on an engraved silver tray. "A hole in one?" he asked, pointing to the ball.

"At Saint Andrews," Walker said, not attempting to conceal the pride in his voice.

Greco could see that the memory of that achievement had relaxed Walker, which was what he had hoped to achieve. Leaning back in his chair, he said,

"I'm trying to form a kind of overall picture of Susan Althorp. What were your impressions of her?"

"Let's start with the fact that I knew her only slightly. She was eighteen or nineteen. I was twenty-four, had a full-time job at Sotheby's, and lived in the city. Besides that, to be perfectly blunt, I was not particularly fond of my mother's husband, Peter Carrington IV, nor was he of me."

"Why did you clash?"

"We didn't exactly clash. He offered me a trainee job in a brokerage firm he owned, where, as he put it, I could eventually make real money and not live on a shoestring. He was contemptuous of me when I declined the offer."

"I see. But you did visit your mother frequently at his home?"

"Of course. That summer, twenty-two years ago, was very warm, and there were frequent pool parties. My mother loved to entertain. She would have their friends over regularly. Peter and Susan both attended Princeton, and their Princeton friends were around a lot. I was usually invited to bring a guest or two. It was very pleasant."

"Were Peter and Susan considered a couple?"

"They'd been dating quite a lot. From what I saw, I thought they were falling in love, or, at least, that he was falling in love with her."

"You mean it was one-sided?" Greco asked, his voice mild.

"I don't mean anything. She was very outgoing. Peter was always quiet. But whenever I stopped by on weekends it seemed as though she was on the estate, playing tennis or lounging by the pool."

"Did you stay at the Carrington home the night of the party?"

"No. I was scheduled to play in a golf foursome early the next morning, and left when the dinner ended. I didn't stay around for the dancing."

"Susan's mother is convinced that your stepbrother was responsible for Susan's death. Do you believe that?"

There was a hint of anger in Richard Walker's eyes when he looked directly at Greco. "No, I do not," he said crisply.

"What about Grace Carrington? You were at dinner at the estate the night she drowned. Actually the dinner was in your honor, wasn't it?"

"Peter traveled a great deal. Grace was the sort of outgoing woman who didn't like to be alone. She was always inviting people to dinner. When she realized my birthday was coming up, she decided that dinner that night would be a birthday celebration for me. There were just six of us there. Peter didn't arrive until nearly the end. His plane was delayed coming home from Australia."

"I understand that Grace drank a lot that evening."

"Grace always drank a lot. She was in rehab several times, but could never quite make it stick. Then, when she was finally able to sustain a pregnancy after several miscarriages, we were all worried about fetal alcohol syndrome."

"Did anyone try to stop her from drinking that evening?"

"She was great at faking it. People thought she was drinking club soda, but it was straight vodka. She was really bombed when Peter got home, and, of course, it drove him crazy to find her in that condition. But when he grabbed the drink out of her hand, poured it on the carpet, and had that outburst, it sort of shook her up. When he stormed upstairs, I remember she said, 'I guess the party's over.'"

"'The party's over' can mean the end of more than a party," Greco said.

"I suppose so. Grace looked very sad. My mother and I were the last to leave. I was staying at Mother's house that night. Grace said she was going to lie down on the couch for a while. I don't think she wanted to face Peter."

"You and your mother left together?"

"We walked to Mother's house. The next morning the housekeeper phoned, hysterical. She had found the body."

"Do you believe that Grace Carrington either fell into the pool accidentally or committed suicide?"

"I can only answer that question one way. Grace wanted that baby, and she knew Peter wanted it. Would she have deliberately taken her own life? No, unless she felt overwhelmed by her inability to stop drinking, and was panicked at the possibility that she had already damaged the fetus."

Nicholas Greco's manner became even friendlier as he casually asked, "Do you think Peter Carrington was angry enough to have helped his wife to end her life, perhaps after she passed out on the couch?"

This time, it was obvious to him that Richard Walker's angry reply was both phony and forced: "That's utterly ridiculous, Mr. Greco."

That's not what he believes, Greco thought as he got up to leave. But it's what he wants me to *think* he believes.

8

Peter Carrington and I were married in the Lady Chapel of St. Patrick's Cathedral where thirty years ago my mother and father exchanged their vows.

The irony for Maggie was that she had been the catalyst that brought us together.

The literacy reception at the estate was a complete success. The housekeeping couple, Jane and Gary Barr, had worked with me and the caterer to be sure that everything was perfect.

Elaine Walker Carrington and Peter's stepbrother, Richard, were very much present, oozing genteel charm as they greeted guests. Except for those beautiful eyes, I was startled at how unalike mother and son were physically. Somehow I had expected that Elaine Carrington's son would resemble Douglas Fairbanks Jr., but nothing could be further from the truth.

Vincent Slater was omnipresent but remained in the

background. With my usual need to figure everything out, I played guessing games with myself as to how he had entered Peter's life. The son of someone who worked for Peter's father? I wondered. After all, I'm the daughter of someone who worked for Peter's father. Or perhaps he was a college friend invited to join the family business? Nelson Rockefeller invited his roommate at Dartmouth, a scholarship student from the Midwest, to work for the family. That man ended up a multimillionaire.

When the brief program began, I introduced Peter. There was nothing in his demeanor to suggest the pressure he was under when he welcomed the guests and talked about the importance of our literacy program. "It's fine to give money to help," he said, "but it's equally important to have people—people like all of you—to volunteer a little time, on a one-to-one basis, in helping others learn to read. As you all probably know, I travel a lot, but I'd like to be a literacy volunteer in a different way. So let's make this an annual event at my home." Then, as the crowd applauded, he turned to me. "Is that all right with you, Kathryn?"

Was that the moment I fell in love with him, or was I already there? "That would be wonderful," I said, as my heart melted. Just that day there'd been another item in the business section of the *New York Times* that asked the question: "Is it time for Peter Carrington to go?"

Peter gave me a thumbs-up, and then, smiling at people and shaking hands with a few of them, he walked down the corridor toward his library. I noticed he didn't go into it, though. I thought he either escaped up the back staircase or even left the house completely.

I had been in and out of the house all day to oversee the caterer and the florist, and to make sure that the people who were rearranging furniture didn't break or scratch anything. The Barrs became my friends that day. At lunchtime, over a cup of tea and a quick sandwich in the kitchen, they made me see the Peter Carrington they knew: the twelve-year-old boy who was sent to Choate after his mother died, the twenty-year-old Princeton senior who was relentlessly questioned about Susan Althorp's death, the thirty-eight-year-old husband whose pregnant wife was found dead in a pool.

Thanks in no small part to the couple's help, everything went perfectly. I waited to be sure the last of the guests were on their way, the cleanup complete, and the furniture put back in place before I left. Though I kept hoping he would, Peter didn't reappear, and in my head I was already trying to frame a way to see him again soon. I didn't want to wait until it was time to plan a reception next year.

But then, inadvertently, and certainly unwillingly, Maggie brought us together. I had driven her to the reception, so of course she waited for me to drive her home. Then, as Gary Barr opened the front door for us, Maggie caught the tip of her shoe in the slightly elevated rim of the door frame and fell hard, almost bouncing off the marble floor of the entrance hall.

I screamed. Maggie is my mother and father and grandmother and friend and mentor, all in one. She is all I have. And she's eighty-three years old. As the years pass, I worry more and more, facing the inevitable fact that she is not immortal, even though I know that she will put up a fight before she goes gentle into that good night.

Then, from the floor, Maggie snapped, "Oh, for heaven's sake, Kay, be quiet. I didn't do any damage except maybe to my dignity." She raised herself on one elbow and began to struggle up, then she fainted.

The events of the next hour are a blur. The Barrs called an ambulance, and I guess they let Peter Carrington know what had happened because suddenly he was there, kneeling beside Maggie, his fingers feeling for the pulse in her throat, his voice reassuring. "Kathryn, her heart seems strong. I think her forehead took the impact. It's swelling."

He followed the ambulance to the hospital, and waited with me in the emergency room until I was reassured by the doctor that Maggie had only a mild concussion, though they wanted to keep her overnight. After she was settled in a room, Peter drove me home to Maggie's house. I guess I was trembling so much from both relief and shock that he had to take the key from my hand and open the door. Then he came in with me, found the light switch, and said, "You look as though you could use a drink. Does your grandmother keep any liquor in the house?"

That question made me start to laugh, a little hysterically, I think. "Maggie claims if everyone followed her regimen of a nightly hot toddy, Ambien would be out of business."

That was when I felt myself trying to blink back tears of relief. Peter handed me his handkerchief and said, "I can understand how you feel."

We both had a scotch. The next day he sent flowers to Maggie and called me to suggest we have dinner together. After that I saw him every day. I was in love and so was he. Maggie, though, was heartsick. She was still sure he was a murderer. Peter's stepmother suggested we wait, warning us that it was much too soon to be sure of ourselves. Gary and Jane Barr, however, were delighted for us. Vincent Slater brought up the subject of a prenuptial agreement and was obviously relieved when I told him that I would sign one. Peter became furious, and Slater stalked out. I told Peter that I had read about agreements where, if the marriage was brief, the settlement would be very limited. I said that was fine with me. I also told him that I wasn't worried about it, because I knew that we would always be together and that we would have a family.

Later, of course, Peter and Slater made peace, and Peter's lawyer drew up a generous agreement. Peter insisted that I have a lawyer of my own review it so that I could be sure that it was fair. This was done, and, a few days later, I signed the document.

The following day, we went to New York and quietly made our wedding arrangements. On January 8th, we were married in the Lady Chapel of St. Patrick's Cathedral, where we solemnly vowed to love, honor, and cherish each other until death do us part.

9

Prosecutor Barbara Krause studied the picture the paparazzi had snapped of Peter Carrington and his new wife, Kay, walking on a beach in the Dominican Republic. Happy is the bride the sun shines on today, she thought sarcastically as she pushed aside the newspaper.

Now fifty-two years old, Barbara had graduated from law school and began her career as a clerk for a Bergen County criminal judge; after one year she moved across the courthouse to become an assistant prosecutor. For the next twenty-seven years, she worked her way up in that office, becoming trial chief, first assistant, and finally, upon the retirement of her predecessor three years ago, was named prosecutor. It was a world she loved, an enthusiasm she shared with her husband, a civil court judge in nearby Essex County.

Susan Althorp had disappeared when Barbara had only been in the office a few years. Because of the prominence of both the Althorp and the Carrington families, the case had been investigated from every possible angle. The inability to solve it or even to be able to indict the number one suspect, Peter Carrington, had been a bone in the throat to Barbara's predecessors, as it was to her.

From time to time, over the years, she had taken out the Susan Althorp file and reviewed it, trying to take a fresh look, circling some testimony, putting a question mark after certain statements. Unfortunately, none of it had ever led anywhere. Now, as she sat at her desk, some of Peter Carrington's statements ran through her mind.

He claimed that he had dropped Susan at her door that night: "She didn't wait for me to open the car door. She ran up the steps to the porch, turned the handle, waved to me, and went inside."

"That was the last time you saw her?"

"Yes."

"What did you do then?"

"I went home. There were still some people dancing on the terrace. I'd been playing tennis all afternoon and was tired. I parked my car in the garage and went into the house through the side door, straight upstairs to my room and to bed. I fell asleep instantly."

See no evil, hear no evil, Barbara thought. Interestingly enough, he used the same story the night his wife drowned in the pool.

She glanced at her watch. It was time to go. She had been sitting in on a homicide trial, just observing. Closing arguments were about to begin. In this case, the identity of the killer was not in question; rather it was a matter of whether the jury would find the defendant guilty of murder or of manslaughter. A domestic quarrel had turned violent, and now the father of three young children would probably spend at least the next twenty-five to thirty years in prison for killing their mother.

Let him! Because of him, these kids have nothing, Barbara thought as she stood up to head back to the courtroom. He should have taken the twenty-year plea we offered him. Nearly six feet tall, and always fighting a weight problem, she knew her nickname around the courthouse was "the linebacker." She reached for a final sip of coffee from the cup on her desk.

As she did, the newspaper picture of Peter Carrington and his new wife again came into her line of vision. "You've had twenty-two years of freedom since Susan Althorp disappeared, Mr. Carrington," she said aloud. "If I ever get a chance to get my hands on you, I can promise you one thing: There won't be any plea to manslaughter. I'll try you for murder and I'll get a conviction."

10

The two weeks we spent on our honeymoon were idyllic. We had married so quickly that we were finding out new things about each other every day, little things, like me always wanting a midmorning cup of coffee, or the fact that he loves truffles and I hate them. I hadn't realized how basically lonely I had been until Peter was there with me all the time. Sometimes I would wake up at night and listen to his even breathing, and think how incredible it was that I was now his wife.

I had fallen so intensely in love with him, and Peter seemed to feel exactly the same way about me. When we'd started to see each other daily, he had asked, "Are you sure you can be interested in a man who is a 'person of interest' in two deaths?"

My answer was that long before I knew him, I absolutely believed that he was a victim of circumstances, and I knew how horrible that must have been, and, of course, continued to be for him.

"It is," he said, "but let's not talk about it. Kay, you give me so much joy that I can really believe there is a future, a time when the answer to Susan's disappearance will be solved and people will know with certainty that I had nothing to do with it." And so, during our courtship, we never talked about either Susan Althorp or Peter's first wife, Grace. He did talk lovingly about his mother—it was obvious they had been very close. "My father was constantly traveling on business. My mother had always accompanied him. But after I was born she stayed home with me," he reminisced.

I wondered if it was after he lost her that the look of pain had settled into his eyes.

On our honeymoon I was somewhat surprised that there were no calls to or from his office. Later I learned the reason.

The paparazzi hung around the gates of the villa he had rented, and, except for one brief walk on the public beach, we stayed on the grounds. I called to check on Maggie every day, and she grudgingly admitted that the stories about Peter had disappeared from the tabloid magazines. I began to hope that Nicholas Greco had run into a blank wall in his investigation of the Susan Althorp disappearance; a blank wall at least as far as Peter was concerned.

I found out soon enough that I was living on false hope.

Home: It seemed impossible to me that I would ever call the Carrington mansion home. As we were driven through the gates on the return from our honeymoon, I thought of the child I had been when I crept upstairs to the chapel, and the trepidation I had felt in late October when I came to ask Peter to allow me to hold a reception here.

I was uneasy when, on the flight back, Peter had become more and more quiet, but I thought I knew the reason. He would once again be in the glare of publicity, and with the demands of his position would not be able to avoid it. I had resigned from the library regretfully, because I loved my job. On the other hand, I had done some serious thinking about how best I could help Peter. I was going to suggest to him that he plan to do a lot of traveling for his company. There would be less interest in Greco's ongoing investigation if the prime target was not around to be followed all the time by the media. Of course I would travel with him.

"Does one still carry a bride over the threshold?" Peter asked as the car stopped at the front door.

I sensed immediately that he would be very uncomfortable if the answer was yes, and wondered if he had carried Grace over the threshold when they were married twelve years ago. "I'd rather walk in hand in hand," I said, and I knew my answer pleased him.

After our blissful two weeks in the Caribbean, that

first evening in the mansion was oddly uncomfortable. In a mistaken gesture of "welcome home," Elaine had ordered a gourmet dinner served by a caterer, relegating the Barrs to the kitchen. Instead of the small dining room that looked out over the terrace, she had ordered it served in the large formal one. Even though she had been wise enough to have us placed opposite each other in the center of the banquet-sized table, with the two waiters hovering around us the dinner felt stilted and awkward.

We were both glad when it was over and we could go upstairs. Peter's suite consisted of two very large bedrooms, each with its own bathroom, divided by a beautiful sitting room. Everything about the bedroom to the right of the parlor made it unmistakably a man's domain. It had two massive hand-carved dressers, a handsome maroon leather couch and matching chairs by the fireplace, a king-sized bed with bookshelves over it, and a television screen that could be lowered from the ceiling at the push of a button. The walls were white, the coverlet had black and white squares, the carpet was charcoal gray. Several paintings depicting different scenes from fox hunting in the English countryside adorned the walls.

The bedroom on the other side of the parlor had always been occupied by the Carrington lady of the house. Peter's wife, Grace, had been the last one to use it. Before that, Elaine had slept there, and before that, Peter's mother, and all his maternal ancestors back to 1848. It was very feminine, with pale peach walls and peach and green draperies, headboard, and bedspread. A love seat and lady chairs near the fireplace made the room look cozy and welcoming. A truly beautiful painting of a garden scene was above the mantel of the fireplace. I knew that soon I would want to put my own stamp on the room because I like more vibrant colors, but it amused me to think that I could have tucked my little studio into it.

Peter had already warned me that he had frequent spells of insomnia, and that when that was happening he would slip over to the other room to read. Since I am sure I will sleep through Gabriel's horn when it finally sounds, I told him that wasn't necessary, but whatever made him more comfortable and more likely to sleep was fine with me.

That night we went to sleep in my room, I with sugarplums dancing in my head at the prospect of really beginning my life as Peter's wife. I don't know what woke me up during the night, but something did. Peter was gone. Even though I knew he was probably in his room reading, I suddenly felt a tremendous sense of anxiety. I slipped my feet into slippers, pulled on a robe, and padded through the sitting room. His door was closed. I opened it very quietly. It was dark, but there was enough early-morning light flickering around the window shades to see that the room was empty.

I don't know what made me do it, but I hurried over to the window and looked down. From there the pool was clearly visible. Of course, in February the pool was covered, but Peter was there, kneeling beside it, resting one hand on the edge, and slipping the other hand under the heavy vinyl covering into the water. His whole arm was moving back and forth as if he was either trying to push something into the pool or drag something out of it.

Why? What was he doing? I wondered. Then, as I watched, he stood up, turned, and came slowly back toward the house. A few minutes later he opened the door to the bedroom, went into the bathroom, turned on the light, dried his arm and hand on a towel, and rolled down the sleeve of his pajama top. He then turned out the light, walked back into the bedroom, and stood facing me. It was obvious he was not aware of my presence, and I realized what was happening. Peter was walking in his sleep. A girl in our dormitory in college had been a sleepwalker, and we'd been warned never to wake her suddenly.

As Peter made his way through the sitting room, I followed him silently. He got back into bed in my room. I slipped off my robe, kicked off my slippers, and gently got in beside him. A few minutes later, his arm went around me and his drowsy voice murmured, "Kay."

"I'm here, dear," I said.

I could feel his body relax, and soon his even breathing told me that he was asleep. But for the rest of the night I lay awake. Peter was a sleepwalker, I now realized, but how often did that happen? And far more important, why, in that altered state, did he go through the motions of trying to push something into the pool or pull something from it?

Something—or *someone*?

11

Nicholas Greco drove through Cresskill, a town near Englewood, watching for street signs and reminding himself once again that it was time to get a navigation system for his car. Frances always tells me that for someone who is so good at solving crimes, I can't make it to the grocery store without getting lost, he thought. She's right.

Nice town, he thought as, following the directions he had taken from MapQuest, he turned right on County Road. He was on his way to interview Vincent Slater, the man who had been called "indispensable" by Peter Carrington's father.

Greco had done exhaustive research on Slater before he'd requested the meeting, but there hadn't been much of interest to learn from it. Slater was now fifty-four years old, a bachelor, still living in the childhood home he had bought from his parents when they moved to Florida. He had commuted to a local college. His first and only job was with Carrington Enterprises. Within a couple years of his employment he had gained the attention of Peter's father and had become a kind of aide-de-camp to him. After Peter's mother died, Slater became a combination of trusted employee and surrogate parent for Peter. A dozen years older than Peter, during the Carrington heir's adolescent years Slater would drive him to Choate, his prep school in Connecticut, and visit him there regularly, stay in the mansion with him on vacations, and take him skiing and sailing during holidays.

Slater's background was interesting, but it was the fact that he had been a guest at the party the night Susan Althorp disappeared that was of primary interest to Greco. He had grudgingly consented to the interview but insisted that it be conducted at his home. He doesn't want any part of me at the mansion, Greco thought. He should know that I've already been there, at least to the gatehouse to talk to the Barrs.

He watched the house numbers and stopped in front of Slater's house, which turned out to be a split-level, the kind so popular in the fifties. When he rang the bell, Slater answered the door instantly. I wonder if he was standing behind it, Greco thought. And without having laid eyes on him before, why do I think he's that kind of guy? "Very good of you to see me, Mr. Slater," he said mildly, reaching out his hand.

Slater ignored it. "Come in," he said curtly.

I could make my way around here blindfolded, Greco thought. Kitchen straight ahead at the end of the foyer. Living room to the right of the entrance, opening into a small dining room. Three bedrooms upstairs. The family room a half level below the kitchen. Greco knew because he had been brought up in the mirror image of this house in Hempstead, Long Island.

It was immediately obvious that Slater's taste ran to the minimal. The beige walls were dull above the brown carpet. Greco followed Slater into the sparsely furnished living room. A modernistic couch and chairs were arranged in a seating group around a wide glass coffee table with steel legs.

Nothing warm and fuzzy about this place or this guy, Greco thought as he sat down in the chair Slater had indicated.

It was too low for his taste. A subtle way of putting me at a disadvantage, he thought.

Before he could make his usual remarks thanking Slater for agreeing to meet him, Slater said, "Mr. Greco, I know why you are here. You are investigating the disappearance of Susan Althorp at the request of her mother. That is praiseworthy, except for one serious problem—your mandate is to somehow prove that Peter Carrington is criminally responsible for Susan's disappearance."

"My mandate is to find out what happened to Susan, and if possible to give her mother peace," Greco said. "I recognize that because he was the last known person to see her before her disappearance, Peter Carrington has lived under a cloud of suspicion for twenty-two years. As his friend and assistant, I would think you would be interested in dispelling that cloud if it were at all possible to do so."

"That obviously goes without saying."

"Then help me. What is your recollection of the events of that evening?"

"I am certain that by now you know exactly what testimony I gave when the investigation was opened initially. I was a guest at the dinner. It was a very pleasant affair. Susan arrived with her parents."

"She arrived with them, but Peter drove her home."

"Yes."

"What time did you leave the party?"

"As you surely know, I stayed over that night. For years I have had my own room in the mansion. Ninety-nine percent of the time I come home to this house, but that night I decided to stay over, as did a number of other guests. Elaine, Peter's stepmother, was planning a ten A.M. brunch, and it was easier to stay there than to drive back and forth."

"When did you retire to your room?"

"When Peter left to drive Susan home."

"How would you describe your relationship with the Carrington family?"

"Exactly as you must have gathered from your various interviews. I never forget the fact that I am their employee, but I am also, I hope, a trusted friend."

"So trusted that you would do anything to help them, especially Peter, who is almost a surrogate son or brother to you?"

"I have never had to worry about doing anything for Peter that would not stand the light of day, Mr. Greco. Now, if you have no more questions, I need to get to Englewood now."

"Just one. You were also present the night Grace Carrington died, weren't you?"

"The night Grace died in an accident, you mean. Yes. Peter had been away in Australia for several weeks. He was expected home in time for dinner, and his wife, Grace, had asked Elaine, her son, Richard, a few local friends, and myself for dinner. Because Richard's birthday was coming up, Grace called it a birthday party for him."

"When Peter came in, he was quite angry at what he saw?"

"Mr. Greco, there is nothing more to add to what you obviously already know about that situation. Peter was understandably upset to see that Grace had been drinking heavily."

"He was very angry."

"I would say upset rather than angry."

"Did you stay over at the mansion that night?"

"No. It was about eleven o'clock when Peter arrived. We were all about to leave anyhow. Peter went upstairs. Elaine and Richard stayed with Grace."

"Were there servants in the house?"

"Jane and Gary Barr had been hired after Peter's mother died. Elaine let them go when she married Peter's father. After his father's death, however, Elaine moved to the smaller house on the grounds, and Peter rehired the Barrs. They've been there ever since."

"But if they had been fired, why were they at the mansion the night Susan disappeared? Peter's father was still alive. In fact, the dinner was really to celebrate his seventieth birthday."

"Elaine Walker Carrington has no hesitation in using people to suit her convenience. Even though she had let the Barrs go because she wanted to hire a fancy chef and butler and a couple of maids, she asked them to help with the serving that evening, and then work the brunch the next morning. They were ten times more efficient than the new staff, and I'm sure she paid them very well."

"Then they were rehired and I presume they served the dinner the night of Grace Carrington's death. Would they still have been up when Peter returned?"

"Both Peter and Grace were very considerate. After coffee had been served, and the cups collected, the Barrs retired to their own place. They had moved back to the former gatehouse on the estate."

"Mr. Slater, I spoke with Gary and Jane Barr last week. We went over their recollection of the dinner party and the brunch the next day. I discussed with Gary something I had noticed in the files. Twenty-two years ago he told investigators that the morning of the brunch, he overheard Peter Carrington tell you that Susan had left her handbag in his car the night before and he asked you to deliver it to her because there might be something she needed in it. He remembered making that statement and having heard that exchange between you and Peter."

"He may remember it, but if you continued to look in the notes, you'd know that at that time I said his recollection was only partially true," Vincent Slater said evenly. "Peter did not tell me Susan had left her purse in the car. He said that she *might* have left her purse there. It wasn't in the car, so obviously he was mistaken. In any case, I don't get your point."

"It's only a comment. Mrs. Althorp is sure she heard Susan close the door of her room that night. Obviously she didn't intend to stay there long. But by then if she had realized her purse was in Peter's car, and she was planning to meet him, she wouldn't be concerned.

Otherwise, if she were meeting someone else, wouldn't it seem natural for her to select another purse, get a compact and handkerchief, the usual things women carry?"

"You're wasting my time, Mr. Greco. You're not seriously suggesting that Susan's mother knew exactly how many handkerchiefs, or, for that matter, how many evening purses were in her daughter's room?"

Nicholas Greco got up. "Thank you for your time, Mr. Slater. I'm afraid there is a development you need to know about. Mrs. Althorp has been interviewed by *Celeb* magazine; the issue will be on the stands tomorrow. In it, Mrs. Althorp specifically accuses Peter Carrington of the murder of her daughter, Susan."

He watched as Vincent Slater's complexion took on a sickly yellow tint.

"That's libel," Slater snapped. "Slander and out-and-out libel."

"Exactly. And the normal reaction of an innocent man like Peter Carrington will be to instruct his lawyers to sue Gladys Althorp. This would be followed by the usual process of interrogatories and depositions until there was either a retraction, settlement, or public trial. In your opinion, will Peter Carrington demand an immediate retraction from Gladys Althorp and, if it is not received, institute a suit against her to clear his name?"

Slater's eyes had turned icy, but not before Greco caught a sudden look of fear in them. "You were about to leave, Mr. Greco," he said.

Neither man exchanged another word as Nicholas Greco left the house. Greco walked down the path, got into his car, and started it. Who is Slater on the phone with now? he wondered as he drove down the street. Carrington? The lawyers? The new Mrs. Carrington?

An image of Kay's heated defense of Peter Carrington when he met her in her grandmother's home came into his mind. Kay, you should have listened to your grandmother, he thought.

12

In the morning, Peter showed no sign of being aware that he had been sleepwalking during the night. I wasn't sure whether or not to bring it up to him. What could I say? That it looked as if he was trying to push something or someone into the pool or pull something or someone from it?

I thought I had the explanation. He was having a nightmare about Grace drowning in the pool. He was trying to rescue her. It made sense, but talking to him about it seemed pointless. He wouldn't remember any of it.

We got up at seven. The Barrs would come in at eight to prepare breakfast, but I squeezed juice and made coffee because we decided to take a quick jog through the grounds of the estate. Oddly enough, up until now we had spoken very little about my father's role as landscaper here. I had told Peter how hard my mother's death must have been on Daddy, and how his suicide had devastated me. I did not, of course, mention the appalling things Nicholas Greco had said. I was infuriated by his suggestion that Daddy might have chosen to disappear because he had something to do with Susan Althorp's disappearance.

As we jogged, Peter began to talk about my father. "My mother never changed the landscaping after my grandmother died," he said. "Then, in fairness to Elaine, when she married my father, she said the whole place looked as if it had been designed as a cemetery. She said it had everything but a sign reading 'rest in peace.' Your father did a beautiful job in creating the gardens that are here now."

"Elaine fired him because of his drinking," I said, trying to sound matter-of-fact.

"That's her story," Peter said mildly. "Elaine always fooled around, even when my father was alive. She made a play for your dad and he brushed her off. *That*'s really why she fired him."

I stopped so suddenly that he was six strides ahead of me before he slowed and came back. "I'm sorry, Kay. You were a child. How could you possibly have known?"

It had been Maggie, of course, who told me that it was Daddy's drinking that cost him the job. She blamed everything that happened on Daddy's drinking: the loss of the job here, even his suicide. I realized I was suddenly furious at her. My father had been too much of a gentleman to give her the real reason he'd been fired, and then, being a know-it-all, she'd decided she knew the reason. Not fair, Maggie, I thought, not fair.

"Kay, I didn't mean to upset you." Peter's hand was in mine and our fingers intertwined.

I looked up at him. Peter's aristocratic face was strengthened by his firm jaw, but always it was his eyes that I saw when I looked at him. Now they were concerned, troubled that he had inadvertently hurt me.

"No, you didn't upset me, not at all. In fact, you've cleared up something important. All these years I've had a mental image of my father stumbling around this place in a drunken stupor, and I've been embarrassed for him. Now I can erase it forever."

Peter could tell that I didn't want to discuss the subject any further.

"Okay, then," he said. "Shall we pick up the pace?"

By running down the stone walks that wind through the gardens, and then reversing a couple of times, we got in a mile, then decided to do a final loop to the end of the west path that ended at the street. High hedges had been planted there. Peter explained that the state had installed a gas line near the curb many years ago, and when my father had prepared the landscaping design, he had suggested moving the fences fifty feet back. Then, if repairs were ever needed, it wouldn't damage any of the plantings.

When we reached the hedges we could hear voices and the sound of machinery beyond the fence. By peeking through we could make out that a Public Service crew was creating a detour on the road and unloading equipment out of trucks. "I guess this is exactly what my father anticipated," I said.

Peter said, "I guess so," then turned and began to run again. "Race you to the house?" he called over his shoulder.

"Not fair," I yelled, as he took off. A few minutes later, out of breath but feeling good about ourselves—at least so I thought—we went back into the house.

The Barrs were in the kitchen, and I could smell corn muffins baking. For someone whose normal breakfast is black coffee and half a toasted bagel minus either butter or cream cheese, I realized that firm discipline would be in order if I was going to stay in shape. But I wouldn't worry about it today, our first breakfast at home.

There's one thing about a mansion: You do get your choice of locations. The breakfast room is like a cozy indoor garden, with painted green and white lattice walls, a round glass top table, cushioned wicker chairs, and a breakfront filled with lovely green and white china. Glancing at the china made me realize again that there were so many treasures in this house, collected since the early nineteenth century. I had a fleeting thought of wondering who, if anyone, kept track of them.

I could tell that there was something troubling Jane Barr. Her warm greeting did not conceal the worry in her eyes. Something was wrong, but I did not want to ask her what it was in front of Peter. I know that he sensed it, too.

The *New York Times* was on the table next to his place. He started to pick it up, then pushed it aside. "Kay, I've been so used to reading the newspapers at breakfast that I forgot for a moment that now I have a very good reason to let them wait."

"You don't have to," I said. "You can have the first section. I'll take the Metro section."

It was after she had poured our second cup of coffee that Jane Barr came back into the breakfast room. This time she did not attempt to hide the concern she was feeling. She addressed Peter. "Mr. Carrington, I'm not one to be the bearer of bad news, but when I stopped at the supermarket this morning they were delivering copies of *Celeb* magazine. The cover story is about you. I know you'll be getting calls, so I wanted to warn you, but I also wanted you to have your breakfast in peace first."

I saw that she was holding the copy of the magazine, still folded in half, under her arm. She handed it to Peter.

He unfolded it, looked at the front page, then his eyes

closed as though he was turning away from a sight that was too painful to watch. I reached across the table and grabbed the tabloid. The banner-sized headline read, PETER CARRINGTON MURDERED MY DAUGHTER. There were two side-by-side pictures beneath it. One was a formal picture of Peter, the kind of stock photo newspapers use when they're running a story on an executive. He was unsmiling, which didn't surprise me. My innately shy Peter is not the kind of man who smiles for a camera. Nevertheless, in this particular unfortunate shot, he did look cold, even haughty and disdainful.

Susan Althorp's picture was next to his, a radiant Susan in her debutante gown, her long blond hair spilling over her shoulders, her eyes sparkling, her beautiful young face joyous. Not daring to look at Peter, I turned the page. The double spread inside pages were just as bad. DYING MOTHER DEMANDS JUSTICE. There was a photo of an emaciated, grief-stricken Gladys Althorp, surrounded by pictures of her daughter at every stage of Susan's brief life.

I know enough about the law to understand that if Peter did not demand a retraction and get it, his only alternative would be to sue Gladys Althorp. I looked at him and now could not read his expression. But I was sure that the last thing he wanted was to hear useless cries of outrage from me. "What are you going to do?" I asked.

Jane Barr vanished into the kitchen.

Peter looked as if he were in pain, as if he'd been physically attacked. His eyes glistened and his voice was agonized when he said, "Kay, for twenty-two years I have answered every question they ever asked about Susan's disappearance. Only hours after they realized she was missing, the prosecutor's office descended upon us, questioning me. Twenty-four hours later, even before they asked, my father gave permission to have bloodhounds sniff the grounds. He allowed a search of the house. They impounded my car. They couldn't come up with one single iota of evidence that suggested I knew what happened to Susan after I dropped her off that night. Have you any idea what a nightmare it would be if I demand a retraction from Susan's mother, don't get it, and institute a suit? I'll tell you what will happen. It will be a three-ring circus for the media and that poor woman will be dead long before it even gets near a court date."

He stood up. He was shaking and fighting back tears. I rushed around the table and put my arms around him. The only way I could possibly help was to tell him how much I loved him.

I think my words gave him some comfort, so that at least he didn't feel totally alone. But then, in a voice that was sad, even a little remote, he said, "I've done you no favor by marrying you, Kay. You don't need this mess."

"Neither do you," I said. "Peter, I think that, horrible as it is, you've got to demand a retraction from Mrs. Althorp, and if necessary file suit against her for libel and slander. I'm sorry for her, but she's done it to herself."

"I don't know," he said. "I just don't know."

Vincent Slater came in as Peter was showering. I knew they were going to Peter's office together that morning. "You've got to convince Peter that he must demand a retraction," I told him.

"That's a subject we'll take up with our lawyers, Kay," he said, his tone dismissive.

We looked at each other. From the first minute I met him, when I came here begging to have the reception in the mansion, I had sensed Slater's animosity toward me. But I knew I had to be careful. He was an important part of Peter's life.

"Peter has been given the chance to clear his name, to show that there isn't a shred of evidence to tie him to Susan's disappearance," I told Vincent. "If he doesn't demand a retraction, he might as well hang a sign around his neck saying, 'I did it. I'm guilty.'"

He did not answer. Then Peter came downstairs, kissed me good-bye, and they were gone.

That afternoon, as they were digging to lay new underground cables, the Public Service crew unearthed the skeleton of a woman, tightly wrapped in plastic bags, buried in the unfenced area at the edge of the Carrington estate. Traces of what appeared to be blood were visible on the front of her decaying white chiffon gown.

Gary Barr was the one who rushed in to tell me what was happening. On his way back from a shopping trip, he had passed the excavation site and was there when the first shout came from the workman whose equipment uncovered the body. Gary told me that he had parked and watched as police cars began to arrive on the scene, sirens blaring.

From the security cameras outside the mansion, I could see a crowd gathering. I don't think that for a minute I doubted that the body would be identified as that of Susan Althorp.

The ringing of the front door reminded me of the pealing of the church bells at the memorial Mass for my father. I can still remember the mournful sound as, my hand in Maggie's, we left the church and stood with friends on the steps of St. Cecilia's. I remember Maggie saying something like, "When and if they find Jonathan's remains, there will be a proper burial, of course." But it had never happened.

As a flustered Jane Barr rushed in to inform us that detectives were here to speak to Mr. Carrington, I had the incongruous thought that soon there would be a proper burial for Susan Althorp.

13

We know he did it, but do we have enough to indict him?" Barbara Krause threw the question out to Assistant Prosecutor Tom Moran, the head of her homicide squad. Six days had passed since the remains of Susan Althorp had been found on the unfenced grounds of the Carrington estate. An autopsy had been performed and positive identification had been established. The cause of death was strangulation.

Moran, a balding and somewhat overweight twenty-five-year veteran of the prosecutor's office, shared his boss's frustration. Since the body had been discovered, the wealth and power of the Carrington family had become evident. Carrington had lined up a team of nationally known criminal defense attorneys, and they were already at work preparing to defend a possible indictment. The cold hard facts were that the Bergen County prosecutor did have enough evidence to establish probable cause to file a murder complaint against

Carrington, and a grand jury would almost certainly indict him. But the odds were that a trial jury, with the burden of proof being beyond a reasonable doubt, would either acquit him or end up a hung jury.

Nicholas Greco was expected at the prosecutor's office momentarily. He had called and requested an appointment with Barbara Krause, and she had invited Moran to sit in on it.

"He says he may have come across something useful," Krause told Moran. "Let's hope so. I'm not crazy about outsiders involved in our cases, but in this instance I'll be happy to give him any credit he wants if he helps us convict Carrington."

She and Moran had spent the morning discussing the strengths and weaknesses of the case, and found nothing new. The fact that Carrington had driven Susan home and had been the last person known to see her was diminished by the fact that both her mother and father heard her come into the house, and that she had called out "good night" to them. When foul play was suspected, Carrington, then twenty years old, had answered all of the questions their office had thrown at him. When he realized that his son was a suspect, Carrington's father had allowed, even demanded, a thorough search of the mansion, the grounds, and Peter's car. The search had yielded nothing.

By the end of the first day that Susan had not

contacted her family, Carrington's summer tuxedo and shoes had been tested for any possible evidence, with negative results. The formal shirt he had been wearing could not be found. He claimed he had put it in the hamper as usual and the new maid had sworn that she had given it to the dry cleaner's pickup service the next morning. The cleaner claimed to have received only one dress shirt, the one belonging to Carrington's father, but that lead had gone nowhere. Investigation showed that the particular cleaner had a long history of mishandling clothing and mixing up orders.

"In fact, the delivery they made when they supposedly picked up the shirt had a neighbor's jacket in it," Krause said, exasperation evident in her voice. "That shirt Carrington was wearing is the piece of evidence we've always needed. Dollars to donuts it had blood on it."

The buzzer on Krause's intercom sounded. Nicholas Greco had arrived.

Greco had met Tom Moran when he initially reviewed the files of the Althorp case. Now he wasted no time in getting to the reason for his visit. "You can imagine how Mrs. Althorp is feeling," he said. "She told me that at least she knows that before too long she and Susan will be lying side by side in the cemetery. But of course the discovery of the body on Carrington property has reinforced her need to see Peter Carrington brought to justice."

"Exactly our reaction," Krause said bitterly.

"As you know, I have been interviewing people close to the Carringtons, including some of the staff. Sometimes memories can be jogged long after the excitement of the initial investigation has taken place. I saw in your files that at the time of the disappearance, you questioned Gary and Jane Barr, the former and present Carrington housekeepers."

"Of course we did." Barbara Krause leaned forward slightly, an indication that she sensed she was about to hear something of interest.

"It's noted in your files that Barr mentioned that the morning of the brunch he overheard Carrington tell Vincent Slater that Susan had left her pocketbook in his car, and he asked Slater to run it over to her home in case she needed anything from it. It seemed to me to be a very unusual request, since Susan was expected at the brunch, and her mother remembers that she was carrying a very small evening bag at the dinner. Slater reported that he looked in the car; the purse was not there. When I pressed Barr, he told me he recalled that when Carrington got that response from Slater, he said, 'That's impossible. It *has* to be there.'"

"The purse was found with Susan's body," Barbara Krause said. "Are you suggesting that Carrington returned it to her after he supposedly went to bed, then forgot that he had done so? That doesn't make sense."

"Was there anything found in the purse that might have been significant?"

"The material was rotted through. A comb, a handkerchief, lip gloss, a compact." Barbara Krause's eyes narrowed. "Do you believe this sudden spurt of precise memory from Gary Barr?"

Greco shrugged. "I do, because I spoke to Slater. He verified the conversation, although with different emphasis. He insists that Carrington told him that Susan *may* have forgotten her purse. I might add two personal observations: The question upset Slater, and Barr seemed very nervous to me. Don't forget, I talked to Barr *before* the body was found. I know that he and his wife helped out at parties at the Althorp home from time to time. So he would have been in contact with Susan there as well as at the Carrington estate."

"Jane Barr swears that after the dinner party she and Gary went directly to their condominium, which was not on the grounds of the estate," Tom Moran told Greco.

"Barr is hiding something," Greco said flatly. "And, I'll bet you anything you want to wager that whether or not Susan Althorp had her purse with her when she got out of Peter Carrington's car is significant, and may have a lot to do with solving this case."

"I'm even more interested in the missing dress shirt Carrington was wearing the night of the dinner party," Barbara Krause said.

"That was the other thing I wanted to discuss. I have a stringer in the Philippines. He managed to track down Maria Valdez, the maid who gave that statement about the shirt."

"You know where she is!" Krause exclaimed. "About one month after our initial investigation, she quit the job, went back to the Philippines, and got married. We know that much. She had promised to keep us informed of any address change, but then we lost track of her. The most we could find out is that she had gotten a divorce and disappeared."

"Maria Valdez is remarried and has three children. She lives in Lancaster, Pennsylvania. I saw her yesterday. I would suggest that someone authorized to make a deal with her accompany me back to Lancaster tomorrow. By that I mean a guarantee in writing that she would never be prosecuted for lying when she was questioned years ago."

"She was lying about the shirt!" Krause and Moran shouted at the same time.

Greco smiled. "Let's say that as a mature woman she can no longer live with the knowledge that her statement twenty-two years ago has kept a murderer from being punished."

14

The funeral for Susan Althorp was front-page news around the country. The picture of the flower-covered casket, followed into St. Cecilia's by her grieving parents, must have sold tons of newspapers and improved the ratings of television stations around the country. Maggie went to the service along with a group of her friends. An alert Channel 2 reporter spotted her and rushed to get an interview.

"Your granddaughter recently married Peter Carrington. Do you believe in his innocence and stand by him now that the body was discovered on his property?"

Maggie's honest answer was fodder for the press. She looked straight into the camera as she said, "I stand by my granddaughter."

"I'm sorry," I told Peter when I heard about it.

"Don't be," he said. "I always valued honesty. Besides, if she hadn't fallen at that reception, you wouldn't be sitting here with me now." He smiled that quizzical smile of his, one with warmth but no mirth in it. "Oh, Kay, for heaven's sake, don't worry. Your grandmother made it clear from the start that she wanted no part of me and didn't want me in your life, either. Maybe she was right. Anyhow, we're doing our best to prove she was wrong, aren't we?"

We'd had dinner and gone upstairs to the parlor between the bedrooms. The suite had become more and more of a retreat for us. With the media constantly camped at the gates, and grim-faced lawyers coming and going, I felt as if we were in a war zone. To go out without being followed by the press was impossible.

There had been a debate this past week between Peter and Vincent Slater and the lawyers as to whether or not Peter should issue some kind of statement expressing sympathy to Susan's family. "No matter what is put out in my name, it's going to be misunderstood," Peter had said. In the end, his brief statement expressing profound sorrow was scorned and torn apart by both Gladys Althorp and the media.

I had talked to Maggie, but hadn't seen her since we'd come home from our honeymoon. I was both angry at her and worried about her. Before we were married, she hadn't budged an inch in her opinion that Peter had killed both Susan and his wife; now she was practically announcing that belief on television.

But there was something else bothering me. The

poison that Nicholas Greco had injected into my consciousness by suggesting that my father might have had something to do with Susan's death had been festering inside me. Then Peter's revelation the morning we jogged through the grounds had only made it worse. My father hadn't been fired because he was drinking. He had been let go because he hadn't responded to Elaine Walker Carrington's advances. And that begged the question: What had driven him to suicide?

I knew I had to find a way to sneak out and visit Maggie without being hounded by the press. I had to talk to her. I knew with all my heart and soul that Peter was not capable of hurting anyone—it was the kind of primal knowledge that is part of our being. But I also knew with equal certainty that my father would never have vanished willingly, and I was more convinced than ever that he had not committed suicide.

It was incredible to me that Peter and I had known such an idyllic time for two weeks, and now, married only three weeks, had been thrown headlong into this nightmare.

We had been watching the ten o'clock news, and I was about to switch off the television when for some reason I decided to check the headline on the eleven o'clock broadcast.

The anchor began, "A source inside the Bergen County prosecutor's office tells us that Maria Valdez

Cruz, a former maid at the Carrington mansion, has admitted she lied when she stated that she gave the cleaner a formal shirt Peter Carrington was wearing the night he escorted Susan Althorp home twenty-two years ago, a shirt that prosecutors at the time thought was a key to the case."

"She's lying," Peter said flatly, "but she's just sealed my fate. Kay, there isn't a chance in hell that I won't be indicted now."

15

At age thirty-eight, Conner Banks was the youngest lawyer in the Carrington dream team of top defense attorneys, but no one, not even his more celebrated—and publicized—peers, could deny his brilliance in criminal court. The son, grandson, and nephew of wealthy corporate lawyers, he had made it clear during his undergraduate years at Yale, to his relatives' collective horror, that he intended to be a criminal defense attorney. When he graduated from Harvard Law School, he clerked for a criminal court judge in Manhattan, then was hired by Walter Markinson, a renowned defense attorney who had defended all types of accused and was especially famous for keeping high-profile celebrities out of prison.

One of Banks's earliest court cases for the Markinson firm had required him to convince a jury that the exotic wife of a billionaire had been mentally ill when she shot her husband's longtime girlfriend. The verdict of not guilty by reason of insanity had been handed down after less than two hours of deliberation, a near-record for any jury deciding a murder case with that defense.

That case had made the reputation of Conner Banks, and in the next ten years that reputation had continued to grow. With his genial manner, large frame, and Celtic good looks, he had become something of a celebrity in his own right, known for his quick wit and for the beautiful women he escorted to high-profile events.

When Gladys Althorp directly accused Peter Carrington of murdering her daughter, Vincent Slater had called Walter Markinson and asked him to assemble a team of top lawyers to weigh the strategy of suing Mrs. Althorp, and then to handle the case if we decided to do it.

Peter Carrington had decided that he wanted the lawyers to hold their meetings in his home rather than in Manhattan, so that he could be present without having to run the press gauntlet outside his home. Now, a week later, Conner Banks had become a regular visitor to the Carrington estate.

The first time they were driven through the gates and they saw the mansion, Conner's senior partner had remarked disdainfully, "Who in the name of God would want to cope with anything that big?"

A passionate student of history, Banks replied, "As a matter of fact, I would. It's magnificent."

When the lawyers reached the formal dining room where the conferences were to be held, Slater was already there. Coffee, tea, bottles of water, and small pastries were laid out on the sideboard. Pads and pens were in place on the table. The other two defense attorneys, Saul Abramson from Chicago and Arthur Robbins from Boston, both in their early sixties and with formidable track records in criminal cases, arrived minutes after Conner Banks and Markinson.

Then Peter Carrington entered the room. To Banks's surprise, he was accompanied by his wife.

Banks was not given to trusting first impressions, but it was impossible not to recognize that Peter Carrington had an aura about him. Unlike his defense team and Slater, all dressed in typically conservative suits, he was wearing an open-necked shirt and a cardigan. Introduced to the lawyers, he immediately said, "Forget 'Mr. Carrington.' It's Peter. My wife is Kay. I have a feeling we're going to be meeting with each other for a long time, so let's dispense with the formalities."

Conner Banks hadn't known what to expect of Carrington's bride. He had already somewhat prejudged her—the librarian who had married a billionaire after a whirlwind romance—as just another very lucky fortune hunter.

He saw immediately that Kay Lansing Carrington did not fit that profile at all. Like her husband, she was dressed casually in a sweater and slacks. But the crimson shade of her high-necked sweater framed a face dominated by eyes such a dark shade of blue that they seemed almost as black as the long hair that was gathered at the nape of her neck and fell loosely past her shoulders.

During that first meeting and the ones that followed, she always sat to the right of Peter, who was at the head of the table. Slater's place was the chair to the left of Peter. By sitting next to Slater, Conner Banks was able to witness the byplay between Peter Carrington and his wife. Their hands often touched tenderly, and the expression of affection in their eyes when they looked at each other made him wonder if it was really all that great to be footloose and fancy-free, as he was.

Out of curiosity, Banks had done some research on the case even before he was hired to help consider the lawsuit. His interest had been piqued because he had met former ambassador Charles Althorp socially on a number of occasions and had noted that he never was accompanied by his wife.

In the first two conferences, which took place prior to Susan Althorp's body being found, the discussion focused on the need for Peter to file suit for libel and slander against Gladys Althorp. "She's never going to retract that accusation," Markinson said. "This is their way to force your hand. You'll have to answer interrogatories and give a deposition. They're hoping to trip you up when you're under oath. As of now, the prosecutor doesn't have enough evidence to indict you. Peter, you were dating Susan, casually. You were longtime family friends. You drove her home that night. Unfortunately, by returning home through the side door, you don't have anyone to support your statement that you went upstairs."

No one? Conner Banks asked himself. A guy, twenty years old, a little after midnight, a party in full swing, and you go to bed? Our client is innocent, he thought, sarcastically. Of course he is. It's my job to defend him. But that doesn't mean I have to believe him.

"I would say that what has helped to keep this case alive is the fact that your dress shirt was missing," Markinson stated. "The fact that the maid said she took it out of the hamper and gave it to the dry cleaner pickup service means that if they try to use the missing shirt as evidence of guilt, it will backfire on them. You don't have anything to lose by filing the suit, and, if it comes to trial, to let the public realize that this case is all about baseless accusations."

The third meeting took place the day after Susan Althorp's funeral, following also the stunning revelation that Maria Valdez, the maid who had claimed to have given Peter's dress shirt to the cleaner, was now retracting her story.

This time, when the Carringtons came into the dining room, the strain on both their faces was obvious. Without bothering to greet the lawyers, Peter said, "She's lying. I can't prove it, but I know she's lying. I put that shirt in the hamper. I have no idea why she's doing this to me."

"We'll try to prove she's lying, Peter," Markinson told him. "We'll look into everything she's been doing for the past twenty-two years. Maybe it will turn out that she's pulled some stuff that would make her a less than credible witness."

Conner Banks initially had strongly suspected that Peter Carrington was guilty of the death of Susan Althorp. Now, adding up the evidence, he was virtually certain. No one had seen Carrington return to the house the night of the party. Twenty years old, he goes straight to bed when there are still guests in the house dancing on the terrace. Nobody sees him park the car. Nobody sees him come in. Susan is missing the next morning, and so is the dress shirt Carrington was wearing. Now her body has been found on his property. The prosecutor is bound to arrest him. Peter, I'll do my best to help get you off, he thought as he looked at the man who was now holding hands with his wife, but I saw some of the footage of that funeral on the news last night. In a way, I wish that I was *prosecuting* this case. And I know that my colleagues feel the same way.

Kay was blinking back tears. She'll stand by her man, Banks thought. That's good. But if he's responsible for Susan Althorp's death, then maybe everyone is right to be suspicious about his first wife's drowning. Is he a psychopath, and, if so, will his new bride get in his way?

Why did he also feel that there was something odd—and perhaps oddly suspicious—about Carrington's rush to the altar with a woman he'd known for such a short time?

16

He's nervous, Pat Jennings decided, as she looked at her boss, Richard Walker. I'll bet anything he's been playing the horses again. For all the money he makes on this place—or *doesn't* make on this place—he might just as well try his luck on the ponies.

Pat had been working six months as receptionist and secretary at the Walker Art Gallery. When she took the job, it seemed like the perfect part-time situation for a woman with two kids in elementary school. Her hours were from nine until three, with the understanding that if a cocktail party was given for a new exhibit, she would come back later. There had been only one such event since she'd been working there, and it had been poorly attended.

The problem was that the gallery wasn't selling enough to even cover the overhead. Richard would be sunk without his mother, Pat thought, as she watched him go restlessly from one painting to another, straightening them.

He's really jumpy today, she decided. I heard him placing bets these last few days; he must have lost a lot of money. Of course, the business of that girl's body being found on his stepbrother's property is pretty upsetting. Yesterday, Richard had turned on the TV to watch live coverage of Susan Althorp's funeral. He knew her, too, Pat thought. Even though it's been a long time, seeing her casket carried into church must bring back a lot of painful memories.

That morning she asked Walker how his stepbrother was reacting to all the publicity.

"I haven't seen Peter," he told her. "I did call and let him know I was thinking about him. All this is happening with him just back from his honeymoon. It's got to be difficult."

Later it had been so quiet in the gallery that when the phone rang, Pat jumped. This place is getting on my nerves, she thought as she reached for the receiver.

"Walker Art Gallery. Good afternoon."

She looked up to see Richard Walker running toward her, waving his arms. She could read his lips: "I'm not here. I'm not here."

"Put Walker on." It was a command not a request.

"I'm afraid he's out on an appointment. I don't expect him back this afternoon."

"Give me his cell phone number."

Pat knew what to say: "When he's at a meeting, he

won't turn it on. If you give me your name and number, I'll—"

The slamming of the phone at the other end of the connection made her yank the receiver from her ear. Walker was standing next to her desk, perspiration on his forehead, his hands trembling. Before he asked, Pat volunteered, "He didn't give a name, but I can tell you this, Richard. He sounds awfully angry." Then, because she felt sorry for him, she offered some unsolicited advice: "Richard, your mother has a lot of money. If I were you, I'd tell her to give you what you need. That guy was scary. And then, a final piece of advice—quit playing the ponies."

Two hours later, Richard Walker was in his mother's home at the Carrington estate. "You've got to help me," he pleaded. "They'll kill me if I don't pay. You know they will. This is the last time, I swear it."

Elaine Carrington looked at her son, fury in her eyes. "Richard, you've drained me dry. I get one million dollars a year from the estate. Last year, between your gambling and the expense of the gallery, you got nearly half of it."

"Mother, I'm begging you."

She looked away. He knows I have to give it to him, Elaine thought. And he knows where, if I'm desperate, I can get whatever amount I need.

17

Former ambassador Charles Althorp knocked at the door of his wife's bedroom. Yesterday, after the funeral, she had come home and gone straight to bed. He did not yet know whether or not she had heard that Maria Valdez, the former maid at the Carrington estate, had recanted the version of events she had given at the time of Susan's disappearance.

He found her propped up in bed. Even though it was nearly noon, Gladys Althorp had clearly not attempted to get up. Her breakfast tray, virtually untouched, was on the bedside table. The television was on, although the sound was turned down so low it was only a murmur.

Looking at the emaciated woman from whom he had been estranged for years, Althorp felt an unexpected and overwhelming wave of tenderness toward her. At the funeral parlor, the casket had been surrounded by pictures showing moments from Susan's nearly nineteen years. I traveled so much, he thought. So many of the pictures, especially the later ones, were just of Gladys and Susan.

He pointed to the television. "You've obviously heard about Maria Valdez."

"Nicholas Greco phoned me, and then I saw it on CNN. He said that her testimony could be the key to convict Peter Carrington of Susan's death. I only wish I could be in court to see him led away in handcuffs."

"I hope you are there, my dear. And I can assure you that I will be."

Gladys Althorp shook her head. "You know perfectly well that I am dying, Charles, but it doesn't matter anymore. Now that I know where Susan is, and that I'll be with her soon, I have to confess something. I've always believed that Peter took Susan's life, but there's also been one tiny doubt in my mind. Did you hear her go out that night? Did you follow her? You were very angry with her. Had the two of you quarreled because she learned that you were involved with Elaine? Susan was so protective of me."

"Elaine was a mistake, and it was over by the time she married Peter's father," Charles said bitterly. "When I saw her, she was divorced and unattached, and that is the truth."

"*She* may have been unattached, but *you* weren't, Charles."

"Isn't it a bit late in the game to discuss that, Gladys?"

"You still haven't answered me. What did you and Susan quarrel about that night?"

"Try to rest, Gladys," Charles Althorp said as he turned and left his wife's room.

18

For the first time, the lawyers were staying for lunch. With skilled fingers, Jane Barr prepared a tray of sandwiches and made fresh coffee. Aghast, she had watched the television reports that Maria Valdez had changed her story. It's all Elaine's fault, she thought. If she hadn't let us go, I'd have been here to pick up the laundry that morning. I would have known *exactly* what was or wasn't in the hamper, and what did or didn't go to the cleaner. How can that Valdez woman dare to change her story now? Who is paying her? she wondered.

It's too bad that I wasn't here when that detective, Nicholas Greco, came by and spoke to Gary. He's been nervous ever since. He thinks he may have done some harm to Peter by telling Greco that Peter was shocked when he learned Susan's purse wasn't in his car.

"What harm can that do?" she had asked Gary at the time, but now she wondered. Maybe that bit of information did have significance. But she knew Peter

Carrington, and it wasn't as though he could ever hurt anyone.

She and Gary had attended Susan Althorp's funeral Mass. Such a sweet, pretty girl she was, Jane thought as she took plates and cups from the cupboard. I used to love to see her dressed up and going out when we would work the dinner parties for Mrs. Althorp.

Outside the church, before the hearse and family limousines left for the private burial, the Althorps had stood in the vestry and accepted the condolences of their friends. Why did Gary duck around behind the crowd instead of speaking to them? Jane wondered. Susan was always so nice to him. At least a half dozen times that last year he chauffeured her to parties when the ambassador didn't want her or her friends to be driving home late on their own. But she knew her husband was not one to show emotion, and perhaps he felt it wasn't his place to be talking to the Althorps with all the dignitaries in the church around them.

Gary had been vacuuming the upstairs hallways while Jane was preparing the lunch. He came into the kitchen in time to save her the trouble of getting him. "Good timing," Jane said. "You can take the plates and cups and silverware inside now. But be sure to knock before you open the door."

"I think I know enough to do that," he said sarcastically.

"Of course you do," she said, sighing. "I'm sorry. I don't have my wits about me. I keep thinking about yesterday and the funeral. Susan was such a beautiful girl, wasn't she?"

As she watched, her husband's face turned a deep shade of red and he turned away. "Yes, she was," he mumbled as he took the tray and left the kitchen.

19

The lawyers didn't leave until three o'clock, following five straight hours of questioning Peter in preparation for what seemed to be the inevitable—a charge of murder in the death of Susan Althorp. We didn't even take a break for lunch, only pausing to nibble on sandwiches and to sip coffee. All the while, every detail of the dinner party and the brunch all those years ago was dragged out.

Occasionally Vincent Slater contradicted Peter about some detail. One in particular surprised me. "Peter, Susan was sitting next to you at the dinner and Grace was at another table."

Until then I hadn't realized that Grace Meredith, the woman Peter married when he was thirty years old, had been at that party. But then, why not? Some twenty of Peter's friends from Princeton had been there. Peter explained that she had come as someone else's date.

"Who was that someone else?" Conner Banks asked.

"Gregg Haverly, an eating-club brother at Princeton."

"Had you met Grace Meredith at any point before that evening?" Banks asked.

I could tell by then that Peter was getting worn down by the constant barrage of questions. "I never met Grace before that evening," he said, his tone frosty. "In fact, I didn't see her again for over nine years. I bumped into her at a Princeton-Yale game. We were both with a group of friends, but neither one of us had a specific date and we paired off."

"Are there other people who know that you hadn't seen her in all those years?" Banks asked.

I guess that Banks saw the expression on Peter's face because he added, "Peter, I'm trying to anticipate the prosecutor. This is the kind of question they'll be asking you. Since your first wife was at the party, they could think that maybe you became interested in her and Susan noticed. Then maybe you and Susan had a fight about it later on and it turned violent."

That was when Peter pushed his chair back from the table and stood up. "Gentlemen," he said, "I think it's time to call it a day." I noticed that he was deliberately cool to Conner Banks when good-byes were being exchanged.

After the lawyers were gone, Peter said, "I don't think I want that Banks character on my defense team. Get rid of him, Vince."

I knew Peter was making a mistake, and fortunately Vincent did, too. He understood that Banks was only preparing Peter for the kind of stinging questions that were coming his way. "Peter, they'll question you about everything," he said. "And they'll make insinuations. You have to get used to it."

"What you're telling me is that the fact that I met Grace that night can be used against me, that maybe I fell madly in love with her and decided to kill Susan?" He obviously didn't expect an answer.

I hoped Vincent Slater would go home; I wanted some quiet time, alone with Peter. We both needed it. But then Peter announced that he was going into the office. "Kay, I have to step aside as CEO and chairman of the company although I will continue to have a major voice in decisions. All my attention has to be given to trying to stay out of prison." Then he added almost helplessly, "That woman is lying. I swear to you, I remember putting my dress shirt in that hamper."

He came over to kiss me. I guess I looked pretty worn out myself because he suggested, "Why don't you try to take a nap, Kay? It's been one hell of a day."

Resting was the last thing on my mind. "No," I said. "I'm going to see Maggie."

I guess the day had really gotten to Peter, because he said, "Be sure to give her my best, and ask her if she'd like to be a character witness for me at my trial."

20

Joining Nicholas Greco and Tom Moran, Barbara Krause flew to Lancaster, Pennsylvania, where they rented a car and drove to Maria Valdez Cruz's home, a modest ranch-style house not far from the airport. It had been snowing there and the roads were slippery, but Greco, because he had already visited the former maid, did the driving. Krause was furious that information about Maria Valdez recanting her previous statement had been leaked to the press. She had vowed to discover the source of the leak and fire the person responsible for it.

"When I was here two days ago, I advised Maria to have her own attorney with her when we come to see her," Greco reminded them as they rang the doorbell.

And it was that lawyer, Duncan Armstrong, a tall, thin man in his early seventies, who answered the door. Once the visitors were inside, he stood protectively next to his petite client and immediately expressed outrage at the leak to the press.

Moran had been present when they questioned Maria Valdez twenty-two years ago. She was a kid then, he thought, nineteen or so, the same age as Susan Althorp. But she had been stubborn, and wouldn't budge from her story that she gave that shirt to the cleaner.

Oddly, the firmness and determination she had shown then was missing now. She seemed nervous as she invited her visitors to sit down in the cozy, spotlessly clean living room. "My husband took our daughters to the movies," she said. "They're teenagers. I told them you were coming, and explained to them that I had made a mistake and lied to the authorities when I was a young girl, but that it's never too late to set the record straight."

"Maria means that she may have been mistaken when you questioned her at the time Susan Althorp disappeared," Armstrong interjected. "Before we do any further talking, I must see what papers you have prepared."

"We are offering Mrs. Cruz immunity from prosecution for her full and truthful cooperation regarding this investigation," Barbara Krause said firmly.

"I'll take a look at those papers," Armstrong said. He read them carefully. "Now, Maria, you know this means that at a trial you'll be called to testify, and the defense attorneys will argue that you're lying now. But the important thing is that you will not be prosecuted on a charge of giving a false statement originally."

"I have three daughters," Cruz replied. "If one of them disappeared and then was found dead, my heart would be broken. When I heard that girl's body had been found, I felt terrible that my statement may have helped her murderer go free. I admit, though, that I would not have had the courage to speak up if Mr. Greco had not found me."

"Are you saying you never saw that shirt, and that you did not give it to the cleaner?" Moran asked.

"I never saw the shirt. I knew Mr. Peter Carrington had said it was in the hamper, and I was afraid to contradict him. I was new in the country, and I didn't want to lose my job. I sent the shirts that were in the hamper to the cleaners, but I was almost certain that his dress shirt had not been there. At that time the police were questioning me, and I thought I could be wrong, but deep down I knew I wasn't. There was no dress shirt in his hamper. But I told the police that it was there, and that it must have been lost by the cleaner."

"The man who owned the laundry always swore they never received that shirt," Barbara Krause said. "Let's hope he's still around."

"If I have to testify, will they think I'm lying now?" Maria asked timidly. "Because I can prove I'm not."

"Prove? What do you mean prove?" Moran asked.

"I quit the job about a month after I was questioned by the police. I went back to Manila because my mother was very sick. Mr. Carrington senior knew that, and gave me a five thousand dollars 'bonus,' as he called it, before I left. He was so grateful I had backed up his son's story. In fairness to him, I believe he really thought I was telling the truth."

"I think you're being too charitable," Krause said. "That money was a payoff."

"I cashed the check, but I was afraid that when I came home with so much money, people might say that I had stolen it, so I made a copy of the check, front and back, before I took it to the bank." Maria reached into the pocket of her jacket. "Here it is," she said.

Barbara Krause took the copy of the check, reviewed it intently, then handed it to Moran. It was obvious to Greco that they believed it to be bombshell evidence. "Now we know that shirt never went into the hamper," Krause said. "It's time to arrest him and go to the grand jury."

21

For the first time in days, there was no media hanging around the main gate when I left. I guess if there had been, they had seen Peter and Vincent leave, maybe even had followed them. I had called Maggie and told her I was on my way to see her. She sounded chastened, probably having realized that what she said to the reporter was a low blow, and that I'd be furious.

But it had been over three weeks now since I'd seen her, and the minute I walked in the door I realized how much I'd missed her. The living room was even more cluttered than usual, but Maggie looked great. She was sitting in her favorite chair, watching Judge Judy, nodding in agreement with the just-rendered verdict, a smile on her face. She loved Judge Judy's outbursts to defendants. The TV was loud because Maggie never will put in her hearing aid, but she heard the door close behind me and sprang up so we could hug each other.

Of course, being Maggie, she got in the first word. "How is he?" she asked.

"By 'he,' I assume you mean my husband, Peter. He's under a great deal of stress and handling it beautifully."

"Kay, I'm worried about you. He's a . . ."

I interrupted her. "Maggie, if you ever use the word to describe Peter that I think you were about to use, I'm out of here, for good."

She knew I meant what I said. "Let's have a cup of tea," she suggested.

A few minutes later I was propped up on the couch and she was back in her chair. We were both holding teacups, and it felt familiar and comfortable and good. I asked about her friends and told her about our honeymoon.

We didn't talk about Gladys Althorp's accusation, or the fact that the former maid had changed her story. I was sure Maggie would be on top of those facts. But I did lead the conversation where I wanted it to go. "Maggie, as awful as it is for the Althorps, I'm glad Susan's body was found. At least it will give her mother some measure of peace."

"It was found on Carrington property." Maggie couldn't resist that one.

"Technically on the property, but outside the fence. Anyone could have put it there." I didn't give Maggie a chance to respond before I said, "Did you know it was

Daddy's idea to move the fence back so that none of the landscaping would be affected if there was any public work in that area?"

"Yes. I remember your dad talking about that at the time. He intended to do something with that property outside the fence, but he never got to do it."

"Maggie, you were wrong about something. Daddy was not fired because he had a drinking problem. He was fired because Elaine Carrington started flirting with him, and when he didn't respond she got rid of him. Peter told me that. Where did you get the idea that it was because of his drinking?"

"I don't care what your husband told you. Your father had a drinking problem, Kay."

"Well, according to Peter, he certainly wasn't drinking when he was working."

"Kay, when your father told me that he'd been fired, he was upset, terribly upset."

"That was only a few weeks after Susan Althorp disappeared, wasn't it?"

"Yes, as I remember it was exactly fifteen days later."

"Then the police must have questioned Daddy as well. He was still working there."

"They questioned everybody who worked on the estate or even visited it. You were staying here with me the night Susan disappeared. Your father had some of his friends in for a poker game at your house. They were at it till midnight, and I gather when it broke up they were all feeling pretty good. That Greco fellow was way off base insinuating your father's suicide had anything to do with Susan Althorp."

"I'm sure of that, but he did have a point. Daddy's body was never recovered. Why were you so sure he committed suicide?"

"Kay, I went with him to the cemetery on the sixth anniversary of your mother's death. That was only a month before he killed himself. Six years and still he broke down and cried like a baby. He told me he missed her every single day, and it wasn't letting up. Something else. He loved working on the Carrington estate. Sure, he had other families up there he worked for, but the Carringtons were the only one who would let him do exactly what he wanted. It was a terrible blow to be thrown out of that job."

Maggie got up from her chair, walked over, and put her arms around me. "Kay, he loved you like crazy, but your dad was in serious depression, and when you drink and are depressed, terrible things happen."

We cried together. "Maggie, I'm so scared," I admitted. "I'm so scared of what may happen to Peter."

She didn't answer, but she might just as well have shouted what she was thinking: Kay, I'm scared of what may happen to *you*.

I called Peter on his cell phone. He was still in the

city and wasn't going to be home until at least ten o'clock. "Take Maggie out for dinner," he said. Then he even laughed when he added, "Tell her it's on me."

Maggie and I went out for "a plate of pasta," as she puts it. Our conversation led her to reminiscences about my mother, and once again she told me the story about how she had stopped the show when she sang that song. She sounded so poignant when she sang that last line, "I heard that song before," Maggie said, her eyes glistening as she hummed the tune, off-key. It was on the tip of my tongue to tell her about my visit to the chapel that afternoon long ago, but I held back. I didn't want a lecture about how foolish I'd been.

Following dinner, I dropped her off at her door, watched until she was inside, then drove home. There were some lights on in the gatehouse, so I assumed that the Barrs were there. I never can tell if Elaine is in, though. Her house is too far away from either the front gate or the mansion to see any lights coming from it.

It was only nine o'clock. The mansion felt really scary to go into alone. I could almost imagine someone hiding inside the suit of armor in the entrance hall. The outside lights sent muted shadows through the stained-glass windows. For an instant I wondered if they were the same lights my father had installed, the ones he'd rushed over here to check that afternoon when he brought me with him.

I got comfortable in a robe and slippers and waited for Peter to get home. I was reluctant to turn on the television, afraid I'd come across another story about the Althorp case and the newest development, the maid who had changed her testimony. I had started a book on the plane coming home and picked it up again. It was no use; the words were meaningless.

I was thinking about my father. All the good memories were flooding my mind. I still missed him.

Peter came in a little after eleven. He looked exhausted. "As of today, I've resigned from the board," he said. "I'll maintain an office at the company."

He said that Vincent had ordered dinner brought into the office, but admitted he hadn't touched it. We went down to the kitchen, and I got some of Jane Barr's homemade chicken soup out of the refrigerator and heated it for him. He seemed to perk up a bit and got up and brought a bottle of red wine and two glasses from the bar. He poured the wine and held up his glass. "Let's offer each other the same toast every night," he said. "We will get through this. The truth will come out."

"Amen," I said fervently.

Then Peter looked directly at me, and his eyes were thoughtful and sad. "Here we are alone, Kay," he said. "If anything happened to you tonight, they'd be sure to blame it on me, wouldn't they?"

"Nothing's going to happen to me," I told him. "Whatever would make you say that?"

"Kay, do you know if I have been sleepwalking since we've been home?"

His question surprised me. "Yes, you were, that first night. You've never told me that you knew you were a sleepwalker, Peter."

"I was as a kid. It started after my mother died. The doctor gave me some medicine, and for a while it pretty much stopped. But I had a nightmare about putting my arm in the pool and trying to get at something, and it keeps sticking in my mind. You wouldn't know if that happened, would you?"

"It *did* happen, Peter. I woke up at about five o'clock and you weren't there. I looked for you in the other bedroom and happened to glance out the window. I could see you at the pool. You were kneeling beside it and your arm was in the water. Then you came back into the house and got into bed. I knew enough not to wake you."

"Kay," he began, his voice hesitant. Then he said something in so low a tone that I could not hear him clearly. His voice broke, and he bit his lip. I could tell he was close to tears.

I got up, went around the table, and cradled him in my arms. "What is it, Peter? What do you want to tell me?"

"No . . . it's nothing."

But it *was* something, and it was terribly important. I could swear that Peter had whispered, "I've had other nightmares, and maybe they really happened . . ."

22

Barbara Krause, Tom Moran, and Nicholas Greco did not arrive back from Lancaster until late afternoon. Krause and Moran went directly to their offices in the Bergen County Courthouse and spent the next several hours preparing an affidavit that summarized the evidence gathered so far in the investigation. The affidavit would be submitted in support of their request that a criminal complaint be docketed and a search warrant be issued. The criminal complaint would charge Peter Carrington with the murder of Susan Althorp, and the warrant would authorize the search of the homes and grounds of the Carrington estate.

"I want them to scour the grounds with the cadaver dogs," Krause told Moran. "How could they have missed finding her twenty-two years ago, when the scent would have been much stronger? Could he have buried her somewhere else and then moved her to the grounds when he believed they would never be searched again?"

"Maybe," Moran said. "I was standing there when those dogs went through the area where she was just found. I don't see how the dogs would have missed the scent, and I can't imagine how our guys, and I include myself, would have missed freshly disturbed soil."

"I'll alert Judge Smith right now," Barbara Krause said, "and request that we be permitted to go to his home at five o'clock tomorrow morning, so he can review the warrants."

"The judge will love that," Moran commented, "but it will give us time to assemble our team tonight and get over there with the warrant by 6:30 A.M., when we're pretty sure Carrington will be snuggled in bed with his new bride. I'll enjoy being his wake-up call."

It was after two A.M. when they completed the paperwork. Moran stood up and stretched. "I don't think we remembered to get any dinner," he said.

"We've both had about eight cups of coffee," Krause told him. "I'll buy you dinner tomorrow night, after we get this guy in custody."

23

I don't think I closed my eyes that night. Peter was so tired that he went to sleep immediately, but I lay beside him, my arm around him, trying to make sense of what I believed I had heard him say. Did he mean that events that he thought were nightmares were actually things that had happened while he was sleepwalking?

Peter woke at six o'clock. I suggested we go for an early-morning jog. I almost never get headaches but was feeling the beginning of one. He agreed, and we dressed quickly. We went down to the kitchen, and he squeezed fresh juice while I made coffee and put a slice of bread in the toaster for Peter. We didn't bother to sit at the table, just stood while we sipped the juice and coffee.

That was the last somewhat normal minute we were to have together.

The insistent pealing of the doorbell made both of us jump. We looked at each other; we both knew what was going to happen. The police were here to arrest him.

It's crazy what you do when something catastrophic happens. I ran to the toaster and grabbed the toast as it popped up. I wanted Peter to eat something before they took him away.

He shook his head when I handed it to him. "Peter, you may not get to eat anything for a long time," I said. "You had almost nothing yesterday."

The door chimes were echoing through the house, and we were talking about food. But he did take the slice of toast from me and began to eat it. With the other hand he refilled his coffee cup and, hot as the coffee was, began to gulp it down.

I ran to open the door. There were at least six men and a woman standing there. I could hear the sound of dogs barking from inside one of the fleet of cars and vans parked in the driveway.

"Mrs. Carrington?"

"Yes."

"I am Assistant Prosecutor Tom Moran. Is Mr. Carrington here?"

"Yes, I am." Peter had followed me into the entrance hall.

"Mr. Carrington, I have a warrant authorizing the search of the houses and grounds of this estate." Moran handed it to Peter and then continued. "You are also under arrest for the murder of Susan Althorp. You have the right to remain silent. Anything you say can and will be used against you in a court of law. You have a right to have an attorney present while you are being questioned. If you choose to answer questions, you can stop the questions at any time. I know you can afford an attorney, so I won't go into the details of having an attorney appointed by the court to represent you."

Intellectually, I had known since yesterday that this probably would happen. But to anticipate something, and then to see it actually take place, is the difference between nightmare and reality. Two detectives walked past me to stand on either side of Peter. Realizing what they were going to do, Peter gave me the search warrant, then brought his hands forward. I heard the click of the handcuffs. Peter's face was dead white, but he was calm.

One of the detectives opened the front door again. It was clear that they were going to take Peter away immediately. "Let me get his coat," I told Moran. "It's cold out."

Jane and Gary Barr had just arrived. "I'll get it, Mrs. Carrington," Jane said, her voice trembling.

"Where are you taking my husband?" I asked Moran.

"To the Bergen County Jail."

"I'll follow you in my car," I told Peter.

"Mrs. Carrington, I would suggest you wait," Moran said. "Mr. Carrington will be fingerprinted and photographed. During that time you will not be allowed to see him. An arraignment before Judge Harvey Smith is scheduled for three P.M. this afternoon in the Bergen County Courthouse. At that time, bail will be set."

"Kay, call Vincent and tell him to be ready to post bail," Peter said. As the detectives urged Peter forward, Gary Barr put a coat over his shoulders, and Peter leaned down to kiss me. His lips were cold on my cheek, and his voice was husky as he said, "Three o'clock. I'll see you there, Kay. I love you."

Moran and one of the detectives went out with him. When the door closed behind them, I stood there, unable to move.

The atmosphere changed. There were at least six detectives still in the foyer. As I watched, all but the female officer put on plastic gloves—the search of the house was beginning. From outside, the barking of the dogs was getting louder; they were starting the search of the grounds. I felt Jane Barr take my arm. "Mrs. Carrington, come back to the kitchen with me," she said.

"I've got to call Vincent. I've got to call the lawyers." My voice sounded odd to me, low, but shrill.

"I'm Detective Carla Sepetti," the officer said pleasantly enough. "I'll need the three of you to stay together, and I'll stay with you. If you wish, we can wait in the kitchen until they are finished searching the rest of the house. Then, we'll have to move. They will want to look through the kitchen, also."

"Let Jane fix you something to eat, Mrs. Carrington," Gary Barr urged.

Food is perceived to be a comfort, to give strength in time of trial, I thought wildly. They're trying to feed me for the same reason I shoved a piece of toast at Peter. I nodded and walked with the Barrs down the long corridor to the kitchen; Detective Sepetti was right behind us. We passed Peter's library. Two of the detectives were there—one of them was pulling books off the shelves, the other rummaging through his desk. I thought of how content Peter had looked that day less than four months ago when I sat in that room with him, admiring its ambiance.

In the kitchen, I tried to drink a cup of coffee, but my hand was trembling so much that the coffee spilled into the saucer. Jane put her hand on my shoulder for a quick second as she removed the saucer and replaced it with a clean one. I knew how much she loved Peter. She had known him since he was a motherless boy. I was sure her heart was breaking, too.

I phoned Vincent Slater. He took the news calmly. "It was inevitable," he said quietly. "But he'll be home tonight, I can promise you that. In New Jersey a judge has to give bail. I'm sure they'll set it in the millions, but we'll have it available."

The lawyers were due to arrive at nine o'clock. For no particular reason, I called Conner Banks rather than any of the other three. "We did expect this, Kay," he said, "but I know it's awful for both of you. We'll get a copy of the arrest warrant, and Markinson and I will be in court at three o'clock. We'll see you then."

When I hung up, I walked over to the window. Rain and sleet had been predicted by noon, but as I watched, I saw the first drops of rain begin to fall. Then pellets of sleet began to hit the window. "Didn't I read somewhere that police dogs don't work if it's raining?" I asked Detective Sepetti.

"It depends on what they're looking for," she said. "If it keeps up like this, I'd guess they'll bring them in."

"What *are* they looking for?" I asked her. I knew there was anger in my voice. The question I really wanted to ask was if they thought Peter was a serial killer and were expecting to find bodies buried all over the estate.

"I don't know, Mrs. Carrington," she said quietly, and I looked at her. She was in her late forties, I would guess. Her chin-length brown hair had a natural wave that softened her somewhat round face. She was wearing a dark blue jacket and black slacks. Earrings in the shape of X's were the only jewelry I could see, although

I'm sure she must have been wearing a watch that was covered by her sleeve.

It was so crazy to focus on details like that, of absolutely no importance to anyone. I turned away from the window. There was a small television in the kitchen, and I turned it on just in time to see Peter leaving the police car and being led into the Bergen County Jail.

"As Carrington is arrested on a charge of murder, evidence continues to pile up against him, our sources tell us," the reporter was saying. "The former maid, Maria Valdez Cruz, has not only confessed that she lied when she claimed she saw Carrington's dress shirt in the hamper, but also has proof that Carrington's father paid her off with a five-thousand-dollar bribe."

I snapped off the television. "Oh, my God," Jane Barr was saying. "I don't believe it. It would never have happened. Mr. Carrington senior was an honorable man. He'd never bribe *anyone*."

Even to save his son's life? I asked myself. What would I have done if I were in his place?

I wasn't sure I knew the answer.

24

Elaine Carrington was still in bed when detectives from the prosecutor's office rang the doorbell of her home shortly after 6:30 A.M. Startled, she threw on a robe and rushed to answer it. Had something happened to Richard? she wondered frantically. Hadn't he satisfied those gambling debts in time? Terrified at what she might hear, she yanked open the door.

When she was handed the search warrant, her immediate reaction was something approaching relief. Then, accompanied by a detective whose presence she ignored, she went to the study and turned on the television.

A few minutes later, the sight of Peter getting out of a car in handcuffs at the Bergen County Jail made her cringe. He's always been good to me, she reflected as she watched him trying to turn his face away from the photographers.

"At age twenty-two, upon his father's sudden death,

Peter Carrington became head of the family empire," the TV anchor was saying.

A picture of father and son, taken shortly before the elder man's fatal heart attack, flashed on the screen, immediately triggering an angry reaction from Elaine. Young as Peter was, he understood what it was like for me to live with that miserable tightwad, she thought. One of the richest men in the world, yet we even argued about money the day of his own birthday party. He was always threatening not to pay bills. "You run them up. You figure out a way to pay them." That was his big speech. In the five years I was married to him, he complained about every nickel I spent, she thought bitterly.

When the segment of the program about Peter was over, Elaine pushed the power button on the remote control. When I married him, everything about this place had been let go for years, she remembered. The only thing he didn't begrudge was the landscaping. Nature boy himself.

She realized that whenever she was nervous or upset, her mind flooded with anger at the stinginess of the prenuptial agreement she had been pressured to sign. Then, a sound from outside made her hurry to the window. Sleet was starting to pound against the panes, but she was hearing something else. "Are there dogs out there?" she asked incredulously of the young detective who was sitting on a chair in the doorway of the study.

"Those are the dogs searching the grounds, Mrs. Carrington," he answered, his tone businesslike.

"They already found Susan Althorp's body. What are they looking for now? Do they think this place is a cemetery?" she snapped.

The detective did not respond.

By noon, the search team had left her house, and Elaine went upstairs to her bedroom. As she showered and dressed, her mind raced with the possibilities raised by Peter's arrest. What will happen if Peter goes to prison for the rest of his life? she asked herself. Would he and Kay decide to sell this place? Can they do it while I'm alive? That might violate my prenup, or at the very least they'd have to buy me out.

The prenuptial she had signed had been the best her lawyer could do. Ten million dollars when Carrington senior died; lifetime residency both on the estate and in the smaller of the two Carrington Park Avenue apartments. Income of a million dollars a year for the rest of her life. But of course there was a catch: the availability of the house and apartment as well as the income would cease upon her remarriage. The ten million has been gone for years, most of it lost in that one lousy investment, Elaine thought bitterly. I should have gotten millions more.

I was wrong to try to talk Peter out of marrying Kay,

she worried as she pulled slacks and a cashmere sweater from the closet. She's bound to be holding that against me. I guess I should have called them when they got back from the honeymoon, but I just didn't feel like looking at her strutting around the mansion.

She turned on the television again. According to the news reports, Peter was going to be arraigned in the courthouse at three o'clock. She picked up the phone. When Kay answered, she began, "Kay, darling, I'm absolutely heartsick for you and for Peter. I want to be with you at the arraignment."

Kay responded instantly to her expressions of concern. "No, don't come to the arraignment," she said, "but assuming Peter is able to come home after bail is posted, it would be nice if you and Richard were here for dinner. I'm going to ask Vincent to be with us, too. I think that Peter needs to look around the table tonight and have the reassurance of being with people who love and support him."

Then Kay broke down and sobbed. "I'm so scared for him, Elaine. I'm so scared for him. I know you are, too."

"Kay, I would do anything, anything, anything in the world to help Peter. I'll see you tonight, dear."

Elaine replaced the receiver. Kay, if only you knew what I've already done to help Peter, she thought.

25

Are you sure you want to do this, Mrs. Althorp?" Nicholas Greco asked. "It's absolutely terrible outside."

"That's what I told her, Mr. Greco." Brenda, the housekeeper, her face creased with worry, was helping Gladys Althorp on with her coat.

"I am going to the arraignment of Susan's murderer, and there will be no further discussion about it. Mr. Greco, we will go in my car. I assume that my driver will be able to leave us near the door of the courthouse."

When she says no more discussion, she means it, Greco thought. He saw that Brenda was about to continue to protest, and he shook his head to warn her off.

The driver was waiting outside, holding an open umbrella. Without speaking, Greco and the driver each took an arm of the frail woman and helped her into the car. When they were on their way, Gladys Althorp asked, "Mr. Greco, tell me how an arraignment is conducted. Does it take very long?"

"No, Peter Carrington will appear with his attorney before the judge. He will have been waiting in a holding cell next to the courtroom. The prosecutor will read the charges that have been filed."

"How will he be dressed?"

"In a prisoner's jumpsuit."

"Will he be wearing handcuffs?"

"Yes. After the charge is read, the judge will ask him how he pleads. His attorney will answer for him. Of course, he will say, 'not guilty.'"

"I would certainly expect him to plead that way," Gladys said bitterly.

Greco could see that his client was biting her lip to keep it from trembling. "Mrs. Althorp," he said, "this isn't going to be easy for you. I wish you had someone in your family with you now."

"My sons could not have made it in time. They both live in California. My husband was already on his way to Chicago this morning when the word came that Peter Carrington had been arrested. But you know something, Mr. Greco, in a way, I'm not sorry to be the only one in my family here today. No one has grieved for Susan as I have all these years. We were so very close. We did so many things together. From the time she was a child, she loved to go to museums and the ballet and opera with me. She was a fine arts major in college, just as I had been. When she chose that major, she joked that it would give us even more in common, as if we needed it. She was beautiful and intelligent and sweet and loving, a perfect, perfect human being. Charles and the boys will attend Peter Carrington's trial. I won't be around to see it. Today is my day in court to represent her. I feel almost as though Susan will be there in spirit, too. Does that sound silly to you?"

"No, it does not," Greco said. "I have attended many trials, and the presence of the victim is always felt as their relatives and friends give testimony about them. Today, when the formal charge of murder is read, everyone in that courtroom will be thinking of the pictures they have seen in the papers of Susan. She will come alive in their minds."

"You'll never know how grateful I am to you for locating Maria Valdez. Her testimony, and the copy of that check from Peter's father, will surely be enough evidence to convict Carrington."

"I believe that ultimately Carrington will be convicted," Greco replied. "It has been an honor to be of service to you, Mrs. Althorp, and I do hope that after today you will find some measure of peace."

"I hope so, too." She leaned back and closed her eyes, obviously exhausted. Twenty minutes later, the car pulled up to the courthouse.

26

Even though he was wearing an overcoat, Conner Banks felt chilled as he hurried from the parking lot to the Bergen County Courthouse in Hackensack, New Jersey. The lot was crowded, and the space he finally had found was about as far away from the courthouse as it was possible to get.

He began to walk faster, and Walter Markinson, his face already wet from the sleet, snapped, "Take it easy. I don't run two miles every morning the way you do."

"Sorry."

"It wouldn't have hurt you to have brought an umbrella."

"Sorry."

On the drive from Manhattan, they had debated the exact wording of the statement they would make to the media. "Mr. Carrington is innocent of this charge, and his innocence will be demonstrated in court." Or, "Our client has steadily maintained his innocence. The case against him is based on supposition, innuendo, and a woman who, after twenty-two years, is recanting her sworn statement."

The way this case is developing, we might as well be defending Jack the Ripper, Conner thought grimly. He had never before been involved in a media circus quite like this one.

There have been some pretty sensational cases tried in this courthouse, he thought, as they finally reached the shelter of the building. There was the so-called Shoemaker, that guy from Philadelphia who marched through Bergen County, attacking women, with his twelve-year-old son in tow. His last victim, the one he killed, was a twenty-one-year-old nurse who had stopped by the house he was robbing to help out with an invalid who lived there. Then there were the Robert Reldan killings. That guy, handsome and from a good family, was reminiscent of Peter Carrington. He abducted and killed two young women. During his trial, he slugged the officer on guard who was taking off his cuffs out of sight of the jury, jumped out the window, stole a car, and had about thirty minutes of freedom. Now, twenty or thirty years later, the Shoemaker is dead, and Reldan is still rotting in prison.

And it is very likely Peter Carrington will spend the rest of his life with him, he thought.

The arraignment was to be held in the courtroom of

the Honorable Harvey Smith, the judge who had signed the arrest warrant for Peter Carrington. As Banks had expected, when he and Markinson got there, the courtroom was already crowded with both spectators and the media. The cameramen were focused on a woman seated in the middle section of the room. To his dismay, he realized that she was Gladys Althorp, the mother of the victim.

He and Markinson darted to the front of the room.

It was only twenty of three, but Kay Carrington was already there, sitting in the front spectator row with Vincent Slater at her side. Somewhat to Banks's surprise, he noted that she was wearing a jogging suit. Then he realized, or thought he realized, the reason for it: Slater had told him that Carrington was about to go jogging when the arrest warrant was served. That's what he'll be wearing when he posts bail and leaves for home, Banks thought. She's presenting a united front.

Markinson's grumpy expression had changed to a benevolent father-figure look. His brow furrowed, his eyes filled with understanding, he patted Kay's shoulder as he said in a reassuring voice, "Don't worry. We are going to take that Valdez woman apart when we get her on the stand."

Kay knows how bad this is, Banks thought. Walter should give her more credit. He caught a flash of anger in Kay's eyes as she looked up at Markinson.

In a voice that was low and strained, she said, "Walter, I don't need reassurances. I know what we're facing. What I also know is that there is someone out there who took that girl's life and who should be in this courtroom right now instead of my husband. Peter is innocent. He is incapable of hurting anyone. I want to feel that that is exactly what you believe, too."

"Blessed are they who have not seen and have believed." The words of scripture ran through Conner Banks's mind as he greeted Kay and Vincent. "He'll be home tonight, Kay," Conner told her. "*That* I can promise you." He and Markinson took their seats. Behind them, Banks could hear the courtroom filling up. It was to be expected—this was the kind of high-profile case that many courthouse personnel stopped in to observe.

"All rise for the court," the clerk announced.

They stood as the judge walked briskly into the courtroom from his chambers and took his seat on the bench. Banks had done his homework as soon as he learned who would be handling the arraignment. He'd learned that the Honorable Harvey Smith was known as very fair, but tough when it came to handing out sentences. The best we may be able to do for Carrington is to drag out the proceedings as long as possible, because once he's convicted, he goes straight to jail, Banks thought. After he is released on bail, at least he can sleep in his own bed until the trial is over.

Peter Carrington's case was not the only one on the docket: there were other detainees awaiting arraignment. The clerk read the charges as, one by one, the others came before the bench. Comparatively petty stuff, Banks thought. The first one was accused of passing bad checks. The second was a shoplifter.

Peter Carrington was the third to be arraigned. When he was led into court, wearing an orange jumpsuit and handcuffs, Banks and Markinson stood and placed themselves on either side of him.

Prosecutor Krause read the charge against him. Cameras clicked and whirred noisily as, looking straight at the judge, his expression grave, his voice firm, Peter entered his plea: "Not guilty."

It was obvious to Conner Banks that Barbara Krause was salivating at the prospect of personally trying this case. When bail was about to be set, she addressed the judge: "Your Honor, this is a defendant with unlimited means at his disposal. He is a very high risk for forfeiting bail and leaving the country. We ask that bail be set in proportion to his resources; that his passport be taken from him; that he be ordered to wear an electronic wrist bracelet at all times, that he be confined to his home and the gated grounds around it; and that his leaving the grounds be confined to attending religious services, visiting his doctor, or conferring with his lawyers, and that these visits take place only after notification to and permission from the monitor of his electronic bracelet."

She's going to be one tough cookie at trial, Banks thought as he looked at Krause.

The judge addressed Peter. "I realize, Mr. Carrington, that with your great wealth, it doesn't matter whether I set bail at one dollar or twenty-five million dollars. Bail is hereby set at ten million dollars." He reviewed the list of conditions the prosecutor had requested and approved all of them.

"Your Honor," Peter said, his voice loud and clear, "I will absolutely abide by all conditions of bail. I can assure you that I look forward to clearing my name at trial and ending this horror for myself and my wife."

"Your wife! What about the wife you drowned? What about her?" The words were shouted, passion in every syllable.

Like everyone else in the courtroom, Banks turned around quickly. A well-dressed man was on his feet in the middle of the courtroom. His face twisted with anger, he slammed his fist on the seat in front of him. "Grace was my sister! She was seven-and-a-half-months pregnant. You killed the child our family will never know. Grace wasn't a drinker when she married you. You drove her into depression. Then you got rid of her because you didn't want to take the chance of having a damaged baby. Murderer! Murderer! Murderer!"

"Remove that man!" Judge Smith ordered. "Remove him at once!" He rapped his gavel sharply. "Silence in this court."

"You killed my sister!" Grace Carrington's brother shouted defiantly as he was rushed from the courtroom.

A hushed silence followed his exit. Then it was broken by the agonized sobs of Gladys Althorp, who sat with her face buried in her hands.

27

It was six o'clock and pitch dark before we finally got home. Outside it was still raining heavily. A police officer stood guard by the roped-off area of the grounds that the dogs had not yet searched.

Thanks to Vincent's quick action, Peter did not have to spend the night in jail. As soon as I phoned to tell him that Peter had been arrested, he had arranged to have whatever amount of bail the judge set wired to a bank near the courthouse in Hackensack. As soon as the arraignment was over, he rushed to that bank, got a check certified in the amount of ten million dollars, and returned to the courthouse to post it with the bail unit.

While he was gone and we waited for Peter to be released, I was allowed to stay with Conner Banks and Walter Markinson in the empty jury room off Judge Smith's courtroom. I think that they were almost as startled and shaken by the attack from Grace's brother,

Philip Meredith, as I was. Then, to have it followed by the pitiful tears of Susan Althorp's mother made it all seem surreal. I watched Peter as he heard Meredith's accusations and Gladys Althorp's sobs. I don't think the expression on his face could have conveyed more pain if he were being flayed alive.

I said that to Markinson and Banks.

They expressed concern that, in the eyes of everyone in the courtroom, everything that happened was prejudicial to Peter, and they acknowledged that the media coverage of the event was going to be absolutely terrible. Even Markinson did not offer his usual conciliatory pats on the shoulder to me.

Then Conner Banks asked a question that absolutely threw me: "To your knowledge, did any member of the Meredith family ever threaten to file a civil suit for wrongful death against Peter?"

I was shocked. "No," I responded immediately. Then I amended my answer: "At least, Peter never told me about one."

"I'm going to be cynical," he said. "Philip Meredith may be a brother lusting for what he perceives to be justice, or he may be looking to extract a settlement from Peter. Actually, it's probably both. He certainly knows that the last thing Peter needs is to have another legal battle going on at the same time as his murder trial."

When Peter was released, Markinson and Banks spoke to him for a few minutes before they headed back to New York. They suggested he try to get as much rest as possible and told him that they would be at the house the next day, early in the afternoon.

Holding Peter's hand, I was aware suddenly of the electronic bracelet on his wrist. We walked down the long corridor toward the car waiting outside. I had hoped naïvely that there wouldn't be any media around when we finally left the courthouse. I was wrong, of course. They were there in force. I found myself wondering if they were the same people who had filmed Peter this morning on his way into jail, or if this was a fresh batch of reporters and photographers.

They began to hurl questions at both of us: "Mr. Carrington, have you anything to say about—?" "Kay, did you ever meet—?"

Vince was standing beside the car, the door open. We rushed into the backseat, ignoring the questions. When we were finally out of sight of the reporters, Peter and I wrapped our arms around each other. We hardly exchanged a word on the drive home.

Peter went straight upstairs. He didn't have to tell me that he wanted to shower and change. I'm sure that after the experience of being in a cell, it was a physical need to have gallons of hot water splash over him.

Vincent was staying for dinner. Saying he had business phone calls to make, he went to his office in the back of the house.

I headed to the kitchen. I would have thought that nothing could lift my spirits, but the heartwarming smell of pot roast simmering on the stove gave me a genuine pickup, if for no other reason than the fact that Peter had told me it was his favorite meal. I was grateful for Jane Barr's thoughtfulness in remembering that and preparing it tonight.

Gary Barr was in the kitchen, watching television. He turned it off as soon as he saw me, but not soon enough. On the screen I could see that Philip Meredith was being interviewed. For a moment I was tempted to find out what he was saying, but I quickly changed my mind. Whatever it was, I had heard enough from him today.

"Where would you like me to serve cocktails, Mrs. Carrington?" Gary asked.

I had almost forgotten that I'd invited Elaine and Richard for dinner. "In the front parlor, I guess."

Elaine and I hadn't discussed time for the simple reason we hadn't known what time Peter would be home, but when I'd been at the house for dinner before Peter and I were married, cocktails were always served around seven.

I hurried upstairs to shower and dress. I wondered

briefly why Peter had closed the door leading from the parlor to the other bedroom, then decided he must have wanted to lie down for a few minutes. It was late, but I took the time to wash my hair. The mirror told me that my face looked pale and tired, so I took special care with makeup, adding eye shadow, mascara, a touch of blush, and lip gloss. I know Peter likes my hair loose on my shoulders so I decided to wear it that way tonight. I thought my black velvet pants with a print silk shirt would seem a little upbeat, although in reality there was nothing to be upbeat about.

When I was ready, I still hadn't heard a sound from Peter. Wondering if he had fallen asleep, I went through the parlor and quietly opened the door of the other bedroom. I gasped when I saw Peter standing at the side of the bed, a bewildered expression on his face, staring down at an open suitcase.

"Peter, what is it?" I ran to him.

He clutched my arms. "Kay, when I got up here, I lay down. I just wanted to rest for a few minutes. I must have fallen asleep. I know I was dreaming that I was going somewhere, and then I woke up. And look."

He pointed to the interior of the suitcase. Underwear and socks were neatly stacked inside.

In the forty minutes since we had been home, he had been sleepwalking again.

28

At seven o'clock, Nicholas Greco was contentedly enjoying dinner with his wife, Frances, in their home in Syosset, Long Island. Normally she would not have asked him about the case he was working on, but after having watched the six o'clock news with the story of the Peter Carrington arraignment, she wanted to know every single detail of what had taken place in court.

She had prepared his favorite meal, a green salad, macaroni and cheese casserole, and baked ham. Greco realized that even though he wanted to put the wrenching day behind him, he owed it to his wife to reflect aloud on his impressions of the day's events.

"If I were Carrington's lawyers, I'd be talking a plea bargain," he said. "That outburst in court made a tremendous impression on people. From what I understand, Philip Meredith isn't given to emotional demonstrations. I had Beth at the office check on him while I was driving home. He lives in Philadelphia, which is where the Merediths have lived for generations. Nice family background, but no real money. He and his sister, Grace, had academic scholarships when they went to college. Philip's a midlevel executive with a marketing company, married to his childhood sweetheart; three kids, two of them in college. He's forty-eight now, his sister was six years younger."

Frances passed the macaroni casserole to him. "Have a second helping. Running back and forth to Lancaster, you haven't been eating properly."

Greco smiled at her and, against his better judgment, reached for the serving spoon. At fifty-five, Frances weighed exactly the same as she had at twenty-five. Her hair was the same shade of ash-blond, but now, of course, was helped along by regular trips to the beauty salon. Even so, in his fond eyes, she hadn't changed much at all in the last thirty years.

"I read about how Grace Carrington's body was found in the pool," Frances said, as she bit into a bread stick. "There were a lot of stories about it four years ago when it happened. *People* magazine did a big spread on it. I remember that they brought up the fact that Peter Carrington had been 'a person of interest' in the disappearance of Susan Althorp. But at the time, I'm almost certain that the Meredith family made a statement to the effect that 'Grace's death is not a mystery. It is a tragedy.' Why do you think the brother is starting to make accusations now?"

Nicholas Greco would have loved to steer the conversation in another direction, but he reminded himself that, as with her figure and her hair color, Frances had retained her lively curiosity.

"From what I understand, Grace Carrington's parents were upset themselves about her drinking, and they also liked Peter very much. They didn't suspect foul play at the time, but now that the father's dead, and the mother is in a nursing home suffering from Alzheimer's, Philip Meredith may have decided that it's time to express his own feelings."

"Well, if you hadn't tracked down Maria Valdez, there wouldn't have been an arraignment today," Frances observed. "I hope Mrs. Althorp appreciates that you were able to do what no one else could."

"Maria had absolutely dropped out of sight when the prosecutor's office was looking to talk to her again. The guy we work with in the Philippines went over her old connections, and it just so happened that she was back in touch with a distant cousin. It took a lot of luck to find her."

"Even so, it was your idea to have Mrs. Althorp accuse Peter Carrington in *Celeb* magazine. All my friends agreed he would sue her for that. If you hadn't located Maria Valdez, you still would have made Peter

Carrington answer questions under oath. And I'm sure he would have tripped himself up somehow."

Would he have tripped himself up? Greco wondered. There was still a nagging and unanswered part of the puzzle: the missing evening purse. Did Susan take it with her when she got out of Carrington's car? For some reason, that question wouldn't go away.

"Thank you for being my number one fan, dear," he told his wife. "Now, if you don't mind, let's talk about something else."

The telephone rang. Frances ran to get it and was back with the receiver on the third ring. "I don't recognize the number," she told him.

"Then let the answering machine pick it up," Greco said.

The message began: "Mr. Greco, this is Philip Meredith. I know you were in court today with Mrs. Althorp. I have been speaking with her. I would very much like to engage you to investigate the death of my sister, Grace Meredith Carrington. I have always believed she was murdered by her husband, Peter Carrington, and if it is at all possible, I want you to find evidence to support that fact. I hope you will return my call. My number is—"

Greco took the phone from his wife's hand and pushed TALK. "This is Nicholas Greco, Mr. Meredith," he said.

29

If anyone had peered into the window that evening and observed us having cocktails in the parlor of the mansion, I am sure they would have thought how lucky we were. Of course Peter and I said nothing about the brief sleepwalking episode but sat side by side on the couch that faced the fireplace. Elaine and her son, Richard Walker, were in the fireside chairs, and Vincent Slater, who always preferred a straight chair, had pulled one over to join the group.

Gary Barr was serving drinks. Peter and I had a glass of wine, the others cocktails. Without being asked, Gary had drawn the doors that separated the parlor into two rooms, making our half more intimate, if you can call a twenty-seven-foot-long room intimate.

On our honeymoon, Peter had told me that he wanted me to hire a decorator to do anything I wanted to refurbish the house. He seldom talked about Grace, but I did remember one comment about her, apropos of decorating: "When Elaine was married to my father, she did a lot of redecorating, and I must say she knew what she was doing. She had a great decorator working with her. Of course she hemorrhaged money in the process. You should have heard my father complain about it. Grace really didn't change anything. She preferred staying in the New York apartment. During the eight years we were married, she spent most of her time there."

All of that was going through my mind as we sat in that lovely room, staring at the fire in the fireplace. Elaine was beautiful as always, carefully made up, her sapphire eyes sympathetic and loving as she looked at Peter.

I liked Richard Walker. He was not good-looking in the traditional sense, but there was magnetism about him that I am sure attracted women. Except for his eyes, you would never have dreamt that, given his rugged features and stocky frame, he had come from the womb of Elaine Walker Carrington. Peter had told me that Richard's father, Elaine's first husband, had been born in Romania and moved to the United States with his parents when he was five or six years old. He anglicized his name when he went to college and was a successful entrepreneur by the time she married him.

"Elaine would never have married a guy without big bucks," Peter had told me, "but in a way she lucked out both times. I gather Richard's father was smart and rather charming but gambled everything away. The marriage didn't last long, and he died when Richard was a teenager. Then Elaine married my father, who was so frugal, the joke about him among his friends was that he still had his First Holy Communion money."

Obviously, Richard must have gotten most of his physical traits from his father, and something of his charm, too, I suppose. Over cocktails, he told us about the first time he had come to the mansion for dinner, and how formidable Peter's father had seemed to him. "Peter was a freshman at Princeton, Kay," he told me, "so he was away at school. I had just graduated from Columbia and had my first job as a trainee at Sotheby's. Peter's father was not impressed. He offered me a trainee job in one of the divisions of Carrington's. I forget which one."

Vincent Slater, who certainly is no conversationalist, began to laugh. "It was probably in the brokerage division. That's where I started."

"Anyhow, I turned him down," Richard said, "and that was the beginning of the end of a beautiful relationship. Your dad always thought I was wasting my time, Peter."

"I know." Peter smiled, too, and I could see that Richard's attempt to divert him from the grim reality of the day was working at least a little.

We went in to dinner, and I was grateful to see that Peter responded to Jane Barr's pot roast by saying, "I didn't think I was hungry, but this looks awfully good."

As we ate, Richard talked about his first tour of the mansion. "Your father told me to have a look around," he said. "He told me about the chapel, and I went up to see it. It's unbelievable to think that a priest actually lived in it in the seventeenth century. I remember wondering if it was haunted. What do you think, Kay?"

"The first time I saw it, I was six years old," I said. Noting his astonished expression, I explained, "I told Peter about it the night my grandmother fell at the reception, and he stayed with me at the hospital and brought me home."

"Yes, Kay was an adventurous child," Peter said.

He hesitated, and I sensed he didn't want to talk about my father. I made it easy for him. "My dad had come back on a Saturday to check on the lighting. There were a lot of guests coming that night for a formal dinner party. I was left on my own for awhile, so I went exploring."

The atmosphere at the table changed. I had stumbled into talking about the night Susan Althorp disappeared. Trying to divert the subject, I rushed on: "It was so cold and damp in the chapel, and then I heard some people coming so I hid between the pews."

"You did?" Vincent Slater exclaimed. "Did you get caught?"

"No. I knelt down. I hid my face in my hands. You know how dopey kids are. 'If I can't see you, you can't see me.'"

"Did you catch a pair of lovers?" Vincent asked.

"No, the people were arguing about money."

Elaine began to laugh, a harsh, sarcastic sound. "Peter, your father and I were arguing about money all over the house that day," she said. "I don't particularly remember that we were in the chapel, though."

"The woman was promising him that it would be the last time." I was desperate to change the subject.

"That sounds like me, too," Elaine said.

"Well, it's certainly not important. I wouldn't have thought about it, except that you began talking about the chapel, Richard," I said.

Gary Barr was standing behind me about to pour wine into my glass. An instant later, to our mutual dismay, the wine was cascading down my neck.

30

As Barbara Krause had promised Tom Moran, the evening of the arraignment they had a celebration dinner at the Stony Hill Inn, one of their favorite restaurants in Hackensack. Over rack of lamb, they discussed the sudden appearance and emotional tirade of Philip Meredith.

"You know, if we could get Carrington to admit to his wife's murder as well as to murdering Susan Althorp, I'd be tempted to offer him a plea," Krause said suddenly.

"I thought that was the last thing you said you'd do, boss," Moran protested.

"I know. But much as I think we'll get a conviction in the Althorp case, it's not a slam dunk by any means. The fact remains that Maria Valdez did flip-flop on her testimony. And Carrington's got the best defense counsel money can buy. It'll get rough."

Moran nodded. "I know. I saw the two of them with

Carrington today. What they're getting paid for one day's work would pay for the braces on my kids' teeth."

"Let's talk about it," Krause said. "If he pled to both Susan's case and to killing his wife, we could offer him thirty years, without parole, on concurrent sentences. Let's face it, we don't have enough to charge him with his wife's death now, but he knows other evidence could develop. He would be released in his early seventies and still have plenty of money. If he took this offer, we would get the convictions and, assuming he lives that long, he'd have the hope of getting out.

"You know perfectly well that I'd love to try this case," Krause said. "But there's another issue. Right now, I'm thinking of the victims' families. You saw and heard both of them today. Mrs. Althorp won't live to see the trial, but if Carrington confesses, she'll probably live to see him sentenced. And there's another angle. If he confesses, it opens the door to civil suits."

"I don't think the Althorps need money," Moran said flatly.

"They're poor millionaires," Barbara Krause said. "Don't you love that designation? It applies to anyone with under five million. I read it in one of the magazines. A civil settlement would mean they could make a significant contribution in Susan's name to a hospital or her college. From what we know about Philip

Meredith, he's never set the world on fire, and he has three kids to support."

"Then you are serious about offering a plea to Carrington's lawyers?" Moran asked.

"Let us say I'm turning it over in my mind. Kind of like being 'engaged to be engaged.' Anyhow, the lamb was delicious. Damn the calories. Full speed ahead. Let's have dessert."

31

I know that dinner relaxed Peter somewhat. As soon as it was over, and we'd had coffee in his library, the others got up to leave. Sometimes Richard stayed over at Elaine's house, but he told us that he was on his way to Manhattan for an after-theatre drink at the Carlyle with a young artist. "She's very gifted I think," Richard told us, "and very pretty, I might add. It so seldom goes together."

"Just don't fall in love, Richard," Elaine said tartly. "And if you decide to have a party for her at the gallery, let *her* pay for the champagne."

When she said that, Vincent raised his eyebrows to Peter and he responded with a trace of a smile. Peter and I walked with the three of them to the door. Both Richard's and Vincent's cars were parked directly in front of the mansion. The men opened umbrellas, and Elaine held on to her son's arm as they dashed down the steps to the cars.

Peter locked the door behind them, then, as we turned to the staircase, Gary Barr appeared. "Mrs. Carrington, we're leaving now. I had to tell you again how sorry I am about your blouse. I can't believe I was so clumsy. I don't think I've ever had an accident like that in all the years I've been serving."

Of course, when the wine spilled on me, I had accepted his apologies, gone upstairs, and quickly changed to another blouse. I think Peter had had enough of the apologizing, because before I could once again reassure Gary, he said brusquely, "I think Mrs. Carrington has made it clear that she understands it was an unfortunate accident. I don't really care to hear any more about it. Good night, Gary."

I had only seen glimpses so far of the formal—make that formidable—side of Peter, and in a way I was glad to witness it. These next months, until the trial, were going to be so humiliating and frightening for him. He had exposed his vulnerability to me because he trusted me. But in that moment I realized that the role I was assuming, less wife than protector, was unworthy of the essence of the man.

As we walked up the stairs, for some incongruous reason, I thought about an evening, maybe ten years ago, when I was home from college. Maggie and I had watched the old movie *To Catch a Thief*, starring Grace Kelly and Cary Grant, on television. During one of the commercials, she told me that Grace Kelly met Prince Rainier when she was making that movie in Monaco.

"Kay, I read about the time the prince came to visit her at her parents' home in Philadelphia. That was when he asked her father for her hand in marriage. The next day her mother told a reporter what a very nice person Rainier was and how easy it was to forget that he was a prince. A society reporter sniffed, 'Doesn't Mrs. Kelly understand that marrying a reigning monarch is not like marrying someone who's just another prince?'"

Today I had seen the hounded Peter in court, followed by the frightened Peter standing over a suitcase that he could not remember having begun to pack. Just now, I had seen an imperial Peter who had heard enough of an employee's explanations. Who is the complete Peter? I asked myself when we were getting ready for bed.

I realized I did not have an answer.

32

The weather the next morning was almost unchanged. The temperature had risen so it was no longer sleeting, but the rain continued, a steady, dismal downpour.

"Looks as though our dogs get another day off," Moran observed when he went into Krause's office a few minutes after nine A.M. "No use having them sniffing around the Carrington estate today."

"I know. It would only be a waste of the taxpayers' money," Krause agreed. "Besides, we're not going to find anything there. I've been going over the little evidence they took from the mansion and the stepmother's house. The entire search seems to have resulted in a big nothing. But I don't suppose we really expected to find much after twenty-two years. If Peter Carrington was smart enough to get rid of his formal shirt right after he killed Susan, the odds are that there was nothing else for him to worry about."

"I'd guess if there had been anything, we would have found it the first time around," Moran shrugged.

"Just one thing kind of interests me. Take a look at this." Krause handed a sheet of paper to Moran. It was a landscaping design sketch.

Moran looked at it carefully. "What about it?"

"It was in a file drawer in a room on the top floor of the mansion. Apparently, over the years, the family has treated a couple of rooms there as an attic, the place where you stick things that you don't want to be bothered going through. The guys tell me that you could furnish a house with the stuff that's up there, from couches and chairs and carpets and china and silverware and pictures and bric-a-brac, to family letters that go back to the nineteenth century."

"I guess they never heard of yard sales or eBay," Moran commented. "Wait a minute, I see what this is. It's a drawing of the outside area of the Carrington estate, the place where the girl's body was found, except that there are plantings on it."

"That's right. Actually, it's a copy of an original sketch."

"What about it?"

"Look at the name in the corner."

Moran held it closer to the lamp on Barbara Krause's desk. "Jonathan Lansing! That was the landscaper, the guy who took a dive into the Hudson not long after

Susan Althorp disappeared. He was the present Mrs. Carrington's father."

"That's right. He was fired by the Carringtons a few weeks after Susan went missing, and he apparently committed suicide. I say 'apparently,' because his body was never recovered."

Moran stared at his boss. "You're not suggesting there's a connection between him and Susan Althorp?"

"No, I'm not. We've got the guy who killed her. What I'm seeing is that Lansing was the one who suggested that the fence be moved those fifty feet back from the street. Looking at this, it would seem as though he didn't intend to leave the area between the fence and the curb untended. This sketch is a design for some perennials to be planted on the outer side of the fence."

"Then he was fired, and the family didn't bother to do anything but throw some grass seed on it," Moran said matter-of-factly.

"Looks like it," Barbara Krause agreed. She put the sketch back in the file folder. . . . "I don't know," she said, more to herself than to Moran. "I just don't know. . . ."

33

On Tuesday morning, the day after the arraignment, Philip Meredith took the train from Philadelphia to New York. Aware that his picture might be splashed on the front page of the tabloids, he took the precaution of wearing dark sunglasses. He had no desire to be recognized and perhaps spoken to by strangers. He did not want sympathy from anyone. He had not laid eyes on Peter Carrington since his sister's funeral. He had gone to court simply for the pleasure of seeing him in handcuffs and charged with murder. His outburst had startled him as much as anyone else in court.

But now that it had happened he intended to follow through on his accusation. If Nicholas Greco had managed to find a key witness against Peter Carrington in the Althorp case, maybe he could find a key piece of evidence that would prove Grace had been murdered as well.

He got off the train at Penn Station on Thirty-third Street and Seventh Avenue and would have preferred to walk the distance to Greco's office on Madison Avenue between Forty-eighth and Forty-ninth streets. But the fact that it was pouring rain dictated that he get in the taxi line. Weather such as this made him think of the day Grace was buried. It hadn't been cold, of course, because it was early September, but it had been raining. She was lying now in the Carrington family plot in Gate of Heaven Cemetery in Westchester County. That was something else he wanted, to bring her remains back to Philadelphia. She should be with the people who loved her, he thought—our parents and grandparents.

Finally he was at the head of the cab line. He got into the next available one and gave the address. He hadn't been to Manhattan in a long time, and was surprised at the traffic congestion. The ride cost nearly nine dollars and he could see that the cabby wasn't satisfied when he didn't add any money to the ten-dollar bill he handed him.

Between the price of the train and cabs back and forth, this day is getting expensive, even before I talk to Greco, Philip thought. He and his wife, Lisa, had already had a blowup about it. "I nearly died when I heard how you carried on in court," she told him. "You know that I loved Grace, but you've been obsessing about this for four years. Hiring a private detective costs money that we don't have, but for God's sake do it. Take out a loan if necessary, but one way or the other be finished with all this."

A narrow building, 342 Madison had only eight floors; Greco's office was on the fourth floor, a suite with a small reception area. The receptionist told Meredith he was expected and promptly escorted him to Greco's private office.

After a cordial greeting and a brief comment about the weather, Greco got down to business. "When you called me at home last night, you said that you may have some proof that your sister's death was not an accident. Tell me about that."

"Proof may be too strong a word," Meredith admitted. "The word I should have used was 'motive.' It went beyond Peter worrying about Grace giving birth to a damaged baby. We're talking about a lot of money as the motive to kill Grace."

"I'm listening," Greco said.

"The marriage was never one of those love matches made in heaven. Peter and Grace were different people. She loved New York society life; he did not. By the terms of their premarital agreement, Grace would have received a flat twenty million dollars if they divorced, *unless*—and this is a *big* unless—she gave birth to his child. Then, in the event they divorced, she would have received twenty million dollars a year so that the child could be raised in a way suitable to a Carrington."

"At the time of your sister's death, Peter Carrington offered to take a lie detector test and passed it," Greco said. "His income has been estimated at eight million dollars a week. Such exorbitant numbers seem incredible to you and me. Nevertheless, even a very large yearly sum payable by the terms of his prenuptial agreement to a divorced wife still is not a compelling motive to kill his unborn child. Even if fetal alcohol syndrome occurred, there would have been plenty of resources to take good care of a child with a problem."

"My sister was murdered," Philip Meredith said. "In the eight years she was married to Peter, she had three miscarriages. She desperately wanted a baby. She would never have committed suicide while she was carrying one. She knew she was an alcoholic and had quietly started going to AA. She was determined to stop drinking."

"Tests of her blood alcohol level showed that she had three times the legal limit in her system when she was found. Many people fall off the wagon, Mr. Meredith. Surely you know that."

Philip Meredith hesitated, then shrugged. "I'm about to tell you something that I had sworn to my parents I would not reveal. They thought it would irrevocably damage the memory people had of Grace. But my father is dead and my mother is in a nursing home. As I told you, she has Alzheimer's disease and is totally unaware of what is going on."

Meredith lowered his voice as though afraid of being overheard. "At the time of her death, Grace was having an affair. She was very careful, in the sense that the baby absolutely was Peter's child. Grace wanted to give birth, then divorce Peter. The man she was involved with didn't have money, and Grace loved the lifestyle she had become accustomed to with the Carrington money behind her. I believe that the night of that party her first drink was spiked, with the goal being to get her drunk, because once she had one drink, it was all over. She couldn't stop."

"Grace was drunk when Carrington got home. Who would have spiked the drink?"

Philip Meredith looked directly at Greco. "Vincent Slater, of course. He would do anything for the Carringtons, and I do mean *anything*. He's one of those sycophants who snuggles up to money and does the master's bidding."

"He spiked your sister's drink with the idea of getting her drunk and then drowning her? That's quite a stretch, Mr. Meredith."

"Grace was seven-and-a-half-months pregnant. If she had suddenly gone into labor, there was a very good chance the baby would have survived. She had already had some false labor pains. There wasn't any time to waste. Peter was not due home until the next evening. I believe that Slater spiked Grace's club soda with vodka, planning to get her drunk, then drop her in the pool after she passed out. When Peter got home, he grabbed the glass from my sister's hand and threw it on the carpet in the same kind of spontaneous reaction I had yesterday in court. I bet he's still kicking himself that he exploded at her. If he'd had time to think, he would have been the benevolent, understanding husband which was his usual role around her when Grace was drinking."

"You are telling me that you believe Slater spiked your sister's drink, and Peter then drowned her in the pool after she had passed out?"

"Either Peter or Slater threw her in the pool, I'm convinced of that. We only have Slater's word that he went home that night. I wouldn't be surprised if Slater helped Peter dispose of Susan Althorp's body, too. I wouldn't be surprised if he got rid of Peter's shirt for him after he killed her. He is that devoted. And that amoral."

"Why don't you go to the prosecutor's office with your theory, now that your mother will not be aware you are breaking your promise to her?"

"Because I don't want my sister's name dragged through the mud, and maybe to no avail. I can supply them with a motive and a theory, but inevitably there'd be a leak and some reporter would get hold of the story."

Nicholas Greco thought of his interview with Slater at his home. Slater was nervous that day, he thought. There's something he's concealing, something that he's afraid will come out. Could it be that he had a role in the death of either Susan Althorp or Grace Carrington, or *both*?

"I am interested in taking on the case, Mr. Meredith," Greco heard himself saying. "I have an idea of your current circumstances and am willing to adjust my fee accordingly. We can include a provision that, if you receive a substantial civil award, then I will receive an additional sum."

34

Almost as if he had been pushed as far as it was possible to be pushed, I saw something change in Peter. We both slept well, out of exhaustion, but, also, I think, because we had a sense that we were in a war. The first battle had been won by the enemy, and now we had to gather our strength for what was to come.

When we went downstairs at 8:30 in the morning, Jane Barr had the table set for breakfast in the smaller dining room, with fresh juice and coffee on the sideboard.

"Why not?" we agreed when she suggested scrambled eggs with bacon, although I did make a firm promise to myself that I wouldn't keep up that menu.

The usual morning papers were not on the table. "Let's look at them later," Peter suggested. "We already know what's going to be in them."

Jane poured coffee for us and then went back to the kitchen to cook breakfast. Peter waited until she left the room before he spoke again. "Kay," he began, "I don't have to tell you this is going to be a long siege. The Grand Jury is going to indict me, we both accept that. Then a trial date will be set which could be a year or more away. To use the word 'normal' is simply ludicrous, but I'm going to use it anyhow. I want our life to be as normal as is humanly possible until I go to trial and a jury renders a verdict."

He didn't give me time to comment before he continued, "I am allowed to leave these premises to confer with my lawyers. I'm going to confer with them a lot, and I'm doing it on Park Avenue. Vince has to be my eyes and ears at headquarters. He'll be spending a lot of time there as well."

Peter took another sip of coffee. In the brief time he stopped speaking, I realized that in less than two weeks I had become so accustomed to having Vincent Slater constantly present that it would seem odd if he weren't around.

"Gary can drive us back and forth to Manhattan," Peter was saying. "I intend to get the necessary permission to go to New York a minimum of three times a week."

There was purpose and direction in the way Peter spoke, and in his expression as well. Then he added, "Kay, I know I could never hurt another human being. Do you believe that?"

"I believe it and I know it," I told him.

We reached across the table to each other and our fingers entwined. "I think I fell in love with you the minute I saw you," I said. "You were so deep into your book, and you looked so comfortable in your big chair. Then, when you stood up, your glasses slipped off."

"And I fell in love with the beautiful girl whose hair was slipping around her shoulders. A line from 'The Highwayman' jumped into my mind: 'And Bess, the landlord's daughter, the landlord's black-eyed daughter, stood plaiting a bright red love-knot in her long, dark hair.' Remember that from grammar school?"

"Of course. The poem's rhythm had the cadence of horses' hooves. But think about it: I was the landscaper's daughter, not the landlord's," I reminded him. "And I don't have black eyes."

"Close enough."

It was odd, but that morning, my father was never far from my mind. I thought of how Maggie had told me only a few days ago that he loved working on the Carrington estate, and he especially loved the freedom of having the opportunity to design the magnificent gardens without regard to cost.

Over scrambled eggs and sinfully cholesterol-filled bacon, I asked Peter about that.

"My father was both a tightwad and burst-of-generosity guy," he said. "Which is what I intend to make our high-priced lawyers realize. If Maria Valdez was going back to the Philippines because her mother was very ill, it would have been like him to write a check to help her out with doctor bills. Yet on the same day he'd go nuts over the price of a set of china Elaine had ordered."

I thought of how Peter had told me to hire an interior designer and do whatever I wanted to redecorate the house. "It doesn't sound as though you're anything like him," I said. "At least not with what you've told me about making changes in the house."

"In some ways I am like him, I guess," Peter said. "For example, he hated it when Elaine hired the chef and the butler and the housekeeper and the maids. Like my father, I'd rather have a couple like the Barrs on a daily basis who go home to their own place at night. On the other hand, I never could see why my father would get upset about money spent on daily life here. I think he must have been a throwback to the Carrington who started out without a shirt on his back and made a fortune in oil wells—they say he was the all-time skinflint. I doubt if he'd have paid for grass seed, never mind acres of expensive plantings."

We finished breakfast and Peter started organizing the day as he had planned it. He called Conner Banks on his cell phone and told him to get permission for him to come into New York that afternoon for a meeting at a conference room in his law firm. Then he spent several hours on the phone with Vincent Slater and executives from his own company.

I realized I was looking forward to going with Peter into the city. At this time, it didn't make sense for me to sit in on Peter's meetings with his lawyers. I wanted to use what time I had to visit my little studio apartment. Some of my favorite winter clothes were still there, and I had some framed pictures of my mother and father that I wanted to have around me here.

Peter got the necessary permission to leave the premises, and we set out for New York in the early afternoon. "Kay, even though your apartment is on the way, I think I'll have Gary drive straight to Park and Fifty-fourth," he said. "If by any chance we're followed by the cops or media, and somebody takes a picture of the car stopped in front of your place, it might raise a question of violating bail. Maybe I'm paranoid, but I can't risk going back to jail."

I understood completely, and that was the way we did it. By the time we got to the front of the lawyers' building, the rain had at last begun to ease up. The weather forecast was for clearing skies, and it looked as though it was actually going to be accurate.

Peter was dressed in a dark business suit, shirt, and tie. His overcoat was a beautifully cut midnight blue cashmere, and he looked every inch the corporate executive that he was. When Gary opened the door for him, Peter gave me a quick kiss and said, "Pick me up at four thirty, Kay. We might as well try to beat some of the rush hour traffic." As I watched him walk rapidly across the sidewalk, I couldn't help thinking how absolutely incongruous it was that less than twenty-four hours ago, he had been standing in an orange jail jumpsuit, his hands manacled, hearing the charge of murder directed at him.

I had not been back to my apartment since the day Peter and I were married. Now on one hand it looked cozy and familiar, and on the other, with new eyes, I saw how small it really was. Peter had been here a few times in our whirlwind courtship. On our honeymoon, he had casually suggested that I just pay off the rest of the lease, and, except for personal items, get rid of everything in it.

I knew I wasn't ready to do that yet. Yes, I had a new life, but some part of me didn't want to completely cut off so much of my old life. I checked my phone messages. None of them was important, except one that had come in just that morning from Glenn Taylor, the guy I'd been dating before I met Peter. Of course, I had told him about Peter as soon as we started seeing each other regularly. "I was just about to take you shopping for a ring," he'd said, with a laugh, but I knew he was only half joking. Then he'd added, "Kay, be sure you know what you're doing. Carrington comes with a lot of baggage."

Glenn's message that morning was just what I would have expected of him—concerned and supportive: "Kay, I'm so sorry about what's happening to Peter. Some way to start a marriage. I know you can handle it, but remember, if I can be of help in any way, let me know."

It was nice to hear Glenn's voice, and I thought about how we had loved to go to the theatre together, and that perhaps one day he and Peter and I could go to dinner and a play. Then I realized that there weren't going to be any evenings out for Peter again unless he was acquitted at his trial. It's my confinement as well, I realized suddenly, because in that moment I knew that I would never leave Peter alone in the evenings.

I gathered some clothes from the closet and laid them on the bed. Almost all of them bore the labels of budget chain stores. Elaine wouldn't be caught dead in any of these, I thought. On our honeymoon, Peter had presented me with an American Express Platinum Card. "Shop till you drop, or whatever that expression is," he'd said with a smile.

I surprised myself by crying. I didn't want a lot of clothes. If it had been in my power, I would have traded all the Carrington money just to have Peter exonerated of the deaths of Susan and Grace. I even found myself wishing he could move into this apartment with me, and be struggling to pay off school loans, just as Glenn was doing. Anything to simplify our lives.

I dabbed my eyes and went over to collect the pictures on the dresser. There was one of my mother and father with me in the hospital right after I was born. They looked so happy together, beaming at the camera. I was wrapped in a blanket, a squished-faced infant, peering up at them. My mother looked so young and so pretty, her hair loose on the pillow. My father was thirty-two then, still boyishly handsome, and with a twinkle in his eyes. They had so much to live for, and yet she had only two weeks of life ahead of her, before that embolism took her from us.

When I learned the circumstances of her death, and that I was still at her breast when my father found her, I had been about twelve years old. I remember that I pursed my lips and tried to imagine what it must have felt like to be nursed by her.

I had showed the hospital picture to Peter the first time he was here, and he had said, "I hope someday we'll be taking pictures like that, Kay."

Then he picked up the picture of my father and me that had been taken shortly before Daddy drove his car to that remote spot and disappeared into the Hudson River. Peter had said, "I remember your father very well, Kay. I was very interested in why and how he chose the plantings. We had a couple of interesting conversations."

Still dabbing my eyes, I crossed to the mantel to get that picture to bring home, too.

That evening, with Peter's assent, I moved his favorite picture of his mother, and one of him as a child with his mother and father, and placed them on the mantel over the fireplace in the parlor of our suite. I added those of my parents that I had brought from the apartment. "The grandparents," Peter said. "Someday, we'll tell our children all about them."

"What should I tell them about him?" I asked, pointing to my father's picture. "Should I say that this is the grandparent who quit on life and on his child?"

"Try to forgive him, Kay," Peter said quietly.

"I do try," I whispered, "but I can't. I just can't."

I stared at the picture of my father and me, and although I know it seems fanciful, at that moment I felt as if he could hear what I was saying, and that he was reproaching me.

The next morning, just as the weatherman had promised, the sun was shining, and the temperature was up in the high forties. At nine o'clock, I heard the sound of barking outside, and realized that the cadaver dogs were back.

35

Nicholas Greco had made an appointment to see Barbara Krause in the prosecutor's office at 3:30 on Wednesday afternoon. "I did not anticipate paying a call on you so soon," he told her when he arrived.

"Nor, to be honest, did I expect to see you," she said, "but you are certainly always welcome."

"I am here because Philip Meredith has engaged me to look into the drowning death of his sister, Grace Meredith Carrington."

Krause had long ago learned to keep a poker face in court, but could not conceal the expression of surprise on her face at this news. "Mr. Greco, if you could come up with anything that could help us to tie that death to Peter Carrington, I'd be most grateful," she said.

"I'm not a magician, Ms. Krause. Mr. Meredith has confided to me a piece of information that I am not at liberty to discuss right now. What I can say is that it provides a compelling motive for Carrington to want to do away with his wife. However, despite that fact, I'm confident that in a court of law no sensible jury would find him guilty beyond a reasonable doubt based just on this information. That is why I would like to see the file you have on the case, and to be allowed to speak to the investigators who went to the scene."

"That's easy. Tom Moran headed up that investigation. He's sitting in on a trial right now, but should be free in an hour or so. If you want, you could wait in his office and read the file there."

"That would be fine."

As she pressed the intercom to send for an assistant to fetch the material, Barbara Krause said, "Mr. Greco, we've been over that file with a fine-tooth comb. We could not find anything that would stand up as evidence in court. From what you are saying, it's obvious that Philip Meredith has been withholding information that would help our case. Whether or not you find something in our file that seems relevant, I would encourage you to urge him to be forthcoming with us. You might remind him that an admission of guilt from Carrington would open the door to a huge civil suit for the Meredith family."

"I am very sure that Philip Meredith is quite aware of that. I also think that, in the end, even if I see nothing else in the file, he can be persuaded to reveal to you what he has already told me."

"Mr. Greco, you are making my day."

For the next hour and a half, Nicholas Greco sat in the one extra chair in Tom Moran's small office, making neat entries in the notebook that was ever present in his briefcase. Of special interest to him in Moran's notes was a reference to the fact that there had been a folded paper in the pocket of Grace Carrington's evening suit, a page from the August 25, 2002, issue of *People* magazine containing an interview with legendary Broadway star Marian Howley. "Howley had just opened in a one-woman show," the notes read. "Although the page was soaking wet, it was identifiable, and contained two words scrawled in Grace Carrington's handwriting: '*Order tickets*.' Page is now in evidence file."

Grace Carrington was planning to attend a Broadway show, Greco thought as he jotted down the date of the magazine. That is not the thinking of a woman contemplating suicide.

There had been another couple at the dinner the night Grace Carrington drowned, Jeffrey and Nancy Hammond, and as of four years ago, they were living in Englewood. Greco hoped they were still there. If so, he would try to talk with them in the next few days.

Gary Barr had served the cocktails and dinner that evening, he noted.

Interesting, that Mr. Barr, Greco thought. He had worked for the Althorps on and off, even as the occasional driver for Susan Althorp and her friends. He had been serving at the formal dinner at the Carrington estate the night Susan disappeared, and at the brunch the next day. He was also there and on the estate in the gatehouse the night Grace drowned.

The ubiquitous Mr. Barr. He may be worth another visit, Greco decided.

It was five o'clock, and Moran still had not returned to his office. He's been in court, Greco thought. He'll want to get home now. I'll phone him tomorrow and set up an appointment for a more convenient time.

He walked down the corridor to Barbara Krause's private office to return the Grace Carrington file. Moran was with her. Krause looked at Greco as though she had forgotten his existence. Then she said, "Mr. Greco, I'm afraid we'll have to put off any further discussions now. Tom and I are on our way to the Carrington estate. It seems the cadaver dogs have dug up more human bones there."

36

Sometimes, when I held a storytelling hour for young children at the library, I would recite one of my favorite poems to them. It was "The Children's Hour" by Henry Wadsworth Longfellow, and begins like this: "Between the dark and the daylight, when the night is beginning to lower . . ."

The daylight was just fading away when I heard the cadaver dogs barking outside, the sound coming from the west side of the grounds. Peter had gone to the lawyers' office in Manhattan again, but I had elected to stay home. I felt overwhelmingly tired, and actually spent a good part of the day in bed, napping off and on.

It was four o'clock when I finally got up. Then I showered and dressed and went down to Peter's library and sat reading in his comfortable chair, waiting for him to get home.

At the sound of the barking, I hurried back to the

kitchen. Jane was coming in from the gatehouse to prepare dinner. "There are more police cars at the gate, Mrs. Carrington," she told me nervously. "Gary went over to see what's going on."

The dogs must have found something, I thought. Not bothering with a coat, I raced out into the cold twilight and followed the footpath that led to the yelping. Detectives were already taping off an area on the near side of the pond that in the summer was stocked with fish. Squad cars were racing across the frozen lawn, their lights flashing.

"One of the dogs dug up a leg bone," Gary Barr whispered to me.

"A leg bone! Do they think it's human?" I asked. Standing there in a light sweater, my teeth were chattering from the cold.

"I'm pretty sure they do."

I heard the sound of approaching sirens. More police are coming, I thought. The media will follow them. Who could be buried there? This whole area was once lived in by Indian tribes. Evidence of their graves has been found from time to time. Maybe it was the bone of one of those early natives they had found.

Then I overheard one of the dog handlers say, ". . . and it was wrapped in the same kind of plastic bags as the girl."

I felt my legs crumbling, and heard someone yelling,

"Grab her." I didn't faint, but a detective held one arm and Gary Barr the other, as they led me back to the house. I asked them to take me to Peter's library. I was shivering when I sank down into his chair, so Jane got a blanket and wrapped it around me. I told Gary to stay outside and report on what was happening. Eventually he came back to tell me that he heard them saying they had found a complete human skeleton, and that there had been a chain with a locket around the victim's neck.

A locket! I had already suspected that the remains might be those of my father. When I heard about the locket, I knew that it had to be the one my father always wore, with my mother's picture inside. At that moment I knew with certainty that the remains the dogs had dug up had been flesh of my flesh, bone of my bone.

37

I don't need any more proof that Carrington killed my sister," Philip Meredith told Nicholas Greco the morning after the skeletal remains of Jonathan Lansing were found on the Carrington property. "My wife and I have talked it over. I'm going to the prosecutor's office and tell them everything. That guy's a serial killer."

Greco was not surprised to get the phone call from Meredith. "I think that is a very wise idea," he said. "And it is possible that there may be no need to make public any information concerning your sister's relationship with another man. If Carrington is persuaded to admit to her death, the public assumption would be that he was trying to prevent the birth of a damaged child."

"But his lawyers would know about it, wouldn't they?"

"Of course. But as you can certainly understand, while they are trying to reach the best possible plea bargain for their client, they would not want the public to know that a man with Carrington's great fortune would commit murder to save money."

"And once he admits to killing Grace, I can file a civil suit?"

"Yes."

"I know it may sound as if my first interest is the money, but it's costing ten thousand dollars a month to keep my mother in her nursing home, and I need help. I don't want to have to move her."

"I understand."

"Thank you for being willing to help me, Mr. Greco. I guess the prosecutor will take over now."

This may be the shortest job I've ever had, Nicholas Greco thought as he amiably agreed with Philip Meredith. But after he replaced the receiver in its cradle, he leaned back in his chair. From the Internet he had obtained a copy of the page from *People* magazine that had been found on Grace Carrington's body the night she was drowned.

Grace was wearing a satin maternity evening suit when she was found in the pool. Why would she put that page in a pocket of the jacket instead of leaving the magazine open on the table? Greco wondered.

Sometimes, when Greco was visualizing a situation, he asked himself, What would Frances have done? In this case, he knew the answer. A fashion-conscious woman would not have taken the chance of creating an unnecessary bulge in the pocket of a satin evening suit. In her own home, if she saw an item in a magazine that she wanted to follow up on, Frances would have put some kind of marker in the magazine or turned it upside down on the table, open to that page.

There was no mention in the prosecutor's file of the magazine being with the evidence the investigators had collected. I must see what day that issue was on the stands or in the mail, Greco thought. And I am even more eager to have a meeting with the outsiders who were present at that dinner, the couple from Englewood, Nancy and Jeffrey Hammond.

I'm going to stick with this, even if I am breaking my cardinal rule, which is never to work pro bono, Nicholas Greco thought, smiling to himself. As Mother always reminded me, the laborer is worthy of his hire.

38

Five days after they found his remains, they gave me the locket they had found around my father's neck. They had photographed and analyzed it for any possible evidence, but then had agreed to let me have it. The lab had cleaned twenty-two years of grime off it, until the underlying sheen of silver appeared. The locket was closed, but the dampness had worked its way inside, and my mother's picture was darkened even though her features were still recognizable. I wore the chain and locket to my father's funeral.

Of course they blamed Daddy's death on Peter. Vincent Slater had driven Peter back and forth to Manhattan the afternoon the remains were found, and they arrived here minutes after the discovery was made. Slater immediately called Conner Banks, who contacted Prosecutor Krause. She told him that she had reached Judge Smith, and he had scheduled an emergency hearing for eight P.M. that evening. She also said that, although she was not yet seeking a warrant for Peter's arrest in this newly discovered homicide, one might very well follow. Tonight she was planning to request that the judge raise Peter's bail and alter the terms of release so that he no longer would be allowed to leave the premises except for a dire medical emergency.

Banks told Vincent he'd meet him and Peter at the courthouse. I wanted to go with them, but Peter absolutely refused to allow it.

I tried to make him realize that after that first terrible shock, my second reaction was one of infinite regret that for so many years I had been angry at my father. I told him that all the anger I had felt at being abandoned had now evolved into pity for Daddy, accompanied by a raging desire to find who had killed him. Sitting on Peter's lap, the blanket still wrapped around me, the library door closed, I told Peter that I knew he was innocent, that I knew it with every bone in my body, with every fiber of my being.

Maggie phoned the minute she heard the story on the local news. When Peter realized she was calling, he told me to invite her to come over. Fortunately, she arrived after he and Vincent left for the courthouse. Then I sent home Jane Barr, who had been visibly upset at the discovery of Daddy's body.

"Your father was a lovely man, Mrs. Carrington,"

she said, weeping. "And to think of him lying out there all these years."

I was grateful that she clearly cared about my father, but I didn't want to listen. I told Gary to go home with her.

Maggie and I sat in the kitchen. She fixed tea and toast; neither one of us wanted anything more than that. While we sipped the tea and nibbled on a few bites of toast, we were both keenly aware that men were continuing to dig in the yard, and we could hear the dogs barking as they were taken back and forth over the grounds.

That night Maggie looked every day of her eighty-three years. I knew she was worried about me, and I completely understood. She thought I was crazy to believe in Peter's innocence, and she didn't want me to stay in the house alone with Peter. I knew that nothing I could say would reassure her.

Vincent called at nine o'clock to tell me that they had increased Peter's bail another ten million dollars, and that a messenger was on his way with a certified check in that amount from Manhattan.

"You'd better get going, Maggie," I said. "I don't like you driving alone at night, and I know you don't want to run into Peter."

"Kay, I don't want to leave you alone with him. My God, why are you so blind and so foolish?"

"Because there's another explanation for everything that has happened, and I am going to find it. Maggie, as soon as we know when Daddy's body will be released, we'll have a private funeral Mass. You must have the deed to the grave."

"Yes, it's in the safe-deposit box. I'll get it. Don't bring your husband to the funeral, Kay. You'd be thumbing your nose at your dad if Peter Carrington was there pretending to mourn him."

It took courage for Maggie to make that statement, knowing that it might cause me never to speak to her again. "Peter won't be allowed to attend Daddy's funeral," I said, "but if he were, he'd be there with me." As we walked to the front door, I said, "Maggie, listen to me. You thought Daddy was fired because of his drinking. That wasn't true. You thought he committed suicide because he was depressed. That wasn't true, either. I know that when Daddy disappeared, you were in charge of selling the house and getting rid of a lot of the stuff in it."

"I moved the living room and bedroom and dining room furniture over to my house," Maggie said. "You know that, Kay."

"And you stuck most of your own stuff in the attic. But what else did you move to your house? What happened to my father's business files?"

"There's just one. Your father was never a saver. I

had the mover put the file cabinet in the attic, too. It was too tall, though, so he laid it down flat. My old couch is upside down on top of it."

No wonder I had never noticed it, I thought. "I want to go through that file soon," I said. We stopped at the guest closet and got her coat. I helped her put it on, buttoned it for her, and kissed her. "Now get home safe," I cautioned. "There still may be some black ice on the road. Be sure to lock the car. And mark my words, one of these days you and Peter are going to be the best of friends."

"Oh, Kay," she said, sighing deeply as she opened the door and let herself out. "There are none so blind as those who will not see."

39

For the last few days, Pat Jennings had not known what to make of her employer, Richard Walker. On Monday he had come in with the familiar look of relief which usually signaled that his mother had paid his gambling debts. That same day, his stepbrother, Peter Carrington, was arraigned on a charge of murder. The next day, on Tuesday, Walker had spoken freely about him: "We had dinner with Peter after he got home," he told Pat.

Pat asked him about the former maid, Maria Valdez.

"Naturally Peter's depressed by what has happened," Walker explained. "It is despicable that that woman changed her story, and now is tainting the memory of my stepfather. I hope they put me on the stand. I'd be able to tell them firsthand how the old man had bursts of spontaneous generosity. I remember one night I was having dinner at 21 with him and Mother. Somebody came to the table to talk about some worthy cause or another, and Carrington senior pulled out his checkbook and wrote a check for ten thousand dollars then and there. Then he stiffed the waiter with a cheap tip."

Walker also talked to Pat about Peter's wife, Kay. "Absolutely wonderful girl," he raved. "Just what Peter has needed for years. From what I've seen, even with all his money, he's never had much happiness."

On Wednesday morning, Walker came into the gallery with a pretty young artist, Gina Black, in tow. Like her predecessors, Gina was introduced to Pat as a brilliant talent, one whose career was going to flourish under Walker's guidance.

Uh-huh, was Pat's reaction.

She had heard about the skeletal remains found on the grounds of the estate on Wednesday night when she and her husband were watching the evening news. The fact that it was the body of Kay Carrington's father was revealed to her the next morning by Walker.

"They're not releasing any details yet," he confided, "but he was wearing a chain and locket with a picture of Kay's mother in it. My mother is freaking out. She was in her New York apartment and heard about it when she turned on the television. She said that when they were searching the grounds with the dogs before the rain started the other day, she asked the detectives if they thought the place was a cemetery."

"*Two* bodies found on the estate," Pat said. "You couldn't pay me to live there."

"Nor me," Walker agreed, as he passed her desk to go into his own office. "I'll be on the phone for a while. Hold any other calls."

Jennings watched as Walker closed the door firmly enough that she could hear a decisive click. He'll be on the phone with his bookie, she thought. He'll be head over heels in debt again in no time. I wonder when his mother will finally throw up her hands and tell him to figure it out for himself.

She reached for her copy of the *New York Post* which she'd tucked in the bottom file drawer in her desk. On the bus down to Fifty-seventh Street, she'd skimmed Page Six, but now she read it line by line. That poor Kay Carrington, she thought. What must it be like to be married to a man who's obviously a serial killer? She must worry that she'll wake up dead someday.

There was only one phone call in the next hour, that one from a woman who gave her name as Alexandra Lloyd. She had called last week and Walker had not called her back. Had he received her message? she asked.

"He definitely received the message," Jennings said firmly. "But I'll remind him."

"Please take my number again, and will you tell him that it's very important?"

"Of course." Thirty minutes later, when Walker opened the door of his office, Pat could see the flush of excitement on his face. There isn't a horse running anywhere today that he hasn't bet on, she thought. "Richard," she said, "I left a note on your desk last week that an Alexandra Lloyd phoned. She just called again and said that it's important you get in touch with her."

She held out the paper with the woman's number. Richard took it from her, tore it up, and went back into his office. This time he slammed the door shut.

40

"The force of the blow that killed Jonathan Lansing was so powerful that the back of his skull was caved in," Barbara Krause said, as she read the autopsy report. "I wonder what Kay Carrington is thinking when she looks at her husband now."

Tom Moran shrugged. "If she isn't getting nervous being alone in the house at night with that guy, I'd wonder if she's legally sane."

"This time we can be sure that Carrington had someone helping him," Krause said. "He didn't leave Lansing's car in that godforsaken spot and then hitch-hike home. Somebody had to drive him home."

"I looked at our file from when Lansing disappeared and was reported as a possible suicidc. The insurance company suspected it was a phony. They had their investigators all over the area where his car was found. A guy like Peter Carrington gets noticed. He has a look about him. I wouldn't care if he was wearing clothes from the Salvation Army, he would have been noticed. No one of Carrington's description got on a bus, or rented a car around there. At the very least, if he drove Lansing's car there, somebody was waiting to pick him up."

"Lansing was supposed to have been fired because of his drinking problem," Krause said, "but suppose there was another reason. Suppose someone was afraid that he was a threat. He was fired two weeks after Susan Althorp disappeared. He supposedly committed suicide two weeks later. By then the police had thoroughly searched the grounds with the cadaver dogs, and I include the property outside the fence."

Krause had the copy of Lansing's landscape design on her desk. "The question is, did he submit it after Susan's body was buried on the site? If so, he signed his own death warrant."

She looked at her watch. "You'd better be on your way. Lansing's funeral is at eleven o'clock. Keep your eyes open to see who's there."

41

I arranged to have my father's funeral Mass in the church nearest to MaryRest Cemetery where my mother is buried. It's in Mahwah, a town about twenty minutes northwest of Englewood. I had hoped to keep the time and place of the Mass and funeral private, but when we arrived at the church, the photographers were there in force.

Maggie and I had been picked up by the driver from the funeral home. On the way down the aisle, I saw familiar faces: Vincent Slater, Elaine, Richard Walker, the Barrs. I knew they were planning to be there, but I didn't want to arrive in a group with them. I was not part of their world when my father died. For these last hours I wanted to separate myself from them. I wanted to keep my father to myself.

In my grief I even felt isolated from Maggie. I knew she had loved my father, and had been very happy when he and my mother were married. I believe that after my mother's death, Maggie had encouraged Daddy to date other women, but knowing her, I am sure she was secretly pleased that he could not or would not do it.

On the other hand, Maggie had always bad-mouthed Daddy to me about his drinking, although I think she exaggerated those stories to help make sense of his disappearance.

The church was sparsely filled, mostly with Maggie's friends, so I knew she hadn't been able to keep her promise not to tell where the funeral would be held. But then I saw the tears in her eyes and my heart ached for her. She had told me once that she never attended a funeral without reliving the grief of my mother's death.

I sat in the front pew of the church, inches from the coffin, my fingers touching the pendant that until now had been on Daddy's body all these years. I kept thinking over and over again, I *should have known* he couldn't have killed himself. He never would have forsaken me.

Maggie began to cry when the soloist sang, "Ave Maria," just as it had been sung at my mother's Mass.

"Ave, Ave, Ave, Maria." How many times over the years had I heard that song? I wondered. I heard that song before. As the last beautiful notes faded into silence, for some reason, I began to think about that episode years ago in the chapel at the mansion. Could the scene between the man and woman possibly have had more significance than I had realized?

The thought passed through my mind, then was gone. The Mass ended. I followed Daddy's coffin down the aisle.

Once outside the church, the media closed around me. One of the reporters asked, "Mrs. Carrington, does it bother you that your husband can't be with you on this difficult day in your life?"

I looked straight into the camera. I knew Peter would have the television on just in case the media did cover the funeral. "My husband, as you must be aware, is not permitted to leave our property. He is innocent of the death of Susan Althorp, innocent of the death of his first wife, innocent of the death of my father. I challenge Barbara Krause, the Prosecutor of Bergen County, to remember the legal and moral principle that in this country, a person is still presumed innocent until found guilty. Ms. Krause, presume my husband is innocent of any crime, then take a fresh look at the facts of these three deaths. I assure you, *I* intend to do just that myself."

That night, when we went to bed, Peter wept as I held him in my arms. "I don't deserve you, Kay," he whispered. "I don't deserve you."

Three hours later, I woke up. Peter was no longer in bed. With a terrible sense of foreboding, I ran through the parlor into the other bedroom. He wasn't there, either. Then from the driveway I heard the sound of screeching tires. I rushed to the window in time to see Peter's Ferrari racing toward the gate.

Fifteen minutes later, squad cars, alerted by the Global Monitor System that tracked his electronic bracelet, converged on him as he knelt on the frozen lawn of the Althorp residence. When a cop tried to arrest him, Peter jumped up and punched him in the face.

"He was sleepwalking," I told Conner Banks later that morning at Peter's arraignment. "He never would have left the grounds otherwise."

Once more Peter was brought into court wearing an orange prison suit. This time, in addition to the handcuffs, there were shackles on his ankles. I listened numbly as the new charges were read: "Bail jumping . . . assault on an officer . . . proven risk of flight."

The judge did not take long in coming to a decision. The twenty-million-dollar bail was forfeited. Peter would remain in custody.

"He's a sleepwalker," I insisted to Banks and Markinson. "He's a sleepwalker."

"Keep your voice down, Kay," Banks urged.

"Sleepwalking in this country is no defense. As a matter of fact, there are two guys in this country who are currently serving life sentences because they killed someone while they were sleepwalking."

42

The shocking tape the police had made of Peter Carrington kneeling on the lawn of the Althorp home, and then attacking the police officer who reached him first, made Nicholas Greco wonder if there was any point in keeping his appointment with Nancy and Jeffrey Hammond, the couple who had been guests at dinner the night Grace Carrington drowned.

Explaining that they had been away, visiting relatives in California, Nancy Hammond called when she heard Greco's message on the answering machine and invited him to stop in.

The couple lived on a pleasant street in Englewood, where most of the houses were older and had wide porches and shutters, the kind of houses that had been built in the late nineteenth century. Greco climbed the five steps from the sidewalk and rang the doorbell.

Nancy Hammond answered the door, introduced herself, and invited him in. She was a small woman who appeared to be in her early forties, with silver hair that becomingly framed and softened her sharp-featured face.

"Jeff just got home a minute ago," she said. "He'll be right down. Oh, here he is," she added.

Jeffrey Hammond was on his way down from the second floor. "That's the way my wife introduces me?" he said with raised eyebrows. "'Here he is'?"

Greco's immediate impression was of a tallish man in his late forties who reminded him of the astronaut John Glenn. Like Glenn, he had smile wrinkles at the corners of his eyes. He was balding, and made no attempt to disguise the fact. A particular peeve of Greco's was to see men not coming to grips with the inevitability of their DNA structure. He could spot a hairpiece a mile away, and even worse in his eyes was to see a man with a comb-over, long strands of hair combed over a shiny pate.

Greco had done a thorough profile on the couple ahead of time, and found the background to be about what he would expect of friends of Grace Carrington. Good solid family on either side: Her father had been a state senator; his great-grandfather, a presidential cabinet member. Both were well educated, and they had a sixteen-year-old son who was presently in boarding school. Jeffrey Hammond was employed as a fundraiser for a foundation. Nancy Hammond worked part-time at the local congressman's office in some kind of administrative capacity.

He had explained in both the message he left and in his telephone conversation why he wanted to talk to them. As he followed them into the living room, he absorbed the details of their surroundings. One of them was obviously a musician. A grand piano with books of sheet music dominated the room. Family pictures covered the surface of the piano. The coffee table had copies of magazines, neatly stacked: *National Geographic*, *Time*, *Newsweek*. Greco could see that the magazines looked as though they'd been read. The couch and chairs were of good quality, but in need of reupholstering.

His overall impression was of a pleasant home with intelligent people. As soon as they were seated, he got to the point of his visit. "Four years ago, you gave statements to the police about Grace Carrington's demeanor at the dinner you shared with her the night of her death."

Jeffrey Hammond looked at his wife. "Nancy, I thought that Grace seemed perfectly sober when we got there. You didn't agree."

"She was restless, even agitated," Nancy Hammond said. "Grace was seven-and-a-half-months pregnant, and had had some false labor pains. She was making an effort to stay off the booze. She was torn. Most of her friends were in the city and were in and out of the apartment all the time. And Grace loved to party. But the doctor had told her to get plenty of rest and I think she felt safer at the mansion than in New York. Of course, then she was bored out here."

"Obviously you knew her very well," Greco commented.

"She was married to Peter for eight years. All that time we were members of the same gym in Englewood. Whenever she stayed at the mansion, she exercised at the gym. We got friendly."

"Did she confide in you?"

"'Confide' is too strong a word. Just one time she let her guard slip and called Peter a rich genius and a stick-in-the-mud."

"Then you don't think she was depressed?"

"Grace was worried about her drinking. She knew she had a problem. She wanted this baby desperately, and she was always aware that she'd previously had three miscarriages. My guess is that she'd already had a drink by the time we got there, then, one way or another, was sneaking others."

For a number of reasons, she wanted her baby to live, Greco thought. Not the least of which, perhaps, was that the baby was her ticket to a lifetime income of twenty million dollars a year. He turned to Jeffrey Hammond. "What do *you* think, Mr. Hammond?"

Jeffrey Hammond looked thoughtful. "I keep going

over that evening in my mind," he said. "I agree that Grace seemed restless when we got there, and then, sadly, in the course of the evening began to slur her words and became unsteady on her feet."

"Did anyone attempt to stop her from imbibing?"

"By the time I noticed, it was too late. She went to the bar and openly poured straight vodka into her glass. Before dinner, she was claiming to be drinking only club soda with a twist of lime."

"That was for our benefit," Nancy Hammond said dryly. "Like most problem drinkers, she must have had a bottle stashed somewhere. Maybe in the powder room."

"Did she expect her husband to be home in time for the dinner?" Greco asked.

"Remember, this dinner wasn't a planned event," Jeffrey Hammond said. "Grace only called Nancy the day before to see if we were free. Early in the evening she told us that Richard Walker's birthday was coming up, so we'd call it a birthday celebration for him. There wasn't a place at the table set for Peter."

"Did Grace refer to an article she had read in *People* magazine about the actress Marian Howley?" Greco asked.

"Yes, she did," Nancy Hammond replied promptly. "In fact, she had it open to that page when we arrived, and she left it open. She commented on what a marvelous actress Marian Howley was, and said that she was going to get tickets to her new play, that she had met Howley at some benefits, and that she had marvelous taste. After dinner, when we were having coffee, she rambled on again about Howley, and repeated herself the way drunks do, going on about what great taste the actress had. Then Grace tore that page out of the magazine and stuck it in the pocket of her jacket, and dropped the magazine on the floor."

"I didn't see her do that," Jeffrey Hammond said.

"By then the rest of you were ignoring her. That was just seconds before Peter walked in, and all hell broke loose. We left a few minutes later."

Greco realized he was disappointed. He had come hoping to glean something further, to learn if there was some significance in the crumpled page in Grace Carrington's pocket. He stood up to leave. "I won't take up any more of your time," he told them. "You have been very kind."

"Mr. Greco," Nancy Hammond said, "these past four years, I didn't believe for one minute that Grace's death was anything but an accident, but after seeing that tape of Peter Carrington slugging the cop in front of the Althorp home, I've changed my mind. The man is a psycho, and I can just picture him picking up Grace when she'd passed out on the sofa, and carrying her out to the pool and dropping her in. I wish I could tell you something that would pin her death on him."

"I do, too," Jeffrey Hammond agreed firmly. "It's just too bad that New Jersey is almost certainly going to eliminate the death penalty."

Greco was about to agree when he saw something that jolted him. It was a look of pure anguish in Hammond's eyes. With the instinct that seldom failed him, Greco calculated that he had stumbled upon the identity of the man who had been Grace Carrington's lover.

43

After the arraignment, the prosecutor allowed me to go back to the holding cell where Peter was being kept before he was transported back to the jail.

He was still handcuffed and shackled, and was standing in the middle of the cell. His head was down, his eyes were closed, and as I studied him, my heart was breaking. His whole body seemed so gaunt that he appeared to have lost twenty pounds overnight. His hair was untidy and his pallor was ghastly white against the stubble of beard on his face.

The cell had a grimy toilet in the corner and an unpleasant odor lingered in the closed area where the cell was located.

Peter must have sensed my presence because he lifted his head and opened his eyes. His voice composed, but his eyes pleading for understanding, he said, "Kay, I wasn't trying to escape last night. I was dreaming that I had to find something, and then I thought someone was attacking me. Kay, I did punch that cop last night. I hurt him. Maybe I am . . ."

I interrupted him. "I know you weren't trying to escape, Peter. We'll make them understand that."

Peter had taken a step back as if he was afraid I would reject him. But then he came forward to the bars, and raised his hands to entwine his fingers with mine. I noticed that the electronic bracelet was gone. It had served its purpose, I thought bitterly, alerting the police that Peter had left the grounds. Money well spent by the State of New Jersey.

"Kay, I want you to divorce me and get on with your life."

That was when I broke down completely, sobbing uncontrollably, angry at myself that I was only making it worse for him. "Oh, Peter, oh Peter, don't say that, don't even *think* that."

He shushed me. "Kay, they'll be here for me in a minute. Listen to me. I don't want you alone in the house. Get your grandmother to stay with you."

I shook my head. "No!"

That was when a sheriff's officer came in. "I'm sorry, Mrs. Carrington, you'll have to leave," he told me.

Still trying to stifle my sobs, I said to Peter, "I'll find out when I can visit you. I'll . . ."

"Kay, you must take care of this immediately," Peter said. "I want you to tell Vince to hire a security firm today. I want a twenty-four-hour guard around the house. *You are not to be alone there without it.*"

It was the statement of a protective husband. Peter was afraid for me.

I looked at him closely. The officer put his hand under my elbow to ease me out of the detention area. I didn't budge. I had something I had to say, and it was perfectly okay for the guard to hear me. "Peter, I'm going to throw one hell of a homecoming party for you when this nightmare is over."

I was rewarded by a sad smile. Then Peter said, "Oh, Kay, would to God I could believe that would happen."

The next morning, the full contingent of Peter's legal defense team gathered at the mansion. Walter Markinson and Conner Banks were there, of course. The other two chief counselors had flown in as well, Saul Abramson from Chicago and Arthur Robbins from Boston.

Vincent Slater took his usual place at the dining table. The Barrs had set out the usual coffee and pastries and bottles of water on the sideboard. Everything was the same, except that Peter was not sitting at the head of the table. I took his place instead.

If the atmosphere had been heavy the previous week, today it was positively grim. Conner Banks opened the discussion. "Kay, if there's any comfort in all of this for you, the police report from the other night indicated that Peter was disoriented and dazed, that he had a blank expression in his eyes, and was unresponsive to their orders to move after they cuffed him. When they were in the squad car he started to ask them what happened and why was he there. He even said, 'I'm not allowed to leave my property, I don't want to get in trouble.' They tested for drugs and there were none in his system, so at least I don't believe they think he was putting on an act."

"He wasn't."

"We've got to get his complete medical background," Markinson said. "Does he have a history of sleepwalking?"

Before I could answer, Vincent Slater said, "Yes, he does."

I could see beads of sweat on Slater's forehead and upper lip. "Horses sweat; men perspire; ladies glow."—Maggie would recite that old chestnut to me during my teenage years if I ever came in after a game of tennis and said something about sweating. To remember it at this moment made me think that I was the one who was in some kind of fugue state.

"What do you know about Peter's sleepwalking?" Markinson was asking Slater.

"As you are aware, I've been working for the Carrington family since the day after I graduated from college. Peter's mother died when he was twelve. At the time I was twenty-four and Mr. Carrington senior appointed me as a kind of big brother to Peter. Rather than have him chauffeured back and forth to prep school, I would drive him and help him get settled. That sort of thing. When there were school breaks, his father would often be away, and if Peter wasn't invited to visit a friend, I would take him skiing or sailing."

I listened, my heart sick, to the story about the boy who had to have someone appointed to keep him occupied during the times when most kids came home to their families. I wondered whether Slater had enjoyed that job, or merely used it to ingratiate himself with Peter's father and then, eventually, with Peter.

"This is something I would never have discussed, except in the hope of helping Peter now," Vincent said. "I witnessed at least three episodes of sleepwalking."

"How old was Peter then?" Banks shot the question at him.

"He was thirteen the first time. It was here, at the house. He had gone to bed, and I was watching television in the room that I now use as an office. I heard a noise and went out to investigate. Peter was in the kitchen, sitting at the table with a glass of milk and some cookies in front of him. His father had warned me that he'd had a few episodes of sleepwalking, and I guessed immediately that I was witnessing one of those episodes.

Peter drank the milk, ate the cookies, put the plate and glass in the sink, and left the kitchen. He passed inches away from me and never saw me. I followed him upstairs and watched him get back into bed."

"Was there ever an episode during which he exhibited violence?" Conner Banks demanded.

"When Peter was sixteen, he and I were in Snowbird, skiing during a school break. We had a two-bedroom suite in the lodge. We'd skied all day and went to bed around ten o'clock. About an hour later, I heard him moving around and looked into his room. He was fully dressed in ski clothes. I realized I shouldn't wake him up, so I followed him to make sure he'd be okay. He went downstairs. There were still people at the bar, but he ignored them and went outside. I had thrown on a heavy jacket over my pajamas, so I followed him out—in bare feet. His skis were locked outside, but he had the key and unlocked them."

"He unlocked his skis when he was asleep?" Markinson asked, his tone incredulous.

"Yes. Then he started to walk toward the lift. I couldn't let him go. I was sure the lift was secured, but, on the other hand, I didn't know what he might do. Remember, I was in my bare feet. I ran behind him and called his name."

I was afraid to hear what Vincent was going to tell us.

"Peter spun around and, much as he attacked the cop last night, he attacked me. I managed to jump aside, but the tip of his ski caught me on the forehead over the eye." Slater pointed to his left eyebrow. "This scar is proof of what happened that night."

"Were there any other episodes of Peter sleepwalking after that?" This time the question came from Arthur Robbins, the defense attorney from Boston.

"None that I'm aware of. I'm only talking about this because maybe in some way it might show a pattern that would be helpful to Peter's defense."

"Was he treated by a doctor after that alarming incident at the ski resort?" Conner Banks asked.

"Yes, by an elderly doctor at Englewood Hospital. That was twenty-five or -six years ago, so I doubt he's still alive, but maybe his medical records are stored somewhere."

"From what I understand, boys are more likely to be sleepwalkers than girls, and I gather that it often starts in adolescence," Markinson said. "However, I'm not sure that making the prosecutor aware of Peter having experienced a violent sleepwalking incident twenty-six years ago would necessarily help him in any way."

"There was another incident last week," I told them. "It was right after Peter got home from the first arraignment." I explained how he had taken a nap, and when I went to check on him, I found him standing up with a suitcase open and partially packed on the bed.

I did not tell them about Peter's sleepwalking incident the night we came back from our honeymoon. I could not put into words the fact that his arm had been in the pool as though he was pushing or pulling an object. I reasoned that these lawyers were being paid handsomely to defend my husband, but also that my information might make them actually believe that he had been responsible for Grace's death.

I was afraid that, even as they worked to acquit him, in their minds they would be thinking, Guilty, as charged.

44

The lawyers are staying for lunch," Jane Barr told her husband when he returned from the errands she had sent him to complete. "Wouldn't you think three straight hours would be enough? Mrs. Carrington looks absolutely terrible. I swear that girl is getting sick."

"It's been a lot of strain on her," Gary Barr agreed as he hung his coat in the closet by the kitchen door.

"I made chicken soup," Jane said unnecessarily. The aroma of simmering chicken and onions and celery was permeating the kitchen. "I'll bake some biscuits and have a salad and cheese. None of them are vegetarians."

Gary Barr knew his wife. For the last two weeks, since Susan Althorp's remains had been found, Jane had been unraveling. He watched as she went over to the sink and began washing lettuce. He came up behind her. "Do you feel okay?" he asked timidly.

Jane swung around, her face contorted with guilt

and rage. "There never was a finer human being in the world than Peter Carrington, and he's in jail right now because—"

"Don't say it, Jane," Gary Barr ordered, his own face mottled with anger. "Don't say it, and don't *think* it. Because it isn't true. I swear on my immortal soul that it isn't true. You believed me twenty-two years ago. You'd better keep believing me now, or else we both may be living under the same roof as Peter Carrington again, and I don't mean on this estate."

45

I did not find any mention in the file of the magazine Grace Carrington had been reading before her death," Nicholas Greco told Barbara Krause as he sat in her office.

"From what I understand, it had been thrown out," Krause told him. "Grace had torn one page from it because she wanted to remember to order tickets to a one-woman show that had just opened on Broadway."

"Yes, so I understand. I have met with the Hammonds, the couple who were at the dinner that night, and we talked about this."

"We questioned them at the time," Krause replied. "In their statements, they both confirmed that Grace had been drinking and that Peter arrived home and made a scene. The Hammonds left shortly after that. It's just unfortunate that Philip Meredith did not tell us four years ago that Grace was involved with another man, even though she never told him who it was."

To Greco it was obvious that Barbara Krause did not share his suspicion that Jeffrey Hammond had been the "other man" Grace had been planning to marry, and it was nothing that he intended to share with her. There was no need to drag Hammond into this. At least not now. His guess was that the man was in his own private hell if he believed that Peter Carrington had learned about the affair, and that knowledge might have contributed to his reason for killing his wife.

"Mrs. Hammond is absolutely positive that the magazine was on the coffee table when they left," Greco told Krause. "I took the liberty of calling Mrs. Barr, the housekeeper, this morning. She distinctly remembers that she did *not* dispose of the magazine, and she says she and her husband went to their residence in the gatehouse before the Hammonds went home. In the morning, she was the one who found the body in the pool. She dialed 911 even before she woke Peter Carrington."

"He would have had time to dispose of the magazine before the squad car got there, but what would be the point of doing that?" Krause asked. "It would be easy enough to get another copy of it. I don't get the significance."

Greco could see that the prosecutor was becoming irritated. He got to his feet immediately. "I must not detain you," he said. "I simply wanted to be sure I had the facts straight."

"Of course." Krause stood up and reached out her hand. "Mr. Greco, you've pulled one rabbit out of the hat. I don't mind telling you that we are following every possible lead to see if we can track down Grace Carrington's lover. Even if we find him, his testimony won't be enough to convict Carrington of her murder, but it certainly gives him a strong motive. The more we know about that situation, the better the chance we have of making Peter come clean, and negotiate a plea."

This isn't about who the lover was, Greco thought. It's about the magazine. He had come to this office today for one reason only—to confirm the fact that the magazine had disappeared either just before or just after Grace Carrington had drowned.

46

It's a time when Kay needs me most, yet she's distancing herself from me, Maggie thought as she aimlessly puttered around the house. If only she'd listened to me and not married Peter Carrington in the first place. Thank God he's in jail, where he can't hurt her. It just made me sick to see the tape the cops made of him when he was outside the Althorps' house, and especially the way he leaped up and attacked that police officer. I hope they put him away for the rest of his life.

It's nine o'clock, Maggie thought. Kay's an early-morning riser—I'll give her a call. Yesterday when I phoned, the lawyers were there, but then she didn't call me back later.

Heartsick at the distance growing between her and her granddaughter, Maggie dialed Kay's cell phone. There was no answer. Maybe she's with the lawyers again, she decided. I'll try the house. This time Jane Barr answered. "Mrs. Carrington stayed in bed this morning," she told Maggie. "I went upstairs to make sure she was all right, and she said she hadn't felt well during the night. The lawyers aren't going to be here today."

"Tell her whether she likes it or not, I'm coming over for dinner," Maggie said firmly.

The front doorbell began ringing as she replaced the receiver. Through the glass panel of the door she could see two men standing outside. When they saw her, both held up IDs identifying them as detectives from the prosecutor's office.

Reluctantly, Maggie opened the door and invited them in. "Mrs. O'Neil," the older detective began politely, "we understand that at the time Jonathan Lansing disappeared, the contents of his home were moved here. By any chance, were there any records or files from his office included in that move, and, if so, do you still have them?"

Maggie thought of her cluttered attic. "I gave away his clothes," she hedged. "The furniture I used. It was better than mine, and after all, his daughter, Kay, was living with me. It made it a nicer home for her." I wonder if they think I stole the furniture, she asked herself nervously. Maybe I should have paid taxes on it.

"Of course, we can understand that," the younger detective said reassuringly. "Were there any business records or personal files belonging to Jonathan Lansing that you may have kept?"

"That's the same thing Kay asked me about. There is one of those old three-drawer steel cabinets that was in the room Jonathan used as an office. It's on the floor of the attic now with my old couch on top of it. Kay says she is going to come over and take a look through it, but I'll have to get someone strong to move things around so that there's room for the couch someplace else, and then he'll have to stand the file upright."

"If you'll give us your consent to examine the contents of that file, we'll be happy to place it where it's convenient for Mrs. Carrington to go through it. You don't have to consent, but we would like to see it."

"I don't see anything wrong with that," Maggie said.

She led the detectives upstairs, then apologized at the mess and the dust. "I always mean to get up here and get rid of things," she explained, as, with minimal effort, they cleared the space around the file and righted it, "but you know how it is. There are some things you never get around to doing. Kay says I'm a pack rat, and she's right."

The detectives did not respond. Each man had taken a folder from the top drawer and was flipping through the contents.

With growing unease, Maggie watched them, wondering if she had done the right thing in letting them come up here. Maybe I should have checked with Kay, she thought. I don't want her to have another reason to be upset with me. On the other hand, if Peter Carrington was the one who killed her father, and they find some proof here, she'd be crazy to waste another minute of her life worrying about him.

"Look at this," the older detective said to his partner as he handed him a sheet of paper. It was a copy of a note and a landscaping sketch sent to Peter Carrington by Jonathan Lansing. The note read:

Dear Peter,

It seems a pity not to complete the project. As you probably know, your father and I discussed creating a simple plan for the grounds beyond the fence. Since I am no longer in his employ, and since I believe Mrs. Elaine Carrington does not care to have me in contact with your father, I wonder if you would be so kind as to pass on this design to him. I enclose the card of a landscaper I know who could execute this plan to your father's specifications.

I have enjoyed our conversations very much, and I wish you well.

Jonathan Lansing

As the younger detective read the note, the older one looked at Maggie. "Never apologize for being a pack rat, Mrs. O'Neil," he said.

47

Conner Banks sat across the table from his client in the small room reserved for lawyer-inmate conferences in the Bergen County Jail. He had been the member of the legal team chosen to review Peter Carrington's options with him.

"Peter, this is what we're facing," he said. "The good news is that while you've been a 'person of interest' in the death of your late wife, Grace, that is a separate issue. It will not be allowed to be mentioned at this trial since they can't connect it to the earlier deaths. However, the fact that the remains of both Susan Althorp and Jonathan Lansing were found on the grounds of your estate means that the prosecution will attempt to try the cases together. Even so, the bottom line is that we think they will not be able to prove guilt beyond a reasonable doubt."

"What constitutes 'reasonable doubt,' given everything that is piling up around me?" Peter asked, quietly.

"I was the last person to see Susan alive. Maria Valdez is going to testify that the shirt I swear I put in the hamper was never there, and that my father paid her to keep her mouth shut. Now you tell me that Kay's father sent me a note with a landscaping design for the area beyond the fence, where Susan's body was found. If I had been guilty of killing Susan, I would have been terrified, because executing that design would have meant her body *would* be found. That would give me reason to get rid of Jonathan Lansing. There's no way out for me."

"Peter, I agree that it looks bad, but listen to me. Somebody else may have intercepted that letter. They have no proof that you received it."

"They have proof my father gave five thousand dollars to Maria Valdez."

"Peter, it's your word against hers that your dress shirt was in the hamper, and don't forget she's refuting her own previous sworn statement. Juries are skeptical of people who change their testimony. And yes, your father gave her a check, but we'll line up other instances of his spontaneous generosity to show that he might have been sympathetic and was helping her because Maria told him her mother was dying."

"The jury won't believe that," Peter said.

"Peter, just remember, we only need to make one juror uncertain of your guilt beyond a reasonable doubt to get a hung jury. If we can't get an outright acquittal, I absolutely believe we *will* get that for you."

"A hung jury—that's not much to hope for." Peter Carrington looked straight at his lawyer, glanced away, then, with an obvious effort, looked back at him. "I did not think I was capable of violence toward another human being," he said, carefully choosing each word as he spoke. "What I did to that police officer makes me understand that simply isn't true. Has Vince Slater told you that I assaulted him when I was about sixteen?"

"Yes, he has."

"What will happen if, despite your best efforts, I do not get a hung jury, and I am not acquitted?"

"Peter, the prosecution would ask for and probably get two consecutive life sentences. You would never get out."

"Suppose somehow they are able to tie me to Grace's death. What would I get in that case?"

"That would undoubtedly be another life sentence. But Peter, there's no way anyone is going to prove that you killed her."

"Conner, give me some credit. There's no such thing as 'no way.' Until now I have absolutely believed in my innocence. I'm not so sure anymore. I do know that I would never willingly harm another human being, but I did serious bodily harm to that cop the other night. I did the same thing years ago to Vince. Maybe I've done it in other instances, too."

Conner Banks felt his mouth go dry. "Peter, you don't have to answer this next question and think carefully before you do. Do you actually believe that, in an altered state of mind, you might have killed Susan Althorp and Jonathan Lansing?"

"I don't know. The other night I thought I was looking for Susan's body on the lawn of her parents' home. I had to make certain that she was dead. Was that a dream, or was I reliving what happened? I'm not sure."

Banks had seen Carrington's expression on the faces of other clients, people who knew they were almost certainly facing a lifetime in prison.

"There's more." Peter's voice lowered and became halting. "Did Kay tell you that the night we got home from our honeymoon, she saw me sleepwalking at the pool, and that I had my arm in the water, under the cover?"

"No, she did not."

"Again, maybe it was just a nightmare, or maybe I was reenacting something that actually took place. I don't know."

"Peter, none of this will come out in court. We'll make a case for reasonable doubt."

"You can keep your reasonable doubt. I want my defense to be that if I committed those crimes, I was sleepwalking and unaware of what I was doing."

Banks stared at him. "No! Absolutely not! There isn't a prayer in hell that you wouldn't be convicted with that defense. You'd be handing the prosecutor your head on a platter."

"And I say there isn't a prayer in hell that I won't be convicted with the defense you're planning. And even if there is, see it my way. My trial will get plenty of publicity. This is a chance to let the world understand that if you are cursed with sleepwalking, and unknowingly commit a crime, you may not be responsible."

"You can't be serious!"

"I have never been more serious in my life. I've had Vince look up the statistics for me. Under British and Canadian law, a crime committed during sleepwalking is called a 'noninsane automatism.' According to the laws in those countries, the deed does not make a man guilty unless his mind is guilty. If at the time of the offense there is an absence of mental control so that any action carried out was automatic, then in law the defense of automatism is possible."

"Peter, listen to me. That may be true in British and Canadian law, but it doesn't work here. I'd be a fool on a fool's errand if I went to court with that defense. We have two cases in this country in which men were convicted of killing people they loved very much while sleepwalking. One man bludgeoned his wife to death, then threw her body in the pool. Another drove miles to his in-laws' home. He was devoted to them, but he was also under great stress. He brutally beat his father-in-law and stabbed his mother-in-law to death. He woke up as he was driving home, went straight to the nearest police station, and told them that something terrible must have happened because he was covered in blood and had a vague memory of seeing a woman's face."

"Vince told me about those cases, Conner. Don't forget, I have lived as a 'person of interest' since I was twenty years old. Even if I'm acquitted, I'll be treated as a pariah who beat the system and got away with murder. I'm not prepared to live like that any longer. If you won't defend me on those grounds, I'll find someone who will."

There was a long silence, then Banks asked, "Have you talked to Kay about this?"

"Yes, I have."

"Then she agrees to it, I gather?"

"Reluctantly, but yes. And she's also agreed to another condition."

"Which is?"

"I'll let her stand by me during the trial. But after I'm convicted, and I understand that I probably will be, she has agreed to divorce me and begin a new life for herself. If she had not agreed to that, I would have refused to allow her to visit me anymore."

48

Maybe it sounds crazy, but after the first day or two, I began to welcome solitude at night. If Peter couldn't be with me, then I wanted to be alone. There was something about Jane and Gary Barr that was making me uneasy. Jane was always fussing over me. I knew she was concerned because I was feeling so rotten, but I still didn't want to feel as though they were observing me like an insect under a microscope.

After the visit from the detectives, Maggie came rushing over in tears, trying to explain that she never would have let the detectives up to the attic if she thought I'd be upset.

I owe her far too much, and love her far too much, to have made her feel any worse than she did. As the lawyers explained to me, even though that letter from my father had been addressed to Peter, there was no proof that it had not been opened by someone else.

During the search of the house, another copy of that design had been found in his father's files.

I managed to reassure Maggie that I wasn't avoiding her, and made her realize why I couldn't let her live with me. She finally agreed that she was comfortable in her own home, in her own easy chair, in her own bed. As I pointed out to her, it was safe here—security guards were ever present at the gate, and on foot on the grounds. Unspoken was the fact that because Peter was in jail, she did not have to fear for my personal safety.

My visits with Peter were heartbreaking. He was allowing himself to become so convinced that he was guilty of the deaths of Susan and my father that his interest in his defense began to take on a curious detachment. The grand jury had voted to indict him on both murders, and the trial had been set for October.

The lawyers, chiefly Conner Banks, were conferring with him in jail, so I now saw less of them. I did begin to hear from people I worked with at the library, and other friends, both from around here and from Manhattan. They were all so careful in the way they spoke to me, solicitous but embarrassed, not knowing what to say.

"I'm so sorry about your father. I would have gone to the service if I had known where it was . . ."

"Kay, if there's anything I can do, I mean maybe you feel like having dinner, or going to a movie . . ."

I knew what was going through the heads of these good people: it's tough to deal with this kind of thing in any rational way. I was Mrs. Peter Carrington, wife of one of the wealthiest men in the country, and I was also Mrs. Peter Carrington, wife of a double—or maybe even triple—killer.

I put off any get-together dates. I knew even the simplest lunch would be uncomfortable for all of us. The one person I regretted not seeing, however, was Glenn. He sounded so normal when he called me: "Kay, you must be going through hell," he said.

Once again, it was good to hear his voice. I didn't try to pretend. "Yes, I am."

"Kay, this may sound dopey, but I've been trying to figure what I'd want if I were in your boots. And I have the answer."

"And it is?"

"Dinner with an old pal like me. Look, I know that's all I've ever been to you, and it's okay. You lead the conversation."

He meant it. Glenn knew it was never "there" between us for me. Actually, I never thought it was "there" for him, either. I still didn't. I'd love to have taken him up on his dinner offer, but, on the other hand, I couldn't even imagine how I would feel if I could reverse positions with Peter, then read that he'd been seen having dinner with a former girlfriend.

"Glenn, it sounds so tempting, but it's not a good idea," I told him, and then was surprised to hear myself say, "at least, not yet."

At what point did I begin to believe that Peter was right, that in an altered state, he had committed the crimes he'd been accused of committing? I began to reason that if he believed it himself, how could *I* not accept it? And, of course, that consideration tore me in half.

I began to picture my father in the last few weeks of his life. Always the perfectionist, he'd been eager to see the last part of his overall design for the estate completed, even though he could not do the job himself.

According to the police report, the blow on his head had been so hard that his skull had been caved in. Had Peter been the one to raise some heavy object and inflict that blow?

Then good memories of my father flooded my mind, memories I had always tried to suppress because I had believed myself abandoned by him.

Memories like: Sunday mornings, when, after church, he would take me to Van Saun Park for a pony ride.

. . . The two of us cooking together in our kitchen. His telling me that Maggie was no cook, that for sheer survival my mother was forced to learn how to follow recipes. Maggie still isn't a cook, Dad, I thought.

. . . The note he had written to Peter: "I have enjoyed our conversations very much, and I wish you well."

. . . The day I had sneaked in this house and gone up to the chapel.

During this time alone, I began to go up to the chapel almost every day. It hasn't changed in all these years. The same nicked statue of the Virgin Mary is there, as are the table that must have served as an altar, and the two rows of pews. I brought a new electric votive candle to put in front of the statue. I would sit there for ten or fifteen minutes, half praying, half remembering that brief quarrel I had overheard that day, twenty-two and a half years ago.

It was there that a possibility began to take root in my mind. It had never occurred to me that perhaps Susan Althorp was the woman I had heard begging for money. Her family was wealthy. I had always read that she had a big trust fund in her own name.

But suppose it *was* Susan? Then who was the man who had snarled at her, "I heard that song before"? After she left the chapel, the man had whistled the last line of the song. Even as a child, I had recognized how angry he was.

It was in the chapel that my desperate hope took root, a hope that maybe I could find another solution, one that would solve the crimes Peter was accused of committing.

I was afraid to give Peter even a hint of what I was thinking. If he began to believe me, and decided that he was completely innocent, then his next thought would be that whoever was guilty might still be nearby. And then he would start worrying about me.

As it was, although he was actively cooperating in preparing his own defense, I could see that the lawyers had convinced him it was hopeless to expect anything but a "guilty" verdict. On my visits to him, he began urging me to move away, to divorce him quietly. "Kay, in your own way, you're as imprisoned as I am," he would say. "I know perfectly well that you can't go anywhere without people looking at you and talking about you."

I loved him so dearly. He was in a cramped jail cell, and worrying that I was holed up in a mansion. I reminded him we had a deal. I could visit him in jail and be with him at the trial. "So don't let's ruin our little time together by talking about my leaving you," I told him. Of course, I had no intention of keeping my part of our so-called deal. If Peter was convicted, I knew I would never divorce or abandon him, or stop believing in his innocence.

But he didn't stop bringing up that subject. "Please, Kay, I beg of you, get on with your life," he said to me during a visit in late February.

I had something to tell him, something I had known

with certainty for a few days now, but hadn't yet decided the best time to tell him. Then I recognized that there would never be a *best* time, but that this was the *right* time. "I *am* getting on with my life, Peter," I said. "I'm having our baby."

49

The part-time job that Pat Jennings had taken at the Walker Art Gallery had begun to make her something of a celebrity. Now that Peter Carrington had not only been charged with murder, but had been caught on tape bail-jumping and assaulting a cop, all her friends were anxious to have any tidbits of gossip that she could pass on about anyone in the Carrington family.

Pat was closemouthed with everyone except Trish, her best friend for the last twenty years. They had been assigned to the same dorm as freshmen in college, and had thought it a riot that each had chosen to be known by a different variation of their shared name, Patricia.

Now Trish worked in the business office of the tony department store Bergdorf Goodman, located at Fifth Avenue and Fifty-seventh Street, only a block away from the gallery. Once a week, the two women grabbed a quick lunch together, and, in deepest confidence, Pat caught her up on the gossip as she heard it.

She confided that she thought Richard Walker was having an affair with a young new artist, Gina Black. "He had a cocktail party for her and it didn't draw flies. When she stops in at the gallery, I can tell she's crazy about him. I feel sorry for her because my bet is that she won't last. From the way he talks, he's had plenty of girlfriends over the years. Think about it—he has two ex-wives, and both those marriages didn't last long enough to have the tea towels washed. I bet both wives got sick of his womanizing and gambling."

The next week, Pat discussed Elaine Carrington: "Richard told me that his mother has been staying in her New York apartment most of the time. Her feelings are hurt because she thinks that Peter Carrington's new wife, Kay, really doesn't want her stopping in the mansion unless she's specifically invited to be there.

"I don't think Richard has gone to New Jersey much, either," she continued. "He told me that he understands how difficult it must be for Kay, knowing that in all likelihood her husband killed her father, even though he may not remember it. Richard said that he believes it must have been like the way Peter attacked that cop. Well, we both saw the tape on television. You could tell Peter Carrington was absolutely out of it. He looked scary."

"He sure did," Trish agreed. "What a shame to marry a guy with all that money and then find out he's insane. Other than that young artist, are there hints of anything new in Richard's love life?"

"Well, there are hints, but I'm not sure it's anything new. There's a woman who's been calling him who must be an old flame. Her name is Alexandra Lloyd."

"Alexandra Lloyd. That's a fancy name," Trish commented. "Unless it's one she made up. Maybe she's in show business. Did you ever meet her?"

"No. My bet is that she's an artist. Anyhow, he's ignoring her calls."

Three days later, Pat Jennings couldn't wait until their next lunch to talk to Trish, so she called her. "Richard is an absolute wreck," she whispered into the phone. "I know he's had a couple of big losses on the ponies. This morning his mother stopped in to see him. When I got here they were in his office with the door closed, and boy, were they going at it! He was telling her that he absolutely had to have money, and she was screaming she didn't have it. Then he yelled something about how she knew perfectly well where she could get it, and she screamed, '*Richard, don't make me play that card.*'"

"What did she mean?" Trish asked breathlessly.

"I have *no* idea," Pat admitted, "but I'd sure love to know. If I find out, I'll call you first thing."

50

The nurse who met him at the door of Gladys Althorp's bedroom cautioned Nicholas Greco not to stay too long. "She's very weak," the nurse told him. "Talking tires her."

His former client was lying in a hospital bed that had been set up next to her regular queen-sized bed. Her hands were resting on the coverlet, and Greco noticed that the wedding ring she had always worn was missing.

Is her finger too thin now to keep the ring from sliding off, or is this one final rejection of her husband? he wondered.

Gladys Althorp's eyes were closed, but she opened them a moment after Greco reached the side of the bed. Her lips moved and her voice was very low when she greeted him.

Greco got right to the point. "Mrs. Althorp, I didn't want to disturb you, but there is something I'd like to follow up on. It might even have to do with someone who may have helped Peter Carrington hide Susan's body."

"I heard the police sirens the night he came here. I made the nurse take me to the window. I saw them drag him into the car . . . and . . ." Gladys Althorp's chest began to heave as she gasped for air.

The nurse rushed to her side. "Mrs. Althorp, please don't try to talk. Just breathe slowly."

I should not be here, Greco thought. He laid his own hand over the woman's emaciated hand. "I am so sorry. I should never have troubled you, Mrs. Althorp."

"Don't go. You came for a reason. Tell me."

Greco knew that it was best to be blunt. "I would very much like to know the names of your daughter's best friends, the ones who used to go with her to parties when Ambassador Althorp had them chauffeured."

If Gladys Althorp was surprised at the request, she did not show it. "There were three other girls. They went to Elisabeth Morrow School with Susan."

Mrs. Althorp was speaking more slowly, giving herself time to take a long breath between every word. "Susan's closest friend was Sarah Kennedy. She married Stuart North. Vernie Bauer and Lenore Salem were the others. I'm afraid I can't . . ." She sighed and closed her eyes.

"Mr. Greco, I really think you must not ask any more questions right now," the nurse said firmly.

Susan would be only forty now, Greco thought. The others would be the same age, within a year or two. He would expect their parents to be in the midsixties to midseventies age range. He wanted to ask Susan's mother if the families of those women still lived locally, but instead he nodded to the nurse and turned to go. Then he saw Gladys Althorp open her eyes again.

"The girls were all at Susan's funeral," Gladys Althorp said. A hint of a smile played at the corners of her lips. "They used to call themselves the four musketeers . . ."

"Then they still live here?" Greco asked quickly.

"Sarah does. When she married Stuart, they bought the house next door. They're living there now."

When Greco left the Althorp home, he doubted that he would ever see Gladys Althorp again. On one hand, he chided himself for disturbing her even for those few minutes. On the other hand, however, he recognized that he felt a growing sense of uneasiness about how neatly everything had fallen into place, which made him believe that there were important pieces of the puzzle that still had not been put in place.

Some of the facts that did not add up were beginning to command all his attention. He had come to the conclusion that Peter Carrington must have had help in hiding Susan's body until after the cadaver dogs had completed their search.

And if Peter *did* kill Jonathan Lansing, he must have had someone follow him to the place miles up the Hudson where he left Lansing's car, Greco mused.

And there was significance to the missing copy of *People* magazine that had been on the table the night Grace Carrington died. He thought he knew what that might have been about. Nancy Hammond saw Grace tear that page out of the magazine. Her husband, Jeffrey, claimed he hadn't noticed her do that. Nancy Hammond said that the attention of the other guests was diverted by Peter's sudden arrival home. She thinks that she is the only one who saw Grace tear out the page and jam it in her pocket.

Did someone who later took that magazine believe that page was still in the magazine?

If so, that would answer a lot of questions.

It would also raise another question, however. Peter Carrington did not know about the magazine. According to all of them—Elaine, her son Richard, Vincent Slater, and the Hammonds, Peter went straight upstairs after he took the glass out of Grace's hand and berated her for drinking.

Greco looked at his watch; it was five o'clock. He picked up his cell phone and dialed information. He had been afraid that the phone number for Stuart and Sarah North would be unlisted, but it was not. He heard a computerized voice saying, "We are dialing

201-555-1570 for you. If you wish to send a text message . . ."

The phone in the North home was answered on the second ring. The woman's tone of voice was warm. Greco hurriedly introduced himself and explained that he had just left Gladys Althorp. "I was hired to reopen the investigation into Susan's death. Are you Sarah Kennedy North?" he asked.

"Yes, I am. And you must be the investigator who located the maid. The ambassador told us about you."

"Perhaps this is an impossible request, but I am in my car outside the Althorp home. I know you live next door. May I stop in now, for just a few minutes? Mrs. Althorp said that you were Susan's best friend. I would very much like to ask you a few questions about Susan."

"I *was* Susan's best friend. Of course you can stop in now. We're the first house to the right of the Althorps."

Three minutes later, Nicholas Greco was walking along the path from the street to the North home. Sarah North was waiting for him, holding the door partially open.

She was a tall woman with wide-set eyes, dark-red hair, and had the look of an athlete about her. She was dressed casually in a sweater and jeans. Her warm smile seemed genuine as she invited him into the study off the foyer. Greco's immediate impression of the interior of the home was that it had been furnished with taste and money.

"My husband doesn't get home until six thirty," North explained as she sat down on the couch and indicated the chair next to it for Greco. "His office is way downtown in Manhattan, and he insists on driving back and forth. During rush hours, as I'm sure you know, it can take forever."

"I understand that in the early twentieth century, Englewood was referred to as 'the Bedroom of Wall Street.'"

"It was, and to a certain extent that's still true. How is Mrs. Althorp doing?"

"Not well, I'm afraid. Mrs. North, I have located the maid whose testimony may help convict Peter Carrington, but I am not satisfied. Some things don't add up, and I now feel he must have had an accomplice. I am interested in that year before Susan died. I understand that, at times, her father hired a chauffeur to drive her and her friends around. Weren't you all old enough to drive yourselves?"

"Sure we were, but if we were going to a party that was any distance away, the ambassador insisted that Susan be driven. My parents loved that idea, of course. They didn't want us riding with teenage guys who might have had a couple of drinks, and would then speed on the way home. Of course, a lot of the time we all were at college, and the ambassador couldn't control what we did there. But at home that was the way it was."

"Yet the night of the party at the Carrington estate, he allowed Susan to be driven home by Peter Carrington."

"He loved Peter. He trusted him. He felt Peter was different. In the summer, when the rest of us were at the club playing tennis or golf, Peter had a shirt and tie on and was at the office with his father."

"So when you were chauffeured, it was Susan and you and two other girls in the car?"

"Yes. Susan sat in front with Gary, and Vernie and Lenore and I sat in the back."

"Gary?" Greco did not want Sarah North to suspect that this was the very person he had come to learn more about.

"Gary Barr. He and his wife would help with dinners when the Althorps had guests. He was also the chauffeur whenever we were driven somewhere."

"What was his manner? Did he become friendly?"

"Oh, yes. Susan referred to him as her pal."

"Was there any chance that there was a . . ." Greco hesitated, "a *romantic* interest there? Did Susan have what in my day we called a 'crush' on him?"

"On *Gary*! Oh, no, *nothing* like that. She said he made her feel good, but by that she meant safe, secure."

"Mrs. North, I hope you understand that I don't

wish to pry when I ask questions that you, as Susan's friend, may not want to answer. But I am just not satisfied. I believe that Peter Carrington must have had help in disposing of Susan's body. Is there anything you can tell me about Susan that may help me to understand why she would have left her home that night after telling her parents she was in?"

"I've spent twenty-two years trying to figure that out," Sarah North said frankly. "It didn't ring true that Peter would be a party to her deceiving her parents. In fact, until I heard the police sirens the night he showed up in the Althorps' yard, I had doubted his guilt. But that night we grabbed our robes and ran outside to see what was going on. I saw the cop he punched. He was badly hurt. It makes sense that the same sort of thing may have happened if he hurt Susan while he was sleepwalking."

"Were you at the party at the Carrington home that night?"

"We all were."

"How late did you stay?"

"Till 12:30 or quarter of one. I had to be home by one o'clock."

"But Susan was Cinderella that night. She was told to be home at midnight."

"I could tell at the dinner that night that her father was furious at her. I think he was just being mean."

"Why was he being mean?"

"I don't know."

"Was Susan upset by her father's attitude?"

"Yes. In fact, Susan was not herself all night. Although, you had to know her well to realize that."

"The ambassador has a reputation for having a very quick temper, doesn't he, Mrs. North?"

"When we were kids, we called him the diplo-NOT. We could always hear him yelling at Susan and her brothers. He's a pill."

"Have you ever wondered what he might have done if he had seen Susan sneaking out of the house?"

"I think he'd have killed her." Sarah North looked startled at her own words. "Of course, I didn't mean that literally."

"Of course you didn't," Greco assured her. He got up to leave. "You have been very kind. May I call you again if I feel it necessary?"

"Certainly. I don't think any of us will be happy until the entire truth comes out about both Susan's death and her father's death."

"Her father's! You mean Mrs. Carrington's father?"

"Yes." An expression of distress came over Sarah North's face. "Mr. Greco, Kay Carrington came to see me. She asked the same kinds of questions you've been asking. I promised her that I would not tell anyone she was here."

"You have my word that I will not reveal it to anyone, Mrs. North."

As Nicholas Greco walked back to his car, he realized he was deeply troubled. He found himself asking the two questions that he always asked himself in the process of solving a case: "Suppose?" "What if?"

Suppose Peter Carrington is completely innocent of any involvement in all three deaths?

What if there is someone else out there, someone connected to the Carringtons, who is the real killer? What would that person do if he learned that Peter Carrington's young wife was asking questions that might lead to the truth being uncovered?

Kay Carrington may not want to speak to me, but I *am* going to meet with her, Greco decided as he got in his car. She *must* be warned.

51

The fact that I was expecting a baby both thrilled and saddened Peter: "It's wonderful, Kay, but you must get plenty of rest. This terrible stress you're under could hurt both you *and* the baby. Oh, God, why did all this happen? Why can't I be home with you, taking care of you?"

He also had decided that the defense he had chosen would help explain him to our child: "Kay, when our child is growing up, I want him or her to understand that the crimes I probably committed happened when I had absolutely no control of myself."

He pressed the lawyers to make a motion to the court to have him tested at a sleep disorder center. He wanted to have it on record that he was, indeed, prone to sleepwalking, and that, while he was in that state, was unaware of his actions.

The issue became a battle between him and his legal staff. "To have it out in open court that sleepwalking is or may be your defense is the same as saying, 'Not guilty by reason of insanity,'" Conner Banks told Peter. "It's skywriting so everyone can see it. 'Guilty. I did it, but I can explain it.'"

"Make the motion," Peter told him.

It meant another day in court before Judge Smith. I pressed my hand against my abdomen, seeking comfort in that tiny being growing inside me, as I saw my child's father led into court once again, manacled and shackled, wearing his orange jail jumpsuit.

It was Conner Banks who made the argument. "Your Honor," he addressed the court, "I know these are extraordinary circumstances, and I am not denying that Mr. Carrington left his premises, which, on the surface, is a violation of the conditions of his bail."

Vincent Slater was sitting with me; I knew he did not approve of having the lawyers make this motion.

"However, Your Honor," Banks continued, "I believe that even the police reports explicitly detailed Peter Carrington's dazed condition at the time of his arrest. Subsequent tests have shown that there was no evidence of either alcohol or drugs in his system. It is imperative to our defense to have Mr. Carrington properly evaluated at a sleep disorder clinic at Pascack Valley Hospital. That would require an overnight stay in which his sleep patterns would be monitored."

"Imperative to our defense," Vincent whispered to

me. "Those are the words that the media is going to leap on."

"We implore Your Honor to allow this test. We would be willing to post twenty-five million dollars in bail if this test is allowed. We recognize that it is not the Sheriff's responsibility to escort the defendant while he investigates possible defenses in his case, and so we would compensate the state for the salaries of the sheriff's officers assigned to guard him. We are also willing to retain a private security firm which will hire several retired police officers who will restrain Mr. Carrington if there should be any attempts to escape, which I assure you there will not be.

"Your Honor, one in two hundred people is a sleepwalker. The potential danger of a sleepwalker to himself and to others has not been recognized or understood by the general population. I doubt that many in this courtroom realize that sleepwalkers are not allowed to serve in the armed forces of the United States. The fear is that they may be a risk both to themselves and to others because they may have access to weapons or vehicles and are unaware of what they are doing when they move about while asleep."

Conner Banks's voice became stronger and firmer as he punched those last words home. Then, when he spoke again after a brief pause, his voice was quieter. "Allow Peter Carrington to establish once and for all that his brain waves indicate that he is the victim of sleepwalking disturbance. Give him this chance."

Judge Smith's face was impassive. I didn't know what to expect. But I knew what Peter was feeling, and it was satisfaction. He was getting his message out. He was beginning to try his own case in the media.

Banks and Markinson were worried; I could see it. During the recess following the request, they came over to talk to me. "The judge is not going to grant this request, and we've tipped our hand. There isn't a person in this room who doesn't think that this is just an insanity defense with a new twist."

The judge returned. He began by saying that in nearly twenty years as a criminal judge, he'd never had an application that included these kinds of circumstances. He said that while the state was concerned about the risk of flight, the prosecutor did not dispute the police report that indicated Mr. Carrington was in a dazed condition when apprehended on the Althorp lawn. He said that on the condition that a member of the defense counsel would always be present, and private security ready to restrain Peter if he attempted to leave, a twenty-four-hour stay at a sleep disorder center was approved.

Peter considered the judge's ruling a victory. His lawyers did not. I knew that even if the medical cause for his sleepwalking was confirmed by experts, it would not make a difference in the verdict at trial. So in that sense, it was a no-win.

After court recessed, I wanted to talk to Banks and Markinson, and asked them to meet me back at the house. Once again I received permission to visit Peter in the holding cell before leaving.

"I know you consider this a Pyrrhic victory, Kay," he said.

"There's only one victory, Peter," I told him fiercely. "We want you home with us. And it's going to happen."

"Oh, love, you look like Joan of Arc. Everything but the sword." For just a moment Peter's smile was genuine, a reminder of the look I saw when we were on our honeymoon.

I wanted so much to tell him that I was digging into every aspect of the evidence surrounding the deaths of Susan and my father, and that I was beginning with the premise that perhaps it had been Susan I overheard in the chapel that day. But I knew that to put those thoughts into words would have a negative effect—he'd only start worrying about me.

Instead, I told him that I was spending time going through the third floor of the mansion. "Peter, those rooms are a refined version of Maggie's attic," I said. "Who was the art collector?"

"My grandmother, I think, although my great-grandmother was responsible for some of it, too. Anything that's any good is on the walls downstairs. My father had everything appraised way back."

"Who collected the china? There's a ton of it up there."

"My great-grandmother collected most of it."

"There's a set of Limoges that's really gorgeous. It's still in the crate. I unpacked a few pieces. I absolutely love the pattern. That's the china I want to use at our dinner parties."

The guard was standing in the doorway. "Mrs. Carrington."

"I know." I looked at Peter. "Of course, if you don't like that pattern, we'll look at the others. Plenty to choose from."

I could see the expression of sympathy in the guard's eyes as I passed him. He might as well have been shouting, "Lady, he's no more going to eat off that china than I am." I wish he *had* said it aloud. I would have told him that when Peter comes home, I'll invite him for dinner.

Conner Banks and Walter Markinson were already at the mansion when Vincent dropped me off. There was a meeting later that day of the board of directors of Carrington Enterprises, and he was sitting in as Peter's representative. Peter now referred to Vincent Slater as "my eyes and ears." He had no voting power, of course, but he did keep Peter apprised of everything that was going on in the multifaceted corporation.

As usual, Jane Barr had brought the lawyers to the dining room, where I joined them. I decided to share with them my growing belief that it was possible that Susan Althorp had been the woman I overheard in the chapel twenty-two years ago.

They had not known about my escapade as a six-year-old, but when they did, their response stunned me. They looked horrified. "Kay, do you know what you are saying?" Banks asked.

"I am saying that it may have been Susan in the chapel that day, and that she may have been blackmailing someone."

"Maybe she was blackmailing your husband," Markinson snapped. "Have you any *idea* what the prosecutor could do with that information?"

"What are you talking about?" I asked, genuinely baffled.

"What we're talking about," Conner Banks said gravely, "is that, if your supposition is true, you have just provided a motive for Peter to kill Susan."

"Did you ever tell Peter about being in the chapel and overhearing that conversation?" Markinson asked.

"Yes, I did. Why?"

"When did you tell him, Kay?" Banks demanded.

I was beginning to feel as if I were being cross-examined by two hostile prosecutors. "I told him the night of the literacy benefit reception in this house. My grandmother fell. Peter went with me to the hospital and waited until she was all right, then brought me home. He came in for a while and we talked."

"That reception was held on December sixth, as I recall," Markinson said, flicking through his notes.

"That's right." I was beginning to feel defensive.

"And you and Peter Carrington were married on January eighth, less than five weeks later?"

"Yes." I realized I was becoming both frustrated and angry. "Will you please tell me what you're driving at?" I demanded.

"What we're driving at, Kay," Conner Banks said—and now his tone was both serious and regretful—"is that we've all wondered about your whirlwind romance. Now you've just given the reason for it. If that was Susan Althorp in the chapel that day, and she was blackmailing Peter, the minute you told him you had overheard the quarrel, you became a threat.

"He couldn't take the chance that you might talk about that encounter to someone else who would put two and two together. Remember, that reception was right after *Celeb* magazine did that big story on him. By rushing you into marriage, he made you unavailable as a witness in case he was ever brought to trial. He could invoke the marital privilege in court, and besides that, he probably worked to make you fall in love with him so that emotionally you'd never give him up."

As I listened, I became so enraged that if I had had something to throw at both of them, I would have done it. Instead I shouted at them. "Get out! Get out and don't come back. I'd rather have the *prosecutor* defending my husband than either one of you. You don't believe that even if he *did* kill Susan and my father, he did it while he was unaware of what he was doing. Now you're saying that his marrying me was pure calculation, just a way to shut me up. Go to hell, both of you!"

They got up to leave. "Kay," Banks said quietly, "if you go to a doctor, and he finds a cancer, but tells you that you're doing just fine, he's a liar. The only way we can defend Peter is to know every possible factor that could influence a jury. You've just delivered a blockbuster that fortunately we are not obliged to share with the prosecutor because it's something that *we* uncovered. We only have to tell the prosecutor if we plan to use it as defense evidence at the trial. Obviously, we won't do that. But for the love of God, please don't tell anyone else what you've just told us."

The fight went out of me. "I already have," I said. "The night Peter came home after he was arraigned."

"You told someone you thought that it might have been Susan in the chapel? Who heard you say that?"

"Elaine and Richard and Vincent Slater were here. I didn't say I thought it might have been Susan. In fact, I told them I didn't know who it was. Elaine even joked that it might have been her and Peter's father because they had been fighting all day about the money she was spending on the party."

"That's a relief. But never mention your visit to the chapel again to anyone. If one of them brings it up, stress the fact that you have no idea who was there because in truth you *don't* know."

I saw the two lawyers exchange glances. "We'll have to talk to Peter about this," Banks said. "I'd like to persuade him to cancel that sleep center business. His only prayer of ever getting home is 'reasonable doubt.'"

I had confided to the lawyers that I was expecting a baby. As they left, Markinson said, "Maybe now that he knows he's going to become a father, he'll let us take control of his defense and have a shot at getting him acquitted."

52

Nicholas Greco sat in the reception room of the Joined-Hands Fund, a charity created to benefit the victims of disasters. Jeffrey Hammond was vice president of the organization, and according to Greco's research, his chief responsibility was not to give away money, but to raise it.

The offices of the charity were in the new Time Warner Center on Columbus Circle in Manhattan, an expensive address that certainly added to the overhead, Greco thought. Hammond made one hundred and fifty thousand dollars a year, a princely salary to average Americans, but not so for those who had a child in a prep school that cost forty thousand dollars a year.

Jeffrey's wife, Nancy, worked part-time in the local congressman's office in New Jersey. Without knowing her actual salary, Greco knew that the amount had to be minimal. He knew also that the congressman's own salary was far too low to allow him to be generous to his staff. It was no wonder that, without personal wealth, many members of congress shared apartments in Washington.

All these thoughts were going through Greco's mind as he sat waiting until the perky young receptionist invited him into Hammond's office. Ninety-nine percent of receptionists were born cheerful, he thought, as he walked down the corridor.

The smile wrinkles at the corners of Jeffrey Hammond's eyes were not in evidence today. His greeting had a forced heartiness to it, and his palm was slightly damp when he shook Greco's hand and invited him to sit down. Then he made sure the door to his office was tightly closed before he went back behind his desk and settled in his swivel chair.

"Mr. Hammond, I asked to see you in your office because I thought it better not to discuss the subject I want to raise in front of your wife," he began.

Hammond nodded without replying.

"I have done a little homework, shall we call it, and find that Grace Carrington had been a great supporter of your charitable fund."

"Mrs. Carrington was very generous to many charities." His voice was carefully neutral.

"Of course. However, she was chairman of your fund for two years, and helped to raise a considerable amount of money, all of which was very beneficial for your position here. To be frank, your job depends on your success in bringing in donations, does it not?"

"I'd like to think that my job is to raise money because that money benefits so many needy people, Mr. Greco."

Perhaps, Greco thought. "Peter Carrington did not attend the many formal dinners that his wife enjoyed, did he?" he asked.

"Peter hated them. He didn't mind what Grace donated to those events as long as he didn't have to attend."

"Then, for several years, you were her escort of choice at a number of these affairs?"

"Yes."

"What did Mrs. Hammond think of that?"

"She thought of it as part of my job. She understood."

Greco sighed. "I think we are beating around the bush. I'm afraid you would not make a very good spy, Mr. Hammond. The inscrutable expression is not in your makeup. When I visited you at your home and we talked about Grace Carrington's death, I looked into your eyes and saw an expression that was nothing short of anguish."

Hammond looked past him. His voice a monotone, he said, "It's true. Grace and I were very much in love. In so many ways we were alike—good family background, good schools, and no money. She never loved Peter. She liked him well enough, and God knows she enjoyed his wealth. She was coming to terms with her drinking problem and wanted to overcome it. In fact, she had joined AA.

"If she had divorced Peter, she would have received a twenty-million-dollar settlement, wonderful money to you and me, but certainly the income on that sum would not have maintained the lifestyle she had come to love: the private jet, the palazzo in Tuscany, the apartment in Paris, all the trappings that Peter Carrington doesn't even bother with, except for the jet, which he uses for business."

"So you intended to have a long-term affair?"

"No. I decided I had to break it off. I know how my behavior must look to you, but believe it or not, I never wanted to be a gigolo. I loved Grace with all my heart, but I also recognized how unfair we were being to both Peter and Nancy."

Jeffrey Hammond bit his lip, got up, and walked to the window, turning his back on Greco. After a moment, he went on: "I called Grace and told her that it had to be ended. She hung up on me, but then called the next morning. She said that she was going to ask Peter for a divorce, that all his money wasn't, after all, what she wanted for the rest of her life. She joked that she was giving up a guy who has money for one who raises money. Peter was away on one of his long trips at the time. My son was graduating from grammar school. We agreed to wait a month before we told Peter and Nancy what we had decided. Before that happened, Grace realized she was pregnant."

"She was planning to divorce Peter before she knew she was pregnant?" Greco asked. "That was quite a change of heart."

"It was Grace's decision. She had been unhappy, and I guess decided that fantastic luxury wasn't compensation for feeling lonely and unfulfilled. But of course, learning that she was pregnant changed everything. She had had three miscarriages in the past and had given up hope of having a baby. But she realized that now, when she gave birth to Peter Carrington's child, she would have not only the baby she had wanted, but would be able to divorce Peter and still have the lifestyle she wanted. So prior to all that, I had been about to tell Nancy that I wanted my freedom, and Grace had been about to tell Peter the same thing. But then we decided to wait."

"Was there any chance that the baby Grace was carrying was yours?"

"Absolutely none. We took every possible precaution to make sure that didn't happen."

"Do you think your wife suspected your relationship with Grace?"

"Toward the end, yes, I think she did," Hammond admitted.

"I would believe that is true. Your wife seems to me to be a very astute woman. Yet she never challenged you about it, either before or after Grace Carrington's death?"

"Never. Early in our marriage, Nancy told me that her father had had a couple of affairs. She believed that her mother was right to pretend she wasn't aware of them. When he was in his fifties he settled down, and he and his wife had a good life together. I think after Grace died, Nancy was hoping that she and I would get closer again."

"Had Grace been drinking much during her pregnancy?"

"In the beginning, yes, but she was trying to stop. She had not had a single drink for the month before she died."

"And then, in the presence of other people, the night of the dinner party, she fell off the wagon. Mr. Hammond, if, as you have just suggested, your wife was aware of your affair, is it possible that she spiked Grace's club soda that night?"

"Unlikely, but I guess it's possible. Somebody did, that's for sure. Grace would never have risked drinking in front of Elaine and Vincent Slater. Either one of them would have told Peter—she knew that."

"You have told me that you went home minutes after Peter went up to bed. Were the gates in the driveway open?"

"Yes. Of course, they can be closed, but they seldom were, even at night. I doubt if Peter and Grace even remembered to turn on the alarm system half the time."

Greco wondered if that was really true, or if Hammond was indicating, for some reason of his own, that both the grounds and the house were easily accessible. "You would have gone home about what time?" he asked.

"A little after eleven. As you have seen, we live quite close to the Carringtons, even though we're not in the estate section of town."

"What did you do after you got home?"

"I went up to bed. Nancy wasn't tired and stayed downstairs to read."

"Do you remember what time she came to bed?"

Jeffrey Hammond's face turned red. "I wouldn't know," he said. "We had had a pretty big row, and I was sleeping in my son's room. He was away at a sleepover with a friend."

"You have been more than candid with me, Mr. Hammond," Greco said. "Frankly, I wonder why."

"I'll tell you why." Suddenly Jeffrey Hammond's voice was filled with the controlled fury Greco had heard earlier when he expressed the wish that the death penalty would be kept in New Jersey. "I *loved* Grace. We could have had a lifetime of happiness together. I want her killer found. If there's one thing I *don't* have it's a motive for killing her. I think you can see that, so I don't have to worry about being a suspect in her death. Maybe she got up, went outside, and lost her balance at the edge of the pool. I know that's possible. But if someone *did* take her life, I want that person found and convicted, even if it means publicly acknowledging our relationship, with all that implies. I love my son, but not enough to let a beautiful woman's life be snuffed out by someone who gets away with it."

"Do *you* think Peter Carrington killed Grace?"

"I do and I don't. Not over the issue of the money—that wouldn't have mattered to him. Peter is not his father's son in that respect. I don't think he'd kill her out of pride, either, the cuckolded-husband outrage. I just don't see Peter doing that. He was frustrated rather than furious when he grabbed the glass out of her hand. From what I know now, I do think it's possible he might have killed her in a sleepwalking state. After seeing that tape of him attacking that policeman, I think that's entirely possible."

"Do you also think it's possible that your wife went back to the mansion, perhaps woke up Grace, and suggested they go outside for a breath of air, and then pushed her into the pool?"

"Nancy never would have done that," Hammond said vehemently. "She's far too clearheaded to lose control that way. She'd never risk going to prison, because then she'd surely be separated from me and our son for good. The ultimate irony has been that she feels about me the way that I felt about Grace. She still hopes that in time I'll fall in love with her again."

"Will you, Mr. Hammond?"

"I only wish I could."

53

After Banks and Markinson left, I went upstairs and lay down to rest. It was almost five o'clock. I knew that a security guard was at the gate and another on the grounds. I had sent Jane home, telling her that I wasn't feeling well, and that I would heat some of her homemade soup later on. Thank God, she didn't protest. I think it must have been evident from my manner that I absolutely wanted to be alone.

Alone in this great, sprawling house from which, hundreds of years ago, in another country, a priest had been dragged out and hacked to death on the lawn. As I lay on the bed in our suite, I, too, felt like I had been hacked to pieces.

Was it possible, I asked myself, that my husband, Peter Carrington, had rushed me to the altar because he needed to make sure I could never testify against him?

Was it possible that all his declarations of love were merely the calculations of a cold-blooded killer who, rather than take the chance of murdering me, married me instead?

I thought of Peter standing in that holding cell, looking at me, with eyes that were alive with his love for me. Behind that expression, had he been mocking me, Kay Lansing, daughter of the landscaper, who had the colossal stupidity to think that he had fallen in love with her at first sight?

There are none so blind as those who will not see, I reminded myself.

I put my hand on my abdomen, a gesture that was becoming almost a reflex reaction to thoughts or situations I did not want to deal with. I was sure the baby was a boy, not because I preferred to have a boy rather than a girl, but because I just knew it was a boy. I was sure I was carrying Peter's son.

Peter *does* love me, I told myself fiercely. There is no other answer.

Am I deluding myself? No. No. No.

Hold fast to what you have, for it is happiness. Who said that? I forget. But I shall and will hold fast to my love for Peter, and to his belief in me. I must, because every instinct tells me that this is truth. This is what is real.

I eventually felt myself calming down. I guess I even dozed a little, because the ring of the phone on the bedside table startled me awake. It was Elaine.

"Kay," she said, I could hear a quivering in her voice.

"Yes, Elaine." I was hoping that if she was in her house, she didn't want to drop in on me.

"Kay, I must talk with you. It's desperately important. May I come over in five minutes?"

I clearly had no choice but to tell her to come. I got up and dashed some cold water on my face, then touched my lashes with mascara and my lips with a light touch of color, and went downstairs. It may sound silly that I bothered to go to that trouble for Peter's stepmother, but I had a growing sense of a looming turf battle between me and Elaine. With Peter in jail and me so new on the scene, she had been getting in the habit of walking in and out of the house as if it were once again her home.

When she came in this evening, however, there was nothing of the lady of the manor reestablishing her position about her. Elaine was ghastly pale, and her hands were trembling. There was no question that she was nervous and terribly upset. I noticed that she was carrying a plastic bag under one arm.

She didn't even give me a chance to greet her before she said, "Kay, Richard is in terrible trouble. He's been gambling again. I must have a million dollars right away."

A million dollars! That was more money than I would have made if I had worked my entire life at the library. "Elaine," I protested, "first of all, I don't have anything like that kind of money, and it's useless to ask Peter for it. He has told me he thinks you're very foolish to keep bailing Richard out. He said that the day you refuse to pay his gambling debt is the day Richard is finally going to have to do something about his addiction to gambling."

"If Richard doesn't pay this debt, he won't be alive long enough to do anything about his addiction," Elaine said. She was clearly on the verge of hysteria. "Listen to me, Kay. I've been protecting Peter for nearly twenty-three years. I saw him come home the night he killed Susan. He was sleepwalking, and there was blood on his shirt. I didn't know what kind of trouble he was in, but I knew I had to protect him. I took that shirt out of the hamper so that the maid wouldn't see it. If you think I'm lying, look at this."

She dropped the plastic bag she was carrying on the coffee table and pulled something out of it. It was a man's white dress shirt. She held it up for me to see. There were dark smudges on the collar and around the top three buttons. "Do you understand what this is?" she asked.

A wave of dizziness made me sink down onto the couch. Yes, I understood what she was holding. I did not doubt for a single instant that it was Peter's shirt, or that the dark stains were Susan Althorp's blood.

"Have the money for me tomorrow morning, Kay," Elaine said.

My mind was suddenly filled with the image of Peter hurting Susan. The antopsy report showed that she had suffered a severe blow to her mouth. That was the way he had flailed out at the cop. My God, I thought, my God. There is no hope for him.

"Did you see Peter come home that night?" I asked.

"Yes, I did."

"You're *sure* he was sleepwalking?"

"I am positive. He walked past me in the corridor and never even saw me."

"What time did he come in?"

"At two o'clock."

"Why were you in the corridor at that time?"

"Peter's father was still ranting about the cost of the party, so I decided to go to one of the other bedrooms. That's when I saw Peter coming up the stairs."

"And then you went into Peter's bathroom to get the shirt. Suppose he had seen you, Elaine. What then?"

"I would have told him that I knew he'd been sleepwalking, and was concerned that he went safely back to bed. But he didn't wake up. Thank God I took the shirt with me. If it had been found in the hamper the next morning, he'd have been arrested and convicted. He'd probably still be in prison."

Elaine started to look relieved. I guess she realized

that I would get the money for her. She folded the shirt neatly and put it back in the plastic bag, as though she were a clerk in a department store, completing a sale.

"If you were really trying to help Peter, wouldn't it have been a good idea to get rid of the shirt?" I challenged her.

"No, because it was proof that I did see Peter that night."

A kind of insurance policy, I thought. Something tucked away against a rainy day. "I'll get you the money, Elaine," I promised, "but only if you give that shirt to me."

"I will. Kay, I'm sorry to do this. I've protected Peter because I love him. Now I have to protect my son. That's why I'm here bargaining with you. When you have a child of your own, you'll understand."

Maybe I do already, I thought. I had not told anyone except the lawyers that I was pregnant. It was too soon, and besides, I didn't want it leaked to the press. I certainly was not going to tell Elaine about the baby now, I thought bitterly, not when I was bargaining to buy the bloody shirt that proved its father was a killer.

54

Vincent Slater had attended a business dinner in Manhattan and was not home in time to respond to Kay's urgent request to call her. "If you don't get back to me this evening, be sure to call first thing in the morning," she told his answering machine.

It was 11:30 P.M. when he got the message. He knew Kay went to bed fairly early, so he wouldn't try to call her now. But what could be so urgent? he wondered. That night, even though he was usually a sound sleeper, he found himself waking up several times.

His phone rang at seven A.M. It was Kay. "I don't want to talk over the phone," she said. "Be sure to stop by here on your way to the city."

"I'm up and dressed already," he said. "I'll be right there."

When he got to the mansion, Kay brought him back to the kitchen, where she had been having a cup of coffee. "I wanted to see you before Jane gets here at eight o'clock," she said. "Last month, that first morning after we got back from our honeymoon, Peter and I went jogging early. I made coffee for us before we went out. It was fun being just the two of us, Mr. and Mrs. Newlywed living in suburbia. It seems a lifetime ago."

In the harsh morning light, Slater could see that it looked as if Kay was losing weight. Her cheekbones seemed more prominent, her eyes enormous. Afraid of what he might hear, he asked what had happened to upset her so much.

"What happened? Nothing very much. It's just that it seems Peter's loving stepmother claims she has been protecting him for years, and now she needs a little help in return."

"What do you mean, Kay?"

"She is willing to sell me an object that could hurt Peter very much if it fell into the hands of the wrong person—meaning the prosecutor. The price is one million dollars, and she must have it today."

"What object?" Slater snapped. "Kay, what are you talking about?"

Kay bit her lip. "I can't tell you what it is, so don't ask me any questions about it. She needs that money today because her wonderful son Richard is deeply in debt after making losing bets. I know Peter opened a joint account for us. How much is in it? Is there enough for me to write a check to her?"

"Kay, you're not using your head. A check takes time to clear. The only way I can get money that fast is to wire it directly into her account. Are you *sure* you want to do this? You know how Peter feels about Richard's gambling. He'd want no part of subsidizing it. Maybe Elaine's bluffing."

"She—is—not—bluffing! She—is—not—bluffing!" Kay shouted, then clasped her hands to her face as a flood of tears rushed down her cheeks.

Startled, Slater watched as she impatiently brushed the tears away in an effort to control her emotions. "I'm sorry. It's just—"

"All right, Kay," he said soothingly. "All right. Don't do this to yourself. I'll wire the money to her."

"I don't want Peter to know," Kay said, her voice low but controlled. "At least not yet. He goes to that sleep disorder center tonight. He's got enough to deal with without having to worry about this, too."

"He doesn't have to know yet. I have power of attorney to transfer money. But realize something: Once that money is transferred, you can't get it back. Will she turn this object over to you before the transfer?"

"I doubt it very much. Let me finish this cup of coffee, then I'll call her. I don't want to sound upset when I'm talking to her."

Slater watched as Kay folded her hands around the cup as if to warm them. They sat at the table for a few minutes, not speaking, both sipping their coffee. Then Kay shrugged. "I'm all right now." She dialed Elaine's number and waited as the telephone rang repeatedly. "There's some satisfaction in knowing that I'm waking her," she said bitterly. "She was falling apart when she first came in here last night, but when I promised to get the money to her today, she managed to cheer up really fast. Oh, here she is."

Slater watched Kay's expression harden as she and Elaine talked. It was obvious, as he listened to one side of the conversation, that Elaine was not parting with whatever it was that she was holding until the money transaction was complete.

What could it be? he wondered.

Elaine was still living in the mansion the night Susan disappeared, Slater thought. The master suite is just around the corridor from Peter's old room.

Was it possible that she saw Peter come home that night wearing a bloodstained shirt?

It was possible, he concluded, nodding slightly.

Slater remembered the sleepwalking episodes he had witnessed years before, when he accompanied Peter on vacation trips. There had been the one incident outside the ski lodge when he woke Peter too quickly and Peter had lashed out at him. The three or four other times he'd witnessed him sleepwalking, when Peter returned to his bed he immediately fell into a deep sleep. Elaine could have gone into his room and retrieved the shirt from the hamper without his even being aware of her presence, he decided.

Kay hung up the phone. "She doesn't trust me. She says her banker will call her the minute the money is in the account, and only then will she come over here with the package I'm talking about."

"Is it the formal shirt he was wearing that night, Kay?" Slater asked.

"I won't answer that. I can't."

"I understand. All right. I'm on my way to New York now. I have to sign some papers to transfer the money."

"Money! That's the cause of most crimes, isn't it? Love or money. Susan needed money, didn't she?"

Slater stared at her. "How could you possibly know that?"

"Oh, of course I *don't* know it." She avoided his eyes by turning her head. Then, in a surprised tone, she said, "Oh, Gary, I didn't hear you come in!"

"I stopped to speak to the guard outside the front door, Mrs. Carrington. I offered him a cup of coffee, then came into the house right there."

Meaning he used the front door, Slater thought. He should know better. Had he been standing in the hall, and if so, how much did he hear? He knew the same thought was occurring to Kay.

Kay stood up. "I'll walk you to the door, Vince."

She did not speak again until they were in the reception area, then in a whisper asked, "Do you think he overheard what we were saying?"

"I don't know, but he had no business coming in the front entrance. I think he saw my car, spotted us through the kitchen window, then backtracked and used that as an excuse to try to eavesdrop."

"That's what I think, too. Call me when the transfer is done and I'll—" Kay hesitated, "and I'll complete the transaction."

At noon Slater called Kay to tell her that the million dollars was in Elaine's bank account.

At twelve thirty, Kay called him back, her voice angry and upset. "She won't give it to me. She said she sold it too cheap. She said her pre-nup was much too small. She wants to discuss an amount that would be appropriate for her future needs."

55

This is one way of getting out of the Bergen County Jail," Peter Carrington observed to Conner Banks as, shackled and manacled, escorted by two sheriff's officers and four private security guards, he was led through the lobby of Pascack Valley Hospital and up to the Sleep Disorders Center on the second floor.

"Not the way I'd necessarily choose myself," Conner told him.

"It's obvious you think this is nonsense," Peter said.

"I didn't mean that. What I meant was that I wish you were going home instead of coming here."

"Well, it seems as if I'm here for the night. Sorry to inconvenience you."

It was eight P.M. Banks had read up on what to expect from this experiment. Peter would be interviewed by a sleep specialist, answer a series of questions, then be put into a bedroom in the testing suite. A polysomnogram recording would be made of his heart rate, brain waves, breathing, eye muscles, leg movement, and all five stages of sleep. A television camera in the bedroom would also monitor him all night. In the morning he would be transported back to jail.

A special bolt and chain had been put on the outside of the door of Peter's bedroom. Banks and three of the guards would sit on chairs in the corridor, while the fourth one, accompanied by a hospital technician, would watch the video monitor that showed the interior of the room with Peter in bed. The sheriff's officers stood outside his door.

At one A.M. the knob on the bedroom door turned. The guards sprang up, but the chain they had installed on the outside prevented the door from opening more than an inch. The tugging from the other side lasted for more than a minute, then the door closed again.

Banks hurried to the monitor; he could see Peter sitting on the bed. He was looking directly in the camera, his face expressionless, his eyes staring. As Banks watched, Peter attempted to reconnect himself to the breathing tube, then lay down and closed his eyes.

"He was sleepwalking, wasn't he?" Banks asked the technician.

"You've just witnessed a classic example of it," the technician replied.

56

For the second morning in a row, Vincent Slater received a seven A.M. phone call; this time it was from Conner Banks. "We've got a problem," Banks said without introduction. "Peter was sleepwalking last night, during his stay at the sleep clinic, and tried to open the door of his bedroom. It could be viewed as a violation of the terms of his release. As soon as the prosecutor hears about it, there'll be another bail hearing. Krause will move to have the bail forfeited."

Slater swung his legs over the bed and sat up. "What do you want me to do?"

"I don't want you to do anything except pray that the judge sees it our way—that Peter didn't know what he was doing. Otherwise you can kiss another twenty-five million dollars good-bye."

"You absolutely *cannot* let that happen!"

"Do you think I won't give it my best shot? Vince, I've been telling you all along that this sleepwalking defense is madness. There is no way that the judge is going to buy it. He certainly wasn't happy with allowing Peter to go to the sleep disorder center, even with the guards. My big worry is that it might look as if this is a stunt to boost Peter's sleepwalking defense at trial. If the judge views it that way, your money is going to help the State of New Jersey reduce its budget shortfall."

"Have you told Kay about this?" Slater asked.

"I didn't want to disturb her yet. The last time I saw her was Monday, and she was pretty upset then."

"I saw her yesterday and she was still very upset. Let me be the one to talk to her."

"I'm sure the prosecutor will ask for an emergent hearing regarding Peter's bail," Banks told him. "You'd better warn Kay. She'll want to be there. I'll let you know what time it's set for."

Warn Kay, Slater thought as he showered and dressed. Yesterday she had me send one million dollars to Elaine's account because she believes Elaine has something that could hurt Peter. Then Elaine upped the ante. Blackmail on top of blackmail.

It's got to be the shirt, he thought.

Or could it be something else?

There was no use going into the Manhattan office today, he decided. If there was going to be an emergent bail hearing, he intended to be there. Rather than going into the city, he would work out of his office at the mansion, then drive Kay to the hearing.

It wasn't easy to phone Kay and tell her what had happened at the sleep center, but he got the job out of the way. An hour later he drove through the gate of the Carrington estate. The security guard gave him a friendly wave. The guard stationed at the house nodded to him as he drove around the mansion and parked his car in the back. He used the key to his private office to enter the house. He was barely inside before his cell phone rang.

It was Nicholas Greco, requesting a brief meeting at his convenience.

"Mr. Greco," Vincent said, "I can see no reason for our meeting, today or any other time. Peter Carrington has been indicted for murder because you located that maid who, for her own reasons, now claims that the sworn statement she made twenty-two years ago was a lie. Why would I be interested in exchanging a single word with you?"

"Mr. Slater, I am not in anyone's employ at this time. For my own sake, I do not like to leave loose ends dangling when I work on a case. I understand that Peter Carrington may admit in court that it is possible he committed those crimes while he was unaware of his actions. But is it not also possible that there is, in fact, another answer? As his close friend and assistant, please give me half an hour. Hear me out."

Without answering, Vincent Slater slammed the phone shut.

"Who was that, Vince?"

He turned around. Kay was standing in the doorway.

"Nobody important, Kay," he told her. "One of those crank callers who somehow manage to get private numbers."

57

When the sheriff's officers reported to Prosecutor Barbara Krause that Peter Carrington had attempted to leave his hospital room by forcibly pulling on the locked door, she immediately requested, and was granted, another emergent bail hearing just as Conner Banks had expected.

At 2:30 that afternoon, she and the defense attorneys and Peter Carrington once more stood before Judge Smith. And as before, the courtroom was filled with the media and dozens of spectators.

I sat with Vincent Slater in the row behind Markinson and Banks. It's difficult to express how I felt. I guess the best way to put it is to say that I felt numb. In the space of a few days—by opening the possibility that Susan had been the woman I overheard in the chapel all those years ago—I had, according to Peter's attorneys, established a motive for him to have murdered her. I had seen the stained shirt he was wearing the night Susan disappeared, and I had paid one million dollars to his stepmother to get it from her. It was blackmail, but I felt I had no choice. And then after paying that money, I'd been held up for more blackmail. I had also visited Susan Althorp's closest friend and learned that Susan had referred to Gary Barr as "her pal." So much was happening, and I was still trying to make sense of it.

I watched as Peter, my husband, my love, was led into the court, emotionally wounded and degraded, wearing shackles and manacles, paraded around for all the world to see on the evening news.

The prosecutor had a triumphant yet outraged air about her as she got up to speak. With every word she uttered, I hated her more.

"Your Honor, this is the second time that this man, who is indicted for two murders, and is a suspect in one other death, has violated the conditions of his bail. The first time, he left his home and went on the property of Susan Althorp's family, which caused them enormous distress. One of the police officers who attempted to arrest him was seriously assaulted. Last night, Peter Carrington attempted to force open the door of his hospital room in yet another attempt to escape. The sheriff's officers reported to me that he desperately pulled on the door for at least a minute. Fortunately, he was not successful."

Peter, I thought, Peter. What are you thinking? Why is this nightmare happening to us?

"Your Honor," the prosecutor was saying, "the state moves that the twenty-five-million-dollar bail posted by Peter Carrington for the purpose of allowing him to go to the Sleep Disorders Center overnight be forfeited. We ask that he now remain in the Bergen County Jail while he awaits trial. It is hard to imagine a person who would constitute a greater risk of flight than he does."

Conner Banks had been waiting impatiently for the prosecutor to finish. Now it was his turn. I watched as he arose from his chair at the defense table and prepared to address the judge. He had a confident air about him that gave me a measure of hope. He glanced at the prosecutor as if he couldn't believe what he had just heard; then he began his argument.

"Your Honor, let's talk about the risk of flight. If Peter Carrington wanted to leave the country, he could have done it over twenty years ago. Instead he has lived in his own home, tried to ignore the scurrilous rumors, cooperated with all the investigations, and now, knowing he would never willingly harm another human being, he has tried to find an explanation for the crimes he may have committed. Or that he may *not* have committed."

It was far too soon for me to have any response from the child I was carrying, but I swear I felt a phantom kick of approval.

Conner continued with his argument: "The entire

purpose of the neurological testing at the sleep disorder clinic was to determine whether Peter Carrington is a sleepwalker, and, if he is, to determine the severity and frequency of this problem. I have been informed by my client's doctors that his neurological readings, when he is asleep, are highly irregular, and clearly indicative of a person with a serious sleepwalking disorder called parasomnia. The doctors who have viewed the tape of this incident have told me that, in their judgment, it was clearly a sleepwalking episode, and that he was totally unaware of his actions."

He's doing a good job, I thought. Please God, let the judge believe him.

"Your Honor," Banks said, his voice rising, "we do not dispute that Peter Carrington got up and attempted to leave the room. However, given the substantial security measures that were in place, of which Peter Carrington was not only aware, but was paying for, it is abundantly clear that this episode was the result of his being afflicted with this terrible disorder. Your Honor, as per your previous order, he spent the night at the center, and now has been returned to jail. It would be a terrible injustice to forfeit the twenty-five-million-dollar bail as a result of actions over which he had no control."

Judge Smith had listened intently to both sides. He looked up, and our eyes locked for just a second before he addressed the courtroom. What did he see when he looked at me? I wondered. Did he see the way I am pleading with him to understand? I felt my heart pounding as he began to speak.

"I can candidly state that this is the most unusual set of circumstances that I have ever encountered with respect to a bail hearing," he said. "I am fully aware that sleepwalking may be an issue in Mr. Carrington's upcoming trial. I, of course, am taking no position at this time regarding the merits of the state's case, or the validity of any sleepwalking defense. The sole issue today is whether Mr. Carrington deliberately attempted to violate the conditions of his bail, and whether he should forfeit the twenty-five million dollars he posted. Defense counsel does not dispute that Mr. Carrington attempted to leave the hospital room in which he was confined."

I looked at the prosecutor. An angry frown was forming on her face. Dear God, let that mean that the judge isn't going to make Peter forfeit that bail. Because if he *does* make him forfeit it, it will mean he believes Peter was putting on an act.

The judge continued: "The defense counsel has proffered substantial indication that the medical testing has revealed a serious sleepwalking disorder. It is also a fair argument that Peter Carrington was fully aware of the intense security surrounding him, which would have made any attempt to escape a virtual impossibility. It is also true, as defense counsel notes, that Mr. Carrington had both agreed to and paid for this intense security. Under all of these circumstances, and again recognizing that the entire purpose of the hospital's evaluation was focused on whether there was or was not a sleepwalking disorder, this court is not convinced that Mr. Carrington consciously tried to escape, or otherwise deliberately violated conditions of his bail. The state's concern about flight is legitimate, and the defendant will remain in jail pending his trial. But given the information before me, I will not order the forfeiture of the twenty-five million dollars bail."

At last we had a sort of victory. I felt myself slump in my seat. Vincent Slater patted my shoulder, an unusual gesture for him to make. "Kay, this is *really* important," he said, his voice full of relief and concern.

Slater so seldom showed any emotion that I was both surprised and touched. I had always thought of him as someone who was efficient and devoted to Peter's interests, but otherwise was basically cold and unresponsive. His reaction offered an unexpected glimpse into the interior Vincent Slater. Of course, I reminded myself, he was undoubtedly thrilled about the return of the twenty-five-million-dollar bail.

I was allowed a few minutes with Peter while he was in the holding cell. "Kay," he said, "last night I was dreaming of kneeling on the Althorps' lawn, the way I was when the cops arrested me. When I was trying to open the door, it was because, in my dream, I had to go there again." His voice dropped to a whisper so that the guard standing nearby could not hear him. "But last night was different." He paused. "I thought that Gary Barr was sitting in the room watching me."

58

Nicholas Greco heard on his car radio that Peter Carrington might have tried to break out of the sleep center. Knowing there would be a bail hearing, he called Barbara Krause's office and learned what time it would be held.

That was why he was in the courtroom during the hearing, and why he waited outside in the hall after it was over, hoping to speak to Carrington's wife, Kay.

When she came out, she was accompanied by Vincent Slater. When Slater saw Greco, he tried to rush Kay Carrington past him, but Greco blocked his way. "Mrs. Carrington," he said, "I would very much like to speak with you. There is a possibility I might be of assistance to you."

"Assistance!" Slater snapped. "Kay, this is the investigator who located the maid and got her to change her testimony."

"Mrs. Carrington, I am seeking the truth." Greco

handed her his card. "Please take this. Please call me." Satisfied that she had slipped it in her pocket, he turned and walked in the opposite direction from the elevators.

He knew by now that he had become something of a familiar figure in the prosecutor's office. Barbara Krause's door was closed, but Tom Moran was standing in the hall outside, talking to a police officer. Greco managed to catch Moran's eye, then waited until Moran came over to speak to him.

Moran waved aside Greco's apologies for dropping in without an appointment. "Come in my office," he suggested. "The boss is not a happy camper after losing the motion for bail forfeiture."

"I understand," Greco said, with a silent prayer of thanks that he had not intruded on Barbara Krause. He knew there was a thin line between her considering him helpful and deciding he was a pest. He also knew that he should not take up much of Moran's time.

Once inside Moran's office, Greco got to the point. "I have been speaking with Susan Althorp's closest friend, Sarah Kennedy North. As you know, Gary Barr used to chauffeur Susan and her friends to parties. But according to Sarah North, it seems he had an unusually close relationship with Susan."

Moran raised an eyebrow. "I'm listening."

"Susan apparently referred to Barr as 'her pal.'

Rather unusual, don't you think, for an eighteen-year-old and a servant who was then in his early forties? Also, the atmosphere in the Althorp home does not suggest familiarity ever existed between the family and the employees. If anything, I would say quite the opposite."

"Mr. Greco, we have always suspected that Peter Carrington had help in both hiding and later in burying Susan Althorp's body. We knew, of course, about the chauffeuring Gary Barr did. The police also spoke to Susan's friends at the time of her disappearance. None of them mentioned Barr as having an unusual relationship with Susan. Perhaps it's time for us to talk to him again. Maybe *his* memory has improved over the years as well."

Greco got up. "I won't take any more of your time. May I also suggest that you thoroughly investigate Gary Barr's background to see if there may have ever been any problem with the law. A possibility has occurred to me which I am not yet ready to share. Good day, Mr. Moran. It is always a pleasure to see you."

59

I despised Elaine for her trickery, but in an odd way, it was also a relief that I was not in possession of the infamous shirt. Even though she was blackmailing us, she also was postponing a moral dilemma for me. As Peter's wife, by law, I did not have to testify against him. To actively withhold or destroy evidence was, however, something else again. But now, I told myself, I was not withholding evidence because I did not possess it.

The media had a field day after the bail hearing. The cover of one of the tabloids had a picture of Peter standing before the judge, his back to the camera. The judge was looking down. The headline was, ZZZZZZZZZZZZZZZ. IS THE JUDGE ASLEEP, TOO? A cartoon in another newspaper depicted Peter with electrodes hanging from his forehead, a breathing tube over his shoulder, and a hatchet in his hand that he was aiming at a door.

I didn't know what access Peter had to the newspapers and didn't ask him. On my next visit, I did question him about the dream he had at the sleep center, when he tried to open the door because he wanted to go to the Althorp home again. "Do you think there was a possibility that you actually *saw* Gary hanging around Susan's house the night she disappeared?" I asked him.

"Absolutely not, Kay! If I had, I wouldn't have let him come within a mile of you!"

Of course he wouldn't. He was convinced it was just a confusing twist to his dream—but I was not.

Our visits were so painful: We looked at each other through a Plexiglas panel and spoke by telephone. He could sit down with his lawyers at a conference table but was not allowed to touch me. I longed to put my arms around him, to feel the strength of his arms around me. It wasn't going to happen.

Conner Banks's suggestion that Peter married me because of what I had heard in the chapel was always in the back of my mind. Then, when I saw the way Peter looked at me, the way his face lit up at his first glimpse of me, I was again certain that he loved me and had loved me from the beginning.

But a few hours later, when I was by myself at home, it did not seem impossible that he and Susan might have been quarreling about money in the chapel that afternoon. Peter was in college at that time. What kind of allowance did he get from a father who was a notorious skinflint? If Susan had something on him, was he driven to desperation—perhaps by fear of his father—to keep her quiet?

These questions haunted me, but when visiting day finally came around again, I felt wretched for ever doubting him.

A dozen times during the weeks after the hearing, I took Nicholas Greco's card from my desk and considered calling him. I had this crazy feeling that somehow he could help Peter. But each time I would remind myself that Peter might not have been indicted had Greco not tracked down Maria Valdez, and I always put the card back in the drawer, and slammed the drawer shut.

We were enjoying a mild February, and I started jogging again, running every morning around the estate. I often stopped at the place where they had found my father's remains. This grave seemed more real to me than the one he now shares with my mother in MaryRest Cemetery. The police had dug at least ten feet in every direction around the spot where the dogs had started their frantic barking. That area had been filled in now, but it still stood out from the dormant grass around it, and I knew the dirt would start to sink when the spring thaw began.

I decided I wanted to plant rosebushes here, but then I realized I was too new in my position as Mrs. Peter Carrington to know who attended to the landscaping.

Sometimes I would stand at the fence and look out at the area where Susan's body had been found. I would try to imagine the twenty-year-old Peter thinking that it was safe to put her body there, because the cadaver dogs had already been through the estate. I even called Public Service Electric & Gas Company. One of their employees told me that there was a gas line near the curb of our property beyond the fence, and that PSE&G had a perpetual easement to service or replace the line. He told me that normally they would never have any need to disturb the ground nearly fifty feet from the curb.

"When there's a suspected leak, we move right in without notification," he said. "The day the Althorp girl's body was found, an odor of gas had been reported, and our people went right over. Our detectors bored test holes much closer to your fence than they might ever do again," he told me.

Which might answer why, even if he were guilty, Peter had not looked particularly upset when he saw the emergency crew digging near the curb.

I thought back to what I knew about that night. Elaine claimed she had seen Peter come in at two A.M. There is no question that he drove Susan home at midnight. Would she have had the nerve to sneak out immediately, or would she wait twenty minutes or half an hour to be sure one of her parents didn't look in on her? I asked myself. And where between twelve thirty and two o'clock in the morning—whether in a sleep-walking state or not—would Peter have managed to hide Susan's body?

And if he did do that, then someone had to have been helping him. My suspicion that Gary Barr was involved in all this was becoming stronger and stronger. It would explain why lately Gary had been acting so nervous, and had been trying to eavesdrop. He must be terribly worried that if, out of loyalty, he tried to help Peter, he might still be charged with being an accessory to murder.

Conner Banks gave me a copy of a tape from The Learning Channel showing reenactments of crimes committed in the United States by two men who were sleepwalking at the time. Both are serving life sentences. The same tape shows reenactments of a homicide and an aggravated assault committed by two men in Canada under the same circumstances. They were both acquitted. Watching the tape, I was heartsick. Two of the men had been bewildered when they were woken by the police, and had no memory of what had happened. The other awoke in his car, and drove to the police station himself because he was covered with blood.

One way that I occupied myself—and it was something that I *did* enjoy—was to make some changes around the mansion. From what Peter had told me, Grace hadn't done anything much to the mansion, but had completely redecorated the Fifth Avenue apartment. I'd only been at the apartment a few times during those weeks between the literacy reception and our wedding. Now, I had no desire to go there without Peter. It's silly, but I would have felt like an intruder. If Peter was sent to prison, I knew that a major decision would have to be made about all the property.

In the meantime, however, I began to make some small changes in this home—my home, I reminded myself. I had Gary bring down the crate of Limoges china that I had told Peter about. Jane washed and I dried the plates and cups and saucers and all the wonderful extra dishes that were used at lavish dinner parties in the late nineteenth century. "You don't see anything like this anymore, Mrs. Carrington," Jane marveled.

There was a magnificent eighteenth-century breakfront in the formal dining room. We displayed the Limoges there, and packed away the china that Elaine had chosen. Good riddance, I thought.

In one room on the third floor, I found a heavy chest filled with blackened antique table silver. When Jane and Gary had polished it, we found that all the pieces were monogrammed. "Whose initials are ASC?" I asked Peter during one of my visits.

"ASC? That's probably my great-great-, whatever she is, grandmother. Her name was Adelaide Stuart when she married my great-great-, whatever, grandfather in 1820. I remember my mother telling me that Adelaide claimed some remote relationship to King Charles, and never let my paternal ancestor forget that she was a cut above him socially. She was the one behind moving the mansion from Wales."

I learned that conversations like this one were the best way to get a smile on Peter's face. He liked the idea that I was putting my own mark on his home. "Do whatever you want, Kay. Some of those rooms are too stiff and formal for my taste. But leave my library just the way it is, and don't even think about recovering my chair."

I also told him that I was going to switch some of the paintings on the walls downstairs with others that I liked better that I'd found on the third floor.

I had Maggie over for dinner a couple of times a week, or else we went out to our pasta restaurant. I knew other diners' eyes followed me when we came in, but I decided I couldn't hide forever, and that eventually, or at least until the trial began, I wouldn't be too much of a curiosity.

I didn't see Elaine for nearly three weeks after her

refusal to give the shirt to me, although I did glimpse her car now and then, passing along the driveway. I'd had all the house locks changed so she could not walk in without ringing the bell. Then one evening after the Barrs had left for the day, I was sitting in Peter's chair reading, and the door chimes began crashing frantically.

I rushed to open the door and Elaine flung herself into the mansion, her eyes wild, her ungloved hands curled like claws. For a moment I thought she was going to close them around my neck. "How *dare* you?" she shouted. "How *dare* you ransack my home?"

"Ransack your home!" I think the shock in my voice and what she must have seen on my face made her realize that I didn't know what she was talking about.

Immediately the anger in her face turned to panic. "Kay," she said. "Oh, my God, Kay, it's *gone*! Someone has stolen it!"

I did not have to ask what she meant. Peter's formal dinner shirt with Susan's blood on it, the shirt that would surely brand him a murderer, was missing.

60

Pat Jennings was spending more and more of her time at the Walker Gallery on the telephone because she had absolutely nothing else to do. In the several weeks since the row with his mother in the office, Richard had been around very little. He told Pat that he was selling his apartment and buying a smaller one, and that he was looking for less expensive space for the gallery. "I think the great romance with Gina Black is over," Pat confided to her friend Trish during one of their frequent phone conversations. "She's been leaving messages for him, but Richard told me to tell her he's out of town."

"How about the other one, Alexandra Lloyd?"

"I guess she's given up. She hasn't called for a couple of weeks."

"Has his mother been in again?"

"No, not once. But I think she lost something. This morning Richard came in and, boy, was he having a fit!

He went right to the phone and called his mother. I heard him tell her that he hadn't slept for one minute after what she'd told him last night because he was so upset. He never seems to understand that when he raises his voice, I hear every word."

"When was that?" Trish asked.

"About an hour ago."

"What else did he say?"

"Something about the utter stupidity of leaving it in the house, and why didn't she just run it up the flagpole for everyone to see? Anyhow, he hung up on her, and she called back ten minutes later. I could tell she was crying. She said she didn't want to talk to Richard. Instead she told me to tell her son that it was all his fault that she had to pull it out now, and his fault that she had it in the house in the first place, and that he should go to hell."

"She told you *that*?" Trish said breathlessly. "Did you give him that message?"

"I had to, didn't I? He just slammed out of here saying he wouldn't be back today."

"How about that?" Trish exclaimed. "You have the most interesting job, Pat. It's so fascinating to be around people like the Carringtons. What do you think Elaine lost?"

"Oh, jewelry, I guess," Pat surmised. "Unless it's a ticket to the Carrington money. Richard could sure use that."

"Maybe it's the 'wild card,' whatever that is," Trish suggested.

They both laughed heartily.

"Keep me posted!" Trish admonished as she hung up.

61

Peter made his point in court at the bail hearing, Kay," Conner Banks said, jabbing his finger at me for emphasis as he referred to his notes. "We have a copy of the tape of him getting out of bed in the sleep center. There's a very clear shot of his face, looking directly into the camera. Anyone can see how glassy his eyes look, and that he's totally unfocused. I think that when the jurors view this, some—maybe all—of them will believe that Peter was in a sleepwalking state at the time, and therefore that he is a sleepwalker. But, Kay, even so, that defense just won't work. If you ever want to see Peter walk into this house again, a free man, you have *got* to convince him to let us attack the state's case, and argue that there is reasonable doubt he killed Susan and there is reasonable doubt that he killed your father."

"I absolutely agree," Markinson said, forcefully.

Banks and Markinson were at the mansion again. It

had been a week since Peter's shirt had been stolen from Elaine's house. I don't know whether Elaine or I was more distraught over its disappearance.

There were only two people I would suspect of having stolen it: Gary Barr and Vincent Slater. Vincent had guessed immediately that the "object" Elaine was using to blackmail me was probably the shirt, and I am virtually certain that Gary overheard our conversation about it.

I could even imagine Vince trying to retrieve the shirt after Elaine was paid the million dollars, especially when she tried to continue the blackmail, but why not tell me that? I confronted him about it and told him that Elaine's "object" was the missing shirt. He absolutely denied he had taken it. I didn't know whether to believe him or not.

If Gary Barr took it, what was he planning to do with it? Maybe he was holding it as insurance for making a deal with the prosecutor, something along the lines of, "Peter was just a kid. I was sorry for him. I hid the body, then helped him bury it outside the fence."

Of course both Vincent and Gary had easy access to Elaine's house. Gary was around all the time; Vince was in and out of the mansion on a regular basis. The guard at the house was almost always at the front door. He'd walk around to the back from time to time, but it would be easy enough for either one of them to avoid being seen by him.

Prior to finding her house had been ransacked, Elaine had spent four days at her apartment in New York. Whoever took the shirt had plenty of time to thoroughly search for it. In addition to Vincent and Gary, there was another possible suspect that entered my mind, although it did seem remote. Elaine had let it slip, when she was frantically telling me that the shirt was missing, that Richard had known about it, too. Would he have taken it as insurance against his future gambling losses? But Elaine said that he didn't know she hadn't returned it to the safe-deposit box in the bank where it had been hidden for twenty-two years, and that he had been genuinely furious when she told him about the loss.

All of these thoughts were whirling through my mind while I was listening to Conner Banks laying out for me, step by step, the factors that he thought were the basis for a "reasonable doubt" defense.

"Peter and Susan were friends, but no one has ever suggested they were seriously involved," Banks was saying. "The formal shirt was missing, but there wasn't a trace of blood on Peter's dinner jacket or pants or socks or shoes, all of which were accounted for."

"Suppose that shirt shows up somewhere?" I asked. "Suppose, for argument's sake, it was stained with Susan's blood."

Banks and Markinson looked at me as if I had two heads. "If there was even the faintest possibility that could happen, I would be bargaining for two thirty-year concurrent sentences," Banks said. "And feel lucky to get it."

Around and around and around we go, where we stop, nobody knows, I thought. Unknowingly, Banks had given me my answer. If the lawyers knew about the existence of the shirt, they would want to plea-bargain, and Peter would never admit to committing those murders just to get a sentence that would give him a possibility—at best—of getting out of prison when he was seventy-two years old.

Our child will be thirty by then, I thought.

"I will not try to persuade Peter to change his mind about the focus of his defense," I told them. "It's what he wants, and I'll support him."

They pushed back their chairs and stood to leave. "Then you'll have to face the inevitable, Kay," Markinson said. "You're going to raise your child alone."

On his way out of the dining room, Markinson stopped at the breakfront. "Magnificent china," he observed.

"Yes," I said, aware that we were now making polite conversation, that Peter's lawyers had as good as thrown in the towel, emotionally speaking.

Conner Banks was looking at one of the paintings I

had brought down from the third floor. "This is outstanding," he said. "It's a Morley, isn't it?"

"I don't know," I confessed. "I'm woefully lacking in my knowledge of art. I just liked it more than the one that was there."

"Then you have a good eye," he said approvingly. "We'll be on our way. We're lining up medical doctors who have treated people who are parasomniacs, and who can testify they are completely unaware of their behavior when they are sleepwalking. If you and Peter insist on this defense, then we'll have to call them as expert witnesses."

It was visiting day at the Bergen County Jail. My waist was thickening and, when I dressed this morning, I had to leave the top button of my slacks open. I had started to wear high-necked sweaters almost all the time; they helped disguise how thin I was, except, of course, for my waistline. I was worried that I was still losing weight, but the obstetrician had told me that that wasn't uncommon in the first few months of pregnancy.

When did it happen that all my nagging doubts about Peter's innocence began to dissolve? I believe it had to do with the file cabinets I started going through on the third floor. I was learning so much about his childhood in what I found in them. His mother had kept a photograph album for each year of his life until she died; he was twelve at the time. I was struck by the fact that his father was in so few of the pictures. Peter had told me that after he was born, his mother stopped accompanying his father on business trips.

She had written notes on some of the pages, loving references to how smart Peter was, how quick to learn, his wonderful disposition, his sense of humor.

I found myself becoming wistful in seeing how very close Peter had been to his mother. At least you had her twelve years, I thought. Then I found a picture taken by the Bergen *Record* photographer the day of her funeral. A devastated twelve-year-old Peter, trying to blink back tears, was walking beside his mother's coffin, his hand resting on it.

His college yearbooks were in one of the files. In one, the caption about him referred to "grace under pressure," and I realized that he was just beginning his senior year at Princeton when Susan disappeared. In the months that followed, the prosecutor's office was constantly pulling him in for questioning.

When I got to the jail that afternoon and Peter was brought in, he looked at me through the Plexiglas for a long minute without speaking. He was trembling, and his eyes glistened with tears. He picked up the phone on his side of the divider. His voice husky, he said, "Kay, I don't know why, but I had a feeling that you wouldn't come today, or ever again, that you've had as much of this misery as you can take."

I felt for a moment as if I were looking at the face of the twelve-year-old boy at the funeral of the person he loved best in the world. "I will never leave you," I told him. "I love you far too much to leave you. Peter, I don't believe you ever hurt anyone. You couldn't. There's another answer, and, so help me God, I'm going to find it."

That evening, I phoned Nicholas Greco.

62

Jane Barr had made beef barley soup in case the lawyers stayed for lunch, but they were gone by quarter of twelve. She was glad that she'd had a reason to cook—she needed something to distract her. Gary had been asked to stop at the prosecutor's office, and he was there now. Why did they want to talk to him? she worried. After all these years, they're not questioning him about Susan Althorp, are they?

Please, don't let it be that, she prayed.

Kay Carrington had a cup of soup before she went to visit Peter at the jail. It's funny about her, Jane thought. She didn't come from money, but she has an air about her, not haughty, but knowing. She's perfect for Peter. And I think she's pregnant. She hasn't said so, but I bet she is.

Where was Gary? she wondered, checking the time. What kind of questions were they asking him? How much was he telling?

After lunch, Jane normally went home to the gatehouse for a good part of the afternoon, then would return to the mansion to turn on lights, draw curtains, and prepare dinner. Today when she arrived home, she found Gary there eating a sandwich and having a beer.

"Why didn't you let me know you were home?" she demanded. "I've been a wreck waiting to hear what they wanted."

"They dug up some stuff about me from the time I was a kid," Gary snapped. "I told you about it. I was in a little trouble when I was a teenager, but the records were supposed to be sealed. There was some stuff in the newspapers at the time, though, and I guess they found out about it that way."

Jane collapsed into a chair. "That was so long ago. They're not holding what happened back then against you, are they? Or are they reading more into it now?"

Gary Barr looked at his wife, something approaching contempt in his eyes. "What do you think?" he asked.

Jane had not yet started to unbutton her winter jacket. Now she reached for the top button and slipped it through the buttonhole. Her shoulders sagged. "I've lived in this town all my life," she said. "I never wanted to be anyplace else. We've worked for nice people. Now all that is in jeopardy. What you did was so awful. Did they ask you about it? Do they know about it? *Do they?*"

"No," Gary replied angrily. "They haven't figured out anything, so stop worrying. The statute of limitations means I'm clear now. They can't file charges because too many years have passed. And even if they try to pin something else on me, I've got an offer for them they can't refuse."

"What are you talking about?" Jane asked, her dismay apparent. "There's no statute of limitations on murder!"

Gary Barr sprang up from his chair and threw the sandwich he was eating at his wife. "Don't ever use that word again!" he shouted.

"I'm sorry, Gary. I didn't mean to upset you. I'm sorry." Tears starting to well in her eyes, Jane looked at the smear of mustard on her coat, the broken pieces of rye bread, the slices of ham and tomato on the floor in front of her.

Clenching and unclenching his hands, Barr made a visible effort to control himself. "Okay. All right. Just remember. It was one thing to be there; another thing to kill her. All right. I'll clean up the mess. Anyhow, that sandwich was lousy. Any of that soup left that you were making this morning?"

"Yes. Plenty of it."

"Do me a favor and get me some, will you? I've had a tough day. And I'm sorry I lost my temper. You don't deserve that, Jane. You're a good woman."

63

Nicholas Greco was pleased to receive an unexpected phone call from Assistant Prosecutor Tom Moran. "That was a good tip," Moran told him. "Barr had a juvenile record that was sealed from the public, but we got access to it. He was arrested for bringing marijuana to school and smoking it in the gym. We also found his high school yearbook and located some of his classmates who still live in Poughkeepsie. Barr had a reputation for having a bad temper. Not exactly your friendly teenage-boy-next-door.

"Of course, that's a long time ago," Moran continued. "It's interesting though, that his classmates remember him as someone with a chip on his shoulder, plus an inferiority complex. He didn't study in high school, didn't want to go to college, then years later, at a high school reunion, whined that he never was given the chance to be a success."

"He struck me as a very insecure, dissatisfied man

who is angry at the world," Greco said. "What you tell me fits the pattern that I have observed."

"Changing the subject," Moran said. "There's something else I know you'd want to hear. Mrs. Althorp died today."

"I am very, very sorry to hear that, but I think for her it is a blessing."

"From what I understand, there isn't going to be a wake, and the funeral will be private. I guess those were her wishes, and you can understand that the family has had enough media coverage for a lifetime."

"Yes, I can understand that," Nicholas Greco said. "Thank you, Tom."

Greco looked at his watch. It was past five o'clock, but he was not yet ready to start home. He wanted to think quietly, and sometimes it was easier to do that after everyone else had left the office and the phones were quiet. Fortunately, it was the evening Frances met with her book group, so she wouldn't mind if he was late arriving home.

He smiled to himself. At the end of the day, Frances was a woman who wanted his attention, full and undivided. Most of the time I give it to her, too, he thought affectionately, but right now I need to enter a brown study. When he had first used that expression in front of Frances, she'd asked what he was talking about.

"It has passed out of the language for the most part,

but in the nineteenth century it was very common," he had told her. "A 'brown study' is defined as a deep, serious absorption in thought, my dear."

"Oh, for heaven's sake, Nick," she had replied, "why not say it straight—you're just trying to figure something out?"

And that's just what I'm trying to do, Greco thought.

Gary Barr was at the top of his list of people and things to consider. Greco sensed that Barr had a chip on his shoulder toward those who, in his mind, had a privileged life. What was his relationship to the Althorp family? he wondered. In the years he and his wife were not working for the Carringtons, they regularly cooked and served dinners for the Althorps. Gary also chauffeured their daughter. How and why did he become Susan's "pal"? I must talk to Susan's friend Sarah again, Greco thought.

The torn page from *People* magazine found in Grace Carrington's pocket was the next thing on the list. It had significance, great significance, of that he was sure. But *why*?

Next was Susan Althorp's evening purse. Why did Gary Barr have such a clear memory of Peter Carrington asking Vincent Slater to return it to her the next morning, and then remembering also that Peter was startled when it wasn't found in his car? Or was Barr making up that story for his own reasons? Slater had confirmed the conversation, but only to a degree. He claimed that Carrington merely asked him to check and see if the purse was in the car, and return it to Susan if it was.

But Susan was expected for brunch later that day. Besides, the bag was small, and could only have held things like a handkerchief, compact, comb, or lipstick. So why make an issue of returning it to her? Was there something special in it that she had needed? Greco asked himself.

All of these pieces are tied together, Nicholas Greco thought, as he sat with his hands folded, not noticing that it was becoming dark outside. But how?

The phone rang. Somewhat irritated at the intrusion, Greco picked up the receiver and identified himself.

"Mr. Greco, this is Kay Carrington. You gave me your card at the courthouse a few weeks ago."

Greco straightened up in his chair. "Yes, I did, Mrs. Carrington," he said slowly. "I am glad to hear from you."

"Can you come see me tomorrow morning, at my home?"

"Of course. What time is convenient for you?"

"Eleven o'clock? Is that all right for you?"

"That would be fine."

"Do you know where I live?"

"Yes, I do. I will be there at eleven."

"Thank you."

Greco heard the click of the receiver being replaced, then hung up himself. Still deep in thought, he got up and walked down the hall to the coat closet. At the last minute, he remembered to leave a note on his receptionist's desk: "Will be in New Jersey tomorrow morning."

64

I hadn't yet told Maggie about the baby because I was sure that she would confide it to several of her friends, and then I'd be reading about it in the tabloids. Maggie categorically *cannot* keep a secret. But I thought I'd been spotted at the obstetrician's office by people who knew me, and since I didn't want Maggie to hear a rumor about it from someone else, I knew I had to tell her.

After I phoned Nicholas Greco and made the appointment, I collected Maggie and brought her back to the house for dinner. Jane had prepared a roast chicken and wanted to serve us, but I had told her to go ahead home, that we'd serve ourselves. The last thing I needed was to have Gary Barr overhear our conversation. I think Jane was getting worried by now about whether or not they were going to lose their jobs, and she started to protest. But then she stopped and very pleasantly wished us a good evening.

The kitchen is large and accommodates a refectory table and benches where the servants used to eat when there was a large staff. Maggie wanted us to have dinner there, but I vetoed the idea. The chairs in the small dining room are infinitely more comfortable. Besides, I know she feels intimidated by the mansion, and I wanted her to get over that.

When we were settled at the table, I told Maggie about the baby. She was absolutely delighted with my news, but then, of course, immediately started worrying about me. "Oh, Kay, it's such a tragedy that your baby's father will never be around to see the little one grow up."

"Maggie," I said, "his name is Peter, and I haven't given up hope. He did *not* kill Susan Althorp, and he certainly did not kill my father. But please, let's talk about something else. Daddy was fired only a few weeks after Susan disappeared. Peter told me Elaine Carrington got rid of him because he wasn't interested in her overtures to him."

"You told me that, Kay," Maggie said contritely. I knew she now regretted that she had jumped to the assumption that the firing had been the result of a drinking problem.

"What was Daddy going to do? Did he have any job offers?"

"I don't know, Kay. It was only a few weeks after he

was fired that we thought he had committed suicide. The last time I saw him was on September thirtieth, twenty-two and a half years ago. We've talked about this."

"Let's talk about it again."

"On September thirtieth, your dad phoned me around five o'clock and asked me to keep you overnight. He said he had an appointment with somebody. You were kind of unhappy about having to come over because he'd promised that the two of you would try some new recipe for dinner that evening. He promised he'd make it up to you. But the next day he didn't come for you and didn't call, and then the police reported his car had been found on the cliff above the river, and that his wallet was on the seat."

"Did they ever investigate to see who he might have been planning to see on September thirtieth?"

"At the time, the police assumed that he'd just made up that story as an excuse to drop you off."

I could tell we were going nowhere with this conversation. I kept hoping that maybe some fragment of a forgotten memory might surface in Maggie's consciousness, but it just wasn't happening.

Over a cup of tea, I decided it was time to finally tell Maggie about the time, all those years ago, that I had crept into this house because I was so curious to see the chapel.

Her reaction, as expected, was that I was always too adventurous for my own good. Unexpectedly, she let it go at that.

Probably because of her reaction, I ended up telling her that I overheard a quarrel between a woman and a man she seemed to be blackmailing, something I had planned to keep to myself. "That's why I knew what the man was whistling, even though it was only one line," I told her, "because you used to hum it for me when you told me about my mother singing it in the school play."

Maggie gave me a look that I couldn't interpret.

"What is it?" I asked her.

"Kay," she exclaimed, "you should have told that to your father! When he and your mother began to date, I told him about the school play and bragged about how well she sang that song. He made her sing it for him. From then on, he called it 'their song.' They even chose it for their first dance at their wedding. You know that."

"Maggie, I knew about the play. But I don't think I remember your telling about Daddy calling it 'their song,' or dancing to it at the wedding," I protested.

"It doesn't matter. But after your father came running over here with you to fix those lights the afternoon of that party, he dropped you off at my house. I remember distinctly how really down he looked. He told me that he had heard someone whistling that song when he was here, and had talked with him. I guess your dad told whoever it was why he was nostalgic about it."

"Did he say who that person was?" I demanded.

"Yes, but I don't remember."

"Maggie, it's so important. Think about it. Please try to remember."

"I'll try, Kay. I'll really try."

There was a question I had to ask. "Maggie, could it have been Peter?"

"No. Positively not," Maggie said firmly. "I'd have remembered if it was Peter Carrington. He was the young prince around here. That's why I was so disappointed to think he killed that poor girl. No, I'm absolutely sure he wasn't the one your dad mentioned!"

She looked at me. "Kay, what's the matter?" she asked. "Why are you crying?"

It wasn't Peter, I thought with relief. It wasn't Peter! It was some other man being blackmailed that day in the chapel. But, dear God, if I had only told Daddy what I heard that day, and he had reported it to the police, maybe he'd still be alive, and Peter wouldn't be in jail, accused of murder.

65

Vincent Slater was convinced that Gary Barr had stolen Peter's dress shirt from Elaine Carrington's house. For a week he had mulled over in his mind the best way to get it back.

The need to recover the shirt had been made even more acute by a call late one evening from Conner Banks, urging him to try to convince Peter to allow his legal team to change the strategy of his defense.

"Vincent," Banks said, "we are more and more convinced that we would have a good chance of a hung jury, and maybe even a shot at an acquittal, if our defense is based on reasonable doubt. An acquittal means that Peter comes home for good. A hung jury means we can argue strenuously for bail, and Peter would probably get to spend at least some time with his child before a second trial. If we got another hung jury at a second trial, the prosecutor would probably give up and drop the charges."

"What would happen if Peter's formal shirt turned up and it had Susan's blood on it?" Slater asked.

"What's going on here? Kay Carrington asked me that same question." There was a long silence; then Conner Banks said quietly, "As I told Kay, if that shirt turns up with Susan's blood on it, Peter had better be willing to plea-bargain."

"I see." It was nine o'clock, not too late to phone Kay, Slater decided. When she answered, she told him she had just driven her grandmother home.

"Kay, my bet is that Gary Barr stole the shirt," he said. "We've got to get it back. There's a set of master keys in a drawer in the kitchen. The gatehouse key is on it. I'll stop by for it at seven thirty, before Jane comes in. Then, I'll phone you at nine as though I'm in New York and ask you to send Gary into the city to help bring some of Peter's private papers home. I'll make sure my people there keep him busy for a while. You just make sure Jane doesn't go home early."

"Vince, I don't know what to think about this."

"I do. I'm not going to leave that shirt in Gary Barr's hands. Let's just pray that he's got it hidden somewhere in the gatehouse or in his SUV. That's something else: I'll tell him that one of our executives may be coming back with him to visit you, so he must be driving one of the family cars."

"As I say, at this point, I don't know what to think,

but I'll go along with you," Kay said. "Vince, I might as well tell you, I have an appointment with Nicholas Greco, the investigator. He's coming here at eleven o'clock tomorrow morning."

Vincent Slater then said something he would never have dreamed he could say to his employer's wife: "The more fool you, Kay. I thought you loved your husband!"

66

Retired ambassador Charles Althorp sat in his late wife's study, a cup of coffee in his hand, an untouched breakfast tray beside him. Already the physical reality of Gladys's death had brought about changes in the house. The hospital bed, oxygen tent, IVs, and seemingly endless medical supplies were all gone. Brenda, the housekeeper, tears flowing, had aired and vacuumed Gladys's bedroom last night.

He had caught the sullen look in Brenda's eyes when she served him breakfast that morning and hoped she had an inkling that she'd better be looking for another job.

His sons had phoned, sad that their mother had died, but glad that all the suffering she had endured was over. "If there's a museum in heaven, Mom and Susan are probably debating the merits of a painting," his younger son, Blake, had said.

Althorp knew his sons disliked him. After college,

they both had chosen to accept jobs far away, giving them an excuse to show up at home only about twice a year. Now they would be back for the second time in a few months. The first had been to attend the funeral of their sister; now it was their mother.

Gladys's body was in the funeral parlor. There would be no wake, but the funeral would not be until Friday, to accommodate his older son, whose daughter had just had an emergency appendectomy. The parents didn't want to leave her.

Neighbors had been calling to express their regrets; he had told Brenda to take messages. But at a quarter of nine, she came into the study and hesitantly told him that a Mr. Greco was on the phone, and insisted on speaking with him.

Althorp was about to refuse, then wondered if Gladys had still owed the man money. It was possible. According to the nurse, the man had been to see her very recently. He picked up the phone. "Charles Althorp." He knew his voice was intimidating. He took pride in that fact.

"Ambassador Althorp," Nicholas Greco began, "let me first express my sincere condolences at the loss of your wife. Mrs. Althorp was a gracious and brave lady, and set in motion the wheels that I think will soon bring a killer to justice."

"What are you talking about? Carrington is in jail."

"That's exactly what I'm talking about, Ambassador. Peter Carrington is in jail. But should he be? Or, to put it another way, should not someone else perhaps be sharing his jail cell? This is a dreadful time to intrude, but may I stop by for a few minutes later today? I have an eleven o'clock appointment with Mrs. Kay Carrington. Would it be possible to call on you at twelve thirty?"

"Be here at noon. I'll give you fifteen minutes." Althorp slammed the phone into the cradle, put down his coffee cup, and stood up. He walked over to the desk where there were pictures of his wife and their daughter.

"I'm so sorry, Gladys," he said aloud. "I'm so sorry, Susan."

67

I was in the kitchen when Vince stopped by for the gatehouse key at seven thirty. Then, as planned, he phoned at nine o'clock. Gary Barr was vacuuming upstairs, and, on cue, I relayed the message to him. "Mr. Slater needs you to drive into the city and get some records from Peter's office," I told him. "There's a possibility that one of the company executives will drive back with you, so take the Mercedes. Mr. Slater will tell you where in the garage to park."

If Barr was suspicious, he didn't show it. He got on one of the extensions and confirmed the parking arrangements with Vincent. A few minutes later, from an upstairs window, I watched Barr drive the Mercedes past the gatehouse and out onto the road.

Vincent must have been watching for him to leave, because almost immediately, his Cadillac pulled onto the driveway and turned left. I guessed he would be parking behind the gatehouse in a spot that couldn't be seen from the mansion. Now it was my job to keep Jane from darting back home for some reason before her usual after-lunch break.

There was a simple way to do it. I told her that I had a headache and would she please answer the phone and take messages, except if Mr. Greco called.

"Mr. Greco?"

I heard the alarm in her voice and remembered that I had been told that after Mrs. Althorp had first hired Greco, he had talked to Gary Barr.

"Yes," I said. "I have an appointment with him at eleven o'clock."

The poor woman looked both frightened and confused. I felt very sure that if Vince was right, and Gary had stolen the shirt from Elaine's home, Jane had no part in that theft. But then I also remembered that she had sworn Gary was home in bed the night Susan disappeared. Had she been lying? By now, I was almost certain that she had.

For the next hour and a half, I was too restless to settle down, so I spent my time on the third floor. I hadn't been through even half the rooms because it took time to untie and remove the covers off the furniture that was stored up there. I was looking specifically for baby furniture, and finally found an antique wooden cradle. It was too heavy to pick up, so I squatted on the floor, rocking it to see if it was steady.

It was exquisitely carved, and I checked to see if it had been signed. It had been, by someone named Eli Fallow, and the date was 1821.

I was sure the cradle must have been ordered by Adelaide Stuart, the posh lady who married a Carrington in 1820. I made a mental note to look up Eli Fallow and find out if he had a reputation as a craftsman. I was finding it fascinating to uncover these treasures, and it at least provided a diversion from my constant worrying about Peter.

That kind of exploring, however, is a dusty business. At 10:30, I went down to the suite and washed my face and hands, then changed into a fresh sweater and slacks. I was barely ready when the doorbell rang promptly at eleven o'clock, and Nicholas Greco entered the house.

The first time I met him had been at Maggie's house, and I had resented his suggestion that my father might have staged his own suicide. He'd even hinted there might be a connection between him and Susan Althorp's disappearance. When Greco spoke to me in the courthouse hallway after the bail hearing, I was so upset that I barely noticed him. But now, as I looked straight at him, I felt that I could detect both warmth and sympathy in his eyes. I shook his hand and led him back to Peter's library.

"What a wonderful room this is," Greco commented as we entered.

"That was my impression the first time I saw it," I told him. Trying to overcome my sudden attack of nerves, brought on by the radical move I was making in meeting this man, I added, "I came here begging the chance to have a literacy cocktail party in the mansion. Peter was sitting in his chair." I pointed to it. "I felt nervous, and not properly dressed. It was a windy day in October, and I was wearing a light summer suit. As I pleaded my case, I was taking in this room and loving it."

"As well you might," Greco said.

I sat behind Peter's desk and Greco pulled up a chair across from it. "You told me you could be of service to me," I told him. "Now explain to me how you would do that."

"I can serve you best by trying to ascertain the entire truth of what has happened. As you are certainly aware, your husband is facing a strong probability that he will spend the rest of his life in prison. It may give him some personal vindication if the world comes to believe that he is innocent—and now I quote—'owing to the act being a noninsane automatism.' That is what might have happened if all this was taking place in Canada, but of course it is not."

"I do not believe that my husband, sleepwalking or not, committed any of those crimes," I said. "Last night I received what to me is convincing proof that he did not."

I had already decided that I wanted to hire Nicholas Greco. I told him that, and then I unburdened myself, starting with my visit to the chapel when I was six years old. "It never occurred to me that I might have overheard Susan Althorp that day," I said. "I mean, why would she need to beg or threaten to get money from anyone? Her family was wealthy. I've heard also that she had a substantial trust fund."

"It would be interesting to establish exactly how much money she had at her disposal," Greco said. "Not too many eighteen-year-olds have access to their trust funds, and Susan's friends tell us that her father had been very angry at her the night of the dinner party."

He asked about the time Peter had jumped bail and been found kneeling on the Althorps' lawn.

"Peter was sleepwalking and doesn't know why he went there, but he thinks it was the same sleepwalking dream that made him try to get out of the hospital room. That second time he thought Gary Barr was in the room watching him," I explained.

I told Greco that I had begun to think that Peter might have been the one who was being blackmailed in the chapel. "Last night, I found out that wasn't true," I said, and, trying not to get emotional, repeated for him what Maggie had told me.

Greco's expression became grave. "Mrs. Carrington," he said, "I have been concerned for you ever since I heard you had gone to see Susan Althorp's friend, Sarah North. Let us presume that your husband is innocent of these crimes. If so, then the guilty person is still around, and I believe—and fear—that person is in close proximity to you."

"Have you any suggestion as to how I can draw out that person?" I asked, aware my frustration was showing. "Mr. Greco, I know I was only six years old at the time, but if I had told my father about being in the chapel, and had recounted what I heard there, he might have gone to the police when Susan disappeared. The same man I heard in the chapel has to have been the man my father heard whistling outside shortly afterwards. Don't you think that knowledge is torturing me?"

"'When I was a child, I thought as a child,'" Greco said, his voice gentle. "Mrs. Carrington, do not be so hard on yourself. This information opens up new avenues, but I beg you, do *not* share with anyone else what your grandmother told you last night, and please tell *her* not to repeat it. Someone might begin to fear both her memory and yours."

He looked at his watch. "I must leave you in a few minutes. I asked Ambassador Althorp to spare me a little time today, and I suggested twelve thirty. Unfortunately, he told me to be there at noon. Is there anything else that you think would be helpful in my investigation?"

I didn't know until that moment that I was going to

tell him about Peter's shirt, but then I decided I had to go for broke. "If I told you something that could seriously hurt Peter's defense, would you feel it necessary to go to the prosecutor with that information?" I asked him.

"What you tell me is hearsay, and I would not be allowed to testify to it," he said.

"All these years, Elaine Carrington has had Peter's formal dress shirt with some stains that appear to be blood on it. A few days ago, she sold it to me for one million dollars, then, after she was paid, refused to give it to me. Since then it has been stolen from her home here on the estate. Vincent Slater believes Gary Barr is the one who took it, and right now he is searching the gatehouse, looking for it."

If Nicholas Greco was astonished at that information, he did not show it. Instead, he asked me how Elaine got the shirt, and how sure I was that it had bloodstains on it.

"'Stains' is too strong a word," I said. "From what I could see, it was more like a smudge, right here." I touched my sweater just above my heart. "Elaine said she saw Peter come home in a sleepwalking state at two o'clock that morning, and while she claims she had no idea what may have happened, she recognized that it was a bloodstain on his shirt and didn't want the maid to see it in the morning."

"So now she uses the shirt to blackmail you, then reneges on the deal. Why did she come forward at this time?"

"Because her son Richard is a compulsive gambler, and she's always bailing him out. This time he apparently needed more money than she could come up with, at least in time to keep him from getting in trouble."

"I see." Greco got up to leave. "You have given me a great deal to think about, Mrs. Carrington. Tell me something. If somebody were to leave something in this house, a personal item of some sort, and your husband thought it might be needed, what do you think he would do?"

"Return it," I said, "and right away. I can give you an example. One night in December, Peter dropped me off at my apartment, then started driving home. He got over the bridge and realized I had left my wool scarf in the car. Can you believe he turned around and brought it back to me? I told him he was crazy, but he said that it was cold, and I had a walk to my car in the morning, and he thought I should have it." I saw what Greco was driving at. "Susan's evening purse," I said. "Do you think that when Peter was sleepwalking that night, he was trying to return her purse?"

"I don't know, Mrs. Carrington. It is one of the many possibilities I shall consider, but it would explain your husband's surprise and distress the next morning when the purse was not in his car, wouldn't it?"

He did not wait for my answer, but instead opened his briefcase, pulled out a sheet of paper, and handed it to me. It was a copy of a page from *People* magazine. "Does this have any significance to you?" he asked.

"Oh, that's an article about Marian Howley," I said. "She's the most wonderful actress. I never miss one of her plays."

"Apparently Grace Carrington shared your enthusiasm for this actress. She tore this page out of the magazine; it was in her pocket when her body was found in the pool."

I started to hand the paper back to Greco, but he waved it away. "No, I downloaded several copies when I got a back issue of the magazine. Please keep this one. Perhaps you could show it to Mr. Carrington."

The telephone rang. I reached for it, then remembered that Jane Barr was supposed to be taking messages. Moments later, as Greco and I were leaving the library, she came running down the hall. "It's Mr. Slater, Mrs. Carrington," she said. "He said it's important."

Greco waited while I went back to the desk and picked up the receiver.

"Kay, I didn't find it," Vince said. "He must have hidden it somewhere else."

There was something in his voice that made me feel sure he was lying. "I don't believe you," I told him.

The phone clicked in my ear.

"Vince Slater claims he didn't find Peter's shirt," I told Nicholas Greco. "I don't believe him. He has it. I'd stake my life on it."

"Does Vincent Slater have a key to this house?" Greco asked me.

"I changed all the locks and gave him a key only to the door that goes from the terrace into his private office. But you can get into the house from the office."

"Then he does have a key, Mrs. Carrington. Have that lock changed immediately. I believe that Vincent Slater may be a very dangerous man."

68

"I've decided to close the gallery at the end of the week," Richard Walker told Pat Jennings. "I know it's short notice, but the building owner has someone who wants the space right away and will pay a bonus to get it."

Jennings looked at him, dumbfounded. "Can you get other space yourself that fast?" she asked.

"No, I mean I'm going to close the gallery *permanently*. As I'm sure you're aware, I'm too fond of horse racing for my own good. I'd like to try a complete change of scenery. I have an elderly friend who has a small but most interesting gallery in London, and he'd very much like to have me go in with him."

"That sounds wonderful," Jennings said, trying to sound sincere. I wonder if Mama has pulled the plug on bailing him out, she thought. I wouldn't blame her. And maybe he's right. It would be a lot better to get away from all the bookies who supply him with all those hot tips. "What does your mother think of all this?" she asked. "I'm sure she'll miss you."

"Even with the Concorde gone, England is just a hop, skip, and jump away, and she has many friends there."

Pat Jennings realized that she was going to not only miss her salary, but also the flexible hours she had here—they dovetailed perfectly with her kids' school schedule. And it had been fun to see Trish regularly, to say nothing about having a seat on the fifty-yard line of the Carrington family saga.

She decided to go for one more tidbit before it was too late. "How is Mrs. Peter Carrington doing?" she asked Richard, trying to sound concerned but not overly interested.

"How nice of you to ask! I haven't seen Kay in several weeks, but my mother tells me they've been in close touch, and we'll be having dinner together before I leave for England."

With a dismissive smile, as if he realized he was being pumped for information, Richard Walker turned to go into his private office. The phone rang. When Pat Jennings answered it, an angry voice snapped, "This is Alexandra Lloyd. Is Richard there?"

Without even asking, Pat knew the answer to give, only this time, she made it more elaborate. "Mr. Walker is on his way to London, Ms. Lloyd. May I take a message?"

"Oh, indeed you can. Tell Mr. Walker that I am very disappointed in him, and he knows what I mean."

This is one message I don't want to give him, Pat thought. I had believed all along that this lady with the fancy name was an artist. Now I'm beginning to think she's a bookie.

It was three o'clock, time to get uptown and pick up the kids. Richard's door was closed, but she could hear the murmur of his voice, which meant he was on the phone. Pat wrote out Alexandra Lloyd's message word for word, and, not happy with the way it looked on paper, tapped on Richard's door, walked in, and placed it on the desk in front of him.

Then, with the haste of someone who knows that a firecracker might explode at her feet at any moment, she grabbed her coat and left.

69

When Nicholas Greco was escorted by the housekeeper into the study where previously he had met with Gladys Althorp, he felt protectively annoyed that her husband had so quickly commandeered the space that so recently had been hers. He saw that her shawl was missing from the chair, and that the blinds were no longer tilted. Sunlight that hinted of an early spring was pouring into the room, destroying the dim and quiet intimacy he had experienced there.

"The ambassador will be with you shortly," the housekeeper said.

Is this a power play? Greco wondered. I asked to come at 12:30; he insisted I be here at noon. Now is hc going to keep me waiting?

Greco remembered how concerned the housekeeper had been about Gladys Althorp. What was her name? he asked himself, then remembered it. "Brenda, I witnessed how solicitous you were of Mrs. Althorp. I am sure you were a great comfort to her."

"I hope I was. I haven't been here that long, but I was very fond of her. And I do know she died happy, knowing that the man who killed her daughter was finally going to pay for his crime. Mrs. Althorp told me that the day she was in court watching Peter Carrington in chains was something she'd prayed for every single day for twenty-two years."

Charles Althorp had come into the room while she was speaking, and had overheard her. "We're delighted to have your opinion, Brenda," he said sarcastically. "You may go now."

Greco took an instant dislike to Althorp. Humiliating his housekeeper in front of another person was probably indicative of the employer-employee relationship that existed in this house, and given Althorp's attitude on the phone, he expected nothing more.

Brenda reacted as though she had been slapped. Her body stiffened. Then, with quiet dignity, she turned and left the room.

Althorp indicated a chair for Greco and sat down himself. "I have a luncheon engagement," he said, "so you do understand that fifteen minutes means fifteen minutes."

"I am aware of the time constraints," Greco said. Deliberately avoiding the use of Althorp's courtesy title, he began, "Mr. Althorp, you were very angry at your daughter, Susan, that last evening. It was noticed and remarked upon by a number of people. Why were you so upset with her?"

"I don't even remember, and it isn't important. Naturally, I have always felt terrible that my last contact with Susan was under those circumstances."

"You and Mrs. Althorp left the dinner party early the night Susan disappeared."

"We left shortly after dinner. As had become usual, Gladys was not feeling well."

"Before you left, you ordered your daughter to be home by midnight. The party, from what I understand, lasted well over an hour after that. Why the curfew?"

"Susan was overtired. I was concerned about her. I wanted her to leave with us. The dancing had just begun. Peter asked if she could stay for a little while; he offered to escort her home."

"You liked Peter."

"Very much, at that time."

"Mr. Althorp, I will ask you again: why were you concerned about your daughter?"

"That is none of your business, Mr. Greco."

"Oh, but I think it is. If what I believe is correct, it is the reason Susan is dead."

Greco watched as Althorp's face turned crimson. Rage or fear? Greco asked himself.

"When Mrs. Kay Carrington was a six-year-old child, she was sitting outside the Carrington mansion waiting for her father, Jonathan Lansing, who, as you know, was the landscaper there. It was the same day as the party. He was attending to a problem concerning the lighting. Kay had heard about the chapel, and, being a typically curious child, went into the house to look at it. While she was there, she heard the chapel door opening and hid between the pews. She did not see the people who entered, but she heard the words they exchanged. It was a couple, and the woman was demanding money from the man."

Greco paused, then, his tone bitingly cold, said, "I believe that the woman in the chapel was your daughter, Susan. I believe that she had developed a drug problem, and that she needed money because she needed more drugs. I believe that you knew of the problem, but wanted to control it your own way, by making sure she had no money, and by keeping such a close watch on her that she would not have access to whoever was her supplier."

"No wonder you have such a fine reputation as an investigator, Mr. Greco. But even if this were true, what does it prove? Why does it matter now?" Althorp's voice was equally cold.

"Oh, I would say it matters very much, Mr. Althorp. If you had sought professional help for Susan, she might still be alive today."

"When she disappeared, I thought she had run away with her dealer. I thought she'd show up again someday," Althorp replied.

"And, thinking that, you committed the unpardonable sin of letting Peter Carrington be a suspect in her disappearance? Despite the fact that you actually thought there was a possibility she might still be alive?"

"I simply didn't know. I couldn't have opened up that possibility. It would have killed my wife," Althorp said. "Susan's mother thought she was a perfect child. The idea that Susan was a drug addict would have destroyed her."

"When did you first suspect that Susan was using drugs?"

"Shortly after she returned from her freshman year at college. There was something different about her that last summer. She'd get irritable, or cry easily, and that was totally unlike her. I didn't know what to believe, but then one evening when she was out, I passed her room and saw that she'd left all the lights on. I went in to turn them off, and spotted something on the floor. It was tinfoil and there was some white powder in it. It appeared to be cocaine. I knew then what was going on. When Susan came home, I confronted her and demanded to know where she was getting the drugs. She wouldn't tell me. That was about a month before she disappeared."

"If you had told the police about Susan's problem, it would have immediately changed the nature of the investigation, and her dealer might have been apprehended. Why did your wife hire me six months ago? It was to find something that could bring your daughter's presumed killer, Peter Carrington, to trial. The arrest and imprisonment of Susan's killer surely would have brought her peace and closure." Greco heard his voice rising. "Was it better to let your wife suffer every day of her life as she did? Was that your idea of being merciful? That is a comfortable excuse for your silence, isn't it? Isn't it true that you hoped to be appointed to another ambassadorship and didn't want any hint of scandal attached to your name? The beautiful debutante presumed to have been murdered by a wealthy young man engendered public sympathy for the family. You were content to leave it at that."

"That is your opinion and I will not dignify it by responding," Althorp said. "Why are you here, Mr. Greco? What difference does any of this make now? It won't bring Susan back, and as my son pointed out to me yesterday, if there is an art museum in heaven, Susan and her mother are there, discussing paintings. It is a scenario in which I find comfort."

"You may find comfort in your scenario, but do you really have the nerve to ask what difference it would make if the truth were told now? Didn't it ever occur to you that Susan may have been murdered by the drug dealer, and not by Peter Carrington?"

"Peter's shirt was missing. I thought that he might have had an argument with Susan that got out of hand."

"It was either a drug dealer or Peter who took her life, and you are content with either answer! I have another theory, Mr. Althorp. You may have heard Susan trying to sneak out that night. You may have been angry enough to harm her yourself. It was noon the next day before anyone realized that she was not in her room. You had plenty of time to hide the body until you could dispose of it permanently."

Charles Althorp gripped the arms of his chair. "That is absolutely preposterous, Mr. Greco! And insulting. Your fifteen minutes are up. Get out!"

"I am going to leave now, Ambassador Althorp," Greco said, emphasizing the title with contempt in his voice. "But I will be back," he said. "I assure you, I will be back."

70

I spoke to Maggie a couple of times in the next few days, and I knew she was concentrating on trying to remember the name of the man my father had heard whistling the tune that was so nostalgic to him. Then something occurred to me. "Maggie, you said that Daddy was down in the dumps when he told you about it. His car was found so soon afterward, and you thought he had committed suicide, do you think you might have talked about that incident to your friends?"

"We certainly talked about how much he missed your mother. I probably did tell them about it. It was an example of how much he missed her."

"Then there's always a chance that you mentioned the man's name, because you said Daddy mentioned it to you."

"I may have, but, Kay, that was over twenty-two years ago. If I can't remember, how do you expect anyone else would?"

"I really don't. But it's just one of those things that are easy for you to do, and may be so helpful to us. I want you to talk about Daddy to your friends. Tell them that, in a way, it's been good for me to know that he didn't willingly leave me. Then you can remind them of that story, and say that it's been annoying you that you can't come up with the name of the man who was whistling that song the day of the party. But talk about it *only* to your friends, please."

"Kay, it's really unlikely that someone will come up with a name after all these years, but I'd do anything to help. It's a visiting day at the jail, isn't it?"

"Yes, it is."

"Will you congratulate your husband—I mean Peter—about the baby?"

"Thank you, Maggie. He'll appreciate that."

Two hours later, I was in the visiting room of the Bergen County Jail, looking at Peter through the Plexiglas. I wanted so much to touch him, to link my fingers with his. I wanted to bring him home and close the door on the rest of the world. I wanted our life back.

But, of coursc, to say any of that now would only make it harder for him. There were so many things I couldn't say. I couldn't talk about the shirt that I thought Gary Barr had stolen from Elaine, only to have it stolen again by Vincent Slater. Vince had continued to deny he found it when he searched the gatehouse and the SUV, but I didn't believe him.

I couldn't talk to him about the money I'd paid Elaine, and I certainly couldn't tell Peter that I'd hired Nicholas Greco.

Instead I told Peter about finding the antique cradle, and how I was going to look up Eli Fallow, the craftsman, and see if I could learn anything about him. "The third floor is like a treasure hunt, Peter."

Small talk. Unsatisfactory. The kind you make with a patient in the hospital when you know you really can't talk about important things because it would be too upsetting. Peter's face lit up at any reference to the baby, but that was followed by worry about me. He noticed my weight loss, and I assured him that the obstetrician said that in the first trimester it was not unusual.

He asked if I saw much of Elaine and Richard. I hedged by saying how shocked I had been when Elaine told me that Richard was pulling up stakes and moving to London. "I gather he's facing his gambling problems, and also the fact that his own gallery is always losing money," I said.

"I think that's a solid direction for him to take," Peter said. "As far back as when Elaine and my father were dating, Richard was into the horses, which, if you knew my father, was absolutely unforgivable. I think one of the reasons my father demanded to see every bill that came into the house during the big decorating siege was because he wanted to make sure Elaine wasn't supporting her son's gambling habit, at least with his money. I think it would be nice if you had Elaine and Richard and Vince for dinner before Richard leaves, Kay."

I couldn't say that was the last thing I wanted to do. Instead I ignored the suggestion and asked, "What kind of allowance did you have as a kid? Was your father generous with you?"

Peter could look so boyish when he smiled. "Actually, he was okay. Fortunately for our relationship, I never went the route of the rich man's spoiled son. I liked to go into the office during the summer and on school holidays. I'm fascinated with the financial world. I'm good at it. That pleased my father. And he honestly had a soft heart for anyone in genuine need, which is why the check he gave Maria Valdez was exactly the sort of gesture he would make, and *did* make to many people."

Then Peter's expression darkened. "And try to convince anyone of that," he added softly.

I knew I only had a few minutes left. I was holding the phone. "Guessing game," I said, and hummed the melody of the song I had heard in the chapel. "Do you recognize this tune?" I asked.

"I don't think so. In fact, I'd say that I don't."

"I had a friend who was a good whistler. Nobody does that anymore. Did you ever know anyone who whistles, I mean, someone, maybe like Vince?"

Peter actually laughed. I realized it was the first time I'd heard him laugh since we came back from our honeymoon.

"Kay, I can as easily imagine Vince whistling as I can see him being a circus barker. Buttoned-up Vincent Slater, whistling a tune for anyone to hear? Come *on*!"

The guard was approaching me. Our visiting time was up. Peter and I pressed our lips against the glass that separated us, and, as usual, I tried not to cry. "How do I love thee?" I asked him.

"Let me count the ways," he whispered. It had become our way of saying good-bye after a visit.

But then he added, "Kay, have a dinner for Richard before he leaves for London. I'd like that. He's always had his problems, but he *is* my stepbrother, and Elaine has always been kind to me."

71

The more I learn, the less I know, Nicholas Greco thought as he drove into the grounds of the Carrington estate. The guard had been told to expect him and gave a casual salute as Greco turned onto the driveway of the gatehouse.

He had phoned yesterday to request this appointment with Gary Barr, and had made it clear that he did not want to have it in Jane's presence.

"I am not aware of how much your wife knows of your activities," he had told Barr, "but unless you have shared all your experiences with her, I suggest you find a reason to schedule our meeting when she is not around."

"I'll be out doing errands until about noon," Barr told him. "Jane is always at the mansion then." In a tone of voice that was both hostile and worried, he'd added: "I don't know why you want to bother with me. I've already told everything I know about that girl's death, and I wasn't even working here around the time the landscaper disappeared."

I hope my strategy to unsettle him by giving him time to worry about the reason for our appointment is working, Greco thought as he parked the car and walked up the path to the gatehouse.

It was a narrow stone structure with leaded pane windows. When Gary Barr answered the door and grudgingly invited him in, Greco was surprised and impressed by the interior of the dwelling. The limited space had been maximized by having the first floor turned into one large room with kitchen, dining, and sitting area flowing together harmoniously. The handsome stone fireplace and high-beamed ceiling imparted a sense of timelessness. How many generations of people have lived here in the four hundred years since it was built in Wales? he wondered.

A comfortable residence for a housekeeping couple, he decided—far more pleasant than the quarters most employees enjoy. He noticed that it was spotlessly clean. In his experience as an investigator, he had sometimes come across housekeepers whose own homes were hardly models of cleanliness.

Without being invited, he selected a straight-backed chair near the couch, sat down, and with a deliberately cool tone, said, "Mr. Barr, I think that we should not waste each other's time this morning. Let's get to the point: You were dealing drugs to Susan Althorp."

"That's a lie!"

"Is it? When you were chauffeuring those young women around, and Susan sat in front with you, you made it your business to become her 'pal.' But there were three other girls in the back. One of them, Sarah Kennedy, was Susan's closest friend. Do you seriously suppose that Susan didn't confide in her?"

It was the kind of tricky question Greco liked to ask, the kind that often brought out a truthful response.

Gary Barr did not respond, but looked around nervously as if afraid someone might overhear their conversation. A chronic eavesdropper is always afraid of someone eavesdropping on *him*, Greco thought with contempt.

"You and your wife worked quite regularly for the Althorps during the years you were not employed by the Carringtons. I have witnessed Ambassador Althorp's attitude toward his employees. You must have resented that very much, didn't you, Mr. Barr? What a sweet revenge it must have been for you to entice the young daughter of the family into drugs, then refuse to give them to her unless she paid for them immediately. After she returned home that last night, she slipped out again because you were going to meet her. Isn't that what happened?"

Gary Barr impatiently brushed away the perspiration

that was glistening on his forehead. "Don't you come here and try to scare me. I know the law. Even if I *did* sell her a little cocaine, that was over twenty-two years ago. The statute of limitations ran out a long time ago. Look it up."

"I don't have to look it up, Mr. Barr. I am quite aware of the statute of limitations, and you are right. Unfortunately, you cannot be prosecuted for selling drugs to that poor girl, but, as I hope you are also aware, there is no statute of limitations for murder."

"*Murder*? You've got to be kidding. I didn't—"

Greco interrupted him. "If I go to the prosecutor and tell what I know, they will undoubtedly open another grand jury investigation. You will be subpoenaed, and you can't take the Fifth Amendment. You can't refuse to testify, because they can't prosecute you. But you can and will be charged with perjury if you lie to the grand jury about your involvement with Susan and anything else you know about her disappearance, so you had better come clean."

"All right! I was there," Barr said, his voice hoarse and hesitant. "It's like you said. She wanted some stuff and I told her I had to have the money up front, and she said she'd have it for me. I told her I'd be outside at quarter of two and to be on time."

"Peter Carrington left Susan at her home at twelve o'clock. Why so late?"

"She wanted to be sure her father was asleep."

"Why didn't you give her the cocaine at the party?"

"She didn't have the cash for me when she left the party. Otherwise I would have given it to her then."

Greco looked at Barr with loathing and disgust. By not giving her what she needed, you signed her death warrant, he thought. Somebody else was going to meet her, supposedly with the money.

"I left here at one thirty and walked over to the Althorps'," Barr said. "I cut across the lawn of the neighbors who live behind their house, and waited under the big tree in the side yard. No one could see me there. She didn't show up at quarter of two. Then, about ten minutes later, I heard a car coming. I waited to find out what was going on, figuring it was someone bringing her the cash, getting there late."

Barr stood up, walked over to the sink, and poured himself a glass of water. He gulped half of it, set the glass down, and came back. "I recognized the car. It was Peter Carrington's. He got out, came around and opened the passenger door, and took something out of it."

"You could see him clearly enough to see what he was doing?"

"There's a streetlight right on the curb in front of the Althorps' house. That's why I was meeting Susan at the side of the house."

"Go on."

"Peter got out of the car and walked across the lawn. Then he knelt down. I kind of crept forward, and I could see he was bending over something. There was just enough light that I could make out that something—maybe even someone—was lying on the ground. Then Peter got back in his car and drove away. I didn't know what was up, but I got out of there and came home."

"You didn't check to see if anyone needed help?"

"Carrington drove away. *He* didn't help anyone."

"And you saw no one else?"

"No."

"Are you sure you didn't meet Susan, have an argument because she didn't have the money, and perhaps, she even threatened to tell her father about you if you didn't give her the cocaine? You strangled her, then heard Peter's car coming and hid. When he drove off, you disposed of the body. Didn't it happen that way, Mr. Barr?"

"No, it didn't. I'll take a lie detector test if you want. I was home at twenty after two. I even woke up my wife and said that I didn't feel so good."

"You mean you wanted a witness, just in case. You're a very self-serving individual, Mr. Barr. I remember your wife offered to take a lie detector test to swear that you were home all night."

"She thought I was."

"We'll leave it at that. By the way, did Mr. Slater find the bloodstained dress shirt after he lured you into New York and searched this house, Mr. Barr?"

It was a satisfaction to Greco to see the dumbfounded look on Gary Barr's face.

"So, *he*'s the one who did it," Barr said heavily "I might have known."

72

Richard was leaving for London on Sunday night. I scheduled the farewell dinner for Saturday evening, more to honor Peter's wishes than to honor Richard, but I did go all out preparing for it. I'm a good cook and I worked with Jane to plan some really special dishes: asparagus with warm cheese as an appetizer, Dover sole, a watercress salad with apples, followed by raspberry sorbet and then an assortment of cheeses with a dessert wine.

"We'll have cocktails in the living room, then after dinner have coffee in Mr. Carrington's library," I told Jane.

"I'll have Gary build a fire in the library," she promised.

Gary Barr was being uncomfortably solicitous toward me, and I knew that before much longer I was going to give him his walking papers. I was very sorry that it would mean letting Jane go, too, but I knew I had no choice, and I was sure she could see the handwriting on the wall.

I had spoken to Nicholas Greco several times, and he had said that my suspicions were totally correct about the missing dress shirt. He told me that Barr had stolen it from Elaine, and Slater had then found it in the gatehouse, and presumably still had it. He warned me that I was not to say or do anything that would indicate *I* was aware of the shirt having been recovered.

"But I was the one who put Gary on the phone with Vincent," I protested. "I set him up for that trip to New York."

"My guess is that Barr is probably thinking that Slater tricked you for his own purposes," Greco said. "You must act as if Gary Barr is still your trusted employee, and I would suggest that when you speak with Mr. Slater, you apologize for doubting his word about the shirt. Certainly Gary Barr would not dare to challenge him on the subject."

Whenever I spoke to Greco on the phone, he continued to warn me: "You must be very careful around both Slater and Barr. We may still find an unholy alliance there. Elaine Carrington is a blackmailer, and her son is always desperate for money. Throw that into the mix and you have a potentially explosive situation."

I told him that Richard was going to live in London.

"I doubt that distance will solve his problems,"

Greco said. "The problem is not in the location; it's in the man."

Greco asked if I had brought the page from *People* magazine to show Peter. I confessed that I had not. "I'm sure he did not see Grace showing her guests that magazine," I said. "Everyone agrees he went straight upstairs after that scene with her."

"I understand your wishing not to cause your husband any further distress, but Mrs. Carrington, someone took that magazine that night. I believe it was taken because that person didn't realize Grace had already torn out the page featuring an article about that actress. It *is* important. Trust my instincts. It is very important."

"I will show it to Peter next time I visit him," I promised. Then I asked Greco if he was making any progress in proving Peter's innocence. His answer did not encourage me: "I am learning why this tragedy was set in motion," he said. "Now it is up to me to put the rest of the story together. It's far too soon and most unfair to offer you unfounded hope."

I didn't want double-talk. "Is there any hope that you can find new evidence so that Peter can be acquitted when he comes to trial?"

"There may be hope, Mrs. Carrington," Greco said. "But until I can offer proof that would stand up in court, it would be impossible to offer you more than just that."

For now I had to be content with that. The problem was, I was missing Peter so acutely that I needed some kind of reassurance that he would come home, even if it would take a miracle.

Planning the farewell dinner for Richard was a diversion, and as I made my selections in the cheese shop, I forced myself to believe that someday soon I would be buying Peter's favorite cheese for him.

I spent time that week having Gary Barr move furniture around in the living room. My first impression of that room had been wholly favorable—it was a beautiful room. But I had come to realize it also was a reflection of Elaine's taste—she had chosen everything in it, and as I got used to being there, I began to feel uncomfortable. Everything seemed too formal, too precise. The room lacked the lived-in feeling necessary to give it comfort and warmth.

I began to exchange the lamps Elaine had chosen with lovely porcelain antique lamps I found on the third floor. According to Jane Barr, Elaine had banished them when she redecorated the mansion. I set framed family pictures on the mantel, and placed photograph albums dating back one hundred years on top of the grand piano.

I once heard a prominent journalist say that in her home, books were the interior decoration. The bookcases by the fireplace in the living room contained expensive but modern tchotchkes. I packed many of them away and replaced them with some of my books which I had shipped to the mansion before the wedding. Peter and I joked that those boxes constituted my dowry. When Elaine came to the house on Saturday, it would be her first visit since I had made my changes. I would be watching for her reaction.

I had told the guests for Richard's dinner to arrive at seven o'clock. It seemed like years had passed since Peter and I had dinner with these same guests the week after we returned from our honeymoon. I decided to wear the same silk shirt and velvet slacks that I'd worn that night. I could tell I wouldn't be wearing those slacks again until after the baby was born. Then I let my hair fall loose on my shoulders. I knew I was dressing for my husband, not these people.

I had left that page from *People* magazine on top of my dresser, hoping that if I kept looking at it I would find the information Greco was sure was there. When I was about to go downstairs, I impulsively picked up that page and took it with me. I placed it on top of Peter's desk in his library, where it would be easy to see when we were having coffee. I had said I wanted to draw out the real killer—if he or she was in that small group. If there really *was* significance to that page, then maybe one of them would react to it.

Frankly, I thought Greco was putting far too much weight on it.

At precisely seven, the chimes sounded, and the first of my guests arrived.

73

"Go easy, Richard," Elaine Carrington cautioned as she watched her son pour a second vodka for himself. "We'll be having cocktails at the mansion, and then wine at dinner."

"I would never have guessed that," Richard said.

Elaine eyed her son anxiously. He'd been on edge ever since he arrived, which meant he probably had placed some bets after getting a few more of his hot tips. But maybe not, she thought, trying to reassure herself. He knows I can't cover his losses anymore.

"What do you think will happen after Peter is convicted?" Richard asked abruptly. "Will Kay just rattle around in the mansion all by herself?"

"She's having a baby," Elaine replied sharply. "She won't be alone for long."

"You didn't tell me that."

"Kay didn't tell me that. I found out because Linda Hauser's daughter ran into Kay at Dr. Silver's office."

"That doesn't prove she's pregnant."

"Trust me. She is. In fact, I'm going to ask her tonight, and I'll bet she'll admit it."

"So we have an heir to the Carrington fortune," Richard said with a sneer. "Isn't *that* wonderful?"

"Don't worry. I plan to be the ultimate stepgrandmother. Kay already understands that I hid that shirt to save Peter, and she's grateful for that. Not giving it to her was a big mistake—she'd have been forever in my debt. Now she sees me as a blackmailer who didn't deliver."

"Which you are," Richard said.

Elaine slammed down the glass of wine she had been sipping. "Don't you dare talk to me like that! If it weren't for you, I'd be living on the interest of ten million dollars as well as a million a year. Between your gambling and your lousy investments, you've drained me dry, Richard, and you know it. You've put me through the tortures of the damned, and now you insult me! Go to hell, Richard! Go to hell!"

Her face crumbled as her son crossed the room in two strides. "Hey, none of that," he said soothingly. "It's you and me against the world—including the whole damn bunch of Carringtons. Right, Mommy?" His voice became teasing. "Come on, Momma-mia, make up with me."

"Oh, Richard," Elaine said with a heavy sigh. "You

remind me so much of your father. Turn on the charm, let's make up. That was his routine."

"You were crazy about my father. I remember that."

"Yes, I was," Elaine said quietly. "But even when you're crazy about someone, at some point you can have enough. Remember that, Richard. And forget that second vodka. Have another at the mansion. It's time to go. We're due at seven."

74

Vincent Slater was the first to arrive for the dinner. As usual, he parked in the driveway behind the mansion and took out his key, planning to enter through the French doors that opened into his office.

The key did not turn—the lock had been changed.

Damn her, he thought, *damn* her! Kay Lansing, the landscaper's daughter—she's now making Peter Carrington's home off-limits to the one person who has protected Peter from the time he was a young boy. And continues to protect him, Slater thought grimly. If she only knew!

If I'd given her the shirt, she would have showed it to that detective, and that would have been it. She puts on an act of being so crazy about Peter, but the way it's going, this will end up with him rotting in prison while she enjoys the Carrington fortune.

Maybe. But then again, maybe not, he thought.

His anger rising with every step, Slater walked

around the mansion, nodded curtly to the guard on duty, and went to the front door. For the first time in nearly thirty years, he pressed his finger on the doorbell and waited to be invited inside.

75

"It was Slater," Gary Barr told his wife as he entered the kitchen. "You can count on him being Johnny-on-the-spot. The clock chimes seven, and there he is, ringing the doorbell."

"Why are you so mad at him? He's always been nice to you." Jane Barr was putting cheese puffs in the oven. She closed the oven door and turned to her husband. "You need to change your attitude, Gary, although it may be too late. I can tell Mrs. Carrington isn't comfortable with you around. That's why most nights she's been telling us not to wait to serve dinner."

"She was the one who got Slater on the phone to tell me to run that fool's errand in New York. She was in on searching the house. She even had you answer the phone so she'd be sure you wouldn't run over there for any reason." Too late, Gary Barr realized that he had said too much. Jane knew nothing about Peter

Carrington's dress shirt, nor did she realize that their home had been searched.

"What are you talking about?" Jane demanded. "Who searched what? Why?"

The doorbell rang again. Saved by the bell, Gary Barr thought as he rushed to answer. This time it was Elaine Carrington and her son Richard.

"Good evening, Mrs. Carrington, Mr. Walker."

Elaine ignored him and brushed by as she headed inside.

Walker paused: "I would suggest that, for your own good, you return what you took from my mother's home. I know more about you than you think I know, and I'm not afraid to use it."

76

Barbara Krause and Tom Moran had stayed in the office long after the rest of the prosecutor's staff had said good night and scurried away for the weekend. After Barbara received the phone call, she told Moran to get out the Susan Althorp file so that they could review the statements Ambassador Althorp had made at the time of his daughter's disappearance.

The ambassador had phoned Barbara, asked for the appointment, and said it was necessary to make it that late because his lawyer would be accompanying him.

"We always considered it possible that he was the one who did it," Moran said, "although it seemed only remotely possible. But now that his wife is dead, maybe he needs to come clean. Otherwisc, why would he bother to bring a lawyer with him?"

Promptly at eight o'clock, Althorp and his lawyer were escorted into the prosecutor's office. Krause's first impression of Althorp was that he looked sick. The ruddy complexion she had remembered when she last saw him was now pasty, and his face had become jowly.

He looks like a guy who just suffered a blow to the solar plexus, she thought.

"My wife has been buried," Ambassador Althorp began abruptly. "I cannot protect her any longer. After the funeral, I told my sons something that I have kept secret for twenty-two years. In turn, one of them then told me something that Susan had confided to him the Christmas before her death, and this new information changes everything. I believe that there has been a terrible miscarriage of justice, and I share responsibility for it."

Krause and Moran stared at him in stunned silence.

"Ambassador Althorp wishes to make a statement," his lawyer said. "Are you prepared to take it?"

77

Elaine did not comment on the changes I had made in the living room, which I interpreted to mean that she was not pleased with them. She carried it off well, although I could understand how she must be feeling. Six months ago she knew nothing of my existence. She had lived in this house for the five years she was married to Peter's father, and after his death had stayed on, running the place until Peter married Grace Meredith. Now it was mine.

"That was when things changed. Mrs. Elaine moved into the other house, and Peter invited us to come back," Jane Barr had confided to me. "Mrs. Grace Carrington took the people on the staff that she especially liked and shifted them to the apartment. That's where she really lived and did her entertaining, so even though there was a new mistress in the house, Mrs. Elaine pretty much had the run of the mansion, even though she didn't actually live here anymore."

In the years following Grace's death, Elaine had become a kind of de facto lady of the house. Then I had come along to spoil it.

I was aware that without me in the picture, she was the closest thing to a relative that Peter had, and it would have been only natural for him to turn to her for comfort if he went to prison. And Peter was generous.

Vincent Slater was either acting very cool to me, or he was afraid of me. I wasn't sure which it was. I couldn't decide whether he felt I had betrayed Peter by hiring Nicholas Greco, or was afraid that Greco would find out something that would incriminate him. Greco had suggested the possibility of an "unholy alliance," as he had put it, between Vince and Barr. I really hadn't had time to give that possibility much thought.

I will say in Richard Walker's behalf that he was the one who made the evening. He told anecdotes about the years he had spent working at Sotheby's when he was in his early twenties, and told us about the elderly art connoisseur in London who had hired him now. "He's quite a delightful guy," Richard said, "and it's a perfect time to make the move. I can get out of my lease for the gallery and even get a bonus in giving up the space. My apartment is in the hands of the broker, and we already have offers on it."

For a little while we avoided talking about Peter, but then at dinner it became impossible to ignore the fact that we were here, dining in his home, while he was in a jail cell. "I did give him some good news," I said. "I told him we were having a baby."

"I guessed it!" Elaine said triumphantly. "I told Richard only a couple of hours ago that I was going to ask—I had my suspicions."

Both Elaine and Richard gave me big, seemingly heartfelt hugs.

That left my other guest, Vincent Slater. Our eyes met, and I saw an expression in his that frightened me. I couldn't read it, but for an instant the image of Peter's other pregnant wife, floating in the pool, flashed through my mind.

By nine o'clock, we were having coffee in the library. By then we had run out of things to say to one another, and there was a kind of forced attitude of civility. I felt so much hostility in the room that I resolved I would never bring these people into Peter's special space again. I could tell that all three of them despised Gary Barr. I knew Elaine suspected him of stealing Peter's shirt. Greco had confirmed that Barr admitted to the theft, and we knew that Vincent had then found it and taken it himself.

I could not be sure if any of them, including Barr, had noticed the page from *People* magazine lying on the corner of Peter's desk. I had placed it in such a way that it was hard to miss. I still didn't understand how it could be important, but if it drew a reaction from one of my guests, then I might have a clue.

At nine thirty, they all got up to go. By then, the stress of the evening had begun to exhaust me. If any of these men was the one I heard being threatened by Susan Althorp all those years ago in the chapel, I was not going to find out about it tonight.

We stood by the front door for a few minutes as Vincent and I wished Richard all good luck in London. He told me that if possible, he would be back for Peter's trial, to lend moral support. "I love that guy, Kay," Richard said. "I always have. And I know he loves you."

Long ago, Maggie had told me that you can love a person without loving everything about that person. "Monsignor Fulton Sheen was a great speaker who had a television program about fifty years ago," she had reminisced. "One day he said something that really impressed me. He said, 'I hate communism, but I love the communist.'"

I think that was a good comparison to the way Peter felt about Richard. He loved the person and despised his weakness.

After I closed the door behind Elaine and Richard and Vincent, I walked back to the kitchen. The Barrs were about to leave. "The cups are all washed and put away, Mrs. Carrington," Jane said anxiously.

"Mrs. Carrington, if you need anything during the

night, you know we'll be there in a minute for you," Gary Barr said.

I ignored his remark, but did say that I thought everyone had enjoyed the dinner very much. I bid them good night and they left by the kitchen door; I double-locked it behind them.

It had become my habit at the end of the day to sit for a while in Peter's library. It made me feel close to him. I could relive the moment I walked into this room for the first time and saw him sitting in his chair. I could smile as I remembered the way his reading glasses slipped from his face when he stood up to greet me.

But tonight I didn't stay there long. I was exhausted, both emotionally and physically. I was beginning to fear that Nicholas Greco would not be able to come up with anything that would help in Peter's defense. He was so cautious when I asked him about what he had learned. Maybe he was even finding information that would *hurt* Peter.

I got up from the chair and walked over to the desk. I wanted to be sure to take the page from *People* magazine upstairs with me. I didn't want to forget it. Greco had been so insistent that I show it to Peter on the next visiting day.

I had anchored the page with Peter's handsome antique magnifying glass, and it was covering a section of the background in the picture of Marian Howley.

Part of the section magnified included a painting on the wall behind Howley. I lifted the magnifying glass and studied the painting intently. It was a pastoral scene, identical to the one I had replaced in the dining room. Taking the page and magnifying glass with me, I ran upstairs to the third floor. I had changed a number of the paintings, and had to dig it out from within a stack I had placed on the floor, each painting covered and carefully wrapped.

The frame was heavy, and I was cautious not to overdo the pulling and lifting, but finally I got it out. I propped it against the wall and then sat cross-legged on the floor in front of it. Using the magnifying glass, I slowly began to examine it.

I'm not an art expert, so the fact that this painting did not in any way stir me was not a test of its value. It was signed in the corner—Morley—with the same flourish as the one now hanging in the dining room. The two paintings were essentially identical in content. But the other one compelled attention; this one did not. The date on this one was 1920.

In 1920, had Morley painted this scene and then gone on to create other similar scenes, only with greater skill? It was possible. But then I saw what could only be visible by careful examination: There was another name under Morley's signature.

"What do you think you're doing, Kay?"

I whirled around. Vincent Slater was standing in the doorway, staring at me, his face white, his lips a thin hard line. He began walking across the room to me, and I shrank away from him.

"What do you think you are doing?" he asked again.

78

In Barbara Krause's office, a court stenographer had been summoned to take down the statement given by Ambassador Charles Althorp. More composed now than he had been when he entered the office, Althorp's voice was steady when he began to speak again.

"At the time of her disappearance, I did not reveal that I had learned my daughter, Susan, had developed an addiction to cocaine. As investigator Nicholas Greco pointed out to me the other day, had I told that to the police when Susan disappeared, the investigation might have moved in another direction."

He looked down at his folded hands as if contemplating them. "I thought that by keeping a tight rein on Susan, and cutting off her allowance, I would force her to stop using drugs. Of course, I was wrong. Greco told me that the afternoon of the party in the Carrington mansion, the present Mrs. Carrington, who was then six years old, overheard a woman blackmailing a man because she needed money. Greco believes—and now I do as well—that it was Susan she heard. Hours later, Susan disappeared.

"For years I have kept the secret of Susan's addiction. I told my sons about it as we stood next to their mother's grave. Had I revealed it earlier, a great injustice might have been avoided." Althorp closed his eyes and shook his head. "I should have . . ." His voice trailed off.

"What exactly *did* you tell your sons, Ambassador?" Tom Moran asked.

"I told them that I believed Susan started taking drugs when she returned from college the beginning of the last summer she was alive, and that she may have been blackmailing someone to get the money she needed. My confession prompted them to open up in turn, telling me things they knew about their sister, things that take on new meaning in context with recent developments.

"My son David had come home for a visit the Christmas before Susan disappeared. Susan had been spending a lot of time at the Carrington mansion. David told me that she confided to him she had noticed that several of the paintings downstairs in the Carrington mansion had been replaced with copies. She was studying art, you know, and knew a lot about the subject. She was sure she knew who was doing the copying, because on one occasion that person invited a young artist to a party in the house, and Susan saw her taking photographs of several paintings.

"David advised Susan to forget what she had discovered and not breathe a word of it to anyone. He said he knew what would happen if Mr. Carrington Sr. found out about it. It would end up as a very messy court case, and Susan might have to testify. David told her that our family had had enough grief with that family because of my earlier affair with Elaine Carrington."

"So Susan did as David suggested, but that summer, when she needed money, she may have used her knowledge of the theft of the art to try to get it," Krause suggested.

"I believe that's exactly what she did," Althorp confirmed.

"Was it Peter Carrington, Ambassador?" Moran asked. "Was he stealing from his own father?"

"No, of course not. Don't you see why this is tormenting me? Peter is in jail right now, accused of killing Susan. He had no reason to kill her. David told me that he believes if Susan had asked Peter for the money, he would have given it to her without question, and then would have tried to get her help. But Susan would never have asked Peter because she was in love with him. David said that my silence has been a curse on Peter. When I spoke to David this afternoon, he said that if I didn't come here tonight, he would never speak to me again."

"Then who was stealing the paintings?"

"Elaine Carrington's son, Richard Walker."

79

Pat Jennings put down the book she was reading, picked up the television remote control, and flipped on the ten o'clock news. "Have to see what's going on in the world," she told her husband, who was dozing over a magazine. Not expecting a response, she turned her attention to the screen.

"We have a breaking news story," the Fox News anchor was saying. "The body of forty-six-year-old Alexandra Lloyd has been found floating in the East River. The victim had been stabbed numerous times. A neighbor and close friend described her as an art teacher who had recently lost her job at a local high school because of budget cuts. Anyone with information should phone the tipster line, 212-555-7000."

"Alexandra Lloyd!" Pat exclaimed, just as the phone rang.

It was Trish. "Pat, I was just watching the news, and—"

"I know," Pat said, "I was watching it, too."

"Are you going to call that tip line and tell them about her calls to Richard Walker?"

"You bet I am, and right now."

"That poor woman. That's so awful, to be stabbed and dumped in the river. My God, do you think he did it?"

"I don't know, but that's for the police to figure out."

"Keep me posted," Trish urged as she hung up.

80

After Charles Althorp had completed his statement and departed with his lawyer, Barbara Krause and Tom Moran stayed in her office, discussing the impact of what they had heard, and assessing how it affected their case against Peter Carrington.

"Even if Walker was stealing good paintings and substituting copies, it doesn't mean that he killed Susan. And much of what Althorp told us is hearsay," Barbara Krause said, flatly.

"And it doesn't answer why Carrington hid his dress shirt that night and why his father handed Maria Valdez a check for five thousand dollars," Moran pointed out. "Anyhow, the statute of limitations has run out on prosecuting Walker for theft, even if we can prove that he was an art crook."

Barbara Krause stood up. "I'm tired. Let's give it a rest."

Her phone rang. "My family probably thinks I ran

off with you," she told Moran as she picked up the phone. Then, as she listened, her expression changed, and she began to pepper the caller with questions: "When did you find her? . . . The secretary is sure she was threatening him? . . . He's leaving for London tomorrow? . . . Okay. Thanks."

She hung up and looked at Moran. "Richard Walker's name has turned up again. The body of a woman who frequently called Walker at work, and who left an angry, almost threatening message a few days ago, has been found floating in the East River. Her name was Alexandra Lloyd. The information about Lloyd calling Walker came from his secretary. My God, I wonder if the two stepbrothers are both killers."

"How did she die?" Moran asked.

"She was stabbed at least a dozen times," Krause said.

"Walker's mother, Elaine Carrington, lives in a house on that estate. He may be there now," Moran said.

"We'll alert the Englewood cops and have them send a squad car over there immediately," Krause replied, a worried tone in her voice. "I know they have some private security outside the estate, but Kay Carrington is alone in that house at night."

81

"What are you doing here?" I asked Vincent Slater as I scrambled to get up from where I had been sitting on the floor. "How did you get in?"

"*How did I get in*? I cannot describe to you the indignity of your asking how I got in. After thirty years of having a key to my own office in this house, after all the years I have spent protecting Peter, including protecting him from prosecution, I arrived here earlier this evening to find that the locks had been changed."

"What do you mean, protecting Peter from prosecution?" I screamed. *"Peter is innocent!"*

"No, he is not. He was sleepwalking the night Susan disappeared. He didn't know what he was doing. I'm sure of that."

"You believe that!"

"His father must have known what happened," Vincent replied. "That's why he paid off the maid. I have the shirt; it has blood on it. That's why I know that he must have done it. You know, Kay, you really had me fooled. At first I thought you really loved Peter, and that you would be good for him. But then you hired Greco, the very man who had located Maria Valdez, whose testimony about a bribe from Peter's father will put another nail in Peter's coffin. Weren't you really hoping that Greco would dig up more evidence, so you could bury Peter once and for all? I know you would have given the shirt to Greco, so that's why I kept it. Admit it. You married Peter to get your hands on his money. Now that you're carrying his child, you've got a lock on it. Or, is it really Peter's child?"

I was too dumbfounded to even respond.

"Or is it the child of the man to whom you've given a key to my office? I just saw someone coming into the house through my office. He left the door open, and that is how I came in. I came back for two reasons: one, because I had to tell you what I thought about your humiliating me by changing the locks, without even a warning."

"And the second reason?" I asked scornfully.

"The second reason," he replied with equal scorn, "is that, if by some remote possibility, I am wrong about Peter having killed Susan, you were inviting disaster this evening by flaunting that page from *People* magazine in the library. I just can't fathom why you did that. I don't know what significance that page has, but I suspect it must have some. Why else would Grace have kept it?"

"Vince, you just told me you saw a man come into this house through your office. Who was it? That door should have been locked."

"It was dark, and I couldn't tell who it was. But I think you know damn well who it was. Where is he now—in your bedroom?"

"No, I'm right here. Kay, you shouldn't have left the new keys in the kitchen drawer."

Startled, we both turned and looked in the direction from which the voice had come. Richard Walker was moving toward us, a pistol in his hand.

82

Deciding not to use the patrol car's overhead lights or sirens that would alert Richard Walker if he was at the Carrington estate, Englewood police officer Steven Hausenstock pulled his squad car up to the gate and spoke to the guard. "Do you know if Richard Walker is here?" he asked.

"He arrived around five o'clock," the guard replied. "He's still here. He sometimes stays overnight at his mother's house."

"Who else is here?"

"Mr. Carrington's assistant, Mr. Slater, left about half an hour ago, but then came back in the last few minutes."

"All right. I need to check on Mrs. Kay Carrington."

"You can drive up to the front door and ring the bell. If she doesn't answer, the other guard is stationed there and has a key. He can let you in."

The officer drove up to the front entrance. He could

see that the only lights visible in the house were on the third floor.

"Is Mrs. Kay Carrington home?" the officer asked the guard.

"Yes, she is," the guard answered. "She had dinner guests earlier. They all left about half an hour ago."

"Who was here?" the officer asked.

"Mrs. Elaine Carrington, her son Richard Walker, and Vincent Slater. Mr. Slater just returned and went around to the back of the house where his office is. He usually enters there."

"Where did Richard Walker go when he left?" the officer asked.

"He walked with his mother toward her house," the guard said, pointing in that direction. "He must still be there, because I haven't seen him. His car is parked outside her house."

Officer Hausenstock got on his car radio. "Richard Walker is here," he said. "The guard last saw him a half hour ago, walking toward his mother's house on the grounds. Send backup units, but don't use sirens or lights. Hopefully he hasn't spotted me yet." Still holding the radio in his hand, the officer asked the guard, "Does Slater's office lead into the interior of the house?"

"Yes," the guard replied.

The officer continued to talk into his radio as he

walked. "I'm going around to the back of the house to see if Carrington's assistant, a guy named Slater, is there. If he is, I'll get into the house that way and check it out. I don't want to ring the doorbell in case Walker has somehow gotten back into the house without the guard seeing him."

Officer Hausenstock turned back to the guard. "Richard Walker may be dangerous, and he may be armed. More police officers will be here soon. If you see Walker, try to avoid any contact with him, and alert the other officers as soon as they get here. He may try to drive out. Tell the guard at the gate what is happening and make sure he closes the gates as soon as the other police arrive."

83

I stood virtually frozen with fear as Richard Walker moved toward us, but then stopped far enough away so that neither of us would have a chance to grab the gun away from him. Vince stepped in front of me; I knew he was attempting to shield me. Richard was pointing the gun directly at us.

"Richard, don't do anything stupid," Vince said calmly. "What is this all about?"

"What is it *about*?" Walker's voice was choked with emotion. "I'll *tell* you what it's all about. It's about the fact that, in the very short time that the present Mrs. Peter Carrington has been here, my life has been destroyed. My mother, for all these years, has protected Peter by hiding that shirt. She saw him wearing it when he came home that night. She could see the bloodstains on it, and she believed he had gotten into some kind of trouble. If she had turned it over to the police the next day, when everybody realized that Susan was missing,

Peter would have spent the last twenty-two years in prison."

The telephone on the table at the bottom of the stairs leading to the third floor began to ring. Walker made a gesture to us to be quiet so that he could hear if a message was left on the answering machine.

I had put the volume on high that afternoon so that I could hear any messages while I was on the third floor. A moment later, Maggie's voice, sounding anxious and frightened, said, "Kay, it's late. Where are you? I just remembered who it was your father told me he'd heard whistling that song. It was Richard Walker, Elaine's son. Kay, wasn't he going to be at your house for dinner tonight? Kay, please be careful. I'm so worried about you. Call me back as soon as you get this message."

I could sense that Richard knew that it was all over for him. I stepped away from Vincent. Whatever was going to happen, I wanted to confront Richard. "It was *you* who killed Susan Althorp," I said, my calm tone masking the fear I felt. "It was you and Susan that I heard in the chapel that afternoon, wasn't it?"

I pointed to the painting I had been examining. "You're the art dealer with the gambling problem. I think you're the one who switched this painting—and God knows how many others. Peter told me that the best art was on the walls downstairs. Well, this one was hung in the dining room, but it's only a copy. The real one can be seen on the wall behind Marian Howley in that *People* magazine article. That one actually belongs in this house, doesn't it, Richard? Grace was on to you, just as Susan had been years before. Susan knew a lot about art. She confronted you about the theft, didn't she? I don't know why Susan would blackmail you instead of telling Peter's father, but she did."

"Don't say anything more, Kay," Vince warned. I realized that Vince was concerned that Richard might lose control and shoot, but I was determined to finish what I had begun.

"Your mother wasn't protecting Peter," I said. "She was protecting *you*. And there's a lot more. My father prepared a landscaping design for the other side of the fence, the area where you had buried Susan. He sent it to Peter so he could pass it on to his father, but Peter was away at school and didn't see it. But I think that your mother did see it, and then she showed it to you. You both realized then that you had to get rid of my father. It wasn't enough that you had already fired him. You were afraid that he might still communicate with Peter's father about the design, and you couldn't let that happen. You made his death look like a suicide, and then you buried my father here on the grounds, because you thought they'd never search these grounds again."

Vince had grasped my arm; I could tell he was frantic to stop me. Richard's hand was shaking. Even though I knew he would probably shoot us, I had to keep going. I was overwhelmed by the emotion of all the years of desperately missing my father, and, even worse, believing that he had abandoned me. I was tortured by the weeks of watching my husband shackled and chained, and it was all because of this man.

In that moment, I became aware of a shadow moving in the hallway behind Richard. I wondered suddenly if it could be Elaine Carrington or Gary Barr, coming to help Richard. Even if Maggie had decided to call the police when I didn't answer the phone, it was probably too soon for them to have arrived here. Whoever it was out in the hallway, I wanted that person to hear what I had to say to Richard Walker.

"You not only killed Susan and my father, you killed Grace, too," I continued. "She had that page from the magazine in her pocket when they found her in the pool. She must have realized that the original Morley painting belonged in this house. And Richard, you might be interested to know that the person you had copy it for you was so proud of her work that she actually signed her own name under the forged Morley signature."

I pointed again to the painting I had been examining. "Tell me, Richard, who is Alexandra Lloyd?"

With a sigh of resignation, a weak smile crossed Richard's face. His hand stopped trembling. "As a matter of fact, Alexandra Lloyd was an artist, but now she's dead. I just heard on the news that her body has been fished out of the East River. Like Susan, the charming young lady who was also a drug addict, Alexandra didn't understand that blackmailing me was a very stupid move. You have also made some serious mistakes, Kay, and now I must deal with you as I dealt with them."

Richard then looked at Vince, and spoke directly to him. "I am sorry, Vince. I did not come here intending to harm you. You have always been decent to me and to my mother. But, unfortunately, you showed up at the wrong time. It's over for me. My luck has run out. The police will eventually connect me to Alexandra, and then they'll figure out the rest of it. I still have a small chance of escaping, though, and so I can't leave you here to notify the police."

Richard turned to me. "But if they do get me, I'll have the satisfaction of knowing, when I'm sitting in prison, that you won't be enjoying yourself on the Carrington money." He aimed the pistol toward my head. "Ladies first, Kay."

As I whispered Peter's name, the shadow I had seen in the hallway became a cop who burst into the room, knocked the weapon from Richard's hand, and tackled him to the floor. “Police!” he shouted to Richard. “Stay down, stay down!”

As the police officer struggled with Richard, Vincent kicked the pistol across the room and then fell onto Richard, trying to help the officer subdue him. Moments later, there was a pounding of feet on the stairs and two more police officers raced into the room. When he saw them, Richard stopped struggling and began to sob.

As if in a trance, I watched as Richard was handcuffed and pulled to his feet. One of the officers retrieved the pistol, and the officer who had been out in the hall turned to me. “I heard everything, Mrs. Carrington,” he said. “Be assured, I heard everything.”

84

At 1:30 P.M. the next day, my husband, shackled and wearing a bright-orange jumpsuit, was brought before Judge Smith. Once again, Barbara Krause would speak for the state, and Conner Banks would stand beside Peter. Once again, the courtroom was jammed with spectators and media. Once again, I sat in the front row. Vince Slater sat on one side of me, and Nick Greco was next to him. Maggie sat on the other side of me, clutching my hand.

Prosecutor Krause addressed the court. "Your Honor, extraordinary events have taken place over the last fifteen hours. Richard Walker, the son of Elaine Carrington, has confessed to the murders of Susan Althorp, Jonathan Lansing, and Grace Carrington. My office has formally charged Mr. Walker with these crimes, and he will be arraigned before Your Honor tomorrow. He has also confessed to the murder three days ago of Alexandra Lloyd, whose body was discovered in the East River in

New York City. The New York Police Department has filed a criminal complaint charging him in that case.

"Your Honor—and may I also address Mr. Carrington—we have profound regret that this gross miscarriage of justice has occurred. Our only comfort is that it was discovered before any further harm was done. We are moving to dismiss the indictment that the grand jury returned against Mr. Carrington. That indictment charged him with the murders of Susan Althorp and Jonathan Lansing. We are also, in the interest of justice, moving to dismiss the bail jumping charges that were recently filed. I note that we had not yet formally charged Mr. Carrington with the homicide of Grace Carrington. Your Honor, the only charge that could possibly remain would be the assault on the police officer when Mr. Carrington returned to the Althorp property, apparently in a sleepwalking state. I have personally spoken to the officer involved, and he has asked me to request the dismissal of that charge, too. He is profoundly sympathetic, as are we, to Mr. Carrington; we believe that he has suffered enough. I move that that complaint be dismissed also."

Judge Smith then motioned toward Conner Banks. "Is there anything that you or Mr. Carrington wish to say?"

Banks and Peter looked at each other, and Peter shook his head. "Your Honor," he said, extending his manacled hands, "please tell them to take these things off me. I just want to go home with my wife."

Judge Smith, visibly moved, said, "I am granting the prosecutor's motion to dismiss all of the charges. Mr. Carrington, I rarely make personal comments, but then, I rarely witness anything like this. I am so sorry that you have been a victim of this tragedy. You will be released immediately."

As the courtroom erupted in applause, I ran to Peter and threw my arms around him. I was too emotional to speak, but he did: "It's over, my love, it's over," he said. "Let's go home."

Epilogue

One Year Later

It has been a year since Peter stood in the courtroom and heard the prosecutor ask that the charges against him be dismissed. The wheels of justice have continued to turn for the people responsible for putting Peter through this ordeal.

Richard Walker pleaded guilty to the murders of Susan Althorp, my father, Grace Carrington, and Alexandra Lloyd. He was sentenced to life in prison in both New Jersey and New York. The prosecutor's office has assured me that he will never be released.

Vince Slater turned Peter's dress shirt over to the prosecutor's office. The bloodstain on it was determined to be consistent with Richard's admission of what had happened to Susan the night of the dinner party. He had promised to meet her outside her house at 1:30 A.M. She wanted it to be that late to be sure her father was asleep. When he met her, she assured him that she was going to quit using drugs and that this would be the last time she would come to him for money. But he didn't believe her. Frightened that she would reveal his theft of the art, Richard decided he had to kill her. To keep her from screaming, he punched her in the mouth, causing her to bleed onto the front of her gown. Then he strangled her. Before he could move the body to the trunk of his car, Richard saw Peter's car pulling up to the curb in front of the Althorp property.

Panicked, Richard had hidden behind the shrubbery, and had watched as Peter got out of the car, retrieved something from the passenger seat, and then walked across the lawn to where Susan was lying. He was wearing his formal dress shirt but no jacket. Richard saw Peter drop an object—which turned out to be a purse—and then kneel down and lay his head against Susan's chest, apparently to listen for a heartbeat. That is when the transfer of blood to his shirt occurred. Peter then returned to his car and drove away.

Richard admitted that during all this, Peter had seemed to be in a daze consistent with sleepwalking.

Elaine Carrington denied any prior knowledge that Richard was going to harm Susan Althorp, but she did admit that he had told her what he had done within hours of its happening. His explanation to her was that he had snapped and killed Susan because she had resisted his advances, even though she had slipped out of her house to meet him.

Elaine confessed that she had advised Richard to hide the body at his fishing cottage in upstate New York, then later helped him to bury it on the property beyond the fence after they were sure that the police searches were over. She also admitted that it had been her idea to have Richard, using a different name, lure my father to an estate that was for sale in upstate New York on the pretext of hiring him as a landscaper.

After Richard murdered my father, Elaine once again helped him bury the body on the grounds. Richard drove my father's car to where it was found near the Hudson River, and Elaine had followed in her own car. She then drove him home.

Elaine denied any involvement in the deaths of Grace Carrington or Alexandra Lloyd. She also claimed to have no knowledge of the art thefts.

Gary and Jane Barr are now divorced, and I am very pleased that Jane has continued to work for our family.

Nicholas Greco has become a regular crime commentator on the Fox News network. I am forever in his debt for his perseverance in helping us to find the truth.

Vince Slater and I have realized that, in very different ways, we were both desperately trying to protect Peter. I shall never forget how he stood in front of me as Richard pointed the gun at us. Vince continues to be

Peter's most trusted aide, and has become my dear friend.

The newest Peter Carrington is now six months old. I can't say "Junior," because he is really Peter Carrington the Fifth. He is the image of his father, and the light of our lives.

Maggie delights in her role as great-grandmother. She and Peter are now very close. She has even convinced herself that in her heart, she had always believed that he was innocent.

Peter is once again the chairman and CEO of Carrington Enterprises, and the company continues to prosper. He will always require medication to prevent sleepwalking, but there have been no further episodes.

A major factor in sleepwalking is stress, and I see it as my job to make our home a safe haven for Peter in every way. When he walks through the door at night and finds the baby and me waiting for him, I can see by the look that comes into his eyes and the smile that lights his face that I am succeeding.

WHERE ARE YOU NOW?

1

It is exactly midnight, which means Mother's Day has just begun. I stayed overnight with my mother in the apartment on Sutton Place where I grew up. She is down the hall in her room, and together we are keeping the vigil. The same vigil we've kept every year since my brother, Charles MacKenzie Jr., "Mack," walked out of the apartment he shared with two other Columbia University seniors ten years ago. He has never been seen since then. But every year at some point on Mother's Day, he calls to assure Mom he is fine. "Don't worry about me," he tells her. "One of these days I'll turn the key in the lock and be home." Then he hangs up.

We never know when in those twenty-four hours that call will come. Last year Mack called at a few minutes after midnight, and our vigil ended almost as soon as it began. Two years ago he waited until the very last second to phone, and Mom was frantic that this slim contact with him was over.

Mack has to have known that my father was killed in the Twin Towers tragedy. I was sure that no matter what he was doing, that terrible day would have compelled him to come home. But it did not. Then on the next Mother's Day, during his annual call, he started crying and gasped, "I'm sorry about Dad. I'm really sorry," and broke the connection.

I am Carolyn. I was sixteen when Mack disappeared. Following in his footsteps, I attended Columbia. Unlike him, I then went on to Duke Law School. Mack had been accepted there before he disappeared. After I passed the Bar last year, I clerked for a civil court judge in the courthouse on Centre Street in lower Manhattan. Judge Paul Huot has just retired, so at the moment I'm unemployed. I plan to apply for a job as an Assistant District Attorney in Manhattan, but not quite yet.

First, I must find a way to track my brother down. What *happened* to him? Why did he disappear? There was no sign of foul play. Mack's credit cards weren't used. His car was in the garage near his apartment. No one of his description ever ended up in the morgue, although in the beginning, my mother and father were sometimes asked to view the body of some unidentified young man who had been fished out of the river or killed in an accident.

When we were growing up, Mack was my best friend, my confidant, my pal. Half my girlfriends had a crush on him. He was the perfect son, the perfect brother, handsome, kind, funny, an excellent student. How do I feel about him now? I don't know anymore. I remember how much I loved him, but that love has almost totally turned to anger and resentment. I wish I could even doubt that he's alive and that someone is playing a cruel trick, but there is no doubt in my mind about that. Years ago we recorded one of his phone calls and had the pattern of his voice compared to his voice from home movies. It was identical.

All of this means that Mom and I dangle slowly in the wind, and, before Dad died in that burning inferno, it was that way for him, too. In all these years, I have never gone into a restaurant or theatre without my eyes automatically scanning to see if just maybe, by chance, I will run into him. Someone with a similar profile and sandy brown hair will demand a second look and, sometimes, close scrutiny. I remember more than once almost knocking people over to get close to someone who turned out to be a perfect stranger.

All this was going through my mind as I set the volume of the phone on the loudest setting, got into bed, and tried to go to sleep. I guess I did fall into an uneasy doze because the jarring ring of the phone made me bolt up. I saw from the lighted dial on the clock that it was five minutes to three. With one hand I snapped on the bedside light and with the other grabbed the receiver. Mom had already picked up, and I heard her voice, breathless and nervous. "Hello, Mack."

"Hello, Mom. Happy Mother's Day. I love you."

His voice was resonant and confident. He sounds as though he doesn't have a care in the world, I thought bitterly.

As usual the sound of his voice shattered Mom. She began to cry. "Mack, I love you. I need to see you," she begged. "I don't care what trouble you may be in, what problems you have to solve, I'll help you. Mack, for God's sake, it's been ten years. Don't do this to me any longer. Please . . . please . . ."

He never stayed on the phone for as long as a minute. I'm sure he knew that we would try to trace the call, but now that that technology is available, he always calls from one of those cell phones with a prepaid time card.

I had been planning what I would say to him and rushed now to make him hear me out before he hung up. "Mack, I'm going to find you," I said. "The cops tried and failed. So did the private investigator. But I won't fail. I *swear* I won't." My voice had been quiet and firm, as I had planned, but then the sound of my mother crying sent me over the edge. "I'm going to track you down, you lowlife," I shrieked, "and you'd better have an awfully good reason for torturing us like this."

I heard a click and knew that he had disconnected. I could have bitten my tongue off to take back the name I had called him, but, of course, it was too late.

Knowing what I was facing, that Mom would be furious at me for the way I had screamed at Mack, I put on a robe and went down the hall to the suite that she and Dad had shared.

Sutton Place is an upscale Manhattan neighborhood of town houses and apartment buildings overlooking the East River. My father bought this place after putting himself through Fordham Law School at night and working his way up to partner in a corporate law firm. Our privileged childhood was the result of his brains and the hard work ethic that was instilled in him by his widowed Scotch-Irish mother. He never allowed a nickel of the money my mother inherited to affect our lives.

I tapped on the door and pushed it open. She was standing at the panoramic window that overlooked the East River. She did not turn, even though she knew I was there. It was a clear night, and to the left I could see the lights of the Queensboro Bridge. Even in this predawn hour, there was a steady stream of cars going back and forth across it. The fanciful thought crossed my mind that maybe Mack was in one of those cars and, having made his annual call, was now on his way to a distant destination.

Mack had always loved travel; it was in his veins. My mother's father, Liam O'Connell, was born in Dublin, educated at Trinity College, and came to the United States, smart, well-educated, and broke. Within five years he was buying potato fields in Long Island that eventually became the Hamptons, property in Palm Beach County, property on Third Avenue when it was still a dirty, dark street in the shadow of the elevated train track that hovered over it. That was when he sent for and married my grandmother, the English girl he had met at Trinity.

My mother, Olivia, is a genuine English beauty, tall, still slender as a reed at sixty-two, with silver hair, blue-gray eyes, and classic features. In appearance, Mack was practically her clone.

I inherited my father's reddish brown hair, hazel eyes, and stubborn jaw. When my mother wore heels, she was a shade taller than Dad, and, like him, I'm just average height. I found myself yearning for him as I walked across the room and put my arm around my mother.

She spun around, and I could feel the anger radiating from her. "Carolyn, how *could* you talk to Mack like that?" she snapped, her arms wrapped tightly across her chest. "Can't you understand that there must be some terrible problem that is keeping him from us? Can't you understand that he must be feeling frightened and helpless and that this call is a cry for understanding?"

Before my father died, they often used to have emotional conversations like this. Mom, always protective of Mack, my father getting to the point where he was ready to wash his hands of it all and stop worrying. "For the love of God, Liv," he would snap at Mom, "he sounds all right. Maybe he's involved with some woman and doesn't want to bring her around. Maybe he's trying to be an actor. He wanted to be one when he was a kid. Maybe I was too tough on him, making him have summer jobs. Who knows?"

They would end up apologizing to each other, Mom crying, Dad anguished and angry at himself for upsetting her.

I wasn't going to make a second mistake by trying to justify myself. Instead I said, "Mom, listen to me. Since we haven't found Mack by now, he's not worrying about my threat. Look at it this way. You've heard from him. You know he's alive. He sounds downright upbeat. I know you hate sleeping pills, but I also know your doctor gave you a prescription. So take one now and get some rest."

I didn't wait for her to answer me. I knew I couldn't do any good by staying with her any longer because I was angry, too. Angry at her for railing at me, angry at Mack, angry at the fact that this ten-room duplex apartment was too big for Mom to live in alone, too filled with memories. She won't sell it because she doesn't trust that Mack's annual telephone call would be bounced to a new location, and of course she reminds me that he had said one day he would turn the key in the lock and be home . . . Home. *Here.*

I got back into bed, but sleep was a long way off. I started planning how I would begin to look for Mack. I thought about going to Lucas Reeves, the private investigator whom Dad hired, but then changed my mind. I was going to treat Mack's disappearance as if it had happened yesterday. The first thing Dad did when we became alarmed about Mack was call the police and report him missing. I'd begin at the beginning.

I knew people down at the courthouse, which also houses the District Attorney's office. I decided that my search would begin there.

Finally I drifted off and began to dream of following a shadowy figure who was walking across a bridge. Try as I would to keep him in sight, he was too fast for me, and when we reached land, I didn't know which way to turn. But then I heard him calling me, his voice mournful and troubled. *Carolyn, stay back, stay back.*

"I can't, Mack," I said aloud as I awakened. "I can't."

2

Monsignor Devon MacKenzie ruefully commented to visitors that his beloved St. Francis de Sales Church was located so close to the Episcopal Cathedral of St. John the Divine that it was almost invisible.

A dozen years ago, Devon had expected to hear that St. Francis would be closed, and he could not in honesty have contested the decision. After all, it had been built in the nineteenth century and needed major repairs. Then, as more apartment buildings went up in the area and older walk-ups were renovated, he had been gratified to see the faces of new parishioners at Sunday Masses.

The growing congregation meant that in the past five years he had been able to carry out somc of those repairs. The stained-glass windows werc cleaned; years of built-up soil removed from the murals; the wooden pews sanded and refinished, the kneeling benches covered with soft new carpeting.

Then, when Pope Benedict decreed that individual pastors could decide to offer a Tridentine Mass, Devon, who was proficient in Latin, announced that henceforth the eleven o'clock Sunday Mass would be celebrated in the ancient tongue of the Church.

The response stunned him. That Mass was now filled to overflowing, not only with senior citizens but teenagers and young adults who reverently responded "*Deo gratias*" in place of "Thanks be to God," and prayed "*Pater Noster*" instead of "Our Father."

Devon was sixty-eight, two years younger than the brother he had lost on 9/11, and uncle and godfather of the nephew who had disappeared. At Mass, when he invited the congregation to silently offer their own petitions, his first prayer was always for Mack and that one day he would come home.

On Mother's Day, that prayer was always especially fervent. Today, when he returned to the rectory, there was a message waiting for him on the answering machine from Carolyn. "Uncle Dev—he called at five of three this morning. Sounded fine. Hung up fast. See you tonight."

Monsignor Devon could hear the strain in his niece's voice. His relief that his nephew had called was mixed with sharp anger. Damn you, Mack, he thought. Haven't you any idea what you're doing to us? As he tugged off his Roman collar, Devon reached for the phone to call Carolyn back. Before he could begin to dial, the doorbell rang.

It was his boyhood friend, Frank Lennon, a retired software executive, who served as head usher on Sundays and who counted, itemized, and deposited the Sunday collections.

Devon had long since learned to read people's faces and to know instantly if there was a genuine problem. That was what he was reading in Lennon's weathered face. "What's up, Frank?" he asked.

"Mack was at the eleven, Dev," Lennon said flatly. "He dropped a note for you in the basket. It was folded inside a twenty-dollar bill."

Monsignor Devon MacKenzie grabbed the scrap of paper, read the ten words printed on it, then, not trusting what he was seeing, read them again. "UNCLE DEVON, TELL CAROLYN SHE MUST NOT LOOK FOR ME."

3

Every year for the past nine years, Aaron Klein had made the long drive from Manhattan to the cemetery in Bridgehampton, to place a stone on the grave of his mother, Esther Klein. She had been a lively fifty-four-year-old divorcee, who died at the hands of a mugger as she was on her daily run early one morning near the Cathedral of St. John the Divine.

Aaron had been twenty-eight then, newly married, comfortably secure in his upward climb at Wallace and Madison Investment Bankers. Now he was the father of two sons, Eli and Gabriel, and a small daughter, Danielle, who bore a heartbreaking resemblance to her late grandmother. Aaron never visited the cemetery without once again experiencing anger and frustration at the fact that his mother's murderer was still walking the streets, a free man.

She had been struck in the back of the head with a

heavy object. Her cell phone was on the ground beside her. Had she sensed danger and taken it out of her pocket to try to dial 911? That possibility was the only one that made sense.

She had to have been attempting to call. The records the police obtained showed she had neither made nor received a call at that time.

The cops thought it was a random mugging. Her watch, the only jewelry that she ever wore at that time of day, was missing, as was her house key. "Why take her house key if whoever killed her didn't know who she was and where she lived?" he had asked the cops. They hadn't had an answer to that one.

Her apartment had its own street-level entrance around the corner from the doorman-monitored main entrance of the building, but as the detectives who worked on the case pointed out, there was nothing missing from it. Her wallet, containing several hundred dollars, was in her pocketbook. Her jewelry box, open on the dresser, held the few pieces of valuable jewelry he knew her to own.

The intermittent rain began to fall again as Aaron knelt down and touched the grass over his mother's grave. His knees sank into the muddy ground as he placed the stone, and whispered, "Mom, I so wish you had lived to see the kids. The boys are finishing the first grade and kindergarten. Danielle is a little actress already. I can just see her in a dozen years auditioning for one of the plays you'd be directing at Columbia."

He smiled, thinking of what his mother's response would be. "Aaron, you're a dreamer. Do your math. By the time Danielle is in college, I'd have been seventy-five years old."

"You'd still be teaching and directing and you'd still be full of spunk," he said aloud.

4

On Monday morning, carrying the note Mack had dropped in the collection basket, I set off for the District Attorney's office in lower Manhattan. It was beautiful out, sunny and warm with a balmy breeze, the kind of weather that would have been appropriate for Mother's Day instead of the cold, wet day that had spoiled any hope of outdoor gatherings.

Mom and Uncle Dev and I had gone out to dinner Sunday night. Obviously the note that Uncle Dev handed us sent Mom and me into a tailspin. Mom's initial reaction was to be thrilled that Mack might be so near. She has always been convinced that he is far away in Colorado or California. Then she became fearful that my thrcat to find him had put him in some kind of jeopardy.

At first I simply didn't know what to think about it, but now I had a growing suspicion that Mack might be head over heels in trouble and trying to keep us away from it.

The lobby at 1 Hogan Place was crowded, and the security was as tight as it gets. Even though I had plenty of identification, without a specific appointment to see someone, I could not get past the guard. As the people on line behind me began to get restless, I tried to explain that my brother was missing, and we might finally have something to indicate where we could begin looking for him.

"Ma'am, you'll have to place a phone call to Missing Persons and make an appointment," the guard insisted. "Now, please, there are other people who need to get upstairs to their jobs."

Frustrated, I walked outside the building and pulled out my cell phone. Judge Huot had been in civil court, and I never had much contact with the Assistant DAs, but I did know one, Matt Wilson. I called the District Attorney's office and was connected to his phone. Matt wasn't at his desk and had recorded the usual answering machine instructions. "Leave your name, number, and a brief message. I'll get back to you."

"This is Carolyn MacKenzie," I began. "We've met a few times. I was Judge Huot's law clerk. My brother has been missing for ten years. He left a note for me yesterday in a church on Amsterdam Avenue. I need help to see if we can track him down before he disappears again." I finished by giving my cell phone number.

I was standing on the steps. A man was going past

me, a square-shouldered guy in his midfifties with close-cropped gray hair and a purposeful stride. I could tell that he had overheard me because, somewhat to my dismay, he stopped and turned around. For a moment we eyed each other, then he said abruptly, "I'm Detective Barrott. I'll take you upstairs."

Five minutes later, I was sitting in a shabby small office that contained a desk, a couple of chairs, and stacks of files. "We can talk in here," he said. "Too much noise in the squad room."

He never took his eyes off my face as I told him about Mack, only interrupting me to ask a few questions. "Calls only on Mother's Day?"

"That's right."

"Never asks for money?"

"Never." I had put the note in a plastic sandwich bag. "I don't know if his fingerprints might be on it," I explained. "Unless, of course, he had someone else drop it in the basket for him. It seems so crazy that he would take a chance on Uncle Dev spotting him from the altar."

"Depends. He might have dyed his hair, could be twenty pounds heavier, be wearing dark glasses. It isn't hard to disguise yourself in a crowd, especially when people are wearing rain gear."

He looked at the scrap of paper. The writing was plainly visible through the plastic. "Do we have your brother's fingerprints on file?"

"I'm not sure. By the time we reported him missing, our housekeeper had dusted and vacuumed his room at home. He shared the student apartment with two of his friends, and like most of those places, there were at least a dozen others who were in and out every day. His car was washed and cleaned after the last time he used it."

Barrott handed it back to me. "We can run this paper through for prints, but I can tell you now we won't get anything. You and your mother handled it. So did your uncle, the monsignor. So did the usher who brought it to your uncle. My guess is that at least one other usher might have helped to add up the collection."

Feeling as though I needed to offer more, I said, "I'm Mack's only sibling. My mother and father and I came in to register with the familial DNA laboratory. But we've never heard from them, so I guess they've never found anyone who could be even a partial match."

"Ms. MacKenzie, from what you tell me, your brother had absolutely no reason to willingly disappear. But if he did that, there was and is a reason. You've probably watched some of these crime programs on television so you probably have heard that when people disappear, the reason usually ends up being an accumulation of problems caused by either love or money. The jilted suitor, the jealous husband or wife, the inconvenient spouse, the addict frantic for a fix. You have to reexamine all your preconceived notions about your brother. He was twenty-one. You say he was popular with the girls. Was there one special girl?"

"No one his friends told us about. Certainly no one who ever came forward."

"At his age, a lot of kids gamble too much. A lot more experiment with drugs and become addicted. Suppose he was in debt? How would your father and mother have reacted to that?"

I found myself reluctant to answer. Then I reminded myself that these were questions my mother and father had undoubtedly been asked ten years ago. I wondered if they had been evasive. "My father would have been furious," I admitted. "He had no use for people who threw away money. My mother has a private income from an inheritance. If Mack needed money he could have gotten it from her, and she wouldn't have told Dad."

"All right. Ms. MacKenzie, I'm going to be perfectly honest with you. I don't think we have a crime here, so we can't treat your brother's disappearance as a crime. You can't imagine how many people walk out of their lives every day. They're stressed. They can't cope, or even worse, they don't want to cope anymore. Your brother calls you regularly—"

"Once a year," I interrupted.

"Which is still regularly. You tell him you're going to

track him down, and he responds immediately. 'Leave me alone' is his message to you. I know it sounds rough, but my advice is to make yourself realize that Mack is where he wants to be, and the most connection he wants to have with you and your mother is that one Mother's Day call. Do the three of you a favor. Respect his wishes."

He stood up. Clearly our interview was over. Clearly I should not waste the time of the police department any longer. I picked up the note and as I did, reread the message. "UNCLE DEVON, TELL CAROLYN SHE MUST NOT LOOK FOR ME."

"You've been very—honest, Detective Barrott," I said, substituting the word "honest" for "helpful." I didn't think he had been helpful in the least. "I promise I won't bother you anymore."

5

For twenty years, Gus and Lil Kramer, now in their early seventies, had been the superintendents of a four-story apartment building on West End Avenue that the owner, Derek Olsen, had renovated for student housing. As Olsen explained when he hired them, "Look, college kids, smart or dumb, are basically slobs. They'll have boxes of pizza piled up in the kitchen. They'll amass enough empty beer cans to float a battleship. They'll drop their dirty clothes and wet towels on the floor. We don't care. They all move out when they graduate.

"My point," he had continued, "is that I can raise the rent as much as I want, but only as long as the common areas look sharp. I expect you two to keep the lobby and hallways looking like Fifth Avenue digs. I want the heat and the air-conditioning always working, any plumbing problems fixed on the double, the sidewalk swept every day. I want a quick paint job when a space is vacated. When the new arrivals come with their parents to check out the place, I want all of them to be impressed."

For twenty years the Kramers had faithfully followed Olsen's instructions, and the building where they worked was known as upscale student housing. All the students who passed through it were fortunate enough to have parents with deep pockets. A number of those parents made separate arrangements for the Kramers to regularly clean the lodgings of their offspring.

The Kramers had celebrated a Mother's Day brunch at Tavern on the Green with their daughter, Winifred, and her husband, Perry. Unfortunately, the conversation had been almost completely a monologue from Winifred, urging them to quit their jobs and retire to their cottage in Pennsylvania. This was a monologue they'd heard before, one that always ended with the refrain, "Mom and Dad, I hate to think of you two sweeping and mopping and vacuuming after those kids."

Lil Kramer had long since learned to say, "You may be right, dear. I'll think about it."

Over rainbow sherbet, Gus Kramer had minced no words. "When we're ready to quit, we'll quit, not before. What would I do with myself all day?"

Late Monday afternoon, as Lil was knitting a sweater for the expected first child of one of the former students, she was thinking about Winifred's well-meant but irritating advice. Why doesn't Winifred understand that I love being with these kids? she fumed. For us, it's almost like having grandchildren. She certainly never gave us any.

The ring of the telephone startled her. Now that Gus was getting a little hard of hearing, he had raised the volume, but it was much too loud. You could wake up the dead with that racket, Lil thought as she hurried to answer it.

As she picked up the receiver, she found herself hoping that it wasn't Winifred following up on her retirement speech. A moment later, she wished it had been Winifred.

"Hello, this is Carolyn MacKenzie. Is this Mrs. Kramer?"

"Yes." Lil felt her mouth go dry.

"My brother, Mack, was living in your building when he disappeared ten years ago."

"Yes, he was."

"Mrs. Kramer, we heard from Mack the other day. He won't tell us where he is. You can understand what this is doing to my mother and me. I'm going to try to find him. We have reason to believe that he's living in the area. May I come and talk with you?"

No, Lil thought. No! But she heard herself answering the only way possible. "Of course, you can. I . . .

we . . . were very fond of Mack. When do you want to see us?"

"Tomorrow morning?"

Too soon, Lil thought. I need more time. "Tomorrow's very busy for us."

"Then Wednesday morning around eleven?"

"Yes, I guess that's all right."

Gus came in as she was replacing the receiver. "Who was that?" he asked.

"Carolyn MacKenzie. She's starting her own investigation into her brother's disappearance. She's coming to talk to us Wednesday morning."

Lil watched as her husband's broad face reddened, and behind his glasses, his eyes narrowed. In two strides his short, stocky body was in front of her. "Last time, you let the cops see you were nervous, Lil. Don't let that happen in front of the sister. You hear me? *Don't let it happen this time!*"

6

On Monday afternoon, Detective Roy Barrott's shift was up at four P.M. It had been a relatively slow day, and at three o'clock he realized that he had nothing to command his immediate attention. But something was bothering him. Like his tongue roving through his mouth to find the source of a sore spot, his mind began to retrace the day searching for the source of the discomfort.

When he remembered his interview with Carolyn MacKenzie, he knew that he had found it. The look of dismay and contempt he had seen in her eyes when she left him made him feel both ashamed and embarrassed now. She was desperately worried about her brother and had hoped that the note he'd left in the collection basket at church might be a step toward finding him. Although she hadn't said it, she obviously thought he might be in some kind of trouble.

I brushed her off, Barrott thought. When she left she

said she wouldn't bother me again. That was the word she used, "bother."

Now, as he leaned back in his desk chair in the crowded squad room, Barrott shut out the sounds of the ringing telephones that surrounded him. Then he shrugged. It wouldn't kill me to take a look at the file, he decided. If nothing else, to satisfy myself that it's nothing more than a guy who doesn't want to be found, a guy who will one day change his mind, and end up on *Dr. Phil* being reunited with his mother and sister while everybody has a good cry.

Wincing at a touch of arthritis in his knee, he got up, went down to the records department, signed out the MacKenzie file, brought it back to his desk, and opened it. Besides the pile of official reports, and the statements from Charles MacKenzie Jr.'s family and friends, there was a legal-sized envelope filled with pictures. Barrott pulled them out and scattered them on his desk.

One immediately caught his eye. It was a Christmas card with the MacKenzie family standing in front of their Christmas tree. It reminded Barrott of the Christmas card that he and Beth had sent in December, the two of them with the kids, Melissa and Rick, standing in front of their Christmas tree. He still had that card in his desk somewhere.

The MacKenzies got a lot more dolled up for their picture than we did, Barrott thought. The father and son were in tuxedos, the mother and daughter in evening gowns. But the overall effect was the same. A smiling, happy family wishing their friends the joys of Christmas and greetings for the New Year. It had to be the last one they sent before the son disappeared.

Now Charles MacKenzie Jr. had been missing for ten years, and Charles MacKenzie Sr. had been dead since 9/11.

Barrott rummaged through some personal papers in his desk and pulled out his family's card. He rested his elbows on the desk and held up the two Christmas cards, comparing them. I'm lucky, he thought. Rick has just finished his freshman year at Fordham on the dean's list, and Melissa, another straight-A kid, is finishing her junior year at Cathedral High and going to a prom tonight. Beth and I are more than lucky. We're blessed.

The thought crossed his mind, suppose something happened to me on this job, and Rick walked out of his dorm and disappeared. What if I wasn't around to find him?

Rick wouldn't do that to his mother and sister, not in one hundred thousand years, he told himself.

But that, in essence, is what Carolyn MacKenzie wants me to believe about her brother.

Slowly, Barrott closed the Charles MacKenzie Jr. file and slid it into the top drawer of his desk. I'll look it over in the morning, he decided, and maybe drop in on some of those people who gave statements at that time. Can't hurt to ask some questions and see if their memories got refreshed along the way.

It was four o'clock. Time to shove off. He wanted to be home in time to take pictures of Melissa in her prom dress with her date, Jason Kelly. A nice enough kid, Barrott reflected, but so thin that if he drank a glass of tomato juice, it would be as visible as mercury in a thermometer. I also want to have a little chat with the limo driver who's picking up the kids. Just to get a look at his license and let him know that he'd better not even think of driving one mile over the speed limit. He stood and put on his jacket.

You take all the precautions you can to protect your children, Barrott thought, as he turned and yelled, "See you," to the guys in the squad room and walked down the corridor. But sometimes no matter what you do, something goes wrong and your kid becomes involved in an accident or is the victim of foul play.

Please God, he prayed as he pushed the button for the elevator, don't let it ever happen to us.

7

Uncle Dev had told Elliott Wallace about the note Mack left in the collection box, and on Monday evening Elliott met us for dinner. Only a flicker of anxiety showed through his typically unruffled exterior. Elliott is the CEO and chairman of Wallace and Madison, the investment firm on Wall Street that handles the family finances. He'd been one of my father's best friends, and Mack and I have always considered him a surrogate uncle. Divorced for years, Elliott is in love with my mother, I think. I also believe that her lack of interest in him in the years since Dad died is one more casualty of Mack's disappearance.

As soon as we were settled at his favorite table in Le Cirque, I handed Elliott Mack's note and told him it made me more determined than ever to find him.

I had really hoped that Elliott would side with me in my decision to try to find Mack, but he disappointed me. "Carolyn," he said, slowly, as he read and reread the note, "I don't think you're being fair to Mack. He calls every year so that you'll know he's all right. You've told me yourself that he sounds confident, even happy. He responds immediately to your promise—or threat—to find him. In the most direct means at his disposal, he orders you to leave him alone. Why don't you go along with his wishes, and, more important, why don't you refuse to allow Mack to remain the center of your existence?"

It was not the kind of question I'd expected from Elliott, and I could see the effort it took for him to make it. His eyes were troubled, his forehead creased, as he turned his gaze from me to my mother, whose own expression had become unreadable. I was glad we were at a corner table where no one else could observe her. I was afraid she would flare up at Elliott as she had at me after Mack's call on Mother's Day, or even worse, break into a storm of weeping.

When she didn't answer him, Elliott urged, "Olivia, give Mack the space he wants. Be satisfied that he's alive, even take comfort in the fact that he's obviously close by. I can tell you right now that if Charley were here, that's exactly what he would be telling you."

My mother always surprises me. She picked up a fork and in an absentminded way, traced something on the cloth with the prongs. I would bet anything it was Mack's name.

As soon as she began to speak, I realized I had been completely wrong in evaluating her response to Mack's note.

"Since Dev showed us that message from Mack last night, I've been thinking somewhat in the same vein, Elliott," she said. The pain in her voice was evident but there was no hint of tears there. "I lashed out at Carolyn because she became angry at Mack. That wasn't fair to her. I know that Carolyn worries about me all the time. Now Mack has given us an answer, not the answer I wanted, but that's the way it is."

Here Mom tried to smile. "I am going to try to consider him an AWOL son—absent without leave. He may live in this area. As you say, he did respond quickly, and if he doesn't want to see us, Carolyn and I are going to respect his wishes." She paused, then added firmly, "So there."

"Olivia, I hope you stick to that decision," Elliott said fervently.

"I'm surely going to try. As a first step, my friends the Clarences are leaving for a cruise on their yacht, starting at the Greek islands this Friday. They've been trying to persuade me to join them. I'm going to do it." She put her fork down in a gesture of finality.

I sat back and pondered this unexpected turn of events. I had planned to talk to Elliott about my appointment with the superintendents of Mack's building on Wednesday. Now, of course, I wouldn't. Ironically, Mom had finally come to accept Mack's situation, as I had begged her to for years, and now I didn't welcome it. As every hour passed, I was more and more convinced that Mack was in serious trouble and facing it alone. I was about to raise that possibility but then clamped my lips together. With Mom away, I could search for Mack without having to cover up what I was doing, or worse yet, lying to her about it.

"How long is the cruise, Mom?" I asked.

"At least three weeks."

"I think it's a great idea," I said honestly.

"So do I," Elliott agreed. "Now, what about you, Carolyn? Still interested in becoming an Assistant District Attorney?"

"Absolutely," I said. "But I'll wait a month or so to apply. If I'm lucky enough to be hired, I won't have any time off for quite a while."

The evening progressed pleasantly. Mom, lovely in a pale blue silk shirt and matching slacks, became animated and smiling, far more than I had seen her for years. It was as though coming to terms with Mack's situation was giving her peace.

Elliott's mood brightened as he watched her. Growing up, I used to wonder if Elliott wore a shirt and tie to bed. He is always terribly formal, but when

Mom turns on the charm, he simply melts. He's a few years older than Mom, which makes me wonder if his head of charcoal brown hair can possibly be natural, but I think it may be. He carries himself with the erect posture of a career military officer. His expression is usually reserved, even aloof until he smiles or laughs, and then his whole appearance lightens up, and you can catch a glimpse of a more spontaneous person hiding behind his ingrained formality.

He jokes about himself. "My father, Franklin Delano Wallace, was named after his distant cousin, President Franklin Delano Roosevelt, who remained Father's hero. Why do you think my name is Elliott? That was the name the president chose for one of his sons. And despite all he did for the common man, remember that Roosevelt was first and foremost an aristocrat. I'm afraid my father was not only an aristocrat but a downright snob. So when I come across too stuffy, blame it on the stuffed shirt who raised me."

By the time we finished coffee, I had decided that I absolutely would not even hint to Elliott that I was going to actively search for Mack. I offered to stay at Mom's apartment while she was away, a fact that pleased her. She isn't impressed with the studio in Greenwich Village that I rented last September when I started my clerkship with the judge. She certainly didn't know that my reason for staying at Sutton Place was to be available if Mack learned that I was still looking for him and tried to reach me there.

Outside the restaurant I hailed a cab. Elliott and Mom chose to walk to Sutton Place. As the cab pulled away, I watched with mixed feelings as Elliott took Mom's arm, and, their shoulders brushing, they went down the street together.

8

Sixty-seven-year-old retired surgeon Dr. David Andrews did not know why he had felt so uneasy after putting his daughter back on the train to Manhattan where she was completing her junior year at NYU.

Leesey and her older brother, Gregg, had come up to Greenwich to be with him on Mother's Day, a tough day for all of them, only the second one without Helen. The three of them had visited her grave in St. Mary's cemetery, then gone out for an early dinner at the club.

Leesey had planned to drive back to the city with Gregg, but at the last minute decided to stay overnight and go back in the morning. "My first class is eleven o'clock," she had explained, "and I feel like hanging around with you, Dad."

Sunday evening, they had gone through some of the photograph albums and talked about Helen. "I miss her so much," Leesey had whispered.

"Me, too, honey," he had confided.

But Monday morning when he dropped her at the station, Leesey had been her usual bubbly self, which was why David Andrews could not understand the gnawing sense of worry that undermined his golf game both Monday and Tuesday.

On Tuesday evening, he turned on the 6:30 news and was dozing in front of the television when the phone rang. It was Kate Carlisle, Leesey's best friend, with whom she shared an apartment in Greenwich Village. Her question, and the troubled voice in which she asked it, caused him to bolt up from the easy chair.

"Dr. Andrews, is Leesey there?"

"No, she isn't, Kate. Why would she be here?" he asked.

As he spoke he glanced around the room. Even though he had sold the big house after Helen's death, and she'd never been in this condo, when the phone rang, he instinctively looked around for her, her hand outstretched to take the receiver from him.

When there was no answer, he demanded sharply, "Kate, why are you looking for Leesey?"

"I don't know, I just hoped . . ." Kate's voice broke.

"Kate, tell me what happened."

"Last night she went out with some of our friends to the Woodshed, a new place we've been talking about trying."

"Where is it?"

"It's on the border of the Village and SoHo. Leesey stayed after the others left. There was a really good band, and you know how she loves to dance."

"What time did the others leave?"

"It was about two o'clock, Dr. Andrews."

"Had Leesey been drinking?"

"Not much. She was fine when they left but she wasn't here when I woke up this morning, and no one has seen her all day. I've been trying to reach her on her cell phone, but she doesn't answer. I've been calling everyone I could think of who might have seen her, but no one has."

"Did you call that place where she was last night?"

"I spoke to the bartender there. He said that Leesey stayed till they closed at three o'clock and then left alone. He swore that she absolutely wasn't drunk or anywhere near it. She just stayed till the end."

Andrews closed his eyes, trying desperately to sort out the steps he needed to take. Let her be all right, God, he prayed. Leesey, the unexpected baby born when Helen was forty-five years old and they had long since given up hope of having a second child.

Impatiently, he pulled his legs off the hassock, pushed it aside, stood up, brushed back his thick white hair from his forehead, then swallowed to activate the salivary glands inside his suddenly dry mouth.

The commuter traffic is over, he thought. It shouldn't take more than an hour to get down to Greenwich Village.

"From Greenwich, Connecticut, to Greenwich Village," Leesey had joyfully announced three years ago when she decided to take early acceptance at NYU.

"Kate, I'll start down right away," Andrews said. "I'll call Leesey's brother. We'll meet you at the apartment. How far is this bar from your place?"

"About a mile."

"Would she have taken a cab?"

"It was nice out. She probably would have walked."

Alone on dark streets, late at night, Andrews thought. Trying to keep his voice from breaking, he said, "I'll be there in an hour. Keep calling anyone you can think of who might have an idea where she is."

Dr. Gregg Andrews was showering when the phone rang, and he decided to let the answering machine pick it up. He was off duty and had a date with someone he had met the night before at a cocktail reception for the launching of a novel by a friend. Now a cardiac surgeon at New York-Presbyterian Hospital, as his father had been until his retirement, he toweled dry, walked into his bedroom, and considered the fact that the May evening had begun to turn cool. From his closet, he chose an open-necked long-sleeve light blue shirt, tan slacks, and a navy blue jacket.

Leesey tells me I always look so stuffy, he remembered, thinking with a smile of the little sister who was twelve years his junior. She says I should get some cool colors and mix them up.

She also says I should get contact lenses and get rid of my crew cut, he thought.

"Gregg, you're really cute, not handsome, but cute," she had told him matter-of-factly. "I mean women like men who look as though they have a brain in their heads. And they always fall for doctors. It's kind of a 'Daddy' complex, I think. But it doesn't hurt to look a little zippy."

The message light was blinking on the phone. He debated whether he should bother to check it now but then pressed the play button.

"Gregg, it's Dad. Leesey's roommate just called me. Leesey is missing. She left a bar alone last night, and no one has seen her since. I'm on my way to her apartment. Meet me there."

Chilled, Gregg Andrews stopped the machine, and pushed the numeral that rang his father's car. "Dad, I just got your message," he said when his father answered. "I'll meet you at Leesey's apartment. On the way I'll call Larry Ahearn. Just don't drive too fast."

Grabbing his cell phone, Gregg rushed out of his apartment, caught the elevator as it was descending from an upper floor, ran through the lobby, and, ignoring the doorman, rushed out into the road to flag down a cab. As usual at this hour, there was none to be seen with the light on. Frantically he looked up and down the street, hoping to spot one of the gypsy limos that were often available on Park Avenue.

He spotted one that was parked halfway down the block and rushed to get in it. He barked Leesey's address to the driver, then opened his cell phone to call his college roommate at Georgetown, who was now Captain of detectives in the Manhattan District Attorney's office.

After two rings, he heard Larry Ahearn's voice instructing the caller to leave a message.

Shaking his head in frustration, Gregg said, "Larry, it's Gregg. Call me on my cell. Leesey is missing."

He checks his calls all the time, Gregg reminded himself as the car threaded its way downtown with agonizing slowness. When they were passing Fifty-second Street, he remembered that in fifteen minutes the young woman he had met last night would be waiting for him in the bar of the Four Seasons.

He was about to leave a message for her when Ahearn called back. "Tell me about Leesey," he ordered.

"She was in a bar or club or whatever you want to

call those places in the Village and SoHo last night. She left alone when it closed and never got home."

"What's the name of the bar?"

"I don't know yet. I didn't think to ask Dad. He's on his way in."

"Who would know?"

"Leesey's roommate, Kate. She's the one who just called Dad. I'm meeting him at the apartment she and Leesey share."

"Give me Kate's phone number. I'll get back to you."

Larry Ahearn's private office was adjacent to the squad room. He was glad that at this moment no one could see the expression on his face. Leesey had been six years old when he visited the Andrews home in Greenwich the fall of his freshman year in Georgetown. He had seen her grow up from a pretty kid to a strikingly beautiful young woman, the kind any guy, never mind a predator, would zone in on.

She left the bar alone when it closed. Dear God, that crazy kid.

They just don't get it.

Larry Ahearn knew that soon he would have to tell Gregg and Leesey's father that in the last ten years, three young women had disappeared in that same SoHo-Village area after spending an evening in one of those bars.

9

On Wednesday morning, as eleven o'clock drew near, Lil Kramer became increasingly uneasy. Ever since the call came from Carolyn MacKenzie on Monday, Gus had been constantly warning her to say only what she knew about Mack's disappearance ten years ago. "Which is nothing," he kept reminding her. "Absolutely *nothing*! Just do your usual stuff about what a nice young man he was, period. No nervous-Nelly glances at me to help you out."

The apartment was always immaculate, but today the sun was especially bright and, like a magnifying glass, exposed the worn areas on the arms of the couch and the chip on the corner of the glass coffee table.

I never wanted that glass table, Lil thought, glad to find an object to blame for her distress. It's too big. It doesn't go with this old-fashioned furniture. When Winifred redecorated her own apartment, she insisted that I take it and get rid of my nice leather-top table that was Aunt Jessie's wedding gift to me. This glass thing is too big, and I'm always bumping my knees on it, and it doesn't match the end tables like the other one did, she thought.

Her mind jumped to another source of concern. I just hope that Altman's not here when the MacKenzie girl comes in.

Howard Altman, the real estate agent and manager for the nine small apartment buildings owned by Mr. Olsen, had arrived an hour ago for one of his unscheduled visits. Gus called him "Olsen's Gestapo." It was Altman's job to make sure that the individual superintendents were keeping everything up to snuff. He never even has the slightest complaint about us, Lil thought; what scares me is that whenever he comes into this apartment, he always says it's a waste of money to have two people living in a big five-room corner unit.

If he thinks I'll ever switch to a pokey one-bedroom, he has another think coming, she told herself indignantly as she adjusted the leaves on the artificial plant on the windowsill. Then she stiffened as she heard voices in the hall and realized that Gus was coming in with Altman.

Even though it was warm outside, Howard Altman, as usual, was wearing a shirt, tie, and jacket. Lil could not see him without thinking of Winifred's scornful description of him. "He's a wannabe, Mom. He thinks getting all dolled up to inspect apartment buildings will make people think he's hot stuff. He was a superintendent just like you and Dad until he started kissing the feet of old man Olsen. Don't let him bother you."

But he *does* bother me, Lil thought. He bothers me because of the way he looks around as he walks in the door. I know that someday he's going to try to make us switch apartments so that he can tell Mr. Olsen he's figured out a new way to make more money for him. He bothers me because as Mr. Olsen got older, he practically turned over the running of all the buildings to Altman.

The door opened, and Gus and Altman came in. "Well, hello, Lil," Howard Altman said heartily, as he crossed the living room with long strides and an outstretched hand to greet her.

Today he was wearing trendy sunglasses, a light tan jacket and brown slacks, a white shirt, and striped green and tan tie. His sandy hair was too short in Lil's opinion, and it was too early in the season to have such a deep tan. Winifred was sure he spent half his spare time in a tanning salon. But all of the above considered, she grudgingly admitted, he was a good-looking man, with even features, dark brown eyes, an athlete's build, and a warm smile. If you didn't know how petty he could be, he could fool you, she thought. He took her hand in a firm grip. He claims he hasn't hit forty yet. I say that he's forty-five if he's a day, Lil thought as she gave him a tight smile.

"I don't know why I even bother to stop by here," Howard said, jovially. "If I could only have the two of you in all our buildings, we could make a fortune."

"Well, we try to keep everything nice," Gus said in the fawning voice that drove Lil crazy.

"You do more than try. You succeed."

"It was good of you to stop by," Lil said, glancing at the clock on the mantel. It was five minutes of eleven.

"Couldn't pass by without popping my head in to say hello. I'll be on my way now."

The intercom rang from the foyer, and Lil was sure it was Carolyn MacKenzie. She and Gus exchanged glances, and he went to the phone on the wall. "Yes, of course, come right in. We're expecting you . . ."

Don't say her name, Lil prayed. Don't say her name. When Howard sees her on his way out, he'll probably think she wants to inquire about an apartment.

". . . Ms. MacKenzie," Gus finished. "Apartment 1B. To the right as you come into the foyer."

Lil watched as the good-bye smile on Howard Altman's face disappeared. "MacKenzie. Wasn't that the name of the guy who disappeared just before I came to work for Mr. Olsen?"

There was no answer except, "Yes, Howard."

"Mr. Olsen told me how upsetting that publicity

was. He felt it really tarnished the image of this building. Why is she coming to see you?"

As Gus walked to the door, he said, flatly, "She wants to talk about her brother."

"I'd like to meet her," Howard Altman said, quietly. "If you don't mind, I'll stay."

10

I'm not really sure what I expected when I walked into that building on West End Avenue. I remember Mack showing me the apartment after he moved out of the dorm at Columbia. He was beginning his junior year then, so I was just turning fifteen.

Because he lived in the city there was no need for our parents or me to visit him there. Instead, he dropped in at home or met us at a restaurant regularly. I know that after he vanished, my mother and father went up to talk to his roommates and other people in the building, but they never let me come with them. That first summer, they made me go back to camp even though all I wanted to do was to help look for my brother.

As it turned out, I was glad that the Kramers couldn't meet me until now. Yesterday, my mother had me out all day with her, doing some last-minute shopping for her cruise. Then the eleven o'clock news last night carried the story of an NYU student who vanished early yesterday morning after leaving a bar in SoHo. There was a shot of her father and brother leaving her apartment building in the Village, and I realized with a jolt that it was right next door to mine. I ached for them.

No amount of money can convince Mom that living in the Village is every bit as safe as living on Sutton Place. For her, the Sutton Place apartment is a haven, a home she and my father joyfully bought when she was pregnant with me. At first it was a large six-room, one-floor apartment, but then as my father became more and more successful, he bought the apartment above us, turned the two into a duplex, and doubled its size.

Now, to me, it seems like a prison where until now my mother has been listening, always listening for the key to turn in the door and Mack to call out, "I'm home." For me, that belief that he might return has become a frustration, a sadness that won't ever go away. I feel so terribly selfish. I loved Mack, my big brother, my pal. But I don't want to have my life on hold any longer. Even the decision to wait before I apply for a job in the DA's office isn't about the fact that being hired means no time off for awhile. It's all about trying to find Mack and, if I fail, promising myself that then I'll get on with my own life at last. I'll spend most of these three weeks in Sutton Place while Mom's away, but that's not to feel safe—it's just in case Mack has some way of knowing I'm beginning to talk to everyone who was ever close to him and tries to call me..

This building where Mack had lived was old, the façade that gray stone that was so popular in New York in the early twentieth century. But the sidewalk and steps were clean, the handle of the outer door polished. That door was unlocked and opened into a narrow foyer where one can either dial an apartment number and be buzzed in, or use a key to open the door to the lobby.

I had spoken to Mrs. Kramer, and I don't really know why, but somehow I expected to hear her voice on the intercom. Instead, a man responded and directed me to their ground-floor apartment.

When I got inside, the door of 1B was already open, and a man was waiting for me who introduced himself as Gus Kramer, the superintendent. As I was going over the file this morning, I remembered what my father had said about him: "That guy is more worried that he'll be blamed for Mack's disappearance than he's concerned that something happened to Mack. And his wife is worse. She had the gall to say that Mr. Olsen would be upset. As if we have to be concerned about the owner of that renovated tenement!"

It's funny that when I was dressing for this appointment, I kept changing my mind about what to wear. I had actually laid out a lightweight pantsuit, the kind I wore to court when I was working for the judge, but somehow it seemed too businesslike. I wanted the Kramers to feel comfortable with me. As much as possible I wanted them to see me as Mack's kid sister, to like me, to want to help. That was why I decided to wear a long-sleeve cotton sweater, jeans, and sandals. As a portent for success, I wore the chain Mack gave me on my sixteenth birthday. There were two gold charms on it, one of ice skates, the other a soccer ball, in honor of my two favorite sports.

After Gus Kramer introduced himself and invited me in, it was like stepping back in time. Despite Daddy's success, he could never budge my grandmother from her apartment in Jackson Heights, Queens. This one had the same velour furniture, machine-made Persian carpet, and leather-top end tables as hers. The only thing that seemed out of place was the glass coffee table.

My first impression of Gus and Lil Kramer was that they were the kind of people who grow to look alike after years together. Her steel-gray hair was exactly the same shade as his. They were a little shorter than average height, with sturdy bodies. Their eyes were a matching pale blue, and there was no mistaking the wary expression in both faces as they offered me a begrudging smile.

Actually, it was the third person in the room who took over as host. "Ms. MacKenzie, I'm so pleased to meet you. I am Howard Altman, the district manager of Olsen

Properties. I wasn't here at the time of your brother's disappearance but I know how concerned Mr. Olsen was—and has been—about it. Why don't we all sit down and let you tell us how we can be of assistance to you."

I could sense the resentment the Kramers had to Altman taking over, but for me it made it easier to deliver my planned speech. I sat on the edge of the nearest chair and addressed myself to him. "As you obviously have heard, my brother, Mack, disappeared ten years ago. There simply hasn't been a trace of him since then. But he does call us every Mother's Day as he did a few days ago. I got on the phone while he was talking to my mother and vowed to find him. Later that day he went to St. Francis, a church in this neighborhood where my uncle is the pastor, and left a note for me to warn me away. I'm so afraid Mack may be in some kind of trouble and ashamed to ask for help."

"A note!" Lil Kramer's exclamation silenced me. I was astonished to see the way her cheeks became flushed and the unconscious gesture with which she reached over and grasped her husband's hand. "You mean he went to St. Francis and left a note for you?" she asked.

"Yes, at the eleven o'clock Mass. Why would that surprise you, Mrs. Kramer? I know over the years that there have been articles about my brother's disappearance and the fact that he contacts us."

Gus Kramer answered for his wife. "Ms. MacKenzie, my wife has always felt terrible about your brother. He was one of the nicest, politest kids we ever had here."

"That's what Mr. Olsen said," Howard Altman told me. Then he smiled. "Ms. MacKenzie, let me explain. Mr. Olsen is so aware of the pitfalls that occur in this day and age with young people, even intellectually gifted young people. He was always around to greet new students. He's up there in years now, but he's told me about how impressed he was with your parents and your brother. And I can tell you, the Kramers have always kept a sharp eye out for heavy drinking, or worse, drug use. If your brother had encountered some kind of problem, it didn't begin or continue under this roof."

This from a man who didn't know Mack, who only knew about him. The message was loud and clear. Don't look here for your brother's problem, lady.

"I don't mean to suggest that anything about Mack residing here triggered his disappearance. But you can understand that it makes sense for me to start searching for him in the last place where he was seen. The brother I knew would never willingly cause my mother and father and me the grief and anxiety we have been living with for ten years." I felt the tears that were always too close to the surface shining in my eyes as I corrected myself. "I mean the anxiety my mother and I experience constantly. I think you may already know that my father was a 9/11 victim."

"Your brother never seemed like the kind of young man who would just disappear without a mighty important reason," Gus Kramer agreed.

His tone was sincere, but I did not miss the glance he shot at his wife or the fact that she was nervously biting her lips.

"Did you ever consider the possibility that your brother may have experienced a cerebral hemorrhage or any other physical condition that might have given him an attack of amnesia or even partial amnesia?" Howard Altman asked.

"I'm considering everything," I told him. I reached into my shoulder bag and took out a notebook and pen. "Mr. and Mrs. Kramer, I know it's been ten years but could I just ask you to tell me what you remember about anything Mack did or said that might have some significance? I mean, sometimes we think of something that didn't occur to us at the time. Maybe as Mr. Altman just suggested, Mack had some kind of amnesia attack. Did he seem in any way troubled or worried, or as though he wasn't feeling well physically?"

As I asked these questions, I thought of how, after the police gave up on trying to find Mack, my father then hired private investigator Lucas Reeves to continue the search. For the last few days I've been reviewing every word of his files. Everything the Kramers told him was in my notes.

I listened as Mrs. Kramer hesitantly, then enthusiastically, told me how Mack was the kind of young man who always held the door open for her, who put his laundry in his hamper, who always picked up after himself. "I never saw him look troubled," she said. The last time she had seen him was when she tidied up the apartment he shared with two other seniors. "Both of the other boys were out. He was working on his computer in his bedroom and told me the vacuum wouldn't bother him. That's the way he always was. Easy. Nice. Polite."

"What time was that?" I asked her.

She pursed her lips. "About ten o'clock in the morning, I would guess."

"That would be right," Gus Kramer confirmed quickly.

"And you never saw him again?"

"I saw him leave the building at about three o'clock. I was on my way home from the dentist. I was putting my key in the lock of our apartment. Gus heard me and opened the door. We both saw Mack come down the stairs. He waved as he went through the lobby."

I watched her glance at her husband for approval.

"What was Mack wearing, Mrs. Kramer?"

"What he had on in the morning. A T-shirt and jeans and sneakers and . . ."

"Lil, you're mixed up again. Mack was wearing a jacket and slacks and an open-necked sport shirt when he left," Gus Kramer interrupted sharply.

"That's what I meant," she said hurriedly. "It's just I keep seeing him in the T-shirt and jeans because that's when I had a little talk with him that morning." Her face convulsed. "Gus and I had nothing to do with his disappearance," she cried. "Why are you torturing us?"

As I stared at her I thought of what Lucas Reeves, the private investigator, had written in his file, that the Kramers were nervous that they might lose their jobs because of Mack's disappearance. Now, nearly ten years later, I didn't accept that reasoning.

They were nervous because they had something to hide. Now they were trying to keep their stories straight. Ten years ago Mrs. Kramer had told Reeves that Mack was just coming out of the building when she saw him and that her husband was in the lobby.

At that moment I would have bet my life that neither one of them ever saw Mack leave this building. Or *did* he ever leave it? That question rushed into my mind and was immediately dismissed.

"I know how long it's been," I said. "But would it be possible to see the apartment where my brother lived?"

I could see that my request startled them. This time both Kramers looked to Howard Altman for guidance.

"Of course, the apartment has been rented," he said,

"but since it's the end of the term many of the students have already left. What is the situation in 4D, Lil?"

"The two who shared the larger bedroom are gone. Walter Cannon has Mack's old room but he's leaving today."

"Then perhaps you could phone and ask if Ms. MacKenzie might stop in?" Altman suggested.

A moment later we were climbing the stairs to the fourth floor. "The students don't mind stairs," Altman told me. "I must say I'm glad I don't go up and down them every day."

Walter Cannon was a six-foot-four twenty-two-year-old who waved aside my apologies for the interruption. "I'm just glad you weren't here an hour ago," he said. "I had stuff all over the place." He explained that he was on his way home to New Hampshire for a summer vacation and was starting law school in the fall.

He's at the same point in time Mack was when he disappeared, I thought sadly.

The apartment coincided with my vague memory of it. A small foyer now stacked with the luggage Cannon would be carrying, a kitchen directly opposite the outer door, a hall to the right with a sitting room and bedroom off it, a bathroom at the end. To the left of the foyer, a second bath and, beyond it, the bedroom where Mack had lived. Not listening to Altman's comments about how well the apartments were maintained, I walked into what had been Mack's bedroom.

The walls and ceilings were off-white. A light flowered cotton spread was tossed on the bed. Matching drapery panels framed the two windows. A dresser, desk, and easy chair completed the furnishings. A wall-to-wall blue-gray carpet covered the floor.

"This apartment, like all the others after they've been vacated, will have a fresh coat of paint immediately," Altman was saying. "The carpet and spread and drapes will be cleaned. Gus Kramer will make sure the kitchen and baths are spotless. We're very proud of our units."

Mack lived here for two years, I thought. I imagined him feeling about it the way I feel about my apartment. It was his own space. He could get up early or late, read or not read, answer the phone or not answer the phone. The closet door was open, and of course it was empty now.

I thought about the Kramers' claim that he was wearing a jacket and open-necked shirt and slacks when he left that afternoon.

What was the weather like that day? I wondered. Was it one of those chilly May afternoons like last Sunday? Or, if it was very warm, and Mack did leave at three o'clock, would wearing a jacket have any significance? A date? A drive to a girl's house in Connecticut, or Long Island?

It's funny but in that room, ten years later, I had a sense of his presence. He was always so laid back. Dad had been competitive, quick to size up a situation, and, with lightning accuracy, appraise and judge it. I know I'm like that, too. Mack was more like Mom. He was always giving everyone a break. Like her, if he ever realized he was being used or treated shabbily, he wouldn't have a confrontation, he'd simply withdraw from the situation. And that, I think, is what Mom is doing now—she views Mack's note in the collection basket as a slap in the face.

I moved to the window, trying to see what he had seen. Knowing how Mack loved to stand at the windows of the Sutton Place apartment and study the panorama, the East River with boats and barges, the lights of the bridges, the air traffic heading in and out of LaGuardia Airport, I was sure he'd often gazed out these windows, overlooking West End Avenue, the sidewalks constantly streaming with people, the vehicle traffic bumper to bumper in the street.

The dream I had had of him after his predawn phone call on Mother's Day replayed itself in my mind. Once again I was walking along a dark path, desperate to find Mack.

And once again he was warning me to stay back.

11

In a weary voice, Dr. David Andrews said, "Detective Barrott, Leesey left that bar at three o'clock yesterday morning. It is now one o'clock Wednesday afternoon. She has already been missing thirty-four hours. Shouldn't you check the hospitals again? If anyone knows how busy emergency rooms are, God knows it's me."

Leesey's father was sitting at the small kitchen table in his daughter's college apartment, his hands folded, his head bowed. Heart-sick, sleep-deprived, and despairing, he had refused his son's plea to go back with him to his apartment and wait for word there. After being here all night, Gregg had gone home to shower and change before stopping at the hospital to see his postoperative patients.

Roy Barrott was sitting opposite Leesey's father at the table. The night my daughter went to a prom, his daughter went to that joint, then disappeared, Roy thought, with a sudden guilty feeling at his own good fortune. "Dr. Andrews," he said, "you have to hold on to the possibility that Leesey may be perfectly all right. She *is* an adult, and has the right to privacy."

Barrott saw the expression on the doctor's face harden into anger and scorn. I sound like I'm suggesting that she's an easy pickup, he thought, and hurried to add, "Please don't think I believe that this is the case with Leesey. We're treating her disappearance as a serious problem." Barrott's boss, Captain Larry Ahearn, had made the urgency of this case perfectly clear already.

"Then what are you doing to find her?" The anger drained from David Andrews's face. His voice was low and halting.

He's only one degree from going into shock, Barrott thought. "We've reviewed the security cameras of the Woodshed, and she *did* leave alone. The only people left in the bar were the band that was playing, the bartender, and the security guard. They all swear that none of them left for at least twenty minutes after Leesey, so we presume none of them followed her. So far, they all check out as okay guys. Right now our people are going over every frame in the security camera at that bar Monday night to see if we can identify any potential troublemakers."

"Maybe someone who was there earlier waited

outside for her." David Andrews knew that his voice was a monotone. Is this detective trying to reassure me? he asked himself. Then the same thought crossed his mind for the thousandth time: I *know* something terrible has happened to Leesey!

He pushed his chair away from the table and stood up. "I'm going to offer a twenty-five-thousand-dollar reward to anyone who helps us find her," he said. "I'm going to put her picture and a description of what she was wearing on posters. You've met my daughter's roommate, Kate. She'll get Leesey's friends to tack them up on every street between that bar and this building. Somebody has to have seen *something*."

As a father that's exactly what I would do, if I were in his shoes, Roy Barrott thought as he got to his feet, too. "Dr. Andrews, that's a very good idea. Give us the picture from your wallet and her height, weight, and hair color. We'll take care of having the posters made. It will be a big help if those posters are up when the bar crowd comes out tonight. I can promise you our undercover people will be in the Woodshed and every other dive around here, talking to people. With any luck we might find a person who saw someone paying a lot of attention to her. But I would suggest, sir, you go to your son's apartment and get some rest. I'll have an officer drive you there."

I'm only in the way, David Andrews thought bleakly.

But he's right—I *do* have to sleep. Without speaking, he nodded.

The door from the bedroom was open. Kate Carlisle had spent a sleepless night, and now after napping briefly, she saw them leaving, with Barrott's hand firmly under the doctor's arm. "Dr. Andrews, are you all right?" she asked anxiously.

"Dr. Andrews is going to his son's apartment," Barrott explained. "I'll be back and forth. Kate, do you by any chance have a more recent photo of Leesey? The one I've seen that was in Dr. Andrews's wallet is more than a year old."

"Yes. I have a good one. I took it only last week. Angelina Jolie and Brad Pitt were walking in SoHo with their kids, and the paparazzi were all around them. I told Leesey to pretend she was a movie star, and I snapped a couple of pictures of her with my cell phone camera. One of them is a terrific shot. She was planning to have it framed for you, Dr. Andrews." Her voice broke. Flustered, Kate ran back into the bedroom, opened a drawer in a night table, grabbed a print from it, and hurried back to them.

In the photo, Leesey had struck a model's pose, her smiling face turned to the camera, her long hair tossed by the breeze, her slender body almost slouching, her hands buried deep in the pockets of her denim jacket.

Barrott's eyes traveled from the lovely girl in the

center to the passers-by in the background. None of the faces was clear. Was it possible one of them had noticed Leesey? he wondered. A predator on the prowl?

I'll get this enlarged, he thought, as he took it from Kate. "This is a very clear picture of Leesey," he said. "I also want you to give me a print of the other picture you took of her. From what I understand, she was wearing a denim jacket the night she went to the club. She's wearing a denim jacket in this picture."

"She was wearing that same jacket," Kate said.

"She bought it two years ago, just before her mother died," David Andrews said. "It has a skirt she wore with it. Her mother laughed and told her that the skirt had strings hanging off it. Leesey told her that was the style. Her mother said if that was considered style, it was time to bring back the hoopskirt."

I sound maudlin, David Andrews told himself. I'm holding up this detective from finding Leesey. I've got to get out of the way here. "Kate, that's a good picture of Leesey. Anyone who saw her could identify her from it. Thank you very much."

Without waiting for her to answer, he started for the door, grateful for the strong hand under his arm. In silence he walked down the three flights of stairs. He was vaguely aware of a camera flashing and someone shouting questions at him as he crossed the sidewalk and was helped into a squad car. He did remember to ask Detective Barrott what else he would do to try to find Leesey. Barrott closed the car door and then leaned down to the window.

"Dr. Andrews, we've already canvassed the people in this building. We know from the security camera here that Leesey didn't get to this door but these houses all look alike. She might have gone to the wrong one. We're going to start door to door, working the whole neighborhood. It will help to have her picture."

"Why on earth would she go to the wrong door? She didn't have too much to drink, you told me that yourself. The bartender and all those other people in the Woodshed swear she was fine when she left that place," David Andrews reminded him sharply.

It was on the tip of Barrott's tongue to reply that, unless it can be proven otherwise, ninety-nine percent of bartenders will swear that a missing patron left the bar sober. Instead he said, "Doctor, no stone unturned. That's my promise to you."

The single reporter on the scene stuck a microphone in Barrott's face as he turned from the squad car. "Look," Barrott said, impatiently, "Captain Ahearn is holding a press conference at five o'clock. He's authorized to give a statement. I'm not."

He walked back into the lobby of the building, waited till he saw the reporter and cameraman get into their van and drive away, then came back out and walked to the next building. Like most of them on this block, the outer door was unlocked, and admittance was gained either by a key or being buzzed in by a tenant.

Barrott's eyes moved up and down the tenant list, then they widened as he spotted one name, "Carolyn MacKenzie." Six degrees of separation? he asked himself. Maybe.

Roy Barrott stood perfectly still, then traced his index finger over Carolyn MacKenzie's name.

The unerring instinct that made him such a superb detective was telling him that somehow, someway there was a connection between the two cases.

12

After I left the apartment building where Mack had lived, I went back to Sutton Place. In the day and a half since Mom had made the decision to go on the cruise, she had been energized, as if after living so long in limbo, she was trying to make up for lost time. She told me she was planning to go through closets and pull out clothing to give away, and then this evening she would be meeting Elliott and some other friends for dinner.

I wondered why she would bother to clean out closets just before she went on vacation, but that became evident. Over a quick lunch, a sandwich and a cup of tea in the breakfast room, she told me that she was listing the apartment with a broker and that as soon as she came back she was going to look for something smaller. "You're never going to move back in," she said, "I know that. I will have call forwarding, just in case Mack decides to phone next Mother's Day, but on the other hand, if I miss his call, so be it. I just may not hang around and wait for it."

I looked at her, astonished. When she said she was going to clean out closets, I was thinking that she meant her own. But now, without asking, I was sure that it was the closets in Mack's room that were going to be emptied.

"What are you going to do with Mack's things?" I asked, trying to sound casual.

"I'll have Dev send someone to get them and deliver them to a place where they'll be put to good use." Mom looked at me for approval and, finding something missing in my expression, said quickly, "Carolyn, you're the one telling me to move on. The fact remains that even if Mack walked through the door today, and even if his clothes still fit him, they'd probably be out of style."

"Don't misunderstand me," I told her. "I think it's a good idea, but I also think that it's the last thing in the world you should be worrying about two days before you're getting on a plane to fly to Greece. Look, Mom, do yourself a favor. Let *me* go through Mack's clothes and sort them out." Even as I spoke, it occurred to me that it was possible that ten years ago, no one had ever carefully explored the pockets of slacks and jackets that Mack had left in this apartment. Lucas Reeves had indicated in his case report that nothing of importance was found in the clothing Mack had left behind in his student apartment.

Without much hesitation, even with relief, Mom agreed. "I don't know what I'd do without you, Carolyn," she said. "You've been my rod and staff through all this. But I know you. You only stopped working two weeks ago, and I can tell you're restless. What will you do while I'm gone?"

She had inadvertently furnished me with a response that was at least partly honest. "We know someone will snap up this place in a heartbeat," I said. "I never intended to stay in the studio indefinitely. I'm going to look around for a bigger place myself. You'll let me have my pick of any furniture you don't take with you, right?"

"Of course. Let Elliott know. A decent one-bedroom is an expenditure he'll certainly approve." Elliott was the trustee of the money my grandfather had left me.

Mom took the last gulp of tea and stood up. "I'd better rush. Helene will have a fit if I'm late for my hair appointment. For the kind of money she charges, she could stand to possess a little more humility." She gave me a quick kiss on my cheek, then added, "If you find an apartment you like, make sure it has a doorman. I never have been comfortable with you living in a place where you have to let yourself in. I've been checking the news. There's no sign of that girl who lived next door to you who disappeared. God help her family."

I was glad Mom had the salon appointment. Now that I was determined to find Mack, I had the sense that I must not lose a minute in my search for him. Geographically, he had been so close to us when he left that note on Sunday. The meeting with the Kramers had left me desperately uneasy. Memories do fade, but when I spoke to them, they had contradicted each other about what Mack was wearing and exactly where they had seen him last. Also, Lil Kramer had been absolutely shocked when I told her he had been at the Mass. Why? Was Mack a threat to them? What did they know that scared them so much?

I had taken the report of Investigator Reeves from the file drawer in Dad's desk. Now I wanted to get the addresses of Mack's former roommates, Bruce Galbraith and Nicholas DeMarco. Nick had kept in touch with Dad regularly, in the beginning. Naturally, as time passed he heard from him less and less frequently. The last time I saw him was when he attended Dad's memorial Mass, but that day is a complete blur to me.

Dad's study isn't large, but as he used to say, it was big enough for what he needed. His big desk dominated the paneled room. To my mother's horror, the faded nine-by-twelve carpet that had been in his mother's living room was on the floor. "Reminds me of where I came from, Liv," he would say after one of her periodic efforts to get rid of it. A worn leather chair with a hassock was his favorite spot in the morning. He always got up very early, made himself coffee, and settled in that chair with the morning papers before showering and getting dressed to go to the office.

Bookcases covered the wall opposite the windows. Scattered on them were framed pictures of the four of us from those happy days when we had been together. Dad had a presence that showed through even in casual pictures: the determined jaw, softened by the wide smile, the keen intelligence in his eyes. He had done everything possible to trace Mack and would still be trying if he were alive. I'm sure of that.

I opened the top drawer of his desk and took out his phone book. On a slip of paper I wrote down Bruce Galbraith's phone number. I remembered he had gone into the family real estate business in Manhattan. I copied both his home and business numbers.

Nick DeMarco, the son of immigrant parents who owned a small storefront restaurant in Queens, had been a scholarship student at Columbia. I remembered that after he got his MBA from Harvard, he went into the restaurant business and, I understand, has been very successful. Both his home and business phone numbers and addresses were in Manhattan.

I sat at Dad's desk and picked up the receiver. I decided to call Bruce first. There was a reason for that. When I was sixteen, I had a fierce crush on Nick. He and Mack were particularly close friends, and Mack regularly brought him home for dinner. I lived for those dinners. But then one night he and Mack brought a girl with them. Barbara Hanover was a senior at Columbia and lived in the same student apartment building, and it was immediately clear to me that Nick was crazy about her.

Even though I was absolutely crushed, I thought I had kept up a good front that evening, but Mack could read me like a book. Before he, Nick, and Barbara left, he pulled me aside, and said, "Carolyn, I know you have big eyes for Nick. Forget it. He's got a different girlfriend every week. Stick to guys your own age."

My angry denial only caused Mack to smile. "You'll get over it," were his parting words to me that night. That was about six months before he disappeared, and it was the last time I stayed home when Nick was coming. I was embarrassed and didn't want to be there. The fact that it was obvious to Mack that I had a crush on Nick made me sure it had been obvious to everyone else. I was grateful neither of my parents ever referred to it.

I got through to Bruce's secretary at Galbraith Real Estate and was told that he was on a business trip until next Monday. Did I care to leave a message? I gave the secretary my name and phone number, hesitated, then added, "It's about Mack. We just heard from him again."

Then I called Nick. His office is at 400 Park Avenue. That's about a fifteen-minute walk from Sutton Place, I thought, as I dialed. When I asked for him, his secretary picked up and crisply told me that if I was from the media, any statement would be coming from Mr. DeMarco's lawyer.

"I'm not from the media," I said. "Nick was a friend of my brother's at Columbia. I'm sorry, I didn't realize he was having legal troubles."

Maybe the sympathy in my voice and the use of his first name was the reason his secretary was so frank. "Mr. DeMarco is the owner of the Woodshed, the place where a young woman was last seen before she disappeared the other night," she explained. "If you give me your telephone number, I'll have him return your call."

13

Aaron Klein had been working for Wallace and Madison for fourteen years. He had started there directly after receiving his MBA degree. At that time Joshua Madison was chief executive of the privately held wealth-management company, but when he died suddenly two years later, his partner, Elliott Wallace, had taken over as chairman and CEO.

Aaron had loved the gruff Josh Madison, but initially he had been intimidated by Wallace, whose formal manner was completely the opposite of his own easygoing style. Then as Aaron continued to rise steadily through the ranks, working with higher and higher-profile clients, Elliott had begun to invite him to lunch in the executive dining room of their office on Wall Street, a clear sign that he was being groomed for a top job.

Ten years ago thcir relationship had taken a giant leap forward when Elliott let down his guard and confided to Aaron the grief and pain he was experiencing at the disappearance of Charles MacKenzie Jr. Elliott had been managing the MacKenzie money for years, and after Charles Sr. died on 9/11, he spoke of Olivia MacKenzie and her children with an air of fierce protectiveness. From everything Elliott had ever said about the missing young man, Aaron knew that he looked on Mack as a surrogate son. The fact that Aaron's mother, Esther, had taught Mack in one of her drama classes at Columbia only strengthened the bond between them.

Then, a year later, when Aaron's mother was murdered during what was determined to be a random mugging, the bond had tightened further still. Now, it was generally accepted in the company that Aaron Klein was the chosen successor of Elliott Wallace.

Aaron had been away visiting clients in Chicago on Monday and Tuesday. Late Wednesday morning he received a call from his boss. "Aaron, do you have plans for lunch?"

"None that I can't change," Aaron said promptly.

"Then please meet me at twelve thirty in the dining room."

I wonder what's up, Aaron asked himself as he replaced the receiver. Elliott isn't usually this last-minute about lunch. At 12:15 he got up from his desk, went into his private bathroom, ran a comb through his sparse head of hair, and straightened his tie. Mirror, mirror, on the wall, he thought sardonically, who's the baldest of us all? Thirty-seven years old, in good shape, not bad-looking, but at the rate I'm going, by the time I'm fifty I'll be lucky if I have six hairs left on my head. He sighed and put away the comb.

Jenny tells me that's part of the reason I've done so well, he told himself. She says I look ten years older than I am. Thanks, honey.

Friendly as they had become, Aaron was always aware that to the blue-blooded Elliott Wallace, the fact that he, his chosen successor, was the grandson of immigrants had to be disappointing. That thought was in his mind as he walked toward the dining room. The kid from Staten Island approaches the privileged descendant of one of the first settlers of New Amsterdam, he thought. Never mind that the immigrants' grandson graduated from Yale in the top ten percent of his class and has a master's degree from Wharton; it still isn't the same as having classy ancestors. I wonder if I'll hear the "cousin Franklin" story again.

Aaron acknowledged that he both hated and was bored by Elliott's oft-repeated anecdote of FDR's having invited a Republican woman to host an event at Hyde Park when his wife, Eleanor, was away. When he was chided by the Democratic chairman, an astonished FDR replied, "But of course I asked her to be my hostess. She is the only woman in Hyde Park who is my social equal."

"That was my father's favorite story about his cousin Franklin," Elliott would chuckle.

As he reached the table and a waiter pulled out a chair for him, Aaron immediately sensed that anecdotes about his revered relatives were the last thing on Elliott's mind today. He looked thoughtful and concerned—in fact, *preoccupied.*

"Aaron, good to see you. Let's order quickly. I have a couple of meetings. I assume you'll have your usual?"

"Cobb salad, no dressing, and iced tea, Mr. Klein?" the waiter asked, smiling.

"You've got it." Aaron did not mind letting his boss think that his salad luncheon was a sign of self-discipline. The fact was that his wife, Jenny, loved to cook, and even her most casual dinners far surpassed the sterile menu of the executive dining room.

Elliott ordered, and when the waiter was out of earshot he got right to the point: "We heard from Mack on Sunday," he said.

"The usual Mother's Day call?" Aaron asked. "I was wondering if he'd stick to form and phone this year."

"He did that, and more."

Aaron did not take his eyes off Elliott Wallace's face as he listened to the account of the written communication from Mack.

"I've advised Olivia to respect Mack's wishes," Elliott said. "But oddly enough, she seems to have come to that conclusion on her own. She referred to Mack as 'absent without leave.' She's going to join some mutual friends of ours for a cruise around the Greek islands. I've been invited to be with them and may go for the last ten days."

"You *should*," Aaron said promptly. "You don't give yourself nearly enough time off."

"And on my next birthday I'll be sixty-five. In a lot of companies I'd be pushed out at that age. That's the benefit of owning this one—I'm not going anywhere for a long time." He paused, as if preparing himself, then said, "But I didn't ask you to join me to discuss vacation plans."

Surprised, Aaron Klein watched as Wallace's eyes clouded with worry.

"Aaron, you've gone through the experience of losing your mother in a random crime. If the positions were reversed, if your mother was the one who had disappeared and then kept in contact, would you respect her wishes or would you feel that you should keep on trying to find her? I find myself absolutely uncertain and troubled. Did I give Olivia the right advice, or should I have told her to renew and redouble her efforts to find Mack?"

Suppose Mom had disappeared ten years ago, Aaron

asked himself. Suppose she phoned once a year, then, when I told her I needed to find her and was going to track her down, she sent me a note telling me to leave her alone, what would I do?

The answer was not hard to reach. "If my mother did to *me* what Mack has done to his family and to you, I would say, 'If that's the way you want it, Mom, so be it. I have other fish to fry.'"

Elliott Wallace smiled. "'Other fish to fry'? That's a strange way to put it. But thank you, Aaron. I needed to be reassured I'm not failing Mack or Olivia . . ." He paused, then corrected himself: "I mean his mother and sister, of course."

"You're not failing them," Aaron Klein said emphatically.

That night, as he was sipping a predinner glass of wine with his wife, Aaron said, "Jenny, today I realized that even stuffed shirts are like schoolboys when they fall in love. Elliott can't mention Olivia MacKenzie's name without getting stars in his eyes."

14

Nicholas DeMarco, owner of the trendy club the Woodshed, as well as an upscale restaurant in Palm Beach, was notified of the disappearance of the NYU coed Leesey Andrews late Tuesday evening while on a golf outing in South Carolina.

On Wednesday morning, he flew home, and by three o'clock Wednesday afternoon he was following a secretary down a long corridor on the ninth floor of 1 Hogan Place to the section where the detectives assigned to the District Attorney of Manhattan worked. He had an appointment with Captain Larry Ahearn, the commanding officer of the squad.

Tall, with the lean figure of a disciplined athlete, Nick walked with long strides, a worried frown on his forehead. Absentmindedly, he passed a hand through his short hair, which, despite his best efforts, curled when it was damp.

I should have stopped home long enough to change,

he chided himself. He was wearing an open-necked checkered blue and white sport shirt, which felt too casual, even with a light blue jacket and dark blue slacks.

"This is the detectives' squad room," the secretary explained, as they entered a large room in which rows of desks were haphazardly clustered. Only a half dozen of them were occupied, although piles of papers and ringing telephones testified to the fact that all of the others were active workstations.

The five men and one woman who were there looked up as he crossed the room, threading his way between the desks after the secretary. He was keenly aware of being the object of sharp scrutiny. Ten to one, they all know who I am and why I'm here, and they resent me. They have me pegged as the owner of one of those raunchy bars where underage kids get drunk, he thought.

The secretary knocked on the door of a private office to the left of the squad room and, without waiting for an answer, opened it.

Captain Larry Ahearn was alone in the room. He got up from behind the desk and offered his hand to DeMarco. "Thank you for coming in so promptly," he said briskly. "Please sit down." He turned to the secretary. "Ask Detective Gaylor to join us."

DeMarco took the chair nearest Ahearn's desk. "I'm

sorry that I wasn't available last night. Early yesterday morning I flew to South Carolina to meet some friends."

"I understand from your secretary that you flew your own private plane from Teterboro Airport," Ahearn said.

"That's right. And I flew back this morning. I couldn't get an early start because of the weather down there. They had heavy storms in Charleston."

"When did your staff notify you that Leesey Andrews, a young woman who left your club at closing time early Tuesday morning, had disappeared?"

"The call came to my cell phone about nine o'clock last night. I was out to dinner with friends and hadn't carried it with me. Quite frankly, as a restaurant owner, I consider people who make or take calls in restaurants pretty insufferable. When I got back to the hotel at about eleven, I checked my messages. Is there any word about Ms. Andrews? Has she called her family?"

"No," Ahearn said briefly, then looked past DeMarco. "Come in, Bob."

Nicholas DeMarco had not heard the door open. He stood up and turned as a trim man with graying hair who looked to be in his late fifties crossed the room with a quick stride. He smiled briefly as he reached out his hand.

"Detective Gaylor," he said, then pulled up a chair

and turned it, facing Nick at a right angle to the captain's desk.

"Mr. DeMarco," Ahearn began, "we are very concerned that Leesey Andrews may be the victim of foul play. Your employees tell us that you were in the Woodshed at approximately ten o'clock on Monday evening and were speaking with her."

"That's right," Nick answered promptly. "Because I was leaving for South Carolina, I worked late at my office at 400 Park Avenue. Then I stopped at my apartment, changed to casual clothes, and went down to the Woodshed."

"Do you visit your club frequently?"

"I would say I *drop in* frequently. I no longer do, nor want to do, hands-on management. Tom Ferrazzano runs the Woodshed for me as both host and manager. And I might add he does an excellent job of it. In the ten months we've been operating, we've never had one single incident caused by an underage drinker being served or an adult being served too much for his or her own good. Our employees are thoroughly checked out before they're hired, as are the bands we book to perform."

"The reputation of the Woodshed is good," Detective Gaylor agreed. "But your own employees tell us that you spent quite a bit of time talking to Leesey Andrews."

"I saw her dancing," Nick said promptly. "She's a beautiful girl and a really excellent dancer. To look at her you would think she was a professional. But she also looks very young. I know her ID had been checked, but if I had to bet on it, I'd have sworn she was underage. That's why I had one of the waiters bring her over to my table and asked to see it myself. She had just turned twenty-one."

"She joined you at your table," Gaylor said flatly. "You bought her a drink."

"She had a glass of pinot grigio with me, then returned to her friends."

"What did the two of you talk about while she was sipping that glass, Mr. DeMarco?" Captain Ahearn asked.

"The usual social-type conversation. She told me she was graduating from NYU next year and still deciding what she wanted to do. She said her father and brother were doctors but becoming a medical doctor wasn't right for her. She said that more and more she was thinking of going for a master's in social work but she wasn't sure. She was going to take a year off after college and then figure out the next step."

"Didn't that seem to you to be a lot of personal information to impart to a stranger, Mr. DeMarco?"

Nicholas DeMarco shrugged. "Not really. Then she thanked me for the drink and went back to her friends.

I would say she was at my table for less than fifteen minutes."

"What did you do then?" Ahearn asked.

"I finished dinner and went home."

"Where do you live?"

"My apartment is on Park Avenue and Seventy-eighth Street. However I recently bought a building in TriBeCa and have a loft apartment there. That was where I stayed Monday night."

Nick had debated about furnishing that information to the police and decided it was wiser to put it on the table immediately.

"You have a loft in TriBeCa? None of your employees told us that."

"I don't share my personal investments with my employees."

"Is there a doorman in your building in TriBeCa?"

He shook his head. "As I told you, my apartment is a loft. The building is five stories high. I own it and have bought out the leases of the tenants. The other floors are now unoccupied."

"How far is it from your bar?"

"About seven blocks." Nicholas DeMarco hesitated, then added, "I am very sure you must have most of this information already. I left the Woodshed shortly before eleven o'clock. I walked to the TriBeCa place and went to bed immediately. My alarm went off at five A.M. I showered, dressed, and drove to Teterboro Airport. I took off at six forty-five, and landed in Charleston at Charleston Airport. I teed off at the club at noon."

"You did not invite Ms. Andrews to stop in for a nightcap?"

"No, I did not." Nicholas DeMarco looked from one to the other of the detectives. "From the news reports I heard driving in from the airport, I know that Leesey's father has posted a twenty-five-thousand-dollar reward for any information leading to her whereabouts. I intend to match that sum. More than anything, I want Leesey Andrews found alive and well, primarily because it would be horrifying if anything happened to her . . ."

"*Primarily?*" Ahearn said, taken aback momentarily. "What other reason do you have to want her found?"

"My second very selfish reason is that a great deal of money has been spent buying the property on which the Woodshed is situated, renovating the premises, furnishing and staffing it. I wanted to create a safe, fun place for young people and not-so-young people to enjoy. If Leesey's disappearance is traced to an encounter she had in my club, the media will hound us, and within six months our doors will be closed. I want you to investigate our employees, our customers, and me. But I can promise you that you're wasting your time if you think I had anything to do with that girl's disappearance."

"Mr. DeMarco, you are one of the many people we are and will be interviewing," Ahearn said calmly. "Did you file a flight plan at Teterboro?"

"Of course. If you check the records, the flying time down yesterday morning was excellent. Today, because of the nearby storms, it was somewhat slower."

"One last question, Mr. DeMarco. How did you get back and forth to the airport?"

"In my car, I drove myself."

"What kind of car do you drive?"

"I usually drive a Mercedes convertible unless for some reason I'm carrying a lot of baggage. Actually my golf clubs were in my SUV, so that was what I drove back and forth to the airport yesterday and today."

Nicholas DeMarco did not need to catch the glance the two detectives exchanged to know that he had become a person of interest in the disappearance of Leesey Andrews. I can understand why, he thought. I was talking to her a few hours before she disappeared. No one can verify that she didn't meet me later at the apartment. I took off early the next morning in a private plane. I can't blame them for being suspicious—that's their job.

With a brief smile, he offered his hand to both men and told them that he was going to make public immediately his offer to match the twenty-five-thousand-dollar reward for information leading to Leesey's whereabouts.

"And I can assure you, we'll be working 24/7 to find her, or if something has happened to her, find the person who did it," Ahearn said, in a tone of voice that Nicholas DeMarco correctly interpreted as a warning.

15

As I was leaving the Sutton Place apartment, my cell phone rang. The caller identified himself as Detective Barrott, and though my pulse quickened, I kept my response to him deliberately cool. He had brushed me off on Monday, so what possible reason did he have for calling me now?

"Ms. MacKenzie, as you may be aware, a young woman, Leesey Andrews, who disappeared last night, lives next door to you on Thompson Street. I am there now, interviewing the neighbors on the block. I saw your name listed on the directory in your building. I'd very much appreciate an opportunity to speak with you again. Is it possible to set up an appointment with you soon?"

Holding the phone to one ear, I signaled to the doorman to hail a cab for me. There was one nearby just discharging a passenger. As I waited for an elderly lady to get out, I told Barrott that I was on my way back to my own apartment and, depending on traffic, would be there in about twenty minutes.

"I'll wait for you," he said flatly, giving me no opportunity to let him know whether that was convenient for me or not.

Some days a cab ride between Sutton Place and Thompson Street takes fifteen minutes. Other days the traffic simply crawls. This was one of those crawling days. It wasn't as though I was in any rush to see Detective Barrott—it's just that once I'm on my way anywhere, I'm impatient to get there, another characteristic inherited from my father.

And that made me think of my father's anxiety when Mack disappeared and the anxiety Leesey Andrews's father must be feeling now. Last night on the eleven o'clock news, holding back tears, Dr. Andrews had held up his daughter's picture and pleaded for assistance in finding her. I thought I could imagine what he was going through, then wondered if that was really true. Bad as it had been for us, Mack had after all seemingly walked out of his life in midafternoon. Leesey Andrews was surely more vulnerable, alone at night, and certainly no match for a strong predator.

All that was whirling through my mind as the cab made its way slowly to Thompson Street.

Barrott was sitting on the steps of the brownstone, an incongruous sight, I thought, as I paid the driver.

The afternoon had turned warm again, and he had opened his jacket and loosened his tie. When he spotted me, in a fluid movement he stood up quickly, tightened the tie, and buttoned the jacket again.

We greeted each other with reserved courtesy, and I invited him inside. As I turned the key in the entrance door, I noticed a couple of vans with TV markings parked outside the building next door, the building where Leesey Andrews lived—or had lived.

My studio apartment is in the rear of the building and is the only one on the lobby floor. I took it on a year's lease last September when I started working for Judge Huot. In these past nine months it has become, for me, a peaceful haven from Sutton Place, where my sense of loss over my father and anxiety over Mack are never totally absent.

Mom was appalled at the size of this place. "Carolyn, nine hundred square feet, you won't be able to turn around," she had lamented. But I have been thrilled by the womblike space. It is a cheery cocoon and I think has been greatly responsible for helping me evolve from a chronic state of inner sadness and anxiety to a surging desire, even a *need*, to have done with it, to get on with life. Thanks to Mom's good taste, I grew up in a home that was beautifully decorated, but I've taken a certain joy in shopping for my studio at bargain sales in home furnishings departments.

My spacious bedroom on Sutton Place has a separate sitting area. On Thompson Street, I have a pullout couch, which, remarkably, has a very comfortable mattress. As Detective Barrott followed me into the apartment, I caught the way he surveyed the room, with its black enamel side tables and bright red modern lamps, small black enamel coffee table, and two armless chairs upholstered in the same stark white of the couch. He let his eyes slide over the white walls and the rug with its checkered black and white and red pattern.

The kitchen is a narrow unit off the living room. An ice cream parlor table and two padded wrought iron chairs under the window are the full extent of the dining facilities. But the window is wide, lets in a lot of light, and plants and geraniums on the sill bring the outdoors in.

Barrott took everything in, then politely refused my offer of water or coffee and sat down opposite me on one of the side chairs. He surprised me by starting with an apology. “Ms. MacKenzie,” he said, “I’m pretty sure you feel that I dismissed your concerns when you came to see me on Monday.”

I let my silence tell him that I agreed.

“I started to look over your brother’s file yesterday. I’ll admit that I didn’t get very far. The call came in about Leesey Andrews and of course that took precedence, but then I realized it would also give me another chance to talk to you. As I told you, we're canvassing the neighborhood. Do you know Leesey Andrews?"

The question surprised me. Maybe it should not have, but I thought to myself that when he phoned and asked to meet me, if I had known her even slightly, I would have said so immediately. "No, I don't know her," I said.

"Did you see her picture on television?"

"Yes, I did, last night."

"And you didn't have any sense of ever having seen her around?" he persisted as though he wasn't sure that I wasn't being evasive.

"No, but of course, living next door, I may have passed her in the street. There are a number of young women students in that building." I knew I sounded irritated and I was. Surely Barrott wasn't suggesting that because my brother was missing I might have some kind of link to this girl's disappearance?

Barrott's lips tightened. "Ms. MacKenzie, I hope you realize that I'm asking you the same questions I, and other detectives, are asking everyone in this neighborhood. Because we already know each other, and because you of all people understand the agony her father and brother are going through, I'm hoping that somehow you can help us. You're an extremely attractive young woman, and as a lawyer you're trained to be very observant." He leaned slightly forward, his hands clasped. "Do you ever walk around this area alone at night, let's say after dinner or a movie, or do you ever go out very early in the morning?"

"Yes, I do." I knew my tone had softened. "Most mornings I jog around six o'clock, and if I'm meeting friends locally in the evening, I often walk home alone."

"Have you ever had a sense of being watched, of someone following you?"

"No, I haven't. On the other hand, I would say I'm rarely out later than midnight, and the Village is still pretty lively at that time."

"I understand. But I'd appreciate it if you'd keep your eyes open for us. Predators, like arsonists, sometimes enjoy watching the excitement they've created. Something else. There *is* another way you might be able to help us. Your neighbor on the second floor, Mrs. Carter, is very fond of you, isn't she?"

"I'm very fond of her. She's terribly arthritic and terrified of going out if the weather is bad," I explained. "She's had a couple of nasty falls. I check on her and pick up odds and ends from the grocery store if she needs them." I leaned back in my chair, wondering where he was going with this.

Barrott nodded. "She told me that. In fact she was singing your praises. But you know how it is with some old people. They're afraid of getting in trouble themselves if they talk to police. My own aunt was like that.

She wouldn't admit it when she saw a neighbor dent another neighbor's car. 'It's none of my business,' was the way she put it." He paused thoughtfully. "I could tell that Mrs. Carter was nervous about talking to me," he continued. "But she *did* tell me she enjoys sitting at the window. She claims she didn't recognize Leesey's picture, but I have a hunch she did. It may only be that she has noticed Leesey walking by and doesn't want to get involved with the investigation in any way, but maybe if you have a cup of tea with her, she might open up to you."

"I'll do that," I said willingly. Mrs. Carter may be old, but she doesn't miss a trick, and she is a window sitter, I thought. She certainly has all the dirt on the neighbors who live on the three floors above her. I considered the irony that I was now investigating for Barrott, when my intention had been to have *him* investigate for *me*.

Barrott stood up. "Thank you for letting me stop in, Ms. MacKenzie. As you can understand, we're working round the clock on this case, but when it's resolved, I'm going to get back to reviewing your brother's file and see if we can come up with some new avenues to follow."

He had given me his card on Monday but probably suspected that I had torn it up, which I had. As I accepted another one from him, he said he'd keep in touch with me. I saw him out, locked the door behind him, and realized that I suddenly felt weak-kneed. Something about his manner made me suspect that Detective Roy Barrott had not been honest. To him, I was not just someone who happened to be a neighbor of a missing young woman. He was trying to create reasons to keep in contact with me.

But why?

I simply didn't know.

16

Lil Kramer had been nervous from the moment Carolyn MacKenzie phoned on Monday requesting a meeting, but on Wednesday, shortly after Carolyn left, had gone into the bedroom, laid down, closed her eyes, and begun to cry silently, tears running down her cheeks.

Lil could hear Gus saying his good-byes to Howard, then he walked into the bedroom and stood over her. At her husband's impatient demand to know what her problem was, her eyes had flown open. "My problem? I'll tell you what it is! Gus, I was in St. Francis de Sales Church at the Latin Mass last Sunday. I've been thinking about going ever since they began saying it again last year. Don't forget, my father was a Catholic and used to take me to church once in a while, back when all the Masses were in Latin."

"You never told me you went there Sunday," Gus snapped.

"And why would I have told you? You have no use for any religion, and I didn't need to hear you ranting that all clergymen are con men."

Gus Kramer's expression changed. "All right, all right. You were there. Hope you said a prayer for me. So what?"

"It was so crowded. You wouldn't believe it. People were standing in the aisles. You heard what Carolyn MacKenzie just told us. *That Mack was there!* I know you won't believe me, but at Mass I had the feeling that I saw someone familiar, just for a moment. But as you know, I'm blind as a bat if I don't have my bifocals with me, and I forgot them when I changed my purse."

"I repeat, so what?"

"Gus, don't you understand what I'm saying? Mack was there! Suppose he does decide to come back! You know," she finished in a whisper, "you know."

As she had expected, Gus had immediately become angry. "Damn it, Lil, that guy must have had his own reasons for pulling the disappearing act. I'm sick of seeing you wringing your hands over him. Knock it off. Stop it. You told his sister just enough to satisfy her. Now keep your mouth shut. Look at me." Roughly he leaned over the bed and raised her chin so that she could not avert her gaze from him. "You're half-blind without your distance glasses. You're jumping to conclusions because of that note Mack supposedly left in the collection. You didn't see him there. So forget all about it."

Lil would not have believed she had the courage to ask her husband why he was so sure. "How can you be so positive that Mack wasn't there?" she demanded in a tense whisper.

"Just trust me," Gus said, his face darkening with anger.

It was the same rage she had seen ten years ago when she told Gus what she had found in Mack's room while she was cleaning. It was that rage that had made her wonder despairingly all these years if Gus could have been responsible for Mack's disappearance.

In a clumsy gesture of affection, Gus ran his calloused hand over Lil's forehead, then, with a heavy sigh, said, "You know, Lil, I'm beginning to think it may be a good idea after all for us to retire to Pennsylvania. If that sister of Mack's starts dropping around here, sooner or later she's going to get you so upset, you'll say too much."

Lil, who loved living in New York and who had dreaded moving to an idle retired life, whimpered, "I want to go right away, Gus. I'm so afraid for us."

17

Bruce Galbraith always checked in with his secretary at the end of the business day. Unlike most of the people he knew, he did not carry a BlackBerry and often turned off his cell phone. "Too many distractions for my taste," was his explanation. "It's like watching a juggler with too many balls in the air."

Thirty-two years old, average height, with sandy hair and rimless glasses, he joked about himself that he was so average he wouldn't even be noticed by a security camera. On the other hand, he was not so self-effacing that he did not know his own worth. He was a superb deal-closer and was considered by his colleagues to have a near-psychic ability to foresee the trends in the real estate market.

The result was that Bruce Galbraith had multiplied the value of the family real estate business to the point where his sixty-year-old father had simply turned over the reins to him. At his retirement dinner his father had said, "Bruce, my hat's off to you. You're a good son and a far better businessman than I ever was, and I was good. Now, you keep making money for us, and I'll pursue my goal of becoming a scratch golfer."

Bruce was in Arizona on Wednesday when he made his daily late-afternoon call to his secretary. She told him that a Carolyn MacKenzie had phoned and left a message that Mack had been in contact again and would Bruce please call her.

Carolyn MacKenzie? Mack's kid sister? These were not names he wanted to hear.

Bruce had just returned to his suite in the hotel he owned in Scottsdale. Shaking his head, he walked over to the minibar and reached into it for a cold beer. It was only four o'clock, but he had been outside in the heat most of the day and deserved it, he assured himself.

He settled in the big armchair facing the floor-to-ceiling window that overlooked the desert. At any other time it was his favorite view, but at this moment he was seeing only the college apartment he had shared with Mack MacKenzie and Nick DeMarco, and reviewing again what had happened there.

I don't want to see Mack's sister, he told himself. All that happened ten years ago, and even then Mack's parents knew I was never close to him. He never once asked me home to Sutton Place for dinner, although he was always taking Nick with him. It didn't even cross Mack's mind that I might enjoy going, too. To him, I was just an unobtrusive guy who happened to be sharing an apartment with him.

Nick the lady-killer; Mack, everyone's choice for the nicest guy in the world. So nice that he apologized for beating me out by a fraction to be one of the top ten graduates of our class. I'll never forget the look on Dad's face when I told him I hadn't made it. Four generations at Columbia, and I was the first not to be in the top ten. And Barbara, God, the crush I had on her in those days. I worshipped her . . . She never even glanced in my direction, he thought.

Bruce tilted his head and finished the beer. I'll have to call Carolyn, he decided. But I'll tell her what I told her parents. Mack and I lived together, but we never hung out together. I didn't even see him the day he disappeared. I got out before he and Nick were awake. So, leave me alone, little sister.

He stood up. Forget it, he told himself impatiently. Just forget about it. The quote that often ran through his head whenever he happened to think about Mack jumped into his mind again. He knew the quote wasn't completely accurate, but it worked for him: "But *that* was in another land, and besides the king is dead."

He went back to the phone, picked it up, and dialed. When his wife answered, he knew his face lit up at the sound of her voice. "Hi, Barb," he said. "How are you, sweetheart? And how are the kids?"

18

After his luncheon with Aaron Klein, Elliott Wallace went back to his office and found himself thinking about Charles MacKenzie Sr. and the friendship they had forged in Vietnam. Charley had been in the army's ROTC and was a second lieutenant when they met. Elliott had told Charley that he was born in England of American parents and had spent most of his childhood in London. He had moved back to New York with his mother when he was nineteen. He had then enlisted in the army, and four years later he had earned his own commission and was side by side with Charley in some of the fiercest fighting of the war.

We liked each other from day one, Elliott thought. Charley was the most competitive person I've ever met and probably the most ambitious. He was planning to go to law school the minute he was discharged. He swore that he was going to be a very successful lawyer and a millionaire. He was actually pleased that he had grown up in a family that didn't have two nickels to rub together. He used to kid me about my background. "And what was the butler's name, Ell?" he would ask me. "Was it Bertie, or Chauncey, or Jeeves?"

As he leaned back in his leather chair, Elliott smiled at the memory. I told Charley that the butler was William, and he was gone by the time I was thirteen. I told him that my father, God rest him, was the most cultivated human being and the worst businessman in the history of the civilized world. That was why my mother finally threw in the towel and brought me home from England.

Charley didn't believe me back then, but I swore to him that in my own way I was just as ambitious as he was. He wanted to become wealthy because he'd never known that world. I was one of the haves who became a have-not and wanted it all back. While Charley was in law school, I went to college and then got my MBA.

We both succeeded financially, but our personal lives were so different. Charley met Olivia, and they had a wonderful marriage. God, how like an outsider I felt when I saw the way they looked at each other! They had twenty-three good years, until Mack disappeared, and after that they didn't have a day that wasn't filled with worry about him. And then 9/11, and Charley was gone. My marriage to Norma was never fair to her. What was it Princess Diana told an interviewer—that there were three people in her marriage to the Prince of Wales? Yes, that's the way it was with Norma and me, only less glamorous.

Grimacing at the memory, Elliott picked up his pen and began to doodle on a pad. Norma didn't know it, of course, but the way I felt about Olivia was always between us. And now that my marriage is a distant memory, after all these years, maybe Olivia and I can plan a future together. She recognizes that she can't live her life around Mack anymore, and I can see that her feeling about me has changed. In her eyes, I've become more than Charley's best friend and the trusted family advisor. I could tell that when I kissed her good night. I could tell when she confided that Carolyn needs to be free to stop worrying about her, and most of all I can tell because she's planning to sell the Sutton Place apartment.

Elliott got up, walked over to the section of the mahogany bookcase that housed a refrigerator, and opened the door. As he reached for a bottle of water, he wondered if it was too soon to suggest to Olivia that a penthouse on Fifth Avenue, down the block from the Metropolitan Museum, might be a wonderful place to live.

My penthouse, he thought with a smile. Even twenty-five years ago, when I bought it after Norma and I were divorced, I dreamed I was buying it for Olivia.

The telephone rang, then the crisp British voice of his personal secretary sounded on the intercom. "Mrs. MacKenzie is calling, sir."

Elliott rushed back to his desk and picked up the receiver.

"Elliott, it's Liv. June Crabtree was coming for dinner and at the last minute she can't make it. I know Carolyn is meeting her friend Jackie. By any chance would you like to take a lady to dinner?"

"I would be delighted. How about having a drink at my place around seven and then going over to Le Cirque?"

"Perfect. See you then."

When he replaced the receiver, Elliott realized there was a slight bead of perspiration on his forehead. I've never wanted anything more in my life, he thought. Nothing must spoil it for us, and I'm so afraid something might. Then he relaxed and laughed aloud as he thought of what his father's reaction would be to that kind of negative thinking.

As dear cousin Franklin said, he thought, the only thing we have to fear is fear itself.

19

Late Wednesday afternoon and long into the night, grim-faced NYU students, scattered throughout Greenwich Village and SoHo, were taping posters on storefronts and telephone poles and trees in the hope that someone might recognize Lisa "Leesey" Andrews and provide information that would lead to her recovery.

The photo that her roommate had taken only a few days earlier of a smiling Leesey, the statistics of her height and weight, the address of the Woodshed, the time she left it, her home address where she was presumed to have been heading, and the fifty thousand dollars reward offered by her father and Nicholas DeMarco were all included on the poster.

"More information than we usually give, but we're pulling out all the stops," Captain Larry Ahearn told Leesey's brother at nine o'clock Wednesday night. "But, Gregg, I'm going to be fair with you. Truth is, if Leesey was abducted, every hour that passes lessens our chances of finding her alive and safe."

"I know that." Gregg Andrews had gone down to headquarters after giving his father a strong sedative and making him go to bed in the guest room of his apartment. "Larry, I feel so damn helpless. What can I do?" He slumped in his chair.

Captain Ahearn leaned across his desk toward Gregg, his expression sober. "You can be a crutch for your father and take care of your patients in the hospital. Leave the rest of it to us, Gregg."

Gregg did his best to look reassured. "I'll try." He got up slowly, as if every move was an effort. He reached for the door of Ahearn's office, then turned back. "Larry, you said, '*if* Leesey was abducted.' Please don't waste your time thinking that she would deliberately put us through this agony."

Gregg opened the door and came face-to-face with Roy Barrott, who was about to knock on the door of his boss's office. Barrott had heard Andrews's statement and realized it echoed what Carolyn MacKenzie had said about her brother in this same office two days earlier. Pushing aside that comparison, he greeted Andrews, then stepped into Ahearn's office.

"The tapes are finished," he said briefly. "Want to look at them now, Larry?"

"Yes, I do," Ahearn said, looking at Gregg's

retreating figure. "Do you think there's any benefit in having her brother look at them with us?"

Barrott turned swiftly to follow Ahearn's line of sight. "Maybe there is. I'll grab him before he gets to the elevator."

Barrott caught Gregg as he was punching the elevator button and asked if he'd accompany them down the hall to the tech room. Barrott explained, "Dr. Andrews, the tapes taken Monday night by the security cameras at the Woodshed have been enhanced, frame by frame, to try to pick out anyone who seemed particularly close to Leesey on the dance floor or who was among the last to leave the club."

Without speaking, Gregg nodded, then followed Barrott and Ahearn into the tech room and took a chair. As the tape ran, Barrott, who had already studied it twice, briefed him and Captain Ahearn on the contents.

"Except for the friends she was sitting with all night, nothing we have seems to show anything significant. The friends all agree that Leesey was with them except for the fifteen minutes she was with DeMarco at his table or when she was on the dance floor. After the rest of her group left at two A.M., the only time she sat at a table was when the band started to pack up. The place had thinned out by then, so we have a couple of pretty clear shots of her until she exited alone."

"Can you go back to that shot of her at the table?"

Gregg asked. Watching his sister on tape sent a wave of sadness through him.

"Sure." Barrott rewound the tape in the VCR. "Do you see anything that we've missed, Doctor?" he asked, trying to keep his voice noncommittal.

"Leesey's expression. When she was dancing, she was smiling. Look at her now. She looks so pensive, so sad." He paused. "Our mother died two years ago, and Leesey's had a hard time struggling with that grief."

"Gregg, do you think that her state of mind would cause her to have a temporary amnesia or anxiety attack that would make her run away?" Ahearn's question was penetrating and demanded a straight answer. "Is that a possibility?"

Gregg Andrews raised his hands and pressed his temples as though trying to stimulate his thought processes. "I don't know," he said finally. "I just don't know." He hesitated, then continued, "But if I had to stake my life, and Leesey's life, on it, I would say it didn't happen that way."

Barrott fast-forwarded the VCR. "All right. In that last hour, whenever the camera scans her, she never has a glass in her hand, which backs up what the waiter and bartender told us, that she only had a couple of glasses of wine all night and wasn't drunk when she left." He turned off the VCR. "Nothing," he said in disgust.

Gregg Andrews got up. His voice strained, he said, "I'll go home now. I have surgery in the morning and I need to catch some sleep."

Barrott waited till he was out of earshot, then stood and stretched. "I wouldn't mind catching some sleep myself, but I'm going to the Woodshed."

"Do you think DeMarco will show up there tonight?" Ahearn asked.

"My guess is that he will. He knows our guys are going to be swarming all over the place. And he's smart enough to know that it will be a big night for him. Plenty of customers will want to get in, out of curiosity, and of course the minor-league so-called celebrities will flock to the place knowing the media will be around. Trust me. The maggots will gather."

"Of course they will." Ahearn stood up. "I don't know if you've checked since you got back, but the track we have on Leesey's cell phone shows whoever has it has been moving around in Manhattan all day. DeMarco only got back from South Carolina late this morning, so if he did it, he has someone in New York working with him."

"It would be nice to think that girl went off the deep end, and she's the one who's running around Manhattan," Barrott commented, as he reached for his jacket. "But I don't think that's the way it's going to turn out. I think whoever grabbed her has already dumped her somewhere and is smart enough to know that when the cell phone is on, we can target that area and start searching there."

"And smart enough to know that by moving her cell phone around, it leaves open the door that she's alive." Ahearn looked thoughtful. "We've checked out DeMarco so thoroughly that we know when he lost his baby teeth. Nothing in his background suggests he'd try something like this."

"Did our guys find anything in the files of the other three girls who disappeared?"

"Nothing that we haven't investigated into the ground. We're checking out the credit card receipts from Monday night to see if we can match any patrons of the Woodshed to the names we have of the people who were in the bars in those cases."

"Uh-huh. Okay, see you, Larry."

Ahearn studied Barrott's face. "You've got someone in mind besides DeMarco, haven't you, Roy?"

"I'm not sure. Let me think about it," Barrott said vaguely. But Ahearn could see that Barrott was focused on something.

20

Jackie Reynolds has been my closest friend since the first grade, when we attended the Academy of the Sacred Heart together as six-year-olds. She's one of the smartest people I know, as well as a gifted athlete. Jackie can hit a golf ball so hard that it would make Tiger Woods blink. The September after we graduated from Columbia, we drove to Duke together. While I was studying law, she was working for a doctorate in psychology.

She has that unmistakable look of the born athlete, tall and firm-bodied, with long chestnut hair that, as often as not, is held together at the nape of her neck with a rubber band. Her extraordinary brown eyes are her dominant feature. They exude warmth and sympathy and make people want to confide in her. I always tell her that she should give cut rates to her patients. "You don't have to drag their problems out of them, Jackie. They walk through your door and spill their guts."

We talk frequently on the phone and get together

every few weeks. It used to be even more often, but now Jackie is getting pretty serious about the guy she's been dating for the past year. Ted Sawyer is a lieutenant in the fire department and a genuinely top-drawer person. He intends to be fire commissioner of New York someday, then run for mayor, and I'd bet my bottom dollar that he'll do both.

Jackie has always been worried about how little interest I've shown in dating. She correctly attributed my lack of interest to the fact that I've felt emotionally burned out. Tonight, if the subject came up, I intended to reassure her that I am now actively working to put all that inertia behind me.

We met at Il Mulino, our favorite pasta place in the Village. Over linguine with clam sauce and a glass of pinot grigio, I told her about Mack's phone call and the note he left in the collection basket.

"'Uncle Devon, tell Carolyn she must not look for me,'" Jackie repeated. "I'm sorry, Carolyn, but if Mack *did* write that note, it suggests to me that he may be in some kind of trouble," she said quietly. "If he weren't under stress and just wanted to be left alone, I think he would have written, 'Please don't look for me,' or simply, 'Carolyn, leave me alone.'"

"That's exactly what I'm afraid of. The more I look at the note and think about it, the more I sense desperation."

I told Jackie about going to see Detective Barrott. "He practically showed me the door," I said. "He wasn't interested in the note. He gave me the impression that if Mack wanted to be left alone, I should respect his wishes. So I started my own investigation by meeting with the superintendents of Mack's apartment building."

She listened to my description of the meeting, interrupting only to query me about Mrs. Kramer. "You say she seemed nervous when you talked to her?"

"She *was* nervous, and she kept looking over to her husband for approval, as if she wanted to make sure she had given the right answers. Then they both changed their story in midstream about the last time they saw Mack and what he was wearing."

"Memory is notoriously inaccurate, especially after ten years," Jackie said slowly. "If I were you, I'd try to see Mrs. Kramer when her husband isn't around."

I made a mental note, then told her about my second conversation with Detective Barrott. Jackie hadn't realized that my studio is right next door to the building where Leesey Andrews lived. I told her about Detective Barrott meeting me there and that I felt there was something behind his wanting to stay in touch with me.

The expression in Jackie's eyes changed. I could read deepening concern in them. "I'll bet Detective Barrott wishes he had taken that note from you," she said vehemently. "I'll bet he'll get around to asking you for it soon."

"What are you getting at?" I asked.

"Carolyn, have you forgotten about the missing persons cases that were in the news just before Mack disappeared? That a bunch of Columbia guys, including Mack, were in the bar in SoHo where that first girl who disappeared had been hanging out? That was just a few weeks before Mack himself vanished."

"I hadn't thought of that," I admitted. "But why would that be relevant now?"

"Because you've handed the DA's office a possible suspect. Mack doesn't want you to find him, which, as I just suggested, could mean that he may be in some kind of trouble. Or it could mean that he *is* the trouble. He called your mother on Sunday and left the note in the collection basket later in the morning. Suppose Mack decided to check out where you now live, maybe to warn you away again. Your address at the apartment is listed in the phone book. Suppose he came by early Tuesday morning and spotted Leesey Andrews on the street walking home. I'll bet that's the way your Detective Barrott is adding things up."

"Jackie, are you crazy?" I began, but the words died in my throat. I was desperately afraid that she had analyzed Barrott's thinking process correctly. In his eyes, and because of me, my missing brother may have become a person of interest in the disappearance of Leesey Andrews, and perhaps of the young woman who vanished ten years ago, only weeks before he did.

Then, in utter dismay, I remembered that not one but three young women had vanished in these ten years before Leesey Andrews failed to return home.

In his wildest dreams, could Barrott possibly be beginning to believe that if Mack is alive he may have become a serial killer?

21

Sometimes the best thing about the moment he took a life was when the scent of fear reached his nostrils. They knew they were going to die, and at that point they stammered out a few words.

One of them asked, "Why?"

Another whispered a prayer, "Lord, receive . . . me . . ."

A third tried to break away, then spat an obscenity at him.

The youngest pleaded with him, "Don't, please don't."

He ached to go back to the Woodshed tonight, to listen to everything they were saying there. It was amusing to watch the plainclothes detectives at work. He could spot them a mile away. Their eyelids always had a hooded look because they were trying to conceal the fact that their bright little eyes were darting around the room.

An hour ago in Brooklyn, he had phoned the number they had on the poster, using one of his unsubscribed phones and prepaid phone cards. He'd made his voice sound excited, and said, "I just left Peter Luger's Restaurant. I saw that girl, Leesey Andrews, having dinner with some guy there." Then he turned off both that cell phone and Leesey's cell phone and hurried into the subway.

He could just imagine the way the cops must have swarmed over there, disrupting the place, annoying the diners, querying the waiters . . . By now they've probably decided that it was just another nutcase calling. I wonder how many crazies have called in to say they've seen Leesey, he wondered. But only one person saw her. *Me!*

But the family wouldn't be sure that it was a crank call. The family never *is* sure until they see a body. Don't count on it, family. If you don't believe me, have a chat with the relatives of the other girls.

He turned on the television to catch the eleven o'clock news. As he'd expected, the breaking news story was being reported opposite the Woodshed. There were crowds of people lined up trying to get into the place. A reporter was saying, "The tip that police received that Leesey Andrews was seen having dinner at a restaurant in Brooklyn has been largely discounted."

He was disappointed that the police had not released the information about the tracking of her cell phone in Brooklyn. But later on, I'll take Leesey's cell phone to Thompson Street for a quick visit, he thought. That will really drive them crazy—thinking she might be being held so near her home.

He almost laughed out loud.

22

It was Friday afternoon before I heard from Nick DeMarco. As luck would have it, when my cell phone rang, I was standing just inside the open door of the Sutton Place apartment, saying good-bye to Mom.

Elliott had just arrived to take her to Teterboro Airport, where she would join the Clarences to fly on their private jet to Corfu, in the Greek islands, where their yacht was anchored.

Elliott's chauffeur had carried the luggage down the hall and was pressing for the elevator. In another thirty seconds they all would have been gone, but I flipped open the phone automatically. I could have bitten off my tongue after I said, "Hello, Nick." Instantly alert, there was no question that both Mom and Elliott guessed it was Nick DeMarco. The statement he gave at a news conference, expressing his deep regret that Leesey Andrews may have met a predator at his club, had been broadcast and rebroadcast in the forty-eight hours since he had made it late Wednesday afternoon.

"Carolyn, I'm sorry I didn't get back to you sooner," Nick said. "As you can understand it's been pretty hectic these past few days. What's your schedule? Are you free to get together this evening or sometime tomorrow?"

I turned slightly away, taking a step back toward the living room. "This evening would be fine," I said quickly, aware that Elliott and Mom were staring at me. They reminded me of the game "Statues" that we used to play when I was about ten years old. Whoever was the leader swung the others around by the hand, and after she let go, you had to stay frozen in exactly the position you were in when you stopped spinning. The one who could last the longest without twitching a muscle was the winner.

Mom's body was rigid, her hand on the doorknob, and Elliott, holding Mom's carry-on bag, was standing statuelike in the vestibule. I wanted to tell Nick I'd call him back but was afraid to let the chance pass to confirm a meeting with him.

"Where will you be?"

"The Sutton Place apartment," I told him.

"I'll pick you up there. Seven o'clock, okay?"

"Fine." We both clicked off.

Mom had a worried frown on her face. "Was that

Nick DeMarco? Why on *earth* is he calling you, Carolyn?"

"I called *him* on Wednesday."

"Why would you do that?" Elliott asked, his tone puzzled. "You haven't had any contact with him since your father's funeral, have you?"

I combined a couple of truths and twisted them into an untruth. "I had a serious crush on Nick years ago. Maybe it's still lingering a bit. When I saw him on TV, I thought it wouldn't hurt to phone him and express my concern that Leesey Andrews disappeared after leaving his club. Result—he phoned!"

I saw an expression of cautious relief on my mother's face. "I always enjoyed Nick when he came to dinner with Mack. And I know he's been *very* successful."

"He certainly seems to have done very well these past ten years," Elliott agreed. "As I remember, his parents had some sort of storefront restaurant. But I must say I don't envy him the publicity he's getting now." Then he touched my mother's arm. "Olivia, we must get started. As it is, we're going to hit all the rush hour traffic, and the Lincoln Tunnel will be a nightmare."

My mother is famous for leaving at the last minute and counting on all the traffic lights to be turning green to make smooth her path. At this moment, I found myself comparing Elliott's gentle reminder with my father's reaction, if he had been here.

"Liv, for God's sake, we're getting a free ride to Greece. Let's not miss it!" would have been his way of hurrying her out.

With a final flurry of farewell kisses and admonitions, Mom got into the elevator with Elliott, her final words, "Call me if you need anything, Carolyn," muffled by the closing door.

I'll admit that I was flustered about this date with Nick, if you can call it a date. I put on fresh makeup, brushed my hair, decided to leave it loose, then, at the last minute, I put on a new Escada suit my mother had insisted on buying for me. Both jacket and slacks were a pale shade of green, and I knew they brought out the red tones in my brown hair.

Why bother? Because after ten years I was still embarrassed by Mack's candid statement that it was obvious I had a crush on Nick. I'm not dolling up for him, I told myself; I'm satisfying myself that I don't look like a gawky adolescent fainting over her idol. But when the concierge phoned from the lobby to tell me that Mr. DeMarco was here, I have to admit that for a nanosecond, I did feel like the sixteen-year-old who had been foolish enough to wear her heart on her sleeve.

Then, when I opened the door for him, what struck me immediately was that the boyish, seemingly carefree Nick I remembered was gone.

When I saw him on television, I had noticed that his

jawline had tightened and that at thirty-two, he already had strands of gray in his dark hair. But face-to-face, there was more. His dark brown eyes had always had a teasing, flirtatious look, but now the expression in them was serious. Even so, his smile, when he took my hand, was the one I remembered, and he seemed genuinely pleased to see me. He gave me a social peck on the cheek but spared me the "little Carolyn, all grown up" routine.

Instead he said, "Carolyn MacKenzie, Juris Doctoris! I heard somewhere that you had passed the bar and were clerking for a judge. I meant to call to congratulate you but never quite got around to it. I'm sorry."

"The road to hell is paved with good intentions," I said matter-of-factly. "Or at least that's what Sister Patricia told us in the fifth grade."

"And Brother Murphy told us in the seventh grade, 'Never put off till tomorrow what you can do today.'"

I laughed. "They were both right," I said. "But clearly you didn't listen." We grinned at each other. It was the kind of banter we used to exchange at the dinner table. I picked up my shoulder bag. "I'm all set," I told him.

"Fine. My car is downstairs." He glanced around. From where he was standing, he could see a corner of the dining room. "I have such good memories of coming here," he said. "When I went home for an occasional weekend, my mother wanted to know every detail of what we ate, and I had to describe the color of the tablecloth and napkins, and what kind of flowers your mother used in the centerpiece."

"I assure you we didn't do that every night," I said, as I fished my key from my bag. "Mom enjoyed fussing when you and Mack were coming home."

"Mack didn't mind showing off this place to his friends," Nick commented. "But I reciprocated, you know? I took him to our place in Astoria for the best pizza and pasta in the universe."

Was there an edge in Nick DeMarco's voice, as though he still resented the comparison? Maybe not, but I wasn't sure. In the elevator on the way down, he noticed that Manuel, the elevator operator, was wearing a class ring and asked about it. Manuel proudly told him that he had just graduated from John Jay College and was scheduled to start at the police academy. "I can't wait to become a cop," he said.

Of course I haven't really lived at home since I started Duke Law, but even so, Manuel and I often exchanged pleasantries. He's worked in our building for at least three years, yet in seconds Nick knew more about him than I ever did. I realized that Nick had the ability to make people open up to him immediately and that that might be why he is so successful in the restaurant business.

Nick's black Mercedes-Benz was parked in front of the building. I was surprised to see a chauffeur jump out to hold the back door open for us. I don't know why, but I never would have visualized Nick as having a chauffeur. This one was a big, heavyset man in his midfifties with the face of a retired prizefighter. His broad nose seemed to have lost most of the cartilage, and there was a scar along his jaw.

Nick introduced us. "Benny worked for Pop for twenty years. Then when Pop retired five years ago, I inherited him. My very good fortune. Benny, this is Carolyn MacKenzie."

Despite his brief smile and pleasant "Nice to meet you, Ms. MacKenzie," I had the feeling that Benny was giving me a very thorough once-over. He obviously knew where we were going, because he set off without waiting for instructions.

As we pulled away from the curb, Nick turned to me. "Carolyn, I'm assuming and hoping that you're free for dinner."

And I was assuming and hoping you'd want to have dinner, I thought. "That would be nice," I told him.

"There's a place in Nyack, just a few miles from the Tappan Zee Bridge. The food is excellent, and it's quiet. At this point, I'm pretty anxious to stay away from the media." He rested his head back on the leather seat.

On the way up the FDR Drive, he told me that he

had been asked to stop at the District Attorney's office again yesterday afternoon, to answer more questions about the conversation he had with Leesey Andrews the night she disappeared. "It was unfortunate that I stayed in the loft apartment that night," he said frankly. "There's only my word that I didn't invite her to stop by on her way home, and I think for lack of anyone else to focus on, I'm in the spotlight."

You're not the *only* one, I thought, but decided not to share with him my certainty that, thanks to me, Detective Barrott also had his sights on Mack as a suspect. I noticed that Nick did not mention Mack's name in the car, and I wondered about that. From the message I gave to his secretary, that I wanted to see him because I had heard from Mack again, he certainly knew we were going to talk about my brother. I wondered if perhaps he didn't want Benny to hear that conversation. My suspicion was that Benny was gifted with very keen hearing.

The restaurant Nick had chosen, La Provence, was everything he had promised. It had been a private home and retained that atmosphere. The tables were far apart. The centerpieces on them were made up of a candle surrounded by budding flowers, and each table had different flowers. Paintings that I guessed to be of the French countryside were hung on the paneled walls. It was obvious from the warm greeting the maître d' extended to Nick that he was a regular customer. We followed him to a corner table with a window that looked over the Hudson. The night was clear, and the view of the Tappan Zee Bridge spanning the river was splendid.

I thought of my dream of trying to follow Mack as he crossed a bridge. Then I tuned it out.

Over a glass of wine, I told Nick about Mack's usual Mother's Day call and then about the note he left in the collection basket. "The fact that he wrote that I must not try to find him makes me feel that something is very wrong in his life," I said. "I'm just afraid that Mack needs help."

"I'm not so sure about that, Carolyn," Nick said, quietly. "I was witness to how close he was to you and your parents. He would know that if he needed anything in a financial way, your mother would provide it on the spot. If he's sick, I would think he'd want to be around you and your mother. I never saw Mack touch drugs, but I don't know, maybe he had started and knew it would crush your father if he found out about it. Don't think I haven't tried all these years to figure out what would make him vanish."

I guess it's what I expected to hear, but even so, I felt as if every door I tried to open was being slammed in my face. When I didn't respond, Nick waited me out for a minute, then said, "Carolyn, you said yourself that

Mack sounded pretty chipper when he called on Mother's Day. Why don't you look at that message not as a plea for help, but as a firm request, or even a command? You can certainly read it that way, too. 'Tell Carolyn she must not look for me!'"

He was right. I know he was. But in a much bigger sense he was wrong. Every instinct in my body told me that.

"Let it go, Carolyn," Nick said. Now his voice was gentle. "When and if Mack decides to surface, I am going to give him one swift kick for the way he's treated you and your mother. Now, tell me about yourself. I guess your clerkship with the judge expires soon. Isn't that the way it works?"

"I'll tell you about that," I said. "But just a little more about Mack first. I went to see the Kramers Wednesday morning."

"The Kramers? You mean the superintendents of the building where Mack and I lived?"

"Yes. And Nick, you may not believe me, but Mrs. Kramer was nervous. She kept looking over at her husband to make sure whatever she told me was all right. I swear to you, she was afraid of making some kind of mistake. What did you think of them when you lived there?"

"To be honest, it's not what I thought *of* them, it's more that I didn't think *about* them. Mrs. Kramer cleaned the apartment, thanks to your mother's generosity, and did our wash once a week. Otherwise it would probably have been a pigsty. She was a good cleaning woman but downright nosey. I know Bruce Galbraith was furious at her. He came in one day and she was reading the mail on his desk. If she was reading his, I figured she was probably reading mine, too."

"Did you challenge her on it?"

He smiled. "No. I did something dopey. I typed a letter, signed her name to it, and stacked it with my mail so that she would find it. It read something like this: 'Darling, it is such a pleasure for me to wash your clothes and make your bed. I feel like a young girl when I look at you. Sometime will you take me dancing? All my love, Lilly Kramer.'"

"You *didn't!*" I exclaimed.

The boyish twinkle I remembered appeared in Nick's eyes for a brief moment. "When I thought it over, I threw it out before she could see it. Sometimes I wish I hadn't."

"Do you think Mack might have had a problem with her going through his mail?"

"He didn't say it, but I have a feeling he was upset about her, too. But he never said why, then he was gone."

"Do you mean it was just before he disappeared?"

Nick's expression changed. "Carolyn, surely you

don't think the Kramers had anything to do with Mack's disappearance?"

"Nick, just talking about them to you brought up something that obviously never came up at the time of the investigation, that Bruce caught her snooping, and that Mack may have been upset with her, too. Give me your assessment of Gus Kramer."

"Good superintendent. Nasty temper. I heard him yelling at Mrs. Kramer a couple of times."

"Nasty temper?" I asked, raising my eyebrows, then said, "You don't have to answer, but think about it. Suppose he and Mack had some kind of confrontation."

The waiter then came to take our orders, and Nick never did answer my question. After that we kept the conversation to catching up on the past ten years. I told him that I was going to apply for a job in the District Attorney's office.

"'Going to apply'?" Now it was Nick who raised his eyebrows. "As Brother Murphy said, 'Never put off till tomorrow what you can do today.' Any special reason for waiting?"

I answered vaguely about taking a little time to find an apartment. After dinner, Nick opened his BlackBerry discreetly and checked it for messages. I asked him to see if there was any update about Leesey Andrews.

"Good idea." He pushed a button, scanned the news briefs, then turned off the BlackBerry. "'Hope is fading that she'll be found alive,'" he said soberly. "I wouldn't be surprised if I'm asked to drop in to the DA's office again tomorrow."

And I may get a call from Barrott, I thought. We finished our coffee, and Nick signaled to the waiter for a check.

It was only later, when he was dropping me at the door of Sutton Place, that he brought up the subject of Mack again. "I can read you, Carolyn. You're going to keep trying to find Mack, aren't you?"

"Yes."

"Who else are you going to talk to?"

"I have a call in to Bruce Galbraith."

"You won't get much help or sympathy from him," he said wryly.

"Why not?"

"Do you remember Barbara Hanover, the girl who came with Mack and me to dinner at your house?"

And how, I thought. "Yes, I remember her," I said, but then I couldn't help adding, "I also remember that you had a big crush on her."

Nick shrugged. "Ten years ago I had a crush on someone different every week. Anyhow, it wouldn't have done me any good. If she cared about anyone, my guess is that it was Mack."

"Mack?" Could I have been so focused on Nick that I didn't notice?

"Couldn't you tell? But Barbara was looking for a ticket to medical school. Her mother had a catastrophic illness that ate up all the money that had been earmarked for Barbara's education. That is why she married Bruce Galbraith. They eloped that summer, remember?"

"That's something else that never came out during the investigation," I said slowly. "Was Bruce jealous of Mack?"

Nick shrugged. "You never knew what Bruce was thinking. But what's the difference? You talked to Mack less than a week ago. You certainly don't think Bruce sent him into hiding, do you?"

I felt like a fool. "Of course not," I said. "I really don't know anything about Bruce at all. He never came here with you and Mack."

"He's a loner. That last year at Columbia, even the nights he'd hit the clubs in the Village and SoHo with a crowd of us, he always seemed to be by himself. We called him 'the Lone Stranger.'"

I searched Nick's face, eager for more detail. "After Mack disappeared, when the investigation started, did the police question Bruce at all? The only thing I found about him in the file was his statement about the last time he saw Mack in the apartment."

"I don't think they did. Why would they? He and Mack never hung out together."

"I was just reminded by an old friend that a week or so before he disappeared, Mack and some other guys from Columbia were in a club the same night as the first girl who went missing. Do you remember if Bruce was there?"

Nick looked pensive. "Yes, he was. I remember because the club had recently opened, and we decided to check it out. But it seems to me that he left early. He certainly was never the life of the party. Anyhow, it's getting late, Carolyn. I've enjoyed it a lot. Thank you for coming."

He gave me a quick peck on my cheek, and opened the door to the lobby for me. There was no mention of getting together again. I walked through the lobby to the elevator then glanced back.

Nick was already in the car, and Benny was standing on the sidewalk, holding a cell phone to his ear, his expression unreadable. For some reason there was something sinister about the way Benny smiled as he snapped the cell phone closed, got back in the car, and drove away.

23

Every Saturday morning, Howard Altman took his boss Derek Olsen out for brunch. They met at exactly ten o'clock in the Lamplighter Diner, near one of the apartment buildings Olsen owned on Amsterdam Avenue.

In the decade during which he had been working for the increasingly testy Olsen, Altman had become very close to the elderly widower, a relationship he carefully nurtured. Lately the eighty-three-year-old Olsen made no bones about the fact that he was becoming more and more disgruntled with the nephew who was his only close relative. "Do you think Steve gives a damn whether I live or die, Howie," he asked rhetorically, as he wiped the last of the egg yolk from his plate with a piece of toast. "He should call me more often."

"I'm sure Steve gives more than a damn, Derek," Howard said lightly. "I certainly give a damn about you, but I still can't persuade you not to order two fried eggs, bacon, and sausage when we get together on Saturdays."

Olsen's eyes softened. "You're a good friend, Howie. It was my lucky day when you came to work for me. You're a good-looking guy. You dress nice. You handle yourself well. I can play bridge with my friends and play golf and know you're out there doing a good job for me. So what's going on in the buildings? Everything up to snuff?"

"I would say so. We've got a couple of kids in 825 behind in their rent, but I stopped in to see them and reminded them that your list of favorite charities doesn't have their names on it."

Olsen chuckled. "I'd have put it a little more crudely. Keep an eye on them." He tapped his cup on the saucer, signaling to the waitress that he wanted more coffee. "Anything else?"

"Something that really surprised me. Gus Kramer phoned me yesterday and gave me two weeks' notice."

"What?" The genial expression vanished from Derek Olsen's face. "I don't want him to go," he said flatly. "He's the best super I ever had, and Lil is like a mother hen to the students. The parents like her, too. They feel good about her. Why do they want to leave?"

"Gus said they're ready to retire."

"They weren't ready last month when I dropped in over there. Howie, I've got to tell you something. There are times when you push to cut corners when it don't make sense. You think you're doing me a favor by trying to kick them out of a big apartment so that you can get good rent for it. I know all about that, but for what I pay them, letting them have more space is a bargain. Sometimes you overstep yourself. This is one of them. Make nice with them. Give them a raise, but make *sure* they stay! And now that we're on the subject, when you deal with them and with the other supers, keep something in mind. You represent me, but you're *not* me. Clear? Very clear?"

"Of course." Howard Altman's vocal cords started to form the name "Derek." Instead he said humbly, "Very clear, Mr. Olsen."

"I'm glad to hear it. Anything else?"

Howard had planned to tell his boss that Carolyn MacKenzie had been in the Kramers' apartment on Wednesday asking questions about her missing brother, but he realized it would be a mistake. In his present mood, Olsen would decide that he should have been told at once, that Howie didn't understand what was important. Besides that, over the past decade whenever Olsen talked about the MacKenzie disappearance, he went ballistic—red in the face, his voice raised sharply.

"That kid takes off in May," he would rant. "The apartments were all rented for the next September. Half of them were canceled. The last place MacKenzie was seen was in my building, so his parents thought there might have been some nut hanging out in the stair-well . . ."

Howard realized that his boss was studying him intently.

"Howie, you look like you have more on your mind. Do you?"

"Nothing at all, Mr. Olsen," Howard said firmly.

"Good. You been reading about that missing girl? What's her name, Leesey Andrews?"

"Yes, I have. It's very sad. I was watching the news before I left this morning. I don't think they expect to find her alive."

"These young women should stay out of these clubs. In my day, they sat home with their mothers."

Howard reached for the check as the waitress placed it beside Olsen. It was a ritual they went through every week. Ninety percent of the time Olsen let him pick it up. When he was annoyed, he did not.

Olsen grabbed the check. "I don't want the Kramers to leave, Howie, understand? Remember last year you stepped on the toes of the super on Ninety-eighth Street? His replacement stinks. If the Kramers leave, maybe you should look for another job. I hear my nephew is out of work again. He's not stupid, in fact, he's pretty damned smart. Maybe if he had your cushy apartment and salary, he'd pay a little more attention to me."

"I hear you, Mr. Olsen." Howard Altman was furious at his employer, but much more so at himself. He had played it all wrong. The Kramers had been as nervous as cats on a hot tin roof when Carolyn MacKenzie showed up the other day. Why? He should have been smart enough to find out what was upsetting them. He made a silent vow to get what it was out of them before it was too late. I want my job, he thought. I *need* it.

Neither the Kramers nor Carolyn MacKenzie were going to cause him to lose it!

24

"Hope is fading that Leesey Andrews will be found alive," Dr. David Andrews read as the latest news report scrolled across the bottom of the television screen. He was sitting on the leather couch in the den of his son's Park Avenue apartment. Unable to sleep, he had gone in there sometime in the predawn hours. He knew he must have dozed off at some point, because shortly after he heard Gregg leave to make his rounds at the hospital, he became aware that a blanket was tucked around him neatly.

Now, three hours later, he was still there, alternately dozing and watching television. I should get showered and dressed, he thought, but he was too weary to move. The clock on the mantelpiece showed that it was quarter of ten. I'm still in pajamas, he thought—that's ridiculous. He looked up at the television screen. What had he just seen on it? I must have read it because the setting is on mute, he realized.

He groped for the remote control, which he remembered placing on the cushion so that he could adjust the volume in an instant if something came on about Leesey.

It's Sunday, he thought. It's been more than five days now. What do I feel right at this minute? Nothing. Not fear, nor grief, nor that murderous anger at whoever has taken her. Right now, at this minute, I just feel numb.

It won't last.

Hope is fading, he thought. Is that what I just read in the news tape on the screen? Or did I make it up? Why does that sound familiar?

A mental image of his mother, playing the piano at family parties and everyone joining in the singing, burst into his mind. They loved the old vaudeville songs, he thought. One of them began with the words, "Darling, I am growing old."

Leesey won't ever grow old. He closed his eyes against the tidal wave of pain. The emotional numbness was gone.

Darling, I am growing old . . . Silver threads among the gold . . . Shine upon my brow today . . . Life is fading fast away . . .

Hope is fading . . . Those were the words that made me think of that song.

"Dad, are you okay?"

David Andrews looked up and saw the concerned face of his son. "I didn't hear you come in, Gregg." He rubbed his eyes. "Did you know that life is fading fast away? Leesey's life." He stopped, tried again. "No, I'm wrong. It's hope that's fading that she'll be found alive."

Gregg Andrews crossed the room, sat next to his father, and put an arm around his shoulders. "My hope isn't fading, Dad."

"Isn't it? Then you believe in miracles. Why not? I used to believe in them myself, too."

"Keep believing in them, Dad."

"Remember how your mother seemed to be doing so well, then overnight the picture changed and we lost her? That's when I stopped believing in miracles."

David shook his head, trying to clear it, and patted his son's knee. "You'd better take good care of yourself for me. You're all I have." He stood up. "I feel as if I'm talking in my sleep. I'll be okay, Gregg. I'm going to shower and dress and go home. I'm absolutely useless here. With your schedule at the hospital, you need downtime when you're here, and at home I'll be better able to keep a grip on myself, I hope. I'll try to get back into some kind of routine while we're waiting to see what develops."

Gregg Andrews looked at his father with the clinical eye of a doctor, observing the deep circles under his eyes, the bleak expression in them, the way in these four days his trim frame suddenly seemed extremely thin. He hasn't eaten a thing since he heard about Leesey, Gregg thought. In one way he wanted to object to his father leaving, in another he sensed that he'd be better off in Greenwich where he volunteered at the urgent care center three days a week and where he was among close friends.

"I understand, Dad," he said. "And maybe you *think* you've given up hope, but I don't believe you."

"Believe me," his father said simply.

Forty minutes later, showered and dressed, he was ready to leave. At the door of the apartment, the two men embraced. "Dad, you know you'll have a dozen people wanting to have dinner with you. Go out to the club with some of them tonight," Gregg urged.

"If not tonight, I will very soon."

After his father left, the apartment felt empty. We've been trying to keep up appearances for each other's sake, Gregg thought. I'd better take my own advice and stay busy. I'll take a long run in Central Park, then try to nap. He had already planned to go back and forth between the Woodshed and Leesey's apartment tonight at three A.M., the same time she had started to make that walk. Maybe I'll find someone to talk to, someone the cops have missed, he thought. Detective Barrott had told him that plainclothes detectives were doing that every night, but the need to help in the search had been building to a fever pitch in Gregg.

While Dad was here I couldn't do it, he thought. He'd have insisted on coming with me.

The day had started overcast, but when he went outside at eleven, the sun had broken through the clouds, and Gregg felt his own spirits lift a bit. Surely on a beautiful spring morning like this, his kid sister, funny, pretty Leesey, could not be gone. But if she wasn't dead, then where was she? Let it be an emotional breakdown or a spell of amnesia, Gregg prayed, as he covered the three blocks to the park with long strides. There, he decided to head north and swing back around the Central Park Boathouse.

Right foot, left foot, right foot, left foot. Let . . . us . . . find . . . her . . . Let . . . us . . . find . . . her . . . He prayed in cadence to the rhythm of the run.

An hour later, tired but somewhat less tense, he was walking back to his apartment when his cell phone rang. With conflicting emotions of hope and dread, he grabbed it from the pocket of his jacket, flipped it open, and saw that the call was from his father.

The words, "Hello, Dad," died on his lips as he listened despairingly. He heard uncontrollable sobbing. Oh, God, he thought, they've found her body.

"Leesey," David Andrews managed to say. "Gregg, it's Leesey. She *phoned*!"

"She *what*?"

"She left a message on the answering machine less than ten minutes ago. I just walked in. I can't believe it. I just missed her call."

Again, Gregg Andrews heard his father's sobs.

"Dad, what did she *say*? Where is she?"

The sobs suddenly stopped. "She said . . . that . . . she loves me but has to be by herself. She asked me to forgive her. She said . . . she said . . . that she'll call again on Mother's Day."

25

I spent Saturday morning in Mack's room in the Sutton Place apartment. I won't say it had a Sunset Boulevard quality to it, but I do know that it no longer held any sense of his presence for me. After Mack had been missing a few days, Dad ransacked his desk, hoping to find some clue as to where he might have gone, but the only things he found were the usual trappings of a college student—notes for exams, postcards, blank personal stationery. One file contained a copy of Mack's application to Duke Law School and his letter of acceptance from them. On it he had scrawled an exuberant "YES!"

But Dad didn't find what he was looking for—Mack's daily calendar—which might have given us a clue to any appointments he had made prior to his disappearance. Years ago, Mom had our housekeeper take down the banners Mack had tacked on the wall and the corkboard covered with group pictures of him and his friends. Everyone in those pictures had been questioned by the cops, and later by the private investigator.

The brown and beige coverlet, matching pillows, and contrasting window treatments were the same, as was the cocoa brown carpet.

There was still a picture of the four of us on top of the dresser. I found myself studying it and wondering if by now Mack had any strands of gray on his temples. It was hard to imagine. He'd had such a boyish face ten years ago. Now he was not only long past being a college student, was probably a suspect in absentia in more than one kidnapping and/or murder case.

There were two closets in the room. I opened the doors of both of them and detected that faint musty odor that grows when no fresh air circulates into a relatively small space.

I took a stack of jackets and slacks from the first closet and laid them on the bed. They all had plastic cleaners' bags over them, and I remembered that when Mack had been missing about a year, Mom had everything he owned cleaned and put back in the closet. I remember at the time Dad had said, "Livvy, let's give them all away. If Mack comes back I'll take him shopping. Let somebody else get some use out of all this stuff."

His suggestion had been rejected.

There was nothing to be found in this sterile clothing. I didn't want to just dump everything in large trash bags. I knew that would make it easier to carry them to the donation center, but it would be a shame if anything got wrinkled. Then I remembered that a couple of Mack's large suitcases, the ones he'd used on our last family trip, were in the storeroom behind the kitchen.

I found them there and brought them back to his room, hauling them up on the bed. I opened the first one and as a matter of habit, ran my fingers through the pockets to see if there was anything in them. There wasn't. I filled the suitcase with neatly folded suits and jackets and slacks, lingering over the tuxedo Mack wore in our family photo that last Christmas.

The second suitcase was a size smaller. Again I ran my hand through the side pockets. This time I felt something I guessed to be a camera. But when I pulled it out, I was surprised to see that it was a tape recorder. I never remembered seeing Mack using one. There was a tape in it and I pushed the play button.

"What do you think, Ms. Klein? Do I sound like Laurence Olivier or Tom Hanks? I'm recording you, so be kind."

I heard a woman's laugh. "You sound like neither of them, but you sound good, Mack."

I was so shocked that I pushed the stop button as tears welled in my eyes. Mack. It was as though he were in the room bantering with me, his voice lively and animated.

These yearly Mother's Day calls and the ever-increasing resentment that was my reaction to them had made me forget the way Mack used to sound, funny and energetic.

I pushed the play button again.

"Okay, here I go, Ms. Klein," Mack was saying. "You said to select some passage from Shakespeare? How about this one?" Then he cleared his throat and began, "When, in disgrace with Fortune and men's eyes . . ."

His tone had changed drastically, had suddenly become ragged and somber.

". . . I all alone beweep my outcast state, and trouble deaf heaven with my bootless cries—"

That was all that was on the tape. I rewound it and played it again. What did it mean? Was it a random selection or had it been chosen deliberately because it suited Mack's frame of mind? When was it made? How long before he disappeared had it been made?

Esther Klein's name was in the file of people the cops spoke to about Mack, but obviously she had offered nothing of consequence. I vaguely remembered that Dad and Mom had been surprised that Mack had been taking private acting lessons with her on the side. I can understand why he didn't tell them. Dad was always afraid that Mack was becoming too interested in his theatre electives.

Then Esther Klein had been fatally mugged near her

apartment on Amsterdam Avenue, nearly a year after Mack went missing. The thought occurred to me that there might have been other tapes that he made while he studied with her. If so, what happened to them after her death?

I stood in Mack's room, holding the recorder, and realized it would be easy enough to find that out.

Esther Klein's son, Aaron, was a close associate of Uncle Elliott. I would call him.

I put the recorder in my shoulder bag and began packing Mack's clothes. When I was finished, the drawers in the dresser were empty, as were the closets. Mom had let Dad give Mack's heavy coats away one particularly cold winter, when the charities were pleading for them.

As I was about to close the second suitcase, I hesitated, then took out the formal black tie I had tied for Mack just before we posed for our Christmas picture that last year. I held it in my hands thinking back to how I had told him to lean down because I couldn't reach high enough to tie it tight.

As I wrapped it in tissue and put it in my shoulder bag to take back to Thompson Street with me, I remembered Mack's laughing response, "'Blest be the tie that binds.' Now, please don't make a mess of it, Carolyn."

26

He wondered if her father had heard the message yet. He could just imagine his reaction when he listened to it. His little girl was alive and didn't want to see him! She said she would call on Mother's Day! Only fifty-one weeks to wait!

Daddy must be twisting in the wind, he thought.

By now the cops undoubtedly had a wiretap on Dr. Andrews's phone in Greenwich. He could just imagine the frenzy they were in. Would they throw up their hands and decide that Leesey has a right to her privacy and drop the search for her? Maybe. It was just the kind of thing people did.

It would be safer for him if they did.

Would they tell the media she had phoned?

I like the headlines, he thought. And I like reading about Leesey Andrews. They've known since Tuesday that she's missing. She's been in all the headlines the last three days. But today the story about her was buried on page four, which was disappointing.

It had been the same thing with the other three girls—within two weeks the story was dead.

As dead as they were.

I'll play around with what to do to keep Leesey on everybody's mind, but for now, he thought, I'll have my fun moving her cell phone around. That must be driving them crazy. "Goosey, Goosey, Gander," he whispered. "Whither do you wander? Upstairs? Downstairs? In my lady's chamber?"

He laughed. All three places, he thought.

All three.

27

"Doctor, you're sure that it *is* your sister's voice on the answering machine?"

"*Absolutely* sure!" Unconsciously, Gregg kneaded his forehead with his thumb and forefinger. I never get headaches, he thought. I don't need one to start now. Three hours after his father called he was downtown in the detective squad section of the District Attorney's office. The message Leesey had left on the answering machine in his father's Greenwich, Connecticut, home had been taken from the wiretap and amplified. In the tech room, Detective Barrott had already played it several times for him and Larry Ahearn.

"I agree with Gregg," Ahearn told Barrott. "I've known Leesey since she was a little girl, and I would swear that's her voice. She sounds nervous and agitated, but of course she may have had some sort of breakdown or . . ." He looked at Gregg. "Or she was forced to leave that message."

"You mean by someone who abducted her?"

"Yes, Gregg, that's exactly what I mean."

"You've confirmed that that call was made from her cell phone?" Gregg asked, trying to keep his voice steady.

"Yes, it was," Ahearn said. "It was bounced from the tower at Madison and Fiftieth. That's why she may be being held somewhere in that area. On the other hand, if she did choose to disappear, I don't see how she can walk outside in that location even to buy groceries without worrying about being spotted. Her picture has been all over the newspapers, television, and the Internet."

"Unless she has some kind of disguise like a burka, that would hide everything except her eyes," Barrott pointed out. "But even that would draw attention in Manhattan." He began to rewind the tape of Leesey's call. "Our tech guys are working on the background sound. Let's concentrate on listening to that."

Larry Ahearn caught the bleak expression on Gregg's face. "I don't think we need to hear it again, Roy."

"What happens now?" Gregg asked him. "If you decide Leesey *did* leave voluntarily, do you give up looking for her?"

"No," Ahearn said emphatically. "Not for one minute. Knowing Leesey as well as I do, even if she disappeared on her own, something is terribly wrong. We're staying on this 24/7 until we find her."

"Thank God for that." There's something else I need to ask them, Gregg thought. Oh, I know. "How about the media? Are you going to tell them that she's contacted us?"

"We don't want anyone to know," Larry said, shaking his head. "That was the first thing I told your father when we spoke to him."

"You told me the same thing, but I thought you meant you wanted to be sure it wasn't a crank call, or someone just imitating Leesey's voice."

"Gregg, we don't want a *hint* of this to get out," Larry Ahearn said urgently. "Awful as this is, it's good to know that as of a few hours ago Leesey was alive."

"I guess I agree. But where *is* she if she's alive? What may be happening to her? The other young women who disappeared after being at one of those clubs in SoHo were never found."

"But neither did any of them call a member of the family, Gregg," Ahearn reminded him.

"Dr. Andrews, there's something else . . ." Barrott began.

"Make it Gregg, please." A hint of a smile crossed Gregg Andrews's lips. "After I got my M.D., if anyone called me at home and asked for Dr. Andrews, it took Leesey months before she didn't automatically hand the phone to my father."

Barrott smiled briefly. "That's the way it is in my

house. If my son gets great marks or some kind of achievement award, his sister thinks it was a mistake. All right, Gregg," he continued, "the last time you saw your sister was a week ago on Mother's Day. Was there anything unusual about that day?"

"That's what absolutely bewilders me," Gregg told him. "My mother's been dead only two years, so naturally it's a pretty low-key day for us. The three of us went to church together, visited her grave, then had dinner at the club. Leesey had planned to drive back to the city with me but at the last minute decided to stay overnight with Dad and take the train home in the morning."

"Before your mother died, was Mother's Day in any way symbolic for all of you, other than the usual sentiment that's attached to it?"

"No, not at all. We celebrated it together, but it wasn't a big deal. When my grandparents were alive, they were with us. There was nothing extraordinary at all about it." Gregg caught the way the two detectives glanced at each other and then the way Larry Ahearn nodded to Roy Barrott. "There's something you haven't told me," he said. "What is it?"

"Gregg, do you know Carolyn MacKenzie?" Ahearn asked.

Now his temples were beginning to pound. Gregg searched his memory, then shook his head. "I don't think so. Who is she?"

"She's a lawyer," Ahearn volunteered. "Twenty-six years old. Her studio is on Thompson Street in the building next door to where your sister lives."

"Does she know Leesey?" Gregg asked quickly. "Does she have any idea where she might be?"

"No. She doesn't know her, but maybe you remember a case ten years ago, when a college student walked out of his apartment and disappeared? His name was Charles MacKenzie Jr. Everyone called him Mack."

"I remember that case. They never found him, did they?"

"No," Ahearn said. "But he calls his mother every year on Mother's Day."

"*On Mother's Day!*" Gregg jumped up. "He's been gone ten years and calls his mother on Mother's Day. Are you suggesting that Leesey might be planning to follow a crazy pattern like that?"

"Gregg, we're not suggesting anything," Ahearn said, soothingly. "Leesey was eleven years old when Mack MacKenzie disappeared, so there's no reason to think that she might have known him. But we thought it's possible you or your father might know the family. My guess is that you travel in some of the same circles."

"Whatever that means." He looked perplexed. "Did Mack MacKenzie call his mother last Sunday?"

"Yes, he did." Ahearn decided not to immediately

share the fact that Mack had left a message in the collection basket. "We don't know what that guy is doing or why he had to go underground. It certainly isn't widespread knowledge that he still phones his family on that one day. It makes us wonder if at some point Leesey might have met him, maybe at one of those clubs in SoHo, and, if she decided to disappear on her own, as he seems to have done, whether she'll stay in touch the same way."

"What do you know about MacKenzie, Larry? I mean if he disappeared voluntarily, was he in some kind of trouble?" Gregg looked pointedly at Larry, searching for answers.

"We couldn't find anything that added up. He had everything going for him and just walked out of his life."

"The same thing could be said about Leesey," Gregg snapped. "Are you starting to think that if she's come across this guy, the next time we'll hear from her is Mother's Day next year?" He looked from one to the other of them. "Wait a minute, do you think that this Mack guy might be a weirdo and has something to do with Leesey's disappearance?"

Larry looked across the table at his college roommate. It's not just his father who aged this week, he thought. Gregg looks ten years older than he did when we played golf last month. "Gregg, we are exploring everyone and every situation that may give us a lead to follow. Most of them will be dead ends. Now do me a favor and take my advice. Go home, get a decent dinner, and go to bed early. Take some comfort in the fact that we know Leesey was alive this morning. You've got a lot of patients who depend on your skill to give them a new lease on life. You can't fail them, and you will if you don't eat and sleep properly."

Not unlike the advice I gave Dad, Gregg thought. I will go home. I will get a couple of hours' sleep and eat something. But tonight I'm going to walk back and forth between that SoHo club and Thompson Street. Leesey was alive this morning. But that doesn't mean that if she's with some kind of nut, she'll *stay* alive.

He pushed back his chair and stood up. "You're absolutely right, Larry," he said.

With a brief wave, he started to leave, but spun around when Ahearn's cell phone rang. Ahearn grabbed it from his pocket and raised it to his ear. "What's up?"

Gregg saw the angry frown before he heard Larry's muttered profanity. For the second time that day, he despairingly thought that Leesey's body had been found.

Ahearn looked at him. "Someone called the *New York Post* a few minutes ago and said that Leesey Andrews left a message for her father today and said she'd call again on Mother's Day. The *Post* wants confirmation." Spitting out the words, he shouted, "Absolutely no comment!" and slammed down the phone.

"Did Leesey make the call?" Gregg demanded.

"The reporter who took it couldn't be sure. Said it was a muffled whisper. There was no caller ID."

"That means that the call wasn't made from Leesey's phone," Gregg said. "She has caller ID."

"That's exactly what I mean. Gregg, I'm going to be brutally honest. Either Leesey had some kind of breakdown and wants publicity, or she's in the hands of a dangerous, game-playing nut."

"Who only calls home on Mother's Day," Roy Barrott said quietly.

"Or who has a loft apartment near the Woodshed and a longtime chauffeur who would do anything for him," Ahearn said bitterly.

28

Howard Altman gave careful thought about how he would approach the Kramers to persuade them to stay on as superintendents. Olsen is right, he admitted. The guy I got him to fire last year in the Ninety-eighth Street apartment house *was* saving us a lot of money. I just didn't get it. Olsen doesn't want to do major repairs there. The property next door is for sale, and when it goes, he's sure they'll make a big offer for his building, too. The old super was keeping things together with chewing gum and kite string. The new one has a list of all the repairs that are needed and keeps telling Olsen it's criminal negligence not to do them immediately.

I should have kept my mouth shut, he thought, but I never could see why the Kramers needed a three-bedroom apartment—the other two bedrooms are never used.

Every so often, when Howard stopped by the

Kramers', he asked for permission to use the bathroom. That gave him a chance to look into the spare bedrooms. Never once in the nearly ten years since he had started working for Derek Olsen had he noticed any change in the placement of the teddy bears on the pillows of the beds. He knew they never used those rooms, but he told himself that what he *should* have realized was that Lil Kramer took a certain lowbrow pride in her big apartment.

And I know all about lowbrow! he thought ruefully. When I was a kid and Pop bought his first brand-new car, the cheapest one on the lot, you would have thought he'd won the lottery. We had to show it off to all the relatives just because Pop hoped they'd be drooling with envy.

I should start a blog and write about my own messed-up family, Howard told himself. I can't let the Kramers retire. Maybe Olsen would get over it if I got some good new people in fast. On the other hand, it would be just like him to fire me and give my job to that sicko nephew of his. In thirty days, Olsen would probably be on his knees begging me to come back, but that's a chance I can't takc. So what approach do I take with the Kramers?

Howard Altman considered possible solutions over the weekend. Then, satisfied with the plan he had come up with, at quarter of ten on Monday morning he stepped into the West End Avenue building where the Kramers lived.

He had definitely decided that pleading with them to stay, offering them a raise, and assuring them that the large apartment would always be their home was exactly the wrong way to go. If Gus Kramer thought that by quitting he could get me fired, he'd do it even if he doesn't really want to retire now.

When he turned the key in the outside door and went into the lobby, he found Gus Kramer polishing the already gleaming brass mailboxes.

Gus looked up. "I guess I won't be doing this much longer," he said. "Hope the next guy you get is half as good as I've been for nearly twenty years."

"Gus, is Lil around?" Howard said, almost whispering. "I need to speak to both of you. I'm worried about you two."

Seeing the look of outright fear in Kramer's face, he knew he was on the right track.

"She's in the apartment sorting stuff out," Gus said. Without bothering to wipe the final cloud of polish from the mailboxes, he turned and walked across the lobby to his apartment. He unlocked the door, pushed it open, and walked in, leaving Howard to grab it before it slammed in his face.

"I'll get Lil," Gus said abruptly.

It was obvious to Howard that Kramer wanted a

chance to talk to his wife and possibly warn her before she saw him. She's in one of the two bedrooms down the hall, he thought. That's where she must be sorting things out. She's finally found a use for that extra space.

It was almost five minutes before the Kramers joined him in the living room. Lil Kramer was visibly agitated. She was rubbing her lips together in a compulsive manner, and when Howard extended his hand to her, she rubbed her own hand on her skirt before she reluctantly responded to the greeting.

As he had expected, her palm was wringing wet.

Do the one-two punch right now, Howard thought. Send them reeling. "I'm going to talk straight from the shoulder," he said. "I wasn't here when the MacKenzie kid disappeared, but I was here the other day when his sister showed up. Lil, you were as nervous then as you are now. It was clear to me as an observer that you were afraid to talk to her. That tells me that you know something about why or how that boy disappeared, or that maybe you had something to do with it."

He watched as Lil Kramer threw a terrified look at her husband and Gus Kramer's cheekbones darkened to an ugly purple-red shade. I'm right, he thought. They're scared to death. Emboldened, he added, "The sister isn't finished with you. Next time she might bring a private investigator or the cops with her. If you think you'll get away from her by rushing to Pennsylvania, you're both crazy. If you're gone when she comes back, she'll ask questions. She'll find out you quit abruptly. Lil, how many people have you told over the years that you don't intend to budge from New York until you're at least ninety?"

Now Lil Kramer was biting back tears.

Howard softened his tone. "Lil, Gus, think about it. If you leave now, Carolyn MacKenzie and the cops will be sure you have something to hide. I don't know what it is, but you're my friends, and I want to help you. Let me tell Mr. Olsen that you've reconsidered and don't want to leave. The next time Carolyn MacKenzie calls to make an appointment, let me know, and I'll be here. I'll tell her in no uncertain terms that the management doesn't welcome her bothering the employees. What's more, I'll remind her that there are stiff penalties for stalking."

He saw the relief on their faces and knew he had convinced them to stay. And I didn't have to give them a raise or promise to leave them in this apartment, he thought exultantly.

But as he accepted Lil's groveling gratitude and Gus's terse expression of thanks, he was burning to find out why they were so afraid, and what, if anything, they knew about the reason for Mack MacKenzie's disappearance ten years ago.

29

Sunday morning I went to the last Mass at St. Francis de Sales. I got there early, slipped into the last pew, and after that tried to study the faces of the arriving congregation. Needless to say, I didn't spot anyone who even vaguely resembled Mack. Uncle Dev always delivers a thoughtful homily, frequently laced with Irish humor. Today, I didn't hear a word of it.

When the Mass was over, I stopped in at the rectory for a quick cup of coffee. Smiling and waving me into his office, Devon said he was meeting friends in Westchester for a round of golf, but they could wait. He poured coffee into two thick white mugs and handed one to me as we sat down.

I hadn't yet told him that I had gone to see the Kramers, and when I did I was surprised to learn that he remembered them clearly. "After we knew that Mack was missing, I went over with your Dad to that apartment on West End," he said. "I remember the wife was all upset at the thought that something might have happened to Mack."

"Do you remember anything about Gus Kramer's reaction?" I asked.

When Uncle Dev gets a thoughtful frown on his face, his resemblance to my father is almost startling. Sometimes that gives me comfort. Other times it hurts. Today, for some reason, was one of the days it hurt.

"You know, Carolyn," he said, "that Kramer is an odd duck. I think he was more upset by the possibility of media attention than he was concerned about Mack."

Ten years later that was exactly my reaction to Kramer, but knowing Devon had to be on his way soon, I didn't take the time to talk that over with him. Instead, I took out the recorder I had found in Mack's suitcase and explained how I had discovered it. Then I played the tape for him. I watched my uncle's sad smile at the sound of Mack's voice speaking to the teacher, then his bewildered frown when Mack began to recite, "When, in disgrace with fortune and men's eyes, I all alone beweep my outcast state, and trouble deaf heaven with my bootless cries."

After I turned off the recorder, my uncle said, his voice husky, "I'm glad your mother wasn't around when you came across that tape, Carolyn. I don't think I'd ever play it for her."

"I don't intend to let her hear it. But, Devon, I'm trying to figure out its significance, if any. Did Mack ever talk to you about taking private lessons with a drama teacher at Columbia?"

"I remember that in an offhand way he did. You know when Mack was about thirteen and his voice was changing, he went through a period where it was really high-pitched. He got unmercifully teased about it at school."

"I don't remember Mack having a high-pitched voice," I protested, then paused to search my memory. When Mack was thirteen I was eight years old.

"Of course, his voice deepened, but Mack was a more sensitive kid than most people realized. He didn't show his feelings when he was hurt, but years later, he admitted to me how miserable he had been during that period." Uncle Dev tapped the side of his mug, remembering. "Maybe some residual of that pain got him involved in the voice lessons. On the other hand, Mack wanted to become a trial lawyer and a good one. He told me that a good trial lawyer must also be a good actor. Maybe that could account for both the lessons and the passage he recited on that tape."

Obviously, we could come to no conclusion. Whether Mack had chosen that dark passage because of his own state of mind, or was simply reciting a prepared text, could only be a guessing game. Nor could we possibly know why he either stopped recording, or erased the rest of the session with the drama teacher.

At 12:30, Uncle Devon gave me a warm hug and went off to his golf game. I went back to Sutton Place and was glad to go there because I no longer felt at home in my West Village apartment. The fact that I lived next door to where Leesey Andrews lived was terribly troubling to me. If it were not for that fact, I thought, I am sure that Detective Barrott would not be trying to connect Mack to her disappearance.

I wanted to talk to Aaron Klein, the son of Mack's drama teacher. It would be easy enough to contact him. Aaron had been working at Wallace and Madison for nearly twenty years and was now Uncle Elliott's chosen successor. I remembered that a year after Mack disappeared, his mother was the victim of a robbery and was murdered, and that Mom and Dad went with Uncle Elliott to visit him when he was sitting shiva.

The problem was I didn't want Uncle Elliott to be involved in our meeting. As far as Elliott was concerned, he believed that Mom and I were planning to accept Mack's request, which, in so many words, was "Leave me alone." If Elliott knew I was contacting Aaron Klein because of Mack, as sure as day follows night he would feel it his duty to discuss it with Mom.

That meant I had to make an appointment with Klein outside the office and ask him to keep whatever conversation we had confidential, then trust him not to go blabbing to Elliott.

I went back to Dad's office, flicked on the light, and went over Mack's file again. I knew Lucas Reeves, the private investigator, had interviewed Mack's drama teacher, as well as other members of the Columbia University faculty. I had read his comments the other day and knew they weren't helpful, but now I was looking specifically for what he had written about Esther Klein.

It was very short. "Ms. Klein expressed her sorrow and shock over Mack's disappearance. She was unaware of any specific problem he may have been having."

An innocuous statement, I thought, remembering the dictionary definition of the word "innocuous": "Pallid; uninspiring; without power to interest or excite."

The few words she and Mack had exchanged on the tape suggested they had had a warm relationship. Had Esther Klein been deliberately evasive when she was talking to Reeves? And if so, why?

It was a question that made me toss and turn in bed that night. Monday morning couldn't come fast enough for me. I took the chance that Aaron Klein was one of those executives who gets to his desk early, and at twenty of nine phoned Wallace and Madison and asked for him.

His secretary had the usual question: "What is this in

reference to?" and seemed miffed when I said it was personal, but when she gave Aaron Klein my name, he took my call immediately.

As briefly as I could, I explained to him that I did not want to upset Elliott or my mother by continuing to search for my brother, but that I had come across a tape of Mack and Aaron's mother, and could I possibly meet him outside the office to play it for him?

His response was warm and understanding. "Elliott told me that your brother phoned on Mother's Day last week and left a note saying that you were not to search for him."

"Exactly," I said. "Which is why I want to keep this between us. But the tape that I found may suggest that Mack was having a problem. I don't know how much your mother may have talked to you about him."

"She was very fond of Mack," Klein said swiftly. "I do understand why you don't want to involve Elliott and your mother. I've always been so sorry about your brother. Listen, I'm leaving early today. My boys are in a school play this evening and I don't intend to miss it by being caught in traffic. I have all the tapes my mother made with her private students in a box in the attic. I'm sure any she made with your brother are there. Would you want to drive up to my house at about five o'clock this evening? I'll give them all to you."

Of course I promptly agreed. I called down to the

garage and told the attendant I'd be picking up my mother's car. I knew it would be hurtful to hear Mack's voice over and over again, but at least if I could be reasonably sure that the tape I found in the suitcase was one of many in that vein, it would end the gnawing fear that he disappeared because he had a terrible problem he could not share with us.

Satisfied that I had made the connection, I made a fresh pot of coffee and turned on the morning news, then listened with a sinking heart to the latest report on the Leesey Andrews case. Someone had tipped a reporter at the *Post* that she had phoned her father Saturday and had promised to call again on Mother's Day.

ON MOTHER'S DAY!

My cell phone rang. Every instinct told me that it was Detective Barrott. I did not answer, and a moment later when I checked my messages, I heard his voice. "Ms. MacKenzie, I'd like to see you again as soon as possible. My number is . . ."

I disconnected, my heart racing. I had his number, and I had no intention of calling him back until after I saw Aaron Klein.

At five o'clock that evening, when I arrived at the Klein home in Darien, I walked into a firestorm. After I rang the bell, the door was opened by an attractive woman in her late thirties who introduced herself as Aaron's wife, Jenny. The strained expression on her face told me that something was terribly wrong.

She brought me into the den. Aaron Klein was on his knees on the rug, surrounded by overturned boxes. Stacks of tapes had been separated in individual piles. There must have been three hundred of them at least.

Aaron's face was deathly pale. When he saw me, he got up slowly. He looked past me to his wife. "Jenny, they are absolutely not here, not one of them."

"But it doesn't make sense, Aaron," she protested. "Why would—?"

He interrupted her and looked at me, his expression hostile. "I have never been satisfied that my mother was the victim of a random crime," he said flatly. "At the time, it didn't seem as if anything had been taken from her apartment, but that isn't true. There is not a single tape of your brother's lessons with her here, and I know there were at least twenty of them, and I know they were there after he disappeared. The only person who would want them would be your brother."

"I don't understand," I said, sinking into the nearest chair.

"I now believe my mother was killed because someone had to get something from her apartment. The person who killed her took her house key. At the time, I couldn't find anything missing. But there *was* something taken—the box that contained all the tapes she had made of your brother."

"But your mother was attacked nearly a year after Mack disappeared," I said. "Why would he want them? What use would they be to him?" Then, suddenly outraged, I demanded, "What are you insinuating?"

"I'm not insinuating," Aaron Klein snapped at me. "I am telling you that I now believe that your missing brother may have been responsible for my mother's death! There may have been something incriminating in those tapes." He pointed out the window. "There is a girl from Greenwich who has been missing all week. I don't know her, but if the newscast I heard coming up here in the car is accurate, she called her father and promised to call again next Mother's Day. Isn't *that* the day of choice for your brother to call? No wonder he warned you not to try to find him."

I stood up. "My brother is not a killer. He is not a predator. When the truth is known, Mack will not be responsible for whatever happened to your mother and Leesey Andrews."

I walked out, got into the car, and began to drive home. I guess I was in such a state of shock that I was on some kind of mental auto-pilot, because my next clear memory is of pulling up in front of our building on Sutton Place—and seeing Detective Barrott waiting for me in the lobby.

30

"Oh, come on, Poppa. You're not really mad at me. You know I love you." Steve Hockney's tone was wheedling as he sat across the table from his elderly uncle, Derek Olsen. He had collected Olsen at his apartment and taken him by cab to Shun Lee West on Sixty-fifth Street for dinner. "We're having the best Chinese food in New York. So we're celebrating your birthday a few weeks late. Maybe we'll celebrate it all year."

Steve saw that he was getting the reaction he wanted. The anger was disappearing from his uncle's eyes and an unwilling smile was hovering around his lips. I've got to be more careful, Hockney warned himself. Forgetting his birthday was the stupidest thing I've done in a long time.

"You're lucky I don't throw you out of your apartment and make you support yourself for a change," Olsen muttered, but without rancor. It always surprised him, the swift rush of emotion he felt when he was with his dead sister's handsome son. It's because he looks so much like Irma, Olsen reminded himself—the same dark hair and big brown eyes, the same wonderful smile. Flesh of my flesh, he thought, as he took a bite of steamed dumplings Steve had ordered for him. It was delicious. "These are good," he said. "You take me to nice places all the time. I must be giving you too much money."

"No you're not, Poppa. I've been doing a lot of gigs downtown. My big break is just around the corner. You're going to be so proud of me. Think about it. My band is going to be the next Rolling Stones."

"I've been hearing that since you were twenty. How old are you now? Forty-two?"

Hockney smiled. "Thirty-six and you know it."

Olsen laughed. "I know I know it. But listen to me: I still think you should take over running the apartments. Howie gets on my nerves sometimes. He irritates people. I would have fired him today, except that the Kramers changed their minds about leaving, thank God."

"The Kramers? They'll never leave New York! Their daughter made them buy that place in Pennsylvania, and I'll tell you why. She doesn't want her parents to be superintendents. Hurts her image with her dreary, stuck-up friends."

"Well, Howie talked them into staying, but you should think about getting a lot more involved in the business."

Oh, please! Steve Hockney thought. Then he suppressed the feeling of irritation. Be careful, he warned himself again, be very careful. I'm his only living relative, but with his moods he could leave everything to charity, or even give a big cut to Howie. This week he's mad at him. Next week he'll be telling me that nobody runs his business like Howie, that he's like a son to him.

He took a couple of bites, then said, "Well, Poppa, I've been thinking that I should be more of a help to you. Look at all you do for me. Maybe the next time you make the rounds of the buildings, I should go along with you and Howie. I'd really like to do that."

"You really would?" Derek Olsen's tone was sharp, his eyes focused on his nephew's face. Then, satisfied with what he saw, he said, "You mean it. I can tell."

"Of course I mean it. Why do I call you 'Poppa'? You took over being my father when I was two years old, after all."

"I warned your mother not to marry that man. He was a no-good. Dishonest, conniving. When you were in your teens, I was afraid you'd end up just like him. Thank God you straightened yourself out. With some help from me."

Steve Hockney smiled appreciatively, then reached

into his pocket and took out a small box. He put it on the table and slid it across to his uncle. "Happy Birthday, Poppa."

Ignoring the last steamed dumpling, Olsen quickly untied the ribbon, tore the birthday wrapping paper, and opened the box. It was a Montblanc pen with his initials engraved on the gold clip. A pleased smile brightened his face. "How did you know I lost my good pen?" he asked.

"The last time I saw you, you were using a cheap giveaway. It wasn't that hard to make the deduction."

The waiter arrived with a platter of mandarin duck. For the rest of the dinner, Steve Hockney carefully directed the conversation to reminiscences of his late mother, and how she had always said that her big brother was the smartest, nicest man she'd ever known. "When Mom was sick, she told me that all she ever wanted me to do was to be just like you."

He was rewarded with the sight of sentimental tears filling his uncle's eyes.

When dinner was over, Hockney hailed a cab and deposited his uncle at home, not leaving him until he was inside his apartment. "Double-lock the door," he cautioned, with a final affectionate hug. As soon as the click confirmed that Olsen had followed instructions, he rushed downstairs, and with rapid steps hurried to his own apartment, ten blocks away.

Inside, he ripped off his jacket and slacks and shirt and tie, and changed into dungarees and a sweatshirt. Time to check out SoHo, he told himself. God, I thought I'd go nuts sitting with that old man for so long.

His ground-floor apartment had a private entrance. When he went out, he looked around, and, as he often did, thought of the previous resident, the drama teacher who had been murdered on the street, only a block away.

That other place I had was the pits, he thought. But after the teacher's death, Poppa was glad to let me have this. I convinced him that people are superstitious. He agreed with me that it was better not to rent it while her death was still in the news. That was nine years ago. By now, who remembered?

I'm never going to leave it, he swore to himself. It suits my purposes exactly, and there are no damn security cameras to keep track of me.

31

Detective Barrott had one good reason for tracking me down. He wanted the note that Mack had left in the collection basket. I had left it in Mack's file in my father's office. I invited Barrott to come upstairs with me, and he followed me into the apartment.

I was deliberately rude, leaving him standing in the foyer while I went for the note. It was still wrapped in the plastic sandwich bag. I took it out and studied it. Ten words in block letters. "UNCLE DEVON, TELL CAROLYN SHE MUST NOT LOOK FOR ME."

How could I be sure that Mack had printed those words?

The paper appeared to be unevenly cut from a larger sheet. When I offered it to Barrott last Monday, he hadn't been interested. He'd said that it had probably been handled by at least one usher, my uncle, my mother, and myself. I don't remember if I told him I had shown it to Elliott as well. Was there any chance that Mack's fingerprints were still on it?

I put it back in the plastic and brought it out to Barrott. He was speaking on his cell phone. When he saw me coming down the hall, he ended the conversation. I had hoped that he would simply take the note and leave, but instead he said, "Ms. MacKenzie, I need to talk with you."

Let me stay calm, I prayed, as I led him into the living room. My knees suddenly felt weak, and I sat in the big Queen Anne wing chair that had been Dad's favorite spot in this room. I glanced up at the portrait of him my mother had had painted, still hanging over the mantelpiece. The wing chair faced the fireplace, and Dad used to joke that when he sat in it, he did nothing but admire himself. "My God, Liv, cast your eyes on that grand-looking devil," he would say. "How much extra did you pay the painter to make me look that good?"

Sitting in Dad's chair somehow gave me courage. Detective Barrott sat on the edge of the couch and looked at me, without a hint of warmth. "Ms. MacKenzie, I've just been told that Aaron Klein, of Darien, Connecticut, has called our office and told us he believes your brother is the person who murdered his mother nine years ago. He said that he always felt that whoever killed her wanted something in her apartment. He now is convinced it was the tapes with your brother's voice. He said you told him you were bringing up a tape to play for him. Do you have that tape?"

I felt as if he had dashed freezing water in my face. I knew how that tape would sound to him. He and everyone else in the District Attorney's office would decide that Mack had been in big trouble and had confided in Esther Klein. I grasped the arms of the wing chair. "My father was a lawyer as I am," I told Barrott, "and before I say another word or give you anything, I am going to consult a lawyer."

"Ms. MacKenzie, I want to tell you something," Barrott said. "As of Saturday morning, Leesey Andrews was still alive. There is nothing more important than finding her, if it isn't already too late. You must have heard the news reports that she phoned her father two days ago and told him she'd call again next Mother's Day. You must surely agree that it defies belief that it's just a coincidence she is following—or being *forced* to follow—your brother's modus operandi."

"It wasn't a secret that Mack phones on Mother's Day," I protested. "Other people knew about it. A year after Mack disappeared, a reporter wrote an article about him and mentioned it. All that's on the Internet, for anyone who wants to look it up."

"It isn't on the Internet that after your brother's

drama teacher was murdered, all the tapes of his voice were stolen from her apartment," Barrott shot back. He gave me a stern look. "Ms. MacKenzie, if there is something on the tape you are holding that might in any way help us to find your brother, your sense of decency ought to compel you to give it to me now."

"I won't give you the tape," I said. "But I *will* swear to you that there is nothing on it that would give you any idea of where Mack might be. I'll go further. The tape is less than a minute long. Mack says a few words to his drama teacher and then starts to recite a passage from Shakespeare. That is it."

I think Barrott believed me. He nodded. "If you do hear from him," he said, "or if something occurs to you that might help us find him, I hope you will keep in mind that Leesey Andrews's life is far more important than trying to protect your brother."

When Barrott left, I did the one thing I knew I had to do immediately—call Aaron Klein's boss, Elliott Wallace, my father's best friend, my surrogate uncle, my mother's suitor, and tell him that by violating our agreement to accept Mack's wishes, I had made my brother a suspect in both a murder and a kidnapping.

32

Nick DeMarco had spent an uneasy weekend. He did not want to admit to himself how unsettling it had been to see Carolyn again. "Pizza and Pasta" had been his code name for himself when he used to have dinner at the MacKenzie home on Sutton Place.

I had zero social graces, he remembered. I was always watching to see what fork they used, how they placed their napkins on their laps. Pop tucked his under his chin. Even hearing Mr. MacKenzie joke about his own working-class background didn't do it for me. I thought he was just being a nice guy trying to help an awkward idiot feel welcome.

And that crush I had on Barbara? When I look back, it was just one more way in which I was jealous of Mack.

It wasn't about her at all.

It was about Carolyn.

I always felt comfortable with her. She was always

funny and sharp. I enjoyed being with her the other night.

Mack's family was my snobby ideal. I loved my own mom and dad, but I wished Dad didn't wear suspenders. I wished Mom didn't give a bear hug to all the regular customers. What's that saying? Something like "Our children begin by loving us; as they grow up they judge us; sometimes they forgive us."

It should be the other way around. "Parents start out by loving us, as we grow up they judge us. Sometimes they forgive us." But not often.

I hadn't wanted Pop to have a storefront anymore. I didn't know what I was doing to him when I put him in charge of my new restaurant. He was miserable. Mom missed being in the kitchen, too. Their high-class son wouldn't let them be who they are.

Nick DeMarco, the big success, voted bachelor of the month, the guy the girls chased, he thought, with an edge of bitterness. Nick DeMarco, the big risk-taker. And now maybe it's Nick DeMarco, the fool who took one chance too many.

Leesey Andrews.

Did anyone hear me offer to help her get a start in show business? It wasn't on the camera when I gave her the card with my address, but did anyone happen to see me slide it over to her?

33

On Tuesday morning, Captain Larry Ahearn and Detective Bob Gaylor, both relatively fresh from six hours' sleep, were back in the tech room of the District Attorney's office, reviewing security tapes from the three other nightclubs in which young women had last been seen before they disappeared.

The cases of all three young women, Emily Valley, Rosemarie Cummings, and Virginia Trent, had been reopened. The grainy photos from Emily Valley's case, now ten years old, had been sharpened and brightened by the latest in cutting-edge technology. In the crowd of students who had entered the club, named The Scene, it was possible to identify clearly Mack MacKenzie and Nick DeMarco.

"When we started looking for Emily Valley, all those Columbia kids came forward in a group after we contacted the ones who signed with credit cards," Ahearn commented, thinking aloud. "It was only a month or so after we talked to all of them that the MacKenzie boy disappeared. Looking back, maybe we should have treated that disappearance as suspicious and tied it to the Valley case."

"He doesn't show up in any security videos of the clubs where the other missing girls were hanging out. Of course, it was three years later that the Cummings girl vanished, and the Trent girl was four years ago. In all that time, he could have changed his appearance a lot. He was heavy into dramatics in prep school *and* in college," Gaylor pointed out.

"I'd have sworn that DeMarco is our guy, but the missing tapes from the drama teacher's apartment and the reference to Mother's Day throw it back into Mack MacKenzie's court," Ahearn said, frustration in his tone and on his face. "How has he managed to hide for ten years? What is he living on? How can he be moving between Brooklyn and Manhattan carrying her cell phone without somebody spotting him? Every cop in New York has an age-enhanced picture of him. And where did he keep Leesey from the time she disappeared till the time she made that call Saturday? And if she's still alive, where is he keeping her now?"

"And what is he *doing* to her?" Roy Barrott asked bitterly.

Neither of his associates had heard him come into the tech room. They both looked up, startled.

"You're supposed to be home getting some sleep," Ahearn said.

Barrott shook his head. "I did. I got as much as I need anyway. Listen, I just stopped at the tech room. They finished enhancing the two pictures that Leesey's roommate, Kate, took of her, including the one we used on the poster. She took these two pictures less than a minute after she snapped pictures of Angelina Jolie and Brad Pitt and their kids. We can now see the faces of the people in the background."

"And what did you find?" Ahearn asked.

"Look at *this* picture. See if you recognize the guy on the left."

"It's DeMarco!" Ahearn said, then repeated it as if he could not believe what he was seeing. "DeMarco!"

"Exactly," Barrott confirmed. "DeMarco never told us he had been in Greenwich Village a week before Leesey disappeared and was across the street when Kate took her picture. He also told us that when he isn't using his SUV, he drives a Mercedes convertible. There wasn't any mention of his chauffeur-driven Mercedes sedan."

Ahearn stood up. "I think it's time we invite this guy back for some more questioning and squeeze him real hard," he said. "It would have been easy for him to have his chauffeur get Leesey out of his loft apartment in the middle of the night and hide her somewhere. Our guys keep coming up with new stuff on him. DeMarco's bought a lot of property, with not much money down. He's on thin ice, financially. If he loses the liquor license from that fancy new Woodshed place, he could end up back in Queens running a pasta joint." Ahearn looked at Bob Gaylor. "Bring him in."

"Ten to one he'll have a lawyer with him," Barrott snapped. "I'm surprised he took a chance on coming in alone last week."

34

Mother was scheduled to fly home from Greece on Wednesday, and my anxiety was mounting. Elliott had come over after my frantic phone call to him on Monday evening to calm me down. There was something intensely comforting to me about the way he took everything that I had to tell him, including the fact that Aaron Klein, his designated successor at Wallace and Madison, now believed that Mack was responsible for his mother's death.

"That's absolute nonsense," Elliott said emphatically. "Aaron forgets he told me at the time nothing had been taken from her apartment. I remember his words clearly—'Why would someone have killed my mother, stolen her key, and not bothered to rob the apartment?' I told him that whoever killed her was probably a drug addict who panicked when he realized she was dead. Aaron has been fixated on trying to find someone to blame for his mother's death for ages, but I'll be damned if he's going to try to pin it on Mack."

There was nothing formal or reserved about Elliott's heated response. Dad himself could not have been more vehement. I think that was the moment when any hesitation I felt about the growing closeness between Mom and Elliott disappeared for good. It was also the moment when I decided to drop "Uncle" and call him Elliott.

We agreed that it was inevitable I would be called in for questioning about Mack and that we had to hire a defense lawyer. "I will not allow Mack to be tried and convicted in the newspapers," Elliott swore. "I'll search around and get the best person I can find."

We also agreed that we had to let Mom know what was going on. "It won't be long before an enterprising reporter links Mack's disappearance with that of the missing girl, because of the reference to Mother's Day," Elliott decided. "Worse yet, I wouldn't put it past the detectives to leak it to the media deliberately. Your mother must *not* look as if she's hiding from them."

Elliott made the call and suggested gently that she head home early. By the time Mom got home on Wednesday evening, everything Elliott had predicted had come to pass. The media, like bloodhounds on a fresh scent, had effectively reopened the cases of the other three young women who had disappeared from nightclubs, and reported the fact that Mack and his college friends had been present at The Scene the night the first girl, Emily Valley, vanished. The Mother's Day connection between Mack's routine phone calls and Leesey Andrews's message to her father was also headline news, of course.

Mom, Elliott's arm around her firmly, had to fight her way past the cameras and microphones when she and Elliott arrived at Sutton Place. Her greeting to me was exactly what I expected but hoped wouldn't happen. Circles under eyes that were swollen with weeping, for the first time looking every day of her sixty-two years, my mother said, "Carolyn, we agreed to let Mack live his own life. Now because of your meddling, my son is being hunted down like a criminal. Elliott has very kindly offered me the hospitality of his home. My bags are still in his car, and I intend to go there. In the meantime, you can contend with the mess out on the streets and make your apologies to our neighbors for destroying *their* privacy. Before I go I want to hear that tape."

Quietly I retrieved the tape, then sat with her in the kitchen and played it for her. Mack's voice, joking with his drama teacher, "Do I sound like Laurence Olivier or Tom Hanks?"—then—the dramatic change in his tone when he began to recite the Shakespeare quote.

When I turned it off, Mom's face was pale with

grief. "There was something wrong," she whispered. "Why didn't he come to me? Nothing could have been so bad that I wouldn't have helped him." Then she reached out her hand to me. "Give me the tape, Carolyn," she said.

"Mom, I can't," I said. "I wouldn't be surprised if we get a subpoena for it. You think it means Mack was in trouble. Another explanation is that he was simply reading a drama assignment. Elliott and I are meeting tomorrow morning with a criminal defense lawyer. I need to have it with me to play for him."

Without another word, my mother turned from me. Elliott whispered, "I'll call you later," before he rushed down the hall after her. When they were gone, I turned on the tape again. ". . . I all alone beweep my outcast state, and trouble deaf heaven with my bootless cries—"

Mack may have been acting, or he might have been talking about himself, but with a combination of pain and bitterness, I thought that now those words were fully applicable to me. A couple of minutes later, the apartment phone rang. As I picked it up and said, "Hello," whoever was on the other end hung up.

35

He couldn't get enough of the new media stories about the other three girls, Emily, Rosemarie, and Virginia. He remembered them all so clearly. Emily had been the first. The newspapers hadn't made too much of her disappearance at the beginning. She had been a runaway, so when she once again didn't come home to Trenton, New Jersey, even her parents conceded it was possible she had simply chosen to disappear.

But when Rosemarie went missing three years later, they began to think it was possible Emily had been abducted. Then, when Virginia vanished four years ago, the media had a field day connecting the three of them.

Of course, it didn't last. Every so often some would-be Pulitzer Prize winner would write a feature story linking the three young women, but with nothing new to report, the public's interest dropped to zero.

Leesey had changed all that. "Mack, where are you now?" was the question on everyone's lips.

Dressed in a hooded running suit and wearing dark glasses, he was jogging on Sutton Place. As he expected, it was crowded with media vans. Wonderful, he thought, wonderful. He removed the small metal box from his pocket, unsnapped it, and took out Leesey's cell phone. Now when he dialed, they'd be able to pin-point his location as being around here. But that's what I want, isn't it? he asked himself with a smile, as he dialed the phone number of the apartment, waited to hear Carolyn answer the call, then disconnected. Then, quickening his pace, he disappeared into the brisk pedestrian traffic on Fifty-seventh Street.

36

Bruce Galbraith and his wife, Dr. Barbara Hanover Galbraith, had, so far as possible, avoided talking about Mack MacKenzie. But finally, on Wednesday evening, after the children were in bed and they had finished watching the ten o'clock news, Bruce knew he had to raise the subject.

They were in the library of their spacious Park Avenue apartment. Whenever Bruce was away on a business trip, the realization of how happy he was in his home and with his family hit him afresh. Barbara had changed to light green pajamas and unpinned her ash blond hair so that it fell loose on her shoulders. He had long since passed the days when he felt clumsy and awkward in her presence, but even so, the sense that he might one day wake up and find he'd been dreaming, that life as he knew it was an illusion, always lingered in his subconscious.

He had witnessed the growing tension in Barbara for

the past few days since the media began linking Mack to the disappearance of Leesey Andrews, the girl from Connecticut, and then to the murder of the drama teacher.

During the broadcast, with the jealousy he had never overcome, Bruce had watched his wife's face when pictures of Mack were flashed on the screen. After he pushed the power button on the remote and watched the screen turn dark, he knew it was time to discuss what needed to be done.

"Barb," he said, "I was in the nightclub the night that first girl disappeared."

"I know, but so were twenty other guys from Columbia, including Nick and Mack," Barbara said, avoiding his eyes.

"Carolyn MacKenzie called me, but I haven't returned her call. I'll bet anything that she follows up on it. As the police investigation widens, it's inevitable they'll look me up. Nick and I were Mack's roommates, after all."

He watched as his wife tried to force back tears. "What are you driving at?" she asked, her voice unsteady.

"I think you and the kids should visit your father in Martha's Vineyard. He's had three heart attacks. No one would question it if you tell people he's in bad shape again."

"What about school?"

"For what we're paying, we can arrange to get lesson plans and a private tutor. The school year is over in a few weeks' time anyhow."

He saw the uncertainty on his wife's face. "Barbara, you joined a practice with two other pediatric surgeons so you'd have a measure of control over your personal life. I would say this is a time to assert that control."

He got up, walked over to her, bent down, and kissed the top of her head. "I could kill Mack for what he did to you," he said quietly.

"I'm over it, Bruce. I really am."

No you're not, he thought. But I've learned to live with that, and there's no way on God's earth I'll let Mack hurt you again.

37

On Wednesday evening, shortly after Mom and Elliott left, Detective Barrott phoned. I had thought that things couldn't get much worse, but I was wrong. Barrott quietly asked if I knew that the call I had just received, that I had thought was a wrong number, had been made from Leesey Andrews's cell phone. I was so shocked that I think it was a full minute before I said something like, "But that's impossible." I paused to digest the fact. "That's absolutely impossible."

Barrott curtly assured me that it was true and did I think it was my brother trying to reach me?

"When I answered it, someone hung up. I thought it had to be a wrong number. Can't you *tell* that I didn't speak to anyone?" I asked him angrily.

"We know that. We also know that this is an unlisted phone in your home, Ms. MacKenzie. Make no mistake. If your brother is the one who has Leesey's phone, and if he tries again to contact you and you do *not* help us find him, you could become an accessory to a very serious crime."

I didn't answer him. I simply broke off the connection.

Sometime between four and seven A.M. on Thursday morning, I decided to phone Lucas Reeves and ask to meet with him as soon as possible. I needed help from someone I could trust to be thorough and impartial. I had already seen, from studying his file on Mack, that he had done a good job interviewing seemingly every possible person who had been close to my brother. The opinion he had given Dad was very clear. "There is nothing in your son's background that would suggest he was experiencing a problem that would cause him to flee. I would not rule out the possibility of a mental illness that he had successfully concealed from everyone."

Elliott and I were meeting at noon at the office of Thurston Carver, the criminal defense lawyer whom Elliott had found to represent us. At nine A.M., I phoned Reeves. He was not in yet, but his secretary promised he would call me back as soon as he arrived. It was obvious that she recognized my name. A half hour later, he returned the call. As briefly as possible, I explained what had happened. "Is there any chance you could see me this morning?" I asked, hearing the desperation in my voice.

His voice was deep and resonant as he answered. "I'll rearrange my schedule. Where is your meeting with the lawyer?"

"On Park and Forty-fifth," I said, "the MetLife Building."

"My phone number is the same, but I moved my office two years ago. I'm on Park Avenue and Thirty-ninth Street, just a few blocks down from MetLife. Can you be here at ten thirty?"

Yes, I could. I was already showered and dressed. The unpredictable weather had served up another blustery day. Looking out the window at people wearing jackets and keeping their hands in their pockets, I changed from the light suit I had planned to wear to a velour running suit, which made me look less like a lawyer and more like somebody's sister. I won't say that it flattered me. It was dark gray, and when I looked in the mirror I could see that it brought out the circles under my eyes and the unusual paleness of my skin. I don't usually bother with much makeup during the day, but I took the time to use foundation, a touch of eye shadow, blush, mascara, and lip gloss. All tarted up in defense of my brother, I thought, then hated the bitterness in my thinking.

If only I had not gone to see Detective Barrott. If only I had not found the tape in Mack's suitcase. Useless thoughts.

I could feel the beginning of a headache, and even though I wasn't hungry, I went down to the kitchen, made a pot of coffee, and toasted an English muffin. I carried it to the breakfast alcove and sat at the table, gazing at the spectacular view of the East River. Thanks to the strong breeze, the current was visibly swift, and I found myself identifying with it. I was being carried by a current I could not fight, and I had to let it take me along until it either overwhelmed or released me.

I had been glad that Mom was in Greece for those few days and I had the apartment to myself. But that was when she was supposed to be somewhere else. It was incredible to me that she was in New York and not staying in her own home, but when I left the apartment, I understood why. The media trucks were there in full force, and reporters rushed to me looking for a statement. This is what happened to her last night, I thought.

I had phoned down to the doorman to hail a cab for me, and he had one waiting. Ignoring the microphones, I jumped into it and said, "Start driving." I didn't want anyone to overhear my destination. Twenty minutes later, I was in the reception room of Lucas Reeves's office. Promptly at ten thirty, he escorted a tense-looking couple, whom I guessed to be other clients, to the outer door, looked around, and came over to me. "Ms. MacKenzie, come right in."

I only remember meeting him once, when he came to Sutton Place ten years ago, so either he remembered my face or, since I was the only one in the waiting room, he assumed I was Carolyn MacKenzie.

Lucas Reeves was even shorter than I remembered. I don't think he was more than five feet four with shoes on. He had a thick head of wiry salt-and-pepper hair that had clearly been dyed to give the illusion of natural graying. His face was creased with small lines around the mouth which suggested to me that he almost certainly had been a serious smoker. His deep, pleasant voice was incongruous coming from such a small man, but it matched the warmth in his eyes and his hearty handshake.

I followed him into his private office. Instead of going to his desk, he led me to a seating area with two chairs, a couch, and a coffee table. "I don't know about you, Ms. MacKenzie," he began, as he waved me to one of the chairs, "but for me it's time for midmorning coffee. How about you? Or, like my British friends, would you prefer a cup of tea?"

"Black coffee would be perfect," I said.

"That's two of us."

The receptionist opened the door and poked her head in. "What'll it be, Mr. Reeves?"

"Two black. Thanks, Marge." Turning to me, he said, "In this day and age of political correctness, I started to make the coffee myself in our little kitchen. My assistant, my secretary, my receptionist, and my accountant bodily threw me out. They said my coffee would peel the paint from a wall."

I was so grateful for his attempt to put me at ease that I felt quick tears rush to my eyes. He pretended not to notice. I had offered to bring Mack's file with me, but he had said he had a duplicate of it. His was on the coffee table. He pointed to it. "Bring me up to date, Carolyn." His eyes never left my face as I explained how, because of me, Mack had become a suspect in both the Leesey Andrews and Esther Klein cases.

"And now they think Mack has Leesey's cell phone. Sure, we have a private number, but it's been the same one since I was a child. Hundreds of people know it." I bit my lip. It was quivering so much I could not go on. The thought flashed through my mind that the reason Mom wanted to stay in the apartment all these years was to be sure she'd never miss a call from Mack.

Listening to me, Reeves's expression had become increasingly troubled. "I am afraid your brother is a very convenient suspect, Carolyn. I will be honest. I could see no reason why a twenty-one-year-old man with his background would choose to disappear. Quite frankly, in the last few days, with all the media attention on him, I have been studying his file and doing some follow-up, purely for my own satisfaction. Your father paid me generously, and I could give him absolutely no help in solving your brother's disappearance."

He looked past me. "Ah, here is the coffee I did not prepare." He waited until the cups were on the table and we were alone again before he continued. "Now I am looking at it from the viewpoint of the police. The night the first girl disappeared, your brother was at that club, The Scene. But so were his two roommates, other Columbia students, and about fifteen more patrons. It was a small club, but there were also, of course, a bartender, some waiters, and a small musical group. That list, as complete as I could make it, is there in your brother's file. Since the police now believe your brother may be involved in that first disappearance, let us think like them. With technology, it is increasingly easy to follow people's lives. I am proud to say that this agency has a technical system second to none. We will begin to update our knowledge of everyone we know to have been in that club ten years ago when all of this started."

He took a sip of his coffee. "Excellent. Strength without bitterness. Admirable qualities, don't you agree?"

I wondered if that was an admonition. Had he

sensed my growing bitterness toward Mack, and even, I admitted to myself, to my mother?

He didn't wait for an answer. "You said you felt that the superintendents, the Kramers, might have something to hide?"

"I don't know whether they have something to hide," I said. "I do know that they seemed terribly nervous, almost as if they were being accused of knowing something about Mack's disappearance."

"I interviewed them ten years ago. I'll have my staff check to see if there was anything out of the ordinary in their lives that might be of use for us to know. Now tell me about Nicholas DeMarco. Trust me with any slight nuance that you may have received from him, either positive or negative."

I wanted to be objective. "Nick is obviously ten years older now," I said. "He's more mature, of course. At age sixteen, I had a crush on him, so I don't know that I could possibly have judged him honestly. He was handsome, he was fun, looking back I think he was flirting with me, and I was young enough to think that I was special to him. Mack warned me away from Nick, and after that, the few times he came to dinner I made it a point to be out with my friends."

"Mack warned you away?" Reeves raised an eyebrow.

"Big-brother stuff. I guess I was wearing my heart on

my sleeve and Mack said that all the girls fell for Nick. Other than that, I would say that when I saw him last, I had the feeling that Nick seemed like someone with a lot on his mind."

"Did you talk with him about the other roommate in that apartment, Bruce Galbraith?"

"Yes. Nick is out of touch with him. Frankly, I don't think he liked Bruce very much. He even called him 'the Lone Stranger.' I told you I left a message asking to meet with Bruce, but so far he hasn't responded."

"Call him again. I doubt that with all the media attention your brother is getting, Bruce Galbraith would ignore your request to see him. In the meantime, I'll get started immediately on updating our files on the others. Because of the reference to Mother's Day, the police were already trying to tie Mack to the disappearance of Leesey Andrews, and by extension to the disappearance of all those young women. *Now* that call to your home from Leesey's cell phone will make them certain of his guilt. Every clue leads conveniently back to Mack. I am beginning to wonder if everything that has happened began that night in The Scene, weeks before Mack disappeared."

I pounced on that. "Mr. Reeves, are you saying that someone else may be deliberately trying to tie Mack to the disappearance of those four women?"

"I think it's possible. As you yourself said, there was

a feature article some years ago that made public the fact that your brother only calls on Mother's Day. Who knows if someone did not tuck that piece of information in his mind and is now using it to deflect suspicion from himself? There are all kinds of identity theft. Following the known pattern of someone who has vanished and chooses not to defend himself may be one of them. Leesey's abductor has her cell phone. He may also have your unlisted number."

It was a possibility that made sense. When I left Reeves's office, I felt that this time I had come to the right person, somebody who would search for the truth without the preconceived notion that Mack had become a killer.

38

Accompanied by his lawyer, Paul Murphy, Nick DeMarco returned to the Detective Squad section of the District Attorney's office on Thursday afternoon. This time, the atmosphere in Captain Ahearn's office was openly hostile. There were no handshakes, no brief expression of thanks that he had promptly responded to the phone call requesting his presence as soon as possible.

But Nick had other problems on his mind. Early Tuesday morning, after a frantic call from his mother that his father was being rushed to the hospital with chest pains, Nick had flown to Florida. By the time he got there, the tests had so far been negative, but his father had been kept in the hospital to guard against the possibility that he was building up to a heart attack. When Nick entered the hospital room, his mother had rushed into his arms and hugged him fiercely. "Oh, Nick, I thought we had lost him," she cried.

His father, an older image of himself, propped up on pillows, his face pale, an oxygen tube in his nostrils and an IV drip in his hand, was clearly unhappy. "Nick, I hate hospitals," was his greeting, "but maybe it isn't such a bad thing this happened after all. In the ambulance, I was thinking about things I wish I'd said to you, only your mother wouldn't let me say them. Now you're going to hear them. I'm sixty-eight years old. I've been working since I was fourteen. For the first time in my life, I feel useless, and I don't like it."

"Dad, I bought a restaurant for you to run," Nick protested. "*You're* the one who decided to retire."

"Sure, you bought a restaurant here, but you should have known it wasn't right for me. I was a round peg in a square hole in that place. It made me sick to see you bleeding money with your fancy overhead and pricey food. I've seen these places come and go. Do yourself a favor and sell that one, or else put some staples on the menu that people can count on when they don't want foie gras and caviar."

"Dominick, don't excite yourself," his mother pleaded.

"I *have* to cxcitc mysclf. I'vc got to gct this off my chest before I *do* have a heart attack. Bachelor of the Month! It was disgusting to watch how pleased you were. You'd think you got the Congressional Medal of Honor. While I'm still around to tell you, cut it out."

"Dad, I hear you. And believe it or not, I'm listening this time. Tell me, what do you want? What can I do to make you happy?"

"I don't want to play golf and I don't want to sit in a pricey condominium where I might get beaned by a golf ball because we're next to the sixteenth hole."

"Dad, all that's easy to take care of. What else?"

Nick had not yet gotten over the look of scorn in his father's eyes. "You're thirty-two years old. Get real. Be the son we were so proud of. Stop running around with the women you meet in clubs. In fact, get out of the club business! You'll get in trouble. Find yourself a nice girl. Your mother and I are pushing seventy. We were married fifteen years before God sent us a son. Don't make us wait fifteen years from now to have a grandchild."

All this was going through Nick's mind as he and his attorney settled themselves in hard, uncomfortable chairs in front of Captain Ahearn's desk. Detectives Barrott and Gaylor were seated on either side of the captain.

It's a firing squad, Nick thought. A glance at his attorney showed him that Murphy was having the same reaction.

"Mr. DeMarco," Ahearn began, "you didn't tell us you have a Mercedes 550 sedan which you only use when you are being driven by your chauffeur."

Nick frowned. "Wait a minute. If I'm right you asked

about cars I drove. I never drive the sedan. It's either the convertible or the SUV when I'm on my own."

"You didn't mention your chauffeur, either."

"I wouldn't have thought there was a reason to mention him."

"We don't agree, Mr. DeMarco," Ahearn told him. "Particularly since your chauffeur, Benny Seppini, has an extensive criminal record."

Without looking at him, Nick knew what Paul Murphy was thinking. Why didn't my client tell me that?

"Benny is fifty-eight years old," Nick told Ahearn. "As a kid, he had no home life and became involved in a street gang while he was in his teens. When he was seventeen, he got sentenced as an adult to prison for burglary and served five years. When he got out, he started working for my father. That was thirty-five years ago. When my father retired five years ago, he began working for me. He is a decent, good man."

"Didn't his ex-wife get a restraining order on him ten years ago?" Ahearn snapped.

"Benny's first wife died young. His second was trying to get him to sign over their condo to her. That was a phony, trumped-up charge and she dropped it the minute she got the condo."

"Uh-huh. Mr. DeMarco, do you do much walking around Greenwich Village in the daytime?"

"Of course I don't. I'm a businessman."

"Did you ever see Leesey Andrews before Monday night a week ago?"

"To the best of my knowledge, absolutely not."

"Let me show you a picture we have of you, Mr. DeMarco." Ahearn nodded to Barrott, who shoved copies of the enhanced photographs Leesey's roommate had taken of her across the desk to Nick and Murphy.

"Recognize the fellow in the background of the second one, Mr. DeMarco?" Barrott asked.

"Of course that's me in the background," Nick snapped. "I remember that day. I was meeting a real estate agent for lunch. I'm interested in buying property in the area near where the old railroad tracks are being developed. Once that development starts, the surrounding property will go sky-high. I saw all the paparazzi in action and looked over to see what was going on. Brad Pitt and Angelina Jolie were there."

"Where were you having lunch?"

"At Casa Florenza, right around the corner from where the picture was taken."

"Then you claim you didn't see Leesey Andrews being photographed by her friend?"

"I not only claim, I *didn't* see her," Nick replied heatedly.

"Do you have the bill for that luncheon?" Gaylor asked in a tone that suggested he would be surprised to see one.

"No, I do not. The real estate broker is trying to sell me property, so he paid. If he succeeds, his commission will keep putting gas in his car for a long time."

"How long will you be able to continue putting gas in all *your* cars, Mr. DeMarco?" Ahearn asked. "You're stretched pretty thin financially, aren't you?"

"What do Mr. DeMarco's business affairs have to do with our presence here?" Paul Murphy demanded.

"Maybe nothing at all," Ahearn replied. "And maybe a great deal. If the state decides to cancel the liquor license of the Woodshed, I don't think your client will make a living selling Popsicles there. And trust me, we *will* find a reason to have it canceled if we even suspect that Mr. DeMarco is not being totally candid with us."

Ahearn turned to Nick. "Do you have the unlisted phone number of the MacKenzie home on Sutton Place?"

"Unless it's been changed, I'm sure I have it somewhere. I remember phoning Mrs. MacKenzie after her husband died on 9/11."

"Do you think Leesey Andrews is dead?"

"I certainly hope not. That would be a tragedy."

"Do you know if she's still alive?"

"What kind of unbelievable question is that?"

"We're out of here, Nick." Murphy was on his feet.

Ahearn ignored him. "Mr. DeMarco, do you own a

cell phone that is not registered to you, one that uses a prepaid card, the kind gamblers and wiseguys use?"

"That's it! We're not going to listen to any more of your cheap insinuations," Murphy shouted.

It was as though Larry Ahearn had not heard him. "And does your troubled chauffeur have a similar phone, Mr. DeMarco? And if he does, did he respond to your frantic call to get Leesey out of your loft apartment? And if she wasn't already dead, did he decide to keep her around for his own amusement? And if that was the case, has he kept you informed as to her welfare?"

Nick, his fists clenched, was almost at the door when he heard Ahearn's final question. "Or are you protecting your college roommate Mack MacKenzie, or perhaps helping his pretty sister to protect him? You had a little tête-à-tête with her last Friday night, didn't you?"

39

After I left Lucas Reeves, I met Elliott at Thurston Carver's office in the MetLife Building. Instantly, I realized that I had seen Carver around court while I was clerking for Judge Huot. He was a big man with a mane of hair that I guessed to be prematurely white—I doubted that he was more than fifty-five years old.

I felt somewhat fortified by my meeting with Reeves, and told Carver the theory he had suggested to me. Mack was missing. That he called every year on Mother's Day was public knowledge, and whoever had kidnapped Leesey Andrews was trying to throw suspicion on Mack by the phone calls he was making.

Elliott, who looked tired and deeply concerned, seized on that possibility. He told me that last night my mother was so upset when they reached his apartment she broke down, crying and sobbing, to the extent that he was desperately worried about her now. "I realized last night that Olivia has always been sure that something must have snapped in Mack's mind to make him disappear like that," he explained to Carver. "Now she believes that if he *is* guilty of these disappearances, he may be completely insane and might end up being shot when the police find him."

"And she blames me," I said.

"Carolyn, she has to blame *someone*. That won't last. You know it won't."

You've been my rod and staff through all this. That's what Mom had said to me last week, after Mack's call on the morning of Mother's Day. I still had every faith that at some point she would understand why I had tried to bring Mack's situation to some kind of closure. In the meantime, she had Elliott to help her, and I realized how deeply grateful I was to him for being there for her now. No matter how this turned out, at that moment, sitting in the elegantly paneled office of Thurston Carver, I surrendered any jealousy I felt at the probability that Elliott would replace my father in my mother's life.

Later that day I called Bruce Galbraith. After I had waited for what seemed an eternity, he got on the phone and grudgingly agreed to meet me in his office on Friday afternoon. "I must tell you, Carolyn," he said, "I have neither seen nor heard from Mack since the day he disappeared. I can't imagine what you hope to learn from me."

I was chilled by the venom in his voice but did not give him the answer that was on the tip of my tongue. *I want to know why you hate Mack so much.*

On Friday afternoon I was ushered into Galbraith's office. It was on the sixty-third floor of his building on the Avenue of the Americas and offered sweeping views of the city. The only comparable view I can think of is from the Rainbow Room in Rockefeller Center.

My memory of Bruce was blurry. Dad and Mom had kept me away from the search for Mack when they were going back and forth to his apartment after he disappeared. I had a vague memory that Bruce had sandy hair and rimless glasses.

His greeting was cordial enough, and he chose to sit, not in what I think would be his usual chair, but in one of the two matching leather chairs on either side of his desk. He began by offering sympathy for the way the tabloids were tying Mack to the disappearance of Leesey Andrews. "I can only imagine what that is doing to your mother," he said. Then he added, after a pause, "And of course to you."

"Bruce," I said, "you can understand how desperate I am not only to find Mack, but whether I find him or not, to clear his name of any connection with the women who disappeared."

"I absolutely understand that," he said. "But the point is that Mack, Nick, and I merely shared an apartment. Mack and Nick were tight. They hung out together, they dated together. Nick was at your house for dinner a fair amount. He's a much better person to ask about Mack than I am. You might as well be talking to the rest of the graduating class at Columbia, for all *I* can tell you."

"What about Barbara?" I asked. "She came to dinner once. I thought she was Nick's girlfriend, but he told me she had a crush on Mack, then she married you after Mack disappeared. Have you ever talked with her about Mack? Would she have any idea what was in his mind before he vanished?"

"Barbara and I have of course talked about Mack with all this recent publicity. She is as bewildered as I am at the idea that he could be involved in any crime. She said that certainly isn't the person she knew."

His voice was calm, but I saw a deep flush creep up from his neck to his cheeks. He *does* hate Mack, I thought. Is it jealousy? And how far would that jealousy have carried him? He was so buttoned up, so contained, an ordinary-looking man, who, judging from his success, was an extraordinarily gifted real estate tycoon. An image of Mack, with his stunning good looks, his wonderful sense of humor, his ever-present charm flooded my mind.

I remembered having heard that Mack beat Galbraith out by a fraction to be in the top ten of the graduating class. That must have been a massive blow to Galbraith's ego, I thought. And after Mack disappeared, Barbara, the girl Nick said had been crazy about Mack, married Galbraith, maybe as her ticket to medical school . . .

"I met Barbara at my house years ago," I said. "I'd appreciate a chance to talk with her."

"I'm afraid that isn't possible," Galbraith said flatly. "Her father is very ill. He lives on Martha's Vineyard. She flew up there with the children to be with him in his final weeks." He stood up, and I got the message the meeting was over. He walked me to the reception room, and I reached out to shake his hand. I didn't miss the way he rubbed his palm on his trouser leg before he reluctantly accepted mine. His was still sweaty and damp. A plain man in an expensive suit, his eyes shuttered.

I remembered that Nick had called him "the Lone Stranger."

40

If there was one person Lil Kramer disliked more than Howard Altman, it was Steve Hockney, Derek Olsen's nephew. That was why when he arrived unannounced on Friday morning, Lil felt thoroughly rattled. Howie's advice to her and Gus—that it would be unwise to rush to Pennsylvania as if they had something to hide—they had originally welcomed with gratitude. But she was totally aware of Olsen's shifting alliances between his nephew Steve and his assistant, Howie, and seeing Steve alone terrified her.

Howie is on the outs with Olsen, she thought, and Steve is going to take over. She was glad Gus had gone upstairs to change the filters in some of the air conditioners. He was in a foul mood after cleaning the staircase between the second and third floors. One of the college kids had spilled beer there during the night.

"They must have been dragging up a keg," he had

grumbled minutes before Hockney arrived. "Spilled beer all over the whole flight. Wouldn't have killed them to have mopped it up themselves."

It's a good thing Gus noticed it before Hockney got here, she thought. He'll probably make a big show of checking out the halls and the staircases trying to find something wrong. A sudden feeling of fatigue overcame her. Maybe, after all, it would be nice *not* to be busy all the time. Trying to sound civil, she invited Hockney in and asked if he'd like a cup of tea. He flashed her a broad smile as he strode past her.

He certainly is good-looking, she thought, and he *knows* it. He always was full of himself, and when he was around twenty, Olsen had to bail him out of a few problems. He almost went to jail. Now there was a certain insolent glitter in his eyes. He declined the tea but settled on the couch, his arm over the back, his legs crossed.

"Lil," he began. "My uncle turned eighty-three last month."

"I know it," she said. "We sent him a card."

"You're better than I am." Steve smiled again. "But I feel it's time that I took over a lot of the management of his affairs. You know him. He won't show that he's feeling his age, but I can see that he is. I also know that Howie Altman is getting on his nerves a lot lately."

"We get along with him," Lil said carefully.

"He's been bullying you about giving up this apartment, hasn't he?"

"I think that's over."

"He's a bully. I know my uncle would listen to you if you made him aware just how nasty Howie has been and can be to you both."

"Why would I cause trouble when it's none of my business what Mr. Olsen thinks of Howie?"

"It's because I want your help, Lil. You seem to forget that I was here in the building when Mack MacKenzie all but accused you of stealing his watch. That was only a few days before he disappeared."

White-lipped, Lil stammered, "He found that watch. He apologized."

"Did anyone *hear* him apologize?"

"I don't know. I mean, no, I don't think so."

Hockney unfolded himself from the couch. "Lil, you're lying about the apology. I can tell. But don't worry. I never told anyone about Mack's watch and I never will. We don't like Howie, do we, Lil? By the way, I'll tell Uncle Derek that this building is the jewel in his crown, thanks to the way you and Gus keep it."

41

Derek Olsen was far from being only the irascible, petulant old man that his nephew Steve and his buildings manager, Howie, thought him to be. He was in fact a shrewd investor who had watched his real estate holdings in strategically chosen apartment buildings turn into a personal fortune worth many millions of dollars. Now he had come to the conclusion that the time was right to begin liquidating his assets.

On Friday morning he called Wallace and Madison and brusquely demanded to be put through to Elliott Wallace. Elliott's secretary, long used to Olsen's behavior, did not bother to tell him that Mr. Wallace was on his way to an urgent meeting. Instead, she asked him to hold, and rushed down the corridor to catch Elliott at the elevator. "It's Olsen," she said.

With an exasperated sigh, Elliott retraced his steps to his office and picked up the phone. "Derek, how are you?" he asked, his tone hearty.

"I'm all right. Your so-called nephew's in a lot of trouble, I see."

"As you well know, Mack has been missing for ten years. It is absurd that the police are trying to connect him to any crime. What can I do for you?"

"He caused *me* a lot of trouble by disappearing when he was living in one of my apartments. Anyhow, that's not why I called. My birthday was last month. I'm eighty-three years old. It's time to sell everything."

"I've been suggesting that for the past five years."

"If I had sold five years ago, I wouldn't get the price I'll get now. I'm coming in to talk to you. Monday morning, ten o'clock, okay for you?"

"Monday at ten would be fine," Elliott said, cordially. When he was sure Olsen had hung up, he slammed the phone down into the cradle. "I'll have to reschedule the entire day," he snapped to his secretary as he hurried back to the elevator.

She watched him go with sympathetic eyes. The meeting that had been scheduled was to decide who would assume Aaron Klein's responsibilities in the firm. After staying home for four days, Klein had phoned in his resignation, saying that it was impossible for him to work side by side with someone who was the champion of his mother's killer.

42

Gregg Andrews had set out a pattern for himself, and he stuck to it. After he left the hospital, he went straight home, grabbed something to eat, and went straight to bed. His alarm was set for one A.M. By two A.M., he was nursing a beer at the bar of the Woodshed and stayed there until closing time. Then, sitting in his car down the street, he watched to see the pattern of how the waiters, bartenders, and band members exited the building, checking to see that they all left within a few minutes of one another, and that no one came out alone, as they'd all claimed about the night Leesey disappeared.

For the last three nights, he had then walked the mile distance between the club and Leesey's apartment, stopping to talk to anyone he saw on the street and asking if by any chance they had been around at the time Leesey vanished and perhaps had seen her. The answer was always negative. The fourth and fifth nights, he drove back and forth covering other streets, just in case she might not have taken the most direct route.

On Saturday morning, at 3:30, after watching the employees lock the door of the Woodshed, he was about to start driving around the neighborhood when there was a rap at the window. A man with streaks of dirt on his face and unkempt hair was staring in at him. Sure it was a request for money, Gregg rolled the car window down only a few inches.

"You're the brother," the man said, his voice hoarse, his alcohol-laden breath sour. Instinctively, Gregg pulled his head back. "Yes, I am."

"I saw her. Will you promise I get the reward?"

"If you can help me find my sister, yes."

"Take my name down."

Gregg reached into the glove compartment and pulled out a pad.

"It's Zach Winters. I live at the shelter on Mott Street."

"You think you saw my sister?"

"I saw her the night she disappeared."

"Why didn't you come forward at once?"

"Nobody believes people like me. I tell them I saw her, next thing they'll be saying I did something to her. That's what happens." Winters put a grimy hand on the car to steady himself.

"If whatever you tell me helps us find my sister, I will

personally hand the reward to you. What do you know?"

"She was the last customer out. She started to walk that way." He pointed. "Then a big SUV pulled up and stopped."

Gregg felt his insides twist. "Was she forced into it?"

"No way. I heard the driver call, 'Hey, Leesey,' and she jumped right in the SUV herself."

"Could you tell what kind it was?"

"Sure. It was a black Mercedes."

43

On Saturday morning he was overcome with one of his periodic episodes of remorse. He felt terrible about what he had done. I didn't think I'd ever kill anyone again, he thought. I was scared. After the first one, I tried to be good. But then it happened again twice. I still tried to stop. But I couldn't. But then *he* made me do it again—and again. And after that I couldn't stop.

Sometimes I feel like telling him. But that would be crazy, and I'm not crazy.

I have an idea that I'm thinking about. It would be dangerous, but then, it's always been dangerous. I know someday I'll be caught. But I won't let them send me to prison. I'll go my own way and take whoever's around with me.

I haven't touched the phone since Wednesday night. I'll make the next phone call on Sunday.

It's such a good idea.
And after that, I'll find someone else.
It isn't time to stop yet.

44

Early Saturday morning, Gregg Andrews called Larry Ahearn's cell phone, the words tumbling from his mouth, to report that someone had seen Leesey get into a black Mercedes SUV the night she disappeared. "And she knew the driver," Gregg insisted, his voice hoarse with fatigue and strain. "He called out her name, and she jumped right in."

In the eleven or twelve days since Leesey had been reported missing, Ahearn had not slept more than four hours a night. When his phone rang, he was at home in a heavy sleep from exhaustion. Now, fighting to awaken, he looked at the clock. "Gregg, it's 4:30 in the morning. Where *are* you?"

"I'm on my way to my apartment. I have Zach Winters, a street person, with me. He's drunk. I'll let him sleep it off at my apartment, then I'll bring him in to talk to you. I'm convinced he doesn't know any more than what I told you, but it's our first solid lead.

How about that nightclub owner, the one who invited Leesey to sit at his table? What does he drive?"

Nick DeMarco was driving an SUV that night, Ahearn thought. He told us he used that vehicle because he was carrying his golf clubs. I'm not sure if he said what color it is. Now fully awake, he sat up, slid out of bed, and walked out into the hall, closing the bedroom door behind him. "DeMarco has at least three different sets of wheels," he said carefully. "Let's find out if his SUV is a black Mercedes. I think I remember that it is. Gregg, we'll also have to check on this witness. You said his name was Zach Winters?"

"That's right."

"We'll look him up, too. If you're bringing him to your apartment, be careful. He sounds like a wino."

"He is. But I don't care. Maybe he'll remember something more about Leesey when he wakes up. *Oh, God!*"

"Gregg, what is it?"

"Larry, I'm falling asleep. I almost hit a cab that cut in front of me. I'll see you around ten o'clock in your office."

A click told Ahearn that Gregg Andrews had disconnected his cell phone.

The door from the bedroom opened. Larry's wife, Sheila, still tying the sash on her robe, said matter-of-factly, "I'll make coffee while you shower."

*

An hour later, Larry was in his office with Barrott and Gaylor. "It sounds fishy to me," Barrott said flatly.

Gaylor nodded. "My guess is that if this guy, what's-his-name, Zach Winters, was on the Woodshed block that night, he was probably too drunk to see, never mind hear what was said. I'll bet anything he's just trying to get the reward."

"That's the way I read it," Ahearn agreed. "But let's start checking him out. Gregg said he'd bring him in here around ten o'clock."

Gaylor was consulting his notes. "When DeMarco was here the first time, he talked about having his SUV in the loft garage because he was going to transport his golf clubs to the plane the next morning." He looked at Barrott and Ahearn. "His SUV *is* a black Mercedes," he said crisply.

"So maybe after he left the club, he went to his loft, picked it up, and decided to go back and try to connect with Leesey." Ahearn's lips were a tight, narrow line. "I think it's about time we put the heat on DeMarco and let the media know that he's a 'person of interest' in Leesey's disappearance."

Barrott was opening the MacKenzie file. "Listen to this, Larry. The first time the father came here after the son had been reported missing, the guys took notes of what he said. 'No reason for Mack to take off. He's on top of the world. Graduated in the top ten of his class. Duke Law School. Bought him a Mercedes SUV as a graduation present. You never saw a kid so thrilled. Only a couple of hundred miles on it when he disappeared.'"

"So what?" Ahearn snapped.

"He left it in the garage when he disappeared."

"Did you ask what color it was?"

"It was black. I'm just wondering if it's *still* Mack's favorite vehicle."

"What happened to the one the father bought him?"

"I don't know. Maybe the sister can tell us."

"Give her a call," Ahearn commanded.

"It's not even six o'clock," Gaylor pointed out.

"We're up, aren't we?" Barrott said.

"Hold on." Ahearn held up his hand. "Roy, did you ask Carolyn MacKenzie to give you the note her brother left in the collection basket?"

"She handed it to me the day she came to see me two weeks ago," Barrott said somewhat defensively. "I gave it back to her. It was a scrap of paper in block printing with ten words on it. I thought it was useless to try to do anything with it. We don't have her brother's fingerprints on file. Her uncle the priest, at least one usher at the church, MacKenzie herself, and her mother had handled it."

"It probably is useless, but I want a subpoena issued

for it, and for that tape she didn't give you the other night as well. Now call Carolyn and ask what happened to her brother's car. My guess is that after a year or two, they sold it."

Barrott admitted to himself that there was some satisfaction at waking Carolyn so early. Her refusal to play the tape or give it to him on Monday evening had convinced him that beyond any doubt she was protecting her brother. He was pleased when she answered on the first ring, suggesting to him that she had not been sleeping well. Neither have the rest of us, he thought. He spoke to her briefly. From the startled look on his face, Ahearn and Gaylor knew he had stumbled onto an interesting development.

When he disconnected, Barrott said, "She'll check with her lawyer. If he agrees, she will turn over the tape and the note. You may have heard me assure her that he will agree."

"What about her brother's SUV?"

"You're not going to believe this. It was stolen out of the Sutton Place garage in the family's apartment building about eight months after Mack took off."

"Stolen!" Gaylor exclaimed.

"Were other vehicles taken?" Ahearn asked quickly.

"No. That was the only one. It's not a large facility. One kid was on duty, asleep in the booth after midnight. Next thing he knew, he had a bag over his head, tape over his mouth, and was handcuffed to the chair. By the time he was found, that SUV was gone."

The three men looked at one another. "If Mack stole his own wheels, it's entirely possible he's still driving it," Gaylor suggested. "My father-in-law has had his Mercedes for twenty years."

"And if he's still driving it, and if the wino's story checks out, there's an equally good chance that Leesey may have driven off with MacKenzie, not DeMarco," Larry Ahearn said somberly. "All right, let's get those subpoenas. Maybe that tape MacKenzie made with the drama teacher will give us something to work with."

45

Howard Altman was well aware of his boss's shifting loyalties, but his first hint that something was seriously wrong occurred when Mr. Olsen did not go out to brunch with him on Saturday morning. He had noticed Olsen using the new Montblanc pen and correctly guessed that it was probably a present from Steve Hockney, Olsen's nephew.

Steve is schmoozing the old man, Howard thought bitterly. It would be just like Olsen to leave everything to him. The first thing Steve would do is fire me. Then he'd sell all the apartment houses and pocket the cash.

The building he lived in on Ninety-fourth Street was one of the smallest Olsen owned. It was four stories high, with only two apartments on each floor. Most of the tenants had been there for years. His apartment was the only one on the lobby floor. Sparsely furnished and immaculately neat, the living room was dominated by his sixty-inch television set. Most of Howard's evenings were split evenly by his two favorite activities, watching movies on television and visiting on the Internet with buddies from all over the world. He found them infinitely more interesting than the people he met in his daily life.

An excellent chef, he always cooked himself a good dinner, watched a movie while he had a couple of glasses of wine and ate from a tray table, then turned off the television set and went directly to his bedroom computer.

Howard loved this apartment, which came with his job. He loved his job, especially now that he was in charge of all Olsen's buildings. I earned it, he told himself, defensively. I got it because I proved myself. I can fix anything that's broken. I can put up a wall to make two rooms out of one. I can replace old wiring and build cabinets. I can paint and wallpaper and scrape floors. That's why Olsen kept promoting me. But what happens if he leaves everything to Steve?

The question persisted in his mind. For once, he could not focus on the movie in his DVD player. How could he get Olsen to sour on his nephew?

And then the answer came to him. He had a master key to all the apartments in the building where Steve Hockney lived. He'd put a security camera in Steve's apartment. I've seen him when he's high, and I've always suspected that he deals in drugs, Howard thought. If I can prove it, that would finish him with his uncle.

Blood is thicker than water. Maybe.

Pleased at finding a possible solution to the impending problem, he turned off the television and went down the hall to his bedroom. He smiled at the familiar whooshing sound he heard as he turned on his computer.

He realized how much he was looking forward to connecting with his friend Singh in Mumbai tonight.

46

I had barely slept Friday night, and the six A.M. call Saturday morning from Detective Barrott finished any hope I had of drifting off again for at least a few more hours.

Why is Barrott so interested in what happened to Mack's SUV? I asked myself, as I replaced the receiver and got out of bed. As usual, I had left the windows of my bedroom open, and padded across the room to close them. The sun had already risen over the East River and it held the promise of a beautiful day. The breeze was cool, but I could see that this time the weather forecasters were right—it would be sunny and pleasant, about seventy degrees by noon. In short, a perfect morning in late May, which meant that right now there was undoubtedly an exodus from the city by people who hadn't already left for their summer place last night. The residents of Sutton Place who didn't have a second home in the Hamptons almost inevitably had one on the Cape, or Nantucket, or Martha's Vineyard, or *somewhere*.

Dad had never wanted to be anchored to one vacation home, but before Mack disappeared we always went away in August. My favorite was the year I was fifteen, when Dad rented a villa in Tuscany, about half an hour from Florence. It was a magical month, all the more so because it was the last time we were all together.

My mind snapped back to the present. Why did Barrott call me about Mack's SUV?

Our garage is relatively small. It only accommodates the automobiles of the residents of the building, with about ten extra spaces for visitors. Dad had just bought the SUV for Mack a week before he disappeared. Mack had parked it in a garage on the West Side, near his apartment. When he'd been missing two weeks, Dad took the spare key and brought the SUV back here. I remember Mack had obviously driven it in bad weather, because it had some mud splatters on the side and on the driver's mat. Dad paid a guy in our garage to clean it, and he did a great job—so great that nothing was recovered when the cops decided to check the car for prints.

When it was stolen, Dad had been sure that one of the garage attendants had spotted it and planned to steal it. He always thought that the guy who had been tied up was in on the scheme, but there was no proof, and he quit soon after that.

Why did Barrott call me about Mack's SUV?

It was a question that kept repeating itself in my mind as I made coffee and scrambled an egg. The newspapers were at the door, and I glanced through them as I ate. The tabloids were still milking the Leesey Andrews disappearance and speculating about Mack's involvement. Aaron Klein's accusation that Mack had killed his mother to recover his tapes was still a hot story. Now, on page three, there was Mack's yearbook picture, but it had been enhanced to show how he might look today. Trying not to cry, I studied it. Mack's face was a little fuller, his hairline slightly higher, his smile ambiguous. I wondered if Elliott had these same newspapers delivered, and if so, had Mom seen them?

Knowing her, she would have insisted on seeing them. I thought of what Elliott had told me at Thurston Carver's office—that Mom had always been convinced some kind of mental breakdown had caused Mack to disappear. Now I wondered if she could be right, and if so, was it possible that Mack had stolen his own automobile? The prospect was so incredible to me that I realized I was shaking my head. "No, no, no," I said aloud.

But I spoke to him two weeks ago, I admitted to myself. He left that message for Uncle Dev. The only rational explanation for Mack's behavior may be that he is irrational. Mother is afraid that if he is responsible for Leesey Andrews's disappearance and is tracked down by the cops, he may be shot if he resists arrest. Is that reasonable, or possible? I wondered.

Neither Mom nor Dad nor I saw any hint of a change in Mack's behavior before he disappeared, but maybe someone else did. How about Mrs. Kramer? I asked myself. Between cleaning and doing the laundry, she was in his apartment regularly. She acted so nervous when I met her. Did she perceive me as a threat? Maybe if I could get her alone, without her husband around, I could get her to open up to me, I thought.

Bruce Galbraith hates Mack. What happened between them to cause that? Nick suggested that Barbara was crazy about Mack. Is Bruce simply jealous, or did something happen that still makes him angry after ten years?

That train of thought made me speculate on Dr. Barbara Hanover Galbraith's trip to Martha's Vineyard to see her ailing father. I wondered how long she planned to stay there. I remembered that Bruce had responded heatedly when I told him I'd like to talk to her. The thought occurred to me that he might have gotten her out of town to prevent my seeing her or the police from looking her up. Her name is in Mack's file as a close friend, I reminded myself.

I put my few dishes in the dishwasher, went into Dad's office, and turned on the computer to see if I could get her father's address and phone number on Martha's Vineyard. There were several Hanover couples, "Judy and Syd," "Frank and Natalie," and one Richard Hanover listed in the Vineyard. I knew Barbara's mother had died just around the time she graduated, so taking a chance, I dialed Richard Hanover's number.

A man answered on the first ring. It was an older voice but certainly cheerful enough. I had planned what I would say. "This is Cluny Flowers in New York. I want to verify the address of Richard Hanover. Is it eleven Maiden Path?"

"That's right, but who's sending me flowers? I'm not sick, dead, or having a birthday." He sounded fit and healthy.

"Oh, I'm afraid I've made a mistake," I said quickly. "The arrangement is for a Mrs. Judy Hanover."

"No problem. Next time they might be for me. Have a good day."

When I disconnected, my first reaction was to be ashamed of myself. I had turned into an outright liar. My second thought was that Dr. Barbara Hanover Galbraith had left New York not because her father had suffered a heart attack, but because she did not want to be around to be questioned about Mack.

I knew what I was going to do. I showered, dressed, and began to throw a few things in a bag. I had to confront Barbara face-to-face. If Mom was right, and Mack had snapped ten years ago, had she witnessed behavior that might have suggested mental illness? I realized that I was becoming frantic to frame a defense for Mack if he was really out there, alive, unstable, and committing crimes.

I called Elliott's cell phone. The fact that he did not say my name and in a low voice promised he'd call me back told me that Mom was within earshot.

When he did call back half an hour later, I could not believe what he told me. "Your Detective Barrott came here looking to talk to your mother. I told him we would have our lawyer present, but then Olivia screamed at him something like, 'Don't you realize my son had a breakdown? Don't you understand he's not responsible for any of this? He's sick. He doesn't know what he's doing.'"

My mouth was so dry I could only whisper, though there was no need to. "What did Barrott say?"

"He verified what your mother said, that she believed Mack may be mentally ill."

"Where is Mom now?"

"Carolyn, she was so hysterical, I called a doctor. He gave her a shot, but he feels she should be under observation for a few days. I'm driving her up to a wonderful sanitarium in Connecticut where she'll be able to get some rest—and, ah, counseling."

"What place?" I asked. "I'll meet you there."

"It's Sedgwick Manor, in Darien. Carolyn, don't come. Olivia doesn't want to see you, and it will only upset her more if you insist on visiting her. In her mind, you've betrayed Mack. I promise I'll take care of her and I'll call you back as soon as she is settled in there."

I could do nothing but agree. Nothing could be worse for Mack than having Mom telling the police again that she's sure he's insane. When I clicked off, I went into my bedroom and got out Mack's tape and played it while I studied the scrap of paper on which he had printed the ten words he had written to Uncle Devon. "UNCLE DEVON, TELL CAROLYN SHE MUST NOT LOOK FOR ME." I listened to his voice: "When, in disgrace with fortune and men's eyes, I all alone beweep my outcast state, and trouble deaf heaven with my bootless cries."

I could only imagine Barrott's reaction if he was able to get his hands on that note and tape after hearing Mother's outburst. I had barely finished that thought when the concierge phoned to say that Detective Gaylor was on his way up. "I'm sorry, Miss Carolyn, he wouldn't let me announce him. He showed me a subpoena he has to deliver to you."

Before the bell rang, I frantically called Thurston

Carver, our criminal defense lawyer, on his cell phone. He told me, as he had when we met at his office, that I could not refuse to turn over what was ordered in the subpoena.

When I opened the door for Detective Gaylor, he handed me the subpoena, his manner professional and impersonal. It was for the note Mack had left in the collection basket and the tape I had found in his suitcase. Shaking with fury, I almost threw them at him. I took some comfort in knowing that I had made a copy of each.

After he left, I slumped into the nearest chair and again heard myself repeating over and over in my head Mack's taped quotation, "I all alone beweep my outcast state . . ." Finally, I got up, walked to my bedroom, and emptied the bag I had started to pack. It was obvious that any plans I had been making to drive up to Martha's Vineyard would have to be postponed. I was so deep into concentrating on what my next logical move would be that I didn't realize my cell phone was ringing. I rushed to pick it up. It was Nick, about to leave a message. "I'm here," I said.

"Good. This would have been a convoluted message. Carolyn," he said, tersely, "I think you should know that I've just been named a person of interest in the disappearance of Leesey Andrews. I see from the papers that the cops' other theory is that Mack has been running around killing people. I might as well tell you that when I was down at the DA's office on Thursday, they even suggested you and I might be cooperating to protect Mack."

He didn't give me a chance to reply before he said, "I'm flying to Florida this morning for the second time this week. My father's been in the hospital. He had a mild heart attack yesterday. I expect to be back tomorrow. Barring any reason I have to stay in Florida, can we have dinner tomorrow night?" Then he added, "It was so good to see you, Carolyn. I'm beginning to understand why I looked forward to being invited to dinner with your family and why it wasn't the same when Mack's kid sister wasn't around."

I told him that I hoped his father would recover quickly, and that yes, tomorrow night was fine. I held my cell phone to my ear for a few moments after Nick clicked off. My mind was a mess of conflicting emotions. The first one was that I acknowledged to myself I'd never gotten over my crush on him, that all week I'd been hearing his voice, remembering the warmth I'd felt sitting across the table from him the other night.

The second reaction was to wonder if Nick was playing some kind of cat and mouse game with me. The DA's office had named him a "person of interest" in Leesey Andrews's disappearance. I knew that was very, very serious, practically an accusation of guilt. But the police also believed he might be helping me to protect Mack. Nick had not contacted me all week, even though Mack's name had been in the headlines. When we had dinner, he had not been even remotely sympathetic to my fear that Mack might need help.

Had Nick really been named a person of interest? Or was it just a device suggested to him by the police to disarm me? And was Nick, close friend of his former roommate-turned-criminal, now hoping to use his influence to persuade me to turn Mack in if he contacted me again?

I shook my head, as if to clear it of all these questions, but they didn't go away.

Worse still, they didn't lead me anywhere.

47

Dr. David Andrews had not left his home in Greenwich since the phone call from Leesey came in. Sleepless, and now a gaunt shadow of the man he had been before his daughter's disappearance, he kept a vigil by the phone, grabbing it at the first ring every time it rang. He always carried the portable receiver from room to room with him. When he went to bed at night, he placed it on the pillow next to his head.

When he *did* get a call, he immediately cut the conversation to a few words, explaining that he wanted to leave the line open in case Leesey called again.

His housekeeper of twenty years, who usually left after lunch, began staying into the evening, trying to get Dr. Andrews to eat something, even if it was only a cup of soup or coffee and a sandwich. He had made it clear to his friends that he did not want anyone to tie up the line, and refused to allow them to stop by and see him.

"I'm better off if I don't feel obliged to keep up a conversation," he told them.

On Saturday morning, Gregg took Zach Winters down to Larry Ahearn's office, but as he sat in while Ahearn interrogated Zach, he saw his story about seeing Leesey get into the black Mercedes SUV begin to unravel. Zach had said that he hung around on that block for about half an hour, but the employees of the Woodshed, who left only a few minutes after Leesey, all swore they hadn't seen him on the street. He admitted that he was a chronic drunk who had once been thrown out of the Woodshed when he came in and tried to panhandle the customers. He admitted that he was angry at Nick DeMarco, the owner, for having him thrown out, and that he knew Nick owned a black Mercedes SUV.

After the lengthy interrogation, Gregg drove Zach back to where he had found him. Exhausted, Gregg went straight to his apartment and fell asleep until nine o'clock Sunday morning. Then, feeling clearheaded and focused again, he showered, dressed, and drove to Greenwich.

The change in his father in the one week since he had last seen him was shocking. His father's housekeeper, Annie Potters, who never came in on Sunday, was there. "He won't eat," she whispered to Gregg. "It's eleven o'clock and he hasn't touched a morsel since yesterday."

"Would you fix some breakfast for both of us, Annie?" Gregg asked. "I'll see what I can do."

After greeting him, his father had immediately returned to his recliner in the living room, the portable phone within reach. Gregg went back into the living room and sat on the chair nearest the recliner. "Dad, I've been walking the streets at night looking for Leesey. I can't do it anymore, and you can't do *this* anymore! We're not helping Leesey, and we're destroying ourselves. I've been down to the District Attorney's office. There is absolutely nothing Larry Ahearn and his people aren't already doing to find Leesey. I want you to come in and eat something, then we're going out for a walk. It's a beautiful day." He got up, and bent down to hug his father. "You know I'm right."

Dr. David Andrews nodded, then his face crumbled. Gregg embraced him. "Dad, I know. I know. Now, come on, and leave the phone here. If it rings, we'll answer it."

He was cheered to see his father eat half the serving of scrambled eggs and bacon Annie put before him. Gregg was nibbling on a slice of toast and drinking his second cup of coffee when the phone rang. His father bolted up and raced from the table, but he didn't reach the phone before the message began.

It was Leesey, unmistakably. "Daddy, Daddy," she wailed, "help me. Please, Daddy, he says he's going to kill me."

The message ended as Leesey began to sob.

Dr. David Andrews lunged for the phone and grabbed it, but by then he heard only a dial tone. His knees buckled, and Gregg was in time to ease him into his recliner before he collapsed.

Gregg was checking his father's pulse when the phone rang again. It was Larry Ahearn.

"Gregg, that *was* Leesey, wasn't it?"

Gregg pressed the speaker button so that his father could hear. "Absolutely, Larry. You know that."

"Gregg, she's still alive, and we're going to find her. I swear that to you."

Dr. David Andrews grabbed the receiver. His voice hoarse, he shouted, "You've got to find her, Larry. You *heard* her! Whoever has her is going to kill her! For God's sake, find her for me before it's too late!"

48

Exhaustion was forgotten as Larry Ahearn played the tape of Leesey's cry for help to the squad. "The call came in at eleven thirty, exactly one hour ago," he said. "It was made from mid-Manhattan. Of course, there is always a possibility that the abductor made a tape of her voice and played it in a different location."

"And if that's the case, he may already have killed her," Barrott said, quietly.

"We're going to go forward under the assumption that she's still alive," Ahearn snapped. "There's no question that whoever has her is on a short leash. He wants attention. I've talked to our profiler, Dr. Lowe. He thinks that this guy is loving the headlines and the way the story is being covered by Greta Van Susteren and Nancy Grace. He's probably also anticipating the uproar when we release the fact that Leesey called her father again and left that message."

Too restless to sit any longer, he stood and tapped his

fingers on his desk. "I don't want to even think this, but it has to be considered. In another five days, maybe seven, the fact that Leesey phoned will stay big news, but without new information, it won't be the headline anymore."

Every detective from the squad room was crowded tightly into Ahearn's office for the briefing. The expressions on their faces became increasingly grave as they followed the thought Ahearn was voicing. "Leesey went to that club on Monday night and disappeared. Her message promising to call again on Mother's Day came the following Sunday, six days later. After a one-week interval, this new call has come in. It's Dr. Lowe's opinion that our guy may not wait another week to give us a new headline."

"MacKenzie's the one doing this," Roy Barrott said emphatically. "You should have seen his mother yesterday when I went to her boyfriend's apartment."

"Her boyfriend?" Ahearn exclaimed.

"Elliott Wallace, the big investment banker. Aaron Klein, the drama teacher's son, worked for him for fourteen years. Klein told me they became really close when his mother was murdered. Wallace was still so distraught about MacKenzie's disappearance the year before that it gave them a common bond. Mack MacKenzie's father was in Vietnam with Wallace, and they became lifelong friends. It's Klein's opinion that

Wallace has always been in love with Olivia MacKenzie."

"Is she living with him?" Ahearn asked.

"I wouldn't call it that. With all the media around Sutton Place, she went home with him. Having said that, Klein wouldn't be surprised if she married Wallace eventually. He sure was quick to stash her away in a private psychiatric residence so she can't keep telling us her son is crazy."

"Is there any possibility she's in touch with her son?"

Barrott shrugged. "I'd say if Mack has contact with anyone in his family, it's more likely with the sister."

"All right." Ahearn turned to address the group. "I still say that DeMarco may be the one behind all this. I want a tail on him 24/7. I want one on Carolyn MacKenzie, too. We'll apply for a wiretap for any and all phones that aren't already tapped: MacKenzie in her Thompson Street apartment, in Sutton Place, and on her cell phone; DeMarco, wherever he works or hangs his hat."

"Larry, I'd like to make another suggestion," Bob Gaylor said. "Zach Winters may be a wino, but I think he saw something that night. He curls up in doorways. The fact that the band members and waiters from the Woodshed didn't see him on the street doesn't prove anything, and I'd swear he was holding back on us when he was here."

"Go talk to him again," Ahearn said. "He lives in that shelter on Mott Street, doesn't he?"

"Sometimes, but when the weather's good, he puts his stuff in a laundry cart and sleeps outside."

Ahearn nodded. "All right. We're cooperating with the FBI, but I want all of you to keep something in mind. I've known Leesey since she was six years old. I want her back, and I want *us* to be the ones who find her!"

49

On Sunday morning, using the service entrance to duck the media, I went for a long, long walk along the river. I felt whiplashed after Elliott's phone call about Mom, and sick with my doubts about Nick—and, let's face it, about Mack.

The day had fulfilled its promise—warm with a light breeze. The current of the East River, often so strong, seemed as mellow as the sunshine. The boaters were out, not too many of them, adding to the scenery. I love New York. God help me, I even love that blaring, intrusive Pepsi-Cola sign on the Long Island City side of the river.

By the end of a three-hour walk, I was physically and mentally exhausted. When I got back to Sutton Place, I stripped, showered, and got into bed. I slept all afternoon, and woke up at six o'clock feeling at least somewhat clearheaded and a bit more able to cope. I dressed casually, in a blue and white pinstriped shirt and white jeans. I didn't care if Nick showed up in a jacket and tie. I wanted no suggestion of little Carolyn dressing up for a date.

Nick arrived promptly at seven o'clock. He was wearing a sport shirt and chinos. I had intended to steer him straight out the door, but his first words were, "Carolyn, I really need to talk with you, and it might be better if we do it here."

I followed him into the library. "Library" sounds impressive. It really isn't that pretentious. It's just a room with bookshelves and comfortable armchairs and a paneled area that opens to disclose a built-in bar. Nick went straight to it, poured himself a scotch on the rocks, and, without asking, a glass of white wine with a couple of ice cubes for me.

"This is what you had last week. I read somewhere that the Duchess of Windsor put ice in her champagne," he said, as he handed me the glass.

"And I read that the Duke of Windsor liked his whisky neat," I told him.

"Married to her, I shouldn't wonder." He gave a brief smile. "Joking, of course. I have no idea what she was like."

I sat on the edge of the couch. He chose one of the armchairs and swiveled it around. "I remember loving these chairs," he said. "I promised myself that if I ever got rich I'd have at least one of them."

"And?" I asked.

"Never had time to think about it. When I started to make money and bought an apartment, I got an interior decorator. She was into the Western look. When I saw it all finished, I felt like Roy Rogers."

I had been studying him, and I realized that the gray around his temples was even more pronounced than I had thought. There were fresh pouches under his eyes, and the concerned expression I had observed last week had now become one of deep worry. He had flown to Florida yesterday because his father had a heart attack. I asked Nick how he was doing.

"Pretty good. It really was a mild attack. They are releasing him in a couple of days."

Then Nick looked straight at me. "Carolyn, do you think Mack is alive? And if you do, is he capable of what the cops think he's doing?"

It was on the tip of my tongue to be honest, to say that at this point, I simply didn't know, but I caught myself in time. "What on earth makes you ask that? Of course not." I hoped that I sounded as indignant as I wanted to sound.

"Carolyn, don't look at me like that. Can't you understand that Mack was my best friend? I never could figure out why he chose to disappear. Now I wonder if something was going on in his head that nobody realized at the time."

"Are you worried about Mack or about yourself, Nick?" I asked.

"I won't answer that. Carolyn, the one thing I beg of you, *plead* with you, is that if he is in contact with you, or if he *does* call you, don't think you're doing him a favor by shielding him. Did you hear the message Leesey Andrews left for her father this morning?" He looked at me expectantly.

For a moment I was too shaken to speak, then managed to say that I hadn't turned on the radio or television all day. But when Nick told me, all I could think of was Barrott's theory that Mack stole his own car. It's crazy, but it reminded me of the day I was five or six years old and Mack suddenly had a terrible nosebleed. Daddy was home, and he grabbed one of the monogrammed towels from a rack in the bathroom to stem the flow. We had an elderly housekeeper at that time who adored Mack. She was so upset that she tried to yank the towel out of Dad's hand. "That one's for show," she shrieked, "it's for show!"

Daddy always got a kick out of telling that story, but he always added, "Poor Mrs. Anderson was so worried about Mack, but to her the fancy towels just weren't disposable. I told her the towels have our name on them, and Mack can ruin them if he likes!"

I could imagine Mack stealing his own car, but not

Mack holding Leesey hostage and torturing her father. I looked at Nick. "I don't know what to think about Mack," I said. "I swear to you and to anyone who will listen that other than those Mother's Day calls, I have not heard from Mack or seen him in ten years."

Nick nodded, and my guess is that he believed me. Then he asked, "Do you think that *I* am responsible for Leesey's disappearance? That I have her hidden somewhere?"

I examined my heart and my soul before I answered. "No, I don't," I said. "But both of you have been dragged into this, Mack because I went to the police, you because she disappeared from your club. If it's neither one of you, then who *is* responsible?"

"Carolyn, I don't know where to begin to look for the answer to that."

We talked for more than an hour. I told him I was going to try to see Lil Kramer alone, because she was afraid to say anything in front of her husband. We went round and round about the fact that, just before he vanished, Mack had been upset with Mrs. Kramer but hadn't told Nick why. I told Nick how Bruce Galbraith had been so hostile about Mack when I saw him last week, and that I thought Barbara had rushed to visit her father in Martha's Vineyard just to avoid being questioned.

"I'm going to drive up there tomorrow or Tuesday," I said. "Mother doesn't want to see me, and Elliott will take care of her."

Nick asked me if I thought that Mom would marry Elliott.

"I think so," I said. "Quite honestly, I hope so. They're very good together. Mom certainly loved Dad, but he delighted in being a bit of a rebel. Elliott is actually more of a soul mate, which of course is a little hard for me to swallow. They're both perfectionists, and I think they'll be very happy together." Then I added words I'd never thought I'd say. "That's why Mack was always her favorite. He did everything right. I'm too impulsive for Mom's taste. Witness going to the police and opening up this whole mess."

I was appalled that I had confided that to Nick. I think he was about to come over to me, maybe put his arms around me, but he must have known that wasn't what I wanted. Instead, he said, his tone light, "See if you can guess this one: 'She sprang full-fledged from her father's brow.'"

"The goddess Minerva," I said. "Sister Catherine, sixth grade. Man, how she loved teaching mythology." I stood up. "You did ask me to have dinner, you know. How about Neary's? I want a sliced-steak sandwich and french fries."

Nick hesitated. "Carolyn, I have to warn you. There

are cameras outside. My car's near the door. We can make a run for it. I don't think they'll follow us."

That was the way it turned out. The camera lights flashed the moment we exited the building. Someone tried to shove a microphone in my face. "Ms. MacKenzie, do you think your brother . . ." Nick grabbed my hand, and we ran for his car. He drove up York Avenue until Seventy-second Street, then turned and doubled back. "I think we should be okay now," he said.

I didn't agree or disagree. My one consolation was that Mom was in a safe place where the media couldn't get at her.

Neary's is an Irish pub on Fifty-seventh Street, a block away from Sutton Place. It's like a second home for many of us in the neighborhood. The atmosphere is warm, the food is good, and the odds are that on any given night, you'll know half the diners.

If I needed moral support, and God knows I did, Jimmy Neary provided it. When he saw me he crossed the room instantly. "Carolyn, it's a disgrace what they're insinuating about Mack," he told me, putting a warm hand on my shoulder. "That boy was a saint. You wait and see, the truth will come out."

He turned, and recognized Nick. "Hey, kid. Remember when you and Mack came in, you bet me that your father's pasta was a match for my corned beef?"

"We never put it to the test," Nick said. "And now my Dad is in Florida, retired."

"Retired? How does he like it?" Jimmy asked.

"He hates it."

"So would I. Tell him to come back, and we'll finally get the answer."

Jimmy ushered us to one of the corner tables in the back. That was where Nick told me more about the visit to Florida. "I begged my mother to keep the New York papers away from Pop," he said. "I don't know what it will do to him if he finds out I've been designated a 'person of interest' in Leesey's disappearance."

Over sliced-steak sandwiches, by unspoken mutual consent, we drifted into neutral territory. Nick talked about opening his first restaurant and how well it did. He hinted that these last five years, he'd moved too fast. "I think I read Donald Trump's success story once too often," he admitted. "I got the idea that skating on thin ice was fun. I've banked an awful lot on the Woodshed. It's the right spot at the right time. But if the State Liquor Authority wants to shut it down, they'll find a way. And if that happens, I'm in big trouble."

We talked cautiously about Barbara Hanover. "I remember thinking how beautiful she was," I told him.

"She is and was, but Carolyn, there's something else about Barbara, a kind of calculated 'What's best for Barbara?' agenda. It's hard to explain. But after we all graduated and I went for my MBA, Mack was gone, and as for Bruce, I didn't care if I ever saw him again."

We both had a cappuccino, then Nick drove me back to Sutton Place. There was just one television van halfway down the block. He rushed me into the building and to the elevator. As the operator held the door open, Nick said, "Carolyn, I didn't do it and neither did Mack. Hang on to that thought."

He skipped the social kiss and was gone. I went upstairs. The message light was blinking. It was Detective Barrott. "Ms. MacKenzie. At eighty forty P.M. tonight, you received another call from Leesey Andrews's cell phone. Your brother didn't leave a message."

50

Lucas Reeves had not taken the weekend off. He had spent it in his office, working with his technicians. Charles MacKenzie Sr. had hired him nearly ten years ago to find his missing son, and the fact that he had never been able to uncover even the slightest hint of what happened to Mack had given Reeves a sense of failure that was never far from his consciousness.

Now he considered it even more urgent that he find the answer, not only to learn what had happened to Mack, but to find the real killer and perhaps save Leesey Andrews's life.

On Monday morning, Lucas was back in his office on Park Avenue South at eight o'clock. His three permanent investigators had been told to get in early. By eight thirty they were seated around his desk. "I have a hunch, and some of my hunches have worked in the past," he began, "so I'm going to act on it. I am going to assume that Mack is innocent of these crimes, and I am going to assume that someone who knew him at least reasonably well *is* responsible. By that, I mean knew him well enough to hear about the Mother's Day calls, and to have his family's unlisted phone number."

Reeves looked from one investigator to the other. "We are going to start by concentrating on the people around Mack. By that I mean his two roommates, Nick DeMarco and Bruce Galbraith. We are going to dig up everything we can learn about the superintendent couple, Lil and Gus Kramer. From there we will concentrate on Mack's other friends from Columbia who were with him in the nightclub the evening that first girl disappeared. Over the weekend, our techs have gathered all the newspaper accounts and media clips that were headlines when each of those other three girls vanished. We have enhanced the faces of everyone caught in those pictures, whether he or she was identifiable or not. Study those faces. *Memorize* them."

Lucas had come in so early that he had made his own coffee. He took a sip, grimaced, and continued. "The media is camped outside Sutton Place. One of you must be in the vicinity at all times. Have your cell phone out, and be using it as a camera. Somebody also has to be on the street when the Woodshed opens tonight, taking pictures not only of guests entering and leaving, but of people hanging around in the streets.

There are a couple of other clubs opening in SoHo this week. Be there with the paparazzi."

"Lucas, that's impossible," Jack Rodgers, his most senior aide, protested. "The three of us can't cover all that ground."

"No one asked you to," Reeves snapped, his normally deep voice several octaves higher. "Get out the list of the guys we use when we need extra help. We must have thirty retired cops available."

Rodgers nodded. "Okay."

Reeves lowered his voice. "My hunch is that the perpetrator loves attention. He may want to be on-site when there's a media rush. The faces that show in every picture you snap will be enhanced in our lab. I don't care how many there are, and I assume there will be hundreds. Maybe, just maybe, one of them will be a match for someone who was around during the media frenzy that followed those other disappearances. I repeat, for the present we are going to assume that Mack MacKenzie is innocent."

He looked at Rodgers. "Why don't you say it, Jack?"

"All right, Lucas, I'll say it. If you're right, we may find a picture of a guy who shows up all over the place. He may be fat, he may be thin, he may be bald, he may have a ponytail. He'll be someone his own mother wouldn't recognize, and he'll be Charles MacKenzie Jr."

51

Detective Bob Gaylor began searching for Zach Winters on Sunday after the squad meeting. He was not at the Mott Street shelter that was his off-and-on home. He had not been seen on the streets since early Saturday morning, when he had been hanging around the Woodshed, and then had gone to Gregg Andrews's apartment. He had been interrogated on Saturday afternoon, then presumably had gone back to his usual haunts. But he had not gone back to the shelter.

"Zach usually shows up at least every other day," Joan Coleman, an attractive thirty-year-old volunteer kitchen worker on Mott Street, confided to Gaylor. "Of course, it depends on the weather. He loves the club area in SoHo. He brags that he gets better handouts there."

"Did he ever talk about being near the Woodshed the night Leesey Andrews disappeared?"

"Not to me. But he's got a couple of what he calls his

'real good buddies.' Let me talk to them." She brightened at the idea of doing detective work.

"I'll go with you," Gaylor volunteered.

She shook her head. "Not if you want to get any information, you won't. I don't usually come in for dinner, but I'm subbing for a friend tonight. Give me your phone number. I'll call you."

Bob Gaylor had to be content with that. He spent the better part of the day wandering through SoHo and Greenwich Village to no avail.

Zach Winters might have disappeared from the face of the earth.

52

True to his word, Derek Olsen arrived at Elliott Wallace's office promptly at ten A.M. His gait stiff, his suit cleaned and pressed, but shiny with age, his remaining tufts of white hair plastered down on his skull, there was a certain buoyancy about him. Elliott Wallace observed him and correctly interpreted that Olsen, if he followed his plan to liquidate all his holdings, was looking forward to telling his nephew Steve, his buildings manager, Howie, and anyone else he could think of, to go jump in a lake.

A cordial smile on his face, Wallace urged Olsen to take a chair. "I know you won't refuse a cup of tea, Derek."

"Last time, it tasted like dishwater. Tell your secretary I want four lumps of sugar and heavy cream, Elliott."

"Of course."

Olsen barely waited for Elliott to instruct his secretary before he said with a satisfied smile, "You and your advice. Remember you said I should get rid of those three broken-down town houses that have been closed for years?"

Elliott Wallace knew what was coming. "Derek, you've been paying taxes and insurance on those dumps for years. Of course real estate has gone up, but if you wish I will show you that if you had sold them and bought the stocks I recommended, you'd be ahead."

"No, I wouldn't! I knew that someday they'd tear down those buildings on the corner of 104th Street and developers would want my place."

"The developers seem to have managed without it. They already broke ground for those condominium apartments."

"The same firm came back to me. I close on the sale this afternoon."

"Congratulations," Wallace said sincerely. "But I do hope you remember that I've made you quite a lot of money investing on your behalf."

"Except for that hedge fund."

"Except for the hedge fund, I agree, but that was quite a while ago."

Olsen's tea and Elliott's coffee arrived. "This is good," Olsen said, after taking a wary sip. "The way I like it. Now let's talk. I want to sell everything. I want to establish a trust fund. You can run it. I want it to be used for parks in New York, parks with lots of trees. This city has too many big buildings."

"That's very generous of you. Are you planning to leave anything to your nephew or anyone else?"

"I'll leave Steve fifty thousand dollars. Let him get a new set of drums or a guitar. He can't look at me over a dinner plate without trying to figure how much longer I'll last. I heard from a couple of my building supers that he announced he'll be taking over Howie's job as my overall manager. He buys me a fountain pen and takes me to dinner, and because I show good feelings to him, he thinks he can take over my business. Him and his gigs. Every time he stops getting jobs at those club dumps, he invents a new name for himself and his loser band, finds the latest kind of weird outfit, and hires a broken-down PR agent. If it wasn't for his mother, my sister, God rest her, I'd have given him the bum's rush years ago."

"I know he's been a disappointment to you, Derek." Elliott tried to maintain his compassionate expression.

"Disappointment! Hah! By the way, I want to leave Howie Altman fifty thousand dollars, too."

"I'm sure he'll appreciate it. Does he know your plans?"

"No. He's been getting pushy, too. I can tell he has the nerve to think he's entitled to a big inheritance from me. Don't misunderstand. He's done a good job, and I thank you for recommending him when that other guy didn't work out."

Elliott nodded, acknowledging the thanks. "One of my other clients was selling a building and mentioned his availability."

"Well, he'll soon be available again. But he's not blood, and he doesn't understand that when you have good workers like the Kramers, you don't squeeze them out of an extra bedroom or two."

"George Rodenburg is still your lawyer, isn't he?"

"Of course. Why would I change?"

"What I meant was that I'll talk to him about setting up the foundation. You say you're closing on the 104th Street property this afternoon. Do you want me there?"

"Rodenburg will handle it. The offer's been on the table for years. It's only the dollars that are different."

Olsen got up to go. "I was born on Tremont Avenue in the Bronx. It was a nice neighborhood then. I have pictures of my sister and me sitting on the steps of one of those little apartment buildings, the kind I own now. I drove up there last week. It's pretty bad. There's a corner lot near where we lived. It's a mess, weeds and beer cans and garbage. While I'm still alive, I want to see it become a park." A beatific smile crossed his face as he turned to the door. "Good-bye, Elliott."

Elliott Wallace walked his client through the reception room, down the corridor to the elevator, returned to his private office, and for the first time in his adult life, went to the bar refrigerator and, at eleven A.M., poured himself a straight scotch.

53

Late on Monday morning, I drove up to Mack's old apartment building. I pushed the Kramers' button on the intercom, and was rewarded after a moment by a hesitant greeting. I knew I had to talk fast. "Mrs. Kramer, this is Carolyn MacKenzie. I need to talk to you."

"Oh, no. My husband is out this morning."

"I want to talk to *you*, not to him, Mrs. Kramer. Please let me come in for just a few minutes."

"Gus won't like it. I can't . . ."

"Mrs. Kramer, you must be reading the newspapers. Surely you know that the police think my brother may be responsible for that girl's disappearance. I need to talk with you."

For a moment I thought she had hung up, but then I heard a click as the door to the lobby unlocked. I went in, crossed the lobby, and rang her bell. She opened it a crack as though to reassure herself that I didn't have an army of people ready to storm the apartment, then opened it just wide enough for me to enter.

The room that had so reminded me of my paternal grandmother's living room in Jackson Heights was in the process of being stripped and dismantled. There were large cartons stacked in the corner. The curtains and draperies had been taken down from the windows. There were no pictures on the wall, and the side tables were bare of the lamps and bric-a-brac I'd seen on my last visit.

"We're moving to our cottage in Pennsylvania," Lil Kramer said. "Gus and I are more than ready to retire."

She's running away, I thought, as I studied her. Even though the room was cool, she had tiny beads of sweat on her forehead. Her gray hair was pulled away from her face and anchored firmly behind her ears. Her complexion was the same dull gray as her hair. I am sure she was unaware that her hands were massaging each other in a fretful, nervous pattern.

Uninvited, I sat on the nearest chair. I realized there was absolutely no use in not coming directly to the point. "Mrs. Kramer, you knew my brother. Do *you* think he's a killer?"

She rubbed her lips together. "I don't know what he is." Then she burst out, "He told lies about me. I was so nice to him. I really liked him. I took such good care of his clothes and his room. And then he accused me."

"Accused you of what?"

"Never mind. It wasn't true, but I couldn't believe my ears."

"When did that happen?"

"A few days before he disappeared. And then he ridiculed me."

Neither one of us had heard the outside door open. "Shut your mouth, Lil," Gus Kramer ordered as he strode across the room. He turned to face me. "And you get out of here. Your brother had the nerve to treat my wife the way he did, and now look at what he's done to those young girls."

Furious, I stood up. "Mr. Kramer, I don't know what you're talking about. I can't believe Mack mistreated your wife in any way, shape, or form, and I would stake my own life that he is not responsible for any crime."

"Keep on believing that, and let me tell you what I'm talking about. My wife is going to have a nervous breakdown worrying that when they catch your killer brother, he'll turn on her and accuse her with his dirty lies."

"Don't call him a killer," I said. "Don't you *dare* call him a killer."

Gus's face flooded with rage. "I'll call him what I want to call him, but I'll give you this. He's a killer who goes to church. Lil saw him the day he left the note in the collection basket, didn't you, Lil?"

"I didn't have my glasses with me, but I'm still sure." Lil Kramer began to cry. "I recognized him. He saw me looking at him. I mean, he had on a raincoat and dark glasses, but it was Mack in that church."

"Just for your information, the cops were here an hour ago, and we told them that," Gus Kramer shouted at me. "Now get out of here and leave my wife alone."

54

On Saturday evening, after he was sure Steve had left for one of his gigs, Howard Altman had let himself into Steve's apartment. Carefully and skillfully, he had placed hidden cameras in the living room and bedroom. The video would be beamed directly into his computer.

Why didn't I think of this sooner? he asked himself, as he set up the surveillance. *Thanks, Steve, for making it so easy for me.* Steve had left lights on in both rooms, as well as in the bathroom. *Derek pays the gas and electric bill for him,* Howard thought resentfully. *He charges me for mine!*

And Steve was a slob. His bed wasn't made. A couple of those stupid costumes he wore to some of his gigs were piled on a chair. The hairpieces and wigs he used when he was acting out some of his characters were tossed in a cardboard box on the floor. Howard tried on one of them, a wig with long dark-brown hair. He stared at himself in the mirror, then ripped it off. He looked like a woman in it, and that made him think of that teacher who had once lived in this apartment and had been murdered.

I don't know how Steve Hockney can live in a place that belonged to someone who was murdered, he thought. I have to get out of here.

On Monday morning, Howard went to pick up Mr. Olsen for one of their scheduled visits to the properties, but he wasn't there. The super in that building told him that Olsen had already been picked up by a car service.

Deeply uneasy, Howard went to their usual first stop, the building where the Kramers were the supers. He was about to unlock the lobby door when it was flung open and a pretty young woman, tears streaming down her cheeks, ran past him.

Carolyn MacKenzie! he thought. What's *she* doing here? He turned and raced after her, catching her a half block away as, remote in hand, she opened the lock on her car door. "Ms. MacKenzie, I'm Howard Altman. We met a couple of weeks ago when you were talking to the Kramers." He spoke in a hurry, slightly out of breath.

He watched as she impatiently brushed away the tears that were still spilling from her eyes. "I'm afraid I really can't talk right now," she said.

"Look, I've been seeing your picture in the papers

and reading all that stuff about your brother. That was before I worked for Mr. Olsen, but I wish I could help you somehow."

"Thank you. I wish you could, too."

"If the Kramers have upset you in any way, I'll take care of them," he promised.

She did not answer, but gave his arm a push to oblige him to get out of the way of the driver's door. Howard stepped back, and with a quick movement, she had opened the door, closed it, and started the car. She did not look at him again as she backed up a few feet, turned the wheel, pulled out of the parking space, and was gone.

His face grim, Howard Altman headed straight for the Kramers' apartment. They did not answer the insistent ringing of their doorbell. He tried to open the door with his key, but the security lock was on. "Gus and Lil, I have to talk to you," he shouted.

"Go to hell," Gus Kramer shouted from the other side of the door. "We're out of here today. You can have this job and this apartment and everything that goes with it. And just so you know, Howie, you'd better watch your back. If Steve has anything to do with it, you'll be looking for a place to live yourself. Now get lost."

Standing there in the hallway, there was nothing Howard could do except leave. Was Steve making the rounds with Olsen? he wondered. Why else would Olsen have ordered a car service this morning?

There was one way he could find out for sure if Steve was around. Howard went back to his apartment and turned on his computer. Scanning the videocam footage, he noted Steve had been in and out of his apartment all day yesterday, but he was always alone. Now there was no one in his living room. So maybe he *was* out with Olsen, Howard thought, but then the bedroom camera showed Steve sitting in his underwear on the edge of the bed, trying on one after another of his wigs. The last one he selected was the one with the long brown hair. The camera caught him smiling at his image and blowing a kiss at the mirror. Then Steve turned and looked straight into the lens.

"Howie, I have my own security cameras installed here," he said. "I need them. Some of my friends aren't exactly trustworthy customers. If you're watching this, or when you *do* watch it, have a nice day."

With trembling fingers, Howard turned off his computer.

55

At noon on Monday, Detective Bob Gaylor received a phone call from the young kitchen worker he'd met at the Mott Street shelter. "Hi, it's Joan Coleman," she said, sounding excited. "I promised to find out what I could about Zach."

The squad room was noisy, but Gaylor blocked out everything but Joan Coleman's voice. "Okay," he said. "What can you tell me?"

"He's on the streets for good. No more shelters, now that it's warm. He showed up with his stuff near the Brooklyn Bridge last night, totally drunk. He was telling his friends that he might get a reward in the Leesey Andrews case."

"He's tried that. I don't think it's going to work."

"My informant, Pete, is a young guy who just might make it. He's an addict, but he keeps trying. He's pretty clean right now, so I trust what he's telling me." She lowered her voice. "He says that Winters claims he has some kind of proof, but can't show it because they'll blame everything on him."

"Okay. So, Winters was in the Brooklyn Bridge area last night?"

"Yes, near some kind of construction site, and he's probably still around there. From what Pete told me, he has a lot to sleep off."

"Joan, if you ever want a job in this department," Gaylor said fervently, "you've got it!"

"No, thanks. I've got enough on my plate trying to do what I can for these poor guys."

"Thanks again, Joan."

Gaylor got up, went into Larry Ahearn's office, and briefed him.

Ahearn listened quietly. "You thought Winters was holding back on us," he said. "Looks as if you could be right. Find him and shake it out of him. Maybe he'll still be drunk enough to spill his guts to you."

"Have you heard any more from Leesey's family?"

Ahearn leaned back in his chair with a sigh. "I spoke to Gregg this morning. He's keeping his father pretty sedated. He won't leave him until this is resolved one way or the other." He shrugged. "Having said that, you and I both understand that we may never know what happened, or what *will* happen to Leesey."

"I don't believe that," Gaylor said. "You were right yesterday when you felt this guy wants attention."

"I'm also beginning to believe he wants to be caught, but in a way that will be a spectacular blowup." Ahearn's hands curled into fists. "Gregg told me an hour ago that he feels so damn helpless. Well, so do I."

As Gaylor turned to go, the phone rang again. Ahearn picked up the receiver, listened for a moment, and said, "Put him through." Waving Gaylor back, he said, "It's Gregg Andrews."

Gaylor listened as Larry Ahearn said, "Of course if your father wants an appeal printed in the media, we'll pass it on to them." He sat down and picked up a pen. "It's from the Bible. Okay." He wrote as he held the phone to his ear, stopping Gregg Andrews once, to repeat something, then said, "I have it. I'll take care of it."

With a deep sigh, he put the receiver down. "This is what Dr. Andrews would like to have read on the television stations and printed in the newspapers so that Leesey's abductor understands just how desperately he needs to have her returned to him safe and sound. It's from the prophet Hosea:

"'When you were a child I loved you . . .
It was I who taught you to walk, took you in my arms . . .
I was to you like those who lift infants to their cheeks.

I bent down and fed you . . .
How could I give you up?'"

Both men's eyes glistened with tears as Detective Bob Gaylor left to search for Zach Winters.

Visions of dollar bills, stacks and stacks of them, were dancing in Zach Winters's brain as he opened his eyes to see some guy standing over him. He had been curled up in one of his favorite spots, a construction site near the Brooklyn Bridge, where the former parking garage had been pulled down, but the new building hadn't been started yet. The board fence had been ripped open, and now that it was warm, he and many of his friends used the site as their home base. Every ten days or two weeks the cops chased them out, but after a day or so they all came back with their gear. Like Zach, they all understood that when construction actually started, they'd be on their way again, but until then, it was a great spot to camp.

Zach had been dreaming about the fifty-thousand-dollar reward he would collect as soon as he figured out a way to collect it without getting himself into trouble, when he felt someone shaking his shoulder.

"Come on, Zach, wake up," a man's voice was demanding.

Zach opened his eyes slowly. A sense of familiarity

seeped its way into his brain. I know this guy. He's police. He was in that room when the brother took me to talk about seeing Leesey. Be careful, Zach warned himself. He's the one who was so nasty that day.

Zach rolled over and slowly propped himself up on his elbows. He had covered himself with his winter jacket and now he pushed it aside. He blinked at the strong afternoon sun, then looked around quickly to make sure that his grocery cart was still there. He had slept with it flat on the ground next to him, his legs straddling the handle so that no one could reach into it without moving him first. It was safe enough, though some of the newspapers he had tucked in at the top were slipping out.

He blinked again. "Whadaya want?" he asked.

"I want to talk to you. Get up."

"All right. All right. Take it easy." Zach groped for the wine bottle that had been next to him when he fell asleep.

"It's empty," Gaylor snapped. He grabbed Zach's arm, and yanked him up sharply. "You've been telling your friends that you know something about Leesey's disappearance, something you didn't tell us the other day. What is it?"

"I don't know what you're talking about."

"Yes, you do." Gaylor bent down, grabbed the handle of the cart, and pulled it upright. "You've been telling your friends you have something that might earn you the reward that's been offered for Leesey Andrews. What is it?"

Zach made a gesture of brushing soil from his jacket. "I know my rights. Get away from me." He reached for the handle of his cart. Gaylor refused to let go of it, and blocked his way.

The detective's tone was angry. "Zach, why don't you cooperate with me? I want you to unload that cart and show me everything in it. We know you couldn't have had anything to do with Leesey's disappearance. You're too much of a drunk to have managed it. If you've got something in your stuff that helps us to find her, you'll get your reward. I promise."

"Yeah, sure you do." Zach reached out and tried to grab the handle from Gaylor. The cart swayed and some of the newspapers fell out. Beneath them, a filthy man's shirt was partially wrapped around what Gaylor instantly recognized as an expensive cosmetic case.

"Where'd you get that?" he snapped.

"None of your business." Zach righted the cart quickly and pushed the papers back into place. "I'm out of here." He began pushing the cart briskly toward the nearest sidewalk.

Staying in step with him, Gaylor grabbed his cell phone and dialed Ahearn. "I need a search warrant to seize the contents of Zach Winters's cart," he said.

"He's got an expensive silver and black cosmetic bag that I'll bet belongs to Leesey Andrews. I'll stick with him until you get back to me. And find out from Leesey's roommate if she knows what kind of cosmetic bag Leesey was carrying that night."

Forty minutes later, backed up by two squad cars, the warrant in his pocket, Gaylor was opening Leesey Andrews's cosmetic case.

"I was scared you'd think I stole it," Zach Winters was whining. "When she was getting in the SUV, she dropped her pocketbook. Some stuff spilled out. She picked most of it up, but when they drove off, I went over there to see if maybe a few dollars had fallen out of her bag. You know what I mean. And I saw this and I took it, and I'll be honest with you, she had a fifty-dollar bill in it and maybe I gave myself a little reward and—"

"And why don't you shut up?" Bob Gaylor interrupted. "If you'd given this to us, even on Saturday, it might have made a difference."

Besides the usual cosmetics typical of a young woman's accessories, he had taken out a personal card. It belonged to Nick DeMarco, and gave the address and phone number of his loft. On the back of the card he had written, "Leesey, I can open some doors for you in show business and I'd be glad to do it. Call me.—Nick."

56

With a satisfied smile, Derek Olsen signed the last of the mountain of papers that transferred the dilapidated town house he owned on 104th Street and Riverside Drive to Twining Enterprises, the multimillion-dollar real estate firm that was building an upscale luxury condominium next door. He had insisted that Douglas Twining Sr., the chairman and CEO of the company, personally attend the sale.

"I knew you'd pay what I wanted, Doug," Olsen said. "It was a lot of baloney that you didn't need my building."

"I didn't need it. I wanted it," Twining said quietly. "I could have done without it."

"And not have the corner? Not have the view? Maybe have me sell it to someone who put up one of those dumb sliver buildings so your fancy people look west at a brick wall? Come on."

Twining looked at his lawyer. "Are we finished here?"

"I believe so, sir."

Twining stood up. "Well, Derek, I suppose I should congratulate you."

"Why not? Twelve million dollars for a fifty-by-one-hundred-foot lot with a broken-down house that I paid fifteen thousand for forty years ago? That's inflation for you." Olsen's gleeful smile disappeared. "If it makes you feel any better, I'm putting this money to good use. A lot of kids in the Bronx, kids who won't grow up in your fancy-schmancy condos and won't go to the Hamptons for the summer, will now have some parks to play in—Derek Olsen parks. So when are you going to tear down the house?"

"The wrecking ball will be there Thursday morning. I think I'll handle it myself. I haven't forgotten how to do it."

"I'll come watch. Good-bye, Doug." Olsen turned to his lawyer, George Rodenburg. "Okay, let's get out of here," he said. "You can buy me an early dinner. I was too excited to eat lunch. And while we're eating, I'll phone my nephew and Howie and let them know that it's coming down on Thursday morning. I'll tell them I just got twelve million bucks for it and it's all going for my parks. I only wish I could see their faces. They'll both have heart attacks."

57

After I left the Kramers', I drove straight into the garage at Sutton Place, passed the flashing cameras, went upstairs, and threw some things in a bag. Wearing the biggest dark glasses I could find, to cover my face, I went back down in the elevator to the garage, this time taking my mother's car to fool them. Then, hoping to God I wouldn't cause an accident, I barreled out onto the street and made a quick turn onto Fifty-seventh Street. I drove up First Avenue as far as Ninety-sixth Street, trying to make sure that I wasn't being followed. I didn't want anyone to have any idea of where I might be going.

Of course, I couldn't be sure, but certainly there was no media van in sight when I turned right on Ninety-sixth and got on the FDR Drive north. The Drive, of course, was named to honor President Franklin Delano Roosevelt. That made me think of Elliott. The chilling thought came to me that if Mack was guilty of all these crimes and was caught, there would be months of publicity and a trial or trials. Elliott had lots of gold-plated clients. I know he's in love with Mom, but would he want to be associated with that kind of publicity? If he were married to Mom, would he want to see her picture in the tabloids during a trial?

Right now, he was her protector, but would that last? If Dad were alive now and Mack ended up in that scenario, I know Dad would be there for him, rock solid and moving heaven and earth to build an insanity defense for him. I thought of Elliott's too often repeated anecdote about FDR—that he chose a Republican to be his hostess when Eleanor was away because there was no Democrat in Hyde Park who was his social equal. I wonder what FDR, or Elliott, would think about having the mother of a convicted serial killer around? The way things were going, I could almost hear Elliott giving a "let's just be friends" speech to Mom.

As I reached the ever miserable cross Bronx traffic, I tried to stop thinking and concentrate on my driving. With traffic slowing to a crawl, I called ahead and managed to get a reservation on the last ferry to the Vineyard from Falmouth. Then I made a reservation at the Vineyard Hotel in Chappaquiddick. And then I turned off my cell phone. I didn't want to speak to or hear from anyone.

It was nearly nine thirty when I arrived on the island

and checked into the hotel. Exhausted but still restless, I went down to the bar and had a hamburger and two glasses of red wine. Then, against all sound medical advice, I took one of the sleeping pills I had found in Mom's night table and went to bed.

I slept for twelve hours straight.

58

At 4:30 P.M. Nick DeMarco was in his midtown office when his phone rang. It was Captain Larry Ahearn with a crisp request that he come to his office immediately. Swallowing over the absolute dryness in his mouth and throat, Nick agreed. As soon as he hung up, he dialed his attorney, Paul Murphy.

"I'll start right down," Murphy told him. "I'll meet you in the lobby there."

"I can do better than that," Nick said. "I was planning to leave in fifteen minutes anyway, which means Benny is probably outside right now circling the block. I'll call you when I'm in the car. We'll swing by and get you."

At five past five, Benny at the wheel, they were driving south on Park Avenue. "The way I see it, it's their way of rattling you," Murphy told him. "The only, and I repeat *only,* circumstantial evidence they can lay at your door are two facts: One, you invited Leesey over to talk with you in the club, and two, you have a black

Mercedes SUV, which makes you one of thousands of owners of a black Mercedes SUV."

He shot a look at DeMarco. "Of course, you could have saved me from being surprised last time we were there."

Murphy had dropped his voice almost to a whisper, but Nick still nudged him with his elbow. He knew Murphy was referring to the fact that Benny's second wife had taken out a restraining order against him. He also knew that Benny had superb hearing and missed nothing.

The traffic was so unbearably slow that Murphy decided to phone Ahearn's office. "Just to let you know that we're in the usual five o'clock rush and can't do a thing about it."

Ahearn's response was simple. "Just get here. We're not going anywhere. Is DeMarco's chauffeur, Benny Seppini, driving the car you're in?"

"Yes, he is."

"Bring him up, too."

It was ten minutes of six when Nick DeMarco, Paul Murphy, and Benny Seppini walked through the squad room to Larry Ahearn's private office. They all noticed the frigid stares from the detectives in the squad room as they hurried through it.

Inside Ahearn's office, the atmosphere was even colder. Ahearn was again flanked by Detectives Barrott and Gaylor. There were three chairs in front of the desk. "Sit down," Ahearn said curtly.

Benny Seppini looked at DeMarco. "Mr. DeMarco, I don't think it's my place . . ."

"Cut the servant routine. You know you call him Nick," Ahearn interrupted. "And sit down now."

Seppini waited until DeMarco and Murphy had taken their places, then lowered himself into his chair. "I've known Mr. DeMarco for many years," he said. "He's an important man, and when I'm not alone with him, I call him Mr. DeMarco."

"That's touching," Ahearn said sarcastically. "Now let's all listen to this." He pressed the play button on a recorder, and Leesey Andrews's voice pleading to her father for help filled the room.

There was a moment of intense silence following the recording, then Paul Murphy asked, "What was the point of playing that recording for us?"

"I'm happy to tell you," Ahearn assured him. "I thought it might remind your client of the fact that as of yesterday, Leesey Andrews was probably still alive. We thought it might stir his better self to tell us where we can find her."

DeMarco sprang up from the chair. "I have no more idea than you do of where that poor girl is, and I'd give anything I have to save her life if I could."

"I'm sure you would," Barrott replied, his voice

dripping with sarcasm. "You thought she was pretty cute, didn't you? In fact, you slipped her your personal card with the address of your cozy loft apartment."

He held up the card, cleared his throat, and read, "'Leesey, I can open some doors for you in show business and I'd be glad to do it. Call me. —Nick.'"

He slapped the card down on the table. "You gave it to her that night, didn't you?"

"You don't have to answer that, Nick," Murphy warned.

Nick shook his head. "There's no reason not to answer it. Those few minutes she was at my table, I told her she was a beautiful dancer, which she certainly was. She confided that she'd love to take a year off after college, just to see if she could make it on the stage. I do know a lot of celebrities. So I gave her the card. So what?" He met Ahearn's suspicious gaze.

"You seem to have forgotten to mention it to us," Ahearn stated, scorn in every syllable he uttered.

"I've been here three times," Nick said, clearly agitated now. "Every time you come at me as if I had something to do with her disappearance. I know you can find some way to have my liquor license suspended at the Woodshed, even if you have to *create* a violation—"

"Stop it, Nick," Murphy ordered.

"I won't stop it. I had nothing to do with her disappearance. The last time I was here, you suggested I'm way overextended. You're absolutely right. If you shut down the Woodshed, I'll be thrown into bankruptcy. I've made some lousy decisions, I don't deny that, but hurting or abducting a kid like Leesey Andrews isn't one of them."

"You gave her your card," Bob Gaylor said.

"Yes, I did."

"When did you expect her to phone you at your loft?"

"My loft?"

"You gave her a card with the address of your loft and the phone number of the landline there."

"That's ridiculous. I gave her the card with my business address, 400 Park Avenue."

Barrott tossed the card at him. "Read it."

Perspiration on his forehead, Nick DeMarco read the print on the card several times before he spoke. "That was two weeks ago today," he said, more to himself than to the others. "I had some cards made, with just the loft address. They came in that day from the printer. I must have put one of them in my wallet. I thought I was giving my office card to Leesey."

"Why would you need an address card for the loft and the telephone number there unless you wanted to slip it to beautiful girls like Leesey?" Barrott asked.

"Nick, we can get up and walk out of here right now," Murphy said.

"That's not necessary. I've got my Fifth Avenue apartment up for sale. I plan to live in the loft. I have too many friends I haven't seen in a long time because I've been too busy trying to be a hotshot restaurant and club owner. Having those cards made was a gesture toward the future." He placed the card back on the desk.

"Is one of the people you want to see in the loft Mack MacKenzie's sister, Carolyn?" Barrott asked. "Cute picture of the two of you, hand in hand, rushing for your car last night. It brought tears to my eyes."

Ahearn turned to Benny Seppini. "Benny, let's talk to you now. The night Leesey disappeared, you had taken Nick's, excuse me, I mean Mr. DeMarco's black Mercedes SUV home with you to Astoria, isn't that right?"

"I drove his *sedan* home." Benny's scarred, rough features began to turn a dull red.

"Don't you have a car? Surely you must get paid enough to have your own wheels."

"I can answer that," Nick interrupted, before Benny could speak. "Last year when Benny told me he was trading his car in, I told him it was stupid for him to be paying insurance and upkeep on a car when I was paying to house three vehicles in a Manhattan garagc, at Midtown prices no less. I suggested that he drive the SUV between his home and Manhattan and then switch to the sedan at the garage when he drove me to appointments."

Ahearn ignored him. "So, Benny, you drove the black Mercedes SUV, which your kindly employer offered you to use as your own vehicle, to your apartment in Astoria two weeks ago tonight, the night Leesey disappeared."

"No. Mr. DeMarco had the SUV in the garage at the loft because he was going to drive to the airport in the morning with his golf clubs. I dropped him off at the Woodshed at about ten o'clock in the sedan, then drove home to my place that night."

"You then went into your apartment, and to bed."

"Uh-huh. That was about eleven o'clock."

"Benny, the parking problem is pretty lousy in your neighborhood, isn't it?"

"Parking's lousy everywhere in New York City."

"But you lucked out. You got a spot for your employer's vehicle right in front of your apartment building. Isn't that right?"

"Yeah, that's where I parked it. I got home and got into bed and turned on Jay Leno. He was really funny. He was talking about . . ."

"I don't care what he was talking about. I care about the fact that the black Mercedes vehicle owned by Nick DeMarco wasn't there the whole night. Your neighbor in apartment 6D saw you pulling into a space in front of the building at about 5:15, when he was leaving for work. Tell us, Benny, where had you been? Did you get an emergency call from Mr. DeMarco? Had there been some kind of problem?"

Benny Seppini's expression became angry and mulish. "None of your business," he barked.

"Benny, do you have a cell phone with a prepaid card?" Ahearn demanded.

"You don't have to answer that, Benny," Paul Murphy shouted.

"Why not? Sure I do. I place a few bets. A hundred bucks here and there. So arrest me."

"Didn't you buy one of those cell phones and prepaid cards as a joke birthday present for Nick, I mean Mr. DeMarco?"

"Keep quiet, Benny!" Paul Murphy shouted.

Benny stood up. "Why should I? I'll tell you what happened that night. I got a call around midnight from a very nice lady who is separated from a drunken bum husband. She was scared. The husband knows she and I like each other. He left a crazy message on her cell phone, threatening her. I couldn't get back to sleep, so I got dressed and drove over there. Her place is about a mile away from mine. I sat outside her building in the car to make sure he didn't show up after the bars closed. I stayed till five o'clock. Then I went home."

"You're a real Sir Galahad, Benny," Ahearn said. "Who is this woman? Who's the guy threatening her?"

"He's a cop," Benny said flatly. "One of New York's finest. She has grown kids who think he's the world's best guy and just has a small problem with booze. She don't want trouble. *I* don't want trouble. So I'm not going to say nothing more."

Paul Murphy stood up. "We've had enough," he told Ahearn, Barrott, and Gaylor. "I'm sure you'll be able to confirm Benny's story, and I know my client would do anything to help the young girl who is missing." He threw them all a scornful look. "Why don't you stop barking up the wrong tree, and go find the abductor of Leesey Andrews and those other young women? And why don't you stop wasting your time trying to put round pegs in square holes while there may still be a chance to save her life?"

The three detectives watched the men depart. When the door closed behind them, Ahearn said, "That story is full of holes. Sure, Benny could have covered himself by being outside his girlfriend's building for a while, but he still had plenty of time to respond to an emergency call from Nick and get Leesey out of that loft."

They looked at one another in an agony of frustration, each man hearing in his head, once again, Leesey Andrews's desperate cry for help.

59

"And the walls came tumbling down . . ." Was that an old gospel folk hymn? Something about Joshua and the walls of Jericho? He wasn't sure. The only thing that *was* sure was that time was running out, fast.

I really, *really* didn't want to end up like this, he thought. It was forced on me. I really did try to stop after the first one. That wasn't counting the *real* first one, of course, the one nobody knew about. But then I wasn't allowed to stop.

Not fair. Not fair.

The end is coming, he thought, feeling his pulse quicken. I can't stop it. It's all over. I'll be found out, but I'm not going to be arrested. I'm going to die, but I'm going to take someone new with me. What's the best way—the most *exciting* way—to do it?

I'll figure it out, he told himself.

After all, he always had.

60

Martha's Vineyard is about three hundred miles northeast of Manhattan, and slower to warm up. On Tuesday morning when I woke up, I looked out the window at the bright cold day. Feeling physically and emotionally stronger, I got out of bed and considered what to wear when I confronted Barbara Hanover Galbraith. It was cool enough for the running suit I had thrown in my bag, but that was not necessarily the outfit I would choose for our meeting.

I didn't want to seem either overdressed or too casual. I wanted no sense of being Mack's little sister when I saw Barbara. She was a pediatric surgeon. I was a *juris doctoris*, an attorney-at-law, and had just completed a clerkship with a civil court judge. My alternative was a dark-green cashmere jacket, white fitted camisole, and white jeans I had taken from the closet at the last minute. Now I was glad that I had the option of wearing them.

Although it was nearly lunchtime, I called room

service to order a continental breakfast, and drank black coffee and nibbled on a cinnamon bun while I dressed. I realized I was so nervous that my fingers were clumsy, fumbling as they unpinned the cleaner's tags from the clothes.

I was perfectly aware that I might be on a fool's errand. Barbara and her children might be back in Manhattan by now. But I didn't think that would be the case. I believed that she was hiding out up here to avoid being questioned about Mack, in which case she'd have stayed put.

I was sure that if I called first she would put me off. But if I simply showed up, there was almost no civil way she could close the door in my face, since she had once been a guest for dinner at Sutton Place.

At least I hoped not.

Checking my watch, I realized I needed to get moving if I wanted to catch Barbara at home. In the car, I set the navigation system. The street where Richard Hanover lived was about six miles away. My plan was to drive to the house and ring the bell. If no one was there, I'd go into the center of town and walk around for a while, then make periodic trips back to the house until she was in.

It seemed like a good plan, but of course the day's events didn't unfold that way. I reached the house at about 12:30. There was no one there. I came back every hour until 5:30. By then, I had decided it was a totally wasted trip, and was as thoroughly disheartened as any human being could possibly be. Then, just as I was making a U-turn, a Jeep with New York plates passed me and turned into the driveway. I caught a glimpse of a woman at the wheel, with a man beside her and some kids in the back.

I drove around for ten minutes or so, then went back to the house and rang the bell. A man in his early seventies answered the door. He obviously had no idea who I was but his smile was cordial. I introduced myself, and said that Bruce had told me his family was visiting. "Come in," he said. "You must be a friend of Barbara's."

"Mr. Hanover," I said, stepping across the threshold, "I'm Mack MacKenzie's sister. I need to talk to her about him."

His expression changed. "I don't think that's a very good idea," he said.

"It's not a matter of its being a good idea," I said. "I'm afraid it's necessary." Not giving him a chance to reply, I walked past him into the living room.

The house was one of those early Cape Cods that had been expanded over the years. The living room wasn't large, but it was charming, with Early American furniture and a hooked rug. Overhead, I could hear the sound of running feet and shrieks of laughter. The children sounded young. I thought I remembered hearing that Barbara and Bruce Galbraith had a boy and twin girls.

Richard Hanover had disappeared, presumably to tell his daughter I was here. While I waited, three little girls came pounding down the stairs, followed by a girl of about eleven. The little ones rushed over to me. Two of them were obviously twins. The girls crowded around me, pleased to be greeting a guest.

"What's your name?" I pointed to one of the twins.

"Samantha Jean Galbraith," she said proudly. "Everybody calls me Sammy, and we took the ferry to Cape Cod today."

They'd been on an all-day excursion to the Cape, I thought. I pointed to the other twin. "What's your name?"

"Margaret Hanover Galbraith. I'm named after my grandmother who is in heaven, and everybody calls me Maggie." Both girls have their mother's blond hair, I thought to myself.

"And is this your cousin or your friend?" I asked, indicating the other little girl.

"This is Ava Grace Gregory, our very best friend," Samantha explained. Ava Grace took a step closer to me and beamed. Samantha turned and tugged at the older girl's hand. "And this is Victoria Somers. She visits us here and sometimes we visit her at her ranch in Colorado."

"I go with them sometimes," Ava Grace told me

earnestly. "And my daddy took all of us to the White House."

"I've never been there myself," I told her. "That's wonderful." I love kids, I thought to myself. Someday I'm going to have at least four of my own, I hope.

"Okay, you guys. Go upstairs and get cleaned up before it's time to go out for dinner." The tone was light and the children were facing me, so they could not see the expression on Barbara Hanover Galbraith's face. She looked at me with such intense dislike that the only emotion I could feel was astonishment.

I had met her once at dinner when I was sixteen years old. I had been heartbroken, because it had looked as if Nick had a crush on her, but now he claims that it was she who had a crush on Mack. Suddenly I wondered if I was reading her expression correctly. Was it scorn that I was seeing in her narrowed eyes and tense body language, or something else?

With a chorus of good-byes, the girls were on their way upstairs. Barbara said, "I'd rather talk in the den."

I followed her down the narrow hall. There was a large country kitchen at the end that spilled into a family room. The den was to the left before the kitchen. If I were to guess, I would say that this was where Richard Hanover spent his evenings when he was alone. It had cheery wallpaper, a patterned carpet, a medium-sized desk and chair, and a recliner that faced a wall-mounted television. There was a reading lamp to the left behind the recliner, and a basket of books and magazines within easy reach.

I could visualize my father in that room.

Barbara closed the door and sat behind the desk, leaving me only the reclining chair, which seemed too big and too deep for me. I knew she was Mack's age, thirty-one, but she was one of those women whose early beauty doesn't last. Her face, which I remembered as being flawless, was too thin now, her lips too narrow. The cascade of blond hair that I had once both admired and envied was now drawn tight in a chignon. But she was still compelling in a slender, autocratic way. I imagined that her commanding presence must be a comfort to the parents of her pediatric patients.

"Why did you come here, Carolyn?" she demanded.

I looked at her, trying to reflect the same hostility that was emanating from her. "Barbara," I said, "from what I understand you and Mack were dating ten years ago when he disappeared. Frankly, I've been told that you were pretty crazy about him. If, as the police believe, and as you surely have read in the newspapers, Mack is committing crimes, there can only be one reason for it, and that is that he's had a complete mental breakdown. I need to know if you saw any sign of it."

She said nothing.

I stared back at her. "I'm telling you right now that

when I met your husband at his office, he showed such hostility about Mack that I was floored. What did Mack ever do to Bruce, and did it have anything to do with his disappearance? What reason do you have for rushing up here to avoid questioning? If you think you can hide out up here, you're wrong. The media is camped outside our home on Sutton Place. Every time I go in or out, they try to shove a microphone in my face. Unless I can get some honest answers from you, and I am satisfied that you know nothing about the reason for Mack's disappearance, then the next time I'm hounded by the media I'm going to tell them you and your husband are holding back information that may be helpful in finding Leesey Andrews."

I watched as the color drained from her face. "You wouldn't *dare* to do that!"

"Oh, yes, I would," I assured her. "I will do *anything* to find Mack and stop him, if he is committing these crimes, or clear his name if he is innocent. For all I know, he's a victim of amnesia and may be living three thousand miles away."

"I don't know where he is, but I *do* know why he walked away." Barbara Galbraith's chin began to tremble. "If I tell you, will you swear to leave us alone? Bruce had nothing to do with his disappearance. Bruce loved me and saved my life. It's because of what Mack did to me that he hates him."

"What did he do to you?" I could almost not form the words. I had been wrong. I hadn't been seeing only hatred from Dr. Barbara Hanover Galbraith. I had been witnessing pain that she had been trying not to unleash.

"I was crazy about Mack. We were going out together. To him, it was casual, I know that. But then I got pregnant. I was frantic. My mother was dying. The health insurance was pitiful, and all the money that had been put aside for medical school had been spent. I had been accepted at Columbia Presbyterian, and I knew I couldn't go. I told Mack."

She gulped to avoid sobbing. "He said he would take care of me. He said we'd get married, and I could defer school for one year, then start."

That sounds like Mack, I thought.

"I believed him. I knew he didn't love me, but I was also sure I could *get* him to love me. Then he disappeared. Just like that. I didn't know what to do."

"Why didn't you go to my parents?" I demanded. "They would have taken care of you."

"Maybe give me a handout to support their son's child? No, thank you." Barbara bit her lip. "I am a pediatric surgeon. I thrill to touch a tiny baby and save its life. I have saved babies so small that they fit in the palm of my hand. I have the gift of healing. But there is one baby I didn't save. My own. I had an abortion because I was desperate." She averted her eyes, and continued. "You know something, Carolyn? Sometimes in the pediatric nursery, when a little one is crying, I go over and pick it up and comfort it, and when I do, I think of the baby I had scraped out of my own womb."

She stood up. "Your brother wasn't that sure about being a lawyer. He told me that he'd get the degree to please his father, but that he'd really have liked to try his hand at acting. I don't think he's crazy—I think he's out there somewhere and maybe even has the grace to be ashamed of himself by now. Do I think he's committing these crimes? Absolutely not. I loathe him for what he did to me, but he is not a serial killer. I'm surprised you'd even give that possibility a second thought."

"I'm going to go, and I promise I will never mention you in any way to anyone, nor bother you again," I said quietly as I stood up, "but I have one more question. Why does Bruce hate Mack so?"

"There is a very simple answer. Bruce loves me. All through Columbia, from the time we were freshmen, I knew that. After I had the abortion, I went to a hotel room and swallowed sleeping pills. And then I decided I wanted to live. I called Bruce. He came rushing to me. He saved my life. He'll always be there for me, and I love him for that, and I've learned over time to love him for himself. Now, do me a favor and get out of this house."

The downstairs of the rest of the house was quiet as

I walked along the hall to the front door. From upstairs I could hear the voices of the children, and my guess was that Richard Hanover had kept them there so that they could not hear what we were saying.

If I could describe my emotions, I would say I felt as though I were in a whirlwind, being slammed back and forth against opposite walls. At last I had the answer to why my brother disappeared. Mack had been unutterably selfish, but he didn't want to go to law school, and didn't love Barbara, and her pregnancy was what galvanized him into running away. Even the quote on the tape made sense. "When, in disgrace with fortune and men's eyes . . . I all alone beweep my outcast state, and trouble deaf heaven with my bootless cries."

In his defense, he must have counted on Barbara going to my parents for support for his baby.

Barbara's flat statement that Mack was not responsible for these crimes, her shock that I would even consider the possibility, was both a reproach and a relief to me. In my mind, I had been trying to form an insanity defense for him. Now whatever fears I had that he was abducting and killing women were over. I knew I would stake my immortal soul on the fact that he was innocent.

Then who was doing this? Who? I asked myself as I got into the car. Of course, I had no answer.

I drove back to the hotel, keeping my fingers crossed that I could extend my stay. The place was really more of an inn than a hotel, and only had eight or ten bedrooms. I had planned to leave at six P.M., and was being billed for a late checkout.

Thank God, my room was available. I didn't think there was any way I could have waited at the ferry and then driven home in my present frame of mind. Driven home to what? I asked myself bitterly. The media at my heels. Barrott's insinuating calls. An absent mother who wanted no part of me. A "friend," Nick, who was probably using me to help clear his own name.

I went upstairs. The room was cold. I had left a window open that the housekeeper hadn't closed. I closed it now and turned up the thermostat, then I looked in the mirror. I looked gaunt and weary. My hair, which I'd left loose, seemed limp on my shoulders.

I grabbed the courtesy bathrobe from the closet, went into the bathroom, and began to run the tub. Three minutes later, I was feeling the warmth of the bathwater begin to permeate the chill in my body. When I dressed, I put on the running suit that, thankfully, I had brought with me. It felt good to be wearing it, zipped high at the neck, only my face and head showing. I twisted my hair back and pinned it, then applied a little makeup to hide the stress I saw in my eyes and expression.

Celebrities in dark glasses at night have always amused me. I often wondered how they managed to read the menu in a restaurant. This evening, I put on the glasses I had worn while I was driving up yesterday. They covered half my face and made me feel shielded.

I picked up my shoulder bag and went downstairs to the restaurant, then was dismayed to see that except for a large middle table with a reservation sign on it, there didn't seem to be anything available. But the maître d' took pity on me. "There is a small table in a corner, near the kitchen door," he said. "I don't like to assign it, but if you don't mind . . ."

"It will be fine," I told him.

I had been settled there long enough to order a glass of wine and review the menu when they came into the dining room. Dr. Barbara Hanover Galbraith, her father, the four girls. And one other person. A boy about nine or ten years old, a boy with sandy hair, whose face I recognized as clearly as I would my own if I looked in the mirror.

I stared at him. The wide-set eyes, the high forehead, the cowlick, the straight nose. He was smiling. Mack's smile. I was looking at Mack's face. My God, I was looking at Mack's *son*!

I suddenly felt light-headed as the realization hit me. Barbara had lied. She *didn't* have the abortion. She never went into any pediatric nursery and longed for the child she had destroyed. She had borne that child, and was raising him as Bruce Galbraith's son.

How much of the rest of her story was true? I asked myself.

I had to get out of there. I stood up and walked through the kitchen, ignoring the stares of the workers. I crossed into the lobby, stumbled upstairs, packed my bag, checked out, and caught the last ferry from the Vineyard. At two A.M. I got back to Sutton Place.

For once, there was no media truck on the block.

But Detective Barrott was standing in the garage. Obviously, he must have known that I was on the way home, and I realized I must have been followed. I was dizzy with exhaustion. "What do you want?" I almost screamed.

"Carolyn, Dr. Andrews received another message from Leesey an hour ago. Her exact words were, 'Daddy, Mack said that he's going to kill me now. He doesn't want to take care of me anymore. Good-bye, Daddy. I love you, Daddy.'"

Barrott's voice echoed through the garage as he shouted, "And then she screamed, '*No, please don't . . .*' He was strangling her. He was *strangling* her, Carolyn. We couldn't save her. Where is your brother, Carolyn? I know you know. Where is that stinking killer? You've got to tell us. Where is he now?"

61

At three o'clock on Wednesday morning, as he was driving around SoHo looking for a vulnerable target, his cell phone rang.

"Where are you?" a tense voice asked.

"Cruising in SoHo. Nothing special." This was his favorite neighborhood. Lots of drunken young women stumbling home at this hour.

"Those streets are alive with cops. You wouldn't try to pull anything stupid, would you?"

"Stupid, no. Exciting, yes," he said, his eyes still scanning. "I need one more. I can't help it."

"Get home and go to bed. I have someone else for you, and she'll make the biggest headlines of all."

"Do I know her?"

"You know her."

"Who is she?"

He listened as he heard the name. "Oh, that's really good," he exclaimed. "Did I ever tell you that you're my favorite uncle?"

62

The horror of the recording of Leesey's final goodbye to her father had shaken even the hardened detective squad to the core. Catching the serial killer before he could strike again had become a burning need for each of them. Over and over, the full squad reviewed every fact that had come to light during the investigation.

On Wednesday morning, they were crowded into Ahearn's office again.

Gaylor was reporting his findings. Benny Seppini's story had checked out. He was seeing Anna Ryan, the separated wife of Walter Ryan, a police sergeant who was known for his heavy drinking and volatile temper. Anna Ryan confirmed that she had been speaking to Benny Monday night two weeks ago and expressed to him her fear of her husband. When told that Benny claimed he had been parked in his car outside her apartment building, she had smiled and said, "That's just what Benny *would* do."

"That doesn't mean Benny didn't get an emergency phone call from DeMarco that night," Ahearn pointed out. "But we'll never prove that."

Ahearn began reading from his notes. In the several days since he had been followed by plainclothes detectives, Nick DeMarco had done nothing unusual. His wiretapped phone conversations had been mostly business-oriented. Several from a real estate agent confirmed that his Park Avenue apartment was for sale. In fact, an offer had been made that he said he would consider. He had tried to phone Carolyn MacKenzie half a dozen times, but she had obviously turned off her cell phone. "We know she was on her way to Martha's Vineyard," Ahearn said. "DeMarco didn't know, and he was getting pretty worried about her."

Ahearn looked up to make sure he still had everyone's attention. "Carolyn went to see her brother's ex-girlfriend, Dr. Barbara Hanover Galbraith, but she didn't stay long. The husband wasn't up there. Then, when the family came into the hotel where Carolyn was staying, she bolted and drove home. Carolyn didn't get any calls in the hotel. She hasn't used her cell phone from thc timc shc lcft town Monday, after she saw the Kramers, till now.

"She was crying when she left the Kramers' Monday morning. We have a picture of her leaving the building. Then a guy followed her to her car. This is a shot of him with her." Ahearn put down his notes and handed photos to Barrott. "We checked him out. His name is Howard Altman. He works for Derek Olsen, who owns a bunch of small apartment buildings, including the one Mack lived in. Altman didn't start the job until a couple of months after MacKenzie disappeared."

The pictures were passed around and put back on Ahearn's desk. "Our guys went back to see the Kramers Monday afternoon." Ahearn's voice was increasingly weary. In his head, he could not stop hearing Leesey's cry, *"No, please don't . . ."* He cleared his throat. "Gus Kramer said he told Carolyn that his wife saw Mack at that Mass when he left the note in the collection basket and that he was a killer and she should leave them alone. Carolyn started crying and ran out."

"The first time we saw her," Gaylor said, "Mrs. Kramer didn't tell us that she saw Mack in church the morning he left the note, because she didn't have her distance eyeglasses with her so she couldn't be sure it was him. Then Monday afternoon she said that now she's convinced it *was* Mack. Do we believe her?"

"I don't believe anything the Kramers tell us," Ahearn said flatly, "but I don't think Gus Kramer is a serial killer." He looked at Barrott. "Brief them on what Carolyn MacKenzie told you when you met her in the garage this morning."

The dark circles under Roy Barrott's eyes had given

way to deep pouches. "We had it out in the garage. She swore that her brother is innocent, that just because Leesey used his name doesn't mean she wasn't made to say it. She said she's going to comb every statement we make or have made and read every word that's been published, and if she finds anything that says her brother is a killer, she will sue until the cows come home." He paused, rubbing his forehead. "She told me she was a lawyer and a damn good one, and she was out to prove it to me. She said that if her brother was guilty, she'd be the first to turn him in before he ends up in a shootout, and then she'd work like hell to create an insanity defense for him."

"Do you believe her?" Chip Dailey, one of the newest detectives, asked.

Barrott shrugged. "I believe she believes he's innocent, yeah. I also now believe she's not in touch with the brother. If he's the one who called her mother's apartment using Leesey's cell phone, it's just another one of his games."

Ahearn's phone rang. When he answered, his expression changed, then he said, "Be sure there's no possibility of a mistake." When he broke the connection, he said, "Lil Kramer spent two years in prison when she was twenty-four years old. She was working for an elderly woman. When the woman died, a lot of her jewelry was missing. Lil was convicted of stealing it."

"Did she admit it?" Barrott asked.

"Never. Doesn't matter. She was convicted at trial. I want her and Gus Kramer brought down here now." He looked around the room. "All right. You all know your assignments." His eye fell on Barrott, who was almost asleep on his feet. "Roy, go home and sleep. You're truly convinced that Carolyn isn't in touch with her brother?"

"Yes."

"Then forget tailing her. We know we don't have enough to detain the Kramers, but once they leave here I want both of them followed."

As the squad turned to file out, Ahearn said something that he had not been sure he was going to share. "I've listened to that recording at least one hundred times. This may sound crazy, but we're dealing with a lunatic. You hear Leesey scream and then a gasping, gurgling sound, but then he disconnected her cell phone. We didn't actually hear her die."

"You seriously think she's still alive?" Gaylor asked incredulously.

"I think the guy we're dealing with would not be above that kind of game, yes."

63

After my shouting match with Detective Barrott, I went upstairs to find concerned messages from both Nick and Elliott on the machine. "Where are you, Carolyn? Please give me a call. I'm worried about you." That was from Nick. His final message had been left at midnight. "Carolyn, your cell phone isn't turned on. When you get home, please call me, no matter what time it is."

Elliott had left three messages, the latest at 11:30 P.M. "Carolyn, your cell phone is off. Please call me. I'm so concerned about you. I saw your mother this evening, and I feel that she is much stronger emotionally, but I feel as if in my concern for her, I may have been failing you. You *know* how dear you are to me. Call me as soon as you get this message."

Listening to all the messages, the concern in both their voices, felt like stumbling into a warm room after an ice storm. I loved them both, but I was hardly going to call either one of them at 3:30 in the morning. I had rushed out of the restaurant in Martha's Vineyard without having dinner, and now I realized I was starving. I went into the kitchen and had a glass of milk and half a peanut butter sandwich. I hadn't eaten peanut butter in ages, but somehow at that moment I craved it. Then I got undressed and fell into bed. I was so wired that I didn't think I would sleep, but the minute I closed my eyes I was gone.

Gone into a maze of mournful dreams and weeping shadows and something else. What was it? What face was I trying to see that was eluding me, taunting me? It wasn't Mack. When I dreamt about him, I saw a boy of ten, with a cowlick and sandy hair and wide-set eyes. *Mack's son. My nephew.* I woke up around eight o'clock, put on a robe, and, still half groggy, went down to the kitchen.

In the morning light, the kitchen seemed reassuringly familiar. Whenever Mom went on a trip, she let our long-time housekeeper have a mini-vacation; Sue would come in only once a week to keep the apartment fresh. All the little signs showed me that she had been in yesterday while I was at the Vineyard. There was fresh milk in the fridge, and the mail that I had dumped on a counter in the kitchen was neatly stacked. I was just grateful that she'd been here the one day I was away. I couldn't have endured having her commiserate with me about Mack.

I didn't have the faintest desire for anything to eat. But my head was clear, and I had some decisions to make. I tried to think them through over three cups of coffee.

Detective Barrott. I honestly thought I convinced him that I was not protecting Mack, but on the other hand, I had not told him about something that might have had everything to do with Mack's disappearance . . .

Barbara had told me that Bruce's anger at Mack was because of Mack's treatment of her. But maybe there was a lot more to it than that. Bruce had always been desperately in love with Barbara. He obviously married her on her terms—"Be my baby's father and send me to medical school." Did he have anything to do with forcing Mack to run away? Did he threaten him? And if so, with what?

That simply didn't make sense to me.

Mack's child. I had to protect him. Barbara didn't know I had seen him. He was growing up as the son of a pediatric surgeon and a wealthy real estate entrepreneur. He had two little sisters. I could never shatter his world, and if I tried to cast suspicion on Bruce, and Barrott began digging into the relationship between Barbara and Mack before Mack disappeared, that could happen.

I needed someone to talk to, someone whom I could trust implicitly. Nick? No. The lawyer we'd hired,

Thurston Carver? No. And then the answer came, and it was so simple I couldn't believe I hadn't thought of it sooner: Lucas Reeves! He had been in on the investigation since the beginning. He had interviewed Nick and Barbara and Bruce and the Kramers. I called his office. It was only 8:30, but he was already there. He told me to come over as soon as I could make it. He said that he and his staff were working on nothing but finding Leesey's abductor.

"Even if it's Mack?" I said.

"Of course, even if it's Mack, but I absolutely do not believe the answer lies with him."

I showered, then turned on the television and watched as I dressed. The police had released to the media the fact that another call had been received from Leesey. "The contents have not been revealed, but a police source confirmed that there is a high probability that she is now dead," the CNN anchor said.

As I pulled on jeans and a long-sleeve cotton sweater, I thought that at least, by not releasing the exact contents of the conversation, Mack's name had been kept out of it.

I like jewelry, and I always wear earrings and something around my neck. Today I chose a thin gold chain with a pearl that Daddy had given to me, and then I fished in the drawer for the earrings that Mack had presented to me on my sixteenth birthday. They were a gold sunburst design with a tiny diamond in the center. I felt close to both Daddy and Mack as I fastened them.

It was about a mile from Sutton Place to Reeves's office, but I decided to walk. After so much time in the car in the last few days, I needed the exercise. The question was how I could avoid the media. I did it by going down to the garage and waiting for a few minutes until a resident of the building came along. Then I begged a ride. He was a distinguished-looking older man. I had never met him. "Could I just hide on the floor of your backseat until we're a couple of blocks away?" I pleaded.

He looked at me sympathetically. "Ms. MacKenzie, I certainly understand why you want to get away without the media, but I'm afraid I'm not the one who should help you. I'm a federal judge."

I almost laughed in disbelief. But then the judge signaled to someone who had just gotten off the elevator. "Hi, David," he said. "This young lady needs help, and I know you'll provide it." Feeling my cheeks burn with embarrassment, I thanked them both.

David whoever-he-was dropped me off at Park and Fifty-seventh. I walked the rest of the way, my thoughts as scattered as the scraps of paper that the breeze was picking up and depositing near the curb. The month of May was almost over. *O Mary, we crown thee with blossoms today, Queen of the Angels, Queen of the*

May. We used to sing that every May at the Academy of the Sacred Heart, and one year, when I was about seven, I got to crown the statue of the Virgin.

Fast-forward to the scene today—me kneeling on the floor of the car to avoid microphones and cameras!

When I got to Lucas Reeves's office, the sight of that small, strong-featured man with the resonant voice helped me to focus again. He pumped my hand vigorously, as if he understood I needed human contact. "Come inside, Carolyn," he said. "I've got quite a setup in here." He led me into a large conference room. The walls were covered with pictures in which faces had been enlarged. Some of them were inside shots, others had obviously been taken outside. "These start when the first young woman disappeared ten years ago," Reeves explained. "We've culled them from newspaper pictures, television clips, security cameras. They were taken in and around the clubs where the four young women disappeared. I have invited the detective squad of the District Attorney's office to come here and inspect them to see if, just maybe, one face will trigger a connection that has been missed so far. Why don't you look at them?"

I walked around the room, stopping when I saw the faces of Mack and Nick and some of their friends at that first club. They looked so young, I thought. Then I walked around all four walls, from one collage to the next, and then to the next, my eyes searching and searching. At one point, I stopped. That looks like—, I thought, then almost laughed out loud. How stupid. I couldn't even see the man's face, just his eyes and forehead.

"Anything?" Lucas asked.

"No. Just the obvious ones of Mack and Nick in that first club."

"All right. Let's go into my office."

We settled in there. The ritual coffee was delivered, and then I told Lucas Reeves what I had learned in Martha's Vineyard. He listened, his expression becoming increasingly grave. "So it now seems that Mack had a very good reason for disappearing. A woman he did not love was bearing his child. He did not want to marry her. He did not want to go to law school. So rather than risk the certain disappointment your parents, especially your father, would have felt, he ran away. The root cause of a vast majority of crimes is one of two factors, love or money. In Mack's case, the primary motive for his disappearance would be his lack of love for Barbara."

Reeves leaned back in his chair. "People have run away for less. If—and I repeat, *if*—Mack was involved in the death of that first young woman, that also might explain the theft of the tapes from his former teacher. When she was interviewed, she could give no explanation for his disappearance, except to say that he would have made an exceptionally fine actor. But perhaps he confided too much to her, and felt he had to retrieve his tapes somehow. I have studied the records. Her death was caused not so much by the blow to her head that rendered her unconscious, but by the fall itself onto the sidewalk. That was what caused the bleeding in the brain that took her life."

He stood up and walked to the window. "Carolyn, there are questions here that we have not yet answered. Even if your brother *is* part of it, I don't think he is *all* of it." He paused, then added: "When I called Captain Ahearn, he did not divulge the full contents of the message Leesey left, but he did say she spoke about Mack."

"Detective Barrott told me what she said." My throat closed as I quoted Leesey's agonizing words, and then I repeated what I had shouted at Barrott.

"And you are correct. She may have been forced to use his name."

"I keep coming back to the fact that Bruce Galbraith hates Mack," I said. "Think how much he must have hated him when Mack was involved with Barbara. Suppose Mack *did* just take off." I started to speculate. "Suppose Bruce is still afraid he'll show up someday, and Barbara will go running to him. She claims she hates Mack, but I wonder if that's true. Mack was such a special human being. He always said that Bruce had zero personality. When I saw Bruce last week, he was openly hostile, so it was obviously not a normal social exchange. But he's a plain-looking guy, and while he may be hugely successful, I bet that on a day-to-day basis, he's still the same dull and boring person. Nick said they called him 'the Lone Stranger,' and he was in the club the night the first girl disappeared." I watched Reeves as he considered all of this.

"I wonder how thoroughly Mr. Galbraith was investigated ten years ago," Reeves said. "I'll look into it."

I got up. "I won't keep you any longer, Lucas," I said. "But I'm glad to have you in my corner." I corrected myself, "In Mack's corner, too."

"Yes, I am." He walked with me through the reception area to the door. "Carolyn, if I may be personal, you are living under a strain that would break the most hardy of men. Is there a place you could get away to, to be by yourself, or with a close friend?" He looked at me with concern.

"I'm thinking about it," I said. "But first I'm going to visit my mother, whether she wants to see me or not. As you know, she's in that private sanitarium in Connecticut, where Elliott brought her."

"I do know." At the door, Reeves took my hand again. "Carolyn, the entire detective squad from the District Attorney's office will be in and out all afternoon. Maybe one of them will spot a face in that sea of faces that will open a door for us."

I walked home. This time I did not try to sneak into the apartment building. The doors of media vans that had been keeping vigil sprang open, and reporters came rushing up to me as I approached our building.

"Carolyn . . . what do you think?"

"Ms. MacKenzie, would you broadcast an appeal to your brother to turn himself in?"

I turned to face the microphones. "I will broadcast an appeal to one and all to presume my brother innocent of any and all crimes. Remember, there is not one *shred* of proof against him. Everything is based on innuendo and supposition. And let me remind all of you that there are libel laws and serious penalties for violating them."

I hurried inside, not giving them a chance to respond. I went up to the apartment and began to return the phone calls I had been ignoring. The first was to Nick. His relief at hearing my voice seemed so spontaneous that I tucked it away in a corner of my mind as something to think about later.

"Carolyn, don't do this to me. I've been a wreck. I even called Captain Ahearn to see if they were holding you there. He said they hadn't heard from you."

"They hadn't heard from me, but they knew where I was," I said. "Evidently I was being followed."

I told Nick that I had seen Barbara in Martha's

Vineyard, but it had been a useless trip. I selected carefully the information I would give him. "I agree with you. She probably married Bruce to get a ticket to medical school, but she seems to be keeping her share of the bargain." I also couldn't resist having a chance to slam her. "She let me know what a devoted and loving pediatric surgeon she is, that sometimes when she walks through the pediatric nursery, she goes over to a crying baby and picks it up to comfort it."

"That would be Barbara," Nick agreed. "Carolyn, how are you holding up?"

"Just barely." I could hear the exhaustion in my voice.

"Me, too. The cops have been raking me and Benny over the coals again. One good piece of news?" His tone brightened. "I sold my Park Avenue apartment."

"The one that makes you feel like Roy Rogers?" I smiled.

"Exactly. The agent tells me the buyer is planning to rip it to the studs and redesign it. Good luck to him."

"Where will you go?"

"To the loft. I'm looking forward to it, if there's anything I look forward to at this minute. We caught a nineteen-year-old with a phony driver's license in the club last night. If we'd served her, we could have been shut down. I wouldn't be surprised if she was planted by the cops to put more pressure on me."

"Nothing would surprise me at this point," I said, meaning it.

"Dinner tonight? I want to see you."

"No, I don't think so. I'm going to drive up and try to visit Mom. I need to see for myself how she's doing."

"I'll drive you."

"No, I have to go alone."

"Carolyn, let me ask you something. Years ago, Mack told me that you had a crush on me and that I should be careful not to encourage it by playing up to you." He paused, clearly trying to keep his tone playful. "Is there any way I could revive that crush, or now is it going to stay one-sided on my part?"

I know there was a smile in my voice. "It was mean of him to tell you."

"No, it wasn't." Nick's voice became serious again. "All right, Carolyn. I'll let you go. But hang on to the thought that we're going to make it through this mess."

I started to cry. I didn't want him to hear, and clicked off, but then immediately wondered if Nick hadn't been starting to say, "together," or did I only imagine hearing that word because I wanted so desperately for it to turn out that way?

Then it occurred to me for the first time that it was possible my cell phone and the telephone line in the apartment were being tapped. Of course they must be, I thought. Barrott has been sure I'm in touch with

Mack. They wouldn't take a chance on not knowing if he called.

Reflecting on my conversation with Nick, I wondered if their ears were burning at his suggestion that they might deliberately try to entrap him with an underaged drinker in the Woodshed.

I hoped so.

64

Lil and Gus Kramer sat nervously rigid in Captain Larry Ahearn's office. Ahearn eyed them carefully, figuring out his approach to them. It was obvious when Gaylor ushered them in that Lil Kramer was on the verge of a total breakdown. Her hands were trembling. There was a distinct twitch at the side of her mouth. She was on the brink of tears. Start gently, or let her have it? He decided on the rough approach.

"Lil, you didn't let on to us that you spent two years in prison for jewelry theft," he snapped.

It was as if he had punched her in the mouth. She gasped, her eyes widened, and she began to moan. Gus jumped to his feet. "You shut up," he yelled at Ahearn. "Look up that case. She was a young girl from Idaho, without a family, caring for an old lady night and day. She never *touched* that jewelry! The old lady's cousins were the only ones who had the combination of the safe in her house. They framed Lil so that they not only had the jewelry but the insurance, may they rot in hell."

"I never met anyone who went to prison who wasn't framed," Ahearn said brusquely. "Sit down, Mr. Kramer." He turned back to Lil. "Did Mack ever accuse you of stealing anything?"

"Lil, don't say a word. These people are trying to frame you again."

Lil Kramer's shoulders sagged. "I can't help it if they do. No one will believe me. Just before he disappeared, Mack asked about his new watch, if I had seen it. I knew he was hinting that I had taken it. I got so upset, I yelled at him. I said the three of you in that apartment are all so careless, then when you can't find something you blame it on me."

"Who else blamed you?" Ahearn demanded.

"That nasty Bruce Galbraith. He couldn't find his college ring, as if I would have anything to do with taking it. What would I do with it? Then, a week later, he said he had found it in the pocket of his slacks. No apology, of course. No, 'I'm sorry, Mrs. Kramer.'" She was weeping now, tired, hopeless tears.

Ahearn and Gaylor looked at each other, knowing they were thinking the same thing: That would be easy to check.

"Then you don't know if Mack found his watch before he disappeared?"

"No, I don't. And that's why I'm so afraid that when he comes back, he'll accuse me again." Lil Kramer began to wail. "And that's why when I thought I saw him in church that day—"

"You *thought* you saw him in church!" Ahearn interrupted. "You told us you were certain you saw him there."

"I saw someone about his size, then when I heard he had dropped the note, I was sure, but then I wasn't sure, and I guess I'm sure now, but—"

"Why did you suddenly decide to move to Pennsylvania?" Gaylor interrupted.

"Because Mr. Olsen's nephew, Steve Hockney, overheard Mack asking me about the watch, and now Steve is holding that over my head," she screamed. "Because he wants us to complain about Howie to his uncle and get him fired and . . . and . . . I can't . . . take . . . it . . . anymore. I just want to die. I want to die . . ."

Lil Kramer leaned forward and covered her face with her hands. Her thin shoulders shook as she sobbed. Gus knelt beside her and put his arms around her. "It's all right, Lil," he said, "it's all right. We're going home now."

He looked up, first at Ahearn, and then at Gaylor. "This is what I think of you two," he said, and spat on the carpet.

65

The other phone call after I finished speaking with Nick was to Jackie Reynolds, my psychologist friend, who had been trying to reach me and whom I'd put off calling. Of course Jackie had been reading the newspapers, but we hadn't talked much since our dinner when all of this began. Remembering my suspicion that the phone might be tapped, I gave very general answers to her questions.

I knew she caught on. "Carolyn, I've had a couple of cancellations," she said. "Have you any plans for lunch?"

"No."

"Then why don't you come up here, and we'll send out for sandwiches and coffee?"

That sounded good to me. Jackie's office adjoins the apartment where she lives on East Seventy-fourth Street and Second Avenue. As I hung up, I realized how much I wanted her guidance about my planned visit to Mom.

Which reminded me that I had not yet spoken to Elliott.

I dialed his office, and was put straight through to him. "Carolyn, I didn't know what to think when I couldn't reach you."

I heard the reproach in his voice and apologized. I knew I owed him that. I explained that I had gone to Martha's Vineyard and the reason for it. Then, keenly aware of the probable wiretap, I said that it was a wasted visit, and that I was going to drive up later this afternoon to see Mom. "If she refuses to see me, at least I tried. I'll get there between four and five," I told him.

"I think that might be good timing," he said slowly. "I hope to get up there around five myself. I want to talk to you and Olivia together."

With that, we left it. What did he want to talk to the two of us about? I wondered. Surely in Mom's fragile state, he wouldn't withdraw his support from her now. Please, God, not that! She needed him. I thought about the night only a few weeks ago, after Mack left the note and at dinner she announced she had decided to let him live his own life. I thought of the way she and Elliott had looked at each other, and how he had planned to join her in Greece. I thought about the way their shoulders were touching when they walked down the street after we left Le Cirque. Elliott could make Mom happy. Mom is sixty-two. She has every chance of living another twenty or thirty good years—unless, of course, I've ruined it for her by blundering into the Detective Squad room and meeting Barrott.

I changed into a jacket and slacks and, as I did last night in Martha's Vineyard, tried to mask the dark circles under my eyes with foundation and added color to my overall washed-out appearance with mascara and lipstick.

I drove out of the garage, this time in my own car, and—surprise! surprise!—for the present, the media vans were gone. I guess they figured they had about as much out of me as they were going to get for the day.

When I got to Seventy-fourth Street, I left the car in Jackie's garage and went upstairs. When she came to the door, we hugged each other. "Nothing like lots of stress as a daily diet," she commented. "I haven't seen you in two weeks, and I bet you've lost at least five or six pounds."

"At least," I agreed as I followed her into her office. It's a medium-sized, comfortable room with a couple of upholstered armchairs facing her desk. I remembered she collects nineteenth-century English prints of dogs and horses, and admired aloud some really wonderful examples framed on the wall. I imagined new patients remarking on them before revealing the problem that had driven them to seek Jackie's help.

We agreed on ham and Swiss cheese on rye with lettuce and mustard and black coffee. She phoned in the order, then we settled down to talk. I told her about my meeting with Barbara, holding back only the fact that she had given birth to Mack's son. Instead, feeling dishonest, I gave Barbara's version, that she had had an abortion.

"It's a viable reason for Mack to escape," she agreed. "But just suppose he had gone to your father and/or your mother. What would either or both of them have done, do you think?"

"Supported them in their decision to marry and have the baby. Put Mack through law school."

"Put Barbara through medical school?"

"I don't know."

"Knowing your father as I did, he certainly wouldn't have put up with Mack taking a crack at acting."

"Now *that* is a certainty, I agree." Then I told Jackie how worried I was that Elliott might reconsider wanting to marry Mom while the present suspicion of Mack existed, or if he ever was arrested and put on trial.

"I'd worry, too," Jackie agreed frankly. "Appearances mean so much to people like Elliott. I know someone like that. He's about Elliott's age, a widower, one of the nicest people you'd ever want to know, but a snob. I joke with him that he'd be caught dead before he'd date anyone who wasn't a socialite, no matter how accomplished and beautiful she was."

"What did he say when you told him that?" I asked Jackie.

"He laughed, but he didn't deny it."

The desk called to say that the delivery was on the way. We settled down to lunch, and Jackie started to remind me that I was planning to apply for a job in the District Attorney's office. Then I knew she could have bitten her tongue. Can you just imagine the District Attorney of Manhattan hiring the sister of an accused murderer?

66

All afternoon, either alone or in pairs, the members of the Detective Squad visited Lucas Reeves's office and studied the photos he had prepared for their inspection. Sometimes they lingered over one or several pictures. They studied the enhanced shot of Mack MacKenzie as he might look today. Some of them held it up to compare with a headshot on the wall, but in the end they all left shrugging their shoulders in disappointment and defeat.

Roy Barrott was one of the last to arrive, at quarter of five. He had gone home and crashed for three hours. Now, freshly shaved and alert, he went painstakingly through the hundreds of stills while Lucas Reeves waited patiently in his office.

Finally, at seven fifteen, as Lucas came in to check on him, he gave up. "They're all starting to look familiar," he said. "I don't know why, but I feel as if I'm missing something over there." He pointed his hand to the far wall.

Lucas Reeves frowned. "Oddly, Carolyn MacKenzie paused at that area as well. I had the feeling that something interested her, but she must have dismissed the possibility. Otherwise I am sure she would have said something."

Barrott stood in front of it again. "It's not going to happen, at least not tonight."

Reeves reached into his pocket and pulled out a card. "I have written down my cell phone number for you. If anything occurs to you and you want to come back here at any hour, call me and I will instruct the security guard to let you in immediately."

"Good enough, and thanks."

Barrott went back to the squad room to find renewed energy crackling through it. Ahearn, his tie pulled loose, his face haggard and weary, was pacing the floor in his office. "We may be onto something," he said. "Steve Hockney, the nephew of the owner of the apartment building MacKenzie was living in, has a sealed juvenile record. We got a look at it, serious stuff, but nothing violent. Dealing marijuana, burglary, and theft. His uncle was able to hire good lawyers who kept him out of a couple of years in a juvenile center. According to Lil Kramer, Hockney was holding it over her head that MacKenzie was missing his watch. That was only a day or two before Mack disappeared. We're looking for Hockney. His band has regular gigs in the

SoHo–Greenwich Village locale, and he uses a lot of costume changes, even wigs and putty to alter his appearance."

"How about the rest of what the Kramers told you?"

"We spoke to Bruce Galbraith. He's one cold fish. He acknowledged that he did ask Lil Kramer about his school ring, but she took it wrong. He wasn't accusing her. He claims he just asked her if she'd seen it when she was cleaning up. She hit the roof and got all upset. Knowing her background, you can understand why she might have been hypersensitive about a question like that."

Bob Gaylor had come in while Ahearn was speaking. "Our guys just reached Hockney's uncle, Derek Olsen, the old man who owns the buildings. He confirmed that there was a rivalry between his assistant, Howard Altman, and his nephew Steve Hockney. He said he's sick of both of them. He's left messages on their phones that he's selling all the property and that the wrecking ball is hitting the 104th Street town house tomorrow morning. We didn't let on that we're hunting for the nephew. We told him we were confirming the Kramers' story."

"What did he say about them?"

"Hardworking, good people. He'd trust them with everything he had."

"Have we got any pictures of Hockney?" Barrott asked. "I want to compare him with a face I saw in Reeves's office just now. I feel as though I've missed something."

"There's one of his publicity pictures with his band on my desk," Ahearn told him. "We've got dozens of them with our guys on the street."

Barrott started rifling through the untidy clutter on Ahearn's desk, then picked up a picture he found there. *"This is the one,"* he said aloud.

Ahearn and Gaylor stared at him. "What are you talking about?" Ahearn demanded.

"I'm talking about *this* guy," he said, pointing. "Where's that *other* picture of Leesey posing for her friend, the one with Nick DeMarco in the background?"

"One of the copies of it is somewhere in that pile."

Barrott rummaged, then, with a satisfied grunt, said, "Here it is." He held up two photos, comparing them. An instant later, he was dialing the cell phone of Lucas Reeves.

67

As I expected, the sanitarium where Mom was staying was about as luxurious inside and out as I would have imagined any place that Elliott would choose for her would be. Thick carpets, soft lights, fine paintings on the walls. I got there around 4:30, and the receptionist had clearly been briefed that I was on my way.

"Your mother is expecting you," she said in one of those professionally melodious voices that seemed to me to fit in with the surroundings. "Her suite is on the fourth floor, with a beautiful view of the grounds." She got up and led me to the elevator, an ornately handsome object with an operator and a velvet seating bench inside.

My escort murmured, "Ms. Olivia's suite, please, Mason," and I remembered hearing that in some of these expensive psychiatric residences last names are not shared. Just as well, I thought. The other guests don't need to know that Mrs. Charles MacKenzie Sr. is in their midst.

At the fourth floor, we got out and walked down the hall to the corner suite. After tapping on the door, my escort opened it. "Ms. Olivia," she called, her voice slightly elevated but still finishing-school modulated.

I walked behind her into an exquisite sitting room. I have seen photos of the suites in the Plaza Athénée in Paris, and I felt as though I was walking into one of them. Then Mom appeared in the doorway from the bedroom. Without another word, the escort was gone and Mom and I looked at each other.

All the conflicting emotions, the roller coaster of emotions that I had been experiencing this last week when Mom took refuge in Elliott's apartment rushed through me as I looked at her. Guilt. Anger. Bitterness. Then they all washed away and the only thing I felt was love. Her beautiful eyes were filled with grief. She was looking at me uncertainly as though she didn't know what to expect of me.

I went over to her and put my arms around her. "I'm so sorry," I said. "I'm so terribly sorry. I guess that no matter how many times I say to myself, 'If only I hadn't tried to find Mack,' I can only tell you I'd give my life to undo that but I can't."

Then her hands began running through my hair the way they did when I was a small child and upset about something. They were loving and comforting, and I knew that she had come to peace with what I had done.

"Carolyn, we'll see it through," she said. "No matter what it turns out to be. If Mack has done everything they say he has done, there is one thing I can be sure of. He is not in his right mind."

"How much have they told you?" I asked her.

"I guess everything. Yesterday I told Dr. Abrams, my psychiatrist, that I didn't want to be protected anymore. I can sign myself out of here anytime, but I'd rather absorb everything that I have to know while I can talk it through with him."

This was the mother I thought I had lost, the one who kept Dad sane when Mack disappeared, the one whose first thought was for me when she knew Dad was lost on 9/11. I had been a junior in Columbia then and had by chance slept home and was still asleep when the first plane hit. Horrified, Mom had watched it by herself. Dad's office was on the 103rd floor of the North Tower, the first one to be hit. She had tried to phone him and actually got through to him. "Liv, the fire's underneath us," he said. "I don't think we'll make it."

The connection had gone dead, and minutes later, she saw the tower collapse. She had let me sleep until I woke up naturally, about forty-five minutes later. I'd opened my eyes to find her sitting in my room, tears streaming from her eyes. Then she'd rocked me in her arms while she told me what had happened.

This was my mother as she was until year after year, the annual Mother's Day call from Mack tore her apart.

"Mom, if you're comfortable here, I wish you'd stay a while longer," I said. "You don't want to be on Sutton Place the way it is now, and once the media got word you were back at Elliott's apartment, they'd be gunning for you there, too."

"I understand that, but Carolyn, what about you? I know you wouldn't come here, but isn't there someplace you can get away from them?"

You can run but you can't hide, I thought. "Mom, I think it's necessary for me to be around and visible," I said. "Because until we have absolute proof to the contrary, I am going to believe and publicly swear that Mack is innocent."

"That's exactly what your father would do." Now Mom smiled, a real smile. "Come on. Let's sit down. I wish we could have a cocktail, but that's not going to happen here." She looked at me, a bit anxiously. "You know that Elliott is coming?"

"Yes. I'm looking forward to seeing him."

"He's been a rock."

I admit I felt a twinge of jealousy and then felt guilty

about it. Elliott *was* a rock. Two weeks ago, Mom had said that I was her rod and staff. My guilt faded as I remembered that Elliott might just be about to announce that he needed to separate himself from our problems. Jackie's words played again in my mind. *Appearances mean so much to people like Elliott.*

But when he arrived, everything I feared turned out to be totally wrong. In fact, in his endearing, formal way, he was looking for my blessing to marry Mom. He sat next to her on the couch, and addressed me earnestly.

"Carolyn, I guess you know I've always been in love with your mother," he said. "I always thought she was a shining star beyond my reach. But now I know that I can offer her the protection of a husband at a very difficult time in her life."

I knew I had to warn him. "Elliott, if Mack were ever to go on trial as a serial killer, you have to be aware that the publicity will be awful. Clients of the caliber you have may not be pleased that their financial advisor is in the tabloids on a regular basis."

Elliott looked at my mother, then back at me. With something of a twinkle in his eyes, he said, "Carolyn, word for word, that is the same speech I heard from your mother. I can promise you this: I would rather tell all my distinguished clients to jump in the lake before I give up one day of being at your mother's side."

We had dinner in one of the private dining rooms. It was a low-key celebration. I agreed with their plan that they would be married as soon and as quietly as possible. I drove home that evening feeling so much better about Mom, but also with the strange sensation that Mack was trying to reach me. I could almost feel his presence in the car. Why?

Again there was no sign of the media on Sutton Place. I went to bed and listened to the eleven o'clock news. A clip with part of my statement to the media was shown, and I sounded strident and defensive. By now it had leaked out, or been allowed to leak out, that Leesey had named Mack as her abductor.

I turned off the television. Love or money, I thought as I closed my eyes. That's what Lucas Reeves said were the causes of the majority of crimes. Love or money. Or *lack* of love, in Mack's case.

At three A.M., I heard the buzzing of the intercom. I got out of bed and rushed downstairs to pick it up. It was the concierge. "I'm so sorry, Ms. MacKenzie," he said. "But someone just handed a note to the doorman and said it was a matter of life and death that you have it immediately."

He hesitated, then said, "With all the publicity, this may be someone's terrible idea of a joke, but—"

"Send it up," I interrupted him.

I stood at the door and waited until Manuel came

down the hall and handed me a plain white envelope. The note in it was handwritten on plain bond paper.

It read, "Carolyn I am sending this by messenger because your phone may be wiretapped. Mack just called me. He wants to see both of us. He's waiting on the corner of 104th Street and Riverside Drive. Meet us there. Elliott."

68

"There he is," Barrott exclaimed, "on the street in front of the Woodshed the night Leesey disappeared. If you look from the angle the security camera caught him, he could see DeMarco's table. And there he is again, in the same frame as DeMarco, watching Leesey when she was posing for her roommate."

Accompanied by the security guard, who had been given permission to admit them, they were in Lucas Reeves's office. They had studied hundreds of pictures in the wall montages, until they could pinpoint the face they were seeking.

"Here's another one that looks like him, but the hair is shorter," Gaylor said, a note of excitement detectable in his voice.

It was half past ten. Knowing they had a long night ahead, they hurried back to the office to begin to process information on one more potential suspect.

69

Lucas Reeves did not sleep well on Wednesday night. "Love or money" was the phrase that ran through his head in a singsong way. At six A.M., as he was waking up, the question that had been eluding him popped into his head. Who would be interested in having a person who is dead seem to be alive?

Love or money.

Money, of course. It was beginning to fall into place like pieces of a puzzle. So absurdly simple if he was right. Lucas, a notoriously early riser, never minded waking up someone when he needed the answer to a question. This time, fortunately, his advisor, a prominent estate lawyer, was also an early riser.

"Can an inheritance trust be broken, or is it always sacrosanct?" Lucas asked him abruptly.

"They're not easily broken by any means, but if there's a good and valid reason for dipping into it, the executor will usually be amenable."

"That's what I thought. I won't disturb you any further. Thank you, my friend."

"Any time, Lucas. But not before seven next time, okay? I get up early, but my wife likes to sleep."

70

I pulled on slacks, slipped my feet in sandals, grabbed a long raincoat to cover my pajama top, and ran for the elevator, shoving Elliott's note into my shoulder bag as I rushed down the hall. In my hurry to get to Mack before he changed his mind about seeing me, I forgot that the garage closed at three A.M. Manuel reminded me of that when I asked for the garage level.

I did the only thing I could do—got outside, into the street, and looked frantically around to flag down a cab. There was none on Sutton Place, but when I turned up Fifty-seventh Street I saw one of those gypsy town cars coming. I must have seemed a wild sight to him as I waved both arms to catch his eye, but he did stop. I got in, and he made a U-turn to go west.

When we got to the corner of 104th and Riverside Drive, there was no one there. I paid the cabby and climbed out onto the quiet street. Then I noticed a van parked down the block, and even though the lights were off, I had a hunch that Elliott and Mack might be in it. I walked closer to get a better look and made a pretense of reaching for a key, as though I were going to the nearest apartment building. Across the street, I could see a large construction site next to a boarded-up old town house on the corner.

Then a man stepped out of the darkened doorway of the next building. For a moment I thought it was Elliott, but then I could see that he was a much younger person, someone whose face was familiar. I recognized him as being the representative of the owner of Mack's apartment building. I had met him that first time I stopped at the Kramers', and he had spoken to me on Monday after I left their apartment in tears.

What on earth was he doing here now, I asked myself, and where was Elliott?

"Ms. MacKenzie," he said hurriedly. "I don't know if you remember me. I'm Howard Altman."

"I remember you. Where is Mr. Wallace?"

"He's with some guy I found camping out in that place. Mr. Olsen owns it. Every once in a while I check on it, even though it's closed." He was nodding toward the boarded-up corner building. "The guy I found gave me fifty bucks to call Mr. Wallace for him, then Mr. Wallace promised me another fifty bucks if I'd write a message for you and deliver it."

"They're inside that building? What does the other man look like?"

"He's about thirty, I guess. He started crying when Mr. Wallace came in. They both did."

Mack was in there, trying to hide in that crumbling ruin. I followed Howard Altman across the street and along the construction fence to the back door of the house. He opened it and gestured me to enter, but as I looked into the darkened interior I panicked and stepped back. I knew something wasn't right. "Ask Mr. Wallace to come out," I told Howard.

His answer was to grab me and pull me inside the house. I was so stunned I didn't resist. He yanked the door closed behind him, and before I could scream or fight to free myself, he shoved me down a flight of stairs. Somewhere on the way down, I cracked my head and lost consciousness. I don't know how long it was before I opened my eyes. It was pitch dark. The air I was breathing was unbearably foul. My face felt caked with blood. My head was splitting and there was something wrong with my right leg. It was bent under me and throbbing with pain.

Then I felt something move beside me, and a whispery voice moaned, "Water, please, water."

I tried to move but could not. I knew my leg had to be broken. I did the only thing I could think to do. I moistened a finger in my mouth, then groped in the dark until I could find the parched lips of Leesey Andrews.

71

With his ever-increasing arthritis, Derek Olsen often woke up during the night, throbbing pain in his hips and knees. On Wednesday night, when his aching joints woke him up, he could not go back to sleep again. The call from the police about his nephew Steve meant, of course, that he was in some kind of trouble again. So much for the fifty thousand I was going to leave him, Olsen thought. He can go whistle for it!

The one bright spot was that in a few hours he was going to have the fun of watching the wrecking ball smash that decrepit old town house into smithereens. Every chip that flies in the air represents money I made on the deal, he thought with satisfaction. I wouldn't put it past Doug Twining to operate the rig himself. That's how mad he is at having to pay me so much.

The pleasurable thought comforted him to the point that sometime before dawn he fell into the deep sleep that normally lasted till eight A.M. But on Thursday morning, his phone rang at six. It was Detective Barrott wanting to know where Howard Altman was. He hadn't returned to his apartment all night.

"Am I his babysitter?" Olsen demanded querulously. "You wake me up to ask me where he is? How do I know? I don't socialize with him. He works for me."

"What kind of car does Howard drive?" Barrott asked.

"When he drives me, he drives my SUV. I don't think he has a car of his own. I don't care."

"Does he ever take your SUV in the evening?"

"Not that I know of. He better not. It's a Mercedes."

"What color is it?"

"Black. At my age do you think I want a red one?"

"Mr. Olsen, we really need to talk about Howard," Barrott said. "What do you know about his personal life?"

"I know nothing. I want to know nothing. He's been working for me nearly ten years. He's done a good enough job."

"Did you check his references when you hired him?"

"He was recommended by an impeccable source, my financial advisor Elliott Wallace."

"Thank you, Mr. Olsen. Have a good day."

"You ruined most of it for me. I'll be tired all day." Derek Olsen slammed down the receiver. But not all of it, he thought as he envisioned the wrecking ball striking a bull's-eye on his piggy bank.

At the other end of the phone, Barrott, unable to conceal his exultation, said, "Elliott Wallace recommended him for the job."

"It ties in with Lucas Reeves's theory," Ahearn agreed. "But we have to go easy. Wallace is a big shot on Wall Street."

"Yes, but he wouldn't be the first executor who dipped into his client's funds, if that's the way it plays," Barrott said. "Any result on the fingerprints?"

"Not yet. We can't be sure the ones we lifted from the outer door of Howard's apartment are absolutely his, but we're running them anyway. I'd swear that guy has a prior record," Gaylor said.

Barrott checked his watch. "The security guard at Wallace's building said he normally gets in at eight thirty. We'll be waiting for him."

72

Once again, Carolyn was not answering her cell phone. Nick phoned her at eight o'clock on Thursday morning with the idea of taking her out for breakfast. He wanted to see her. I *need* to see her, he thought. On the late news, he had watched the clip of her on television, passionately defending Mack.

He wanted to know how she had made out on the visit to her mother. He knew how hurt she had been by her mother's refusal to see her.

At least her cell phone was on. It was ringing. It had been turned off Monday afternoon and all day Tuesday. A gnawing sense that something was wrong made Nick decide to stop at Sutton Place, and make sure that she was home.

The morning concierge had just come on duty. "I don't think she's back yet," he said, when Nick asked for Carolyn. "I understand she had an emergency message at about three A.M. and went rushing out.

Whoever handed the note to her doorman said it was a matter of life or death. I hope everything is all right."

Everything *isn't* all right, Nick thought frantically. He began to dial the now familiar number of Detective Barrott.

73

"Thank you for seeing us, Mr. Wallace," Barrott said politely.

"That's all right. Is there any news of Mack?" Elliott asked.

"No, I'm afraid there isn't but we do have a few matters you can help us clear up."

"Of course." He gestured for the detectives to take a seat.

"You know Howard Altman?"

"Yes, I do. He is the employee of my client Derek Olsen."

"Didn't you actually recommend Altman to Mr. Olsen ten years ago?"

"I believe I did."

"How did you happen to know Mr. Altman?"

"I'm not really sure. As I recall, a former client had sold some real estate and was looking to place him." Elliott's expression was blank.

"Who was that client?"

"I'm not even sure I can remember. I dealt with him only briefly. But it was one of those coincidences. Olsen had been in and mentioned he was having a terrible time getting good help, and I passed Altman's name along to him."

"I see. We'd certainly appreciate having that client's name, and I'm sure you'd want to find him. Altman may be a suspect in the abduction of Leesey Andrews, which of course would clear the name of Mack MacKenzie."

"Anything that would clear Mack's name would be priceless to me," Elliott told Barrott, his voice shaking with emotion.

Barrott studied him, taking in the beautifully tailored suit, the crisp white shirt, the handsome blue and red tie. He watched as Wallace took off his glasses, polished them, then put them back on. What is it about this guy that I'm seeing, he asked himself. It's the eyes and the forehead. They looked familiar. Then he wondered: *Is it possible? My God, he resembles Altman.* He signaled to Gaylor to take over the questioning.

"Mr. Wallace, isn't it a fact that you arc thc cxccutor of Mack MacKenzie's estate?"

"I am the executor of all the MacKenzie family trusts."

"The *sole* executor?"

"Yes."

"What are the terms of Mack's trust?"

"It was set up by his grandfather. He was not to receive income from it until he reached the age of forty."

"In the meantime, of course, it continues to grow."

"Certainly. It has been carefully invested."

"What would happen if Mack died?"

"The trust would go to his children, and if he had none, to his sister, Carolyn."

"Could Mack have asked for an advance from his trust for what you as executor deemed to be a responsible reason?"

"It would have to be extremely responsible. His grandfather wanted no playboy heirs."

"How about the fact that he was about to get married; that his future wife was pregnant with his child; that he no longer wanted his parents to pay his way; that he would put himself through college and would want to pay for his wife to go to medical school? Would all that be good and sufficient reason to dip into the trust?"

"It might be, but that situation did not occur." Elliott Wallace stood up. "As you can understand, I have a busy calendar and—"

Barrott's cell phone rang. It was Nick DeMarco. Barrott listened, determined to keep an inscrutable look on his face. Carolyn MacKenzie was missing. The new victim, he thought.

Wallace, holding an arm out, was attempting to usher them out of his office. Lucas Reeves is right, Barrott thought. It all fits into place. He decided to trick Wallace with false information.

"Not so fast, Mr. Wallace," he said. "We're not going anywhere. We have Howard Altman in custody. He's bragging about the abductions. He's bragging about working for you." He paused for a moment. "You didn't tell us you were *related* to him."

Finally, Wallace's unruffled exterior showed signs of strain. "Oh, poor Howie," he sighed. With one hand he leaned on his desk, and with the other he reached into the top drawer. "He's totally delusional, of course."

"No, he isn't," Barrott snapped.

Elliott Wallace sighed again. "My psychopathic nephew promised to die in a breathtaking fashion and take Carolyn and Leesey with him. He couldn't even handle that well."

In a single, quick motion, Elliott Wallace removed a small pistol from his desk drawer and held it to his forehead. "As Cousin Franklin would have put it, 'My fellow Americans, farewell,'" he said, and pulled the trigger.

74

Larry Ahearn was in the squad room when the call came in from Barrott. "Larry, we were right about Wallace. He just blew his brains out. Before he did, he told us that Altman is his nephew. He said that Altman has Carolyn and Leesey and he's going to kill them and then kill himself. But he didn't tell us where they are."

With icy calm, Ahearn absorbed the stunning information. "As of the last few hours, neither trace we have on those phones is giving us anything," he said. "Either the phones are turned off or they're in an area where we can't get reception. What about Altman? He must have a cell phone. I'll call his boss, Olsen, on another line. Hang on."

75

Derek Olsen, camp chair in hand, was about to go out and walk down the block to see the wrecking ball destroy his old town house. Irritated at the second phone call from the detectives, he was even more irritated at the reason for it. "Sure Howie has a cell phone. Who doesn't? Sure I know his number. It's 917-555-6262. But I'm telling you something. That's the one I pay for. I get the bill. I watch it like a hawk. Business only. I guess he has another. How should I know? I'm on my way out for some excitement. Good-bye."

As Barrott waited on the line for Ahearn to check with Olsen, Detective Gaylor moved swiftly to secure the premises. With one hand he locked the door of Wallace's office and with the other dialed 911 on his cell phone.

Then he heard Barrott explode as he reacted to what Ahearn was telling him. "The business cell phone that

Olsen gave you for Altman is turned off! But wait a minute. Wallace would never have been stupid enough to call Altman on that line anyway. There must have been another number that he used to reach him. Hold on, Larry."

In two strides Barrott was across the room and kneeling beside Wallace's body, rummaging through his pockets. "Here it is!" He yanked out a small state-of-the-art cell phone, opened it, and scrolled through the directory. This has got to be it, he thought, as he spotted the initials "H.A." He pushed 5 and then the send button and, breathing a prayer, held the phone to his ear.

It rang twice and then was answered. "Uncle Elliott," an edgy, high-pitched voice said, "we did our good-byes last night. I don't want to talk anymore. There's only a few minutes left."

The connection broke. Within seconds, Barrott was back on his own phone, giving Howard Altman's number to Ahearn, who was frantically waiting to pass it on to the phone technicians who would trace it.

76

He came down to the basement three times during that long night. As I lay next to Leesey on that clammy dirt floor, pain vibrating from my leg, my face crusted with dried blood, my fingers entwined in Leesey's, he alternately cried and laughed and moaned and giggled. I dreaded the sound of steps on the stairs, not knowing if this would be the time he would decide to kill us.

"Remember the Zodiac Killer?" he sobbed the first time he came down. "He didn't want to keep going. Neither do I. He wrote a letter to a newspaper that he knew could be traced to him. I wrote one, too, but I tore it up. I am tortured, but I don't want to go to prison. The first girl was when I was sixteen. I had put that behind me. Then it happened again. I was the caretaker on an estate, and the housekeeper's daughter was so pretty. When they found her body, they suspected me. My mother sent me to New York to be with her dear older brother, my uncle, Elliott Wallace . . ."

Elliott Wallace! Uncle Elliott! But that's impossible, I thought, that can't be.

I felt his breath on my cheek. "You don't believe me, do you? You should. My mother told him he had to help me or she'd expose him for the fraud that he was. But even before I met him, it happened again, right after I got to New York, the first girl in the nightclub. I weighed her body down and threw it in the river. Then I met Uncle Elliott, and I told him about it and said I was sorry, and he had to get me a job or I'd go to the police and turn myself in and tell the newspapers he was a phony."

Altman's voice became sarcastic. "*Of course*, he said he'd find me a job." His lips touched my forehead. "You believe me now, don't you, Carolyn?"

Leesey's breath had become a soft, terrified whimper. I squeezed her hand. "I believe you," I said. "I know you're telling the truth."

"Do you know that I'm sorry?"

"Yes. Yes. I know that."

"That's good."

It was so dark I couldn't see him but sensed that he had moved away from us. Then I heard him going up the stairs again. How long would it be before he came back? I asked myself frantically. I had been so foolish.

No one knew where I had gone. It might be hours before someone looked for me. Nick, I thought, Nick, be worried. Know that something's wrong. Look for me. Look for us.

I think a couple of hours passed, and then I screamed. He had been so quiet that I had not heard him come back. His hand covered my mouth.

"It doesn't do any good to scream, Carolyn," he said. "Leesey screamed in the beginning. I'd come down here and tell her about her picture being in the newspapers. She didn't want to record those messages for her father, but I told her that if she did, I might let her go. But I didn't mean it. Now don't scream again. If you do, I will kill you."

He was gone again. My head was pounding. The pain in my leg was unbearable. Would Lucas Reeves or Detective Barrott try to reach me? Would they and Nick realize that something was wrong?

The last time he returned, I had the sense that it was morning. I could see his shadow on the stairs. "I was never going to commit another crime, Carolyn," he said. "I really did like managing those buildings, and I loved the friends I made on the Internet. I still thought I could stop. I really tried. Then Uncle Elliott said that *now* I owed *him* a favor. He needed me to get rid of your brother. Mack went to Elliott. He wanted to tap into his trust fund. His girlfriend was pregnant, and

Mack wanted to get married and pay for his own education and hers, too. But Uncle Elliott had cleaned out most of the income from both of your trust funds. He'd invested tons of money in something that fell apart. He tried to put Mack off, but he knew that Mack was suspicious. I had to kill him."

I had to kill him. I had to kill him. Mack is dead, I thought bitterly. They murdered him.

"Elliott had to keep everyone thinking Mack was alive so that the trust funds wouldn't be examined. I made Mack say the words that you heard on the first Mother's Day phone call before I shot him. Then a year later Elliott made me kill the teacher and steal the tapes she had of Mack so he could make new Mother's Day calls. Elliott is a technical genius. For years he mixed what Mack had said on those tapes for the calls. Your brother's buried right here with the other girls. Look, Carolyn."

He directed the thin beam of a flashlight across the basement floor. I raised my head.

"See where the crosses are? Your brother and the other girls are buried there next to each other."

Mack had been dead all these years that we had been hoping and praying for him to come back to us. The reality that Mack was buried here in this miserable, filthy basement filled me with an overwhelming grief. Somehow I had always believed I would find him. Mack. Mack. Mack.

Altman was laughing, a high-pitched giggly sound. "Sure, Elliott was born in England. His mother is from Kansas. She was a maid with an American family that was transferred to England. She got pregnant in London and was sent home after the baby was born. She helped him make up all those stories about being a relative of President Roosevelt. They made them up together. She helped him get that swanky English accent. He's good with voices. The last three years he's even been doing Mack's voice himself. He knows you already had compared Mack's real voice with home movies. Had you fooled, didn't he?"

Altman's voice was becoming more and more shrill. "We only have fifteen minutes before it's all over. They're going to demolish this building. But I want to tell you. I dropped that note in the collection basket. Uncle Elliott was worried that you were going to start looking for Mack. Elliott had me leave it there. Lil Kramer saw me in church. I saw her look at me a couple of times. But then she thought I was Mack because you told her he'd been at that Mass. Good-bye, Carolyn. Good-bye, Leesey."

For the last time, I heard his steps retreating. Fifteen minutes. This building was going to be demolished in fifteen minutes. *I am going to die*, I thought, *and Mom is going to marry Elliott . . .*

Leesey was trembling. I was sure she understood

what he had said. I kept holding her hand and moistening her lips, talking to her, begging her to hang on, that everyone was looking for us. But now I did not believe what I was saying. I believed that Leesey and I would be the final victims of this madman and Elliott Wallace. In that moment I thought that at least I would soon be with Mack and Daddy.

77

"We've got him. He's on 104th and Riverside Drive," Larry Ahearn yelled.

An alarm went out to all the squad cars in the vicinity. Sirens wailing, they rushed to the scene.

The wrecking ball was in place. A delighted Derek Olsen saw that his business rival Doug Twining was inside the cockpit of the crane.

"One." Derek jumped up and began to count.

"Two." Then his triumphant cheer died on his lips. Someone was pushing open the boarded window on the second floor of the old town house. Someone was swinging his legs over the sill and waving. Altman. It was Howie Altman.

The wrecking ball was swinging toward the house. At the last instant, Twining spotted Altman and swung the controls so that the ball missed the house by inches.

Squad cars, tires screeching, were rounding the corner.

"Come back! Come back!" A screaming Howie Altman was running along the roof of the porch, waving his arms at the crane. As he began to jump up and down, the rotted wood caved in and the house began to crumble, floor by floor toppling into each other. Seeing what was happening, Altman dove back through the window in time to have tons of debris crash down on him.

Police poured out of the squad cars. "The basement," one of them yelled, "the basement. If they're there, it's their only chance."

78

The ceiling was falling around us. I pulled myself up and tried to throw my body over Leesey, who was now barely breathing. I felt a chunk of plaster hit my shoulder and then my head and arm. Too late, too late, I thought. Like Mack and those other girls, Leesey and I were doomed to end our lives here.

Then I heard the sound of the outside basement door being pulled open, and shouting voices approaching me from above. That was when I let myself drift off and escape from the pain. I guess they sedated me pretty heavily, because it was two days before I really woke up. Mother was sitting on a chair by the window of the hospital room, watching over me as she had done on 9/11. As we had that day, we cried together in each other's arms, this time for Mack, the honorable young man, son and brother, who had died because he wanted to accept his responsibilities.

Epilogue

One year later

When the books were checked, we learned that Elliott had robbed us of a fortune. It was clear, as Altman had ranted, that Mack had realized something was wrong with his trust fund, and the realization had cost him his life.

It was a miracle that Leesey was still alive. She had been tied up on that dirt floor for sixteen days and nights, unable to move, Altman alternately threatening to kill her and then taunting her about jumping into the SUV outside the Woodshed when he told her Nick had sent him to drive her home. He had given her only a few sips of water each day. Starving and dehydrated, she was in extremely critical condition when she arrived at the hospital. Just as Mom had kept her vigil at my side, Leesey's father and brother kept theirs in her hospital room, coaxing and begging her back to life.

The Andrews have become our very good friends.

Dr. David Andrews, Leesey's Dad, regularly invites Mom and me for dinner at his club in Greenwich. Their friendship has been a great comfort as Mom and I struggle with the pain of Mack's death. I know we have been a help to Leesey as she recovers emotionally from her terrible ordeal. Mother sold the Sutton Place apartment and now lives on Central Park West. I notice that Dr. David comes down frequently to go to dinner and the theatre with her.

We managed to keep from the media the full story of Mack's reason for becoming suspicious that his trust fund was not in order. Of course, I told Mom about Mack's son. It was not my place to keep it from her. Dr. Barbara Hanover Galbraith came to see us and told us how much she regretted believing that Mack had abandoned her. Even then she was not completely honest. She did not admit that she had borne Mack's child until I confronted her. Then she begged us to wait until he is older to tell him the truth, and we have reluctantly agreed. Mom and I wish with all of our hearts that we could know and be close to Mack's son. We have quietly attended plays and concerts at his school, St. David's, and it is like seeing Mack again. They called him Gary. To Mom and me he will always be Charles MacKenzie the Third.

The Kramers are enjoying life in Pennsylvania. When they learned the truth about Mack's disappearance, they came to apologize to Mother and me. Lil told us that because she had gone to prison for stealing when she was a young woman, she was hypersensitive when Mack asked her about his watch. It was found in Howard Altman's apartment. We'll never know whether he stole it from Mack's college apartment or took it after he killed him.

Lil also explained what she had found in Mack's room that had made Gus so angry. "It was a silly note making fun of me, saying that I wanted him to take me dancing, but it hurt my feelings," she said. That, of course, was the note Nick had written and then thrown away. Obviously he had been right about the fact that Lil was a bit nosey. When I asked him about it, he said he had crumpled it and thrown it in the wastebasket near Mack's desk. That is why Lil thought Mack had written it.

I'm happy to report that I'm one of the busy Assistant District Attorneys of Manhattan and regularly work with the detectives who started by suspecting me and now are my close friends and colleagues.

Nick and I were married three months ago. We have turned the loft into a charming New York apartment. The Woodshed is doing well. One of our favorite eating places is his father's newly reopened Pasta and Pizza in Queens. I've always said I would have four children, and we're looking forward to having the first one before too long. I hope it's a boy. His name will be Charles MacKenzie DeMarco.

We'll call him Mack.

Turn the page to read a gripping extract from
Mary Higgins Clark's latest novel . . .

ALL BY MYSELF, ALONE

1

The magnificent cruise liner *Queen Charlotte* was about to leave on her maiden voyage from her berth on the Hudson River. Promised to be the epitome of luxury, she was compared to both the first *Queen Mary* and even the *Titanic*, which had been the height of luxury one hundred years earlier.

One by one the passengers filed aboard, checked in and were invited to the Grand Lounge, where they were met by white-gloved waiters offering champagne. When the last guest had come aboard, Captain Fairfax gave a speech of welcome.

"We promise you the most elegant voyage you have ever or *will* ever encounter," he said, his British accent adding even more luster to his words. "You will find your suites furnished in the grand tradition of those of the most magnificent ocean liners of yesteryear. *Queen Charlotte* was constructed to accommodate precisely one hundred guests. Our eighty-five crew members are committed to serving you in every possible way. The entertainment will be worthy of Broadway, Carnegie Hall and the Metropolitan Opera. There will be a wide range of lectures to choose from. Our presenters include celebrity authors, former diplomats, and experts on Shakespeare and gemology. The finest chefs from around the globe will conduct farm-to-table cooking presentations. And we know that cruising is thirsty business. To remedy this hardship, there will be a series of wine tastings hosted by renowned connoisseurs. In keeping with the spirit of this cruise, one day there will be a lecture from the book of Emily Post, the legendary social arbiter of a century ago, illuminating the delightful manners of the past. These are only a few of the many activities you may choose from.

"In closing, the menus have been chosen from the recipes of the finest chefs the world over. Now, once again, welcome to your new home for the next six days.

"And now I would like to introduce Gregory Morrison, the owner of the *Queen Charlotte*. It was his vision that this ship would be perfect in every detail, and that is why you will enjoy the most luxurious cruise you will ever experience."

Gregory Morrison, a stout, ruddy-faced, silver-haired man stepped forward.

"I want to welcome all of you aboard. Today is the realization of a young boy's wish that began over fifty years ago. I stood next to my father, a tugboat captain, as he guided the most magnificent cruise ships of his day in and out of New York harbor. Truth be told, while my father was looking forward, toward where we were heading, I was looking back, watching in awe as spectacular cruise liners sliced elegantly through the gray Hudson River water. Even then I knew I wanted someday to build a ship even more awe-inspiring than the vessels I admired all those years ago. *Queen Charlotte* in all her majesty is the realization of the dream I dared to dream. Whether you are with us for five days to Southampton or stay with us for ninety days around the world, I hope today marks the beginning of an experience you will never forget." Raising his glass, he said, "Anchors away."

There was a smattering of applause, then people turned to their nearest fellow passengers and began to chat. Alvirah and Willy Meehan, celebrating their forty-fifth wedding anniversary, were relishing their great fortune. Before they won the lottery, she had been cleaning houses and he had been repairing overflowing toilets and broken pipes.

Thirty-four-year-old Ted Cavanaugh accepted a glass of champagne and looked around. He recognized some of the people on board, the chairmen of General

Electric and Goldman Sachs, several Hollywood A-list couples.

A voice next to him asked, "By any chance would you be related to the ambassador Mark Cavanaugh? You bear a striking resemblance to him."

"Yes, I am," Ted smiled. "I'm his son."

"I knew I couldn't be wrong. Let me introduce myself. I am Charles Chillingsworth."

Ted recognized the name of the retired ambassador to France.

"Your father and I were young attachés together," Chillingsworth said. "All the girls in the embassy were in love with your father. I told him no one deserved to be that good-looking. He served as ambassador to Egypt for two different presidents as I recall, then to the Court of St. James's."

"Yes, he did," Ted confirmed. "My father was fascinated by Egypt. And I share his passion. I spent many years growing up there. Then we moved to London when he became ambassador to Great Britain."

"Have you followed in his footsteps?"

"No, I am a lawyer, but a good part of my practice is devoted to recovering antiques and artifacts that have been stolen from their countries of origin." What he did not say was that his specific reason for being on this voyage was to meet Lady Emily Haywood and persuade her to return her famed Cleopatra emerald necklace to its rightful owners, the people of Egypt.

Professor Henry Longworth overheard the conversation and leaned in closer to hear the exchanges better, his eyes sparkling with interest. He had been invited aboard as a lecturer. A renowned expert on Shakespeare, his presentations, which always included renditions of passages, never failed to delight his audiences. A medium -sized man in his sixties, with thinning hair, he was a sought-after speaker on cruises and at colleges.

Devon Michaelson stood a short distance apart from the other guests. He had no need or desire for the banal small talk that was the inevitable result of strangers meeting for the first time. Like Professor Longworth, he was in his early sixties with no outstanding height or remarkable facial features.

Also standing by herself was twenty-eight-year-old Celia Kilbride. Tall, with black hair and sapphire-blue eyes, she did not notice, nor would she have cared about, the admiring glances that were cast at her by her fellow passengers.

The first stop on the round-the-world voyage would be Southampton, England. That was where she would disembark. Like Professor Longworth she was an invited lecturer on the ship. A gemologist, her subject would be the history of famous jewels through the ages.

The most excited passenger in the room was fifty-six-year-old divorcée Anna DeMille of Kansas, who had been the grand-prize winner of this trip in a church-sponsored raffle. Her dyed black hair and matching eyebrows were bold against her thin face and body. Her prayer was that this would be her opportunity to meet Mr. Right. *Why not?* she asked herself. *I won the raffle. Maybe this is finally going to be my year.*

Eighty-six-year-old Lady Emily Haywood, famed for her wealth and philanthropy, was attended by the guests she had invited: Brenda Martin, her assistant and companion over the last twenty years, Roger Pearson, who was both her investment manager and the executor of her estate, and Roger's wife Yvonne.

When interviewed about the cruise, Lady Emily had stated that she intended to bring her legendary Cleopatra emerald necklace and wear it in public for the first time.

As the passengers began to disperse, wishing each other "Bon voyage," they could not know that at least one of them would not reach Southampton alive.

2

Instead of going to her cabin, Celia Kilbride stood by the railing of the cruise ship and watched as she sailed past the Statue of Liberty. Her time on the ship would be less than a week, but it was long enough to get away from the glaring media coverage of Steven getting arrested on the night of their rehearsal dinner, twenty-four hours before their wedding. Was it really only four weeks ago?

They had been toasting each other when the FBI agents walked into the private dining room of 21 Club. The photographer who had been taking pictures had snapped one of them together, and another focusing on the five-carat engagement ring she was wearing.

Handsome, witty, charming, Steven Thorne had cheated her friends into investing in a hedge fund that was created only to benefit him and his lavish lifestyle. Thank God he was arrested before we were married,

Celia thought, as the ship sailed into the Atlantic. At least I was spared that.

So much of life is chance, she thought. It was shortly after her father died two years ago that she had been in London for a gemology seminar. When Carruthers Jewelers provided a business-class airline ticket, it was the first time she had flown other than in coach.

She was in her seat for the flight back to New York, sipping a complimentary glass of wine, when an impeccably dressed man put his briefcase in the overhead compartment and slid into the seat next to her. "I'm Steven Thorne," he said with a warm smile as he extended his hand to her. He explained that he was returning from a financial conference. By the time they landed, she had agreed to meet him for dinner.

Celia shook her head. How could she, a gemologist who could find a flaw in any gemstone, so misjudge a human being? She inhaled deeply and the wonderful scent of the ocean seeped into her lungs. I'm going to stop thinking about Steven, she promised herself. But it was hard to forget how many of her friends had invested money they couldn't afford to lose because she had introduced them to Steven. She had been forced to sit for an interview with the FBI. She wondered if they believed that she was involved in the theft, despite the fact that she had invested her own money in the scheme.

She had hoped not to know any fellow passengers, but it had been widely publicized that Lady Emily Haywood would be on the ship. She regularly brought pieces from her vast collection of jewelry to Carruthers on Fifth Avenue to be cleaned or repaired, and insisted that Celia check each one for any chips or scratches. Her assistant, Brenda Martin, was always with her. And Willy Meehan, the man who had come in to buy a forty-fifth wedding anniversary gift for his wife, Alvirah, had told her all about the fact that they had won forty million dollars in the lottery. She'd liked him immediately.

But with so many people on the ship, it would be easy to have plenty of private time, aside from the two lectures and one Q&A session she would be giving. She had been a guest speaker several times on Castle Line ships. Each time the agent in charge of entertainment events told her that the passengers had voted her the most interesting lecturer. He had phoned her only last week to invite her to fill in for a lecturer who had become ill at the last minute.

It had been manna from Heaven to get away from the sympathy of some friends and the resentment of the others who had lost money. I'm so glad to be here, she thought, as she turned and went down to her cabin.

Like every square inch of *Queen Charlotte*, the exquisitely furnished suite had been designed with meticulous attention to detail. It was a sitting room, bedroom and bath. It had roomy closets, unlike the older ships she had traveled on where the concierge suites were half this size. The door opened onto a balcony where she could sit outside when she wanted to feel the ocean breezes without being in the company of others.

She was tempted to go out on the balcony now, but decided to unpack and get settled instead. Her first lecture would be tomorrow afternoon and she wanted to go over her notes. The subject matter was the history of rare gems, beginning with ancient civilizations.

Her phone rang. She picked it up and heard a familiar voice on the other end of the line. It was Steven. He was out on bail before his trial. "Celia, I can explain," he began. She pressed End and slammed down the phone. Just hearing his voice made a wave of shame wash over her. I can detect the smallest flaw in any gem, she thought again bitterly.

She swallowed against the lump in her throat and impatiently brushed tears from her eyes.